She turned her back to him and undressed. When she was naked she put her hands over her breasts and turned back. 'My God,' he said, 'Titian should have painted you. That wonderful hair. "Girl into Woman" he would have called it.'

She felt brave suddenly. She felt wanton. She spread her arms and let him see all of her, let him be the first man ever to look at her body in lust. She bent and picked up her glass again, scooped into the champagne and drank. Hot eyes, watching her. 'You sweet temptress,' he whispered.

When he began kissing she thought she would drown, when he touched her naked flesh she moaned as if in pain. She lay and waited for him, lay and longed for him. This man, this stranger. He was looking down at her, his face almost distant. 'My lady. My beautiful one. The end of your innocence.'

Olga mitchell

Hallmark

Elizabeth Walker

HEADLINE

Copyright © 1991 Elizabeth Walker

The right of Elizabeth Walker to be identified as the Author of the Work has been asserted by her in accordance with the Copyright, Designs and Patents Act 1988.

First published in 1991
by HEADLINE BOOK PUBLISHING PLC

First published in paperback in 1992
by HEADLINE BOOK PUBLISHING PLC

10 9 8 7 6 5 4 3 2

All rights reserved. No part of this publication may be reproduced, stored in a retrieval system, or transmitted, in any form or by any means without the prior written permission of the publisher, nor be otherwise circulated in any form of binding or cover other than that in which it is published and without a similar condition being imposed on the subsequent purchaser.

All characters in this publication are fictitious and any resemblance to real persons, living or dead, is purely coincidental.

ISBN 0 7472 3659 3

Typeset by Medcalf Type Ltd, Bicester, Oxon

Printed and bound in Great Britain by
Collins, Glasgow

HEADLINE BOOK PUBLISHING PLC
Headline House
79 Great Titchfield Street
London W1P 7FN

Acknowledgments

Hallmark could not have been written without the help of many, many people in the silver trade. It was not always easy to persuade them to talk; silver is a secretive business from start to finish, with lovely, precious things changing hands almost furtively, in battered suitcases and brown paper bags. Nonetheless a number of people were tremendously kind:

The auction houses, Phillips and Sotheby's. Robert Miller of Sotheby's in Chester was great fun, while Mr Culme in London, when asked to recommend suitable reading, studiously omitted to mention the wonderful books he has written on silver. Fortunately I discovered them for myself, and his lucid and enthusiastic explanations did much to help my understanding.

David Newbould of Hill Brothers (Silversmiths) Ltd, in Sheffield. He was kind enough to educate me in the mysteries of smithing, the almost magical process by which beautiful things are produced from fire and dirt. Thanks to him and all his staff.

Mr Jack Koopman of The Silver Vaults, Chancery Lane, whose lovely silver is breathtaking. He made me aware of the vast international market that exists for silver, and the close-knit world of the dealers in that trade. Mr Koopman's daughter is one of the few women in silver today, and the time they gave me was very much appreciated.

Mr Jack Shaw and his son, of The Old Grammar School, Ilkley, where I live. They must rue the day their stock of antique silver first caught my eye, because I have bombarded them ever since with questions. Unfailingly courteous, they are due my grateful thanks.

One last point: ordinary people today consider sterling silver to be beyond their reach. They don't buy silver tableware any more, and content themselves with plate or stainless steel. But hallmarked silver holds its value — and nobody ever sold a stainless steel set at a profit! Small, good pieces of silver are not that expensive and in today's world they don't even need much cleaning. Find a good dealer, ask his advice, and buy something lasting and beautiful.

Hallmark

Chapter One

Matilda Winterton gazed distastefully down at her long legs. Muddy and blotched from the cold, they protruded from a knee-length voluminous grey skirt like the fossilised relics of a past civilisation. A graze marked one shin, and she dabbed at it with the corner of a towel.

'Honestly, Matty! That's my towel, it's got my name on.' A tall, angular girl pointed at the label, 'The Hon. Griselda Lemming-Knott' in sloping script. 'You've covered it in blood.'

'You can't complain, you're the one who maimed me,' retorted Matty. 'And, Grizzle, we were supposed to be on the same team.'

Griselda folded herself on to the wooden bench at Matty's side. 'Sorry. But Miss Matthews was screaming at me and I panicked. It's a family trait, my great-great-grandfather went to pieces in the Crimea.'

A third girl drifted in from the field. 'I hope he wasn't playing hockey. Not in a battle, anyway.'

'Actually, Lorne, he was commanding a cavalry unit. He turned and ran, which was jolly sensible of him, all things considered. But he ended his life in shame.'

Gathering the regulation school duffel coat around her Lorne joined the others on the bench. Her long hair swung like a length of black silk, and her brown, almost sooty eyes looked out with lazy confidence from a heart-shaped face. She looked what she was, a rich girl from Southern Carolina, half frozen to death. 'I absolutely despise hockey,' she declared.

'I don't know why,' said Matty. 'You never play. It's me and Griselda who have to turn out every Thursday and risk permanent damage to our health.'

1

'But why do I have to watch?' complained Lorne. 'One of these days I'll catch a fatal chill and die. My daddy will have to fetch me in a coffin lined with lace.'

'He might not bother,' said Matty. 'He might leave you here, mouldering in the sick room. I swear there are three corpses in there already.'

'My daddy would certainly come,' said Lorne. Then she grinned. 'Unless he was buying a horse.'

Griselda got up stiffly and went over to the showers. She turned taps with vigour and shouted, 'You should try living at Peregrines, it's always cold. We eat supper with our coats on until at least April. Oh, damn! There isn't any hot water.'

'There must be.' Matty limped across and put her hand under the flow. It remained icy cold. 'I don't believe it!' she exclaimed. 'The money it costs to keep us here and the water isn't even lukewarm!'

'I always thought the English liked cold showers,' remarked Lorne. 'To suppress their desires.'

'All I desire is some hot water,' said Matty. 'Oh, how I hate this place! Everything ugly, everything uncomfortable. It's like some ghastly experiment in deprivation.'

Griselda, whose home life was very little different, said bracingly, 'Come on, girls! It's not that bad!'

'It's an abuse of human rights,' said Lorne, and huddled deeper into her coat. Matty, faced with an icy shower, let out a little sob.

The door burst open and a plump girl charged in. She had a key on a tattered piece of string. 'Stop! Don't do it! I've got the key!'

'So I see,' said Matty. 'What for?'

'The cupboard with the water heater. Idiot Matthews forgot to turn it on, and when she remembered she couldn't be bothered to trail over here so I grabbed the key and came to the rescue. I couldn't bear the thought of Matty and Grizzle's suffering.'

'Henrietta, you're wonderful!' Matty hugged her and Henrietta beamed.

'I've got something else too,' she confided. 'Look!' From the capacious pocket of her duffel she extracted a bottle of rum.

'By the spirit of America!' Lorne fell on her knees.

'By the honour of the Lemming-Knotts!' Griselda seized the bottle and wrestled with the top.

'By the gorgeous muscles of the man who fetches the laundry!' Matty flung open a locker and searched frantically for paper cups.

By six the scene had drifted towards debauchery. Clouds of steam from the showers had turned the place into a Turkish bath, and Griselda and Matty lounged on the benches, each wearing nothing but a towel. The others had merely taken off their coats, but Lorne was standing in the middle of the floor, paper cup in hand, declaiming.

'Come, fellow members of our loyal band, stand with me and declare your loyalty.'

'What to?' asked Matty blearily. 'Rum? I'm very loyal to rum. And even loyaller to hot water.'

'You can't be loyaller, it isn't good English,' said Henrietta.

'To each other!' Lorne looked irritably at Matty. 'We're loyal to each other. Don't you ever take anything seriously?'

Matty looked aggrieved. 'Like what? I'm not going to become anyone's blood brother, if that's what you're getting at.'

'Blood sister,' said Griselda. 'You could only be someone's blood sister.'

'Whatever it is, we should be it,' said Lorne. 'We ought to have an oath or something. We've stuck together through thick and thin over all these years. Soon we're going to leave, and what then? We'll drift apart and forget each other. We need an oath.'

'I won't swear on anyone's dead grandmother,' warned Matty. 'And even if I did, it wouldn't make the slightest difference. We'd still all forget to write.'

'You don't have to write to remain friends,' said Griselda.

'No.' Henrietta sat up, saying earnestly, 'If we didn't see each other for years we'd still be friends, if we didn't write or talk on the telephone or anything. If one of us went to the moon and didn't come back until she was an old old lady, we'd still remember her. We'd still come and say hello.'

3

'We could swear on the rum bottle,' said Griselda, looking down her beaky nose at the object in question.

'And swear by the spirit,' giggled Matty. 'All right then, hands together on the rum bottle.'

The girls put their hands one on top of the other.

'Where did the rum come from, Henry?' asked Matty curiously.

'My aunt sent it by mistake,' said Henrietta. 'It was meant for my cousin in the navy. I suppose he's got my fruit cake.'

'She can't be at all like your mother,' said Griselda. 'She only ever sends you further supplies of regulation knickers.'

'I suppose it's because my mother's the eldest. She thinks my aunt's terribly irresponsible.'

'Can we have your attention?' asked Lorne with exaggerated patience. 'Oaths are not occasions for general chatter.'

'Definitely not,' said Griselda.

Matty added, 'By the legs of my own, at this moment absent, pair of regulation knickers, no sir!'

There was a silence. 'I can't think of an oath,' said Lorne.

'It was your idea,' said Matty.

'I know, but I can't think of anything. You try, Matty. Something Shakespearean.'

'Oh, all right.' She closed her eyes to concentrate. Then she sparkled at her friends. 'I know! Puck's speech.' She had played him in the last school play, with just the right air of grinning charm.

> '"Over hill, over dale,
> Thorough bush, thorough brier,
> Over park, over pale,
> Thorough flood, thorough fire"

– we have not served the Fairy Queen, but instead the jewel of friendship. And we shall serve it always.'

'Always,' said Lorne and Griselda.

'Forever,' said Henrietta.

They withdrew their hands and passed the rum bottle round once more. 'I wrote to my mother twenty times in my first term here, asking to be taken home,' said Henrietta

4

plaintively. 'She never takes any notice of anything I say.'

'You wouldn't have known us if you'd quit,' said Griselda. 'Did you want to go home, Matty?'

Matty looked down at her slender feet. 'Not home, exactly. My mother had just died, I wanted to get away from home. But anywhere else would have done. The food!'

'Ugh! The food!' Lorne shuddered. 'We should all be bundles of wobbling flab.'

'I am,' said Henrietta mournfully. 'It isn't fair.'

'You're only plump,' said Matty owlishly. 'Anyway, the laundry man fancies you, he watches your breasts bouncing up and down in your gym slip.'

Henrietta sighed. 'My mother won't buy me a proper support bra. She thinks my muscle tone will go. I haven't got any muscle tone! But it's you he fancies really, Matty. He leers at you from his van.'

'And I leer back! Oh, what it is to be reduced to mooning after the laundry man!'

'Well, he is rather decent,' said Griselda. She hiccupped.

'Actually he's sweaty and not very bright. That's what I like about him.' Matty wrapped her arms round herself and sighed.

'We must all try and write when we leave,' said Lorne firmly.

'You're the one that won't,' said Matty.

'But of course I will! I never forget to write letters. Do I?'

'Yes,' said her friends. Without their help Lorne would long since have been expelled for indolence.

A distant bell sounded from the main school. Griselda peered out of the misty window and saw girls bustling in to tea. 'We're going to be late,' she said. 'That's another black mark.'

'If we hurry it'll be all right.' Matty cast aside her towel and began hunting for her bra.

Henrietta sat down, saying, 'I feel all dizzy. Like being seasick. I can't face fish paste sandwiches.'

'We shouldn't have to eat them,' said Lorne. 'What would happen if we rose up in a body and refused?'

'We'd starve,' said the others in unison. Lorne sighed. It was probably true.

5

They ran from the changing rooms trailing a miasma of rum and equally illicit perfume. Griselda, over six feet tall, led easily, and she was followed at some distance by Matty, making up in grace what she lacked in speed. Lorne, who considered exercise only acceptable in the company of a well-bred horse, followed lackadaisically, while Henrietta puffed her way in the rear, golden curls bobbing. As they careered one after another into the magnificent polished wood entrance hall, they each slithered to a halt.

'We do apologise, Miss Saunders,' said Griselda with dignity.

Miss Saunders, a small grey woman entirely dwarfed both by Griselda's height and her manner, folded her prim hands. 'Hardly the conduct we expect of our sixth form. It can be no surprise to anyone that none of you girls was considered fit to be appointed a prefect this term.'

'You were very wise,' agreed Matty. 'The good name of this school ought not to be brought into disrepute by people like us.'

Miss Saunders blinked. 'Er — yes. In fact, Matilda, I wish to speak with you. Confidentially. Come to my office.' She turned to lead the way.

The girls exchanged alarmed glances. A summons from the headmistress was never a trivial affair. Too often it meant bad news from home. Miss Saunders paused at the foot of the sweeping staircase. 'Come along, Matilda! I don't have time to waste. You others can go into tea. At once!'

With a sense of advancing doom, Matty followed the headmistress up the stairs. She was sure the fees had been paid this term. Had the cheque bounced? It would have done so before now. Perhaps her father had withdrawn her for next term, but he would have told her, surely, before he spoke to Miss Saunders. Was it Simon? Her heart went cold with fright. 'It isn't Simon, is it? My brother?'

Miss Saunders turned and looked down at the girl's white, anxious face. She was a pretty child. Too pretty. Hair like a polished chestnut, and clear grey eyes. She had been wonderful as Puck, an electric spirit. But she had a defiant streak, for all her pretend obedience. 'As far as I know your brother is quite well.'

'My father then? Is it him?'

'Come into my office, child.'

Matty followed her into the room. It was large, with windows opening on to a wide verandah from which favoured pupils could watch matches in summer. Matty had never been so favoured. There was a goodish desk, but the woodworm had been active for as long as Matty had known it, and there was a nice little bureau in the corner. Matty fancied that one of the legs had been replaced, the colour was always a trifle odd. And a couple of the portraits were by noted provincials of the nineteenth century. Her father would have valued this room in five minutes flat, perhaps less. If you asked him what someone was like, he never said 'Nice chap', but 'Sheraton copy in his study, and a damned good dining table. Very early.'

Matty perched on the edge of the visitor's chair. Miss Saunders arranged herself at the desk, her fingers toying with a paper knife.

'Is it the money again?' blurted Matty.

'Not the money, no.'

They looked at each other, the worn older lady, her hopes and ambitions shrunken away, and the glowing girl, as fresh as a flower on a fine spring morning. Suddenly Miss Saunders could find no words. She could think of nothing to say. But the words had to come, the girl was sitting there, her eyes wide with expectation.

'I'm sorry, Matilda,' she said tightly. 'The police have informed me of an accident. Your father's dead. He killed himself at eleven o'clock this morning.'

In the bedroom cubicle that was all the privacy the school afforded, Matty sat hunched on her bed. Girls were clattering out of the dining hall, but she could face no one yet. And tomorrow she would go home.

She shuddered, a spasm that was repeated every minute or so. She couldn't quite believe any of this. Dad gone, Dad giving up, Dad letting her down in this terrible, final way. He had gassed himself in his car, a couple of miles from

7

one of his favourite small town auction rooms. He might even have bought something. But then on the way home, suddenly, he wouldn't have wanted to go on. Oh, she knew how it was. Nothing had ever been the same since her mother died, there was no joy in going home. And he was always impulsive, acting on some hunch, some inspiration, not stopping to think. But even so − he hadn't been that miserable. The three of them, she, Simon and Dad, they had managed, put together a life for themselves.

There was a perfunctory rattle of the curtain and Griselda swept in, her long face longer still with anxiety. 'Matty? Is everything OK at home?'

One look at her friend and she knew the answer. She sat on the bed, taking Matty's cold hand in her own. 'Oh, my poor dear. Don't tell me if you don't want.'

Matty took another, shuddering breath. 'I do want. Grizzle, it's so awful I can hardly believe it. Let's wait for the others. I'll tell you all at once.'

Lorne and Henrietta arrived together. 'Are you going home, Matty?' demanded Lorne, sweeping the curtain aside with a flourish. 'I've brought you a sandwich. It's disgusting, but if you're to travel you'll need it.'

'Hush up, Lorne, do,' muttered Henrietta. 'Can't you see Matty's upset?'

Lorne paused. 'Oh. Yes. I do see. We should have brought the rest of the rum.'

'I don't want rum. I just want − something. I don't know what to do, you see.'

'Wait.' Lorne brushed through the curtains again, returning moments later with quilts from neighbouring beds. 'You're in shock, you've got to be warm. Put this on your shoulders, Matty. You can tell us everything. Everyone else is downstairs, no one but us can hear.'

Matty looked round at her friends; Griselda with her horse face, the delicious Lorne, and plump little Henrietta looking years younger than seventeen. 'I couldn't bear it if you weren't here,' she said throatily.

'Well, we are here,' said Griselda in bracing tones. 'No need to get dismal, Matty.'

'I think there is.' She took another of those long, painful

breaths, that seemed to sear a trail of anguish down her throat. 'My father killed himself this morning. A hose through the window of his car. The other end was connected to the exhaust pipe.'

The others gasped, startled for once into silence. Matty couldn't bear the silence. She dashed on recklessly, 'I don't know why, you see. Or at least — it can't have been the money. He hasn't been doing well lately, no one in the antiques business has, but I've only got another two terms here, and if the worst came to the worst I could have left and Simon could — well, we'd have thought of something.'

Her friends sat motionless, still stunned. After a moment Henrietta said, 'Is Simon all right? It wasn't anything to do with him?'

Matty shook her head. 'I don't think so. Miss Saunders telephoned his school for me. His housemaster's wife is fussing over him tonight. We're both going home tomorrow. I just can't think what's going to happen. He's only ten, and his mother's dead and his father's gone and —'

'Now, now,' said Griselda. 'No need to go to pieces. I imagine you'll find there's been a business problem of some sort. That's usually the way.'

'There are always problems with antiques,' said Matty irritably. 'The showroom staff kept leaving, we couldn't afford to buy really good stuff and we lost money over a few things. We got landed with some fake Minton that Dad bought on trust from another dealer. He shouldn't have rooked us but he did. It was upsetting. Annoying. No more than that.'

'Could you not sell the china on?' asked Lorne. 'Let the buyer beware and all that?'

Matty shook her head, fiercely upset. 'Of course we couldn't! In antiques you've only got your reputation, nothing else. Dad was honest, honest as the day is long. He didn't do a crooked thing in all his life, not knowingly! If he sold something that wasn't right it was an honest mistake. Anyone can make a mistake, can't they?' Her clear grey eyes, fringed with chestnut lashes, were wide and questioning.

Griselda took out one of her father's ancient

9

monogrammed handkerchiefs and blew her nose. 'I take it he'd been accused of something?'

'You didn't tell us, Matty,' said Lorne in a singsong of accusation.

Loyally, Henrietta said, 'I don't suppose it's the sort of thing you do tell.'

Matty looked miserably round at them. 'I would have told you. I wanted to. But I thought − everyone thinks dealers are crooks, don't they? And you don't know my father. You − didn't know him. But he was absolutely straight, he prided himself on it. He didn't ever sell fakes, not knowingly. Even if there was a let-in piece, some late restoration, he always had to say. But − but there was this ring, an auction ring, people banding together to keep the prices low, deciding beforehand who was going to get what. Things like that happen, at auctions, usually because of stupid private buyers who pay too much and cut out the dealer, and I absolutely know he would never − ' She gulped, swallowing down tears. 'There was an investigation. An auction ring was operating on most of the big northern sales. I found out before Christmas, the police were looking into things. And he promised me he hadn't done anything. They'd asked him of course, the others in the ring, they wanted him to join. It only works if everyone's in. All the important, respected dealers. And he was respected. Terribly.'

Suddenly she seized Griselda's handkerchief and buried her face in it. Sobs shook her slim shoulders.

'I could go and get the rum,' offered Henrietta. 'I hid it in the cricket locker.'

'Not yet,' said Lorne. 'Matty, not everyone's honest. My father sold a horse once − he knew if you put it in a pasture you wouldn't catch it for a week − but he sold it. My mother was so angry I thought she'd explode.'

'And my father's in the City,' added Henrietta. 'Everyone knows that's crooked. At least − I mean, all those shares and things. I bet Daddy sometimes does something wrong.'

Matty gasped and mopped her eyes. 'You know perfectly well he's completely honest,' she said breathily. 'And I bet your father didn't lie, Lorne. He just left something unsaid.'

10

'But he was lying by omission!' declared Lorne, who was something of a philosopher. 'He was morally in the wrong.'

Griselda said, 'Actually, I don't think there's an awful lot to be said for honesty these days. Look at us, stuck at Peregrines, hardly a bean left after centuries of honest toil. Your father didn't do anything terribly bad, Matty. He didn't beat up old ladies.'

'He might as well have done,' she said thickly. 'He joined a ring to buy their furniture for less than it was worth. He didn't want to do it, but everyone else joined in. And these schools are so terribly expensive, and he so much wanted to keep the house. He felt — it was all we had, you see, after my mother died. She'd made it so lovely. It was as if she was still there in a way, with her cushions and all her pretty things. He kept it for her.'

Henrietta's pink face suddenly crumpled. 'I do think it's so terribly sad!' she wailed. 'Poor Matty. Poor Simon. And poor us, because Matty's going to leave and we'll all be left alone!'

They all looked at each other. 'Perhaps we had better get the rum,' said Griselda.

They talked long into the night. For once, in view of Matty's tragedy, they were spared the visits of officious staff and remained, crouched on Matty's bed, talking in low voices. Matty found that the rum helped, dulling reality's edge. She would have given anything for a moment's escape, back into careless youth. The morning, the future, stretched before her like a black chasm.

'There won't be any insurance,' said Griselda. 'There isn't, with suicides.'

'I do so hope you don't have to sell the house,' said Henrietta.

Matty swallowed. 'I think we will. That's all there is, and we've got to live. The shop's just rented, and we haven't much stock right now. There's a foul table Dad bought from an old lady, he was sorry for her and paid too much, and he's got a stuffed bear, all moth-eaten and glassy-eyed. He was buying the strangest things —' she drifted off, tearfully.

'You'll stay for your exams, won't you?' asked Lorne.

'The money won't allow,' said Matty tightly. 'I'm almost

sure it won't. There may be debts. I shall have to get a job, though there isn't anything I can do. Why don't they teach you to type in this place? They don't teach us anything useful. I could be a swimming pool attendant, I suppose, I've got my lifesaving badge. And I can drive. But I've got to keep Simon, pay his school fees and everything. And if he hasn't a proper home, they'll take him into care, and teach him to be a mugger or a rapist or something!' Her voice rose in panic.

'Now you're just being silly,' said Griselda. 'There must be lots of jobs you could do. Come on, everyone, let's think of some.'

They sat in silence for long minutes. Matty put her head on her knees, her shining hair cascading down mournfully. She groaned.

'Stop that, do!' commanded Griselda. 'We've lots of ideas, haven't we?'

There was a long pause. 'You could learn to type,' said Henrietta fearfully.

'She'd starve,' said Lorne flatly. 'How about being a model?'

'I'm too short,' said Matty. 'You have to be six foot or so. Griselda's height.'

They fell silent again. There was no need to say that Griselda was never going to be a model.

'You should build on what you know,' said Griselda thoughtfully. 'Couldn't you be something in antiques? After all, you've grown up with them. We can't take you anywhere without having you price half the furniture.'

Matty sighed. 'Dad was in antiques for twenty years and he never made any money. It's so difficult. You need capital. If you want to be properly established you have to buy only the best, even if it's just the best of something ordinary, like old cooking pots. And I couldn't possibly afford anything decent. I'd be a glorified junk shop owner, no more.'

Lorne rested her chin on her fists. 'It's certainly the age of the specialist,' she said thoughtfully. 'If you get to know everything there is to know about something people come knocking at your door. People pay you to write books about it, give lectures, everything.'

12

'I'm not an expert in anything,' said Matty. 'Neither was my father. He knew quite a bit about a lot of things, that's all. He sort of drifted into antiques, after the army. He learned as he went along.'

'But you could specialise,' said Henrietta. 'You could be a world expert on something. Get a job with an auction house. Pictures, or jewels, or horrible old books that nobody wants to read.'

'Or carpets, or porcelain, or old glass,' added Griselda, with mounting enthusiasm.

Lorne picked up the rum bottle and drained the last into her own paper cup. 'Silver,' she said.

They wouldn't listen to her at first. They were used to Lorne's exotic ideas, and seldom credited them with practical point. But whatever else they considered couldn't divert the girl. 'All right,' said Matty at last. 'Why do you think I should learn about silver?'

Lorne shrugged the quilt gleefully over her shoulders. 'Because it's beautiful. No point learning about something you don't even like. And it's glamorous, it leads to a glamorous lifestyle. Nobody who isn't somebody buys good silver. You could marry a millionaire!'

'I want a job, not a husband,' flared Matty. 'I want my own money.'

'Any money would be useful right now, it seems to me,' said Griselda. 'Is there much trade in silver, Lorne? We've had our stuff at Peregrines for centuries; it sort of hangs around, waiting to be cleaned.'

'I imagine it would – at Peregrines,' said Lorne. 'But in America, silver's big business. My father was talking about investing in it last time I was home. English and early American, they're the thing.'

'My mother's looking for a good silver teapot,' said Henrietta. 'Georgian or something. Everybody's getting them.'

'It's going to be a craze,' said Lorne. 'You bet!'

Matty considered. 'I wouldn't know where to start. Perhaps you have to do a fine arts degree or something.'

'Oh, you only have to read books and look at things,'

said Griselda airily. 'Buy a few pieces, some spoons or something.'

'I can't buy anything! I'm broke.'

'There'll be money left from the sale of the house,' said Lorne. 'Bound to be. You'll have to travel, see the best at first hand. Private collections, museums, that sort of thing.'

Matty's head whirled. Problems, exhaustion and misery crowded in on her like great weights. The girls could play their games, weave their fantasies, but she was in the midst of it, facing the truth. Suddenly she couldn't take any more. 'Would you mind going away?' she said abruptly. 'I think I want to get some sleep.'

When they had gone Matty laid her head down on the cold pillow. She felt a hundred years old instead of seventeen. If only, when she woke, everything could be as before, cold showers and all. If only she could go home and see her father. She closed her eyes in the dark, but even so tears seeped from under the lids and ran down her temples into her hair. Against her will she let out one anguished, strangled sob.

Henrietta's voice came from the next cubicle. 'Matty? Please don't cry. I know it's going to be all right. We'll make it right, honestly.'

Matty lay in the dark and said nothing.

Chapter Two

Matty sat on the old chintz sofa, looking out into a garden that in summer overflowed with larkspur, Sweet William and roses. Now the birdbath was iced over, the lawn frosted and the only colour was in holly berries, brilliant as blood.

'I don't know what he was thinking of,' she said thickly. 'He must have known what a mess he'd be making for us.'

Gerald Connolly, the family solicitor, said, 'Actually Matty, I don't imagine he was doing much thinking. When he knew the case would come to court he was very distressed. He was deeply implicated, not just in this ring affair but a lot more besides. A prison term was almost inevitable, you know.'

Matty's fingers clenched. 'He wasn't dishonest! They must have ganged up on him, made it impossible. He never took a penny that wasn't his in his whole life.'

Connolly reached out and gripped her shoulder. 'I know, my dear. Believe me, I do know. But can you pull yourself together a little? A car's just arrived. Simon's here.'

Matty nodded and took a long, steadying breath. She went out into the narrow hall that she had always considered cramped and now knew was nothing of the kind. This was a perfect house, the only house she ever wanted to live in. You saw things differently when you knew you were going to lose them.

Simon, tall for his age with hair as shining brown as his sister's, walked stiffly into the room. He was wearing a school blazer, and looked absurdly smart. 'Hi,' he said to Matty, and as she leaned to kiss him he pushed her away. 'Don't fuss, please. Everyone's been making the most terrible scenes. I'm not ill.'

15

Matty took a long breath. 'They all think we're going to go to pieces.'

'I won't.'

She felt her heart twist with worry. He looked so white and strained. He pushed past her into the kitchen. 'Any biscuits? Bet there aren't. Dad wouldn't have thought of doing the blasted shopping, I suppose. He's even left the dishes in the sink.'

They stood looking down at the remnants of their father's last meal, something quick no doubt, out of a packet.

Suddenly Simon said, 'You'd think he'd have given us a chance. I mean, we could've talked him out of it, anything. He didn't have to go right ahead and do it, just like that. Whatever he'd done.'

Mr Connolly said gently, 'I imagine he was very, very ashamed.'

Simon looked up, his eyes fierce despite the tears. 'Was he? Then why did he do it? If he was going to be a crook he could've been a rich one, and gone to prison with loads of money in the bank. Then we'd have been all right. He didn't have to kill himself. He didn't have to go off and leave us in the lurch!' His voice was shrill with gathering hysteria, fuelled by the strain of those hours at school, when he had to pretend to be fine. Matty went to him, and gathered him up. In the first seconds he fought her, and she hung on, avoiding his kicks. Gradually, as resistance faded, Simon relaxed into sobs.

'Er – I think I'll come back later,' said Mr Connolly.

Later, when they were calm, they had lunch, washing up everything briskly right away. They changed into jeans and old darned sweaters, and sat before a crackling log fire. It was hard to believe that their father wasn't out in the garage, fiddling with some saleroom purchase. Suddenly everything seemed normal.

Matty said, 'We're going to have to sell this place.'

'But where will we live?'

'I don't know. A flat, perhaps. Somewhere cheaper.'

'I bet there isn't anywhere. Everyone in my year lives somewhere grander than this.'

But at that moment there seemed nowhere more desirable

than their own shabby house. Matty wondered if she was going to cry again, but forced the tears back. If anyone needed strength then she did, for Simon if no one else.

'What about school?' he asked.

'We'll pay somehow,' said Matty, trying to sound confident. 'There's bound to be enough left over.'

'Wouldn't it be better if I went to the local one?'

His sister shook her head. 'If I'm working you'll have to board. I must get a job, you see. We'll manage.'

She smiled at him, her brave, slightly roguish grin. 'It'll be fun, once we get over all this. We can look after ourselves. I'll be working, instead of slogging away at exams and university, and in the holidays we can go hop picking or something, and get gypsy brown in the sun.'

'Suppose it rains?' said Simon.

'And suppose it doesn't? We'll have a nice little flat somewhere with a window box, and instead of mowing the lawn all summer we'll go swimming instead.'

He laughed, bravely, and she put out her hand and grasped his. 'It will be all right, love. I promise.'

But the next day, there seemed no room for optimism. Mr Connolly sat at her father's desk and drew up a schedule of debt. 'You realise there was a second mortgage on the house?' he said. 'I felt it was unwise at the time, but your father didn't want to close the shop, and it did tend to lose rather a lot of money from time to time. So you are going to receive very little of the proceeds from the house sale. Do you have any antiques here that might be valuable?'

Matty sighed, rubbing her fingers over her forehead. 'No. We only kept the junk. Some things look all right but aren't, for instance that desk. Dad got some good moulding from a collapsed cabinet and stuck it on. The dining chairs don't match and the table needs restoring and the grandfather clock lost its works a hundred years ago. We haven't anything.'

'Oh. Oh, I see.'

Mr Connolly scribbled notes on the pad before him. Matty mentally crossed off the cracked pair of vases on the mantelshelf, the oil paintings by second-rate Victorians, even

17

the iron bootjack that was a nineteenth-century Elizabethan fake. If they sold everything it might raise two thousand pounds, and even that estimate could be wildly optimistic.

'When should we move?' she asked.

Mr Connolly looked up. 'As soon as possible. You mustn't incur more interest on the loans than is absolutely necessary, so we can't waste time. If you and your brother could pack everything you wish to keep, then I'll contact a saleroom. The estate agent tells me he already has some interest in the house, so we could have everything cleared up quite soon.'

'Oh.'

Matty got up and went to the window. Over the last few days the frost had given way to mud and rough breezes. The house would never make what it ought to at this time of year. They should sell in the summer, when the trees were heavy with leaf and the borders thick with summer scents and drowsing bees. Simon was to return to school, but she had nowhere. Where could she go?

The telephone rang, breaking into her thoughts. Mr Connolly said, 'Shall I?' but Matty shook her head. She went into the hall to take the call in private. At once she recognised Griselda's voice.

'Matty? Are you all right?'

'Hello, Grizzle. I'm fine. At least – I will be. We're in turmoil, you see, selling everything.'

'Yes, we thought you might be. Do you realise it's half term next week?'

'Is it? Damn. I was hoping to send Simon back to school, get him away when everything's being picked over. He's finding it very tough.'

'That's what we thought. Well, you'll be glad to hear that we've come up with a plan. You and Simon are to come to Peregrines. We'll all be there, even Henrietta. Fortunately the old battleaxe she calls a mother is only too delighted to have Henry slumming it with us. She thinks we're the right sort.'

Matty gurgled with sudden laughter. 'And so you are. We shall love to come.'

'Don't expect it to be comfortable. We don't normally

have guests in winter, you have to be bred here to endure the cold. Bring hot water bottles. Oh, and Lorne is convinced she's right about the silver thing. She's been talking to everyone, got it all organised. Apparently you have to go to Russia, they've an amazing collection of Elizabethan silver. Peter the Great bought it, and it hasn't been cleaned since.'

'Russia? Oh.'

'Don't you want to go to Russia?'

'I — I'll have to think about it. Thanks, Griselda, I'll see you all next week.'

She replaced the receiver and stood for a moment, thinking. There would be no career in silver, no real career at all, just a job. Perhaps in time, when Simon was older, she would go back and take her exams, but for the moment her only consideration had to be cash. Mr Connolly came out of the room behind her.

'Matty, I wondered if you wanted to keep this?' He was holding out a long slender ladle.

'I don't know. Are you sure it's ours? Where did it come from?'

'Actually, it was the last thing your father bought. He went to that sale, picked this up and then — decided. It's silver, you know. The real thing.'

'Is it?'

Matty took it and felt the weight. It was heavy, well balanced between bowl and tapering handle. The metal reflected the light, a soft glow that defied the afternoon gloom. The piece was plain, quite without ornament, and as far as she knew it was the only piece of silver her father had ever bought in his life.

'The proverbial silver spoon' said Mr Connolly, with a heavy attempt at good cheer.

Matty didn't look at him. She closed her hand on silver, feeling a great rage against her father, heat that by rights should melt the thing in her hand back into nothing. It remained hard against her palm. She would not be influenced like this, she decided, she would not allow some chance purchase to make her think of destiny.

She glanced up at Mr Connolly. 'He never bought silver,

you know. But I'd better keep it. It's useful, for one thing.'

'Yes.' Mr Connolly looked ill at ease for a moment. 'If you do decide to sell, Matty, I'd be happy to take it off your hands. Silver looks so good on the table, doesn't it?'

Her head came up. 'I suppose it does. But I won't sell just yet, if you don't mind.'

He looked slightly aggrieved. He had imagined taking it back home, and delighting his wife.

Upstairs, packing for the week at Peregrines, Matty listened to Simon throwing toys roughly into a box. He was ridding himself of so many childish but still loved possessions. When he was asleep she would go back and rescue his fluffy rabbit and his teddy bear, as well as his toy cars. Although she must grow up at once surely he need not; there was time enough yet for childhood. As she stood up the ladle caught her eye. Reaching out, she tossed it almost inconsequentially into her case.

Peregrines was a large, cold Victorian mansion set on a windy heath. The girls sometimes visited, Lorne more than the rest, when a holiday was too short to justify a return trip across the Atlantic. They all habitually brought their extra woollens and packets of biscuits, like seasoned travellers in Siberia, for Peregrines had no central heating and an aged and erratic cook. It also had no mistress but Griselda, since her mother had long since absconded with a family friend. She had left an air of muddle behind her, which seemed to offend no one.

On this occasion Griselda's father, Lord Knelworth, made a special effort to greet Matty and Simon as they arrived. A tall, spare, rather disordered man, he looked embarrassed and fiddled in his waistcoat pocket. 'Sorry to hear of the upset,' he managed, jogging from foot to foot. 'Very distressing. Grizzle says you're really up against it. Bad business. Anything I can do – take you shooting this afternoon if you like, young feller.'

Simon gaped until prodded by Matty. 'Thank you, sir. Thank you very much.'

Lord Knelworth wandered away and Simon turned to his

sister. 'He's going to take me shooting! I don't know how! What am I supposed to do?'

'I don't know,' said Matty, wondering if she ought to ban shooting. It was bound to be dangerous.

'Oh, he'll show you all that,' said Griselda. 'He loves teaching boys to shoot.'

She showed Matty and Simon to their rooms, a connecting pair on a draughty landing. Simon went off to explore, leaving Matty and Griselda to unpack, and before they were half finished Henrietta charged through the door, followed more elegantly by Lorne.

'Darling Matty!' declared Henrietta, hugging her. 'Has it been terrible?'

She tried to smile. 'Everything's being sold,' she admitted. 'House, contents, everything. The solicitor thinks we may have ten thousand left when it's done.'

Lorne looked appalled. 'But that's nothing!'

'Better than nothing,' said Matty bravely. 'I shall invest it for Simon. I might be able to find an economical school.'

'We tried one of those for Charlie,' said Griselda, whose brother was now an officer cadet. 'They staffed the place with drunks and mental cases.'

'Oh dear.' Matty grimaced. 'Well, perhaps I'll send him somewhere good and hope to earn enough to keep him there later on.'

Lorne arranged herself elegantly on the bed. 'Which brings us to the point. We've all done a great deal of research on your behalf. I can't tell you how many charming men I've telephoned. Everyone's been so kind.'

Matty giggled. Men dissolved at the first hint of Lorne's lazy Southern drawl. 'Everybody recommends the same man, a Mr Chesworth. He's a silver dealer, and he's the man to train you. I've persuaded him to see you in London, and that was not easy. It's a strange business you're getting into, Matty.'

'I haven't agreed to get into anything.'

'It really is best,' burst in Henrietta. 'I've drawn up this schedule. I've been through every catalogue of every silver sale for the past six months, in London and New York. Would you believe it, the stuff is going up in price every

21

day! Honestly, you can't lose. You buy it, you sell it, and you treat yourself to lovely things with the profit. Wouldn't you like to do that, Matty? Wouldn't you like to study to do that?'

They all beamed at Matty, waiting for her approval. All at once she felt much older than her friends, like an adult about to pour cold water on some brilliant but impossible childish scheme. 'It's awfully kind of you all to go to such trouble,' she said carefully.

'It wasn't any trouble,' said Lorne.

Henrietta confided, 'I got a detention for going through silver catalogues in prep.'

Griselda, more perceptive than the others, said, 'You don't want to do it, do you, Matty?'

She sank on to the Jacobean chest under the window, automatically noting that the original lock had long since been broken off. 'It isn't that! I can't afford to do it. This Mr Chesworth won't pay me to train, and as for buying and selling silver — I haven't got a bean! Ten thousand pounds has got to keep me and Simon indefinitely. I've got to find something that pays really well. So it looks as if I'm going to have to be a call girl.' She stared defiantly at her friends.

Henrietta sat down beside her with a bump.

Lorne said, 'You know you always fall asleep at midnight. It would never work.'

'They'd all be smelly and fat,' said Henrietta with a shudder. 'Politicians, probably.'

'It hasn't got any long-term prospects,' said Griselda. 'And think of the drawbacks. Old men, unsocial hours, and nobody ever inviting you for a weekend without expecting you to cavort naked in the swimming pool — I mean to say, Matty, I can understand your reasoning, but it won't do.'

'I could give up when I was rich. Think of the champagne. Beautiful clothes. Men adoring me.'

'We'd only ever be able to see you at lunch,' said Henrietta, as if the thought were too terrible to bear.

Matty chuckled. 'I do love the moral rectitude of my friends. Don't you think it's wrong to sell myself to the highest bidder? To lie on perfumed sheets and let some gorgeous man sate himself with my virgin body?'

22

'It wouldn't be virgin long,' interposed Lorne practically. 'And, as Henry says, the gorgeous ones would be thin on the ground. If you want to sell yourself, do it once and marry an oil well or a shipping line or something. You can clean him out when you divorce.'

Griselda fixed Lorne with a look of amazement. 'You really are an incorrigible romantic, Lorne,' she murmured.

Lorne flushed. She and Griselda got on least well of all the girls. Lately they had taken to the occasional scratchy exchange. 'I'm only being practical. If you're selling yourself you should put a decent price on the goods.'

'I'd much rather she went into trade with inanimate objects,' said Griselda. 'You haven't met Mr Chesworth, Matty. He may be charming. He may pay you zillions.'

Lorne let out a yelp, but it was strangled at birth by Griselda's iron gaze.

Matty sighed. 'I suppose you're right. Anyway, wouldn't it be dreadful to be a call girl who never gets called? I might be the least successful one ever. We haven't had any training for sex. They ought to run courses.'

'I think it sort of — comes naturally,' said Lorne. She smiled to herself, one of her lazy, inscrutable smiles. Sometimes she seemed almost catlike.

'Are you going to tell?' demanded Henrietta. 'I think it's very mean of you not to say.'

'It's a secret,' said Lorne, but she blushed slightly. 'I don't want to talk about it. I don't want people to know.'

'You've told us the important bit,' said Griselda. 'Who was he?'

'There isn't any "was" about it,' flared Lorne. 'He's always been around, I've known him forever. His name's Greg. Greg Nelson Berenson.'

'Nelson, eh? Has he got one of everything?' asked Matty wickedly.

'I knew you'd be horrible,' shrieked Lorne, and smothered her face in a pillow.

The others looked stricken. 'We're sorry,' said Matty softly. 'We won't make fun. Is he nice, Lorne? Is he young? Does he ride horses?'

'Yes.' Lorne looked up, tearfully. 'He's the son of our

next-door neighbour. They've got the property that borders ours, by Little Creek. I've loved him forever, right from when I was tiny. He's tall, and blond, and all the girls want him. But he wants me. Can you believe it?'

'Yes,' said Griselda bleakly. From the vantage point of her own stringy, beaky-nosed, mousy-haired self, Lorne was supremely beautiful. Her creamy skin had the texture of a peach, speckled with dew. Her eyes were heavy-lidded and lustrous, looking out at the world with lazy sensuality. Of all four girls, she was easily the loveliest.

'Have you — you know?' asked Matty urgently.

Lorne flushed dark red. 'Yes!'

'What was it like?' demanded Henrietta. 'Oh, Lorne, you never told us! Why didn't you tell us?'

Lorne said, 'It was private. Special.'

The girls were silent. Was this going to happen to all of them? Sooner or later there would be men, and suddenly their friendship would be secondary, lost to that other world. Each would experience it separately, and they wouldn't tell. They would be seduced, not just in body, but in mind.

Suddenly Lorne giggled. 'It was so big!' she chortled. 'I couldn't believe it. You don't think it's going to be that big.'

'Did it hurt?' squeaked Henrietta, screwing up her face. 'I can't imagine anything more horrible.'

'It hurt the first time,' confessed Lorne. 'Not after that. Anyway I was worried the first time, we were in a bedroom at a party and I kept expecting someone to walk in. We did it in his barn after that. I got all scratched with the straw.'

'What was it like?' asked Matty, almost wistfully. 'Was it very exciting?'

Lorne looked away. 'Yes,' she said shyly. 'It's strange. When you're getting undressed and everything you can't imagine what he's going to do, it's just impossible. Then when he — you know — it's right. It seems the best thing to be doing. At the start I tried to keep quiet and things, I thought he wouldn't want me to holler, and then I couldn't help it. I behaved like an animal. But I think that's how it's supposed to be. Greg didn't mind. He liked it. He said we'd be two wild animals together. He kissed me — everywhere.' Her long, slender hands fluttered across breasts and crotch. Even the remembered excitement seemed to touch her with light, her lips and eyes glistening with the memory.

Griselda said, 'He seems to have made the most of his opportunities.'

'I wish someone would kiss me,' moaned Henrietta. 'But not there, if you don't mind. I bet nobody ever kissed my mother there.'

'Are you sure I can't be a call girl?' murmured Matty.

Somewhere in the distant reaches of the house, a gong sounded.

'Luncheon,' said Griselda. 'I'll persuade Father to open some wine, as a treat.'

The meal was patchy, with watery soup followed by excellent salmon and then bread and butter pudding made with cream. Matty was suddenly sparkling, entertaining Lord Knelworth with ease. He said, 'Good idea, that of Grizzle's, the silver thing.'

'I thought it was my idea,' murmured Lorne, but her host failed to hear.

'That sort of thing's always useful for a girl,' he went on. 'Everyone's got silver to sell now and then. It's nice if a pretty young girl can give them an idea about it. The professionals are a shifty lot. Ask them in to value a bookcase, they try and buy a dozen paintings and half the furniture.'

'We have to buy new furniture a lot,' said Lorne. 'It's the parties. My cousins ride horses up the stairs.'

'They used to do that sort of thing in India, I believe,' mused Lord Knelworth. 'Perhaps that's why they built bungalows.'

'Do you have low stairs or very fit horses?' enquired Griselda.

Lorne chuckled. 'Neither. Just very drunk cousins.'

Lord Knelworth climbed reluctantly to his feet. 'Come on, young feller,' he said to Simon. 'Let's leave the girls to their party. We've got to see about finding you a decent gun. Single barrel at your age, I think.'

Simon scrambled up, pink with embarrassment. 'Do be

careful,' said Matty anxiously, and he gave her a withering look.

When they had gone, Griselda said, 'You're getting to be a terrible mother hen, Matty.'

Defensively Matty said, 'He needs someone to worry. People ought to have other people to worry about them.'

'And you've got us,' said Henrietta happily. 'We've all got us. I think that nothing terrible can happen ever as long as we all still care.'

The four looked around at each other. At that moment they felt very close, as if no barriers, no misunderstandings, could ever stand between them.

'This is no time to lie around getting drunk,' said Griselda crisply. 'We've got to decide about Matty.'

'You know, Grizz, I can see you as a Miss Saunders type in later life,' said Matty naughtily. 'Ordering dishevelled young girls to smarten up.'

'There's nothing wrong with being organised,' said Griselda. 'Now, have a look at that candlestick. Henrietta, grab that jug off the side table, and Lorne, scrabble around in the drawer and see if you can find some of those wine label things. Dreadfully pretentious, I always think, but they're very old. Just shows, pretension isn't the prerogative of the twentieth century, or even the smug Victorians. Were there pretentious Romans, do you suppose?'

'I imagine they gilded their chariots,' said Matty dispassionately. 'You are raving, Griselda. At this rate you'll be dotty by twenty-five.'

'Oh, earlier,' said Lorne, flourishing three silver wine labels. One said 'Cavice', one 'Whiskey' and one 'Madeira'. 'These are very pretty. You should use them.'

Matty took them from her and studied them. They were indeed pretty, elegantly scrolled with leaf and berry decoration. The Madeira label had a panther's head above the word. She turned them over to look at the marks, but they were very small. She could just make out the lion, sideways on, his head turned and his paw raised as if he were waving. It was the sterling mark, the centuries-old guarantee of high quality silver. Matty put the labels on the table cloth.

'I really don't know anything about these things. They're silver. They might be very valuable.'

'Oh, probably,' said Griselda airily. 'Wouldn't you like to learn about things like that? Wouldn't you like to understand them?'

'Quite possibly,' said Matty, nearing exasperation. 'Girls, I can't see any way in which it can help me make a living!'

'Look at this jug,' coaxed Henrietta. 'Don't you think that's nice?'

Matty grimaced. The piece was extremely strange, an odd shape covered in lumpy silver foliage. 'It looks as if it's had a bad accident,' she complained.

'Perhaps it has,' said Griselda. 'We've had it forever. The candlestick's a bit better, isn't it?'

Matty picked it up. The remains of old wax fell out of the top. The metal felt oily, not entirely cold. But it was a very ordinary candlestick, unadorned and heavy. 'This is nice,' she said emphatically. 'You should have it valued.'

'Now.' Griselda leaned her chin on her hands. 'What would you say if we asked you to sell this for us?'

'I'd say no,' retorted Matty. 'Honestly, you're not that hard up. And I don't want charity.'

'It might not be charity. We might sell it, if we knew what it was worth. The Lemming-Knotts have flogged the silver in times of need for centuries past. We buy it back when we're flourishing. We never get rid of everything, just the odd bits. We've only got one of those candlesticks, nothing else will match.'

Matty felt beleaguered. 'I can't start dealing when I don't know a thing about the subject,' she said crossly. 'And I certainly can't waltz off to London. Who would look after Simon?'

'We would,' said the girls in chorus.

'And he can come to us in turns in the holidays,' said Henrietta breathlessly. 'We've thought it all out. He can go to Griselda first, then me, and then Lorne. He'll love it.'

Matty blinked at her. 'Lorne lives in America.'

'He'll have to come for the whole summer,' said Lorne. 'It'll be great! And as for the ticket, if we both travel tourist

27

it should cost the same as one first-class seat. Remember, you're going to owe me a lot of champagne.'

Matty tried another tack. 'But Henry's mother won't have him. You know she won't.'

'I've asked her,' said Henrietta defiantly. 'She says Simon can come. I'm afraid she does think — well — that he's rather young. About five, actually.'

'She'll try and put him in a cot!' Matty was appalled. She got up from the table. 'It's just the most stupid idea.'

'It would be fun,' said Griselda.

'You'll get to travel,' said Lorne.

'And I'm sure you'd make pots and pots of money,' said Henrietta.

Matty put her hands up to the sides of her head. 'All right, all right, all right! I'll go down and see this man in London. Will that do?'

'And take the silver,' said Griselda. 'It will give you something to talk about.'

Chapter Three

Matty stepped off the London train feeling nervous. She carried not only the silver but the burden of her friends' expectations, and they were much heavier. It was up to her to sample life, to drink from the forbidden cup and report back with her experiences. Still trapped in the almost convent existence of school, hemmed in by parents, exams and conventions, the girls were sending Matty out as a scout, to discover if life was as they hoped. She must bring back a sign, some evidence of adventure, like the dove with the olive twig, telling Noah of land.

Whenever she had been in London before she had been in Henrietta's care and they always travelled by taxi. Today, husbanding her money, she went by tube, and became lost in the maze of tunnels and signs. Buskers sang in the wells of escalators, and the walls resonated with wailing renderings of 'Blowing in the Wind' or 'It's Been a Hard Day's Night'. Buskers always sang old hits, she thought, the old faithfuls. A girl, no more than fourteen, with a child hanging on her skirt, held her hand out for money. Struck by terrible fellow feeling, Matty gave her two pounds, more than she could afford.

At last she came out into light and air at Chancery Lane. A man selling newspapers distractedly grunted directions from the corner of his mouth and she said 'Thank you — yes' although she barely understood him. She set off across the road, and the man yelled at her. She blushed but followed his pointing arm, turning left, fighting her way into a paved courtyard against a tide of formless humanity.

The entrance to the silver vaults was poorly advertised. Only a couple of swing signs marked the London Safe

Deposit Company and Silver Vaults. They were indeed vaults, Matty realised, with access down a single wide staircase. The doors, at present standing wide, were of grey metal almost a foot thick, as if this were a warship in danger of flood. No one took any notice of her. In fact there were few people around. She followed signs into a wide corridor, on either side of which were more of the metal doors, each leading to rooms she could only glimpse, but which were clearly crammed with silver. She felt nervous and unsure of herself, stepping into a world so unfamiliar. Although these seemed to be shops there were no shoppers, just herself and a few young men, scurrying purposefully here and there.

She peered into a shop that she thought was unoccupied. A plump woman, almost hidden behind a cabinet, said, 'Can I help you?' and Matty jumped.

'I was just looking,' she said hastily, and the woman smiled and went back to writing her notes. Most of the people that came here were tourists, there weren't many that truly came to buy. This was a huge dealing cellar.

But the silver dazzled Matty. It gave an odd air of newness to the place. Everything shone, as if it had been made yesterday, there was none of the tat that so characterised other sections of the antique trade. She wondered if she simply did not know what tat in silver meant, and acknowledged that was probably the case. To her, everything looked wonderful.

She left the shop and stepped into another, and after that another. It was hard to believe there was so much silver in the world as was gathered here, in this vast underground storeroom. She felt bewildered by the profusion. In any one shop there might be a polished table displaying cutlery, cabinets filled with jugs and decanters, hundreds of mugs, teapots, coffee pots — everything the ingenuity of man had ever considered making in a beautiful metal. Finally Matty stopped. A glass table was home to wine labels. Hundreds were laid out beneath the glass, and more were clustered in the cabinets around the walls. A small man with neat hands was leafing through a catalogue.

'I was looking for Mr Chesworth.'

The man's head jerked up. 'Sammy? He's not down here. By the entrance, there's a bell.'

'Oh.'

The man went back to his catalogue. Matty turned to go, but on impulse she said suddenly, reaching into her plastic bag, 'I wonder if you can tell me something about these? I was going to show them to Mr Chesworth.'

The wine labels lay on the counter between them. 'I don't know anything about silver,' said Matty ingenuously.

'No. Not many people do.'

He was small and balding. As he turned the labels in his hands Matty felt her hackles rise. She had to curb the urge to snatch the pieces back, and keep them safe in her bag. He looked up with a blank, unyielding stare. 'Give you ten pounds each. The stuff's good enough. I won't make much on it.'

'Thank you.' Matty scooped the three labels deftly away. 'I'll see what Mr Chesworth offers. I may come back.'

'Make it twenty for the whiskey one. It's a nice piece.'

'Is it? I'll see Mr Chesworth.'

She walked away, feeling him watching her. If that man wasn't trying to swindle her then she wasn't her father's daughter. She had known the minute he touched the labels, deliberately controlling his sudden shake of excitement. Not for nothing had she sat night after night listening to her father and his friends talking about deals: the good picture behind the nineteenth-century copy; the brooch hidden at the back of the desk. But her father hadn't been crooked. He hadn't robbed people, not really.

Mr Chesworth's office was approached via a security lock. She stood on the worn step, pressing a buzzer. Eventually, after many clicks, she pushed her way into the hall to be confronted at once by a steep stair. She climbed up, noting the utilitarian carpet and blank cream walls. If the girls could see this, she thought. Where was the glamour now, in this workaday office inches from the roaring traffic of London?

A substantial lady was seated behind a desk. At her side on the floor was a vast silver pot, big enough to bath a baby. On her desk were three teapots, and a side table held a forest of silver spoons on a green baize cloth. The lady was typing

31

a letter on a machine that would not have been out of place in a museum. She smiled at Matty.

'Miss Winterton? I'm Emily. Mr Chesworth is expecting you.'

'Thank you.'

Feeling a little flustered, Matty pushed the only other door in the room. Polished mahogany she noticed. And up here the thin carpet had given way to thick green pile, like a wonderful lawn. Things were improving, Matty decided, sniffing the rich scent of pipe tobacco.

She entered a room lined with shelves, most of them crammed with books. The desk was huge, with one or two pieces of silver stacked on the corners, simply parked there with no intent to display. The man who sat behind the desk was small, greying, with a pipe clenched between his teeth, although he was at the same time muttering down a telephone and making notes on an auction catalogue. He hunched his shoulder to jam the telephone receiver against his ear and gestured to Matty to sit down. The only chair was of worn leather, low and comfortable. Matty wished she could stand. The chair left her at a disadvantage.

Mr Chesworth fixed her with a sharp eye, muttering, 'Talking to New York. Sell a lot of good silver there. Buy a lot too. All right, Ed, all right! I'll come over. Goodbye.'

He slammed down the telephone, grumbling to himself. Then he looked beadily at Matty. 'Are you the young woman that's been pestering me?'

'No. That's my friend Lorne. She thinks I should learn about silver.'

'And become one of those nuisances at country house sales, no doubt, deluding your rich friends about their pieces. I told that girl a dozen times, I don't want you.'

Matty said, 'Oh. Oh, I see.'

They stared at each other for a moment. She felt an unreasonable urge to cry, and instead burst out, 'I don't mind, actually. I mean, I don't really want you either. My friends thought I should work in silver, that's all. They have the romantic idea that I'll make my fortune. They don't know anything about business.'

'And you do, I suppose?'

Matty flushed. 'I know a bit. I know you don't make your fortune just because you buy and sell expensive things. It's the turn that counts.'

'So it is. So it is.'

Some of his grumpiness seemed to have gone. Matty said bravely, 'Would you mind if I showed you some wine labels? I spoke to a man in one of the shops a moment ago and I'm quite sure he was trying to rook me. He offered ten pounds for these two and twenty for the whiskey one, but I think it's worth a lot more than that. I'm sure the dealer thought it was special.'

Sammy Chesworth picked up the label. He smiled for the first time, a brief flicker of pleasure. 'Oh, yes,' he said. 'Yes, indeed.' He held it in his hand, feeling the weight; he rubbed his fingers gently over the contours of leaves and panther's head. Finally he turned it over, his free hand reaching for his eyeglass with a movement born of long practice. Finally he looked up. 'Paul Storr. It bears his mark. A very fine piece from one of our finest silversmiths. Worked for many years with Rundell, Bridge and Rundell, a fascinating alliance. And if there's more where this came from, you're a very lucky girl.'

'It isn't mine. But I thought that man was a cheat.'

'It's easy to cheat the ignorant. Some people deserve it, pretending to know what they don't, but little girls shouldn't have their good silver taken away for nothing.'

'You needn't worry about me,' said Matty, getting to her feet. 'I can spot his sort a mile off. I'll ask my friend if she wants to sell the label. Oh, I've a candlestick here as well. And a nasty jug.'

At the sight of the jug Chesworth made a face. 'Young lady, this is a false piece. It is also illegal. See the rim? It used to be a tankard. The lip was let in later, and badly let in, you can see solder everywhere. All this chasing is Victorian addition, of course. Very common, sadly.'

'What do you mean, it's illegal?'

He looked at her over his spectacles. 'I mean that, technically, to buy or sell this piece is to commit an offence. Dealers do, of course, but they shouldn't. Apart from anything else it weakens the trade.'

'But why isn't it allowed? I don't understand.'

He almost glared at her. 'That does not surprise me. Young woman, the assay laws of this country forbid alteration of a piece, involving the addition or removal of silver, without that piece being touched at the silver hall. That is, having it stamped as of proper standard. Look at this jug.' He turned it round, exposing the rim. 'There is the sterling mark, and you can see from this letter next to it the date on which the piece was stamped. 1720 as it happens. The leopard's head shows that it was touched in London, but the maker's mark is that of a man who worked in Kent. This was a decent piece once, belonging to some country squire no doubt. I imagine there was a lid, but it broke off or was melted down at some time. A lot of silver got sold for melting, tons of it during the Civil War. That's why we have so little remaining from before that date.

'Because silver is all about money, you can never lose the intrinsic value of the stuff. It isn't like pot, or wood, or marble. Silver is first of all money, and only then a work of art. And the standard has to be upheld, as it has been for centuries, since the middle ages. Silversmiths made the laws and they've stood by them, because it was in their interest to do so. Not something to let go lightly.'

Matty blinked at him. He seemed unduly agitated it seemed to her. He tossed the jug aside and picked up the candlestick. Matty said, 'Actually, that is rather nice. Griselda only has one though, which is a pity.'

'Why?' Again that beady gaze.

'Because two would bring a better price, I suppose. But even if she wasn't selling, one looks a bit sad on its own. And this stick is so deliciously unfussy.'

Chesworth put down the candlestick. He picked up his pipe instead and waved it at Matty. 'Sit down, girl, sit down. What's all this about?'

'I'm sorry?'

'I may be old but I'm not senile! You know far more than you pretend. You arrive with a Paul Storr wine label and a Queen Anne candlestick of Britannia standard and expect me to believe you're a beginner? Where could you find such things, eh?'

'At Peregrines,' said Matty simply. 'Do you know it? My friend is Griselda Lemming-Knott. Honestly, I don't know anything about silver but the things you've told me today. I know what I like, though.'

'Indeed. You seem to like everything that you should.'

His mouth seemed grim suddenly. Matty put out her hand for the jug and the candlestick. 'I'd better be off,' she said. 'You don't want to train me and actually I can't spare the time to be trained. I've got my brother to support. So it was a silly idea, really. My friends just thought a career in silver would suit me.'

'Perhaps they know you better than you know yourself.'

She paused, looking at him with enquiry. 'I'll give you fifty pounds a week for the first year,' he said gruffly. 'Plus commission on personal sales. You're not worth a penny more while you're learning. You will live with my wife and myself. If we're still together at the end of a year then we'll talk again, but I warn you, I won't stand for lateness, stupidity, sloppy dressing, romance, eating garlic, rubbing hallmarks, or dishonesty in any shape or form. Do I make myself clear?'

'I'm not sure.' Matty felt a little breathless. 'Do I get time off?'

'Naturally. I'm not an ogre. You will be free every evening after supper. If you're at a loss for amusement I will lend you some books. And you can read this one while you get yourself organised. I'll expect you here on Monday.'

She took the book, heavily bound in worn leather. The title was *Britain's Gold and Silversmiths*. 'Thank you,' she muttered.

As she stepped from the taxi at Peregrines the girls descended on her.

'Well?'

'I've got a job,' said Matty, still somewhat bemused. 'He's giving me fifty a week. But I have to stay with him and his wife and he's the oddest man. Says I mustn't eat garlic.'

'We must allow the rich their idiosyncrasies,' said Lorne.

'I don't think he is all that rich. He might be though. Silver everywhere, tons of the stuff. He's short and smokes a pipe and he said he was on the 'phone to New York, but I didn't believe him.'

Griselda said, 'You don't suppose he's a conman, do you?'

Matty shook her head. 'I just wonder if he isn't a bit mad. He's given me a book to read, and it's going to take me months.'

'It doesn't sound at all exciting,' said Henrietta, visibly crestfallen. 'Weren't there any Arabs in the place?'

'Not one,' said Matty. 'But I walked down Bond Street and there were hundreds there. And loads of silver in the shops. I wondered if I ought to go in and ask for a job there, but I didn't have the courage.'

'You'll do much better with Mr Chesworth,' said Lorne. 'Trust me, Matty!'

They dined that night to the accompaniment of Simon talking guns with Lord Knelworth. 'Did you think I was getting better, sir? I was hitting the clays right in the middle. I hope I don't have to wear an eye patch like you said. I mean, I'd look stupid.'

'You haven't hurt your eye, have you, Simon?' asked Matty fearfully.

'We had some trouble deciding on his lead eye, that's all,' said Lord Knelworth.

'Starting at my age, I could be an Olympic shot, couldn't I, sir?'

'Of course you could, Simon. There's no reason at all why not.'

He was a very kind man. As her own father had been — kind. Matty ducked her head suddenly. There was no point in endowing her father with qualities he had never possessed. Kindness he had in full measure, but he hadn't spent enough time with his son. Work had interfered, and his own restless nature. Not for him long hours tramping the park with a garrulous ten year old; he would have gone indoors for a whisky and soda within the first five minutes. He hadn't listened when Simon talked either, he had a telltale glazed expression, and would interrupt in the middle of some story to say, 'Did you see the cabinet, Matty? Got it for a song.'

Her brother's mind was working along the same lines, it

seemed. That night, when she went to tuck Simon up, he said, 'I wonder if Dad would have liked me more when I grew up?'

'He liked you pretty much anyway,' said Matty. She smoothed Simon's rich brown hair.

'Not as much as you. He thought I was a pain. Lord Knelworth doesn't care how much time I spend with him. He even took me to see one of his tenants yesterday, and I said he needn't. I listened to all the business talk and everything.'

'I expect he misses his own boys. They're all grown up now.'

'If Dad wanted me grown up he should have waited. Now he'll never know if I was a decent sort or not.'

As she rose to leave Simon caught her hand. 'You're not to worry about me, Matty,' he said. 'I mean, it must be a drag having to think about paying for me and things.'

'It isn't a drag at all,' she replied. 'I'd hate it if I was on my own. You wait, in no time at all we'll have a new house and lots of money and nothing to worry about.'

'Yes. In no time at all.'

He grinned at her over the top of the sheet. She felt choked suddenly with love and responsibility. He must never know how he dragged at her heels, forcing her to abandon university in favour of a lowly job and reliance on her friends' goodwill. If the girls had failed her she didn't know what she would have done.

She went to join murmuring voices in the library. The girls were kneeling on the worn rug, telling fortunes by the flickering light of the log fire. 'Oh, Matty,' said Henrietta, looking up. 'We've been reading Tarot cards. I'm going to have dozens of children.'

'More than three, anyway,' said Lorne. 'Griselda's cards won't come out. They're different every time.'

'What about you?' Matty sat down, crossing her legs easily.

'Lorne won't, she doesn't want to know,' said Henrietta. 'Let's try you, Matty.'

Matty placed the strange cards in front of her, face up, one after the other. She didn't understand them, but Lorne clucked in surprise. 'This is for power — and this is for love — and this is for money! You will be strong and rich, with a wonderful lover.'

'But will I be happy?' asked Matty.

In the firelight Lorne's face seemed to lose flesh. Her eyes glittered and her lips seemed touched with a dark glow. The hollows of her cheeks were infinite. 'Will any of us be happy?' she breathed softly. 'Surely you can have happiness if you choose. Do any of us choose? Or are there things we will always want more?'

'There can't be anything we would want more,' said Henrietta.

'Money. Excitement. Power. Revenge.' Griselda almost whispered. 'That's what you mean, isn't it, Lorne?'

Her black hair swung. 'Oh, yes. Life isn't only about mornings. It's about night, and dark desires.'

Suddenly the light switched on. 'What are you all doing, sitting here in the dark?' said Lord Knelworth.

They blinked, like owls in the sun.

Matty bumped her suitcase up the stairs of Sammy Chesworth's office with a feeling close to gloom. There seemed so little to excite her about the bare walls and dull paintwork, and the mundane reality of Emily in the outer office. She was making tea and said brightly to Matty, 'Do you take sugar, dear? Best to find out straight away, isn't it? Mr Chesworth isn't in today. He said you were to start cleaning.'

Matty's heart sank still further. 'Cleaning?'

'The silver, dear, yes. He's very strict about it. No rubbing the marks, and watch for good chasing — that blurs very easily, especially bright-cut. Warm water and soft cloths, that's what Mr Chesworth likes. Take your tea now, will you?'

Matty took her cup and followed Emily through to the main office. Silver was piled all over the desk: candlesticks, teapots, chafing dishes and jugs. Forks and spoons littered the side table, and a pile of knives, the blades pitted and rusting, lay discarded on the floor.

'We'll be getting new blades put in those,' said Emily.

'Never last, knives. Do you see that sugar caster? It's Lamerie.'

'What?' Matty looked enquiring.

'Made by Paul de Lamerie. Perhaps the greatest silversmith of all time. 1722 that piece, I think. Not his most rococo period, but lovely all the same. George I, of course. Queen Anne popped off in 1714. I do like a good piece of Lamerie.'

Matty took up the caster and inspected it. There was a heaviness to it, a depth of sheen that was very pleasing. 'You'll notice it's slightly dented,' said Emily. 'Mr Chesworth may decide to have that knocked out. But, of course, that would ruin the patina. For myself, I'd get rid of the dent − another two hundred years will put the patina back after all. Dents don't get better with time.' She moved to a door hidden in part of the panelling. Behind it was a small room with a sink and a table. 'Get going, dear,' said Emily brightly. 'You can have most of this done by lunchtime.'

By evening Matty's hands were red and sore. She resolved to buy herself a pair of rubber gloves, whenever time permitted. There might well be no time. Emily allowed her twenty minutes for lunch and no more. She was a skivvy, rubbing up teaspoons and polishing pots, with Emily constantly droning on at her. And what would be her fate when, presumably, she graduated from this task? She didn't know where Mr Chesworth was, or what he was doing. For that matter, she didn't know where she was supposed to spend the night.

'End of a good day's work,' said Emily finally. She covered her typewriter, put on her hat and gathered up the post.

'I think I'm supposed to stay at Mr Chesworth's,' said Matty.

'Oh.' Emily looked surprised. 'He didn't say anything to me.'

'I don't know where he lives.'

'No? He's got a house in Holland Park. You can get the tube.' She gave Matty some perfunctory directions.

Out in the streets London was emptying, like a great

pitcher suddenly full of holes. Tiredness hung in the air, and Matty drank it down, her suitcase banging against her legs. She and Emily parted at the post box. 'See you tomorrow then, dear.' Matty joined the hordes making their blind, inhuman progress down to the tube.

Disgorged into the leafy avenues of Holland Park, Matty wondered if Emily had given her the wrong address. Elegance abounded, from the matching bay trees beside flights of Georgian steps, to the well-lit drawing rooms full of excellent furniture. She spotted a card table in a window, the sort of piece her father could never afford. Even the plant set down upon it grew in expensive and elegant form. Every house sported an elaborate and obvious burglar alarm.

She stopped, finally, before a dark blue polished front door. It was a town house, large, stately and quietly imposing. She knew at once that Mr Chesworth could not possibly live here, that she would knock, be sent away, and spend her night under the arches until in the morning she could slink to the office and confess her stupid mistake. Was there perhaps a bedsit she could find? A cheap hotel? She only had fifty pounds, mostly Henrietta's. She had lied to her mother about needing a new school skirt. Reluctantly, already blushing, Matty ascended the steps and knocked.

'Ah! You must be Matty.' The lady who greeted her was tall, with ash-blonde streaks in her greying hair. 'I'm Delia Chesworth. I wanted to send the car for you but Sammy said you were very capable, and wouldn't have any trouble finding us. I hope you're not too tired. We've some people dining tonight.'

'I can always eat in my room —'

'Goodness me, child, you're included. Now, have you a nice dress to wear? Sammy said you were just out of school, and wouldn't have anything but neat skirts and jumpers. But you could have a dozen ballgowns for all we know, couldn't you?'

'I haven't brought much,' said Matty breathlessly.

'Dear me, it won't do Sammy any good to be proved right! I'll find you something from Patricia's clothes. That's our daughter. She died, you know. Cancer.'

Matty fumbled for something to say but Mrs Chesworth was leading the way upstairs, and Matty followed her in a daze. Her feet sank into deep ruby carpeting. Portraits covered the wall, eighteenth century she guessed. They were dark and somewhat lowering.

'Sammy collects these,' said Delia, waving an explanatory hand. 'He likes to pretend they're ancestors. Heaven knows where the real portraits are, somewhere in Europe. The war, you know. Most of the family went to Buchenwald.'

She made it sound like a holiday camp. Matty studied her from behind, noting slender legs topped with generous hips. The woman turned and beamed at Matty, a friendly, open smile. Matty smiled shyly back.

'Do you want to wash or anything? Dear me, look at your hands! Sammy's had you cleaning that dreadful silver. Come into Patricia's room, I'll find you some hand cream. And a dress, you must have a dress.'

She bustled Matty into a room. It was pink and white, full of airy, gilded furniture. A French four-poster bed dominated the centre, and everywhere stood photographs and cards. They were get well cards, Matty noticed.

With the utmost diffidence, she said, 'Did your daughter die recently?'

Delia smiled at her. 'No. Ten years ago, now, when she was twenty. But I keep it like this. I like to remember her, I don't want to rub her away.'

Matty caught her breath. Yet Delia seemed so wholesome, so normal, and when she opened the wardrobes and took out old-fashioned dresses, Matty felt no repugnance. She said, 'Isn't it strange? You don't realise how fashion changes.'

'Do you think it has?' Delia looked anxious. 'If you don't want to wear them I shall quite understand.'

'I don't mind. Really. It's very kind of you.'

They were beautiful clothes. A white linen trouser suit had stood the test of time, and an embroidered cocktail dress in blue shantung silk.

Matty fingered the dress. 'Would this be right, do you think? It might not fit.'

'Patricia wasn't as tall as you. But we can try, can't we?'

Matty nodded.

She put the dress on in the privacy of her own room. Should she have refused to wear it? she wondered. It would have seemed so rude, in the face of Delia's smiling welcome, yet it seemed even odder to be wearing someone else's clothes. She looked at herself in the long mirror on the wardrobe door. Her room was furnished with oak, more suitable for a man than a girl, and she had a bathroom with brass taps like ship's capstans. It was a very serious room, with a large and imposing desk. On the top, clearly displayed, were three items of silver.

A bell sounded to summon her to dinner. She went slowly down the stairs, feeling strange in the borrowed dress, its skirt inches above her knees. Everything about the house was strange. Why did Sammy Chesworth have such an ordinary office when he lived here, in luxury? The only mark of Sammy's trade was the silver on the desk in her room. He might have been a wealthy industrialist, a stockbroker, anything.

'Oh, it does fit!' Delia caught her shoulder in a brief hug. Beyond her stood Sammy, small and nondescript in a dark suit, and a middle-aged couple. 'What do you think, Sammy?' Delia pushed her forward.

He grunted. 'Very nice. Harry, Janet, this is my new assistant. I don't remember her name – Matilda or something.'

'Matty,' she said.

'Ah, yes. Matty.'

She knew he would never remember.

They sat down and drank sherry, served by a Filipino maid in a frilly white apron. Matty was embarrassingly aware of her legs, protruding endlessly from the hem of the dress. Harry was staring at them.

'Where do you come from, Matty?' asked Janet. 'Are your parents alive?'

Sammy said, 'Questions, questions! Where does anyone come from? Her father was in antiques, she's an orphan. A waif, a stray, the sort of girl anyone would take from the street. I took pity on her. She can clean my silver and be grateful.' Everyone laughed.

42

'She's a great deal too pretty to be left out on any street,' said Harry.

Matty mentally cursed Lorne. She had told Sammy everything. Was that why he had spoken about honesty? Did he think that she too would be persuadable, open to a few quid on the side, a bit of pressure? She watched him with hot eyes, and suddenly he was looking at her, an old, understanding gaze. He glanced at her raw hands, and smiled to himself.

The chatter went on without her. They began dinner, and suddenly, over the soup, Sammy said: 'Right, girl. The piece on the left of the desk in your room. What is it?'

Matty swallowed convulsively. She'd stared at the thing for minutes wondering what it was for. It was like a very large napkin ring, with pretty beaded edges and the outer surface heavily patterned with dogs and hares. 'It's a potato ring,' she said in a strangled voice. 'You put a hot dish on top to stop it marking the table. It's got nothing to do with potatoes, except that it comes from Ireland.'

'That isn't Irish, it's American,' snapped Sammy. 'You can tell by the workmanship, it's slightly finer. Same extravagance, better quality. And the marks would have told the tale.'

'I don't look at the marks,' said Matty.

Harry let out a yelp of laughter. 'She's a silver dealer and she doesn't look at the marks!'

'She'll never be a good one if she does,' said Sammy with emphasis. 'Marks can be faked, it's the piece that tells the story. Later, she'll confirm her thoughts by the marks.'

'It seems too easy, just looking up the marks,' said Matty breathlessly. 'Like going by the catalogue at an auction, and not looking at the pieces at all.'

Sammy yawned. 'It's what most of us do. We're all fools, we silver dealers. We need life simple.'

'Rogues, the lot of you,' said Harry cheerfully. 'You could tell people like me anything and we'd believe you.'

Sammy looked at him with veiled contempt. 'It is never wise to buy out of total ignorance,' he said thinly. 'A little study never goes amiss.'

Over the beef, a veritable baron, when Matty was

43

struggling with a plate heaped high at Delia's insistence, Sammy said, 'And the piece in the centre, Matty? No problem there, I trust?'

She had a mouthful of beef. She swallowed it down, and it settled like a rock under her breastbone. 'Adam-style cup,' she muttered. 'Horrible twiddly little handles.'

'Date?' demanded her inquisitor.

'Late eighteenth century, round about the French Revolution. Adam style gone off.'

Sammy grunted in satisfaction. Janet said, 'You're giving the poor girl indigestion, Sammy.'

'She must have some more wine,' said Delia, and fussed over Matty's glass.

'Got yourself a star, Sammy,' said Harry, and winked in Matty's direction. 'How many more pieces are there on this desk?'

'Only one other,' said Matty.

'And what about that one other?' Chesworth's beady eyes bored into her with almost leprechaun intensity.

Matty laughed. 'Silver plate,' she said lightly. 'But a nice pot for all that.'

'Did you look at the marks?'

She shook her head. 'I didn't need to, it's worn through near the lid. Too much polishing.'

Her party-turn completed, Matty was allowed to eat in peace. But her appetite had vanished. She wondered what would have happened if she had left looking at the silver until later. He might have thrown her out, then and there. He was such an odd man.

She went to bed as soon as the meal was over. No one tried to detain her, presumably because they would discuss her when she was gone. She felt like a zoo animal, kept for the amusement of others. Vague feelings of resentment vied with disorientation. This morning she had left Peregrines, tonight she was amongst strangers in a strange life.

The telephone in her room buzzed once. She picked it up. 'Hello?'

Sammy's voice barked at her. 'In the morning, you put on the schoolgirl skirt and jumper. We are going to

Pickering's, the auctioneers. I wish to hear not one word
from you during the whole of our stay, no talking at all until
we are back in my office. Understand?'

'Yes, Mr Chesworth.'

He hung up.

Chapter Four

They took a taxi to the saleroom, and on the way Sammy tossed a catalogue at Matty. 'I want the Charles I apostle spoons, I can sell those anywhere. Also the silver and glass dressing case — it's Austrian. I don't normally touch Continental silver, but this is very fine. I've a client will buy this in an instant.'

'Do you often buy for clients?' asked Matty.

He glanced at her. 'I buy for anyone who'll pay. I've got a reputation. When it's passed through my hands they know it's a good piece. Sometimes if I'm bidding the other dealers follow just because it's me. They think I must be on to a good thing. So, when you've learned a bit, you'll bid for me.'

'Me?' Matty was aghast.

'Yes, you, miss. We'll get you out of your schoolgirl rig and make you work. For today, you keep quiet.'

So strictly did Matty adhere to this instruction that she didn't even apologise when she bumped into someone. The silver had been on display for some days previously, and now was to be sold in a small, intimate room with dark green walls. A horseshoe table ate into a third of the room's space, and around it sat the major dealers. The silver was displayed within the horseshoe, one lot at a time, under the unwavering scrutiny of experts. Sammy took his seat at the table with a brief nod to acquaintances. No one challenged his right to sit there, although others, whether through nerve or ignorance, were discreetly asked to move elsewhere in the room. Matty found herself a seat three rows from the front, perched on a hard chair.

Two women sat next to her. 'If I don't get the dressing case I shall die!' said one to the other. 'All the dealers are after it.'

'You can afford to pay more,' said her friend. 'They'll never go too high, they have to sell it on.'

Matty felt her heart sink. Her father had so often been beaten on a piece by the private buyer, prepared to pay anything to have something they wanted. What would Mr Chesworth do? She wondered if failure at an auction made him very bad-tempered. He never seemed anything other than cross, as it was.

It was a mixed sale, with many Continental lots to be sold before the English and American silver made its appearance. Matty watched intently. She wished she had had a chance to view. But there was a definite look about the foreign pieces, she decided. Even when designs were similar, the shapes of handles, an odd flower on a lid, proclaimed them different. Two or three specialists at the table bid for almost everything, sharing it out between them, it seemed. There was a brief spat over an incomplete service of dessert knives and forks, and it realised well over the estimate. But then most things did, Matty noticed. The auction house was under-pricing to tempt eager buyers.

The arrival of the dressing case caused a flutter in Matty's near neighbours. They were glamorous women, both she suspected with face lifts. The bidder was clenching and unclenching massively ringed fingers. 'Lot thirty-three, a most attractive Austrian dressing case, approximately dated mid to late nineteenth century. Some fourteen pieces in the original silk-lined case. A thousand pounds, am I bid?' Matty's neighbour waved her catalogue.

'One thousand two hundred – three hundred – four –'

A man at the table was bidding against. He was one of the Continental specialists, and the small price increases seemed to be annoying him. He rattled a pen on his catalogue in a little gesture of irritation.

Two thousand pounds was reached in an instant. At two thousand four, Matty's neighbour began to squeak, and jumped in eagerly, waving her catalogue. They were at two thousand five. The specialist shook his head and sat back.

'Do I hear two thousand six?' enquired the auctioneer, in manicured tones. Matty's eyes fixed on Sammy. 'Three thousand,' he said.

The woman on Matty's left collapsed with a groan. Her friend hissed, 'Can't you beat him? Don't you want it?' But the woman shook her head. Her husband could well afford such a price, but she knew he would not tolerate it. After all, the auction guide gave a maximum of two thousand two hundred pounds, and her husband would think she had gone mad.

One of Sammy's neighbours murmured something to him, but he did not reply. He sat at the table, quite inscrutable, showing no pleasure at his purchase. He came in again for a single mustard pot, part of a long separated set, and again paid over the odds. His last bid was for the apostle spoons. Matty leaned forward to see, but as they were barely seven inches long, she could hardly make them out. Each spoon had the figure of an apostle topping the handle, according to the catalogue James the Less, whoever he was, and St Paul.

'Two very fine spoons,' said the auctioneer. 'Do I have three thousand pounds?'

Three dealers nodded. The bidding raced to four thousand, and then hung in suspension. Sammy lifted his head, almost idly. If he had placed a bid Matty didn't see it, but the bidding was away again, to four thousand five. 'Sold,' said the auctioneer, regretfully. His little palmheld gavel cracked down.

Afterwards Matty waited for Sammy in the foyer. 'I'm sorry you didn't get the spoons,' she said.

He glared at her, and she remembered her vow of silence. She looked round warily, wondering which of the throng might be dealers who would need to know that Chesworth had been after the spoons. It was like being in the secret service, she reflected, watching Sammy and his fellow dealers make discreet contact with officialdom, trying to imply that they had bought nothing of consequence, nothing at all in fact, they were merely applying for the next catalogue, when, God willing, things would improve.

'We'll collect later,' muttered Sammy, and bustled Matty out. 'You can come back in a taxi.'

'I might get mugged,' she protested.

'For a few thousand pounds? Anyway, it's insured. Don't leave it in the cab.'

She returned in the afternoon, and asked almost shiftily for the silver. This was a neurotic trade and no mistake. Sammy had given her a letter of authority, and it disappeared into the office for long moments before she was given the goods. She sat in the reception hall, leafing through catalogues of glamorous house sales overseas.

She was imagining going to view an Italian villa complete with amphitheatre and stage when the door opened and a tall young man appeared, struggling with an enormous brass hat stand. He was wearing a brown suit with pale pink checks, a tie in a darker pink, a shirt in dazzling white and an expression of pained forbearance. 'Put some muscle into it, damn you,' he complained, and his partner, less able to cope, heaved his end into the foyer.

'It weighs a ton,' he complained breathlessly. 'Give us a break, Sholto.'

'I can't imagine why we're selling it,' commented the first young man, taking a rest. 'It has no artistic merit whatsoever.'

'Queen Victoria used it at Osborne.' The second young man was wearing a tie in flamboyant purple, and at that moment it was dangling in the dusty mouth of some sort of writhing gargoyle.

'No wonder Albert died. Perhaps she asked him to shift it. My God, the thing must be filled with lead.'

At that moment the acorn top of the stand came loose from its moorings and plunged floorwards. Her reactions honed by the hockey field, Matty shot out a hand and caught it.

'I say! Well held.' The man in the brown suit abandoned the stand to his partner. He loomed over Matty, flicking back a shock of black hair with a dusty hand.

'I think it's broken my finger,' complained Matty.

'Has it? Don't worry, you may have lost a finger but

you've acquired a slave. If I'd dented the thing I should have been booted out of here before I could say oops. And I've only been here a month.'

Matty hugged her bruise. 'If my finger's broken I'll be unemployed,' she remarked. 'And I've only been in my job two days.'

The man took the brass acorn from her lap and tossed it to his partner, and then took hold of Matty's hand. He had a tan and her fingers looked pale as string.

'What an elegant hand,' he said. 'It doesn't look broken.'

'Would you prefer it to be obviously mangled?' she enquired. 'Blood and sinews and that sort of thing?'

He grinned, and squatted down, putting his face on a level with hers. He had the most horrible scar distorting one cheek. She felt a sense of unhappy shock. He said, 'Don't worry, I've a very strong stomach. Does this hurt? Or this? You know, some people might say the only thing to do in a case like this is kiss it better.' He lifted her fingers to his lips.

Matty snatched her hand away, her face flaming. He was laughing at her, showing strong white teeth in a nut brown face. He must have been abroad very recently, to be so brown. The scar was dark red in contrast. His hair was falling over his forehead again. 'Let me buy you lunch,' he said. 'To make up.'

'Er – no thank you,' said Matty. She could almost hear the girls chorusing in the background, 'Matty! You didn't say no? Oh, you coward!'

'I don't have a very long lunch hour,' she confided.

'Don't you mean lunch break? A lunch hour is, by definition, sixty minutes long.'

'I was using the Julian calendar,' muttered Matty, obscurely. 'Don't be pedantic. And hadn't you better move your hat stand? Someone really will break something if you leave it there.'

'But something's broken already!' He put a hand theatrically on his chest. 'My heart!'

'Try Superglue. You can list it in the catalogue as "well restored".'

He let out a great crack of laughter. The girl at the

51

reception desk came back to her post. She gave Matty's persecutor a very old-fashioned look and said to Matty, 'We have Mr Chesworth's items for you now.'

'Thank you,' said Matty, and rose with as much dignity as she could muster. She felt breathless, as if she had been running. Why, oh why, didn't she go to lunch, even if it did lose her the job?

'Sure you won't change your mind?' He was looming over her. Her head was on a level with the knot of his strange pink tie.

'I regret –' Matty inclined her head graciously.

'If only you truly did. Au revoir, my sweet.' He picked up his end of the hatstand and manoeuvred it out through the door.

'We're learning to live with our Mr Feversham,' said the girl at the desk, sardonically. Then she caught Matty's eye, and grinned. 'He's a great deal too charming for his own good.'

'Or anyone else's,' said Matty. She opened the large oilskin bag that Mr Chesworth had given her. The girl popped in the dressing case, the small mustard pot and the pair of apostle spoons. Matty opened her mouth to protest and then closed it again. How had he managed to get those? She hadn't seen him bid. The old fox. She zipped the bag shut, signed the receipt and made her exit.

The next day Sammy sat her before a pile of silver. 'All for cleaning,' he said flatly. 'But first you sort it into date order. No checking with the books, I want you to date it by style alone. You have an hour.'

Matty stuck her tongue out at the door as it closed behind him. There was no way she could get it absolutely right, and no doubt he would crow over her mistakes. She glowered at a small teapot, prettily decorated with fine chased borders on the body and lid. She had no idea of the date. Picking it up she almost gasped, there was no weight there at all. This was rolled silver, a technique of the industrial revolution applied to the silversmith's art. It meant that each item required far less metal, and in this case perhaps far too little. But it was a delicate and pretty piece. She peered at the maker's mark. HB. Hester Bateman then, one of the most famous of the women silversmiths, working in the eighteenth century.

She put the pot in the middle of her line and began arranging pieces either side of it. The apostle spoons she knew were Charles I, so they were easy, but an elaborate epergne, or table centrepiece, left her puzzled. It was wildly extravagant, festooned with little baskets, the hooks for which were the leaves and tendrils of some fantastic plant. Breaking her own rule again she peered at the marks, but other than establishing that it was made in Birmingham she could go no further. To read the date letters for the different assay halls without a guide needed true expertise.

She moved things up and down, one here, one there, gradually following the flow of design through the centuries. First, there was solid English craftsmanship, which reeled under the impact of Huguenot silversmiths driven out of France. The two strands lived side by side for a while, finally fusing into the great age of English silver, the wonderfully fluid, imaginative rococo work that combined the best of both worlds. When that became overblown it was superseded by Adam, which in turn degenerated into flimsy, slight, trivial little pieces. Back again came heaviness and solid worth, and so the wheel rolled on.

She was still moving things about when Sammy came back. Silent, he inspected the line, shoulders hunched, neck stretched out, while Matty stood humbly aside. It was like school again, only worse. Sammy Chesworth was judge, jury and executioner.

He sniffed, and moved the epergne. 'This isn't as early as it might appear. Look at the workmanship. The leaves are cast, not hammered. They were probably made in a die, like spoons. You know from the marks it's from Birmingham, and they were masters of this sort of thing. Lots of nice little nutmeg graters and so on come from there. But can't you see your provincial squire, with his money, wanting something different from the newfangled flimsy tat? He wanted his moneysworth, and he got it. 1770, Adam's heyday.'

Matty nodded, and winced as Sammy seized on the Hester Bateman teapot. 'Very popular maker, our Hester,' he declared, ringing his finger against the thin metal. 'Good businesswoman too. But don't get it into your head that she did the work. I suppose she might have done something, but basically she took over when her husband died, doing the books, overseeing the men. In my view she got pushed too far by popular taste, but she does some things very well. Very feminine, all her work.'

Matty nodded. Then she put out a hand and touched a square box tea caddy. The sides were decorated with the raised figures of Chinese mandarins. 'I got stuck on this,' she admitted.

Sammy put his thumbs in his belt. 'You've made a good guess, it's 1766. George III, the one who went mad. But Chinoiserie came and went. We had it with Charles II, it hung around on a few formal things in the eighteenth century, and surged up again towards 1750. And of course the Victorians flirted with it, when they could overcome their urge to put deer and harebells and lilies on everything. A Chinese pigtail should make you think, and personally I get rid of 'em. Never could put up with it.'

Finally the row was arranged to Sammy's complete satisfaction. Matty was exhausted, and her head swam. Sammy took his pipe from his pocket and started the long ritual of lighting and tamping. 'And why should anyone at Pickering's be sending you flowers?' he enquired.

Matty's head came up. Her eyes turned to circles of amazement. 'He didn't!'

'No, he didn't,' agreed Sammy. 'I returned them.'

Matty almost gibbered. 'But – but – that's not fair! I might have sent them back myself! Or not. I don't know.'

Sammy chuckled to himself. He seemed to be enjoying the situation.

She said, 'You had no right to send the flowers back.'

He looked at her beadily. 'I had every right. I will not have you chatting indiscreetly to some dilettante fop who spends his days writing rubbishy catalogue notes and selling to amateurs. We have secrets here. I want them kept.'

'I always keep secrets,' said Matty hotly. 'And the reason you don't like catalogue notes is because they give an awful lot away. They tell people what you'd like to keep to yourself.'

He waved his pipe at her. 'And why shouldn't I? I've got a living to earn. And so have you! The fewer people know you're working for me the better, and the first time I send you to Pickering's you come home with some dandy hot on your trail! I should never have taken on a girl. And never a pretty one.'

Matty tossed her head. 'Then you'd have lost a great opportunity. One of these days you'll find out how good I am at this. I'm going to be the best!'

He let out his cackle of a laugh. 'I quake in my shoes! Girl, you haven't even begun!'

'I know that,' said Matty coldly. 'If you want to get rid of me you can. I'll go and work for some other dealer, and find out all he has to say. I'm sure you're not the only expert around here.'

'I'm sure you're not the only expert around here!' He mimicked her, waggling his head from side to side. 'Get on with your work, girl! All this needs cleaning. When that's done you can write me a valuation list, referring to recent catalogues and price reports. I haven't time to spend squabbling!'

He bustled out, leaving Matty angry and shaken. Ought she to have been so rude? But he should never have sent the flowers back. Why, she had a bruised finger to consider, and besides no one had ever sent her flowers before.

A pall hung over the office all afternoon. It was relieved slightly around four when Mr Chesworth departed on some nameless errand, leaving Emily and Matty in peace. Emily put the kettle on. 'Some very pretty blooms there were,' she said archly. 'A very well-chosen bunch of flowers if I may say so.'

'I only wish I'd seen them,' said Matty. She stripped off her rubber gloves. 'It was wicked of him to send them back.'

'You know Mr Chesworth,' said Emily, perhaps meaning that she knew Mr Chesworth and that Matty ought to learn.

'He never likes people getting chatty. I was amazed when he took you on, dear, I never thought he would.'

'No.' Matty hunched on the rickety office chair. 'I like it, really,' she confided. 'Mrs Chesworth fusses a lot, but otherwise it's fun.'

'You're a natural, that's why,' said Emily. 'I suppose Mr Chesworth spotted it. That's his skill, you see, he can always detect quality.'

'We're two select pieces, then,' said Matty, and she and Emily laughed.

'Here.' Emily opened her desk drawer and tossed a small white envelope across. 'You might as well see what he said.'

'Oh, Emily!' Matty's eyes grew round once again. 'He'd be furious if he knew!'

'Well, he doesn't know,' said Emily. 'And he won't, if we don't tell him.'

In a heavy black pen the card read: 'To Broken Fingers from Cracked Ventricle. Can we share a tube of Superglue some day? Yours, Sholto Feversham.'

Three weeks later she wrote to Simon.

'Are you having fun? I am. Mr and Mrs Chesworth are very kind. If I ate all the food they give me I'd be fat as a cow. I'm getting terribly knowledgeable, so watch out. I'm in danger of becoming a silver bore.'

A knock sounded on the bedroom door. 'Come in,' called Matty cautiously, knowing full well who it was. Delia came into the room, with a Liberty's carrier bag.

'Matty darling, you're not resting are you? I keep telling Sammy not to work you so hard, it's cruel. Look, I was in Liberty's today and I saw this lovely summer skirt. Just the thing for dinners or parties, or even going to work if you were somewhere a little more pleasant than that terrible office. Oh, and I picked up some perfume I thought was so you. Young and pretty. Do try it!'

Matty tried to frame the words. 'You really shouldn't, Delia!' she managed.

'But of course I should! A little mothering is just what you need. I love to buy you things. Try the perfume, dear, just a little spray on your wrist. Will you try it? For me?'

Reluctantly Matty extended her wrist. This was getting completely out of hand. First it had been lending her clothes, and however often she returned them they moved inexorably into Matty's wardrobe. Then it was toiletries, some soap, some talcum powder, graduating to lipsticks and eyeshadows that Delia thought Matty might like. Clothes and expensive perfume were new additions to the gift list, but Matty had no doubt that unless checked Delia would soon be buying her diamonds. And, wish as she might for diamonds, she did not want them from the sad, love-starved hands of her childless hostess.

'I can't take these things, Delia,' she said desperately. 'It isn't right.'

'Nonsense, child. You know how much I like shopping for you. It gives me pleasure.'

'I know, but — really, these things are so expensive. It puts me too much in your debt.'

'Dear Matty!' Delia reached out and hugged her. 'As if you could be in my debt! You've brought so much fun and happiness to my home, darling. You can't imagine how it's been since Patricia died. How lonely I've been. I've tried so hard, you know, to be brave about it. Not to be one of those terrible, childless hags. I have Sammy, and my friends and my home, and I had twenty marvellous years with Patricia, but still, it's a loss. To have you, now, so young and so much in need — well, it's a blessing.'

Matty swallowed hard. What was she to say? 'But I'm not in need, Delia.'

'Darling, of course you are! No clothes, no parents, no money — you could be starving if I wasn't here to care for you. You need me. You need looking after. Soon, when you're older, we'll start inviting some nice young men for you to meet. Tall, handsome men with prospects. It's going to be such fun. And when I think of your wedding, I can hardly wait! We'll get the dress from a top designer, I haven't quite decided who, but someone we both like. Don't worry, I won't force some terrible creation on you! I learned better than that with Patricia. You girls will have your own way. But something lovely. Something to set you off to perfection.'

She kissed Matty fleetingly, a brush of lips against her cheek. She smelled sweet and wholesome, a warm and lovely woman. A woman yearning for her child once again. She pressed the skirt into Matty's hands. 'Wear it for dinner, darling, there are people coming. Wear it for me.'

Matty wore the skirt. She sat quite silent at table while Delia babbled and Sammy grunted and the nice, well-intentioned guests did their best to bring her into the conversation. Matty couldn't respond. She felt Sammy watching her, but she wouldn't meet his eye. Work was one thing; they communicated in brief, frank exchanges there, talking of nothing but silver. Here, each revolved around Delia, and their orbits never crossed. They never talked at home.

As soon as the meal was over Matty excused herself.

'Do stay, darling,' said Delia pleadingly.

Matty said, 'I won't if you don't mind, Delia. I'm a little tired.'

As she left she heard Delia say, 'Poor Matty, I think she's got a headache. She's the most charming child normally, you've no idea. I've quite fallen in love with her.'

It wasn't yet ten and Matty felt wide awake. She sat on her bed, barely glancing at the three new pieces of silver Sammy had placed ritually on her desk. Irish pieces this week, with a higgledy piggledy set of marks. As always he was hoping to trap her.

She wondered if he had intended quite so vicious a trap. He couldn't have known how Delia would be. Or was she like that with everyone, every girl who might have been Patricia, give or take years, inches, colours, anything that a grieving mother might mourn?

A knock came on the door. Matty paused. Then she called out cautiously, 'Who is it?'

'Me.' Sammy. Matty got up and turned the key to let him in.

'I'm surprised you feel the need to lock your door.'

'I have to. Otherwise she comes in and leaves things on the bed.'

'They're things that you need. She loves to give them to you.'

Matty said nothing.

After a moment Sammy said, 'You like these American pieces, then?'

Matty said, 'Irish, with crazy marks. Too easy.'

'I'm making everything too easy! You've got a job, a home, money, lovely things! What do you want — hunger, neglect?'

'She's even talking about finding me someone to marry!' Despite herself Matty found her voice shaking. 'To begin with I didn't mind, but she's getting worse. I'm not her daughter. I can't pretend to be. You've got to speak to her. You can't go on closing your eyes and saying it doesn't cause harm, because in the end she's going to be badly hurt.'

In a sad, dead voice he said, 'There's no hurt worse than she has suffered already. None.'

'I can't make up for it. Really, I can't.'

He spread his hands. 'Does it cost so much, a little tolerance? Does it take so much endurance to accept some pretty things? I'll talk to her, tell her to be sensible. She was sensible with Patricia. "Don't be extravagant, money doesn't grow on trees, do you think your father works his fingers to the bone just for you to fritter it on clothes?" And then she was gone. My wife relives every harsh word and wishes it unsaid. They weren't even harsh, just the love of a mother. Patricia was always greedy, she had everything and she wanted more. I wonder sometimes, did she know? She lived every day to the full.'

Matty said, 'It's not that I don't understand — I do. And I want to help. I wouldn't mind if we went shopping together, and bought things with my money, perhaps. But I haven't any money to spend. I save it for my brother. When she gives me things it makes me feel like a sponger, like some sort of parasite. It isn't honest.'

'You have a very naive view of honesty, girl.'

She looked at him with clear grey eyes. 'I'm sure you don't find that so surprising. You know all about my father.'

59

Sammy said, 'I think you should know something — your friend told me only that he was in antiques, his business failed and he died. She told me no more than that.' He went to the desk and lifted one of the expensive, elaborate pieces of silver. He weighed it in his hand. 'The good pieces sing to you,' he murmured.

On impulse Matty crouched down and pulled her suitcase from under the bed. She flung open the lid, and there was the spoon. She held it out to Sammy. 'The last thing my father ever bought,' she said. 'And as far as I know, the only silver. What do you think he paid?'

Chesworth grimaced. 'At present prices, £250 perhaps. A good early piece, with clear marks. But unremarkable.'

'He paid £50.' Matty took the spoon back. She rubbed her fingers against the bowl, and just the touch comforted her. As Sammy said, good pieces had their own song. 'He got it cheap because of an auction ring,' she said jerkily. 'The police knew, they were staging a crackdown. He'd been doing it for a while, getting more and more involved. And afterwards he couldn't bear to live with himself. So he stopped. Living, that is. So don't tell me that I'm naively honest — I'm just honest. I don't blur the edges, I don't pretend that a little bit of cheating doesn't count. Because it does. Because in the end you buy good spoons for peanuts and die of the shame.'

Sammy watched as she replaced the spoon, shutting the suitcase with determined clicks of the locks. 'My wife doesn't ask for you to love her,' he murmured.

'But if I don't, it's cheating.' Matty sat back on her heels. 'And you're cheating her. We both are. We humour her and do nothing to help. You should take her on holiday, spend some time making her happy.'

'And leave my business in your capable hands, no doubt.'

From downstairs they heard Delia calling. 'Sammy? Sammy, are you all right? You've been ages.'

'Coming, Delia.' He glared at Matty, making her the focus of all his irritation. 'All right then! Have it your way. You can go to New York on Monday, I've some pieces to show to my private clients. I shall take Delia to France.'

Matty sat in her room, listening to Delia and Sammy

squabbling mildly over the length of time he had been upstairs. 'You shouldn't keep sale catalogues in the bathroom,' Delia was saying. 'When you stay in there so long I think you've died. One day I'll call the fire brigade.'

'Men with helmets and axes, all for a little old chap with his trousers round his ankles,' retorted Sammy. There was a ripple of laughter.

Matty got up and shut the door. New York on Monday, he had said. Her very first time abroad. She hadn't even got a passport.

Chapter Five

Standing in front of her in the immigration queue was an extremely large black man wearing a jungle camouflage jacket, army boots and an empty ammunition bandolier. Matty could not imagine such an obvious terrorist being admitted without question into the United States, but when she looked around her there seemed any number of dubious characters; the man in the floor-length fur coat, sporting mirrored glasses, the woman in tight white pants and a red top that bared her cleavage from throat to waist. They all looked extremely suspicious aliens.

She shifted her weight from one foot to the other, wishing she had resisted Delia's persuasion and worn something more sensible herself. High heels and a sharp black suit undoubtedly gave her an air of sophistication, but the discomfort after hours on a plane was something else.

An unassuming man carrying a briefcase and a tennis racquet was ushered away to a private room. Drug smuggler? Mafia boss? Matty barely heard the woman officer call her forward.

'It says here that you're a silver dealer. What exactly is that?'

'I − er − I deal in silver. Antique silver. My boss does. Buying and selling.'

'And you're hoping to do deals in New York?'

'I don't know − not me, really. I'm here to show some silver to some people. It was sent separately, with all the documents. Mr Chesworth said it was all in order.' Her voice rose in panic. She could visualise herself in a room next to the man with the racquet, admitting, denying, guilty.

The woman officer was smiling. 'You don't sound all that

confident,' she murmured. 'Is this your first business trip?'

Matty nodded. 'And it's my first time abroad. I don't think Mr Chesworth realised.'

'No need to tell everybody, hon. You go out there and make it. Have fun!'

Matty was through. Perhaps it was going to be fun after all. Perhaps people would go out of their way to help her. There were notices everywhere. She read them in a daze, forgot her suitcase, remembered it again, caught her heel in a grating and wished she'd worn flat shoes. But the taxis stood in line, and the driver surprised her by helping with her luggage, and soon she was speeding away, into a brand new country.

The hotel was grand. Sammy had said, 'I suppose you'd better have my suite. My customers won't want to look at silver laid out on your bed. Just don't expect luxury every time.'

But Matty had never seen such luxury. Three wonderful rooms, with floor-length windows, banks of fresh flowers, and electric blinds. She kicked off her shoes and curled her toes in the thick carpets: she swung open the cocktail cabinet and poured herself a glass of house champagne. She giggled suddenly. If the girls could see her now! But only Griselda would be impressed. Lorne and Henrietta lived lives of seamless luxury themselves, and only suffered at school. But, if it wasn't for them, she'd never have got here.

Matty lifted her glass. 'To the girls,' she declared. 'At this moment sitting down to lumpy mashed potatoes and stew. May I do as much for them some day.'

The silver arrived in large leather boxes an hour later. Matty had lost a night's sleep, but champagne and excitement revived her. She unpacked straight away, littering the small sitting room with tissue and card, setting each item carefully on to the deep blue cloth that the hotel always provided for Sammy's visits. When the display was finished she stood back and looked at it.

Somehow she wasn't satisfied. The silver looked jumbled and dull on a simple table, and the overhead light reflected back in a painful glare. Elegance, form, extravagance, colour, all these the silver possessed. But they belonged to an age of candlelight, mahogany and satin dresses, not this stark display. Each wonderful piece had lived its life commanding its own isolation, and in competing against each other all were defeated.

Matty turned on table lamps, moving them around the room, and then began to break up the collection into smaller, more cohesive sections. She rang down and asked for some small tables, and some more cloths. She stood the tables one on the other, in banks, and arranged important pieces on top, two or three lower, and then the spoons and forks and coasters flat on the bottom. She gave a little Scottish sugar caster unusual prominence, because it was small and simple and she liked it. A set of candlesticks, worth ten times as much, that she considered well made but stylistically dreadful, were consigned to the floor.

Finally, when all was done, the room tidied and locked, the outer door chained and bolted as Sammy had been careful to instruct, the alarm set for dawn and the curtains drawn against the bustle of the New York night, Matty fell into bed. But hunger pangs stopped her from sleeping. Getting up again she raided the fridge, eating chocolate and nuts, crisps and some cocktail cheese. She began to worry, about burglars, or bouncing cheques, or making a bad impression on someone Mr Chesworth considered important. What's more, it was two weeks since Simon had written from school. He might be miserable, bullied, anything. But at last, just when she had decided that she would never go to sleep, she did.

'Ed McKeogh. Good to meet you.'

Matty shook the proffered hand. Mr McKeogh was a New York dealer, and he and Sammy often worked together, each sending the other things they thought would go better in a different market. He looked around the large sitting room, all neat and tidy, with notepads and bill folders spread ready on the desk. 'Sammy told me to take care of you, but it seems to me you're all set,' he remarked. 'How in the world did you persuade him to let you come? He's never had an assistant before, let alone a pretty one.'

'His wife needed a holiday,' said Matty. 'Would you like to see the silver?'

'Yup.'

He inspected her display in silence, piece by piece. Then he stood back and looked at the whole. 'He knows what he's doing, does Sammy. He hired a professional. This looks real good.'

'I hope so.' Then Matty said breathlessly, 'The only thing that worries me is stealing. I mean, suppose someone took something? Teaspoons, or a wine label. It's rude to hover as if I think they are thieves, but if I don't, they could be!'

Ed nodded. 'It's best if you don't have to go out of the room much,' he admitted. 'Keep anything you might need close to hand — notepads, reference books, that sort of thing. But with Sammy's clients you should be safe. He's known them all a long time.'

She scanned the list in her hand. The first appointment was in ten minutes' time, and she wasn't sure if it was ethical for Mr McKeogh to stay. But he guessed her dilemma. 'I'll take you to dinner tonight,' he said, tapping her on the arm. 'We can talk business.'

'I don't think I can.' Matty was apologetic. 'Mr Chesworth said I was to keep this evening free, in case someone wanted to come back. He says they often do.'

He looked irritated. 'They often don't! Sammy's an old woman. You don't want to do everything he says.'

'It is my first trip,' said Matty apologetically. 'I'm sorry.'

'Yeah. Some other time perhaps.'

She hoped she hadn't upset him. Would Sammy have expected her to go, despite what he said? She might have irrevocably insulted his friend. Matty gnawed on a fingernail and felt nervous, wondering what she should do if no one came. But her first client arrived minutes later.

Mr Rittorno was a small, Italianate man in a white suit. He was balding, smiled a lot showing gold teeth, and was delighted with Matty. 'Mr Chesworth knows when he's on to a good thing, huh?' He took her cheek between forefinger and thumb and pinched it. 'What a beauty!'

She retreated behind her desk. 'Perhaps you could tell me what sort of items you had in mind?' she said coldly.

66

'I have no idea! Something beautiful. Something feminine. Something warm.' He leered at her.

'If you'd like to come this way.' She picked up her keys and led the way starchily to the showroom. If he pinched her bottom she'd hit him with one of the ugly candlesticks.

But he loved the candlesticks. He purred over every unnecessary lump laboriously crafted by some unartistic journeyman in years gone by.

'Such beautiful pieces,' he declared. 'Such weight!'

'They are very heavy,' agreed Matty, wondering why the man didn't just buy silver ingots and be done with it. But if he wanted wealth he could display, with solid ostentation, then the candlesticks would do.

'How much?' he asked throatily, stroking the metal as if it was alive.

'A hundred and fifty thousand dollars,' declared Matty. Sammy had told her to take no less than a hundred and twenty, so she was leaving herself room to manoeuvre.

'I take them,' said Rittorno.

As she was wrapping the pieces he said, 'I shall take you to dinner, my dear. To show my appreciation.'

'I'm afraid I already have an engagement.'

'Then you must cancel it. Believe me, I'm very generous.'

Matty was taken aback. He was leering at her, and she was suddenly aware that she should have fastened her black suit up to the neck. What's more the skirt was too short. She watched in frozen fascination as Rittorno reached out his hairy little hand and felt down her jacket for her breast. 'The silver excites me,' he whispered.

Matty fell back against the desk. 'If you'd like to take your candlesticks, Mr Rittorno,' she said shrilly, 'I have another client arriving in a minute.'

'Are you a virgin? I'll pay you. As much as the candlesticks. More. Believe me, I'm a very rich man.'

He was pressing against her, his hands fumbling, his breathing harsh.

She lifted the last unwrapped candlestick, closed her eyes and braced herself to hit him over the head. Suppose she killed him? Her upraised arm shook for a vital second, and in that instant a knock came on the door.

'My next client,' said Matty. Rittorno peeled himself away, sparing a surprised glance for the threatening candlestick. Matty bundled it up with the others and thrust them at the man.

'Tonight —' he ventured.

'Goodbye, Mr Rittorno,' said Matty firmly.

'Goodbye — goodbye.' He tried to take her hand and kiss it, but she put it firmly behind her back.

She held the door as he left. Her stomach was churning, she longed for a few moments to collect herself. Keeping her eyes on the floor, without a glance at the man waiting to be admitted, she ushered him into the room. Let him not be another Mr Rittorno, she prayed. She consulted her list. 'Mr Wolfson.'

'Sadly, no. I don't have an appointment.'

She looked up then. She knew him. Her mind whirled, trying to place someone tall, black-haired, with amazing blue eyes in a horribly scarred face. It was the man from Pickering's. The man who had sent her flowers. Sholto Feversham.

'What on earth are you doing here?'

'Rescuing you from lecherous customers, if appearances are anything to go by. You should watch Rittorno, spending money excites him. He'll jump on anything, he's notorious.'

She gulped. 'Oh. Oh, I am glad, I thought it was just me. Sammy might have warned me!'

'I don't suppose he knew. He restricts it to women, thank God.'

Matty giggled. 'I was going to hit him with a candlestick. You saved me from murder.'

'Take more than that to finish off Rittorno. He had a doberman set on him once, I seem to remember. You ought not to see strangers alone. It isn't safe.'

'Are you safe?'

He grinned. 'What a very silly question. Of course not.'

She went and sat on the sofa, crossing her legs in her elegant skirt. 'I'm not supposed to let anyone but clients through the door,' she told him. 'You don't want silver, do you?'

He shrugged. 'I don't know. Can I look?'

'No. You might steal something.'

'I won't. Brownie's honour.'

'You still can't. I've someone coming.'

'As the actress said to the bishop.'

She choked on a giggle. The girls made jokes like that, but never in front of people they didn't know. She said primly, 'I think you should go away.'

He stood over her, looking down. 'I don't think I will. I would like to see the silver, actually. I'm a picture specialist, and I'm doing a valuation, and my client asked if I'd come here and view the silver on her behalf. She's very old. She'd prefer me to tell her if there's anything she might like.'

'You won't know!' declared Matty.

'I think I might.'

She sighed angrily, and glanced down her list of clients. 'Who are you representing?'

'Mrs Waterman. She's twelve o'clock.'

'Oh. Oh yes, I see.' Mr Chesworth had written in pencil, 'Charming old lady. Crippled. May not feel well enough to attend.'

As she unlocked the room she said crisply, 'I can't imagine why anyone would need someone from London to look at their pictures. New York's full of art experts.'

'I specialise in Renaissance art. I spent a lot of time in Italy as a boy, I tend to get asked here and there to look at things.'

'Are you saying you're a world expert?'

'I wouldn't dream of being so immodest. I'm not that good. There just isn't anyone else who's any better.'

Matty shot him an enraged glare, and he chuckled.

Her opinion of him mellowed as he looked at the silver. He knew what he was doing, Matty decided, watching him instinctively discard the pieces she herself disliked. Her eyes kept drifting to that scar, a pucker extending the length of one cheek, dotted on either side with jagged stitch marks. Without it he would be terribly good-looking.

He turned to her. 'You'll have to help me. I like that wine cooler, but shouldn't there be more than one? A pair perhaps?'

'The other's in a house in Kent,' admitted Matty. 'They were split in a Will at some time, and the liners got lost. The other cooler might come up one day, you never know.'

'If you give me the address of the Kent people, I'll take it. Mrs Waterman might like to write and see if they'll sell.'

Matty hesitated. Sammy would be thrilled if she sold the cooler, it was a wonderful piece. But it was unethical to give names to strangers. It was the sort of thing that caused burglaries.

'I really can't say,' she said regretfully.

'Are you sure?' He picked up the little sugar caster and inspected it. 'I like this. Very pretty. I'd give you commission if we managed to buy the other cooler as well.'

'That doesn't sound awfully proper.'

'Do you think not?' He grinned at her. 'You may be right. Look, why don't I come and pick you up this evening, with the cooler and this other piece, and we can visit Mrs Waterman. Then she can make up her own mind. Afterwards we can go somewhere and eat.'

'You're the third person to invite me out tonight. I said no to the others.'

'Third time lucky, perhaps. It is business.'

He was standing nowhere near her, but still her knees shook. He was so tall. His suit hung on him like an unconsidered rag, though she could tell it was expensive. His tan had faded since last they met, and his teeth seemed less white. He wasn't all that good-looking, she realised with surprise. Quite apart from the scar his skin was pitted with the dead craters of teenage acne. Matty was almost relieved. She had been starting to think that he was the most attractive man she had ever seen in her life.

'I can't let the silver out of my sight,' she prevaricated.

'She'll probably buy it. So you'll only have to worry for an hour or so.'

'If you really think there's a chance —'

'More than a chance. If I tell her to get it then she will. She likes me.'

'How very unwise.'

He chuckled and said, 'So you did send the flowers back?

70

I thought it was Sammy Chesworth. Someone told me he was trying to pretend you weren't working for him.'

'The flowers were unnecessary,' said Matty. 'And I don't think we should discuss Mr Chesworth.'

'No, we can talk about him tonight. Six o'clock, OK?'

'No. No, I don't think −'

A knock came on the door. Feversham tossed the sugar caster to Matty and she barely caught it. 'Losing your touch, I see. Six tonight.'

The day went well. Mrs Waterman's absence at twelve meant that Matty had time to write up her records and eat a sandwich off a tray. She had sold the candlesticks to Mr Rittorno, some wall sconces to her next caller, and a multitude of odd spoons and forks to the next, an avid collector. 'Always a pity when you can't make up a set,' he said regretfully, running his fingers down a pretty silver and ivory fork. 'You can't even get modern stuff to match. You'd think someone would make it.'

'I didn't know people did make silver today,' said Matty curiously. 'I thought it was all electroplate.'

He nodded. 'A lot of it is. But the skills are still there. They just don't apply them like they did. See you again, Miss Winterton, it's been a pleasure.'

Most of the expensive pieces remained. Anything unsold was to be placed in a vault until Sammy could next travel over, and personally approach those buyers who could usefully include some of the things in their collections. Quality would always sell, but there was a skill in finding the right time, the right person, the right price. Matty dreaded to think how much money was invested in Sammy's hoard of silver. He would hold on to something for as long as it took to get his price, and sometimes it seemed he would buy at any cost, provided what he bought was the best. Yet he prospered, neatly fitting his niche in the market, the man who bought the best and sold the best, the rich man's trusted friend. Sammy lived off the world's millionaires.

It was past five. The hotel room suddenly seemed claustrophobic. She could be anywhere, she was experiencing nothing. Thank goodness she had some excuse for going out and disobeying Sammy who thought he could rule every second of her life. He thought he owned her.

She ran a bath and lay in it, wasting time she did not have. Halfway through washing her hair the telephone rang. She picked up the bathroom extension.

'Hello?'

'It's Sholto. Ready?'

'Er – no. I'll be ten minutes.'

'OK. I'll wait for you down here.'

She rinsed her hair wildly and leaped from the bath. She had wasted nearly an hour, and had no idea what to wear. She ran to the wardrobe and stared desperately at the clothes hanging within, almost pleading for something to leap out and demand to be worn. There was the trouser suit – Patricia's trouser suit – damn Delia, she would pack it! But it would do.

She caught sight of herself in the mirror, red from the bath, her hair a damp tangle. Nothing could be done until it was dry, and she ran into the bathroom and started frantically dragging a brush through the strands, deafened by the roar of the hotel drier. Gradually she became aware of a noise. Someone was knocking on the door.

She opened it on the chain. A blue eye confronted her. 'I thought you'd been murdered. I came up here to save you.'

'You couldn't if I was dead. I'd be beyond help.'

'I imagined you at your last gasp. Are you one of those boring girls who always takes a day to get ready?'

'No, of course not! It was just – I lost track of time. Do you want to come in and wait?'

'Good heavens, no! I'll just sit on the floor out here, guarding your door. I realise I should be a eunuch, but that does seem a little unnecessary. I don't think we want too much authenticity.'

'Why don't you just come in?'

Matty closed the door and unlatched the chain. When she opened it again Sholto's face creased in a delighted grin. 'Well! What a lovely view.'

Following his gaze Matty glanced down at herself. One

breast was peeping over her towel. Her face flamed and she raced for the bathroom.

She became still hotter under the drier. But gradually her hair assumed its usual sleek fall, shining with deep, coppery colour. Her nerves settled too. She was grown-up now. There was no need to be embarrassed. The door opened a crack and she squeaked, clutching her towel to her chin. A hand appeared, holding a champagne glass.

'Here. I hate to drink alone.'

'Is that my champagne?'

'Unless strangers leave bottles in your fridge. You are now thirty minutes late.'

'Oh.' She took the glass and sipped it. 'Thank you,' she said.

'Not at all.' The hand withdrew.

Matty did her make-up. At school she had experimented with everything, including a Gothic phase of dead-white skin and black lips and eyes. In London she had confined herself to understatement in deference to Sammy, but here – what should she do here?

Grey eyes stared back at her from the mirror. She picked up a brush and outlined them in sparkling dazzle dust. Glitter settled on her lashes and freckled her nose, and she did not brush it away. Rose pink lipstick looked a little weak in comparison, so she covered it with sticky gloss. Her reflection surprised her, heavy-lidded, pouting, almost sultry.

'Don't look,' she called out. 'I'm going into the bedroom.'

'My eyes are fixed on the fire regulations,' replied Sholto. 'We've got to get in the bath together. Shall we practise?'

'No.'

Matty scuttled across to her bedroom. Champagne on an empty stomach was making her woozy. She struggled into her underclothes and then into the suit. It smelled of Delia, expensive and slightly sad. The jacket was long and narrow, buttoning close around Matty's hips, and the trousers were skin tight. Looking at herself, Matty blinked. An inch of cleavage showed above the jacket, and when she breathed the top button visibly strained. The whole suit was a size too small and by rights she should change, but she couldn't, there wasn't time — Matty thrust her feet into black heels, picked up her small black bag and was ready.

Sholto Feversham put down his champagne. 'You were definitely worth waiting for,' he said throatily.

'We mustn't forget the silver,' said Matty. 'It is business.'

'Is it? Er — yes. We could always go later.'

'But we've got to go now.' She blinked at him, her lashes like glistening curtains. Her hair shone as if it were still wet.

'Come on,' he said abruptly.

In the taxi, the wine cooler resting between them like an enormous pet, he said, 'Do you often wear that suit?'

Matty shook her head. 'Delia packed it. That's Sammy's wife. Don't you think I should have put it on?'

'That depends. Mrs Waterman may be a bit surprised.'

Matty glanced down at herself. 'But it's very demure. At least — I thought it was.'

'Suggestive is the word I'd use. Tell me, how do you come to be working for Sammy Chesworth? All silver dealers are secretive, but he wouldn't tell the angel of death whether he preferred heaven or hell.'

'He doesn't tell me much. Except about silver, and he never stops doing that. He's a walking encyclopedia, and he can spot a good piece at a hundred paces. He took me on because — well, because of his daughter, if you must know. She died.'

'Good God. You don't have to sit in a high chair, do you?' He was gazing at her in surprise.

'Of course not. She died when she was twenty, ten years ago. And she was extravagant and wild, and Sammy adored her. So did Delia. Actually I'd have liked her too I should think, she must have been great fun. I'm not in the least like her.'

'I bet you are. I bet you're anything but goody two-shoes.'

Matty considered. 'I was wild once,' she admitted. 'But now I'm reliable and conscientious and thrifty. Terribly dull.'

'Terribly. And I don't believe you. Not in that suit.'

Mrs Waterman's house was large and dark. Sholto rang the bell with assurance, while Matty looked into the shadows and wondered what she would do if someone leaped out to steal her wine cooler. Then the door opened and yellow light flooded the steps. An elderly black lady was welcoming them.

'Good evening, Miss Digby,' said Feversham. 'We're a little late. I hope Mrs Waterman won't be inconvenienced.'

'Not at all, Mr Feversham. She loses track of time. If you'd come this way?'

They followed her stately progress. The hall was hung with chandeliers of the finest Italian crystal, reflected again and again in gold-framed mirrors. A very small painting hung above a walnut side table, a pale, almost pastel execution of the Madonna and child. Sholto stopped before it, and stood, hands in pockets, absorbed.

'Sholto,' hissed Matty, because Miss Digby was waiting.

'Yes − yes.' He reluctantly came away. Miss Digby turned the heavy knob of a door. An old lady sat in a high-backed wing chair, a rug across her knees and her hands folded upon them. She had hair of the purest white, and eyes, once blue, now misted with age. A small fire burned in the grate, and every surface, every table, every wall was covered with pictures and sculptures and beautiful things.

'Mr Feversham and friend, ma'am.'

'Mrs Waterman − may I introduce Matilda Winterton, Mr Chesworth's assistant?' Sholto put his hand under Matty's elbow.

The old lady smiled delightedly. 'What a pretty young thing you are! No wonder Sholto insisted you come and see me. He knows I like pretty things.'

'Then I'm sure you'll like my silver,' said Matty.

'Told you she was a professional,' said Sholto. 'But why are you keeping the Giorgione in the hall? You can't see it there.'

'I thought it looked fine, over the table,' defended Mrs Waterman. 'Don't you think it looks good?'

'You never go in the hall. You should have it in here, instead of that ghastly Dürer.' He waved a dismissive hand at a painting full of lumpish figures.

'But I like that! It has reality.'

'Ugliness, you mean. Giorgione is about beauty and

75

purity. He transcends the mundane. I'll bring it in here.'

Under Matty's amazed stare Sholto went back into the hall and detached the Giorgione from the wall. An alarm began to squawk. 'Turn that off would you, Miss Digby?' He wrestled with the electric cable to which the picture was linked.

Mrs Waterman was laughing. 'Don't mind him, my dear,' she said to Matty. 'I'm used to him. He's never yet agreed with anywhere I've put a painting he bought for me.'

'Won't the police come?' asked Matty, as the alarm squawked on.

'Oh dear me! I'd better telephone them.'

She picked up the phone next to her chair, stabbing at the numbers with twisted arthritic fingers. Then she murmured and laughed, and murmured again. 'I'm so sorry — it's so silly of me — an oversight, no more. The password? I really can't remember it — Digby, what is our password? They think I might be being held to ransom.'

Miss Digby paused in the doorway. 'Rubicon, ma'am.'

'Ah, yes. Rubicon. So you see, no one has a gun at my head. Thank you. Thank you so much.'

The alarm was suddenly silenced. Sholto brought the picture triumphantly into the room and prepared to remove the Dürer.

'Don't you dare!' said Matty. 'You'll start the alarm again. Find somewhere else for the blessed thing.'

'It is indeed a blessed thing,' said Sholto. 'Look at the colour. I discovered this painting. Before it was cleaned it was nothing but a dark blob. Don't you love her expression, the way she keeps her eyes averted? Modesty, of course, but also an unwillingness to recognise the truth. Because of what her child is, she must lose him.'

'You can put it on an easel,' said Matty practically.

Mrs Waterman clapped her twisted little hands. 'What a wonderful idea! Digby, have we an easel? Mr Feversham won't rest until he has his picture displayed as he would like.'

When the easel came Sholto put it up in a corner of the room, assessing light from the window and the evening effect of lamps.

Matty went across to him. 'We are supposed to be selling my silver!' she hissed.

He glanced up. 'Then sell it! This painting's more important than some lump of metal.'

'Really!'

She turned on her heel and flounced back to Mrs Waterman. She dragged the wine cooler into the old lady's view. 'This is the main piece,' she said breathlessly. 'There's a pair to it, but the other's not for sale as far as I know. It's very fine — mid-eighteenth century — and would go wonderfully on the table in the hall.'

'There's a pair, you say?' Mrs Waterman was looking sharp.

'Yes.'

'If I could get the pair — do you think I could do that, Sholto?' She called across the room to him.

'I'm sure you could.' He was distracted, placing his painting just so.

'You must tell me exactly where the other cooler is,' declared Mrs Waterman, and her eyes sparkled with delight.

'I really can't,' said Matty. 'I mean — I don't know.'

'But you must tell me,' coaxed Mrs Waterman. 'Otherwise I shan't buy this lovely piece. And a pair shouldn't be parted, it's all wrong. If I bought them, they'd be together again. And when I'm dead someone else will have the pleasure of owning a proper set. We shouldn't betray lovely things by taking their friends away, it isn't kind.'

'My own sentiments exactly,' said Sholto, coming back from his painting, the better to admire it.

'It's not ethical to give that sort of information,' blustered Matty.

'Neither is it ethical to keep good sets apart. We're not going to steal the piece, Matty, merely ask for it.' Sholto kissed the top of her head in passing. Matty felt as if she had received an electric shock. She almost put up her hand to touch the spot.

'I couldn't without asking Mr Chesworth,' she said desperately.

'Coward,' said Sholto.

'Mr Chesworth always tells me things like that,' said Mrs

Waterman, although he did not. Matty knew he did not. She looked askance at Mrs Waterman, realising that under her sweet old lady façade resided a rapacious and fanatical collector. She held out her poor little sugar caster. 'Wouldn't you like to look at this instead?'

'But I want my wine coolers!'

'I know, but — if you took the one, I'd see if Mr Chesworth could obtain the other. I'd have to go through Mr Chesworth, it's only right.'

Mrs Waterman made a face. 'I hate buying odd bits,' she said crossly. 'I have to have some guarantee that I'll get the pair.'

'I can't give you any sort of guarantee,' said Matty.

It was clear that Mrs Waterman was upset. A good half hour of coaxing got Matty nowhere, she would sell nothing tonight. The old lady wouldn't even look at the caster, and every time her eyes fell on the wine cooler she moaned piteously: 'How much I should like a pair! I've always wanted a pair!'

They left soon after, with Matty cradling the silver against her breasts. It felt cold and heavy, as disappointed as she.

'That was a complete balls-up,' said Sholto in the taxi. 'You could have sold both pieces. Mrs Waterman loves a chase, she'd have written a charming letter to those people in Kent, and they'd have said no, and she'd write again — it's the sort of thing she loves.'

'Mr Chesworth would have sacked me,' said Matty defensively.

'And he'll sack you anyway, for not selling enough. Let's go and eat.'

They stopped at a small, discreet restaurant. The silver was a nuisance, like a baby up beyond its bedtime. The man in the restaurant couldn't understand why they had it with them, and at the same time couldn't resist goggling at it. 'This is wonderful!' he kept saying, running his fingers over the rich embossing of the cooler. 'Magnificent!'

They put it under the table and after some anxious kickings with her toe in case it had been stolen Matty took her shoes off and put her feet in the thing.

'I have never before dined with someone using a foot bath,' said Sholto.

'There's a first for everything,' said Matty, who had never before dined with a strange man at all.

He ordered champagne and lifted his glass to look at her through the haze of bubbles. 'I like your breasts,' he murmured. 'They verge on the voluptuous. You should eat more.'

'Do you like fat women then?' Matty's throat felt dry and she gulped at her champagne.

'I like generous women. Reckless women. Goddesses, grabbing handfuls of pleasure from life's laden board.'

'You think I'm a prude.'

'No, I don't. Prudishness is dragging at you, that's all. You'll shake it off.'

She laughed and leaned forward, entranced by his odd smile, caught up at one corner by the badly stitched scar. 'We'll decide over coffee,' he said.

'Decide what?'

'If we're going to sleep together. I'm savouring the question of that button. Will it or will it not give way? The thought of your nipples in the soup is exciting me utterly.'

Matty almost gasped. 'If that happens we definitely won't sleep together. It sounds terribly painful.'

'This place is renowned for its chilled soups.'

She laughed at him again. She felt drunk, and kept pressing her feet against the cool silver under the table, trying to sober herself. She had only met this man twice. Was she really going to give him her virginity? Of course not. Certainly not.

They were served more quickly than was necessary. It was a pity, Matty liked the pauses between plates, when they sipped wine and sparred with each other. 'You take advantage of Mrs Waterman,' she said.

'Nonsense. I abet her in her quest for the beautiful. She's a wonderful collector, very discerning. It's what keeps her alive.'

'All those Italian paintings. Are you Italian or something?'

'Not in the least. One of my aunts has a house in Venice,

I was consigned to her at one time. Only the paintings kept me sane. It shouldn't be possible to live like an English spinster amidst the glories of Italy, but she managed it. By God, she did.' His face changed. For a moment he looked bleak.

Matty said, 'Oh, look, here's the coffee.'

She sipped at hers, he left his untouched. She felt his eyes on her, like blue glass, flintglass. He said, 'I know it's your first time. And you know you may never see me again. I just feel it's something we should do together, tonight, creating a memory. We'll never forget it.'

She met his eyes. 'I'm only supposed to go in for mature and meaningful relationships. It says so in the book. Won't I ever see you again?'

He shrugged his shoulders. 'God knows. I'm not in the least reliable. I don't think you can look to me for a trip to the movies every Saturday night.'

'What can I look to you for?'

He said suddenly, 'I should have brought the Giorgione. I'd put it at the head of the bed and deflower you while the Madonna looked away. I should like that.'

'I shouldn't! I think that's rather horrible.'

'Sex can be horrible. And it can be beautiful, and inspiring, and wholly, carnally engrossing. Let's go.'

She left the restaurant barefoot, her shoes inside the wine cooler. Sholto cradled it like their beloved child, a giant and beautiful baby. In the taxi it sat on the seat between them, and they were silent. They didn't speak again until the hotel room door had closed and they were alone.

She said, 'I'm not sure this is such a good idea.'

'Oh, but it is! Let's fill this cooler with champagne.' He went to the fridge and took out three bottles, the entire stock. He emptied them one after another into the giant silver bowl.

'It's going to lose all its fizz,' said Matty wonderingly.

He scooped some up in a glass and drank it. 'Actually, it's divine. The bubbles are running riot.'

It was true. Freed from the confines of their bottles, the gases were exploding themselves in hectic death. Matty gulped the stuff down, feeling drops run down her chin.

Sholto lifted his glass and poured half of it down her cleavage. 'Undress. We'll both undress.'

She was drunk and she knew it. This man, this stranger, flung his clothes on the ground and stood naked before her, distended and shocking. But she wasn't shocked. 'I knew you were my sort of girl,' he said softly. 'You want life.'

'I want — this. I want to know what it is.'

'Open your box, Pandora.'

She turned her back to him and undressed. When she was naked she put her hands over her breasts and turned back. 'My God,' he said. 'Titian should have painted you. That wonderful hair. "Girl into Woman" he would have called it.'

She felt brave suddenly. She felt wanton. She spread her arms and let him see all of her, let him be the first man ever to look at her body in lust. She bent and picked up her glass again, scooped into the champagne and drank. Hot eyes, watching her. 'You sweet temptress,' he whispered.

When he began kissing she thought she would drown, when he touched her naked flesh she moaned as if in pain. His erection troubled her, it was aggressive and without place. She touched it and pushed it down, her fingers shuddering at the dampness, the strange solidity. It wasn't like flesh. He pulled away and fitted a condom, breaking the wonderful, endless rhythm. It was an intrusion, an unwelcome brush with reality. She lay and waited for him, lay and longed for him. This man, this stranger. He was between her legs, and she was urgent, wanting, desperate for she knew not what. He was looking down at her, his face almost distant. 'My lady. My beautiful one. The end of your innocence.'

The thing crushed down her defences. It troubled her no more.

Chapter Six

She was awake in the dawn. He lay beside her, spreadeagled on the bed. He was long, smooth, with a narrow stripe of hair running down the centre of his chest, to his belly and beyond. He had beautiful hands, she realised, with fingers that tapered to a point, like an elegant monkey. But at rest, without the electricity of his waking self, the face was scarred, damaged, almost unhappy. She would have loved him less if his face had been perfect, she thought. For she did love him. After the night, she could do nothing else.

If this was all she ever knew of love, it would be enough. Her body was at peace with itself, each single part felt settled and content. He had loved her like a man tasting the finest wine, he had made her believe that she was lovely. Pushing his face against her skin, licking her sweat, glorying in all her curves and hollows, he had awakened her to herself.

She got up quietly and went to bathe. Loving such a man was madness. Suppose she never found anyone else to give her such a night, and such a morning? She might pass the rest of her days unhappily, because she had learned too early about bliss.

After a while, lying in the suds, she opened her eyes and saw him leaning in the doorway, watching her. 'I've rung down for breakfast,' he said. 'We deserve it.'

Sitting up, Matty said, 'I don't think we do. After our night of sin.'

'Rubbish. Thou shalt not fornicate is not one of the ten commandments. I was loving my neighbour.'

Matty giggled. 'I think you're immoral. I think I should be affronted.'

83

'Don't be. I'd find you very boring and be off like a shot. I don't approve of morality.'

'Why do you keep talking as if you're about to make a run for it? You don't have to. I'm not trying to cling on.'

'No. No, I can see you're not.'

Later, they sat and ate breakfast, either side of a small table. It was very companionable, each glancing at a newspaper, toying with orange juice, toast, eggs and hash browns. Sholto lounged comfortably back, his long legs stretched out, his shirt open at the neck. Matty was wearing one of the dresses Delia had bought at Liberty's, a soft silk print in dark pinks and mauves. She felt soft today, with a newly discovered femininity. She felt beautiful.

A knock came on the door. They looked at each other. Suddenly Matty gasped, 'Oh no! The clients! I forgot! Now Sammy's bound to sack me.'

'No need to panic. We're having a breakfast meeting. Just let me get a tie.'

Matty waited as long as she could, but at the third knock she opened the door. Sholto was still in the bedroom, she could think of no way of explaining that. She struggled with her composure. 'Mr and Mrs Shilworth? Do come in.'

They were in their late thirties and affluent. He wore a sharp suit and she a satin two-piece in an aggressive shade of blue. Mrs Shilworth looked askance at the breakfast table. 'I wasn't aware you were busy, Miss Winterton.'

'I'm afraid my breakfast meeting over-ran somewhat,' said Matty with a deprecating wave of her hand. 'May I offer you some coffee? I'll ring down for some croissants and toast.'

'Coffee will be fine' said Mr Shilworth, casting an eye around for the invisible guest.

As if on cue, Sholto emerged from the bedroom. He was wearing his tie and jacket, and carried the sugar caster. 'I've called my client and he's agreed,' he said smoothly. 'We'd like an authentication certificate, of course.'

'Of course,' said Matty, wondering what on earth he was talking about.

'If you'll wrap the caster, I'll take it with me now.'

Matty blinked. 'Er — perhaps I'd better keep it until the certificate's drawn up.'

'Not at all! I wouldn't dream of troubling you when you're so busy. You can send it on at your convenience.'

'That's a very pretty piece,' said Mrs Shilworth, as Matty enfolded the little caster in tissue paper.

'Scottish,' said Matty. 'If you look at the mark you can see it's a tree with a bird in the branches, over a dolphin. Nicely idiosyncratic. 1762.'

'We have Scottish ancestors,' said Mr Shilworth wistfully.

'What a good thing I called so early and pre-empted you,' said Sholto, and bared his teeth in a wolfish smile.

Matty was starting to panic. What was he doing taking her caster? Was he going to steal it? He hadn't produced a single penny to pay, and she dare not say so, not now. When the caster was wrapped he shook hands all round and prepared to go. 'We must talk this evening,' said Matty firmly. 'You'll want your certificate.'

He laughed at her. 'As I said, you can always post it on. Thanks for all your help.'

He was gone, and so was her caster. Matty almost ground her teeth in rage. She excused herself for a moment and went back into the bedroom. The wine cooler sat on the floor with some underwear draped rakishly over its lovely sides. Flat champagne lay in a puddle in the bottom. Matty threw the clothes to one side and emptied the champagne into the waste bin, drying the vessel with a handful of tissues. It was time the cooler went back under lock and key, where people like Sholto could not abscond with it. When she emerged, cradling the thing in her arms, the couple were impressed. For a mad moment Matty wondered if they would buy it, because surely then Sammy would forgive the loss of his caster, but it didn't happen. The Shilworths lived in an apartment and had no place for something so vast.

'We wanted some nice forks — and some fruit knives,' said Mrs Shilworth doubtfully. Matty nodded. She might have guessed as much. They had dressed up for their visit, and had only a limited budget. But they wanted good silver on their table. If she handled them well they could be clients for life, coming to Sammy for piece after piece as they grew in affluence. They would leave their children a lovely collection.

She took them into her showroom, and in half an hour had sold them a canteen of King's pattern cutlery and some Georgian serving spoons. Their departure coincided with the arrival of the next customer, and so it went on, throughout the day. Finally, at six, she was done. There was no one left to see. What's more, the silver that remained was all in the wine cooler class, large and expensive. Sammy would be disappointed in sales there, he had hoped for more.

Matty slumped on a sofa and kicked off her shoes. She had a headache. Where was Sholto, and where was her caster? If this was his way of repaying her honesty, her trust, then she despised herself. What idiot gullibility. She should have known what sort of man he was.

The telephone rang and she picked it up. 'What about my certificate?' demanded Sholto. 'I demand my money back!'

Matty went weak with relief. 'You give me my caster back! I could have sold it today.'

'I sold it for you. And I would like a certificate. You know the sort of thing, nice paper, copperplate writing, giving a potted history of the piece. Made in Scotland, 1762, by whoever it is, French overtones in style as with so much Scottish work.'

'If you know so much, why don't you write it?'

'Don't be peevish. Look, I'll come over.'

He arrived twenty minutes later, and dropped a cheque in Matty's lap.

'But this is from Mrs Waterman!'

'Yes. Without the wine cooler to distract her she decided she liked it after all. I knew she would.'

Matty lifted her chin. 'Do you want me to thank you?'

'No. Just give me the address of the people in Kent.'

'You'd make money if I did.'

'And so would you. Or are you so content to live as Sammy Chesworth's surrogate daughter that you'll forgo your independence?'

Matty's cheeks flamed. 'That isn't fair. I don't get anything I don't work for. Except – except for the things

86

Delia gives me, and I try to say no and she won't have it.'

'Sounds like sponging to me.'

She picked up her discarded shoe and threw it at him, but anger spoilt her aim and she missed. Her fists were clenched, her eyes like grey glass. The skin was drawn tight across her nose and she was dead white except for two round spots of colour high on her cheeks. She was a creature of sudden rages. They came like tropical storms, fierce and then gone. 'You beast!'

'If the cap fits,' said Sholto calmly.

'Pig!' She turned her back on him and bit her own hands, because otherwise she would murder him. He came up behind her and took them away from her mouth, holding each clenched fist in his own.

'Stop that. Why are you getting so cross?'

'I don't sponge! I don't take what isn't mine! I've got my young brother to support and I have to stay with Sammy.'

'How old's your brother?'

The thought of Simon swept through her like a rush of cold water. She stopped struggling. 'Ten. Nearly eleven. He's only got me. I try to earn enough to pay his school fees, they're so expensive. And I want to get a flat, so he can have somewhere for the holidays. There's nowhere for him, you see. It isn't good for him.'

'No.' As her hand relaxed he unfolded it and studied the damage. She had left deep imprints of her teeth on the knuckles.

'What a nasty temper you've got. Poor little orphan Annie.'

'Don't waste your time feeling sorry for me,' snapped Matty. 'I don't need sympathy. And I don't need you trying to wheedle things out of me. If people thought that asking Sammy Chesworth to look at their stuff was tantamount to advertising it on the open market, then he'd never get a look at a private collection again.'

'Nobody need ever know I got the information from you.'

She turned and stared at him. 'They'd guess. And I should know. Sammy might never trust me again. How can you ask me when you know I'd be risking my job?'

'And you're such a good little girl.'

'Don't patronise me!'

She crossed the room away from him, rubbing her hands on her upper arms, as if she was cold. She didn't love him, not at all. Last night seemed a lifetime away, and as he stood there, the scar on his face like a crease of sardonic laughter, she wondered if it had ever happened.

'I was so sure you were generous,' he murmured.

'You're asking for something that isn't mine. You must see that.'

'I need the money, Matty! So do you.'

'You can't expect auction houses to pay you much at first. I'm sure you can manage.'

His blue eyes seemed to glitter. 'I shall certainly manage, my dear. Without your assistance, it seems. Just remember to mention to Sammy that the caster was sold to Mrs Waterman due to my good offices. Although I imagine you won't.'

'I will! Of course I will.'

His expression said clearly that he didn't believe a word. Matty's knees felt shaky, all her rage had gone and she was left full of tears. If only she could do what he asked. It seemed to him so little to ask and it wasn't, it wasn't! Even if Sammy never discovered what she'd done, she would know she'd betrayed his trust. He had taken her into his home, she could not deceive him.

Sholto was going. But first he made her sit down at the desk and write out a description of the little sugar caster, neatly, in fountain pen, on thick white paper. Her hand shook and she could not write, tears fell on to the ink and smudged it.

'I'll do it,' said Sholto abruptly. 'Tell me what to write.'

She dictated the note, her voice trembling. He knew enough to write it himself, she felt sure. 'Many casters might once have been part of a set,' she said waveringly, and watched his hand write. 'Pepper pots are common. But this little sugar shaker stands by itself as an attractive piece, largely because of its charming simplicity of design and the lack of later alteration.'

He wrote in a large, sloping hand, long black strokes

against the white paper. He put down the pen. 'It doesn't have to be like this. We started so well.'

'It wasn't going to last. You said so.'

'Yes.'

She wished he would go away. She wanted to cry, because love had come and gone in the twinkling of an eye. It was to be expected of course. Matty didn't expect happiness to oblige her just yet. She had sipped from a cup which was at once taken away, and he wasn't the man she had thought him, not at all. Her love was her own again, to keep for someone worthy. How she wished he would go away.

He stopped at the door. 'Are you packing tonight?'

She nodded. 'I'm getting an early flight. The silver has to go in a vault.'

'Give the wine cooler my regards. Remember, you could have sold it. Sammy would have been delighted.'

She turned away, but did not close the door. She heard him go down the hall to the elevator, and when she looked again, he was gone.

Holland Park seemed almost homely after New York. Matty felt battered by experience, as if she had been in a fight and had lost. Since her father's death she had swung from depression to wild confidence at dizzying speed, but lately she had lodged somewhere in between. Now, in her first real test of independence, she had failed. Virginity gone, lover gone, and no great selling coup to report.

She drew a breath of dusty, fume-laden London air, mixed with the scent of trees in the park. Familiar surroundings brought some measure of comfort, and not everything had to be confessed. Sammy would get one story, the girls quite another. There would be some small amount of boasting. After all, Sholto Feversham wasn't someone of whom she need be ashamed.

Delia welcomed her in with cries of delight. 'Dear Matty! I was so worried about you. Sammy said I was to enjoy myself, but as I said to him, how, when poor Matty's all alone in New York with those muggers and murderers and silver thieves?'

'None of the silver got stolen,' said Matty. 'I was fine, honestly.'

Delia considered her. 'You don't look fine. You look tired, and you've lost weight. It's those airline meals. I'll get you something tasty, something nourishing.' She bustled off, and Matty leaned her head against the hall cupboard and let out a low groan.

Sammy, descending the stairs, said, 'Don't tell me you've got a hangover. I send a girl to see my best customers and she drinks too much.'

Matty straightened. 'I'm just tired, that's all.'

She and Sammy eyed each other. He said, 'Come into the study. Tell me the worst.'

She gave him her expurgated tale. He blew down his nose now and then, making pertinent comments. 'You should have had dinner with Ed McKeogh. He'd have taken some of the big stuff off your hands. He drives a hard bargain, but he's straight.'

'You didn't tell me,' accused Matty. 'I wasn't sure if I was supposed to talk money with him.'

'You're a dealer, you talk money with everyone. We sell most to other dealers.'

She went on with her tale. When she explained that Sholto had arranged the sale of the sugar caster, Sammy put his fingers together and stared at her over them. 'I should have remembered he was thick with Mrs Waterman. Buys her Italian paintings. He'll be trying his best now he's lost his job.'

Matty gaped. 'I didn't know that. What happened?'

Sammy shrugged. 'There was a row. A picture was brought into the auction house, supposedly by Tiepolo. I know nothing of painting, but it was taken to be genuine — the owner had some expert or other at his elbow. Feversham disputed the provenance. Said the thing was a good eighteenth-century forgery. There was a great fuss, the value of the picture was in serious doubt, the reputation of the expert was in doubt, no less. And Feversham's considered too young to be much of an authority. Still at the dogsbody stage. The usual thing in these cases is for the painting to be considered by a few more eminent judges, and a consensus drawn. The consensus was that the painting was genuine. Feversham wouldn't agree, made a colossal fuss and wouldn't back down. He became obnoxious and was asked to leave.'

'But if he believed he was right –' said Matty in amazement.

Sammy snorted. 'Right or wrong, he was upsetting people. These things are bought for investment. It's not what the picture is that counts, but what people believe it to be. Probably it was what he said, but no one wanted to agree, too much was at stake. Of course rumour got out and the painting didn't reach its reserve. It was all very messy.'

Matty said nothing for a moment. No wonder he had been so anxious to do Mrs Waterman a favour. 'Should I have told him where the other wine cooler is?' she asked.

Sammy's eyes flashed. 'Of course not! As yet they don't want to sell. When they do, they'll come to us. We don't want every Tom, Dick and Harry making them offers they can't refuse. Mrs Waterman's dangerous, always snatching things from under people's noses. The sooner she dies the better.'

'I rather liked her,' said Matty.

'She's a very charming woman, but when it comes to collecting she has no scruples. Do anyone down. As for Feversham, I'll give him commission on the sale, he got a good price. And next time I go to New York I shall go and see Mrs Waterman myself. She'll buy that cooler. I shall tempt her with the promise of the other. It's going to come up, one of these days.'

He chuckled to himself and Matty, feeling herself dismissed, rose to go. Sammy picked an envelope off his desk and tossed it at her. 'Letter for you. Came two days ago. And that friend of yours has been telephoning. I told her you were abroad.'

'What was it about?' Matty felt a vague anxiety, and Sammy waved a dismissive hand. 'Something and nothing. Your brother. She said you weren't to worry, she was doing all that she could.'

Matty turned and fled upstairs. In her room she slammed

the door and ripped open her letter. It was in Simon's handwriting.

Dear Matty
This is to tell you I'm running away. I'm going to stay with Lord Knelworth, because he likes me and no one else does. I hate them too, there isn't anyone nice. I keep getting detentions, which isn't fair when I get top marks all the time. Don't worry, I told the school you were hunting kangaroos in Australia, so they won't ask you where I am. You'd better not visit, the police could be on my trail.

Lots of love
Simon

Matty dropped the letter and grabbed the bedside 'phone. She dialled Peregrines' number with frantic fingers. Why was there no letter from Lord Knelworth? Had Lorne meant that they were all joining in a search? Simon was missing, she was sure of it, lost in the vast hinterland between Peregrines and his school.

Lord Knelworth himself answered the 'phone. 'Hello. Hello. Who is this?'

'It's Matty Winterton. Have you got Simon?'

'Matty? Oh yes, Matty. I should say we've got Simon! And while he's a charming boy, quite charming, it really is time you got something sorted out about his school. Sounds an awful place by all accounts. The boy tells me there's a master comes and leers at them in the bath.'

'What?' Matty squawked with horror.

'I know things can be pretty rum at these schools, but that sort of thing can't be tolerated. I've a good mind to turn him in myself. Imagine! Boys of that age. Could affect them for life!'

She stammered promises and apologies. 'I'll come up and see him,' she promised. 'It's so kind of you to take him in.'

'No trouble, dear girl. Nice boy. Very keen to learn to shoot.'

In deference to Matty's supposed undernourishment, Delia served high tea. Confronted with scones and sandwiches, cake and jam, Matty felt slightly sick. In contrast Sammy and Delia were tucking in, seemingly delighted to have her home again. She felt such a fraud. When they looked at her they saw Patricia, her place filled again. Matty was forced to be an imposter.

'I wonder if I could have a couple of days off?' she ventured.

They both looked at her in surprise. 'You get days off,' said Delia. 'Our shopping days. Is there something you want to do, Matty? I can help you, do let me.'

'It's my brother,' she said, feeling as if she was struggling through the cloying treacle of Delia's affections. 'I've got to go and see him. There's trouble at his school, I don't know what.'

Sammy looked irritable. 'I've got work for you to do. I can't manage, you can't go.'

'Sammy!' Delia admonished him. 'If Matty wants to do something we can't stand in her way. She's fond of her brother. She's a very affectionate girl.'

'He's only got me,' said Matty.

Delia made a face. 'And in no time he'll be off in the world and you won't get even a card at Christmas. Boys are so independent these days.'

'Simon's still awfully young. Only ten.'

'Is he, dear? Then of course I shall go with you. I'll be able to help.'

'I really must insist on going by myself,' said Matty firmly.

Sammy waved a hand theatrically. 'Insist! She insists! In my time, she insists!'

'You can dock my wages if you want.'

Sammy grumbled and groaned, although Matty knew he had given in. But Delia was offended. When tea was over she went upstairs to lie down, saying she had a headache. Matty knew it was in her power to put things right, just by letting Delia come, and she was tempted, if only for the money. Delia would pay the train fare, hire a car, smooth Matty's path until there was nothing to obstruct or confound her anywhere. And Matty couldn't bear it.

In the morning she took her overnight bag and went to

catch the train. Delia was still in bed, suffering from a migraine apparently. Reproach hung heavy in the corridors, and Sammy left a large box of silver in the hall. 'If it's stolen, so be it,' he muttered. 'I've no time to be concerned with such things. My assistant should deal with them.'

'I'll look at it as soon as I get back,' promised Matty.

'What use is that if it's been stolen? It comes from a great country house, and it's going to be lost. They'll sue me for millions.'

Matty closed the door firmly behind her.

It was Friday, and the ticket cost nearly fifty pounds return. 'I only want second class,' stammered Matty.

'That is second class. They don't come no cheaper. Peak travel on Fridays.' The man behind the glass glowered at her. She should have let Delia come, thought Matty, writing a cheque. Despite her best efforts money seemed to trickle away, because although she bought almost nothing for herself Simon needed trousers, or guitar lessons, or had become inveigled into backing someone's sponsored swim. Was he really so miserable at school? She couldn't bear to think of it.

Two changes of train later she arrived at her stop. There was no one to meet her and no taxi, so she wrestled with the station 'phone box for ten minutes and managed to ring a mini-cab firm who promised to send someone in due course. After thirty minutes she rang again, and eventually a battered Ford turned up. Matty climbed in the back, full of gloom and despondency. She had eaten nothing since the evening before and she felt cold and tired.

Peregrines was not welcoming on a chill spring afternoon. The wind raced across the park and shook the new leaves on the oaks. New-born lambs crouched down in the grass while their foolish mothers wandered about bleating for them. When Matty rang the bell Lord Knelworth came himself, looking careworn.

'Hello, Matty. Grizzle's just rung. She and her friends are coming for the weekend, they've broken out. Some company for you, I dare say. But I don't know what they'll eat.'

Matty's face remained set. 'Is Simon here? He is still here, isn't he?'

Lord Knelworth nodded. 'Good Lord, yes. And showing no sign of leaving. That school deserves a stiff letter if you ask me. Very stiff.'

Simon was in the kitchen, making biscuits. When he saw Matty he went pink. There was flour in his hair.

'You do look a sight,' said Matty.

'Can't help that. Lord Knelworth likes me to do things. I'm very useful.'

Matty looked round, but her host had tactfully withdrawn.

'You can't stay here, Simon,' she said reproachfully.

'Yes I can! The house is big enough. He doesn't mind.' But his voice tailed off. Lord Knelworth's assumption that his stay was temporary had been disconcerting. Clearly he liked Simon, but there had been signs that he was finding him a little wearing. It wasn't what the boy had imagined, at school. Vaguely, without clear thought, he had expected a limitless welcome, because after all, it seemed to him, the old man led a very boring existence. Simon was prepared to exert himself to brighten his tedious days.

'Did you tell fibs about your school?' asked Matty.

Simon was sulky. 'No! I hate it there. They hate me.'

'You told Lord Knelworth that the masters leer at you in the bath. You're not going to tell that to me, are you?'

'They do!' He struggled for defiance. 'They're a load of perverts.'

'And you're a liar. Really, Sim, you ought to know me better by now. I can always tell when you're lying.'

He screwed some biscuit dough into a ball and splatted it down. 'It used to be true. There was a crackpot they had to sack.'

'About fifty years ago,' said Matty. 'What's the real trouble? Is it the work? You never had any trouble before.'

'I can do the work. I come top. By miles.'

'Oh. Oh, I see.'

Matty's heart sank. How well she knew the ruthless dynamics of a boarding school, of any school. The clever children were so often desperately lonely.

'Did you talk to your housemaster?' she asked.

'What, Batty Bateman? He made me join the stamp club. I hate stamps.'

'So what did you do?'

Simon looked at her from under his lashes. 'I set fire to the sick room. I didn't mean it! Honest! It was only the bin. But it set the smoke alarm off and the fire brigade came. So I ran away.'

The biscuit dough was breaking into dry pellets. Matty picked one up and nibbled at it, wondering what on earth she was going to do. Ought she to ask Delia if Simon could come to London? She knew it wouldn't work. Delia had little time for boys and in that neat, polished household he would wreak havoc. Should she send him back to school? He had never been truly happy there. Matty suspected that they didn't stretch him enough, because they had many less able boys demanding attention. Perhaps he needed a more academic environment.

The girls arrived at nine, just as Matty was despatching Simon to bed. A long blue Jaguar drew up at the door, its horn sounding insistently. Lorne was at the wheel, Griselda at her side and Henrietta in the back. They were all waving.

'Where did you get the car?' demanded Matty.

'Daddy,' said Lorne, extricating herself elegantly from the car. The effect was incongruous, for she was still wearing her school uniform. 'It was a present.'

'Some present,' said Matty, much impressed.

'My mother's bought me a Mini, for town driving,' said Henrietta breathlessly. 'Hello, Matty. You've no idea how dull school is without you. Nothing but work, and exams next month. Mummy's taking me out straight after for the Season. I've been to two parties already.'

'Sounds appalling,' said Griselda. She looked down her beaky nose at Matty. 'You look harassed. Let's get inside, it's freezing out here.'

The girls made for the kitchen, and cooked up baked beans on toast and mugs of cocoa. They sat around the big pine table, enjoying the merciful warmth of the range. Griselda found some elderberry wine from years ago and they sat sipping the dark liquid and talking.

'I feel so strange,' said Matty. 'As if I've been away for years.'

'You forgot us,' said Henrietta dismally.

'Of course she didn't!' Griselda thumped the table. 'We've all been busy, that's all. We'll have reports. Everyone must say what they've been doing. You first, Lorne.'

The dark girl tossed her hair back. The fine bones of her face were infinitely lovely. 'You know what I've been doing! I've been driving my beautiful car. Sometimes I go up to London and shop in Knightsbridge, and mostly I take my good friends out to tea. And when I was home last Greg made love to me three different ways. I think we're going to get married.'

'This could end in tears,' said Matty dubiously. 'Aren't you a bit young, Lorne?'

'I don't know. How young is young? My mother got married at twenty.'

'You're not eighteen,' said Griselda.

Henrietta said, 'You two are just being beastly. Lorne's in love. I think it's wonderfully romantic. I bet he gives her flowers and chocolates and compliments.' She sighed dreamily, wrinkling her plump little nose, imagining.

'Does he?' demanded Matty.

Lorne coloured. 'He's kind of practical,' she confessed.

'I'm sure he thinks romantic thoughts,' insisted Henrietta, shifting in her seat. She had put on weight again, thought Matty. Her golden hair framed an apple face, and her breasts were stuffed into a blouse a size too small. The blouse was in turn anchored by a straining school skirt, giving the effect of two dumplings, one on top of the other, with arms, legs and head as appendages.

Matty said, 'Have you got a romance then, Henry?'

Henrietta sighed and shook her head. 'No. I haven't anything to tell. My mother's furious because I look so dreadful in the dresses she wants me to wear. I keep telling her, I'm never going to be tall and thin, not if I starve for a hundred years.'

'It wouldn't suit you to be thin,' said Matty, half out of loyalty and half out of truth. Henrietta would always be rounded and soft, and it wasn't unattractive. She exuded comfortable happiness and good health, and if underneath she was ridden with angst, she hid it well. She took after her father, whose phlegmatic personality enabled him to live harmoniously with a managing wife. But then he spent his days in the City, and didn't have to endure the endless battles, as Henry did. She wasn't quite as happy as usual, Matty decided.

'What are you doing after the Season?' she asked. 'University?'

'We're leaving that to Grizzle,' said Henrietta ruefully. 'You've dropped out, Lorne's going to be a sex object in America, and I'm too dim.'

'I'm not a sex object,' said Lorne.

'Of course you are.' Griselda sloshed more wine into glasses. 'But, being you, I imagine you can't be anything else. Let's hope that in time you develop into a sensible human being.'

There was a stunned silence. The girls never attacked one another, it was part of their loyalty. Any criticism was to be expressed as gently as truth allowed.

'You bitch,' said Lorne.

'She didn't mean it,' said Matty hurriedly. 'Did you, Grizz?'

Griselda had gone slightly pink. 'No. Of course not. Sorry, Lorne.'

To fill the gap in the conversation, Matty said, 'Actually I've got something to tell.'

Three heads turned to look at her. 'You haven't,' said Henrietta in awed tones. 'Matty, you didn't!'

She took a deep breath. 'It was when I was in New York. I stayed in a fabulous hotel, in a suite. And one night – this man stayed with me. His name's Sholto Feversham. We had a row and I'm never going to see him again,' she added.

'Oh, Matty,' breathed Henrietta. 'That is romantic!'

'Was he rich?' asked Lorne. 'Don't throw yourself away on a pauper, Matty! You can't afford to.'

'He isn't rich, but it doesn't matter. We had an argument and that was that. He wanted me to do something dishonest.'

98

'You'd already been immoral, what's a bit of dishonesty between friends?' asked Griselda.

Matty chuckled. 'He doesn't equate fornication with immorality. He really is — incredible.' She sighed gustily.

As the night wore on the level in the wine bottle inexorably sank. The talk got more ribald. They began imagining any number of ways in which Matty could ensnare a millionaire. 'You could have cards printed,' suggested Lorne. 'Matilda Winterton, almost new, good service guaranteed. Offers invited in excess of one million dollars.'

'If it's dollars, make it five million,' said Griselda. 'She's a silver expert now, she can't be undersold.'

'I might be an expert in ten years,' said Matty, sinking her chin in her hands. 'Working with Sammy, I only ever see good silver. There's tons of rubbish about. I can value Lamerie at a glance, but I don't know a thing about Victorian tat.'

'Who needs to?' Lorne yawned expansively. 'When you've hooked your millionaire, you'll only see the stuff when the maid puts it out at dinner. Look, I'm going off to bed.'

The others got up to follow. But Griselda caught Matty's arm and held her back, waiting until they were alone. 'It hasn't been the same without you,' she said jerkily. 'Lorne drives me mad. She's so trivial.'

Matty chewed her finger. 'She isn't really. It's just her way.'

'And it's annoying me. Suddenly it's annoying me, and I hate myself for it. She's rich and pretty and generous and kind — and she dances through life without a single problem. She's going to marry her rich next-door neighbour and be happy forever. I have to confess to being despicably jealous.'

'She hasn't got Peregrines,' said Matty.

'No.' Griselda leaned back against the door frame. 'Perhaps it'll be better at university. There might be more of a place for ugly women there.'

'You're not ugly! You're different, that's all. A different style.'

Griselda laughed. 'I haven't got any style, and you know

it. By the way, how was Simon? Pop sounded rather strained on the 'phone.'

Matty said, 'Simon thinks he's going to stay here forever. He was intending to adopt your father as a new, improved parent. Don't worry, he's going back to school. I just don't know which one.'

'Awfully clever kid, I always thought,' said Griselda.

Matty nodded. 'Too clever. He needs an academic sweatshop. And he needs a home and security. I don't know where he's going to go in the holidays.'

'One of us will have him,' said Griselda. 'We all agreed.'

Matty smiled tremulously. 'Thanks, Grizz, but I won't bring him back here for a while, if you don't mind. He's getting too attached.'

Things were better the next day. Griselda organised a boat trip and picnic, and they took ancient rowing boats down the river. The picnic was dull and damp, so they took refuge in a pub instead and ate pasties and chips. Simon glowed with happiness.

'Great, isn't it, Matty?' he said, his cheeks shining red.

She nodded. He had a fishing rod Lord Knelworth had found for him and rummaged about on the riverbank while the girls sipped cider, watching him through the window of the pub.

'Don't look so anxious, Matty,' said Henrietta. 'I'll tell Mother he's coming to us for the holidays.'

'Forget it,' said Lorne flatly. 'With all due respect, Henry, a dose of your mother wouldn't be good for him. He'll come to me. I've got a cousin about the same age. They can ride and make fires in the woods. He'll have a great summer.'

'We really couldn't impose,' said Matty, and Lorne gasped.

'Did you say that? Did I really hear you say that? Since when did helping each other mean we had to be polite?'

They were all looking at her in accusation and Matty blushed to the roots of her hair. 'I'm sorry! Really I am. Yes please, Lorne, if you can manage it, then I'd love Simon to come to you.'

There seemed no end to her friends' generosity. On the Sunday Griselda pressured her father into telephoning schools, arranging for Matty and Simon to visit that afternoon. Transported in Lorne's Jaguar, they stood on the edge of playing fields and watched little boys get muddy, and took tea with headmasters and discussed maths. They chose the school that made no bones about excellence. 'You have to work here,' said the headmaster, fixing Simon with a cold eye. 'No shenanigans of any sort. We only like clever boys.'

Matty left him there, promising to send the uniform on. It would cost over two hundred pounds. Sitting next to Lorne in the car on the way home, she was silent and miserable.

'He'll love it, you know he will,' encouraged Lorne. 'He's not like us, he likes doing Latin half the night.'

Matty stirred herself. 'It's not that. I just feel I'm wasting time. The fees are more than before. I've got to earn money – for Simon, for a house, everything.'

'Honey, you will. You'll make a good living.'

'Yes, but when? In ten years? Simon needs it now.'

Lorne said nothing. She had the vague sense that Matty might be luckier than she knew. At least Matty had a purpose in her life, a single, driving need that must be satisfied. Lorne had no need of anything. Her path was strewn with primroses, any one of which she could pick, and the primroses stretched on and on, perhaps into infinity. She felt cold suddenly, and turned up the heating in the car. Matty's journey might be hard, but in comparison Lorne's was nothing but an aimless ramble. Then she felt the warm breath of comforting air, and she turned on the radio and found an upbeat pop station. There was nothing to worry about. Schools made her neurotic, that was all. Life was all about fun.

Chapter Seven

Sammy looked up from the papers on his desk. 'Did you get it? What price?'

'Six fifty.' Matty slumped into the chair opposite him. 'One of the other dealers asked me if I was working for Mr Chesworth, and I pretended I was deaf.'

'Why didn't you say no?'

'You know I won't lie.'

Sammy held out his hand for her parcel and she gave it up. It was a set of table salts, each lined in blue glass and standing on exquisite paw-shaped legs. There was something fantastical about them but they were so small and pretty that they were quite without menace. Sammy chuckled at them, and prepared to throw away the paper. But there was something else wrapped up. 'What's this?'

'Just some forks. They were cheap.'

'Cheap? They needed to be. You'll never match them.'

'We can keep them, can't we? They're lovely.'

He sniffed, weighing the forks in his hand. They were elaborately handmade, covered in scrolls and whorls. 'If you go on like this, Matilda, you will soon be able to tell people that you are definitely not working for Mr Chesworth. I tell you again, you are not to bid on your own account! I decide what we'll buy, not you.'

She said nothing. The forks had been an impulse, because yesterday she had despatched Simon to stay with Lorne and even if his fare was paid she had spent more than she intended on clothes and presents. Spending Sammy's money on forks he did not need seemed somehow an irrational consolation. Simon worried her so much, and it was better to have Sammy cross with her and worry about that.

He tossed the forks to one side. 'You'd better get off. My wife telephoned, she wants you at home.'

Matty took in her breath. 'I've work to do,' she said.

'I let you off, go. My wife wants to lunch at Harrods or some such thing. It's a fine day, be off with you.'

In the outer office Matty stood disconsolate. Emily said, 'Better get off, dear. Mrs Chesworth was most insistent.'

'I bet he didn't stand up for me, did he?' Emily always listened in on interesting calls.

Emily made a face. 'He tried. As much as men ever try. She was in one of her states, making a terrible fuss. Kept talking about Patricia.'

'Yes, she does. She didn't like it that I spent time with my brother. Made her furious.'

There was nothing for it. Matty put on her coat and prepared to go. Emily said, 'If she's buying you perfume, I'm getting a little low at the moment. And I could do with some bath oil.'

Matty nodded. 'OK. But she's trying to buy me balldresses just now. You don't want one of those, do you?'

'Not on your life! And neither do you. Where does she think you're going to wear them? Really, that woman gets odder and odder. Sammy ought to do something.'

The door to the inner office opened. 'Ought I indeed?' he demanded.

Emily went bright red. 'Sorry Mr Chesworth,' she muttered.

'I'm just off,' said Matty, and fled.

It was the usual difficult afternoon. Delia was in spendthrift mood, and nothing Matty could say would check her. If she wouldn't try a dress on Delia would attempt to buy it anyway, and when it came to the balldress they were reduced to an unseemly tug of war.

'I don't want it! Delia, put it back,' insisted Matty.

'Oh please, Matty! Darling, it'll be lovely, I promise. Trust me, trust my good taste. I know what suits you, I always have. Don't make me miserable, darling. Sammy won't like it.'

The assistant stood in mute protest as Delia tried to thrust the dress towards her and Matty hauled it back to the rail.

It was dark, almost midnight blue, tight to the hip before swirling out to the floor in a riot of diamante. It would indeed suit the girl, and she must have thought so too, because suddenly she gave up. With a cry of triumph Delia rushed the dress to the till. 'We'll have it! You must try it on at home, Matty, we'll go at once. I can't wait to see how lovely you'll look.'

Next morning Matty slammed a bottle of perfume on to Emily's desk.

'Oh dear,' said Emily. 'We did have a bad day. Not the ball dress?'

Matty nodded. 'I gave in. We were fighting over it and suddenly I looked up and saw all these people watching. What must it have looked like? We could have been a couple of dogs. And you could tell the assistant was going to regale the whole staff canteen with the story. I couldn't bear it.'

'Did you have a word with Sammy?'

Matty shook her head. 'He kept out of my way, all evening.'

But in the office he couldn't escape. He tried, going out first thing to an auction and buying teaspoons, but eventually he had to return to base. He made a lot of noise, demanding cups of tea and the instant despatch of faxes to Italy. 'I've got an epergne to send them, the one with the cupids, Matty. Have you done the paperwork? I told you a week ago.'

'But you keep sending me off shopping.'

'Shopping? Shopping? Girls give their eye teeth to go shopping. Get it done now, girl, now!'

Matty followed him into his office and shut the door. Sammy sat down at his desk and began a restless rummage through his papers. Finally he stopped. 'Don't expect me to take her on another holiday,' he declared.

Matty sank down on the chair, and let out her breath in a long sigh. 'I'm wondering if you can find me another job.'

'Don't be ridiculous, girl! You're not trained. You know nothing. Who'd employ you?'

She shrugged. 'Someone you know, perhaps. And if not that, then I'll get another job entirely. Something outside silver. Something that pays enough to let me get a flat.'

He looked at her. 'Patricia wanted a flat. We wouldn't let her.'

'Oh. I didn't know.'

He linked his hands together on the worn leather of his desk. 'I missed a silver-mounted decanter this morning,' he murmured. 'I was thinking of Delia, my mind wandered. I'm getting old.'

'It's not that I don't like her,' said Matty. 'I do. Very much.'

His beady eyes bored into her. 'Do you have to be so straitlaced? Do you have to be so rigid? I pay for the things, I don't care how much they cost. Or take them back to the shops, get the money. It's nothing to me. For my wife's health, it's cheap.'

'It does nothing for her health! She gets worse and worse. She's never accepted Patricia's death and if she goes on like this she never will. You pander to her, you don't help. It's got to stop.'

He dropped his eyes. 'I'll think of something. Believe me, I will.'

'I want you to do something now.'

'Now, now! I give her the best training in the world and she wants it yesterday. I tell you I'll think, no more!'

'Then I resign.'

'I don't accept it. Go on and work, you've work to do.'

'I'll go to an agency, I'll do filing or something.'

'If you want to file you do it here. Since you give Emily perfume, I'm sure she'll let you file!'

'Sammy, you know I've got to get away!'

They were both shouting. When they fell silent the air hummed with the echo of their voices. 'You can go and see Don Paolo de Caruzon,' said Sammy sulkily.

'Who?'

'Look him up, look him up! He wants to sell his silver. He wrote and asked me to visit. You can go. Mexico, on Friday.'

'This morning you wouldn't let me buy three forks on my own initiative!'

'You can always telephone me. You've got a good eye – too bad it's not commercial. I'll take Delia to a doctor, get an opinion. When you come back we'll talk.'

Matty reeled out of the office. Mexico! Sammy amazed her. Emily rattled the carriage of her typewriter. 'Paolo de Caruzon, no less,' she said smugly. 'Take the ball dress, dear, we're talking high society.'

Mexico. Towering mountains, yellow as sulphur, and above them the dry blue air. Fat women sat at the roadside, shaded by umbrellas, selling melons, mangoes, peaches. The taxi was headed towards the sea, and they passed through the groves of this or that, climbing, falling, then climbing again until they teetered on a crumbling cliff road, praying they did not meet a truck. The driver sang wailing songs and flashed dark eyes at Matty. Every now and then she would try to read her guide book, but reality seduced her, taking her gaze again and again to the window and the heat beyond.

At last the taxi turned between huge white pillars, up a tree-lined drive. Flowers rioted in the undergrowth, a profusion of growth, and Matty began to feel violently nervous. The de Caruzons were immensely wealthy, and said to be immensely proud. Who was she to give an opinion on their wonderful silver?

The drive expanded into a huge circle, in the midst of which stood a fountain. Beyond it the house itself was tall and whitewashed, consciously imposing. Two men carrying rifles leaned idly on the parapet of a whitewashed sentrybox. Matty got out of the car and stood uncertainly while the driver unloaded her luggage.

'Preetty good, eh?' he enquired. 'Preetty special. They got everything, own beach, own chopper. How long you stay?'

'I don't know.'

Matty fumbled in her bag for cash and paid the man. As a last friendly gesture he ran up the steps and pulled on the bellrope, while she tried to smooth the travel creases from her skirt. She had chosen to wear a white suit in a linen mixture, supposed to resist crushing, but she felt dishevelled and unprepared. Her grey silk camisole was damp with sweat. She had the uneasy feeling that it was clinging to her.

When she looked down she saw that it clearly outlined her nipples.

The door opened. She pulled her jacket across her breasts and ascended the steps. 'My name's Matilda Winterton. I'm Mr Chesworth's representative.'

A Mexican woman of statuesque proportions inclined a dignified head. 'Come in, Miss Winterton.'

Before Matty could stoop to pick up her luggage, a boy scuttled out and grabbed it. She followed the woman's swaying bottom into the house, crossing marble floors. Behind her the boy struggled with the cases, and from somewhere in the house a woman's voice called, 'Where is Conchita? I can't do my hair without Conchita.'

Matty's guide drifted towards a marble staircase, with twin gilded arms separating to embrace the hall. Between them hung an enormous picture of Christ on the cross. The expression was terrible, heart-rending, made all the more awful by lights directed right into the figure's eyes. Matty stopped and goggled at it.

'If you would hurry,' said the woman. 'My mistress is calling for me.'

Matty ran up the stairs. Someone had lit the candles in tiny holders against the wall, as if this were a church. But suddenly two small boys crashed through a door on to the landing and raced down the stairs, making shooting noises. One of them turned his fire on Matty and she pretended to die, clutching her heart and gurgling. He shrieked in delight and raced on, still firing.

The woman smiled at Matty. 'Boys,' she murmured. 'They all like guns.'

'Yes.' Plucking up courage Matty said, 'Ought I to say hello to Mr de Caruzon?'

'At dinner. Don Paolo never sees guests before dinner. You should wear good clothes, silk or lace.'

She opened a door and Matty followed her through. A four-poster bed stood in the centre of the room, and French doors led to a balcony. Beyond, at the foot of a tumble of rocks, the sea lapped and thrashed tirelessly, and birds dipped and swung in the warm air rising from the cliffs.

'Do you wish me to run your bath?'

Matty turned. 'Oh, no. Not at all. But if you could advise me on what to wear?'

The woman smiled again. The boy with the cases was slumped at the top of the stairs, recovering. She went to him and snatched the bags from his hands, moving them effortlessly into Matty's room. Snapping open the catches with her large, strong fingers she began to sort through all Matty's carefully chosen clothes.

The ball dress gave her pause. She smoothed it reverently, and laid it on one side. 'That is very beautiful,' she said.

'Yes.'

She held up a sheath in grey-blue satin. 'But you will wear this tonight.'

'Are you sure?' The dress was tight, low-cut and seductive. If everyone else was wearing neat cocktail dresses, Matty knew she would die.

'Don Paolo always asks that his guests should dress for dinner. He admires beautiful clothes.'

The voice came again, floating along the corridors in querulous demand. 'Conchita! Conchita, my hair!'

'I must go.' The woman rose and made her stately way to the door. Then she turned. 'I am Conchita,' she said unnecessarily.

'Yes. Thank you.' They each inclined their head.

The dinner gong sounded at seven exactly. Matty, waiting in the dress, felt weak with hunger and nerves. Unlike a hotel there was nothing at all to eat in her room, and she had even taken to eyeing the enormous flower arrangement that stood on the centre table, in case some of it might be edible. But now that the moment had come she hesitated. The dress was so revealing — one of Delia's wilder and more insistent purchases. The bodice was strapless, held up with the minimum of boning. Matty's breasts swelled over the top because Delia always bought things a size too small, Patricia's size. The whalebone was rigid against her flesh and the tight skirt restricted each step to a mincing wriggle. It was the sort of dress that led to seduction, thought Matty. She did not look like a silver expert.

She plucked up her courage and opened the door. A man was passing; brown hair, brown eyes, wearing a dinner jacket. He stood back to let her pass. 'How do you do.' he said. 'Have we met? I am Luca de Caruzon.'

'Matilda Winterton. I'm here on business.'

'Then for once business will surely be a pleasure.'

He put his hand under her arm as she descended the stairs, holding her a little too close. Matty said, 'Are you the Don's son, perhaps? I'm sorry, I don't know who anyone is −'

'I am his son-in-law. At the Don's request I have taken his name. My wife is Eleanor, the Don's daughter. His only child.' There was an edge to his voice, a touch of bitterness. She looked at him cautiously, not sure what to expect. He had a soft mouth, she thought, a weakness in an otherwise handsome face.

Together they walked across the hall, Matty's heels sounding like rifle shots on the marble. Beyond, through enormous double doors, stood the main salon, a riot of gilding and buttercup yellow. A tall, grey-haired man was holding court in its centre, and Luca steered Matty towards him.

'Father, may I present Matilda Winterton. She tells me she is here on business.'

Don Paolo nodded. 'Indeed. Our silver expert. How do you do, Miss Winterton.'

'How do you do.' She resisted the urge to curtsey.

'I wasn't expecting a beauty. Mr Chesworth has never been all that much of a ladies' man, to my knowledge.'

Matty swallowed. 'Mr Chesworth and I − Mr and Mrs Chesworth have been very kind,' she managed. 'My parents are dead.'

'An orphan. How exotic!'

Matty turned. A woman was sitting in a chair, her little feet resting on a stool. She was dressed in a froth of red lace and her hair was piled high on her head, glossy black coils held in place with diamond pins. But her skin was stretched tight across her bones, like fine creased leather on an embroidery frame. A woman no longer young, thought Matty. A woman desperate to be young again.

'My wife,' said Don Paolo, waving a dismissive hand. 'Doña Maria.'

Matty murmured her greeting, although Don Paolo had turned his back on the woman and was drawing Matty aside.

'Look at this,' he said, and lifted a giant candelabrum from a glass-topped table. 'Mexican silver. So heavy – feel the weight of metal.'

Matty's nose instinctively twitched. Here was another one, equating weight of silver with quality. Finesse was lacking. She quite disliked the piece. The artistry of good silver rendered its bullion value insignificant, but a piece like this she would gladly see melted. She put it down and instead lighted on a nutmeg grater under the glass in the table itself. 'That's a good specimen,' she murmured. 'I imagine it's American.'

'But so small,' said Don Paulo.

He drew her a little to the side. She felt a tremor of apprehension, aware that he had quite the wrong impression of her and that in this dress she had given it to him. 'I am so glad to have you here,' he murmured. 'I wasn't aware that Mr Chesworth understood me so well.'

'I really think – I'm not at all sure –' Matty stammered incoherently.

'You have beautiful breasts, my dear.'

Doña Maria's voice rang out. 'Conchita! Conchita, I must have champagne. And my hair is falling. Why did you not do my hair as you should? Conchita!'

'You are so young,' murmured Don Paolo. 'The young have so much to learn.'

'Mr Chesworth has taught me a great deal about silver,' she prevaricated.

'But I am talking about love.'

To Matty's intense relief, Luca crossed to them. 'Perhaps Miss Winterton would like to sit next to me?' he asked.

Don Paolo said, 'What are you about, Luca? Do you wish to make Eleanor jealous?'

'If I might be privileged to know my own wife,' said Luca tensely.

The Don observed Matty beneath lowered lids. He shrugged. 'I give her to you. But remember, I am the old bull and I still have the pick of the cows.'

Matty felt her temper snap. 'I am not a cow,' she said,

111

in a low, furious voice. 'Don't you dare speak of me like that! I'm here to look at the silver. No more.'

Both men looked at her in surprise. 'You will sit with Luca,' said Don Paolo distantly.

'Thank you,' said Matty. She and Luca moved away.

He took her in a circuit of the room, introducing her to some of the dozen or so people there. Suddenly the door opened and a tall, pale woman came in. She stared around the room, unmistakably her father's daughter, proud, black-eyed, but at that moment crackling with tension. She saw Matty with Luca and at once came across.

'Who is this?' she demanded. 'What are you doing?'

'Eleanor.' Her husband tried to meet her eye, but inevitably his gaze fell. 'A girl,' he said feebly.

'I see that! What girl? Why are you here?'

Matty said, 'I'm Matilda Winterton, here to do a silver valuation. Were those your boys I saw earlier? They were like you. Very good-looking.'

For a moment Eleanor hovered between rage and good manners. But to Matty's relief she relaxed suddenly, and lit up her sombre face with a smile. 'My boys. They are beautiful, so full of life. They should not have to live here, it is not good for them.'

'Your father feels —' said Luca, and she turned on him.

'What does it matter? I want to live where I want to live, why can't you stand up for me for once? You're not a man. You can't do what a man does, you don't know how! Weakling!'

Her words carried across the room. Matty was uncomfortably aware of Don Paolo's lifted head, of his wife's repeated parrot screeching, of the hushed conversations around them.

'I like living in the country,' said Matty inanely.

'This is not living,' said Eleanor. 'To be here is a living death.'

The announcement of dinner came none too soon. Matty sat between Luca and an aged and silent de Caruzon relative. He ate with determination, occasionally asking why Matty was there. Each time he listened to what she said, nodded, and forgot. Across the table Luca's wife sat watching with burning eyes. At the head was Don Paolo, toying elegantly with his food. At the foot Doña Maria was a dressed up doll, endlessly wailing: 'Conchita!'

'We are surprising you,' murmured Luca.

'It's a beautiful house,' fenced Matty. 'Many fine pictures.'

'You can see Doña Maria is a religious fanatic. She cannot resist the depiction of religious suffering.'

'Many collectors have strange whims,' said Matty.

'She is hardly a collector. To be honest, I despise her. She simply buys gory paintings, no more. She is quite without discernment.'

'Are you an expert?' asked Matty.

'To a degree. To quite a degree.'

He reached under the table and touched her thigh. 'Please don't,' said Matty.

'But you wish to buy our silver.'

'Any deals must be strictly above board,' said Matty, frightened into stiff formality. 'I never enter into any sort of relationship with clients.'

'But I am not your client. Do you want money perhaps? I will pay you to come to my room.' His hand fumbled in her lap, defeated by the tightness of her dress.

Almost hysterical, Matty said, 'Mr de Caruzon, your wife is sitting across the table!'

'Yes. She cares nothing for me. And you excite me so.'

Matty resorted to school-mistress severity. 'Then control yourself! I didn't come here to be used. I came to look at the silver, and that's all.'

She seemed to be getting through to him. Looking defeated he withdrew his hand and took a generous helping of the next course. Conscious that across the table Eleanor de Caruzon was sneering, Matty again tried to make conversation with her other neighbour, but it came to nothing. Suddenly Luca caught hold of her hand and drew it down under the table, she struggling to resist. His wife's eyes looked at him with contemptuous amusement. The table cloth surged as Luca and Matty battled.

'You are not a cold woman,' whispered Luca. 'I know

these things. Feel how you excite me.' He pressed her against him. His eyes were glistening, he was breathing in shallow breaths to contain himself. Suddenly Matty closed her hand on him, gripping with vicious intent. He lurched, gasped, and fell forward.

'It is his heart,' yelled Doña Maria. 'Conchita, call the doctor.'

Matty's other neighbour staggered up and began loosening Luca's tie and trying to pull him back from the table. Luca fought him off, panting, his face suffused with colour. 'I'm all right. I'm all right, I tell you! I'll go and lie down.'

Suddenly Eleanor burst into peals of ribald laughter. Luca left the room, bent over, the laughter ringing about his ears.

'Eleanor!' snapped Don Paolo 'That is enough!'

'Even that girl's more than enough for a chimpanzee like him,' retorted Eleanor. 'He can't even get a little trade girl into bed!'

Colour rose in Matty's cheeks, not in embarrassment but rage. She wanted to put her hands under the table and tip it over, heave it on top of all of them, and be done. Instead she picked up her fork and tried again to eat. Don Paolo sat like a judge above her, watching her every move.

After the meal the windows were opened. People wandered out to walk in the gardens, with the exception of Doña Maria. She remained sitting in her chair, wailing for Conchita. Matty left the others as quickly as she could, striking out down a side path between banks of flowering shrubs. She took long breaths of the scented evening air, and with it came relief. For a moment or two she was free of them.

She rounded a corner. There, on a stone bench, sat Luca's wife. She was crying. 'Er – I'm sorry,' said Matty stiffly, and prepared to back away.

'Oh, it's you. Please stay and talk to me.'

'I don't think I wish to,' said Matty, and Eleanor laughed.

'You were offended at dinner – don't be. It wasn't about you. My father's a bully, as with all powerful men, and he married me to a weakling. I make him weaker, I think. I ask him to do what he cannot. I ask him to challenge my father.' She laughed a little. 'I want to go to Europe, Paris, anywhere. They keep me a prisoner! Did you see the men with guns at the gate? They are not our protectors. They are there to prevent my escape.'

Matty said, 'Was your husband trying to impress you?'

Eleanor shrugged. 'I don't know. Perhaps not. I won't have him in my bed nowadays. I tell him to do what he likes, but you see, he can only do it under my eye and even then he fails. I hate him. I hate him to touch me.'

'Then why did you marry him?'

A long, weary sigh. 'Why indeed? Because my father wished it. Luca is my father's right hand man, and it was advisable. I used to think my father cared what happened to me, that he wanted the best for me. Now I know he only wants what is best for him, Don Paolo. He cares nothing for me.'

Eleanor turned a handkerchief in her fingers, endlessly twisting it. 'I have no one I can tell,' she burst out.

Filled with curiosity, Matty said: 'Tell what?' in a non-committal tone.

'What happens! What he does!' The woman turned to Matty and took her hands. 'The dealers all come with their paintings and their silver and their pottery. My father buys many things, he sells many things, always buying and selling. You understand?'

'Yes,' said Matty, who did not.

'He does not ask where anything comes from. But sometimes I know. So many lovely things come into this house, and they stay, for years sometimes. Until they are forgotten. Until the world has stopped wondering. Sometimes pictures, but not often. Other things.'

'Is – is the silver stolen?' asked Matty, wide-eyed.

Eleanor shrugged. 'I do not know. Some, perhaps. But now you know you must avoid incrimination, must you not?'

The woman smiled in cold self-congratulation. Matty's mind raced. Was she lying? Was she simply trying to put her off buying Don Paolo's silver? Or could it be true?

'What is your father's business?' she asked cautiously.

But Eleanor sat on the garden bench and said nothing. Her dark eyes burned into Matty's in utter silence.

They walked back to the house together, and parted on the terrace. Matty was exhausted. She couldn't wait to take herself off to bed. The great house seemed to have swallowed its inhabitants. There was no one anywhere in the bright rooms and corridors. She paused at the foot of the stairs, wondering if there was someone to whom she should bid goodnight. In a household like this, set on shifting sands, her only refuge seemed to be in punctilious good manners, a careful pretence that she hadn't noticed what was going on.

A door in the hall stood ajar. She thought she heard noises and went to peep inside. It was a little chapel, with an altar, burning candles and a row of embroidered kneelers. Lying across the kneelers was the half-dressed body of her host, Don Paolo de Caruzon, and astride him, naked and heaving, was Conchita. She plunged up and down, her great breasts swinging in arcs, Don Paolo's thin, aristocratic hands cradling her giant buttocks, his long muscled legs protruding beneath her.

'Conchita!' he was murmuring.

Unseen and quite still, Matty watched wide-eyed. She wanted to look away but the scene was comically, grotesquely erotic. The woman started to grunt, like an animal, and suddenly Matty was disgusted. She turned and ran up the stairs.

She slept badly that night. The faces of the women kept intruding, Doña Maria, Eleanor, Conchita. Paolo de Caruzon was not a pleasant individual, added to which, Matty was scared of him. That in itself annoyed her: she hated to think she was so much a coward. In all the escapades of her schooldays she had been the one to crawl across the roof on a night-time dare, the one to run the gamut of disapproval when she smuggled booze into the prep room. She was used to thinking of herself as brave, and yet, so far from home, she was frightened.

Conchita's advice on clothes was studiously ignored next morning. Matty resurrected her severe black suit, and tied her hair up in a black and white bow. But she need not have worried. Don Paolo's exertions with Conchita had exhausted him. He sat at the breakfast table in a state of weary relaxation. His only companion was the silent relative, working steadily through a plate of porridge.

'Good morning, Miss Winterton. Today we will speak of silver.' Don Paolo waved her to a seat.

'Indeed.' Matty sat down, and was instantly enveloped in a huge damask napkin, flung across her lap by a servant. Fruit, breads and yoghurts were all served to her, and she devoured everything. She glanced at her knife. It was stainless steel, just like last night. It puzzled her. If Don Paolo had so much silver she would have expected at least a silver handle, even if the knife was modern. Old knives rarely survived as usable pieces. She looked at the forks, the spoons. Not a piece of silver there.

'You don't use table silver, Don Paolo?'

'Certainly not. My pieces are not to be mauled by indigent relatives.' His eyes passed coldly over the old man, now scoffing bacon.

'Don't you feel that half the pleasure of good silver is that it's useful?'

'The pleasure of good silver is in its value. Come, you will see.'

She got up and followed him from the room. They went through a door and down a flight of stairs to the cellars, but even here there was soft carpet and mirrors. He removed a bunch of keys from his pocket and unlocked a door. Within was another door, this time locked with a combination. He put his eye to a spyhole, turned the tumblers and opened up.

The room was lined with silver. It stood on tables, under tables, on shelves and on the floor. A silver chandelier hung with its chain pulled short, a dozen epergnes ranged underneath it, each with its full complement of sweetmeat dishes hanging round the edge. And yet everything was black with dirt.

'Don't you ever clean it?' asked Matty.

'Why, no. Cleaning ruins the marks.'

'I see. What a pity none of this can be enjoyed.'

She walked around the room, touching things, inspecting the pieces that interested her. Sammy had told her to buy whatever de Caruzon wished to sell, but at a price, only at a price.

She turned to Don Paolo. 'Which pieces?'

'All of them.'

Matty blinked. 'It could take me a week to value all this! I'd have to telephone Mr Chesworth.'

'Then do so. The entire collection is for sale.'

All Matty's instincts rose up and assailed her. 'Why don't you auction it?' she asked bluntly. 'Some of this stuff could make fabulous prices.'

He raised his brows in quelling style. 'My name must never appear as the owner of any of this. Mr Chesworth knows my views on confidentiality, and I trust he will impress them on you. I never advertise my possessions.'

If they were his possessions, thought Matty. How much of this was recorded on mouldering police lists in far-off countries?

When he left Matty settled down to work. It was absorbing. She felt like Aladdin counting rubies in a cave full of treasure. There was so much that was interesting and complicated: a set of sconces, for instance, with overstruck marks, indicating that one maker had begun the work and another finished it off. But it could be an attempt to make something ordinary seem more important. She glared at the metal through narrowed eyes, willing it to tell her the truth. On balance, they were genuine, but Sammy would know best.

One bowl she left until last, like the favourite sweet in a box of chocolates. She fancied it might be Lamerie, although the decoration was a little more free and swirling than she might expect. Who then? Storr perhaps? Achambo? She wasn't sure.

The bowl itself was medium-sized, heavy, with a wonderful acanthus leaf and mask decoration. Matty peered at the marks, ready to be amazed, although at first she didn't recognise anything. NS — she knew of no maker with that mark except one and Sammy had told her never to expect to see it. She looked again, struggling to make the S into a B, then N into an H or something similar. But the mark was quite clear and unmistakable. This bowl had been made by Nicholas Sprimont.

118

She felt dizzy. To her knowledge Nicholas Sprimont had made only about eighteen pieces, and this was not known to be one of them. She peered at the marks again, wondering if the piece could be forged, but it sang to her of authenticity in weight and balance, in sheer artistic merit. Sprimont had been a wonderful silversmith, but had abandoned his craft to become a jeweller, leaving behind only a few tantalising remnants. He must have hated the job, thought Matty. All that hammering to raise one single pot. And yet he was brilliant.

She put the bowl on one side, looked away and then looked back. Was she deceiving herself? No. Even blackened and neglected it was the finest possible piece of work. All the horrors of the house and its inhabitants suddenly seemed as nothing, compared with the privilege of handling this one Sprimont bowl. She hugged herself gleefully. Sammy was going to be amazed.

Don Paolo came to collect her himself at lunchtime. He locked up the room with a great clanging of bolts. 'Do you have a catalogue of any sort?' asked Matty. 'It would help.'

'I never keep lists of my possessions.'

Matty's suspicions were like gremlins, whispering in her ear.

Luca was at lunch, sitting next to his wife. Matty saw him touch her hand at one point, but she ignored him. Don Paolo was watching them, his eyes hooded and inscrutable, and at the other end of the table Doña Maria sat and squeaked for Conchita.

Eleanor looked at Matty. 'Are you enjoying the silver?'

'Very much. It's beautiful. A wonderful collection.'

'I have not seen it in years.'

'Good heavens. Perhaps this afternoon — ?' She looked enquiringly at Don Paolo.

'I fear not. You have too much work. Some other time.' There would of course be no other time. Eleanor met her eye. 'You see?' her look said. 'You see how it is? Now you must understand.'

All afternoon Matty struggled, listing, assessing, weighing each piece on her silver scale. Sammy would need a bank loan to afford so much, and when she was released at around six she went straight to telephone him.

'Sammy? It's me.'

'Matilda. You should have called yesterday. Anything good?'

'You bet! A Sprimont bowl, and I'm sure it's right. And everything else — Sammy, not counting the bowl, at a guess it's a million and a half, perhaps two.'

He sucked in his breath. 'Sprimont? Off your head. You're valuing rubbish, you must be. I should have taught you about rubbish.'

'Sammy, every piece is good. He's got some bad Mexican stuff in the house, and a few nice American pieces here and there, but this is all English and it's all locked up.' She dropped her voice to a whisper. 'He's laundering money, Sammy. Is he in drugs? I'd bet my life he's a crook.'

Sammy's voice snapped out: 'Be quiet, Matty! Remember where you are!' He went on, more calmly, 'Don't ask questions. Take photographs, list everything, and make him an offer. We can sort out your fake Sprimont later. I want a copy of the list faxed to me as it's drawn up. You are weighing everything?'

'Of course. Some of the bigger stuff's a problem but the maker's weight's scratched on lots of things. It's all filthy, you know.'

'The man has a right to do as he wishes with his own silver. He has a right to do as he wishes with his money. Remember that, Matty.'

She went out into the gardens before dinner, in her white suit. A rough path led down the cliffs to a tiny private bay, with a boat house and a single shower. Matty took off her shoes and paddled in the lapping waves, watching a crab dash from side to side, eyes swivelling madly. The light was pure, lending the surrounding cliffs and even the horizon the clarity of a well-focused photograph. Tomorrow she would bring her costume and swim, decided Matty. This was a strange and disturbing household, but it need not disturb her.

The cliff was steep and difficult to climb. She wasn't as fit as at school, with no hockey to exhaust her, and she rested every hundred yards or so. A seat had been positioned halfway up and she collapsed on to it, shading her eyes against the fierce sun. Suddenly she noticed a summerhouse, hidden in the trees further up. A movement caught her eye; it was Eleanor, running from the building. Even at this distance Matty could see that her lip was cut and bleeding. A few moments later Don Paolo appeared, and walked slowly and languidly after her.

Eleanor did not appear at dinner, and Luca sat in silence, eating nothing. Even the aged relative appeared to notice an atmosphere, and muttered to Matty, 'The air's close tonight. We'll have a storm.' Doña Maria held her rosary and clicked the beads, muttering to herself. She had brought a small painting into the room and it was propped on an easel so all could see. It was the inevitable blood-soaked crucifixion.

The meal seemed to drag, and Matty watched clouds building in the sky beyond the window. The stillness of the evening should have warned her, it was the calm before the storm. Luca left before the coffee was served, and a few moments later they heard Eleanor screaming in hysterics. Suddenly, alarmingly, there was silence. There came the hiss of rain, striking the hot stones of the terrace, the sudden rush of scent caused by the cooling of an overheated day. The room was darkening, and no one moved to switch on the light. Dimly, in the distance, came the sound of the front door bell, and minutes later the dining room door opened, letting in a flood of light. Standing there, tall, rain-soaked, wearing a bush jacket with jagged rents where the sleeves had once been, was Sholto Feversham.

Chapter Eight

He was like the storm itself, electric and disturbing. Don Paolo got up from the table and held out his hand. 'Sholto. I expected you tomorrow.'

'I got an earlier flight. Doña Maria. How is Conchita?'

'She is well. Very well. Will you take wine?' The woman made a sad attempt at a sparkle. She must once have been lovely, thought Matty, and could be still. How she hated de Caruzon.

She felt Sholto's eyes upon her and lifted her head. He stared at her, and she stared back, saying nothing.

'Miss Winterton,' said Don Paolo. 'To buy silver. Mr Feversham is here to buy paintings.'

'How do you do.' Matty inclined her head.

'How do you do.'

He turned away and she felt a stab of chagrin. He should be pleased to see her. Why wasn't he pleased? She tried to remember what she had last said to him. Surely she hadn't let her temper get the better of her? Once she lost her temper it was hard to remember what she had said.

Doña Maria held out her hand and in tinkling tones demanded that Sholto look at her little picture, here, on the easel. He came across and inspected it. 'Divine,' he said, waving a theatrical hand. 'Such passion.'

'Such anguish!' corrected Doña Maria. 'I like to look upon anguish.'

'Divine anguish,' said Sholto, and Matty wondered if she should laugh. But everyone here was so humourless. Sholto shot her a brief glance, and she knew he had said it for her benefit. Damn the man. He found it so easy to make her feel that she held a special place in his affections, and yet

123

Doña Maria felt that, and Conchita, simpering by the door, and no doubt Eleanor, and Mrs Waterman, and any woman of Sholto's cosmopolitan acquaintance. Matty wished she had never slept with him. She wished she could regret it more.

Sholto went to his room to change, with Conchita promising that food would be brought up to him. Rain was drumming on the ground, and the thunder rumbled ever closer. A cat, soaked to the skin, ran hectically past the window.

'Conchita,' said Don Paolo, 'have my daughter and her husband join us in the salon. I insist on it. We will drink together.'

Doña Maria was excited, arranging lamps and candles to illuminate her paintings in the salon. The walls seemed alive with writhing figures, blood, pain. Don Paolo was setting a bottle of tequila on an ugly tray of Mexican silver, with glasses and a small pot of salt. The aged relative called for port and they gave him a half tumbler of the stuff. He quaffed it in one.

To Matty's surprise Luca came in with his wife. Eleanor was white, under an apparently unbearable strain, even her lips were shaking. But still she looked out at them all as if she would burn them up with her stare. She was like a bird, thought Matty, a captured bird of prey.

'Luca! Come here,' commanded Don Paolo.

The man hesitated. He didn't want to obey like a dog and increase his wife's scorn, but he did not dare resist. The hesitation collapsed into compliance. He went quickly to the Don's side.

'You must go away for a few days,' said Don Paolo. 'I've some business I want you to do.'

Luca licked his lips. 'I can't leave Eleanor. She's ill.'

'My daughter makes herself ill. A man can't live, tied to a woman's apron strings. She'll have everything here, all possible care. You can go in the morning.'

Eleanor sat in a chair, eyes black with anger. 'You want to destroy me,' she said bitterly.

Matty found herself suddenly speaking. 'Perhaps Eleanor could go as well?' she said. 'Why not?'

124

Don Paolo gasped in surprise. When he found his voice he said, 'I wasn't aware we needed your advice on anything except silver, Miss Winterton.'

'You know us experts,' said Matty with an attempt at bravado. 'We gather evidence and make our judgements. Sometimes it's hard to confine those habits to one field.'

Sholto's voice cut across them. 'Personally I find it very easy. Doña Maria, you have acquired a Montagna since last we met. Most interesting.'

She simpered at him, while Eleanor sat in tense silence in her chair. Matty went across to her.

'You don't have to stay here,' she said in a low voice. 'I really think you should leave.'

'You should not take my part,' said Eleanor. 'He'll revenge himself on you. He allows me no friends, no allies. He wants to crush me!'

'Perhaps he doesn't realise —'

Eleanor almost laughed. 'Oh, but he does! He knows so well how to torture me. It's a pleasure with him. He puts no limits on his pleasure.'

'But you could leave!' insisted Matty. 'He can't keep you prisoner. Of course you can leave.'

Eleanor reached out and touched Matty's hand. 'You are so young and so strong,' she said gently. 'I should like to be like you again. I should like not to be what my father made me. And that weakling I married.'

Matty was embarrassed. She did not understand.

Sholto and Don Paolo were drinking tequila together. The laughter was wild, and getting wilder. Glasses were beginning to be smashed.

'Mind my paintings!' wailed Doña Maria. 'Oh, look! The rain is full of red soil. It's almost like blood.'

Luca went to take his wife's hand but she shook him off. The aged relative was drinking yet another tumbler of port. He staggered back against a painted screen and sent it crashing to the floor.

'Mind my paintings!' yelled Doña Maria. 'Conchita, Conchita, come and see!'

Matty could bear no more. She turned on her heel and went to bed.

No one but Matty took breakfast next morning. She sat alone at the white cloth and was served toast and fruit juice, coffee and ripe peaches. The storm had scrubbed the day clean, its only legacy a delicious freshness in the air and a deluge of fallen petals on the grass. But the absence of Don Paolo left Matty with a problem; she could not get into the strong room to continue her inspection of the silver. After waiting for half an hour, with no sign even of Conchita, let alone Don Paolo or Doña Maria, she collected her swimming things and took herself off for a walk.

An old gardener smiled at her as she brushed through the damp flowers. Last night's cat was sunbathing on a step, licking its coat into silken submission. Evil seemed far away. She was reading too much into a simple family conflict. Even as she thought it she knew it wasn't true. Don Paolo had created Paradise, complete with serpent.

The cliff path was slippery after the rain and she often had to hold on to twigs and branches. She wondered if Don Paolo intended to offer his silver elsewhere, because Mr Chesworth had chosen someone so difficult to value it. Sammy would be furious. But she could not stand by and watch that man, that terrible man, imprisoning his daughter like this.

Luca was going away. Was it drugs? Was Don Paolo a drug baron, washing his money in the gloomy pool of the world's art markets? He bought lavishly, waited a long time and sold again, and no one asked questions because no one dared. There was no money in rocking the boat. Should Sammy be buying his silver at all? The thoughts preoccupied her. When she reached the beach she stood for a moment looking out at the limpid blue sea. A slow swell was a reminder of last night's storm, rolling in from the horizon like the product of an eternal machine. Matty kicked off her shoes, pulled off her skirt and pants, and in one quick movement dragged her shirt and bra over her head. Naked, she reached down for her swimming costume.

A voice said, 'Please don't bother. I really don't think you should spoil it.'

126

Matty spun round. Sholto was sitting on the sand by the boat house and he was without a stitch of clothes.

'How could you!' She snatched up her skirt and held it in front of her.

'How could I what? Sit here? Take my clothes off? Watch you? All very pleasurable activities.'

Matty grabbed at her things. 'I'm going back up.'

'Bit prudish, isn't it? I was gazing on your lovely flesh with pleasant recognition.'

'I think you're vile,' said Matty.

'At least I'm prepared to remember it. Your virginity was lost one wonderful, unregretted night. I can't give it back to you. I wouldn't if I could.'

Matty didn't know what to do. When she thought about it, prudishness did seem out of place. 'I'm going to swim,' she said, and turned and ran naked into the waves.

He came after her. She ran like a hare, like a gazelle, feeling the water slowing her legs, her body, dragging her down until she felt it take all of her, sending shockwaves through her warm flesh. She took a stroke, another, and suddenly his arms were round her waist. He held her, naked, against him.

'Let go,' hissed Matty. She pushed her hands against his chest, trying to remove her breasts from contact.

'Never.'

'Because I let you once, it doesn't mean you can do it always.'

'You don't give me permission to have you! We do it together. We take our pleasure like two adult, wanting, seekers after beauty.'

He was nudging at her body, and the waves pulled at her, pushed at her. She let the sea move her, let it take her to the shallows, his body hot on her cold skin. The shock of him inside her made her cry out. She fell back and her head was under water. He pulled her shoulders close to him and a circle of feeling ran from her womb to her breasts, returning in a rush of hot blood. Her orgasm came powerfully; it was a wave, a wave of joy. Like silver, love could be ugly, and like silver again it came near to spiritual perfection.

127

She lay on the sand, panting. 'I hate you,' she said lazily.

'Of course you do. Don't expect me to admit that we've met.'

'I wouldn't dream of it. You're too busy making up to Doña Maria. The woman's insane.'

'Fixated, more like. But she's got some wonderful paintings. Perhaps when she looks at Don Paolo she imagines him crucified. An end too good for him, I should think.'

'I thought he was a great friend?'

Sholto lay back, sloshing salt water over his groin. 'Perhaps he is. I don't know what makes a friend. Someone you're pleased to see, I should think, for whatever reason. He pays me. That makes me wonderfully enthusiastic.'

Matty said, 'I heard you'd lost your job. You should have said.'

'Why? I don't like people to know my little desperations.'

'Were you desperate? Eleanor is.'

'Eleanor is making a lot of fuss. She should take a leaf out of Conchita's book, and humour the old boy. Just one of those things, just one of those tiresome necessities.'

'You don't know a thing about women. We can't be like that.'

He rolled over on his stomach and his blue eyes bored into her. 'What can you be like?'

Matty got up. She fetched her towel and began drying herself, knowing that each movement made him want her. She felt powerful, tempting.

'When did you go on the pill?' he asked.

Matty looked blank. Then horror dawned. Sholto's face became a picture of anguish. 'I don't believe it! You bloody fool!'

'I didn't plan this. It wasn't my idea!' Matty almost backed away, he looked so fierce and grim.

'Just don't expect me to support you! Don't think you're going to trap me like that!'

'I haven't trapped you at all,' snapped Matty. 'I had my period until two days ago, so it's almost bound to be all right. Unless you've got Aids of course. Calm down.'

But he was dressing, in careless haste. It was as if he was desperate to escape.

'I wish you'd trust me,' said Matty suddenly. 'You've no reason not to but I feel you don't.'

He stopped then, and looked at her. 'I don't trust anyone. This is a very lonely world, Matty. We come together in brief moments of need. It means nothing. Sometimes we just have to take the risk.'

'Don Paolo's into drugs,' said Matty timidly. 'He's asking us to wash his money clean.'

He grinned. 'Is that your conclusion? Sorry, you're wrong. He's an arms dealer. Off the shelf missiles and so on. But it's nothing to do with you, and the silver is. Forget your conscience, forget your principles. If it's truth and beauty you want, then look for it in art. Man puts it there to keep it safe. He knows it can't survive anywhere else.'

She recoiled from his intensity. He went up the cliff first, almost running. Matty couldn't keep up, and when she reached the top there was only the old gardener, still hoeing, and the cat washing its paws.

Luca went away the following day, leaving Eleanor brooding. She went into the garden sometimes with her children, playing games with them, throwing the ball too hard. When they cried she seemed not to know how to comfort them, and Matty felt a great rage. Misery was like an inheritance, handed down through generations, never ending. There ought to be an end of Don Paolo. Powerful men ruled only because others were too timid to stand up to them.

She threw herself into her work. Each lunchtime and evening she would emerge from her cellar and join the family at meals. Sholto ignored her, talking to Eleanor instead, sharp, clever conversations that made even her smile. Other than that he talked only of art.

Much discussion centred on one particular painting. It wasn't a favourite of Doña Maria's, containing little in the way of gore, and lurked in a dark hall, unlit. Doña Maria wanted to sell it, but Sholto was reluctant. What would she put in its place? He only had this or that to show her. He pulled out postcard-sized photographs of pictures, offering them to the lady like dishes on a menu. One delighted her, of Christ much mauled, staggering under the weight of the cross. 'Take that other and let me have this,' she pleaded. 'I must have this!'

Sholto prevaricated. The new painting was bigger, better, worth more. He didn't want a boring little saint-encrusted square: no one else would buy it. But if she wanted the new one so much — if she truly didn't mean to be without it — Sholto named his price.

Matty's spoon froze in her pudding. She felt Don Paolo's eyes on her and forced herself to continue eating with every appearance of calm. How could he? How could Sholto sit there and smile? She knew, instinctively, that Sholto wanted the painting with every fibre of his being, that it was special. All the reluctance was so much moonshine, when this painting was worth far, far more than he seemed ready to pay.

Doña Maria was bargaining now, trying to take something off the price of her new acquisition, but Sholto wouldn't budge. He talked of statistics, market trends, downward turns. The deal was as good as done.

Matty waited until the evening. After dinner, at around nine, Doña Maria went to bed, Don Paolo went off to one of his women and guests were left to themselves. Normally Matty worked, checking reference books and auction prices, but tonight she waited in the hall. Sure enough Sholto appeared. He was wearing soft shoes and a jacket.

'Are you going for a walk?' asked Matty.

He shook his head. 'Into the village. I've a car booked and usually it turns up. Coming?'

She nodded. They couldn't talk here.

They walked down the drive and after a while a taxi appeared. Sholto waved at it and held the door for Matty to get in. 'Do you often do this?' she asked curiously.

He nodded. 'Most nights. Anything rather than spend the evening there. I cringe every time Eleanor fixes her blistering gaze on me. I can't decide if she really wants an affair or just fancies spiting Luca, or her father, or someone. Hellish family.'

'I thought you liked them! You behave as if you do!'

'People don't sell to people they don't like. You should remember that.'

Matty snorted. He had a remarkable capacity to annoy her. The taxi hurtled on, racing down the cliff road, sending showers of pebbles over the edge into infinity. Inevitably the passengers were flung against one another. Sholto said, 'I'm amazed the old boy hasn't taken to visiting you after hours.'

Matty glowered. 'He'd get a meat hook in his neck if he did. And he knows it.'

'What a she-cat! I thought it was more your desperate bid to blend into the wallpaper. I wouldn't have believed you could look so dull.' Matty glanced down at her black suit. Nowadays she wore it buttoned high, with flat shoes, no jewellery and little make-up.

'It isn't dull, merely businesslike. I don't know why, but in this profession you daren't look sexy. A little intimate chat about hallmarks so quickly degenerates into hands on knees.'

Sholto put his hand up her skirt. 'Or hands up all those who want a good night.'

'Stop that! Just stop it!'

Sholto laughed and let her go.

The village was beautiful. Small white-washed houses huddled together, occupying the scant few yards between the cliffs and the beach. Fishing nets were draped over the rocks and sea birds called. A girl laughed, and there was the smell of seaweed and fish cooking. The sun was dying, a red orb sinking into the sea. Matty got out of the taxi and stood, transfixed.

'Preetty good, huh?' said the taxi driver, used to awestruck tourists.

'Sure thing,' said Sholto, tossing him some cash. 'We'll go back in an hour.'

They wandered down the street. There was one café, with battered iron tables out in the sun. The proprietor offered them bowls of fish soup, and Sholto accepted. Matty drank tequila and dipped tacos into Sholto's food. It was delicious.

'You're going to be ill in the morning,' said Sholto. 'Don't drink so much.'

'I don't care. This is fabulous.'

He munched on tacos. 'Thought you wanted to talk.'

'I didn't say that.'

'You've been glowering at me. It's no use, I can't wean Doña Maria away from blood, and I don't intend to try. It's not my moral duty, whatever you say.'

Matty looked at him over her glass. In the twilight the scar on his face cast a shadow. 'How did you hurt your face?' she asked.

He met her eyes. 'None of your business.'

'Did you have acne too? It must have been horrible.'

He shrugged. 'Not particularly. Rather like being a leper, I should think. Social ostracism. Gave me lots of time to do interesting things like learn about art. It went away, it wasn't terminal.'

'But everybody hates spots.'

'No use hating what you cannot change. Have another tequila.'

Matty did. She had a strong head for booze. 'I think that painting you're trying to buy is an unsigned Titian,' she announced. 'Or at least from his school. Or something.'

Sholto's spoon paused in its journey to his mouth. 'Shut up,' he said shortly.

'You're paying her peanuts because she doesn't know. And I know they're wicked, and I know they're rich as hell, but it's not the sort of thing you should do. It gives dealers a terribly bad name and it's bound to affect your reputation.' She leaned forward confidentially. 'Look, there's a Sprimont bowl in the silver. I mean, I ask you, Sprimont! An unknown piece and I'm sure it's genuine. I could pass it off as just this or that, it wouldn't matter, Don Paolo couldn't check. But if I did and he found out — and he would find out, the moment we sold it on — Sammy wouldn't do any more business with him. And I'd never get asked to value anything, or buy anything, because people would think I was one of them. Someone like you — a cheat.'

His face became set, the blue eyes hard as glass. 'Don't call me a cheat.'

'You're not, yet. But if you buy the painting you will be. You can still get it a bit cheap, it isn't verified.'

'I wouldn't get it at all if she knew. The old boy wouldn't let her sell.'

'But you still shouldn't! It's dishonest.'

'And selling guns isn't, I suppose?'

Matty struggled to see through her own confusion. 'If I had my way, Sammy wouldn't do any deals with the man. When I set up on my own I won't touch a thing that isn't straight, and if it costs me money then I'll get used to being poor.'

'You'd have to. You wouldn't make a brass farthing.'

His hair fell in a black wing across his face. Matty reached out and pushed it back for him. 'Please don't do it.'

'Don't be stupid, I need the money. I'm buying on credit as it is. Will you tell?'

She shook her head. He said, 'Let's go along the shore. We can make love. Or won't you do it with a cheat?'

'I – just won't do it tonight. It upsets me. It makes me want to be in love with you.'

'And you don't fall in love with cheats!'

She considered. 'I don't know. Probably not.'

His expression barely changed. Matty watched him, waited for him to say something, wondered why he made no effort at persuasion.

'You know what's in that painting?' he said suddenly. 'It's so filthy you can hardly see, but it's the virgin, surrounded by a bunch of the most worldly saints you're likely to see. She's beautiful and she's voluptuous, and yet we're supposed to believe she's beyond sexuality. But even the cherubs are leering! Who do you think she was? It's an early work, we can assume the fires were burning pretty bright. Do you suppose he put his brushes down and started on her? But it doesn't matter if he did or if he didn't, because that's gone, they're gone. Only the picture is still here. So don't give me that stuff about you'll only do it if you're in love, if he's a good sort, if the wind's in the east and the dog's been fed, because it won't wash. You're just denying pleasure. Denying life. And if we went over there and did it a hundred times it wouldn't matter. It's the art that's important. We don't matter at all.'

Matty felt uncomfortable. If he asked her again she'd say yes. Her groin ached suddenly, and she shifted in her seat, aware of painful desire. What Don Paolo did with Conchita, whatever anyone did that had caused the billions and billions of people in the world, was nothing like what she and Sholto did together. It was nothing like anyone had ever done before.

They walked in silence along the beach. The taxi was waiting, and the sun was dying, falling headlong into the sea. They neither spoke nor touched.

Matty woke with a start. She had heard something. The curtains in her room were blowing in the draught from her open window, and beyond were the dark, silent gardens. Had they broken that silence? What had she heard? Whatever it was Matty's conscious self couldn't remember it, but her subconscious told her to be afraid.

She got out of bed and put on her robe. She went to her door and opened it, listening intently. Quiet pressed in on her, like a suffocating blanket, and then suddenly, chilling her blood, she heard it again: a long, suffering wail.

It was Eleanor. Matty knew it was. Without giving herself time to think she pulled her robe closed and ran down the corridor, up a flight of stairs and along again. Then she stopped. She was lost. Where had that noise come from?

The door next to her opened and a hand caught her wrist. She opened her mouth to scream, but Sholto's voice said, 'Shush! Don't make a sound.'

Disobeying, Matty hissed, 'Did you hear it? That terrible noise.'

'I heard something. And in this house it's not wise to enquire further. Go back to bed.'

'I can't. It was horrible.'

'Then stay here.'

'No!'

She pulled away from him. The house ached with quiet, and unquiet misery. And again someone wailed.

Matty turned to Sholto. 'Come with me. Don't make me go by myself.'

'You shouldn't go at all.'

But she turned to look at him, her grey eyes alight with youth and hope, and an idealistic faith in goodness. If he had ever had such faith he couldn't remember it. Yet he couldn't stand by and watch it destroyed in her.

'Come on, it must be Eleanor.' He led the way up a short flight of thickly carpeted stairs. Some part of Matty's mind registered that he was wearing black silk pyjamas. No wonder he had no money, she thought. He always wore such terribly expensive clothes. Even the collapsing ones were designer distressed.

Sholto paused outside a thick, mahogany door. Matty could hear muffled sobs, and then the wail again, that terrible, heart-stopping cry of an animal in pain. Casting Matty a look of burning reproach, Sholto knocked and called out softly: 'Eleanor? Eleanor, can we help?'

After a moment the door opened a crack. Conchita's large, benign face stared at them. 'She is sick,' she whispered. 'I cannot make her well.'

'Can I do anything?' Matty pushed forward. She was determined to enter that room.

Conchita put up no more than a token resistance. Matty and Sholto swept through, to face whatever horror might be there. But all they saw was Eleanor, her lace nightdress hanging like a rag from her shoulders. She sat hunched on her bed, crying and wailing, all her defiance gone. When she saw her rescuers she put her hands over her face and hid from them.

'Eleanor! Eleanor, what is it? Please let me help.'

'No one can help. No one but him.'

Matty knelt on the bed beside her and drew her hands down. 'Do you mean Don Paolo? Do you want to run away? I can help you. I promise I won't let you down.'

'He won't ever let me go. I will never be free.'

'Yes, you will! We'll help her, Sholto, won't we?'

'No.'

Matty turned on him. In a rage, she turned on him. 'How can you? How can you stand there and look at her and say

135

that? You haven't any heart, you haven't anything that passes for human feeling. No wonder you have to bury yourself in art — at least paintings can't demand anything. And God forbid that anyone should ever ask anything of you.'

His face didn't change. The scar made it seem as if he might almost be smiling. 'Look at her arms, Matty,' he said. 'She's a heroin addict.'

Eleanor flung herself down, sobbing wildly. Conchita said, 'Don Paolo says she is to have no more. Her husband, he is weak, he gives it when she cries. She goes mad for it. Don Paolo says it is his curse. Now he says she is not to have any more. She is to stay here for all the time it takes to stop her.'

Matty stared at Eleanor. 'Did you lie to me?' she asked shrilly. 'All those things you said — were they true?'

But the woman moaned and thrashed about. Sholto took hold of Matty's shoulders. 'I've been wondering about her for a while. She looked so damned odd.' He turned to Conchita. 'When did she start?'

The woman spread her hands. 'A long time ago. When she was at school. Don Paolo had her cured, but last year she went back to it. Her husband gives in too much. She is kept here to stop her, but still she tries. She is stupid.'

Suddenly the woman on the bed sprang into life. Imbued with sudden strength, she leaped at Conchita, her fingers spread into claws. 'You can give it me!' she shrieked. 'You know how to persuade him and you won't, you won't! I'll give you anything. I've got things, money, anything you want. If I have it I can be well!'

Conchita reached out a massive hand and dealt her a solid slap across the face. Eleanor fell back, her cheek flaming. Her breathing was laboured and painful. But she reached out her arm to Sholto. 'Please,' she whispered, 'I can be good for you. We can have fun together, I know a lot of things a man like you will like.'

Sholto said, 'Not just now, Eleanor. Thanks all the same.'

On the way downstairs Matty started to cry. Although the tears fell silently, every now and then she let out a strangled sob. 'Be quiet,' hissed Sholto. 'We don't want the old man knowing we know.' But Matty couldn't be quiet. When they reached Sholto's room he bundled her inside and closed the door.

He produced a bottle from his bedside drawer and poured a measure into a tooth mug. 'Brandy,' he said shortly. 'Come on, you look as if you need it.'

She took the glass and gulped half the contents. It burned a fiery trail down her throat, lodging as an ember near her heart.

Sholto took the glass and drained it himself. His face became quizzical. 'I think it's pretty funny, actually. I think I might believe in divine vengeance. And all the time I thought she was after me for my body alone.'

Matty said, 'I'm going to ask Sammy not to deal with the man. It isn't right.'

'You can't do that! You know you can't let Sammy down.'

Matty turned on him. 'Don't you mean that if I take a moral stand you might feel you have to as well? And you're not even doing honest business.'

'I'm taking a shyster for a ride. So what?'

'It isn't right! You can't. When you do something that's wrong it leaves a stain you can't ever wash away. And the next bad thing doesn't seem so bad, and the one after that, until you're nothing but a crook with no real goodness left.'

She was looking straight at him, her eyes like clear pools, the lashes their dark, sheltering reeds. He hated her to look at him like that.

'You and Doña Maria would make a wonderful pair. Fanatics both. I am not the unstained soul you would like me to be, Matty. I let old ladies stagger across busy roads as a matter of course.'

'No you don't.'

'Matty, you don't know me at all.'

She got up to go, but Sholto caught her hand. 'Stay, Matty. Stay with me.'

His fingers were long and warm. They had the power to enslave her. If she wished, this man and she could lie together, blotting out thought with a compulsion so much more ancient and instinctive. But they had been given thought, like an unwanted present, and she would not set it aside. She exerted the slightest pressure against his hand. He let her fingers fall. 'I'll telephone Sammy in the morning,' she said. 'Then I'll tear up the catalogue and go.'

Chapter Nine

The dust blew in clouds along the road, dimming the purple flowers that grew at its edges. Matty stood with her cases at her feet, waiting for a taxi. She wondered if Don Paolo was making things difficult. The man on the gate had promised the car would come, but he had been vague, as Mexicans were. One hour, perhaps two – it would come, sometime.

She sat on the more robust of her bags. It was hotter than Hades and her stomach hurt, as it often did when she was worried. Don Paolo's face came back to her, the skin drawn smoothly over uncaring bones, his eyes like flints, unblinking. He hadn't believed anything she had said. She didn't know what he thought.

A motorbike passed, the girl on the back sitting sideways, clutching a bag of plastic bottles. A beat-up little car followed close on their heels, and overtook them in a cloud of choking yellow dust. Then, for a long time, nothing. Just the heat, heavy as an overcoat, and the thick, cicada silence.

Someone was coming. Footsteps sounded ringingly clear on the sunbaked drive. It could be Don Paolo, anyone. She stood up, wondering if she should hide. He knew that she knew, he knew everything. Perhaps he had listened on the telephone. What did men like that do when people judged them?

She faced the drive, her sunhat held as an inadequate shield in front of her. When she saw the tall, gangling figure approaching between the massed banks of flowers she felt an absurd relief. He was carrying his suitcase. She put her sunhat on her head.

'What are you doing here?'

He gave her a grim stare. 'Studying philosophy.'

'But − has he thrown you out?'

He put his suitcase down beside hers. 'I think you can assume that.'

'Oh. I'm sorry. I knew you were hoping − I suppose the deal must have been very important.'

'Yes.' His eyes narrowed as he stared into the distance. 'Never mind. Something else is bound to turn up.'

She sat on her suitcase again, timid and silent. This was her fault. Don Paolo had turned against Sholto because of her. After a while, when they had been passed by a man on a donkey and another on a bicycle, she said, 'I don't know when this taxi's coming. Perhaps it won't.'

'Then we'll catch the bus. There's always one in the evening, going to town.'

'Oh, I didn't know. That makes me feel better.'

He turned to her with a grin. 'They don't have wolves in Mexico. Don Paolo wouldn't come out and devour you.'

'I bet he would. I keep expecting to be shot. At least − I can't decide if he's sinister or if I just think he is. I saw him, you know, with Conchita. In the chapel.'

Sholto said, 'Not surprised. Anyone married to Doña Maria would need some sort of outlet.'

'You're not feeling sorry for him, are you?'

He shrugged. 'Yes, a bit. Drug addict daughter, batty wife, weakling son-in-law. A silver expert of unimpeachable morality must have been more than he could stand. And as far as his business is concerned, who knows how he got into it? He might only have been trying to get ahead. I can sympathise.'

'If you want to get ahead, get a hat,' intoned Matty.

An hour passed. The sun was getting low in the sky. Matty was terribly thirsty. She got up and began marching up and down, up and down, irritating Sholto. Then she resigned herself, and flung herself back on her case with weary patience. 'What are you going to do then?' she demanded.

He pushed her spare suitcase flat and lay back against it, stretching out his long legs. 'I was hoping you'd have a suggestion. You got me into this.'

'Me? I'm out of a job. When I phoned Sammy he said

– he was furious. He was absolutely, thunderously livid. He told me to go and boil myself in a vat of chilli sauce and never darken his door again.'

'Did he mean it?'

Matty grimaced. 'No idea. Perhaps not.' She let out her breath in a long, anxious sigh. 'Anyway, my brother's staying in Carolina with a friend of mine. A best friend, from school. I thought I'd cash in my plane ticket and go and see her. I can take my brother home after the holidays. Sammy might have calmed down by then.'

'Carolina? Never been. Right, I'll come with you.'

Matty gaped at him. 'No,' she said at last.

'Thanks a lot. I throw up the chance of making my fortune, all because of your wretched principles, and you won't let me come on a bus ride.'

'But he sacked you. That was what you said.'

'I did not. I decided – well, let's say it was in everyone's interest for me to decline the sale. You were right. It would have played hell with my reputation. I am now Honest Feversham, straight as a die. Not Feversham the Fraud, who you can't let through the door because he never tells the truth. I'm on the path of righteousness and you should be proud of me.'

Matty considered. 'Actually I'm astounded. I never thought you'd do it.'

'Sweet maiden, neither did I.'

At that moment the bus came roaring round the bend in the road. Sholto leaped up and stuck out his arm, waving madly. Matty got to her feet, feeling confused. She had been at the roadside so long she felt as if she must belong there. But the bus panted to a halt, and stood shuddering and belching out fumes, like a monster. Inside it smelled of sweat and fish, and the passengers stared at them out of creased brown faces. Matty and Sholto sat squeezed together at the back, and he took her hand and cradled it in his own. 'Here we are then,' he said cheerily. 'All aboard the Skylark.'

Days passed. They travelled on bus after bus, until the days became weeks. Matty had one of her bags stolen, the one with all her everyday clothes. She was left with the jeans she stood up in, her balldress, her black suit and no clean pants. Sholto lent her his spare underpants and she wore them bunched at the waist with a safety pin holding them together. The slit in the front made them seem strangely erotic, as if, in wearing them, she was associating with him, indecently. He seemed to catch her thought. When she came out of one ladies' room he said, 'Strange to think that my Y-fronts have made it into your jeans. It gives me quite a thrill, thinking of what they're up to.'

'Don't be disgusting,' said Matty, putting on her most puritan expression.

They were beginning to run short of money. Matty used up several dollars trying to telephone Lorne and warn her that she was coming, but when she got through to the house Lorne was always out. It never seemed possible to tell distant strangers that she was about to descend upon them, complete with man. 'Is Simon there?' is all she would say, and they assumed she was checking up and said, 'He's out right now. But he's fine — a real boy. We'll get him to call you.' It sounded oddly hesitant.

'Your English politeness is going to choke you one of these days,' said Sholto, after another abortive call.

'I don't see you seizing the phone and yelling, "We're coming to stay, put the kettle on,"' retorted Matty sourly. 'They're looking after Simon, they've been good enough already.'

'Don't undersell yourself. We're an asset to any party. Good-looking, witty, and antiques experts. How in heaven's name did you know that was a Titian? I nearly missed it myself.'

'One of my many talents,' said Matty, but then she giggled. 'I didn't guess a thing till I saw your face. Then, when I stared at the picture, I thought it would have to be someone Venetian, because that's your speciality, and then someone terribly famous, because you looked so wolfish, and then someone who was going to make you millions because I could see pound signs where your eyes should be. I only know Titian.'

'You gave me heart failure. I may never recover.'

'Poor you.'

She rested her head against him. They were waiting for yet another bus. They had eaten yet another hamburger, drunk yet another milkshake and chewed desultorily on what seemed like their hundredth Hershey bar. Occasionally they would leave the bus depots and walk in ordinary streets, passing ordinary houses. The smells of real food drifted out to them, and twice Matty had forcibly restrained Sholto from getting into conversation with a passing housewife, in the hope that she would invite them home to dinner.

'You have the most tiresome principles,' he complained. 'Why don't they ever mean that we have fun?'

'We have to earn our fun,' said Matty. 'We can't get it on the cheap.'

'You mean to get it from your friend.'

Matty flushed. 'That's different. She's my friend. And if I'm begging from her I'd better not do it from anyone else, in case I get in the habit.'

'The only habit you're likely to get into is a nun's,' muttered Sholto.

In the night, sometimes, on half-empty buses, they kissed. They pressed their bodies against one another, fumbling in jeans and under shirts, hot, excited, knowing they couldn't be satisfied. When she first met Sholto, Matty had thought him a man of the world, but on the buses, in the small hours, they were as young as the new day. He wasn't a lot older than she. He wasn't all that experienced. Sleeping, leaning against one another with a hot southern wind blowing in every time the driver opened the door, Matty sometimes felt absurdly happy. For once her life held no complications, just Sholto, the bus, and the night.

But the day came when the driver deposited them on a long, empty road. 'It's down there aways,' he said, chewing an indigestion tablet. 'Two, three miles. I used to live around here.'

As the dust settled again and the road became hot and quiet, Sholto picked up the cases. 'Come on. We might as well start.'

'We look like tramps,' muttered Matty. 'I didn't realise. I hope I don't look as bad as you.'

'Worse. It doesn't matter. She's a friend, isn't she?'

The countryside was lush and wooded. Horses grazed beneath spreading trees and sometimes a drive led away to a wooden house, with smoke drifting up from a chimney. The road crossed a small river, and then crossed it again. A man with a hound dog waved to them and said, 'Howdy.'

They heard the car coming minutes before it passed them. As it came round the bend Matty turned to look. It was a big station wagon, crammed full of people. One of them shrieked, and the car lurched to a sudden stop. It reversed back with a grinding squeal.

'Matty! By all that's wonderful, Matty! What are you doing here?'

'Hello, Lorne. We were coming to see you.' She pushed a hand through her sticky hair. As Lorne scrambled from the car Matty saw she was wearing cut-off jeans, a skimpy top and a wonderful tan. Her hair fell down her back like a waterslide. 'You look fantastic,' said Matty truthfully.

'And you look like hell. And — aren't you going to introduce me?'

Lorne fluttered her batlike eyelashes in Sholto's direction. Matty felt her heart shudder.

'Sholto Feversham,' he said, and held out his hand. 'You must be Matty's fairy godmother. Sorry to land on you like this but when we tried to phone, you were out. Find a shed for us somewhere.'

'I never put handsome men in sheds,' said Lorne, bridling.

'No doubt they lock themselves in voluntarily when you spurn them,' said Sholto. He and Lorne both laughed. His teeth were every bit as white as Lorne's, thought Matty.

The car was full of Lorne's cousins, ranging from a pert nine year old called Francine to a boy of twenty. 'Simon couldn't come out,' explained Francine as Matty squashed in next to her. 'They grounded him.'

'When I phoned it sounded — hasn't he been good, Lorne?'

She met her friend's eyes in the driving mirror. How had Sholto managed to get the front seat? Lorne said, 'He's been great. What's a few rosebushes between friends? We don't approve of formal gardens.'

144

'He let some pigs into the garden,' explained Francine. 'It was a joke. There was a party and everyone had to run out in their good clothes and chase pigs.'

'It was a wonderful joke,' said Lorne. 'Really nobody cared.'

Matty felt sick.

Lorne's family home was a tall Colonial mansion, its pillared portico extending into a vista of grassland, grazing horses and distant hills. Creepers mantled the walls, thick as blankets, and two or three old men were hoeing flowerbeds and trimming shrubs. Around the corner of the house Matty could see an enormous garage and a swimming pool. And here she was, inflicting herself on this sumptuous household, like some tramp, some graceless sponger.

'What do you think?' Lorne confronted her, smiling her dazzling smile. 'The old homestead.'

'Beautiful,' said Matty. 'I hate to drop on you like this, Lorne.'

'I'll tell Aunt Susan we have visitors,' said Francine, and gambolled away into the house.

Lorne said, 'Don't look so worried, Matty. Come to my room. We can talk while you bathe.'

'Can I talk while you bathe?' asked Sholto innocently.

Lorne eyed him. 'This is girl-talk. Besides, I don't think time with you should be wasted talking. Go along with Cousin Campbell, you can teach him the rudiments of sophistication.'

The cousin flushed to the roots of his carroty hair and said, 'Shucks, Lorne!' But she just smiled and winked and left him bewildered.

Submerged in a steaming tub of water, watching days of grime float away, Matty said, 'I knew you'd like Sholto.'

Lorne widened her eyes and held out a martini for Matty to sip. 'Is there a woman living who wouldn't? Matty, he's gorgeous. And too much for you, my dear. That is one dangerous man.'

'Oh, Miss Experience! He's nice.'

'Matty! Nice, he ain't. Good-looking, charming and sophisticated, sure. He's nice like sharks are nice.'

145

'You haven't said two words to him. He's nice. And he isn't good-looking. His face is a mess.'

Lorne swallowed a gulp of the drink. 'If it wasn't, he'd be pretty. Are you sure you want him, hon? He's much more my type.'

Matty sank beneath the suds. 'Lay off,' she murmured. 'Anyway, what about your boyfriend? As far as Sholto's concerned, I haven't finished yet.'

Lorne sighed. 'Well, you'd better tell me everything,' she said at last. 'And I mean everything. All about Mexico, all about the silver, and all about bed. No shy blushes, please.'

Matty giggled and sat up. 'I saw this man,' she confided. 'The man who had the silver. He was flat out on the floor and this woman, the maid, absolutely enormous, was on top and you know – doing it!'

'Yuk!' squawked Lorne. 'Fat people. I hate to think.'

'It wasn't yuk. Just a bit funny, watching all that flab gyrate. In a way it was liberating, because if they could do it then so can everyone else. Fat, thin, old. . . it doesn't matter.'

'No one over thirty should do it at all,' declared Lorne. 'There should be a law.'

'Fascist.' Matty yawned. 'Is it still Greg then?'

Lorne nodded. 'Everyone's kind of assuming – well, it makes sense. Their property running so close to ours and all. And his family's big in state politics, they're really influential. I know my dad's keen.'

'What happened to the romance?'

Lorne flashed her brilliant smile. 'He's a nice guy, Matty. You wait, you'll really like him. And what would I do if I didn't get hitched? Sleep with a lot of men not half as nice as Greg, and then find he's married someone else. He's twenty-six, Matty, he won't wait forever.'

'You could travel. Anything,' said Matty.

'Sure. Greg says he'll take me to Rome.'

An unspecified anxiety nagged at Matty. Lorne had everything: looks, money, sparkle, brains. The world was hers if she would only reach out to take it. But she was lazy. Too often Matty and the girls had had to bully her into action, otherwise she just drifted along with the tide. Lorne liked to oblige people. She obliged them right to the point where she woke up and discovered she had obliged herself into an unpleasant mess.

'Why don't you get a job.' Matty heard the familiar nag in her voice and, predictably, Lorne looked bored.

'What is the point, Matilda? I'm living a wonderful life. Just wonderful. Parties, friends, everything. Why should I give it up to satisfy your Puritan ideals? Besides, everyone would be sad if I went away. Mom, Dad, Greg, everyone. And I'd be sad. I'd miss my horse.'

Matty let it go. Perhaps Lorne was right and she was too intense about things. If you could rest in idleness beside still waters, not hurting anybody, not spoiling anything, why take the rugged pathway at all? But she knew that would never be enough for her. She had to test herself against life, find out what she and it were made of, discover problems which she could overcome. There was no greater nightmare for Matty than Lorne's paradise of unchallenging, endless serenity.

Washed, brushed, in a white dress of Lorne's and wearing Lorne's make-up, Matty felt better. She descended a wide flight of stairs, a breeze scented with a thousand flowers wafting around her legs. Lorne was right to wallow in her good fortune. This was luxury, this was family living as she had never experienced it. Laughing voices came from the terrace, the cook was singing in the kitchen and Lorne's mother was in the hall, arranging an armful of flowers.

Matty put out her hand. 'Mrs Shuster? How do you do. I'm Matty Winterton.'

The woman was tall, greying, with delicate skin that was crumpling into wrinkles at the corners of her eyes. Her smile was immediate and welcoming. 'Call me Aunt Susan,' she said. 'Everyone does. You're just as I expected, Matty, Lorne's told me so much. You were very kind to her at school. It's good to repay some of that.'

Matty blushed, too British to accept compliments easily. 'I hope Simon hasn't been too much trouble,' she managed.

Aunt Susan made a little face. 'He's a boy, my dear. It's hard without a father's hand. Don't you have a relative or someone could see to him? Sometimes he seems very wild.'

'Oh. I am sorry — he's had such a lot of changes. And there isn't anyone except us. But I'll speak to him. He isn't usually naughty.'

'He's a nice boy,' said Aunt Susan, bravely. 'He has wonderful manners at table.'

Matty's heart sank still further. If that was the best that could be said of him then things were really bad. 'I think I'll go and find him,' she muttered.

He was at the pool, diving with some of the cousins. There seemed to be dozens of them, mostly boys, all tall and blond and athletic. Next to them Simon's ten-year-old skinniness looked laughable. When Matty called, 'Simon! Simon!' hardly able to contain herself, he tossed his copper hair from his eyes and said gruffly, 'Hello, Matty.'

She had to stop herself hugging him. Then, seeing the strange looks, she realised that she should have hugged him. It was only in cold grey England that you pretended you didn't care. She put out her arms and squeezed.

'Get off, Matty! You smell of soap.'

'And you smell of swimming. You're so brown. Has it been fun, love? You haven't been lonely?'

He shook his head. 'The guys let me hang out with them everywhere.'

'"Hang out", indeed! You make it sound like a load of bats.'

'Ha-ha. Did you sell lots of silver? Are we rich?'

She shook her head. 'Actually, I've lost my job.'

'Oh. Oh, I see.'

He looked down at the floor. All at once Matty realised how much he had longed for her to succeed. Left here with strangers, trespassing on their good will, however freely given, he was without pride.

'If you don't hurry up, I'll be the one to make a fortune,' he said grimly. 'You're not trying very hard, are you?'

'I'm doing my best.'

'And I get dumped here!' He dropped his voice to a fierce whisper. 'They all think I'm a beggar or something. They think my father's in prison!'

'You can tell them he isn't. Tell them he's dead.'

Simon tossed his hair back. 'What's the point? He

would've been in prison. If you don't get some money soon, Matty, I'm going to rob a bank. I bet you can't even pay my school fees.'

She could, but only just. Their meagre store of capital was disappearing fast, and she had to pay for their tickets home. 'Don't worry about the money,' she said tightly. 'It's going to be all right. But it won't be if you don't behave yourself. What have you been doing? Why?'

He made a face. 'It wasn't much. They made a fuss about nothing. They went into huddles and talked about sending me to a behaviorist or something. It was funny.'

'Not my idea of a joke,' said Matty.

He looked up at her through his mop of hair. She felt a desperate love for him, full of panic and responsibility. If only she was older, if only she was richer!

'Good Lord, Matty, you look gorgeous.' It was Sholto, wearing swimming shorts. Next to the Shuster cousins his skin was pale, biscuit-coloured, but the flat, contoured muscles of his chest and belly made her swallow. Lorne was right. Without the imperfection of his face he would be an impossibly beautiful man.

'Are you Simon?' he went on. 'How do you do.' He put out a hand, and Simon shook it.

'Are you Matty's boyfriend?'

'Yes. Sort of. She can be a bit of a pain.'

'You bet!'

'Thanks a lot,' said Matty, peeved. 'You're nothing but a couple of rogues.'

'I'd rather be a rogue than a bore,' said Sholto, and Simon chuckled.

'Would you? So would I. And it's boring being neat and polite and − grateful!' He almost spat the word.

Sholto laughed, but the sound choked off suddenly. He turned away towards the pool, saying over his shoulder, 'Get a move on, Simon! Race you to the end.'

Matty stood watching. It was no contest. Sholto's dive took him halfway, and the skinny child next to him flailed sticklike arms in vain. But when he reached the far side Sholto made a racing turn, coming back at Simon in a welter of bubbles and foam. He seized the boy round the waist, roaring, playing sharks. The race ended in wild laughter.

In the Shuster household, children ate early, leaving the adults to a civilised repast later on. The cool of the evening heightened Matty's sense of peace and gracious living. Doves called in the woods nearby and a strange red bird flitted around the house, eating peanuts from nets hung at the windows. She helped Aunt Susan prepare small white flower arrangements for the long table. There were fourteen to dinner that night, a houseful.

Matty had little to change into, so she stayed in the white dress. Lorne wore a wrapped blouse of navy silk, with a black silk skirt nipped into her tiny waist. The blouse revealed her cleavage, and she put on a padded bra as well. 'If it's boobs the men want we might as well oblige,' she said to Matty. 'I wish mine were as big as yours. Do you think I should get an implant?'

'Don't they go hard as rock?' said Matty.

'Not if you massage them. I'd have to make it every night, with lots of foreplay. But I'll have babies first. I don't want some poor kid sucking out lumps of silicone, do I?'

Matty chuckled. 'I take it Greg's the prospective father? When am I going to see him?'

'He's coming to dinner tonight. Don't expect him to be – you know.'

'No? What shouldn't I expect?'

Lorne looked uneasy. 'Someone – someone like Sholto. Sophisticated. Up to everything. Never lost for words. Greg's more natural, he knows about natural things. Horses, farming, the neighbourhood.'

'You mean he's dumb!' squawked Matty in horror. 'Are you really going to marry this farmhand?'

'He isn't a farmhand! His folks own a place that's almost twice as big as ours. They're so rich! And he's really well thought of, everyone says he'll be in politics one day. He's been to the best schools, and he's travelled, everything.'

'But he still talks about cows.'

Suddenly Lorne giggled. 'Yes. And horses. But I like cows and horses! And around here, they win lots of votes. So don't try and despise him, Matty. I know you. You'll set out to make him seem a real hayseed.'

Matty prepared herself for the absolute worst. But when he came striding through the door, huge and blond, like an enormous golden dog, she was taken aback. Greg Berenson exuded masculinity like aftershave. His teeth were large and square, and when he saw Lorne he beamed, flung out his arms and said, 'Hi, honey.'

Encircled, Lorne stood on tiptoe to kiss him. 'Hi.'

He enfolded her and transformed her affectionate peck into passion. When he let her go he said, 'You've been keeping away from me. Where were you today? I waited an hour out riding.'

Lorne raised her eyebrow provocatively. 'I was busy. My friends came. Matty and Sholto.' She leaned back against Greg's arms, wanting to be free. Reluctantly he released her, and focused on Matty.

'Good to meet you,' he said absently.

'And Sholto,' insisted Lorne.

Sholto stepped forward, hand outstretched. His height was within an inch of Greg's. His eyes, intensely blue, made Greg's seem made of glass. And was that a laugh, or merely the effect of his scar? Sholto's quizzical grin was always misleading. 'How do you do,' said Sholto, in almost a parody of politeness.

Greg eyed him up and down. 'Hi. Are you a friend of Lorne's?'

'A passionate acquaintance. No more than that.' Sholto put his hand on his heart.

'What do you mean?' Greg hesitated, halfway between polite amusement and suspicion. Inevitably, Sholto pushed him the wrong way.

'What can a gentleman say? Would he sully a lady's name? Even though what's passed between us will haunt me all my days.' He sent a lingering, soulful glance in Lorne's direction.

Greg swung round to confront Lorne, and saw she was laughing. Matty too was grinning. 'What does he mean?' demanded Greg. 'How well do you know him?'

'We only just met,' said Lorne, putting her hand on Greg's arm. She reached up to brush his cheek with her lips. 'Don't be silly.'

'Sholto's a fool,' said Matty. 'Ignore him.'

'But many a true word is spoken in jest,' said Sholto, and the lift in his voice gave the phrase a disquieting ambiguity.

Matty hustled him away. 'He'll thump you,' she muttered.

'What, that ape? He couldn't hit a barn door with a broom. And why does he keep mauling your friend? One mighty hand remains firmly stuck to her backside.'

'Yes,' said Matty dubiously. 'Lorne says he's very natural.'

'Does she mean simple? Or simply sexually undisciplined?'

'I think he's the sort that would look really, really good on television.'

'Oh, Christ, yes! That inane grin – he'd go down a bundle.'

Matty glanced at Sholto dubiously. She didn't like such an absorbed interest in Lorne's escort. 'Would you like to be mauling Lorne? Is that it?' she asked tensely.

Sholto didn't look at her. 'Don't mind me,' he murmured. 'I get vicious sometimes. When I see someone that rich, that untroubled and with a face that perfect, I get an urge to smash it with an iron fist. And failing that I use my rapier wit. Unattractive, don't you think? I do.'

Matty glanced from Greg to Sholto. 'I think you're very good-looking,' she said.

'Oh, for Christ's sake! Don't humour me, Matty.'

Sholto walked away from her. He went to talk to Aunt Susan, and soon she was laughing and going pink. In contrast Greg kept Lorne pinned firmly to his side, looking down at her with fierce concentration. Matty thought he was very much in love, completely obsessed himself and demanding obsession in return. She could see why. Lorne was exquisite tonight, and all at once Matty felt her own brand of envy. She would have given anything for Sholto to be so much in love.

But, at dinner, Sholto seemed to have shed his bad temper. He took Matty's hand beneath the table and squeezed it. 'Nice people,' he murmured. 'Here, you can take good deep breaths and know you're not going to get poisoned.'

152

She knew he was thinking of the de Caruzons. 'Are you glad to be out of it?'

'Yes. But not so glad to be minus the cash. I want to live in a place like this one day. I want a home like this. And I haven't even begun.'

His fingers traced the lines of veins on the back of her hand. It was warm, affectionate, close. Suddenly he let go and turned to talk with animation to the girl on his other side. In a reflex, to hide her hurt, Matty picked up her spoon and checked the marks. As she had thought, nineteenth century; but the serving spoons were a great deal older, and probably Scottish. She craned her neck to see them.

Lorne's laughter rang out. 'Go on, Matty! Have a look. And Dad's got a couple of coffee pots he wants to sell. He'll show you later.'

Matty blushed. 'I don't need any favours, Lorne. No more, at any rate.'

'No favours, just business,' said Drake Shuster. 'I should get rid of some stuff. The place is getting like a museum.'

'You should get into Venetian art,' said Sholto with decision. 'The only thing this house lacks is some really good pictures.'

'We used to have a Monet sketch,' said Aunt Susan doubtfully.

'Modern tat,' declared Sholto. 'When we've eaten I'll show you some photographs. I promise, these pictures will transform your lives. When you actually see them, they provide a standard of excellence which you can never lose. A yardstick for judging life, I promise.'

He returned to his meal, leaving everyone breathless. 'What do you think of these paintings, Matty?' asked Aunt Susan.

She considered. 'They are wonderful. Very expensive. They're a bit out of fashion, of course, so they're probably a good buy if you like that sort of thing. Italian nobles, saints, virgins and so on. Quite a bit of breast feeding.'

Sholto snorted. 'Have you seen La Vierge au Coussin Vert in the Louvre? The virgin's breast comes out of her armpit. Hilarious! Don't take painting too seriously, please. You either like it or you don't.' He resumed talking to the girl on his other side.

Matty nudged him. 'Sholto, you are either in or out of this conversation. Don't keep jumping in, like a demented spaniel in a pond.'

Lorne said, 'You always did that, Matty! You would read a book and talk as well. You were a pain.'

'Henrietta was worse! She daydreamed.'

'And Griselda slapped her,' agreed Lorne. 'God, Griselda was a bully.'

'No, she wasn't.'

'Of course she was,' said Sholto. 'An impossible woman.'

Matty glared at him. 'You don't know her!'

'No,' he agreed, 'but if you will have this tedious chat about old schoolchums nobody else knows, then you can't be surprised if the rest of us use some imagination. Personally I was shocked when Henrietta ran off with the games mistress, but there you are.'

'She didn't! Did she?' Aunt Susan's eyes were enormous. 'I've spoken to her mother on the phone, a most sensible woman.'

'Of course she didn't,' Matty spluttered. 'Ignore him. He's uncontrollable.'

'A demented spaniel. A badly trained gundog. A pain in the arse,' agreed Sholto mournfully.

Drake Shuster leaned across to his daughter and said in badly muffled tones, 'Who did you say he was?'

Everyone collapsed in laughter.

There was dancing after dinner. Greg enveloped Lorne in a close embrace, and they sidled across the floor together. Cousin Campbell danced with Matty while Sholto cornered Drake and Susan with his collection of photographs. Matty could see him talking animatedly, discarding this or that, stopping at one and jabbing his finger forcefully at the print. He was never anything but forceful about painting. It was his passion.

'Is he a bit — unstable?' asked Campbell, guiding Matty carefully round the improvised floor, past a coffee table and a lamp standard.

'Not in the least,' said Matty. 'He's just Sholto. I've never met anyone like him.'

'I should think not,' said Campbell. 'He's weird.'

It was probably true. Matty relaxed into Campbell's embrace, feeling him breathe with immature passion down her neck. She knew she ought not to get too involved with Sholto. He was, as Campbell said, weird.

Lorne and Greg Berenson were sneaking out of the French windows. Matty looked to see if Aunt Susan was watching, but she appeared engrossed in the photographs. Then Lorne stopped. 'Turn the music off, someone,' she called. 'I can hear something.'

She flung the window wide. In the sudden silence there came a high, thin, childish shrieking. Matty's heart leaped into her throat. 'Simon!' she wailed, and ran.

The men overtook her easily. She was wearing thin sandals and couldn't run, she kept catching her heels in the pasture. In the moonlight, by the paddock fence, she could see a small figure, and horses, running. The shrieks weren't Simon's, she realised, they were Francine's. Where, oh where, was Simon? She prayed, exerting every ounce of mental power. Please God, let him not be dead. Without Simon, darling Simon, she would have no one.

The men were amongst the horses. She could hear them calling, 'Whoa, whoa, steady now, steady.' Drake Shuster caught his good saddlehorse, and Greg faced down a big grey and used his belt to tie it up. Horses reared against the pale night sky, splitting the air with wild whinnies. Sholto was kneeling in the middle of the field, tending something.

She couldn't run the last yards, her heart was beating so violently it wouldn't sustain her. 'Is he dead? Has he killed himself?' She was almost whispering.

'Nothing more than a broken arm,' said Sholto. 'Sit up, Simon. Your sister's about to die of fright.'

In the pale light his face was like chalk, the eyes glassy, his hair dulled to blackness. 'I fell off,' he said, and his voice wobbled.

'I should think you did, son,' said Drake. 'That horse ain't even broke.'

'Francine said he was all right,' said Simon. 'It would have

155

been OK but when I fell off she started screaming and that frightened them. They were galloping everywhere, I didn't dare move. And then she screamed more. I suppose she thought I was dead.'

'I suppose she did,' said Matty. 'Oh, Simon!' She sank down beside him, put her head on her knees and burst into tears.

Sholto put her to bed. He took her upstairs and tucked her in, saying, 'Would you like a bedtime story?'

She nodded. 'Something cosy. Nothing horrid.'

'There aren't any nice ones. The nice part is knowing they're not real.'

'Reality seems nightmarish just now,' said Matty. 'Why is he doing these things, Sholto? He likes it here. I don't understand.'

He stood looking down at her. His face was odd. Sometimes he could look as if he was remembering something cold and unlovely. 'I'll explain it to you one day,' he murmured. 'It isn't hard.'

'Tell me now,' pleaded Matty. 'I can't sleep for thinking about him. Please.'

He touched her hair in utter gentleness. For a moment she thought he would stay. But he pulled away from her restraining hand and left her.

Chapter Ten

Morning brought an atmosphere heavy with guilt. Francine was confined to her room, and Simon, arm in plaster, was lying feverish in bed. Matty went to see Aunt Susan. 'I'll take him away at once,' she said tearfully. 'I'm so sorry – I don't know why he does these things. I wish I could say it was just high spirits, but it isn't. Do you really think he should see some kind of psychologist?'

The older woman sighed. 'Don't worry too much about it, Matty. It's the fashion these days to have our children looked at and worried over. Mostly, they grow out of these things. The boy's had too much trouble, we can't expect him to be as if none of it had happened. He needs to be settled. Don't take him yet, dear, not while he's sick.'

Matty nodded, dumbly. Simon needed a home, and she hadn't got one to give him.

She went to talk to Lorne. 'I should have been a call girl. Simon could have lived in a flat full of pink chiffon and poodles.'

'Call girls go out to do it, they don't have to have chains on the bed,' said Lorne practically. 'Don't be too hard on Simon, he did me a favour last night. Did you see Greg, being so manly? When he flexed those giant muscles I went weak with desire. I'll go and see him today. He can have me on toast.'

'You don't mean you're going to marry him, do you?' Matty was apprehensive. She didn't like Greg all that much.

'No! Not yet, anyway. I just want him – in the haybarn – all muscle and sex.'

She had the desired result of making Matty laugh. It was becoming harder and harder to do nowadays. Little lines of worry were appearing between her fine, chestnut brows and she had developed the habit of cocking her head to one side, as if she was listening to some sound that no one else could hear. It was her conscience, thought Lorne. Matty was tormented by her own failure.

Lorne looked at her own, heart-shaped face, reflected in the mirror. It was a delicate face, implying fragility and sweetness. In contrast Matty's was wide, with well-spaced eyes tapering to a firm chin. They made a handsome pair, and of the four schoolfriends they were by far the best looking. Matty had better colouring, thought Lorne, more original. Her own dark hair and white skin seemed dull beside Matty's chestnut and ivory. Who had the better body? She was thinner and smaller, but Matty had that swelling, vibrant bosom.

She dressed in tight jeans and a figure-hugging tee-shirt, ready to go and see Greg. The thought of the pleasure to come made her colour come up. It was like starting all over again, although she had known him since she was old enough to know the difference between boys and girls. And she had known he was hers. But then, all the boys around here might have been hers if she had wanted them. The interruption, sudden and hard to take, had been school. It had felt like being wrenched from the Garden of Eden, and flung naked into a cold and cruel world. Now, coming back, it wasn't the same. They should never have sent her away, she thought. If she had never seen the world beyond this valley then she would have lived forever in rural content. She wouldn't now wake up in the mornings and feel as if she was acting a part.

Going out to her car, she met Sholto. 'Walking?' she asked.

He nodded. 'Driving?'

She nodded back, laughing. 'You ought to go and see Matty. She's all stewed up about her brother. He's a funny kid.'

'Most of them are. But most you don't notice.'

She made a face at him. 'Says the sage.' As she was about to go, she turned back to him, surprised at herself. 'Do you think I'm beautiful? Or just pretty?'

158

He never hesitated. 'Beautiful. You should get yourself painted. Before you run to fat. At the moment, you're exquisite.'

Lorne almost gasped. 'Better than Matty?' she asked quickly.

'Better than? Now, that's a difficult judgment.' He studied her. 'The problem is, I know what Matty looks like in the flesh, so to speak. And I don't think I'd better ask you to strip off so I can give a comprehensive comparison, pleasant as that would be. Objectively, I'd say that you are twenty per cent more beautiful than Matty. But that might alter in the future. Matty – Matty glows.'

She knew what he meant. Simon had it too, that same glorious inner light. It came of a certain spiritual tension, the same tension that sometimes exploded in Matty's terrible rages, in Simon's escapades. For some reason Matty's long-dead mother, known only to Lorne from faded photographs, and her dusty, inconspicuous father, had combined to imbue their children with a glow.

'You're a very odd man,' said Lorne to Sholto.

'Am I?' He laughed. 'You just don't know me. I've travelled an odd road, that's all. Where are you going? To screw the gorilla?'

Taken aback, Lorne said, 'Yes. If it's any of your business.'

'We both know it isn't. Have fun. You'd better make sure the sex is good because he's got no sodding conversation. He'll make a wonderful politician.'

He lifted a casual hand in a wave. Lorne stood for a long moment, looking after him. Had she said he was odd? The man was verging on the insane.

The Berenson place lacked the grace of her own home. The house was low and ranchlike, with unpleasant modern furniture. If she owned this house, thought Lorne, she would do something about the decor. It was the fault of Mrs Berenson, a woman Lorne privately considered stupid. She trailed around in the wake of her husband, Sherwood, watching him make up to other women at official receptions. He had a certain steely charm, Lorne acknowledged. When people talked about Sherwood Berenson they often forgot he even had a wife.

The dairy herd was grazing close by the house. The paddock exuded a delicious blend of grass, dung and flowers, a scent that spoke to Lorne of richness and plenty. It was a smell she associated with childhood, when the Shuster place had been deep in pedigree cattle. This country, her own familiar land. She wondered how it was that year by year her father's enterprises seemed to go, sold off here and there, whittled away. The Monet sketch, the pedigree herd, the good silver. But the spending never stopped. A small cold thought entered her head, spoiling this perfect afternoon. She put it away, put it resolutely out of her mind. The sight of cattle tearing grass began to soothe her and she remembered why she was there. It would be a waste not to enjoy this wonderful day.

He was waiting for her, pretending to work on a tractor. He had grease on his hands and he wiped them perfunctorily on a dirty cloth. Huge hands, brown and roughened with work, a man's hands. Suddenly urgent, she ran to him and put her arms around his neck. He lifted her up, holding her tight enough to crush bones. 'Oh, Lorne,' he murmured. 'You're just the best.'

She drew back to stare at him. 'This is the best,' she whispered.

When would she ever want more than this? As she lay in the hay, watching him rip off his jeans, she half remembered the other times. It was always good. She couldn't imagine a time when this would fail to please her. At the beginning it had almost been more her than him, she had felt driven by her own need. They said women grew passionate under the sun, and she had been passionate, a passionate girl. A girl who needed a man. He came down on her, his body hot and heavy. His big hands cradled her breasts and she stretched herself under him, revelling in the feel of another's warm skin. This would never end. This was home, this was pleasure, this was pinsharp, hectic excitement.

When it was over she folded up under him, like a house cat. She was full of gentleness suddenly. 'You're one hell of a woman,' he said.

She reached out and touched the sweat beading his cheek. 'Thanks.'

'So, when are we going to get married?'

She blinked at him, wondering why he was raising that now. She put her arm over her face, she was too sleepy to talk. He caught her wrists and confronted her. 'Come on, Lorne, no point taking years over it. Pa wants us to get on and I've waited long enough. If we fix it for next spring that gives us time to get a house fixed up. There's the place in five acre, we've been keeping it free.'

'It's a nice house.' She stretched back in her hay bed and he reached out and tangled his fingers in hers.

'I won't let anyone else have you. You know that.'

'But why be in such a hurry? I've only just got home.'

His face darkened suddenly. 'A girl like you should have a man to look after her. You're the wife a man like me should have and I won't have you messed about.'

'What do you mean? Messed about?'

'You know what I mean, Lorne. Men. That friend of yours. You need to be married. People around here know me. You'll get respect. Greg Berenson's wife won't have a moment's trouble.'

She laughed at him and put her arms around his neck to bring his head down to hers. 'I don't want to get married. Not yet. I'm having far too much fun.' She tickled his face with her kisses and he began to laugh, rolling his head from side to side. 'Lorne, stop it. Lorne — Lorne, you stop tickling like that! You're the sweetest girl — if we get hitched there won't be a man in the county won't envy me.'

He rolled on top of her, ready again. She put her hands on his heavy shoulders. He was as thickset as a prime beef bull.

'Say you love me,' she teased.

'You know I do! I can't say it pretty but I do. Don't expect me to be like your clever friends. I'm just a dumb old boy from the sticks.'

Her heart went out to him. He was a good man, a loving man. One day she might marry him, but not yet.

When they came out of the barn they had hay in their hair.

The afternoon was ending, the cattle moving in slow file to the milking shed. Sherwood Berenson stood on the step of the farmhouse, watching them. 'Lorne,' he said.

'Hi, Mr Berenson.' She felt awkward, as she always did with him. He always seemed to know what she had been doing.

'How's things at your place?'

'Fine. Mr Berenson. Just fine.'

'You come along in and talk awhile.'

He turned on his heel and led her into the house. She didn't want to go but refusal seemed impossible, with Sherwood at the front and Greg behind. She went into the sparse, unfriendly house and accepted a glass of sour lemonade.

'I'll go help outside,' said Greg suddenly. Lorne glanced at him in panic. Why was he leaving her? Was this planned? Of course it was. Sherwood Berenson had something he wished to say.

It was quiet without Greg. Sherwood stared at her unblinking, and she looked at the floor. The man unnerved her more than a little. He never felt the urge to fill silence with conversation; neither did he feel uncomfortable when silence was all there was. To Lorne, brought up with polite chatter, it was unbearable. 'The cows look well,' she said at last.

Sherwood moved his chair a little closer to her. Instinctively she leaned back. 'You think I'm going to hurt you?' asked Sherwood.

'Er — no, Mr Berenson. But I'm wondering why you wanted to talk to me.'

'You've been in the barn with my son almost every day since you got home from school. Don't you think that's a good reason?'

Lorne's face flamed. 'What Greg and I do is our business, Mr Berenson.'

'You do it with other boys? Or is he the only one?'

She flailed for an answer. 'I — we — you've no right to ask that! But of course I don't — I'm no whore, Mr Berenson!'

He grunted. 'Never thought you were. You're a lovely

162

young girl with a woman's natural needs. But a man has to be sure. I want Greg and you to wed.'

'Yes. So he said.'

He got up and went to pour some more lemonade, only this time he added spirits from a small, clear bottle. He handed Lorne her glass.

'You'll find that more to your taste, I guess. Shusters never did like the plainer things in life. Always did have fancy ideas about living. Pity of it is, they never could make it pay.'

Lorne's fingers felt ice-cold on her glass. Sherwood went on, 'Thing is, your family's thought well of around here. A Shuster's better than a Berenson and always has been. Two generations back we were nobody. But Shusters have always been somebody. Important. Respected. Take your daddy now. Much admired, a gentleman of stature. And his daughter's so pretty and so well connected she could have her pick of a dozen fine young men.'

'I don't mean to marry anyone just yet, Mr Berenson,' said Lorne stiffly. 'Now, I really must be getting back —'

'No, Lorne, you sit right there. You're a girl I admire, straight-talking, sensible. I'll talk straight to you. Now, you know I want you to marry Greg. He needs a girl like you — pretty, clever, showing him how to go on at cocktails in New York. He needs a woman with class and, Lorne honey, you got it.'

'I'm very fond of Greg,' she prevaricated. 'But —'

'But nothing! Now, I know you're young and I know you're trying your wings. But it would do your daddy more good than you know if you married my son.'

'My father? He only wants me to be happy.'

'I saw him last night and he wants a hell of a lot more than that. You don't measure happiness in dollars and cents.'

She took a gulp of her drink and choked. He was telling her something that she was too stupid to understand. 'Are you saying my father's in trouble with money?'

Sherwood leaned back in his chair. 'Been in trouble since the day he was born. And now he's in deep trouble. The deepest. Damn near broke.'

163

She looked at him in horror. How could he know, this big, quiet man with his farmer's hands and small, clever eyes? Her father wouldn't tell him a thing. He always said Sherwood Berenson was too full of other men's business for anyone's good. 'You're lying,' she said jerkily. 'My father bought me a Jaguar car for my last birthday. He's going to buy a great Italian painting, the deal's almost done.'

'He won't buy a damn thing,' said Sherwood. 'He asked me for the money and I said no. That's not an investment, Lorne, not the sort I like.'

'Why should he ask you?' she asked, and her lips felt stiff and bloodless.

'Same reason he's asked me all the times before – I'm the only one that'll pay.'

He talked on, for almost an hour. In the early days Drake Shuster had suffered dips in his fortunes, when the price of beef dropped, or horseflesh was out of fashion. Each time the pendulum had swung back to prosperity. But then there had been one or two setbacks, with disease in the stock and a serious fire, but always the bank had lent money to tide him over. Naturally they lent to him, he was Drake Shuster, after all. The Shusters lived as they had for generations, with lavish hospitality and Southern charm. Sadly, luck had turned away. A venture into an airfield had failed, and another with a new strain of rye, and the day came when the bank would lend no more.

'I'll give this to your pa,' said Berenson. 'He didn't ask for a cent. I gave it, freely. He's a man of honour and I knew he'd do the right thing. Trouble is, the last year or so the right thing's been darned pricey. He can't afford to pay my interest, and that's a fact.'

'What's he going to do?' asked Lorne.

Sherwood looked at her and smiled. 'Lorne honey, that depends on you.'

By the time she came out the milking was done. Greg was leaning on the fence, looking at the cattle walking back into the meadow, back to their grass and a peaceful night. Did he know? Lorne wondered. He must. His father had collected all the loans Drake Shuster had incurred over years, and if he so wished he could take the Shuster place tomorrow. If her father sold everything he had he couldn't pay him back. They were ruined, and she alone had the power to put it right.

'I'd never foreclose on my own kin,' the man had said. 'Why, as long as it gets to be Berenson land in the end, it's no concern. The day you wed Greg is the day I forget all about those loans. But don't you take that into your decision. Marriage is important. It's your own life. Your parents have made their choices, it's up to you to make yours.'

She felt a small shiver run up her spine, although the day was warm. But she had intended marrying Greg in the end, hadn't she? When she had settled again, when home seemed familiar and safe. Berenson's words seemed to sound again and again in her head, making her doubt everything she had once thought certain. If only she could go to her parents and ask if all this was true. But if it was they would never let her marry Greg to save them, and if it wasn't – why, if it wasn't, had the Monet sketch been sold, and the good racehorse, the quality bull, the patch of land on the south side where Pa used to go shooting? It was all true. What's more it was time to stop denying it. She had to face up to her future and to what she must do.

'I think you should be a little more experienced. It's a big step. You don't know anyone else.'

'I don't want to know anyone else. I'm happy. And you should be happy for me.'

Lorne lay on her bed, wearing nothing but bra and pants, extending her hand to admire her solitaire diamond. Matty was wrapped in a towel, fresh from the shower, and downstairs could be heard the bustle of last minute preparations for Lorne's party.

'Your mother doesn't like him,' declared Matty. 'Quit now, it's not too late.'

'My mother does like him! She's known him since he was a baby.'

'Perhaps she's hated him since he was a baby. You know she's worried. Didn't she ask you if you wanted to wait?'

'She didn't mean it.' Lorne sat up and hunched a

shoulder. 'Perhaps it is a bit rushed, but it's what we want. I don't want people talking about me. They talk about anyone around here.'

'You don't have to marry someone just because you sleep with them!' said Matty in horror. 'I don't understand you, Lorne.'

The other girl wrapped her arms around her knees. 'And I forgot what it's like around here. Everyone knows what Greg and I have been doing. They've all been talking, and if we didn't get married they'd say I was a tramp. It isn't like the big city, where you can do what you like and walk away from it. Here it follows you all your life. So we're going to get married. Soon.'

She was determined. Matty said doubtfully, 'If you're sure —'

And Lorne replied, 'I'm sure. Double, double sure.'

Matty flung down her towel and began to get dressed. She was to wear her balldress tonight, because Simon had said, 'Thank goodness you don't have to borrow. It's like being a beggar.' So she would wear her extravagant dress, appropriate or not. The sequins glittered like stars in a winter sky. It was a stunning frock. But, looking at the party preparations, she realised it would be just the thing. The people of this neighbourhood made the most of celebrations and dressed up.

Lorne said, 'I love it here. It's heaven. And now I'll live here forever.'

'Just remember, you can always come to me,' said Matty.

'Starving in your garret,' mocked Lorne. 'We can starve together. Or make a threesome with the divine Sholto.'

'Oh, very funny.'

Matty pulled a brush through her chestnut hair. At the moment she was cross with Sholto, for being so unreasonable about his picture. He had insisted the Shusters buy it, long beyond the bounds of reason, and at the last they had suffered the embarrassment of having to refuse. It shouldn't have been necessary. But Sholto was at his most flamboyant when selling pictures, Matty realised. His performance was so amazing that his victims seemed to feel it would be sacrilege to interrupt by saying no. The bemused

Shusters had almost found themselves the owners of a minor Venetian masterpiece that would cost a fortune to insure, whether they liked it or not.

For her own part, she was feeling guilty enough about buying their coffee pots. She wasn't even sure that they really wanted to sell, but they had seemed so wistful and had been so brave about her modest valuation, that she increased her offer, for friendship's sake. Tomorrow she and Simon were going back to England, Simon to school and she to see Sammy. He wouldn't be impressed with those coffee pots. She felt sick with apprehension.

Lorne was dressing in a confection of ruby satin and lace. Flounces and frills served to emphasise her excessive fragility, turning what should have been a fruitcake of a dress into the petals of a flower. Her dark hair was in ringlets, cascading over her shoulders. Tonight, chastened, she was the archetypal Southern belle.

'Want to borrow some earrings?' she offered.

'No thanks,' said Matty automatically.

Lorne sighed. 'You're taking this independence kick too far, Matty. You're getting badly hung up. That dress needs earrings. Wear my sapphires.'

As always it was rude to refuse. Grudgingly Matty took the offering. 'I wish the others were here,' she said suddenly.

Lorne considered. 'I don't. Griselda would be mean. I can hear her now: "I know you Americans have mysterious tastes, Lorne, but do you really want to spend the rest of your life with a man whose only concession to civilisation is some little command of the English language?" And ever after I'd see Greg as some sort of neanderthal.'

'What a good thing you don't,' said Matty weakly.

'I like neanderthals!'

When she went down Sholto was waiting at the bottom of the stairs. 'Where's Simon?' asked Matty, and he grimaced.

'Is that all I'm good for? Nursemaiding? He's in the kitchen, making one-handed canapés. Stop ignoring me, Matty.'

'I don't ignore you.'

'Then for God's sake meet my eye!' He swung her round

167

to face him, tipping her chin up with a firm hand. 'OK, they don't want to buy. I've accepted it. Hold that picture for two years, less, and they'd make thousands. But leave that aside. It's not all that, is it?'

She sighed, and unable to escape him any other way, shut her eyes. Tears tried to squeeze under her lashes. 'I'm just frightened. For me and Simon.'

'Do you think I don't know?'

'I haven't any money.'

'I've a bit. Not a lot, but some.'

'That's your money.'

'And we're staying with your friend. OK, we split it. What's a thousand quid between friends?'

She felt a great and rising rage. She put up her hands and grabbed handfuls of her hair, yanking it painfully. 'I hate people giving me things! I hate all this stinking charity!'

'Which is why you're wearing Lorne's earrings, I suppose.'

She wrenched them from her ears and threw them across the room. They bounced against the wall and tinkled to the ground.

'Oh, look,' said Sholto cheerily. 'You've broken the setting. Well done.'

It was so awful she wanted to cry. But somehow laughter began to choke her. She hung on to Sholto's arm and roared with mirth. He began to laugh too. They were holding each other up, screaming with laughter. 'We are just so damned poor!' chuckled Sholto. 'So pathetically, desperately poor!'

'I've still got my principles!' gasped Matty.

'And I haven't even got those.'

Gradually the laughter subsided. Sholto said, 'Oh God, that's better. Let's pick up the earrings and be sensible. You've been so tense lately I thought you would snap.'

'I didn't think you'd noticed,' said Matty distantly.

He lifted his brows. 'I didn't think you wanted me to notice.'

Suddenly she put her arms round his neck and put her face up for his kiss. He enfolded her, his mouth hot and welcoming, tasting of wine and toothpaste and him. Matty gave a soft moan.

'Oops! Do excuse me.'

It was Lorne, coming down the stairs. They parted, Matty flustered, Sholto unconcerned. 'You have just witnessed my rehabilitation on Matty's Christmas card list,' he remarked, 'And where is your heart-throb, young Lorne? On this of all nights?'

'He'll be here soon.'

'She says gloomily. Can't say I blame you. Back out tomorrow, Lorne, while the presents still have labels. But at least wait until then, your mother's worked so hard on the food. You could chuck him after the buffet, I suppose. A wonderful end to a party.'

The girls put up their hands to hide their giggles. It always seemed a mistake to laugh too uproariously at Sholto, he simply got worse. The kitchen door opened to a flurry of maids bringing trays of glasses and jugs of punch across the hall, and the door bell rang. It was Greg himself, dressed to the nines in a tuxedo and holding a bunch of red roses. Sholto sighed. 'Hi, Greg,' he said patiently.

'Hi.' Greg looked a little surprised to be politely acknowledged. He had been intending to ignore Sholto with acid point. He turned to Lorne, offering the roses. 'For you, Lorne honey,' he declared. 'The rose in my heart.'

Sholto reached out and plucked one of the roses, presenting it theatrically to Matty. 'For you, Matty honey,' he mimicked. 'The weed in my vegetable patch.'

Lorne's polite acceptance of the flowers dissolved in laughter. Greg's face flamed. He thrust the flowers at her and turned on Sholto, his hands lifted. 'What do you mean?' he said softly.

'Not a lot,' said Sholto. 'It was a joke.'

'I don't like your sort of joke.'

'Come to that, I don't like your sort of compliment. But I can give you some guidance. Now, poetry's always a good bet, John Donne's a winner. "Come live with me and be my love" and all that. A tasteful verse, carefully penned, can so often obviate the need for the embarrassing verbal cliché.'

'You motherfucker!' snapped Greg.

'Is that any way to speak to the woman you love?' asked Sholto.

Greg's great fist swung, Sholto sidestepped, and at that moment Aunt Susan came into the hall. 'Ah,' declared Sholto, 'say hello to your hostess, Greg. She's gone to a lot of trouble for your party.'

Greg's inner torment was comical. His bunched fist turned into a reluctant handshake. He looked daggers at his tormentor.

Lorne fought against riotous laughter, saying, 'Come along, Greg, see what Mother's done for us. Everything's lovely. You can talk to Sholto later.'

She dragged him forcibly away. Aunt Susan said, 'Have you been upsetting that boy, Sholto?'

He grinned. 'I don't think he's too bright.'

'Oh, he's bright enough. I've no worries on that score.' She grimaced slightly.

Matty said, 'They don't have to get married soon, anyway.'

Aunt Susan sighed. 'I don't like his father, and that's a fact. Drake and he are good friends, but I don't like that sort of friend. And the mother's a nonentity. Greg was always very proud of his father, I recall. I can't forget how serious he was.'

'Well, I was an ugly little brute,' remarked Sholto. 'And I've improved to the beautiful thing you see today.'

It was self-mocking, but held an underlying edge. So much of Sholto's conversation did. Matty said, 'You're a stunner. Beautifully battered.'

'Oh, for God's sake! Don't massage my poor bent ego, I'm not that pathetic.'

'You're never pathetic,' said Aunt Susan. 'Please, you two, talk to Lorne. Ever since she came home she's been getting further and further away from me. I want to know she's sure about this. Sometimes I think she forgets what's really important.' She looked anxious and worn.

When she had gone to check on glasses and plates, Sholto said, 'Ironic really. Any self-respecting orphan would give their eye-teeth to have her as a mother. But not Lorne.'

'She adores her,' said Matty. 'Half the trouble, I think. She can't bear to let her down.'

He took her hand. 'And you and I, my sweet, have no one to let down but us. We should think ourselves lucky.'

The guests were beginning to arrive. Matty stood in her beautiful gown and admired them. She had never been to so grand an occasion. There were dowagers in pearls, children in velvet trousers, the stylish young and the elegant middle-aged. They came in cars as big as buses, by plane to the airstrip, and one arrived in a horsedrawn carriage from a farm twenty miles away. Lorne was becoming ever more white and brittle. She leaned on Greg's arm and smiled and talked, while he reached down now and then to put his arm around her. A buzz of approval enveloped them like warm milk. There was no doubt at all that they made a wonderful couple.

'Do you think he's marrying her for the money?' murmured Sholto. They were dancing a waltz.

'Aren't they rich as Croesus?'

He shrugged. 'Apparently. According to Drake Shuster they own half the county. So it must be love. Lorne's a catch, but she's bound to be difficult. Much too sexy and highly strung to be a farm wife forever.'

'She won't be a farm wife. He's going to be in politics and he wants Lorne as his glamorous ornament. Anyway, she thinks she likes farming.'

'I know. Odd how people can be so ignorant about themselves. Now you, Matty, would be quite at home tilling the soil. About your level actually. Good, honest toil. No nasty commerce to worry about, you could live on potato soup.'

'Don't be mean,' she said. 'It's too good a party.'

The house vibrated with people and laughter. Drake Shuster called for silence and made a speech, asking everyone to toast the engaged pair. 'It's always good to be friends with your neighbours,' he said, 'and we've known the Berensons all our lives. Sherwood Berenson's stood by me in all manner of times for years now. They're good people and they've been good friends, and now they can be family. Greg's a lucky man, luckier than he knows, but we're glad too, because we're welcoming a good man into our home. We know he'll take care of her.'

Applause fluttered across the room. Greg bent down and kissed his bride-to-be and Sherwood Berenson clapped loudly, making appreciative noises, preparing to make his own speech. Lorne was watching him, her face set as if in concrete.

A movement caught Matty's eye. She stepped an inch or two back, to get a better view of the window. It was Simon, his plaster cast immobilising one hand but the other fiddling in his pocket. Matty reached out and caught Sholto's wrist, squeezing hard. He followed her line of sight.

'Wait here,' he said softly, and slipped out of the door. Matty couldn't wait. She followed him, attracting surprised glances, breaking the thread of Berenson's speech. 'I always knew I was a bad speaker,' he said, pausing amidst laughter.

The dress slowed Matty's steps, catching on roses and terracotta pots. She dragged at it ruthlessly, feeling the bodice tight as a corset, finding it hurt to breathe. In the shadow of the bushes, twenty feet from the window, were Sholto and Simon.

'Sholto? Have you stopped him? What was he doing?' Her voice was shrill with accusation.

'I wasn't doing anything,' said Simon sulkily.

'Much,' supplied Sholto. 'Don't panic, Matty, it wasn't dangerous. He was about to set off a stink bomb.'

'What? In Aunt Susan's house? During the party? When she's been so kind? Simon, you're a creature from hell!' Matty turned away, putting her hands to her midriff, trying to breathe.

'It wouldn't matter. Lorne doesn't really want to marry him,' muttered Simon.

'Whether she does or not, how could you think of such a thing? Oh, it's no good. I'll have to get him a behaviorist or whatever it is. I can't cope.'

She sank down on the grass, her head on her knees. Sholto said, 'Now look what you've done,' in a high-pitched, jokey voice, and Simon giggled.

Matty looked up at them. 'Can't either of you take it seriously? Or are you as stupid and childish as him, Sholto?'

'He isn't stupid and he isn't childish.'

'I don't know what else I'd call it. He's a stupid little boy!'

'Shut up, Matty. You're making things worse.'

'They can't be any worse! Everything's a mess. If he'd behaved he could have come here every summer, and now – I don't know what's to happen.'

She was hyperventilating in short, gasping breaths. Sholto squatted down beside her, his hand resting on her back. After a moment he unhooked her dress and slid the zip open. Matty gasped, pressing her head against her knees. Gradually her breathing slowed.

'You can't blame him for hating charity,' said Sholto softly. 'You hate it as much.'

'There isn't anything else,' she puffed. 'Hating it doesn't matter.'

'At the very least you should leave him his pride. Do you want him humble and beaten and afraid?'

'I'm not afraid,' said Simon.

'I was,' said Sholto. 'Same age as you. Dumped. And from then on every mouthful of food was tainted with bloody gratitude. I was afraid of getting used to it. And I was so afraid of what would happen if one day I went too far that I almost *wanted* to go too far. To get it over with and find out.'

'Were your parents dead?' asked Simon.

'No. My father ran off with another woman and my mother went into a depression. She died in a mental hospital a year later. Suicide, probably. I was dumped on my father's sister in Venice. And I never, for one moment, behaved well.'

Matty scrambled up, holding the dress in front of her. 'You're just encouraging him. If he was good, people would want to have him to stay.'

Simon glared at her. 'Lord Knelworth didn't.'

'You weren't one of the family! You were a guest. Don't you understand, Simon? You've got to behave carefully.'

'You've got to crawl,' said Sholto, his tone objective. 'On your knees, but not too humble, grateful but not obsequious, at home but not as if you were born with your feet under the table. The art of sponging, or how to survive as the unwelcome guest. I'm surprised at you, Matty. You, of all people.'

'Shut up, will you? Shut up! You're just encouraging him.'

'Well, perhaps I didn't get enough encouragement. Thinking back on it, I don't think I got any.'

He walked away, into the dark. After a moment Matty said, 'Don't listen to him. He's mad.'

'He's great. I wish I could go and stay with him.'

'He hasn't got anywhere to live either! And I think that should tell you something. Simon, Simon, I'm doing my best! Can't you at least help a little, and not make everything so hard?'

He dropped his head. 'You don't hear what they say. And even when they don't say it you know what they're thinking. Everyone. The people here.'

'Couldn't you try not to take any notice?'

It was futile. She was asking him to give up everything, including his pride. He wasn't a parcel, to be delivered here, there and everywhere, courtesy of his sister's friends, and he could no longer be treated as one. She had run out of time.

She sent him to bed, and kicked the stinkbomb into the leafmould under a bush. It almost made her smile, imagining the consternation if it had exploded in the midst of the elegant party. She knew she should go back in, but there was no one to fasten her dress. Where had Sholto gone? She followed the path through the garden and down to the wood, listening to the nightbirds calling, letting the cool air soothe her unquiet spirit.

He was leaning against a tree, his white shirt clear in the dark. 'I could shoot you,' said Matty. 'Like an Indian. Perhaps I should.'

He reached out and took hold of her hands, pulling them down. The dress fell around her waist, leaving her breasts naked. They were butter heavy, the nipples erect with anticipation. She could feel his anger, like a flame.

'Was she horrible? Your aunt?'

He took a long, remembering breath. 'Yes. She wasn't just unkind, she was cruel. Emotionally cruel. Tempting me with the promise of affection. If I did this, and that, and the other, then she would love me. And I did everything — and she never did. She laughed at my need of it. Mocked my silly teddy bear, my sad little photograph of my mother, my pathetic gifts to her. But she taught me — oh, she did that. I learned to look at pictures with her — she had a relatively good eye. No vision, of course. No one that cold could possess it. And she taught me to hate.'

Matty put up her hands to defend herself from his stare. 'Don't look at me like that. I'm not her. Simon's not you.'

'You couldn't be her. She's still alive, living in her huge house, the canal lapping at the windows, rats gnawing at the walls. But Simon could be me. He fights the way I fought. To be himself. To grow up respecting himself. And his lovely, lovely sister can't bring herself to do a bit of business just to give him a chance.'

'I'm doing my best!' Matty shrieked at him. 'You won't help and you won't even give me credit for trying! I'm going to go and beg Sammy to let me have my job back. I kept the de Caruzon catalogue because I couldn't bear to tear it up, so I'll give him a copy and let him deal if he sees fit. And it still won't make me anything like enough money to buy so much as a shoebox that Simon could call his home!'

He was smiling his wicked smile. 'Your breasts flush pink when you're angry. Did you know?'

'No. Do me up, I want to go back. I've had enough of you.'

'Of course you haven't.'

They made love on a mossy bank, the dress hanging from a tree next to Sholto's jacket. At Lorne's instigation Matty was on the pill, and she felt careless and wild. She was too young to be weighed down by responsibility: she hadn't time to waste in worry and strain. Looking up into Sholto's face she wondered if she would ever forget him. He smiled down at her, as if he knew what she was thinking, and she knew that she never would.

Matty woke with a pounding headache, dry mouth and shivering skin. She was desperately hungover. Groping into the bathroom for a drink of water she passed her crumpled dress on the floor, her shoes separated by yards of carpet, Lorne's earrings in a reproachful handful on a chair.

Last night had been wild. She and Sholto had fulfilled every appetite: sex, dancing, food, fun. At dawn some of the cousins had mounted horses and tried to ride up the stairs, while Aunt Susan put her hand to her head and said, 'I can't bear it! Do they have to? Again?' Sholto, rejecting the stairs, had jumped Drake's quarterhorse over a table.

It was late. Blinking at the day, Matty tried to focus on the clock. It was almost three in the afternoon, and she had intended to leave before twelve. Now what?

The bedroom door swung open and Matty squinted and lifted her head. Simon stood there, wearing jeans and sweater, ready to travel. 'Sholto says we can still make the flight if you hurry.'

'I can't hurry. I'm dying.'

'Sholto says no one ever died of a hangover.'

'Sholto can say what he likes.'

None the less she staggered up. All preparations had been made yesterday. She had only to fling the balldress and shoes into her case and put on her jeans and shirt. Only. . . it was impossible. She could barely see.

'Here, I'll do up your buttons.'

It was Sholto, looking pale. 'Aren't you ill?'

'I didn't drink the brandy. Or at least, not half a bottle. You were a very silly girl, Matilda.'

'Don't gloat. Are you ready?'

'Sure thing.'

He put his hand in his pocket and produced a cheque. 'One picture sold,' he said. 'To a Shuster cousin with taste. Not a great work, nor a great price, but we get the commission. Want your share or not?'

Matty swallowed down bile, and with it her anxious conscience. 'Yes.'

'Good girl. This is the first day of your sensible life. Put your shoes on.'

As she struggled to put her feet swollen by dancing into shoes that seemed a size too small, she saw Sholto pocket the earrings.

'Put them back. They're Lorne's.'

'And we'd better get them mended. We'll post them and say they were taken in error. Or we can write and tell her to collect in person. She'll need an excuse to get away from the gorilla.'

'Did he really — ?' Matty grimaced, trying to remember.

Sholto nodded. 'Yes. It was he who swung from the chandelier, swiping the early Wedgwood bowl a terminal blow. 'Twas he. Never mind, if it gives Lorne good reason to dump him, the Shusters will think it worth every penny.'

'His father tried to grope me,' commented Matty.

'Did he? Surprised you remember, you were so drunk.'

Matty blushed. Her only consolation was that she wouldn't be alone in cringing at the antics of the night before. Guests had thrown up in the flower beds, had swum naked in the pool, had been discovered in amorous clinches with the wrong people. 'What was the worst thing I did?' she asked fearfully.

He considered. 'You told Drake Shuster that the coffee pots he had sold you were not really the sort of items you stooped to consider under normal circumstances. One had an added lid and the other had been bashed about by the Victorians.'

Matty put a hand to her head. 'I didn't! I did?'

'You did.'

The scene downstairs put her shame into perspective. The chandelier hung on trailing bare wires, and a crack extended the width of the ceiling. The fragments of Wedgwood bowl had been gathered into a sorry pile in the middle of a scratched table, and the carpet was covered with hoof marks. In one corner there was a large, hoof-sized tear. Aunt Susan was surveying the horror, looking pale and tragic.

'Er — I do apologise,' said Sholto humbly.

'It wasn't you, was it?' She looked at him wearily. 'After a while I couldn't bear to look.'

'It wasn't him,' said Simon, sending Sholto a look of fierce loyalty.

'Perhaps we should have done something,' said Matty feebly.

Aunt Susan sighed. 'Matty dear, no one has ever been

able to do anything when the Shuster boys party. We should hold it in a barn or somewhere, they shouldn't come into a decent house. I hate to think how much all this is going to cost.'

Their shame at being part of the débâcle kept them silent. Maids and caterers were moving carefully around, like medical orderlies in the aftermath of battle. Outside, floating in the swimming pool, were high-heeled shoes, panties and a set of false teeth. Matty, Sholto and Simon made their farewells, and Aunt Susan kissed and hugged them, reserving special warmth for Simon. 'We've loved to have you,' she assured him. 'Don't think we didn't.'

'He doesn't think that,' said Matty, and there was an embarrassed moment. They all knew that he did.

At the last minute Matty's headache cleared enough for her to remember Lorne. She stood under her window calling, and after a moment Lorne leaned out. She drooped over the sill like a debauched nymph, her eyes sooty with weariness and old mascara.

'Remember to come and see me when it all falls through,' called Matty.

'Just send me the address of the garret,' retorted Lorne. 'You were rude about our coffee pots.'

Matty went red. 'I'll find you some better ones. I'm sorry, Lorne.'

The girl yawned capaciously. 'Don't be. Have fun, Matty. Don't get serious.'

'I'll remember that,' said Sholto, grinning up at her.

'It's about time you started to get serious,' retorted Lorne. 'Go away, I'm asleep. Good luck. Be seeing you.'

One of the gardeners took them to the train in the station wagon. Simon was whistling to himself through his teeth. 'Don't be so cheerful,' said Matty. 'You didn't do so well.'

'They didn't mind.' Simon settled in his seat, thinking happily about going back to school. It unsettled Matty. She had never in her life wanted to go back to school.

The swaying of the car was making her ill. She rested her forehead against Sholto's arm and tried to imagine what she would do when she returned to London.

'What are you going to do when you get back?' she asked him.

He yawned, sleepily. 'Dunno. Book a room somewhere, and spend this money.'

'You should put it to one side. You might want to start a business or something.'

Slumping down in his seat he said, 'Don't be boring.'

But later, in the night, when they sat on a train that clacked endlessly towards the airport from which they would fly home, he sat staring out of the window into the dark. Simon was asleep, all innocence and peace, his head propped uncomfortably on his grass-stained plaster cast.

Sholto said, 'Suppose I did start a business? Would you come in with me?'

Matty sat up a little. She felt terribly thirsty. 'What sort of business?'

'Dealing. Broking. Buying for people on commission. Good silver, good pictures. We both know what's what.'

'You might. I don't know anything except what Sammy taught me.'

'You know a damn sight more than most.'

She said, 'I'd made up my mind to go back to Sammy. I'll have to go and see him.'

He turned from the window, grinning at her. 'You do that. And I'll go and see my aunt.'

'What, the one in Venice?'

'No. The one in Bournemouth. She refused to have me live with her, told me she'd never liked my father and saw no reason to make his life any easier than it was already by taking on his responsibilities. She thought he'd have to rescue me from Venice. She's been feeling guilty for years about leaving me there. I shall do the decent thing and allow her to expiate that guilt with money.'

Matty said nothing. Experience had taught her the futility of reasoning with Sholto over things like that. But what was she to do? It wouldn't be tactful, or even wise, to dump Simon at school and then turn up at Sammy's with her suitcase. No, she would simply have to go and stay with Henrietta.

Chapter Eleven

The house was tall and imposing, sheltered from the street by a sliver of a garden edged with iron railings. It overlooked a square, iron-railed again, with only the residents permitted to own keys. The more elderly took the air amongst the bushes on fine days, and sat on benches, reading *The Times*. Dogs were not allowed.

Matty had visited only once. The unassailed dominance of Henrietta's mother had made her uncomfortable; the woman appeared to rule even sunrise and sunset within the confines of her house.

'Don't mind her,' Henrietta had said, but it was hard not to. She missed nothing, commenting on every torn fingernail and laddered stocking. When Matty broke a tooth mug, even though she hid the pieces in the cupboard, she knew Mrs Giles would find out. And on the last day, with nothing said, the broken pieces had been displayed in a pile on Matty's dressing table. She had left a silent pound in payment.

But she was an adult now. She was a woman. Grown women didn't cringe when they met formidable people. They looked them in the eye, extended a firm hand and said, 'How do you do.' Matty rang the bell and waited. She expected the maid to answer the door, and when instead she found herself confronting Mrs Giles she opened and closed her mouth, quite wordless.

'Good heavens — Matilda. What a surprise. Do come in.'

'Er — yes — thanks awfully.' Matty gulped and blushed.

The hall was large and imposing, just like Mrs Giles. She had grey hair permed and tinted into an enormous steely shell, an immovable frame for her large, strong face. It suited her, as did the jacket and skirt in tailored navy wool,

181

the heavy pearl earrings and her pearl brooch. A handsome woman, people would have said. Terrifying, thought Matty.

'I wondered – is Henry in? I mean, Henrietta.'

Mrs Giles sighed. 'I always hate the way you girls shorten names. It's sloppy. And so are your clothes. Why are you wearing such a tired suit, Matilda?'

Matty glanced down at herself. Her black suit had a shadowy stain on the skirt and was in desperate need of pressing. 'I had a suitcase stolen in America,' she said apologetically. 'I've only got this and some evening clothes.'

'Then I suggest you go shopping.' Mrs Giles raised an eyebrow and led the way upstairs.

Henry was lying on her bed, reading *True Confessions* and eating sweets. When she saw Matty she leaped up, squealing with delight. The sweets disappeared under the pillow with a practised flick of the hand. 'Oh, Matty! Darling Matty! How wonderful.'

'Don't squawk, darling,' said Mrs Giles automatically. 'I hope you weren't eating sweets.'

'Of course not.' Her guilt was obvious.

But her mother was feeling indulgent. 'Henrietta's had a cold,' she told Matty. 'It's very nice for her to have a friend. Now, you girls are bound to have lots to talk about. I'll bring up a tray.'

When she had gone the two girls bounced on the bed, just as they had when they were fourteen. Matty almost fell off, and choked on a shriek. It was like school again, with authority looming, ready to pounce.

'You look exhausted,' said Henry breathlessly, flopping back.

'I am. I've come from America. I left my suitcase at the station but I'm so hoping you'll invite me to stay.'

Henrietta sat up. 'You haven't lost your job? Oh, Matty, how could you?'

'Not without difficulty. I'm ashamed of myself. By the way, Lorne's got engaged to the strangest man. He's very good-looking and a bit Old Testament. The sort of man who could be president, all front and no back. Except I think he might be a pig.'

Henry's eyes widened. 'How do you know?'

'I don't. But he looks it. And he tried to hit Sholto, except Sholto is never where you expect him to be and he missed.' Matty lay back on the bed and closed her eyes. 'Oh, this is bliss! I could go to sleep.'

'No you couldn't! Matilda Winterton, you're to wake up and tell me everything. Every last bit.'

They talked for two hours, and Mrs Giles came in and out, checking on them and supplying more tea and crispbread. Finally she extended the longed-for invitation. 'Would you like to stay the night, Matilda? You and Henrietta seem to have so much to talk about.'

'That's awfully kind of you, Mrs Giles. Thanks.' Just the right degree of girlishness. Matty felt a fraud.

When she had gone, she said, 'How are you getting on with her these days?'

Henrietta shrugged. 'OK. Quite well, actually. We still have rows over clothes, of course, but nowadays I give in and just go out looking a fright.'

'Quitter.'

Henry bit into a Mars bar from a secret hoard. 'You'd quit too if you had to face up to her when she's in full flood. She has this vision of what I should look like. Alice in Wonderland or something. Blue dresses, sashes, button boots, or the nearest thing to it you can get in Harrods.'

'You look nice in blue,' prevaricated Matty.

'Not in sashes I don't.'

To demonstrate she flung open her wardrobe doors and pulled out dress after dress. They were all waisted, lacy, and of necessity huge.

'Oh dear,' said Matty. 'I suppose Lorne could wear that sort of thing. But then, she's so thin.'

'And I'm not! I'm not getting any thinner either. She's relaxed the diet a bit, thank God. For one whole week she served me watercress at every meal. Then she found I was sneaking out to buy chips and she was furious. Daddy had to stand up for me.'

'But you could lose a bit, couldn't you? Sensibly, I mean.'

Moodily Henrietta brought out another Mars bar. 'I suppose so.' She bit into it vengefully.

Henrietta had been confined to the house for a week with

her cold. She had missed three parties, two lunches and a
race meeting, but she didn't seem to mind. Matty had the
feeling that Henrietta liked staying at home, reading her
magazines and eating. It worried her.

'What are you going to do when the Season's over?' she
asked bracingly. 'Get a job, perhaps?'

'I don't know. Something. Mother's hoping I'll be
a receptionist in an art gallery. That way I'll meet all
the people I should know. She thinks some knight in
shining armour will ask to marry me and that will be
that.'

'No knights?' Matty looked enquiring.

'Not even a snotty little squire. I suppose it's my shape.
Matty, the whole world's thinner than me. Nobody likes
fatties and I just get fatter and fatter. Soon I'll swell up and
explode, like an over-inflated balloon.'

Looking at her, Matty found the thought far from absurd.
Henry was more puffed up than she had ever seen her. She
stood up and went to open the bedside drawer. It was empty.
But Matty knew her friend too well.

'What do you do with the evidence?'

Wordlessly, Henry pulled up the mattress. A treasure
trove of sweet papers nestled there, glowing like jewels.

Matty put her chin in her hands, staring at her friend.
'Do you want to be thin, Henry?' she asked. 'Or would you
be happy the way you are, if your mother stopped nagging?
I mean, if you don't want to diet then say so.'

'I don't want to diet.' But then Henry sighed. 'I do want
to be thin, though. Isn't there any other way?'

'You know there isn't. I suppose it might be possible to
run round the park while eating, and wear it off faster than
you take it in, but otherwise starvation's the only choice.
Look, what you need is some autonomy.'

Henrietta made a face. 'Will I like it? Does it hurt?
Honestly, you and Griselda always were too clever by half.
What is autonomy?'

Matty suppressed a yawn. 'All I mean is that you should
be in charge of your own life. Eating what you want, because
you want it, not because it's a good card to play against
your mother.'

'I don't do that. I eat because I like food. I like it more than anything.'

Matty brightened. 'There you are then! All we have to do is find you things you like better. Sex is good, but you can't do it three times a day, and drink's smashing, except it's fattening. How about roller coaster rides?'

'Don't they give you brain damage? I mean, they would if you did them constantly.'

'Yes.' Matty thought again. 'You need a job,' she decided. 'Something to get you out of the house. Something useful.'

'I'm supposed to be doing the Season!'

'But you're not, are you? You're eating. So you could have a job and go to parties in your time off. You'll have no time to eat, you'll get so thin all those dresses will have to be taken in.'

Henrietta screwed up a Mars bar wrapper and hid it under the mattress. She eyed Matty speculatively. 'And what are you going to do? You haven't got a job or a Season. Or a weight problem,' she added dismally.

'Hmmm.' Matty got off the bed. 'I'm going to get my suitcase. Tomorrow I'm going to see Sammy Chesworth and the day after that I'll decide what I'm going to do. Come on, Henry, give me the sweets.'

'No! There'll only be fish for dinner.'

'Sharks live on it. That and the odd leg.' Matty gnashed her teeth.

'And I can't.'

Matty held out her hand, schooling her face into disapproval. But Henry clung to her little store of chocolate. She wailed softly, like a goose with a nest full of eggs. Then, as Matty shrugged and turned away, she thrust the whole lot into a paper bag. 'Go on then! Take it! And see if I care.'

'That's the spirit,' said Matty. 'Isn't it better being bullied by me instead of your mother? Don't worry, soon you won't have time to feel hungry.'

Despite all her insecurities Matty felt strangely calm the next day. London seemed like home, a familiar stamping ground. She gave up her suit to Mrs Giles and it was returned in almost better condition than the day she bought it. Mrs Giles also telephoned a shop and had three white blouses sent round. 'You'd better buy them, Matilda,' she advised. 'You can't go around like a tramp. And this shop is very good value, with excellent workmanship. All seams are double sewn.'

She was the most managing woman. But the blouses were lovely, made from heavy cotton that would wear forever. Mrs Giles should have run a company, thought Matty, looking round at the well-ordered house, with desks covered in lists and orderly files. She could have run ICI and still found time to discuss the shape of canapés for the NSPCC cocktail party. Matty ruefully paid her hostess for the blouses.

The trouble with Mrs Giles was that you dared not confess to weakness. She had none herself and didn't understand it in others, so poverty, unemployment and greed meant nothing to her. Matty speculated on abandoning her on some famine-struck African plain and seeing what would happen. She suspected the Giles Programme for Famine Relief would be in progress before twenty-four hours had elapsed, with anyone disobedient enough to die sent elsewhere to do it, to keep the statistics up to scratch.

She went to look for Henrietta. Inevitably she was in the kitchen, about to disgrace herself in the fridge.

'Oh well, if you're going to cheat all the time . . .' said Matty.

Henry slammed the door shut. 'I wasn't cheating! I was thinking about it.'

'Aren't you coming out? We're job hunting, remember?'

'Have you told Mother?'

Matty made big eyes. 'Don't be daft! We'll tell her later. When you're employed.'

They went into town, to an employment agency. It seemed farcical, seeking a job for Henrietta when it was Matty who needed the money. As the girl behind the desk ran her finger down the vacancies Matty's heart sank. Something like this might suit Henry, but not her. Everything was so badly paid. Working for Sammy had shielded her from the reality of the job market, where no one wanted an unskilled, inexperienced girl. Henrietta was being considered for a job as a receptionist, but the pin-thin clerk eyed her bulk with reserve.

'They do want someone with good dress sense,' she murmured, with a distinct lack of tact.

'Henry's got dress sense,' declared Matty. 'It's her mother that hasn't.'

Henry got up, muttering confused thanks. Matty followed her into the street. 'I don't want to be a blasted receptionist anyway,' said Henrietta. 'I don't even want to work in an art gallery.'

'What then?' Matty stood squarely in front of her, barring Henry's automatic path to the confectionery kiosk.

'I want to be a shop assistant!' She stared longingly at the banks of extra strong mints and Opal fruits.

'No can do. Unless it's a television shop or something. And even then, not if it's next door to a sandwich bar.'

'You're worse than my mother,' snapped Henry.

Matty grinned. 'Yes, aren't I? It's because I know you better. I know your appetites.'

Henrietta's stomach was rumbling. She didn't think she had ever been so hungry in her life. All she had eaten the entire day was a bowl of muesli and a cottage cheese salad. Matty had managed two slices of toast at breakfast and a piece of ham pie with her salad at lunch, not to mention hot bread and butter. No wonder she was so smug.

'I'm going to have a coffee,' declared Henrietta.

'Henry! No!'

'Just a coffee! With a sweetener. Nothing to eat, not even a Danish.'

'Especially not a Danish! Henry, you know if you go in one of those places you'll crumble. You'll apple crumble. You only have to see food to want it. Henry, have some sense.'

Henrietta's soft blue eyes became positively cold. 'You sound just like my mother,' she said distantly.

Matty fell silent. If Henrietta was determined to find a coffee shop there was nothing she could do. 'One day,' she muttered, trailing behind her friend. 'Not even one day!'

'Shut up, Matty,' said Henrietta. She stomped ahead, her

feet incongruously small at the end of plump legs. It wouldn't be hard for her to lose some weight, thought Matty. She was fatter than she had ever been. It couldn't be good to be so heavy.

They were walking away from the shops, into one of the endless London hinterlands of houses, offices, car parks and nondescript warehouses. A couple of tramps were slumped against huge steel doors on the other side of the street. Matty's spirits rose. This wasn't coffee shop territory. Henrietta had been so preoccupied she had got lost.

But Henry wasn't to be beaten. She stopped outside a church, one of the barely functioning relics that still exist in London, whose congregation has long since moved away both physically and spiritually. A sad privet hedge grew at its side, and a small, handwritten sign said 'Tea, coffee, 20p. The crypt'. There was an arrow pointing to a door.

'We'll go in here,' said Henry.

Matty eyed the door dubiously. 'If you ask me, they're shut.'

Henrietta went and tried the door. To her own considerable surprise, it opened. 'Come along, Matty,' she called. 'We can have our coffee.'

It was a dark, dingy church hall. Some trestle tables stood across one end, sporting an urn and some cups. A plastic tray of wrapped chocolate biscuits stood beside it, with some sugar and plastic spoons. The tables and chairs were the type used for whist drives, liable to fold up on themselves at any moment. The only people present were three tramps, sipping tea out of cups held in gloved hands, and the vicar.

He was fresh-faced and exuberant. He had dark hair, green eyes and a dog collar that was slightly too big. 'Hello, girls,' he called. 'Want a cuppa?'

'No thanks,' said Matty.

'Yes please,' said Henrietta. 'Two coffees, please. And – just two coffees.'

'Can't tempt you with a biscuit, can I? And I think we've got some Mars bars somewhere.' He rummaged in a box on the floor.

'I'm on a diet,' said Henrietta.

He stopped rummaging in his box. 'Oh well, just the two coffees it is then.'

Henrietta produced her 40p and she and Matty went to sit down. The coffee was lukewarm but not unpleasant. Henrietta ostentatiously clicked a sweetener into hers. The tramps slurped their tea and muttered to themselves, and after a while the vicar came and leaned on the wall to chat.

'Sure you don't want a Mars bar? We make a better profit on them than anything.'

'They're bad for you,' said Matty virtuously.

'Not for our clients they're not. About the only thing they eat, really. Makes some headway against the fag ends and meths.'

Henrietta giggled. 'Do you get many tramps?'

'Nothing but, usually. And we don't call them tramps. "Dossers" is just about acceptable, but we try and be more polite.'

'Yes. Of course,' Henry looked chastened.

The vicar pulled up a chair and sat astride it the wrong way round.

'What are you doing here then? Is it a school project or something?'

'We have left school,' said Matty coldly. 'Can't you tell? We're brimming with brittle sophistication.'

'Overflowing with it,' agreed Henry. 'From our well-cut hair to the tips of our perfectly veneered nails.' She rattled her own nails on the table. She had beautiful hands. 'Actually we got lost,' she admitted. 'I've been job-hunting. And I couldn't walk another step.'

'Didn't you get anything, then?' the vicar grinned encouragingly. He did everything encouragingly, thought Matty.

'I'm too fat to be a receptionist,' said Henry. 'And too useless to be anything else.'

He didn't contradict her. Instead he nodded and sighed. 'I know what you mean. I knocked about a bit before I joined the church, and it's amazing the things you need to know nowadays. You've got to be best friends with a computer before you can apply for the dole.'

'Did you go on the dole then?' Henrietta leaned forward, alight with interest.

He went a little pink. 'No actually, I didn't. I got work teaching little boys Latin. But I kept it quiet, it didn't do a thing for my street cred.'

Henrietta let out a gurgle of laughter. Matty, bored, gathered up the cups. 'Shall I wash these for you?' she asked.

The vicar leaped to his feet. 'No, no, washing up's all in the price.'

'You ought to have someone to help,' said Henrietta.

'What, to wash up two cups? No, the time I need help is midnight, when we do the soup run. And that's when nobody wants to come.'

Matty smiled politely and began to drift to the door. Henrietta hung back. 'I'd help,' she said. 'When shall I come? Tonight?'

The vicar said, 'Don't be daft! It's cold, dirty and a bit dangerous. And I can't pay.'

'I wouldn't mind that. Would it be all right if I turned up at half-past eleven?'

He hesitated. 'You might get mugged just getting here.'

'No I wouldn't. I've got − I can borrow my mother's car. I could try for one night and see if I minded, couldn't I?'

'Well − yes, I suppose you could. And I do need the help. All right then, half-past eleven it is. Wrap up, it can be freezing.'

Outside, on the pavement, Matty said, 'Henrietta, you have gone stark, raving mad! You can't possibly spend the night running about London chatting up tramps − your mother would have a fit. The ones in there were bad enough, and at night they'll all be drunk and filthy. You could be murdered.'

'What do you think his name is?' asked Henrietta dreamily.

'Who?'

'The vicar of course! Do you think he's married? I'll die if he is. Did you ever meet anyone so fantastically gorgeous in all your whole life?'

Matty choked on a giggle. The vicar was thin and

somewhat sparky, but by no stretch of the imagination could he be called gorgeous. What's more, he had the worn, over-darned appearance of the seriously poor.

'He's probably got fourteen children,' she said discouragingly.

'Oh no!' Henrietta looked stricken. 'He wasn't wearing a ring or anything? Did you see a rattle in his pocket?'

Matty relented. 'No, of course I didn't. He's young, he probably isn't married at all. But, Henry, you can't moon about after a vicar. Your mother won't like him one bit.'

'I don't care what she thinks. He's gorgeous. He's got the most lovely eyes of anyone I've ever seen. I wonder if I could take his photograph without him noticing?'

Losing her patience, Matty said, 'Do stop it, Henry! Come and have a Mars bar.'

'No!' Henrietta's soft face was set with determination. 'I shall never eat a Mars bar again. From now on it's watercress and nothing else. He thinks I'm a schoolgirl lump, and he's right. I'm going to get thin and I'm going to get clever. He's awfully clever. Do you think he reads the *Guardian*?'

'Sure to,' said Matty. She felt bewildered. 'Henry, I know he's nice, but couldn't you fall for someone more suitable? Someone you could see in daylight?'

'I go where my heart leads me,' said Henry theatrically, and ran along the pavement, her hands clasped to her breast.

'Oh, the wonders of love!' Matty ran after her, arms outstretched, and passers-by crossed the street, in case they were mad.

They parted at the underground. 'I'll come with you if you want,' said Henrietta, which was kind of her. She was anxious to get home and try on jumpers to look fetching for the soup run.

'I'd better go by myself,' said Matty, who would much prefer not to go at all. The thought of seeing Sammy had depressed her all day. She had to see him and get it over with.

As she neared the silver vaults she stopped and checked her appearance in a shop window. She seemed very pale, her skin almost as white as the new blouse. She was wearing flat shoes and looked like a shop girl, as unlike the dead daughter as it was possible to be. Patricia would never have looked anything other than stunning.

Emily gasped when Matty buzzed the door. 'Come up, dear,' she whispered noisily, and Matty heard her kick Sammy's door shut. Creeping up the stairs like a criminal, she wondered what she would do if he raged at her. Ought she to gather the rags of her dignity and withdraw? The familiar churning of her stomach became sharply painful, she wondered if she was going to be sick. If she was to grow out of anything she wished it could be that. She longed to be of an age when she could face things without keeping half her mind on the bathroom.

Emily was waiting wide-eyed. 'He's going to be furious,' she mouthed.

Matty hissed, 'What shall I do? Shall I just go in?'

'He's been hoping you'd write. Every day he goes through the post looking for a letter.'

'I didn't know what to say.'

'He wouldn't have minded. Anything would have done.'

Matty gathered her courage. She had made such a mess of this, had taken all Sammy's kindness and cast it in his face. All she could do was apologise. She reached out and knocked with intended firmness on Sammy's door. It came out as a feeble little knock, hardly audible, and she tried again, making no more sound.

'What are you doing, Emily?' called Sammy. 'Are you cleaning the door?'

Matty took hold of the door knob and went in.

Sammy was at his desk, a catalogue open in front of him, covered in his scrawled writing. He looked up at Matty for a long moment, then down at the catalogue. 'Have you seen this?' he demanded. 'The Dana collection's for sale. That man in Mexico can keep his stuff, this is marvellous.'

'There was the Sprimont bowl,' whispered Matty. 'I should at least have got that.'

'Well, we know where it is. We'll get it one day.'

Matty sank into the chair and burst into tears. 'Oh, Sammy,' she sobbed. 'I'm so sorry! I made such a terrible mess of everything. But he's an arms dealer and horrible, and Eleanor's a heroin addict, and the whole place was evil. I couldn't do business with them.'

'I could forgive you anything but tearing up the catalogue,' he said morosely.

'I didn't tear it up. I kept it. I made a copy. For you.' She put the list on the desk between them. Attached to it were photographs, including several of the Sprimont bowl.

Sammy spread his hands. 'I forgive you – everything. Blow your nose, you look like an orphan.'

'I am an orphan!'

'So you are. And so am I, it's only to be expected. We can face everything in life, provided it's expected. By the way, Delia's in therapy.'

Matty gulped. 'Oh, I'm – glad.'

He nodded. 'I wasted too much time. Far too much.'

Emily brought in a pot of tea, and they sat and gossiped about silver and the trade with rare warmth. Matty felt safe, back in the bosom of this, her surrogate family. She didn't have to worry about what was to happen, what she was going to do. She could come back to Sammy and be safe.

Then Sammy cracked his Rich Tea biscuit into fragments and said, 'And where are you going to work then, Matty?'

She felt as fractured as the biscuit. 'But – I thought – aren't I coming back here?'

Sammy sighed. 'I sacked you. I meant it.'

'I know you did, but that was then. You said you'd forgiven me.'

'Matty, Matty – it isn't a question of forgiveness. There are practicalities. With Delia as she is you couldn't come back to live at home, and on the money I pay, what else could you afford? If I paid you more I should need more from you. And who could tell when your principles would choke you once again? This is a naughty world, Matilda, full of naughty people. Silver isn't just art, it's money, and where there's money there has to be corruption. I cannot risk another débâcle.'

'I wouldn't do it again,' said Matty in a small voice. 'I'd do just what I ought.'

'And if next week there was another de Caruzon? His dirty money, his crazed wife, his wonderful silver?'

'I – I don't know.'

He said no more. There was no more to be said. Matty got up and Sammy fumbled with his cheque book. 'I owe you a bonus,' he said gruffly. 'You sold some good things while you were here, you did good work.'

'You don't owe me anything.' Matty was tearful. 'You taught me everything.'

'I don't know everything. No one does.' He put down his pen and looked sorrowfully into her face. 'Go to an auction house. It's the only place for knowledge without capital. I'll give you a good reference.'

'Would you?'

He nodded. 'You've got a good eye, my girl. You impressed me, and I'm not the impressionable sort.'

'Do you think I could deal, Sammy? Do you think I've got the knowledge?'

He looked surprised. 'Of course. What have I taught you otherwise? But the knowledge counts for nothing – what will you use for money? I've taken a lifetime to be able to go to a bank and demand money for big pieces, and I started with something. You have nothing. It would take you two lifetimes. What are you going to do, trade in teaspoons?'

She nodded. 'Yes. If I have to.'

'You could do it after the war, but not now. You'll never make a bean.'

When she went into the outer office, Emily was crying. 'You can always come and sleep on my floor,' she offered, bravely.

'It's all right, Em,' promised Matty. 'I'm not destitute. I'll manage.'

'We were all so happy here! It should have gone on. He's being a stubborn old fool.'

'He's being sensible. He's right.'

Out in the street, Matty took a deep breath, filling her lungs with the end of the day. A door had closed behind her in more ways than one, but she wasn't quite without hope. She had a place to stay, however briefly, she had a little cash, a very little, and there was Sholto. She wished suddenly that he was different, reliable, stable, rich. But he was as he was. It seemed there was only one course open to her. They had to start that business.

Henrietta was wearing jeans. They had fitted her last summer, when she wasn't so fat, but this year they were excruciating. She could only fasten them by lying on the floor and when she stood up rolls of flesh hung over the waistband. What's more they were painful, almost cutting her in two. She covered her unseemly waistline with a huge sweater in the inevitable royal blue. It was redeemed by a black V arrowing down from shoulders to waist, which detracted somewhat from her girth. She looked in the mirror and made a face. Sometimes she hated herself, hated the soft nose, soft pink cheeks, soft blue eyes, soft mouth, soft everything. But at least, she thought, sighing, she didn't look like Griselda.

There was no question of telling her mother where she was going. The thought never even entered her head. Instead she had agreed with Matty that they would go up to bed at eleven, or rather Matty would, while Henry sneaked out of the door. Matty would then carol 'Goodnight, Henrietta' several times, while running a bath, banging a door and drawing Henry's curtains. A bolster in the bed and all was done. Childsplay, after boarding school. But, of course, returning would be more of a problem. Matty would have to be awake.

The evening was tense. Matty alternated between solid gloom and wild optimism, causing Mrs Giles to ask her if perhaps she was running a temperature. Henry knew that on the following day her mother would question her closely about Matty's habits, in case she was on drugs. Mrs Giles had read all about the signs. She would have Matty undergoing rehabilitation ten seconds after discovering the first piece of tinfoil. Henry wished the house contained something stronger than aspirin. Valium, perhaps. But nerves apart, she wanted nothing to dull her perceptions of the night.

In the hall, preparing to go upstairs, Matty hissed, 'Just don't get knifed by a meths drinker. Your mother would hold me personally responsible.'

195

'The only thing you're responsible for is letting me back in,' whispered Henry. 'You've got to wake up.'

'I'll set the alarm under my pillow,' promised Matty.

'You don't know when for.'

'I'll set it every hour. How's that for devotion?'

Henry squeezed her hand. She crept out of the door under cover of Matty's loud, one-sided conversation. 'Actually, Henry, I thought dinner was delicious — very filling — you can't still be hungry — have a glass of water —'

She wished Matty wouldn't talk about food. She was so hungry she felt ill, and every now and then a great wave of dizziness came over her. But imagine, if the vicar ever extended his wiry hand towards her and encountered rolls of flab . . .? She would die. The shame would definitely be terminal. She probably weighed more than him, and he was at least six inches taller.

It was still quite early for London and the streets were far from deserted. She drove her little Mini along, wondering where all the tramps would be. Dossers. Down and outs. Perhaps she should copy the vicar and call them clients? As she left the main roads and began wending her way down side streets to the church, there ceased to be anyone much around. There was the odd prostitute, with high heels and white handbag, but no one else. Thankfully there was a light over the church door, illuminating the fateful sign: 'Tea, coffee, 20p'.

She parked the car next to a van, checked her face in the mirror, and got out. It was deathly quiet. Suppose he wasn't there, suppose it was just dossers, filthy and menacing? How good it would be to be at home now, in bed and safe. They'd had self-defence lessons at school but they had stopped at screaming and running. No one ever thought you'd be stupid enough to put yourself in a situation that needed more.

The door to the crypt wasn't locked. It opened to show the vicar, wearing jeans and sweatshirt, assembling boxes of bread and urns of soup. 'Hi,' he called. 'I didn't think you'd come. Glad you have though. Could you cut up those pies? They're from the supermarket, past the sell-by date. We don't often get as much as this.'

Delighted to be doing something, Henrietta chopped up

196

pie. The vicar was loading the van, piling it to the roof with food and blankets. Sharp on twelve, he started the engine. 'Can't be late,' he said. 'They're expecting us.' Henry got in.

'What's your name?' he asked as he drove. 'I'm Peter Venables.'

'Henrietta. Henrietta Giles. Henry.'

'You're much too feminine to be a Henry. Does your mother mind your coming out like this?'

'Oh no,' lied Henry, whose heart was singing. He thought her feminine! 'She does a lot of charity work. She likes me to get involved.'

'Good for her. You'd be surprised the number of people won't touch this sort of thing. Look, most of the blokes are fine, but one or two of the meths drinkers can be a bit difficult. Keep close to me.'

He stopped the van at the end of an alley. In the narrow beam of the headlights Henrietta saw a jumble of cardboard boxes along both sides, with men, young men, standing or sitting around. They were expecting the van and came sauntering forward to collect their food.

'Pie today,' said Peter, swinging open the back doors. 'Anyone need a blanket?'

Henrietta silently handed out pie and soup. Most of the men took bread as well, putting it in their pockets to eat later. They were young, she realised, some younger than she. On the whole they weren't badly dressed, though one or two smelled sour and dirty. They were people she might pass any day on the street and not notice.

One of the men had a form he wanted to show Peter. It was an application for a job. 'Put down my address,' said Peter. '5 Inkerman Terrace. If they write there, I can always find you.'

Henrietta memorised the blessed words. Inkerman Terrace – a name filled with romance.

As they got back in the van Peter said, 'If he gets a job he might be able to get a room.'

'I thought they'd be tramps. Not like that.'

'We've got tramps as well.'

They had everything. On a patch of wasteland near a power station there were ragged men clustered around a bonfire. 'Mostly patients from long stay mental hospitals,' said Peter. 'Stay close to me.' The flickering light created shadows and horrors. Peter knelt to a bundle of rags, within which huddled a man. 'You a nurse?' demanded one of the men of Henrietta. She shook her head. But he showed her his hand anyway. It was burned and suppurating, but he swore when she suggested he go to hospital. She looked in the van and found a first-aid kit and gently, doubtfully, applied a dressing.

'All right?' asked Peter, as they moved on.

'Sure. More all right than them, anyway.'

'Good girl.'

He was right about the meths drinkers. They surged about the van, aggressive and unpredictable. Peter was jostled and put up his hands to show he held no weapon. 'I'm only here to help,' he said gently. 'I've got no drink and no money.'

'You know what you can do with your fucking soup,' said one, and sank back beside his fire, in a welter of filthy rags.

Boldly, Henrietta took him a piece of pie. She held it out to him and he took it, mumbling it against rotted teeth. She felt inspired suddenly, and triumphant – and yet she wanted to cry.

They returned to the church at three. Utterly weary, she nonetheless thought she would never sleep; her mind was racing, full of new things. 'This city's a mess,' she said suddenly. 'I never realised.'

'I think all cities are the same.' He got down from the van. 'Thanks. You were a great help. Make sure you have a bath – some of those blokes are the last refuge of the human flea.'

She shuddered. 'Same time tomorrow, then? Today?'

He stopped and looked at her. 'Are you sure? I thought you wanted a proper job?'

'I do. But in the meantime I can help here. It is all right, isn't it?'

'More than all right. You're a blessing. Look, could you bring a few things? Bottles of water, cotton wool, that sort of thing. Antiseptic. We often have to dress wounds. Whatever you can.'

'I'll bring all that. I think I'd better mug up on first aid, hadn't I?'

'Good idea. Thanks, Henry. Thanks.'

It was half-past three when she got back and Matty was fast asleep. Presumably she had set her alarm for three and then four, and Henry had arrived back in the doldrums. Ten minutes of stone rattling at last roused her, and she came down to open the front door.

'How was it?' she asked blearily.

'Great. But I'll have to get a key to the back door and come and go through that.'

'You're not going again, are you?'

Henry nodded. 'Every night. I think Peter's been doing too much. I'm going to suggest he lets me drive the van.'

'Bully for you.' Matty smothered a yawn.

'I'm starving,' said Henrietta, making her way upstairs.

'I bet you've got a Mars bar,' grumbled Matty.

'I haven't anything of the sort! Look, I've got to have a bath, I've probably got fleas.'

'Then keep away from me! Honestly, Henry, I think you've gone batty.'

'It could be you in a cardboard box one day,' said Henrietta sagely. 'It could be any of us.'

Matty crawled back to bed, wondering what Henry would say if her mother woke up and found her taking a bath in the middle of the night. This could never last more than a week, whatever the charms of the vicar. She sank back into slumber, only to be roused seconds later by the alarm going off under her ear. It was four o'clock and she had forgotten to turn it off. The morning threatened, and she would be leaden with weariness, on a day when she would need all her wits. She was going to see Sholto.

Chapter Twelve

Sholto had scribbled his aunt's address on the back of a Hershey bar wrapper. Matty stood on the seafront, wrapper in hand, buffeted by wind and gusting rain. A few hardy souls were marching along the beach, their mackintoshes swirling about them and their dogs racing madly, ears pinned flat to their heads by the gale. England, at the end of summer, was no place for the faint-hearted.

Matty turned her back on the beach and studied the tall houses. They retained a certain elegance, despite, or perhaps because of, the decampment of the British holidaymaker to warmer climes. Bournemouth was still clement enough on average to sport cacti in the hotel gardens, and the well-heeled elderly had been making their homes here for generations. On a day like this, though, they shut their Regency front doors and hid.

The wind tugged at her as she began to walk, counting off the numbers of the houses. She had no winter coat, and she had given up her umbrella when it blew inside out twice in ten minutes. She was wet through and freezing cold, and quite suddenly her spirits plummeted to the depths. She stopped and leaned against a railing. Where was the point of it all? Why was she bothering? Wouldn't it be easier to put Simon in care and throw herself in the sea and be done with it?

A voice behind her said, 'Are you trying to freeze to death, Matty? I take it I'm supposed to discover your corpse clinging to the doorknob, expiring in the storm.'

She looked up. Sholto was standing at a front door, wearing gold slippers, a gold silk smoking jacket and trousers in plum-coloured wool. 'I take it you are auditioning to be the genie of the lamp,' she said meanly. 'Where do you find your clothes?'

'Come in, Matty. You're making me feel sorry for you.'

'God forbid.'

She trudged soggily up the steps and into the blessed shelter of the house. It smelled of polish and still, warm air. It was very dark, with heavy green wallpaper in the hall, and a dark brown ceiling.

'My aunt takes Victoriana very seriously,' said Sholto. 'It's all rather tiring.'

But it was warm. Matty allowed herself to be led into the parlour, where a fire was raging in the grate. She thawed before it, and steam rose from her shoes. Sholto took her jacket and hung it on a chair.

'Do cheer up, Matty,' he said. 'I keep feeling this manly urge to take you in my arms and protect you from bandits. And there aren't too many bandits in Bournemouth.'

'Oh, Sholto!' She looked at him mournfully. 'I don't think we should start this business. We're bound to fail.'

He poured her a whisky. 'So why begin? I see your point. Why go through all the anguish when we could nip round to the bankruptcy court right now and save all the hassle in between? It's a good policy. Let's get dying over with, that's what I say!'

Matty laughed. She remembered how much she liked the way he could always make her laugh. 'I suppose we might make our fortune,' she conceded.

'No might about it. Now, my aunt's promised to put up the money for premises. We have to pay interest and so on, but we can handle that. I thought somewhere near London. OK by you?'

She wrinkled her nose. 'Not really. Everything's so expensive. I thought we might go north. I know the scene a bit better there, and it's nearer Simon.'

'It doesn't matter to me. It's just a base. With any luck I'll be travelling a lot of the time.'

'Oh God, I knew it!' Matty ran her hands through her wet hair. 'We haven't moved in and already I'm sick of doing the housework. You're never going to lift a finger, are you?'

'Don't be trivial. We'll get someone in. And I'll cook.'

'I refuse to iron your shirts!' declared Matty.

'All right, all right! Don't you have any domestic urges? Even I can pass the odd five minutes polishing bathroom taps.'

'Good. I have no domestic talents whatsoever.' She put out her feet and toasted them deliciously. Her spirits always rose when she was with Sholto. He had the ability to make her see life as an elaborate and ridiculous joke.

'She's lending us two hundred thousand pounds capital,' said Sholto.

Matty's jaw dropped. 'She can't be! She must be mad!'

'It's not a gift. Bank rates of interest, and repayment in five years. We have to make it work, Matty.'

'Oh, no! Please, no! Repay that and a house as well? You didn't tell her we could?'

He shrugged. The sardonic smile played fleetingly around his mouth. 'What else was there to say? You never know.'

She held out her glass for more whisky. He joined her and they sat either side of the fire, saying nothing. It was madness to accept such a deal; they would have to make thousands of pounds a year just to pay the interest, and then they had to live and trade and build up a business.

'Does she know the risks?' asked Matty feebly.

'Oh yes. I told her it's my only chance. I said she owed it to me. She's giving the minimum I consider necessary to start a quality concern.'

'Sammy can spend that in one day.'

'Sammy's not going to be spending it. We're going to cut our cloth, Matty my sweet. And we'll have fun. If nothing else, I can wake up in the mornings and adore you. I do so like your erratic spirits.'

He came and loomed over her chair and she laughed up at him. His face came down to hers. She wondered if he knew how much she needed him, and hoped he did not. He didn't want someone to cling. But when he kissed her, when he held her like this, she wanted to cling as tight as she could hold.

Sholto's aunt appeared at dinner. He cooked, resolving to

prove to Matty his promised competence, and the meal was rich and extravagant. He threw in wine and cream as a matter of course, and crushed handfuls of fresh herbs which he tossed into sauces quite at random. The result was magnificent.

'Very good, Sholto,' said his Aunt Enid. 'Say what you like, Italy did you a great service.'

'As the actress said to the bishop,' said Sholto. His aunt looked nonplussed and he gave her an innocent grin.

She was a woman who had once been tall. Age was steadily shrinking her, and she constantly told Sholto she couldn't remember him being so enormous. She walked with a cane, and wore a shawl draped across her shoulders. Clearly she had no time for sentiment. 'It's about time you had something done about that scar,' she remarked. 'It quite ruins your looks.'

Sholto laughed. 'I think I can live with it now, Aunt. I found it most trying when it was almost as red as my spots. People kept trying to take me to hospital — they thought I'd just been run over.'

'How did it happen?' asked Matty, knowing Sholto wouldn't tell her.

He said, 'Don't be curious,' and poured her more wine.

'It was an accident,' said Aunt Enid.

'Oh, don't disillusion her!' said Sholto. 'Matty would much rather imagine me fighting a maniac knife killer. Wouldn't you, Matilda?'

'Was it your fault?' she asked.

He leaned back and put his feet on the table. 'Of course. When is anything not?'

'There's a certain amount of truth in that,' said his aunt. She eyed him with cold judgment. 'Sholto fell through a glass roof at my sister's house in Venice. Some prank or other. My sister, in her wisdom, had him stitched up by the local quack — as a punishment no doubt. The man was an alcoholic, failed to administer a proper anaesthetic, and in fact made a botch of the whole thing.'

'She certainly did believe in object lessons,' said Sholto, and laughed.

Matty felt slightly stunned. How could anyone do such

a thing? Her brave attempts at sophistication seemed to crumble in the face of such a horrible crime. To invoke a lifetime's retribution for a moment's silliness seemed the height of cruelty. And every day, when he looked in the mirror, he would remember. After a moment, Matty said, 'Did you say she was still alive?'

'Who, Aunt Theresa? I should say so. At the last count. There must be someone who counts the devil's slaves.'

'Don't be bitter, Sholto,' said Enid.

Matty said 'I think you ought to shoot the old cow. Or, better still, drop her through the roof and not stitch her up at all! She could do it herself, with paperclips.'

Aunt Enid said, 'Good heavens!' and seemed to notice Matty for the first time. Anger made her worth noticing. In the light of the table candles her eyes seemed to flash clear fire, and her hair was like flame itself.

'Don't be angry over me,' said Sholto. 'I'm not worth it.'

'You are! Don't say things like that! I hate the woman!'

Enid sighed. 'She acted according to her lights. I shouldn't have left him there. I know that now.' Her hands closed on her napkin in one small, tense gesture. She turned to Matty. 'I hope your partnership goes well. Do ensure that Sholto keeps me informed.' She got up, slowly, and left the room.

'And I hate her too!' said Matty, fiercely. 'Why can't she just give you the money?'

Sholto said, 'She thinks prosperity would be bad for me. She might be right.'

'Don't be so reasonable! Don't accept that people don't have to love you, it isn't right.'

He was eyeing her with hard concentration. 'Matty, stop it.'

'Stop what?'

'Fighting my battles. Taking my side. I don't need it and I don't want it.'

Her breath left her. She groped for words. 'But I want it. For me.'

'One of life's nasty little lessons is that other people aren't just like us. I'm grown up, Matty, all the way through. All right, I had a miserable childhood, but it's gone, it's done.

The old bat might have achieved her end, you never know.
I'm tough as old boots. And a hell of a lot tougher than
you.'

'You're telling me not to get attached, aren't you?' said
Matty.

He lifted the wine bottle and refilled both their glasses.
'Oh, I want you attached — to an extent. There's business
and there's bed, and a fair amount of attachment is
inevitable there, it seems to me. But don't accept party
invitations on my behalf.'

'You don't want to be a couple, you mean.'

He looked at her over his glass. His eyes were so blue and
his hair so black. 'Right.'

She took the train back to Henrietta's. It was still raining,
and Sholto came to the station and held his umbrella over
her head. If he had asked, if he had hinted, she would have
stayed with him. The journey back was cold and lonely, with
too much time to think about the future. Perhaps he was
going to insist on separate bedrooms. The thought made her
fold her lips on a groan. She didn't want to be the one
wanting most, needing most.

It was just after midnight when she arrived back. She
knocked, suddenly realising that Henry would be out. Mrs
Giles answered the door. 'Matilda! I assumed you were
staying overnight.'

'Er — I thought I'd better not. I hope you hadn't gone
to bed.'

'We were just going up. Henrietta went very early, she
was exhausted, poor girl. But I'm surprised the knocker
didn't wake her. I'll go in and see if she's all right. Her cold
pulled her down, you know.'

'She's probably taken a sleeping pill,' said Matty
urgently.

'I should think she has not, Matilda! Where would
Henrietta get such a thing?'

'Well — she probably hasn't.' Matty looked wide-eyed
at her hostess.

As Mrs Giles moved again towards the stairs, Matty said,
'Mrs Giles — I wonder — if you could — I wonder if you

wouldn't mind taking my temperature? I feel dreadfully under the weather.'

'Have you been taking sleeping pills? What have you been taking?'

'Paracetamol. For a headache.'

Mrs Giles sighed enthusiastically. Sickness was meat and drink to her; she revelled in aspirins, lemon drinks and crisp pillowcases. Nothing gave her greater satisfaction than to instal a thermometer in a glass of antiseptic at a bedside. 'Go straight up, Matilda,' she instructed, heading briskly for the kitchen, 'I'll bring you a drink. Borrow one of Henrietta's winceyette nightdresses — I do not want to see you in that ridiculous nylon. You may well be coming down with flu.'

Matty nipped into Henry's room and found the nightdress. Then she gulped a glassful of hot water, straight from the bathroom tap. When Mrs Giles came up, armed with her medicinal supplies, she said innocently, 'Henrietta's fine, Mrs Giles. She said I interrupted her dream and I was to turn off the light.'

'Did she? Then I won't disturb her. Open your mouth, dear.'

Matty sat in the bed, willing the thermometer to show something credible, reflecting that Henry would never know what sacrifices were being made on her behalf. Not only was Mrs Giles about to rub her back with Friar's Balsam, she was also armed with syrup of figs. But there was something reassuring about the fuss. Matty leaned back in the bed, feeling a child again, knowing that for once someone else was in charge. Being a competent adult was so very tiring. Perhaps she was ill after all. She looked up at her firm, confident mentor. Mrs Giles had never had a moment's doubt or indecision in her life, and at that moment Matty worshipped her. 'Thank you, Mrs Giles,' she mumbled.

The brochure said 'Interesting Tudor farmhouse with outbuildings. Suitable for a variety of uses'. The garden was a jungle of wild roses and thorns, and the outbuildings consisted of two long, almost windowless barns. An old tree house was leaning crazily in an apple tree, and the windfalls were feeding a goat. It watched them with yellow eyes, crunching apples efficiently.

'What do you think?' Sholto climbed over the gate and wandered down the path, hands in pockets.

'Simon would love it.'

Sholto grinned. 'Yes. So he would.' He struggled with the rusting front door key, and finally forced an entrance. 'The place smells disgustingly damp,' he shouted.

'It's been empty for years.'

Matty followed him, wrestling with herself. She loved the house. More than that, she adored it. The moment they turned down the lane she had known she wanted it, that this was the ideal house, the only house. There were trees and birds and bushy, unkempt hedges, and as far as the business was concerned it was only five minutes from an enormous main road, and – she wanted it.

She followed Sholto into the kitchen. 'Oh God, what a mess,' he said, turning the tap and sending a shower of rust into the cracked old sink. 'Why do they send us to these places? They know we don't want to spend half a lifetime turning the place into a dream home. We've got a business to run.'

'The barns look ideal,' said Matty. 'Wonderfully secure.'

'You realise it's got four acres? We'd have to run cows.'

'Hens,' said Matty. 'In the country you've got to keep hens.'

Sholto snorted. 'If there's one thing I'm not wasting my time with, it's bloody farming.'

They went upstairs. The roof was low and the windows in the bedrooms were within a foot of the floors. You could only stand upright under the central truss, from which ancient bunches of herbs still hung, long since dried to disintegration. There was one big room and two smaller.

'One of these could be the bathroom,' said Matty. 'That leaves one room for Simon and one for us.' Was she assuming too much? She glanced at him.

He said, 'We'd need a four-poster bed. Couldn't live in a place like this without one. That's the trouble with good houses – you have to worry about suiting them and it costs a fortune. An arm and a leg. Now, a ghastly modern box would be much better. Functional.'

Matty decided to put her cards on the table. 'I don't want to be functional.'

'Don't you? Then what do you want?'

She took a deep breath. 'This.'

He said nothing for a long moment. Then he chuckled. 'Your face! Ever since we turned into the lane. A little girl wanting a dolly.'

'But it is gorgeous! You know it is. It's convenient, and beautiful, and it's got these lovely low windows, and look, there's a view right across the fields, and a stream, and who do you suppose owns the goat? You wouldn't mind having a goat, would you? If it came with the house?'

'I'll hit my head every time I get out of bed.'

'Then you'll just have to stay in bed. I'll make it worth your while. Promise.'

He came and stood in front of her. She put her arms around his neck. 'Oh, Matty, Matty,' he murmured. 'When you look at me like that I can't think straight. We don't need a house like this.'

She nuzzled his neck. 'Yes we do. We'll enjoy it. We'll do it up just perfectly, and I'll make curtains and cushions and things. I know all the auctions around here — we won't have to pay much for furniture. And if we make a hash of things and Aunt Enid throws us out, then we'll have had fun! Wouldn't you rather fail here than in your functional modern box? Anyway, a box won't have barns. We've got to have barns.'

He held her buttocks and moved her against him. 'The only thing I've got to have right now is you.'

They made love in the dust of the bedroom floor. He was very aroused, but then they made love only rarely. He restricted himself, she thought, giving in to her attraction only when he could no longer resist. He reared up on her, his face convulsing in a rictus of pleasure. Emptying into her, he sank down. A moment later he said, 'Good?'

'Quite good. Too short. We should do it more often.'

'Do you mean that? Or is it unsubtle persuasion?'

'I mean it.'

She had a vision of nights in the four-poster bed, closer than this, learning about closeness. She closed her eyes to hide her thoughts from him. He didn't want the things she needed, he had told her so. But they might be things he could learn to want. If she gave them to him, then in time they might even be things he would need. The urge to say 'I love you' was almost overpowering. She didn't say it, because for one thing it might not even be true. Moments like this seemed unfinished without it, that was all. It ought to be said. She rested her face against him, and the words seemed so loud in her head that she might have whispered them. Had she? 'You're lovely,' said Sholto. 'Lovelier than you know.' And it had to do.

The year was turning colder. They moved in on a day of hard frost, with the house full of damp new plaster that wouldn't dry. Matty walked from room to room, her footsteps echoing and her breath forming clouds. When they lit fires the windows ran with condensation, like thick curtains hiding them from their surroundings. They might have been anywhere.

Sholto was busy in the barns. Matty had been surprised to learn that he had pictures all over the place, stored in attics and furniture warehouses, waiting for him to find time for them. He was gathering them together, putting up battens from which they could hang, installing spotlights and alarm systems. He had collected them over years.

For her part, her only quality piece was her silver spoon. She took it out of her suitcase and laid it on the beam that served as a mantel in the sitting room, but looking at it upset her. She didn't want to sit there in the evenings and think about her father. She thought about him too much, and never reached any conclusions. So the spoon became the first piece in her own barn, the silver barn. She put it in the drawer of an old stained table Sholto had found.

The first evening was strange. They had almost no furniture and sat on upturned tea chests before the fire. Logs crackled energetically, sending shadows leaping over the walls. Night lurked at the uncurtained windows, tapping with twiggy fingers. Sholto said, 'You won't like it here alone.'

'I don't mind it. I'm not going to be alone.'

'But I'm not going to be here much, Matty! I shall be travelling. I'm going to Italy on Friday.'

She was silent. She hadn't understood. Then she said bravely, 'I shall travel too. Auctions, people to see, that sort of thing. But I won't start yet. I'll see to the house first.'

'I thought you weren't domesticated?'

She opened her eyes wide. 'I'm not. But I can't live in a mess. Besides, it's nice to have a home. It's been ages. I want to wake up in the mornings and see things that I want to see, not somebody else's idea of good taste. And when Simon comes at Christmas I want him to step through the door and — and know that he's at home.'

Sholto said, 'Toughen up, Matty. You'll never make it as anything if you cling to all these teddybears.'

'I suppose if it was up to you the place would stay as it is,' she flashed. 'You're frightened of making a home. You think you might get to like it.'

His smile mocked her. Then he got up and fetched a bottle from a packing case in the corner. She watched him as he poured, dressed in drainpipe jeans that made him seem taller and thinner than he was. He hated encumbrances of any sort, she realised. Like a soldier in a war zone, he remained at all times free and aware. But he understood her and her needs, although he would not join her in them. He seemed to assume that she would grow out of them, as he had, or be forced to give them up.

The wine was thick and cold. It made Matty dizzy. 'Henry will be out with her vicar now,' she said sleepily.

'I like your friend Henry,' said Sholto.

'You don't know her.'

'I like the sound of her. Tremendous guts, risking her mother's wrath. What's more, she sounds cuddly. Warm.'

'You're going to love it if I get fat.'

'Will I?' His face twisted a little. She never quite knew what he was thinking. He put out his hand to her. 'You'll do as you are. Since we haven't got our four-poster bed, let's go and lie down on our humble mattress and think about being rich enough to get fat.'

*　　*　　*

The van was running very badly tonight. Peter kept cursing under his breath, which showed that he was relaxed with her. He never used to swear in front of people; he thought it unbecoming in a vicar.

Henry wriggled her toes in her fleecy lined boots. Her mother had been reluctant to let her buy them, because they weren't much use normally, but for nights like this they were invaluable. The heater had broken again, although Peter said he'd fixed it. He was quite good at things mechanical, provided they had a little more life left in them than this van. At that moment it wheezed to a standstill.

'Shit!' Peter banged a gloved hang on the steering wheel.

'Perhaps it's the plugs,' said Henrietta helpfully.

'I think it's the petrol feed. There's a blockage. We'll never get it fixed tonight.'

'What can we do?'

His face was a white blur, with only a flash from his eyes. 'We'll get you a taxi and send you back. I'll try and do some of the round on foot.'

'I can do that too. We'll carry twice as much.'

He argued with her, but to no avail. Besides, he wasn't arguing with conviction, she thought gleefully. He needed her to help him. He was relying on it. She loaded up bags with rolls and some almost-off cream cakes. They'd have to do without soup tonight. It wouldn't matter, even though it was cold. Sometimes she thought the main purpose of the run was to show people that the world hadn't forgotten them, that someone cared.

'I don't know what I'd do without you,' said Peter, and she looked up and beamed.

'I like helping.'

'I know. It's a rare quality. Most people want at least thanks, and the dossers don't even give you that. Sometimes I feel myself getting angry, but you never do. I so admire that.'

Henrietta wanted the ground to open up and swallow her. How could he think she got no reward? Only to sit next to him in the van was enough. She watched his hands as he drove, wiry hands, with a seg on his third finger where he held his pen to write his sermons. She had never heard one

212

of his sermons, although she longed to. Apparently there were only half a dozen old ladies who came regularly to his services, and if she was one seventh of the entire congregation she could hardly go unnoticed. And there would be time enough for him to notice her when she was thin.

The bags were heavier than she realised. Peter strode on and she struggled in his wake, having to rest every few yards. They were heading towards the fire in the centre of the waste ground, and on this cold night the meths drinkers were crouched at its foot, silhouetted against the blaze. They probably wouldn't want the food at all, she thought dismally. But the food was the necessary introduction.

The absence of the van made her feel quite vulnerable, trotting in Peter's wake. From the very first night, all those weeks ago, there had always been the option of staying in the van, retreating to the van, getting in the van and driving quickly away. Now she was on their level. She had nothing to distinguish her from the people on the ground. Wishing that Peter wouldn't go so fast, she hurried on.

As they approached, unfamiliar without their transport, a couple of men got up and came aggressively forward.

'It's only us,' called Peter. 'The van's conked out. We've brought what we can.'

The men began to gather round. Henry could sense their lack of trust; they disliked even the most minor deviations from routine. Perhaps in their fuddled brains only the simplest, most repeated events had meaning.

She saw a man with a cut eye. She had treated him last week. She went across and looked at it, delighted to see that the patch she had washed still remained perceptibly cleaner than the surrounding skin, and what's more, the cut was healing. 'What you bloody doing?' the man growled, and she stepped away. No use looking for thanks, as Peter said.

A police car went past a block away, its siren wailing. The men became unsettled, and the big, young one Henry had never liked grabbed Peter's arm and yelled, 'You setting them on us? You bloody setting us up?'

'Don't be daft,' said Peter, tapping the man's tense hand.

'They're going across the river, most like. Have some grub. On a night like this you could do with it.'

It seemed to Henrietta that the man was about to let go. But then, unexpectedly, they saw an approaching blue light. The car was driving across the waste ground towards them, bouncing and plunging across the uneven surface. The dossers began to shout, and one of them picked up something from the floor and ran with it to the far side of the fire, into the shadows. The man who held Peter yelled thickly, 'You bastard!' He swung his fist into Peter's gut. Henrietta screamed.

'No, no, no,' wailed one of the dossers, but the young one came at Henry, put his face within an inch of hers, and spat.

The police found her in tears, feebly wiping spit from her face, and Peter doubled up in agony. 'Good thing we came,' said one. 'Saw your van and thought we'd give you a hand.'

'It was all your fault,' sobbed Henrietta.

'It might have happened – anyway,' gasped Peter. 'Don't like – changes in routine.'

'Best get you to hospital, mate,' said one of the policemen. 'You could have a ruptured spleen.'

He sounded hopeful, thought Henry. He was delighted at having something to enliven a dull night. She looked around at the bags, spilling their contents on to the ground, and at the little crowd of dossers cowering away on the far side of the fire. She picked up some of the cakes and took them across. 'Here,' she said. 'You might as well have them. No point in having everything go wrong tonight.'

The police left them both at the hospital. Henry went into the lavatory and washed her face four times. She couldn't rid herself of the thought that the man might have been carrying some horrible disease. When she came back, Peter said, 'He spat at you, didn't he? You'd better get some vaccinations, to be on the safe side.' He was feeling better. When the doctor examined him he found only an enormous spreading bruise, and he ended up waiting for Henry to have her injections. On the way out they passed a dosser, bleeding heavily from a headwound, but they didn't recognise him. By mutual consent they continued on their way.

214

They got back to the church as it was getting light. Henrietta had her Mini to collect, and she offered to give Peter a lift home, since the van had packed up. 'I'm sorry it's been such a terrible night,' he said ruefully, locking the door of the crypt. 'I bet you won't come again.'

'Would you mind?' She looked up at him wearily. Tiredness was making things very easy between them.

'You know I would.'

His hand met hers, somehow. Henrietta smiled shyly and he said, 'I didn't know my luck the day you walked in here. Incredible.'

'Was it?'

'Yes. Dear, dear Henry.'

They stood quietly holding hands. Henrietta found herself thinking that she was probably in heaven, except that she was too tired to realise. A great yawn threatened to engulf her and she took her hand away to smother it.

'You're exhausted,' said Peter.

'So are you.'

'Yes. And I've got to go hospital visiting at eleven.'

'You'll be OK once you've had some sleep. It isn't six yet.'

They went out to the car together. She wondered if he would kiss her and hoped not. She wasn't thin enough yet. She started the car and drove out of the road. No sooner had she turned left down the High Street than a police car leaped forward and crowded them into the kerb.

Peter said, 'They've got it in for us. Twice in one night!'

Henry wound down the window, and gazed up fearfully at the police officer. It was the same one as before. 'What have we done?'

'I don't know.' He looked puzzled. 'Is this your car?'

'Yes. It's — my mother bought it.'

'Henrietta Giles, are you? Your mother's reported you missing. Dragged from your bedroom by a masked intruder. There's a countrywide search on for you.'

Slow colour surged up into Henrietta's face. 'What on earth's going on?' said Peter.

'I think you'd better both accompany me to Miss Giles's home,' said the policeman. 'Come along now. Follow me.'

Mrs Giles was in her sitting room. She was fully dressed,

although her make-up was somewhat faded. Henry's father was also there, but dishevelled, as if he had endured a terrible night. As indeed he had. When he saw Henrietta he let out a strangled sob and embraced her. 'We found a balaclava on the floor. We thought you'd been abducted.'

'That was silly, Daddy. The balaclava's mine, I'm quite all right.'

'I think we shall be the judge of that! Henrietta, where have you been?'

At the sound of her mother's voice all Henry's resolution turned tail and fled. She desperately wanted to go to the lavatory. Peter said, 'I'm sorry. We should of course have telephoned.'

Focusing on his dog collar, Mrs Giles flinched. 'Something terrible has happened. Henrietta, tell me at once.'

Looking up into her mother's face, Henrietta took the coward's way out. 'We've been to hospital,' she whispered.

'Not much of an incident,' said Peter. 'Just the usual sort of thing. A run-in with some of the dossers. It wasn't serious.'

'Dossers?' Mrs Giles looked angrily from one to the other. 'What do you mean?'

Peter rubbed wearily at the stubble on his chin. 'I don't know. Whatever you people call them. Tramps. Homeless men. This lot were meths drinkers — they're not all as bad. I'm sure Henry's told you.'

Mrs Giles took a shuddering breath. 'Henrietta has told us nothing,' she said softly.

'But I'm sure — Henry said — normally of course — it was unforeseen —' Even Peter's usual ebullience was suffering steady extinguishment under the considerable force of Mrs Giles's personality. He looked worriedly at Henrietta. She didn't meet his eye.

'Just as long as you're all right,' said Mr Giles, embracing his daughter again.

His wife snapped, 'Shut up, Geoffrey. I want to hear what Henrietta has to say.'

Henry could say nothing. She opened and closed her mouth in feeble panic.

216

'It's only the soup run,' said Peter with an attempt at bracing cheer. 'She comes every night. I'm sorry. I thought you were aware.'

'Every night?' said Mrs Giles, with gathering menace. 'Do you mean to say, Henrietta, that you have been deceiving us for some time?'

Henrietta whispered, 'Yes.'

'What on earth for?' interposed her father. 'Henry darling, you could have been hurt.'

'It isn't a very great risk,' said Peter. 'You see, in London today –'

'Be quiet, sir!' snapped Mrs Giles, as if he were a dog. Peter subsided.

Henrietta started to cry. 'If you found the resolve to undertake this task then I think you can find enough not to snivel about it,' said her mother. 'We have wasted a great deal of police time. What's more, we are lunching today in Cavendish Street. I expect you to be sensibly rested. As for you, sir –' she cast Peter a look of loathing ' – kindly take yourself off. You can find someone else's daughter to fumble under the protection of your calling.'

Henry's face flamed. Peter stammered, 'I can assure you – I would never – Henrietta has never –'

'Then I suggest you go away,' said Mrs Giles in withering tones.

When he had gone Henry ran upstairs and fell sobbing on her bed. Her mother came in after her. 'Take your clothes off, Henrietta. They smell disgusting.'

'It's only antiseptic. We had to go to hospital.'

'I don't wish my house to smell of antiseptic. I shall talk to you later about this. Be assured that in future I shall be locking your bedroom door. Contact me on the extension 'phone if you need something.'

As she left the key turned in the lock. Henrietta's mouth dropped open, in impotent astonishment. She had really done it. Her mother had really locked her in.

Chapter Thirteen

Matty moved the cupboard a little more tidily into the corner and stood back to admire it. She was pleased with herself. It had cost thirty pounds at auction, which was a snip whichever way you looked at it. The beading had been detached at some time and people had been put off, but years of helping her father had given her skills enough to tackle that. She had glued the pieces back into place, eradicated some marks with a little judicious rubbing with spirits of wine and glasspaper, and the piece was almost as good as new — except that antiques should never look new, she reflected. Good restoration meant knowing when to stop.

The house was coming together nicely. She had painted most of the rooms white, enlivening them with stencils. The bedroom had pink roses marching around the window and along the edges of the beams and skirtings. She had bought heavy white fabric for the curtains, because it was dirt cheap, and tied it back with huge tarnished gold bullion cord she had discovered in a tea chest at a sale.

The telephone rang, and Matty ran downstairs to pick it up. 'Hello?'

'Matty! It's me.'

'Henry! What's the matter? You sound upset.'

'I am. It's terrible. I've escaped.'

'From where? Have you been kidnapped?'

Henrietta sobbed. 'No. Imprisoned. By my mother.'

Matty heard herself let out a long, low groan. She could have foreseen this. She dropped her voice. 'Can she hear you?'

'I hope not. I'm in Littlebury.'

'You mean – Littlebury village? That's two miles from here!'

'Yes. I've escaped and I'm coming to stay.'

Climbing into the aged estate car they had bought for the business, Matty felt a growing sense of doom. Sooner or later Mrs Giles would follow hot on Henrietta's trail. And it would probably be sooner. Like a hound of hell, Mrs Giles would descend on the wrongdoers, ready to drag them down. No one she had ever met was a match for Mrs Giles when she had her mind set.

Henrietta was standing outside the station. She was wearing an old red anorak and she was snivelling into a handkerchief.

'Do stop it, Henry,' said Matty, embracing her. 'Your mother can't actually kill us.'

'It's not that. It's Peter. I miss him so.'

'Oh. Peter.' Matty fully understood. Last night she had found one of Sholto's more extreme waistcoats stuffed in a box. It had smelled of him. He had been gone weeks now, and had sent one scrawled postcard, giving nothing away. She was beginning to think he was never coming back.

Henry told the story as Matty drove. 'It was torture. She kept bringing me huge meals, like roast beef and Yorkshire pudding. And chocolate cake. And then she'd come and lecture me, and Daddy wasn't allowed in because she said he was gullible and wouldn't make me see the error of my ways. She said I wasn't to come out until I promised never to see Peter again as long as I lived.'

'So you climbed out of the window,' said Matty.

'No! I promised, of course. Then I ran away.'

Matty laughed. Henrietta was ever the pragmatist. 'I definitely don't think you should marry Peter,' she remarked. 'I mean, he must be full of Christian principles. And you're a heathen.'

'You don't understand. You don't know what he's like. I haven't even kissed him yet!' She burst into tears.

Henrietta drooped dismally into the cottage, quite ignoring the beauty of the place. Matty felt aggrieved. 'Don't you like it?' she said finally.

Henry gave it a cursory glance. 'Yes. Very pretty. You

always did know how to decorate and things, Matty. How's the business?'

Matty said nothing. Instead she went rather pink and began fiddling with the tassel on one of the comfortably shabby chairs. Henry said, 'You haven't done anything, have you? You've been painting walls and putting up curtains. Oh, Matty.'

'I will do something,' said Matty desperately. 'Soon. It's just — I don't know where to start. Sholto dashed off straight away, he knows everyone. I don't know anyone. I don't know what to do.'

'Aren't you supposed to go to auctions? Special ones for silver?'

'Yes. But I went to one and I didn't like a thing. Sammy's given me too high standards. He taught me about the best, when the world's full of tarted up teapots and fakes.'

She sank her chin into her hands, allowing her spirits to plunge. It was a wonderful relief. She had crammed her days full of activity, refusing to let herself think, because thought brought panic hard on its heels. It had seemed so easy before, when the idea first began. The world had seemed full of opportunities. But somehow she hadn't imagined being here alone, she hadn't expected Sholto to go away and leave her to begin.

'You do get all the sale catalogues?' asked Henrietta. 'Surely that's the start.'

'But I need contacts! I need people to know about me. I want to be offered silver from people's own houses. I don't want to fight at auction for every teaspoon.'

'Then you should advertise.'

Matty blinked at her friend. Not for nothing was Henrietta her mother's daughter. She was essentially practical. 'What a good idea. I could start with the local paper.'

'And a few others. Newspapers are all syndicated these days, with a good advert you could cover half the country. If you combine visits with going to sales it should be worthwhile.'

'Would you like to write the advert?' asked Matty meekly. 'Sure.'

221

Henrietta got up and took off her jacket. Matty's mouth dropped open. Where once there had been folds of plump flesh, now there were simply folds of baggy jeans. Even with her jumper tucked in there was still plenty of room. She was holding her trousers up with a belt.

'Henry! You've shrunk.'

'Yes, I know. But I'm still awfully fat.'

'I don't think you're fat at all.' Matty got up and went to prod and poke. Henrietta was still rounded, certainly, but much of that was her natural shape. The mountains had become hillocks, but they would not and should not disappear. Within her dreadful clothes resided a very creditable figure.

'You are still eating, aren't you?' enquired Matty. 'You're not going to die of anorexia?'

'My mother thinks I'm in the throes,' said Henry gloomily. 'She's been trying to make me diet for years and when I do she hates it. On Tuesday she made me go to this lunch. I ate the salmon, and she boomed at me down the table, "Henrietta, I've had enough of this faddiness. Unless you can eat properly I shall be forced to send you to a clinic." And the man next to me looked appalled and offered me his bread roll. I had to eat it with everyone looking.'

'It wasn't quite solitary confinement then,' said Matty.

Henry's eyes went huge. 'Yes! Every night. I couldn't see Peter.'

That night Henry slept in Simon's room, on a rather attractive military-style iron bed that Matty had picked up. Matty retired to her mattress, reflecting that the house seemed so much more pleasant now that she had company. It was hard living alone. She had never been quite alone before in her whole life. There was a certain terror in it, as if it would take only the slightest loss of concentration for the existence to become pointless and unsustainable. When she got up each morning it was so easy to do things for the house and forget all about any greater ambitions. She had been wasting time and money, and it was fortunate indeed that Henry had brought her to her senses before Sholto did.

They went out first thing in the morning to place the

advertisement. It read: 'Sterling Silver wanted. Anything considered. Advice and valuations in your own home by reputable expert'.

'I don't think even Sammy calls himself an expert,' said Matty ruefully.

'False modesty doesn't pay,' said Henry. She stopped outside a baker's window to torture herself with desire. Her golden hair blew about her face in the chill wind and a passing lout came up close and muttered, 'Wotcher, darling,' in her ear. Henry took no notice.

'You've changed,' said Matty in admiration. The time was not so long past when Henry would have blushed scarlet. But only a little time ago the man wouldn't have bothered muttering at all. Losing weight had turned the girl's face from a blob into a cheery, snub-nosed circle with a delicate pink and white skin.

'You should hear what the dossers say,' said Henry. 'The worst ones, that is. The ones that are just homeless are quite polite really.'

They drove back through Littlebury. Standing at the station in the taxi queue was Mrs Giles.

'Oh my God!' Matty stamped on the accelerator and squealed down the road like a bank robber making a getaway.

Henrietta dived for cover. 'We can't go to the house! We can't go anywhere! What shall we do?'

Matty drew the car to a halt. The two girls looked at each other. 'Perhaps she's prepared to be reasonable,' said Matty.

'She won't be.'

'You don't know that. Perhaps now she realises how strongly you feel.'

'She thinks I want to do good works. So does Peter. My mother virtually accused him of sexual abuse, but he's never touched anything more than my hand. I wish he had.'

Matty looked sympathetically at her despondent friend. They both knew there was nothing for it. She turned the car round and went back to collect Mrs Giles.

'Would you like a cup of tea, Mrs Giles? A biscuit? Some sherry?' Matty hopped from foot to foot, anxiously. After a brief but pungent fracas with her mother Henrietta had run upstairs to hide.

'Tea, I think, Matilda. And an explanation. No doubt Henrietta's confided in you, and I should be grateful if you would enlighten me. Why is she so eager to get out at night? Is it drugs? Men? Has she been taken over by one of those sects, the Moonies perhaps? She seems so preoccupied – this weight loss – she hardly seems to eat any meat!'

'She's on a diet,' said Matty.

'I'm in half a mind to send her to a psychiatrist.'

'Oh! But – I don't think that's necessary.'

Matty struggled with herself. Confidences between friends could never be betrayed, but Mrs Giles was like an unguided missile. Unless directed she would explode in all the wrong places. 'I think – Henrietta's very inspired by Peter's – the vicar's – work,' she managed. 'She wants to do something to help alleviate suffering. She felt she was making a real contribution.'

'It was unsafe,' said Mrs Giles decisively. 'For a girl her age it was madness. I've made enquiries about the man, of course. I spoke to the bishop. Apparently he's a known hothead.'

'I didn't think they appointed that sort as bishops,' said Matty naughtily, but Mrs Giles withered her with a look. She would never have suffered a moment's disquiet at the hands of the lower fourth.

'Of course she's probably infatuated with him,' said Mrs Giles. Matty was dumbstruck. Mrs Giles saw her face and allowed herself a wintry smile. 'I'm not entirely without understanding, Matilda. I can only hope she hasn't been foolish. Pregnancy. Some horrible disease.'

'He's a vicar!' gasped Matty. 'They don't – he wouldn't – all they do is give out soup and buns.'

'Men can't be trusted with young girls,' said Mrs Giles firmly. 'It was lucky we caught it when we did. Which reminds me, Matilda. Are you living with this man you're in business with? If you are then it must stop. Not only is it wrong, but it sets your brother the worst possible example. A child that age. Three, is he? Four?'

'Er – a bit older than that.'

'Really? I felt sure Henrietta said that he was attending playgroup. But a boy of any age shouldn't be exposed to looseness. You can both show restraint, Matilda. And if the man's not capable of it then he's not much of a man. I'll fetch Henrietta now.'

There was no resistance. Henrietta came meekly downstairs and followed her mother out to the car. Matty drove them both back to the station.

Dawn came late on autumn mornings. Matty packed the car with cardboard boxes, in case the things she was going to see might actually be things she might buy. Besides, it looked better to have an apparently full car. She wanted to appear established, prosperous, not a beginner with a copy of the price guide in her pocket.

She had bought a new suit, grey flannel. It was businesslike, she felt, without being intimidating, and she wore a dark green shirt underneath, fastened at the neck with a Victorian clip. It was the sort of thing she imagined a silver dealer would wear.

A strange feeling came over her, almost as if she was impersonating herself. Was this the real Matty, smart and well groomed, with a head full of facts and figures? Or was she still a little girl, nervous and hot tempered, liable to fly off the handle at any real or imagined injustice? Strange thoughts proliferated when she was alone. Doubts multiplied. To begin like this, on a cold dark morning, seemed impossible.

As she drove the grey sky lightened. Wintry trees stood well back from the motorway, and crows rose like ragged blankets, inauspiciously. The letter had come from someone a hundred miles away and it sounded so promising. Matty had telephoned just to make sure, because she wasn't travelling all that way for a bit of silver plate. People barely seemed to know the difference any more, and wasted their money on valueless tat, when the real thing was only a little more expensive. The only exception she would consider would be old Sheffield plate, made when plating technique was new, with a rough and extravagant brilliance. Sammy wouldn't touch it, but she thought she might. If she had the opportunity.

The miles rolled by. She flicked channels on the radio, searching for something to amuse her, but she could only find the news. There was an earthquake somewhere, and trouble in the Gulf. Then the newsreader said, 'Police in Switzerland are to decide today whether to release a British art dealer, Mr Sholto Feversham, held on suspicion of fraud. Mr Feversham purchased a painting a week ago, The Martyrdom of St Christopher, from Mr Luca de Caruzon, a member of a family influential in world art. The painting was believed to be a copy of an earlier work, but members of the family now maintain that Mr Feversham was aware of the painting's true significance, as a fifteenth-century original, and was guilty of fraud. Mr Feversham has so far declined to divulge the painting's whereabouts.'

Matty stamped on the brake and brought the car to a shuddering halt on the hard shoulder. Her heart was beating furiously. Fraud. Arrested on a charge of fraud. She might have known he'd do something underhand. He and Henry would make a great team, not a scruple between them. How had he bought from Luca? Why? No wonder he was in prison. What was she to do?

After a while the thudding of her heart seemed to ease. There was nothing to do but drive on, although sitting here the maelstrom of speed on the motorway seemed terrifying. She started the car and drove along the shoulder, waiting for a gap in the traffic, but in the end she was forced to slot in between two lorries, the driver behind flashing her and bullying her on. If only she could go home, she thought. She felt better in her little house, more secure. Out in the world there was danger and dishonesty, the sort of double-dealing that landed people like Sholto in gaol.

Escaping the motorway at last, she struggled to relax. Her hands felt wet on the steering wheel and she stopped for a moment in a wood, to walk about a little and calm herself. She tried to lash herself into some sort of urgency, because time was getting on, she would be late.

Her customer lived in a tall, ivy-covered house down a dank lane. Leaves lay in wet drifts everywhere, and the place smelled of rotting vegetable matter. An old man was standing in the garden, wearing a sports jacket that had seen very much better days over a hand-knitted pullover covered in egg stains. Matty began to feel calm again.

'Mr Mountjoy? I'm Matilda Winterton.'

'Yes. Indeed. Yes. You were a little late –'

'I had some trouble on the motorway.'

He was nervous, more nervous than she, and she smiled to put him at his ease. He said, 'I hope it's not been a wasted journey – one hardly knows – it is very old, you see.'

'How old?' Some people equated 1910 with antiquity.

'My mother always said it was eighteenth century.'

Matty's heart began to thunder within her breast. This felt right. The old man came of a formerly rich family, he lived in a house that would once have been plush, and now, in old age, he was selling the family treasures. 'Don't you have anyone you would like to leave your silver to?' asked Matty jerkily. He probably only wanted a valuation.

He stopped in his tracks, looking slightly guilty. 'I have no family,' he said, almost as if he expected Matty to disapprove. 'I live alone.'

'So do I,' said Matty. 'It's difficult, really.'

'Yes.'

The house smelled of old age. Most of the curtains were drawn against the sun, although there was none. Everything was dusty and disordered, with the cold that comes from lack of use rather than lack of heat. He ushered Matty into the dining room. On the table, gleaming faintly beneath layers of tarnish, was the silver.

'Could you put the light on, please?' Just seeing it gave her a great surge of confidence. She knew what this was. It greeted her like an old and familiar friend. Two teapots with stands, a set of silver-handled knives with the blades all to hell and three sweetmeat dishes. She tutted over the knives; the hallmarks had been rubbed, no doubt courtesy of some past butler. But they were saleable, and new blades would transform them.

She turned to the teapots. They were fine – very fine. One was by a maker she knew, the other was more obscure, and perhaps less good. For long moments she simply explored them, enjoying the feel of cool metal. She had missed the silver. Every piece you picked up was the beginning of an elaborate puzzle, and you might have all the bits to solve that puzzle or never fill in the gaps.

The old man said, 'My mother always believed them to be valuable.'

'Your mother was right. They're lovely. Excuse me a moment.'

She dived for her price guide. Her own feeling was that she might sell for perhaps £5,000, which meant she couldn't give much more than £4,000. It seemed mean, taking so much. It was possible of course that she could get more for the pots, especially if she sent them abroad — her mind began to sort possibilities. Sammy had contacts abroad, and she did not. It was best to assume she would be selling at home.

'Four thousand two hundred pounds' she said. 'And five hundred for the knives.'

'Good heavens.' He sat down in a worn leather chair opposite her. 'I didn't imagine — so much.'

'You could always auction them,' said Matty, knowing she was cutting her own throat. 'But then there'd be commission. And the uncertainty.'

'You never know what might happen at auctions. Rings and so on. We've always avoided them, as a family.'

'Very sensible.'

His eyes were brightening as he thought of all the money. 'You seem so young to be an expert,' he confided.

'I've been very well trained. Mr Chesworth in London. He's been in silver all his life.'

'My mother often went shopping in London. Years ago, of course, when one could afford the train. Will you take tea?'

She declined. She had to be going.

The pots were parcelled up, and then he said, 'Dear me, young lady! You've forgotten to pack the bowls.'

Matty looked at him. 'But I haven't quoted for the bowls.'

'Haven't you? But I thought — surely that covers everything?'

She shook her head. 'Mr Mountjoy, I'm about to pay you £8,900 for two teapots and a set of knives.'

228

'But the pots were £4,200!'

'Yes. Each.'

He put his head in his hands. He was shaking. 'Forgive me, young lady, but are you sure? You are very young. You could get into terrible trouble. I'm sure you can't pay so much.'

'But they're worth that, Mr Mountjoy. Look, one of them is dated 1720, the other a little later. They still have the original stands, the lids are original and the marks are very clear. I assure you, I know what I'm doing. And if you want to sell the bowls as well I'll give you ten thousand pounds for the lot.'

Mr Mountjoy let out a groan. She was showering him with unlooked for riches. 'I shan't know what to do!' he exclaimed. 'Good heavens, I could eat pheasant every night!'

'You'd lose the taste for it,' said Matty. 'Now, I should like to write you a cheque, but obviously you'll want to telephone my bank to have it authorised. I've brought one of the manager's cards with the number.'

'Not at all, not at all, young lady. I wouldn't dream of doing anything so untrusting. We must have something — some sherry — something to celebrate. Won't you join me in a sherry?'

Matty accepted and they sat either side of the table, drinking out of glasses that must themselves have been two hundred years old, even though she knew almost nothing about glassware. The old man was soon flushed and happy, confiding details of his desperate finances that would now be quite restored by his windfall. When she left, the box cradled under her arm, he stood at the door, waving.

She drove round the corner and parked. She needed to collect herself, she was shaking. Her nerves were playing up again, this time because thievery had been so close to hand she could have reached out and put it in her pocket. He would have accepted a thousand or two for his whole magnificent collection, and thought himself lucky. She could have robbed him blind.

Her father would have done it. So would Sholto. She could remember her father saying, 'In this business it's the strong that survive, the nice men go to the wall.' But if she had to survive by cheating people like old Mr Mountjoy then she'd starve. How else was she to live with herself? Fairness must be her policy, because the alternative was horrible. She thought of the silver spoon. Things bought by deceit could never give you pleasure.

She drove home slowly, listening to the radio, hoping to catch more news of Sholto. At last, at four o'clock, the announcer said, 'The art dealer imprisoned in Switzerland on suspicion of fraud has been set free. Mr Sholto Feversham was found to have no case to answer, despite pleas from the de Caruzon family for him to be held in custody pending an appeal for export restrictions to be placed on the disputed painting, the Martyrdom of St Christopher. Mr Feversham is returning to England immediately.'

Matty's heart did a little jig. He was coming home! He would see her silver and think she was wonderful, she need never tell him how little it might have cost. He would admire the house. Tonight, or tomorrow if he couldn't get a flight, they would have a candlelit dinner and make love.

The traffic was heavy at that time of day, and she didn't reach home until six. She got out of the car in a fluster, anxious to light the fire and make everything welcoming. But the door opened before she could reach it, and there was Sholto, already. He was wearing a white suit. He had the most wonderful tan. Matty flung herself at him, sobbing.

'Hey, hey, what's the panic? I haven't returned from the dead.'

'You were in prison! It was on the news. I was planning to come and rescue you.'

'But I was enjoying myself! Private room, colour television, food a little on the dull side, but then freedom has to have some point. What's more it kept me out of the clutches of the de Caruzons, and that has to be an advantage.'

'If you will swindle people.'

'I swindled no one. I took advantage of their unattractive greed, no more than that. Any parcels arrived for you?'

'No. Should there be some?'

'I damn well hope so. I sent you the picture.'

Matty's eyes became very large. Then she began to rummage beside the front door, behind the tangled web of creeper. The postman sometimes left things there. Sure enough, she unearthed a small parcel, the bottom inch soaking wet, the address barely legible. 'M. Winterton, Larkspur Cottage, Back Lane, Littlebury. Handle with Care'.

'Oh, Christ,' groaned Sholto. 'You've left fifty thousand pounds standing outside the front door.'

'You didn't pay that, did you?'

'No. Five. And you needn't look at me like that. Maisie de Caruzon may be very old but she is also very nasty. One of the nastiest women I have ever met. Savages her servants as a matter of course.'

'You're making excuses,' said Matty coldly.

'I don't have any to make. I told her I thought the thing was original, and the old bat cackled away at me. Thought she'd teach me that she knew best. She said if I was so sure then I could have it for five thousand, and we both knew that was two thousand over the odds, if the thing was copied. I decided not to touch it but she insisted. Positive she was right and I was wrong. Wouldn't let me look at another thing. So in the end, when she'd yelled at the butler for flinching when she screamed, told me I was the ugliest art dealer she'd ever seen and her maid the most stupid woman in history, then I bought the painting.'

Matty took the parcel inside and began ripping off the paper. Sholto had wrapped it in cardboard from a shirt box. 'I see you found time to buy clothes,' she remarked.

'The odd five minutes. You don't go to Italy and not buy clothes. Now, look at that. How can that horrible old woman not have seen what this was? Blinded by too many diamonds, I suppose.'

'Did she wear diamonds?'

'Laden with 'em. A veritable Christmas tree. She's the old Don's sister, you know. Thought her money gave her the right to spit on the rest of human kind. When she discovered the truth she set the dogs on me, of course. The whole mewling pack of the de Caruzon clan. Eleanor's finally got Luca to bring her to Europe, so presumably she's cleaned up her act since last we met. Did the old boy ever sell his silver, by the way?'

Matty said, 'Not that I know of. The market's dropped. Because of me he missed the boat.'

'Glad to hear you can take some of the blame, then. I got mixed up in a family squabble that brings in a lot of old scores.'

'Sure it wasn't just you?' asked Matty.

He shrugged. 'God knows. Perhaps the old man's dropped dead. Luca's got his hands on the reins, that's for sure.'

He was without stillness, moving tensely here and there. As Matty took the last of the wrapping off the picture he stopped. His face became a mask of concentrated interest. After a moment he said, 'Now you can see I was right. It's a copy all right, but just about as old as the original. Mantegna. If these things weren't so unfashionable I'd get half a million for it.'

Matty squinted at the picture. The colours were dark with centuries of dirt, and there were cracks across one corner. A small piece of paint had chipped off. 'It's a bit of a mess, isn't it?'

'No. There are hundreds worse than that. I know a man in America who'd buy this over the 'phone, in any condition. But then he knows what he's doing. He restores them himself, he's brilliant.'

'Another dealer, then.'

'Good God, no. He collects. Unlike silver, in this game you don't get the mugs. My lot know what they're doing, by and large. And so do I.'

It was a very Italian picture. Crowds of people milled amidst marble columns and decorated cornices, and a vine seemed to be growing over a pergola in the middle of the street. The body, if that's what it was, lay hugely prone, one muscled leg held up by a saviour or assailant, it was hard to tell.

'Worth a few days in gaol, don't you think?'

'I don't know. Perhaps.' She went through to the kitchen, to put on the kettle and start to cook.

Sholto said, 'Let's go out somewhere. We're making money, I want to celebrate.'

'Tonight? Your first night home?'

'Yes.'

She didn't want to go. Suddenly the perfect evening would have been to stay just here, with Sholto, before a log fire. She wanted him to love her in the firelight, the rough skin of his face raking against her breasts. At that moment he came towards her, taking the lapels of her suit in his hands. 'You look intimidatingly businesslike,' he murmured. 'Not my sort of wench at all.'

'I bet you found some luscious Italian girls,' whispered Matty, surprising herself. Until that moment she hadn't known she was jealous. But she was. Who wouldn't be jealous of Sholto?

He didn't reply. He simply lifted her skirt, sliding his hands into her pants and tights to pull them down. In one smooth movement he unzipped and put himself into her, and the pleasure was so sharp and unexpected that she gasped. His height made it hard for him to move in her, and he pushed her back against the table. She hung on him, staring straight into his face, and when she came, a second later, she felt her teeth clench violently. His fingers probed into the cleft of her bottom and gripped her. He held her hard against him, grinding, bludgeoning her into orgasm again. Her legs went to jelly and she collapsed on him, she didn't want any more. She realised, thankfully, that he was done.

They went to a restaurant in Littlebury. It was small and not very good, with the vegetables frozen and the main courses lacklustre.

Sholto ordered champagne and put them into a panic, and suddenly Matty began to enjoy herself. They began to act, pretending to be world-weary Londoners, appalled by this provincial lack of style.

'One would imagine they'd have langoustines,' complained Matty.

'At the very least,' agreed Sholto. 'If not lobster. One can have it flown in nowadays, packed in ice.'

Matty thought she might believe him. 'Doesn't the lobster object?'

'I should think not! What lobster wouldn't prefer to die

233

in splendour, rather than live out his life in obscurity? They positively throw themselves into the pots.'

'Then, for the lobster's sake, they should have lobster,' agreed Matty, flourishing her champagne glass.

'And certainly langoustines.'

They laughed at each other, and the waitress threw them alarmed glances. The only other diners were the local auctioneer and his wife, who whispered about them audibly. 'Big London dealers — trying to wipe us out — won't last five minutes.'

'By the way,' said Sholto, 'the house looks fine.'

Matty went pink. 'Oh. I wasn't sure if you'd like it.'

'It's all very cottagey. Suits the place. Oh look, here are the puddings. Straight out of the freezer cabinet in Tesco's.'

They giggled together over Black Forest gâteau. Matty said, 'Do you think the de Caruzons are going to bear a grudge? We seem to be getting in their way rather a lot.'

He nodded. 'Luca doesn't like me, I'm afraid. Tried to bribe the guards to give me a good thrashing, which isn't the Swiss thing at all.'

'Do they thrash people over there?'

'Shouldn't think so. Beat them to death with sweet reason, if you ask me. You have to come back to dear old England for a bit of corrupt violence.' He grabbed her hand and pretended to savage the inside of her wrist. Matty squealed but he held on, and when she stopped struggling he touched her skin with a long, sensuous kiss.

'I feel like Olive Oyl,' she whispered. 'With real geese swimming up my arm.'

'Thanks. I always wanted to look like Popeye.'

He paid the bill with a few casually discarded notes. Matty said, 'I bet you've overtipped. You waste money, Sholto.'

'Don't be boring, my little hausfrau.'

She kicked him on the ankle and he yelped, leaving the restaurant hopping. 'Serves you right,' snapped Matty. 'I haven't just kept house. I've bought some lovely silver and you haven't been interested at all. You can be so self-centred at times.'

'I didn't see any. There's just one vast, empty barn.'

'It's in the car.'

'One lot? Haven't you been busy.'

Sholto hadn't locked the car, but the silver was still there. Matty got it out and showed it to him by the light of a street lamp.

'How much are you going to make?' he asked.

She shrugged. 'I'm not sure. Three thousand perhaps. In comparison with you that's pretty small beer.'

'If we go on like this we'll be millionaires in six months.'

She touched his silk tie. 'If you go on like this we'll need to be.'

His eyes glinted in the darkness. He felt in his pocket and brought out a small parcel. 'I brought you a present. Here.' It was a silk scarf in deep russet and yellow.

Matty wrapped it extravagantly around her throat, saying, 'I'm not going to be neat any more. I shall be arty.'

'You are anyway. When you're at your neatest you look like a whore in school uniform. Deliciously sexy.'

'Is that why you keep assaulting me?'

'Too right.'

The night was turning colder. They drove home watched by a hazy moon, the last dregs of cloud like fingers across a face. Suddenly, with a sense that she was living in a narrow band of joy, Matty felt wildly happy.

Chapter Fourteen

Griselda was working in her room. Books and papers were spread all over the desk and her hand moved steadily, filling a page with neat writing. From time to time she would pause to push her reading glasses further up her nose, and then she would write again. Once she stopped to make herself some coffee, but then she returned to the desk and the writing. There was something remarkable about her grim concentration, she worked as if she was shutting something out.

The room should have been wonderfully tranquil. It was one of the best rooms, looking out over trees and flat fields on which cows grazed in summer. Now the grass was rimed with frost and the trees were leafless, shuddering in the teeth of a brisk autumn gale. Sometimes, at the height of a gust, the window rattled, but it wasn't that which disturbed her. Far from it. It was the sound of laughter and the chink of glasses, the unmistakable shrieks of girls having fun. Somewhere on the floor below someone was having a party. Griselda, once again, had not been invited.

Soon the essay was finished. Griselda replaced the cap on her pen, knowing she had done a good job. The one positive thing about university was the marks; if she impressed none of her fellow students at least she had caused a stir amongst the tutors. Yet how much better it would have been if she hadn't overheard Glamourboy Somers say, 'That horsy one − Lemming-Knott, the one with the boot face − there's a good brain in there somewhere, thank God.'

The 'thank God' had puzzled her. Did he mean that at least she had some saving graces? That she wasn't totally repulsive, both inside and out? Or was he seeing it from her point of view, as something that redeemed the terrible affliction of ugliness? Whatever it was, his words had stabbed her.

Now that the work was done, her room felt like a trap. She knew she should go out, but the thought of inflicting herself on people who didn't want to know was almost unbearable. She could see herself gatecrashing the party, embarrassment making her speech even more appallingly plummy: 'Hello, can I come in? The name's Griselda – awful I know, but what can one do?' They would all look at her, amused, disguising their lack of welcome.

Never in her life had she imagined she would long to be back at school. But she did, oh, how she did. The enforced years of proximity had broken down all barriers, the girls knew each other through and through. There she had known she had friends. There she had been free of the terrible, skinless vulnerability of loneliness.

It would not get better if she stayed here all day. She got up and went to the mirror, fiddling inexpertly with mascara and eye shadow. Matty had always done her eyes, and now somehow Griselda couldn't do them herself. The confidence had gone, of course. Once you had that you had everything, but knowing it didn't make it any better. She was wearing a tweed skirt, red woollen tights and a red sweater. It was almost the college uniform, the sort of thing all the girls here wore, but it looked different on everyone else. Griselda was tall and gangling, she resembled a wading bird with endless thin red legs.

A major effort of will got her out into the corridor, and from there she could pretend she was on her way somewhere, anywhere. She followed the noise to the floor below, and stood for long seconds outside the room, praying for the door to open and someone to say, 'Hi! Come on in.' But nothing happened. The people inside began singing and Griselda crept silently away.

But she would not go back to her room. Instead she would go into town and have a coffee. As it turned out, she should have returned to her room, at least for a coat, and she had to run through the freezing wind, her eyes watering from the cold, no doubt ruining her already messy make-up. She cannoned breathless into the nearest coffee shop, one to which she had never been before. Wiping her eyes with the back of her hand, she sat down and tried to collect herself. There was only one other person in the shop.

'Hello, Griselda,' he said.

'Good Lord! Bertie!' She looked across into the plump face of Bertram, Duke of Brantingham, their immediate next-door neighbour at Peregrines.

He came across and sat awkwardly down at her table. He was a couple of years older than she, and already his hair line was receding. None the less the sight of him revived Griselda miraculously.

'I'd forgotten you were up,' she said. 'I'd have called on you if I'd remembered. It really is the most ghastly place.'

'Do you think so? Everyone seems to be having a marvellous time.'

'Yes. They do, don't they?'

The waitress came over and took orders for tea and toasted teacakes. When she had gone, Bertie said, 'Not having too much fun then?'

Griselda shook her head. 'I expected too much. I thought there'd be parties and things. You know.'

'We seem to have quite a few parties. I just never seem to know what's going on at them. I sit in a corner and try not to get noticed.'

He grimaced, and Griselda said, 'I don't believe you! And at least you get invited.'

'Never to the right ones, though. It's the classic thing, isn't it? The laughter always in the next room. It's my own fault, of course. I took a year out to see to the estate when my father died, and now everyone here seems just out of nappies. And it doesn't help having a title. The world's got so damned egalitarian.'

'I should have joined more societies,' said Griselda dismally.

'I joined everything,' said Bertie. 'Couldn't keep half of them up. And the Christian thing was a big mistake. Kept getting people round wanting to pray with me.'

She chuckled, relaxing for what felt like the first time in weeks. She'd always quite liked Bertie, although as a little

239

boy he had been cast in the shade by his noisily drunken father. It was rare for the old duke to be invited on a shoot unless children and dogs had been warned and a spare keeper designated to flatten him if he tried to shoot anything he shouldn't. On one occasion he'd peppered Lord Knelworth himself after the whistle.

'How are things at home?' she asked.

'Oh, you know. Frugal. The old boy ran through the money, of course.'

'You're not going to have to sell up, are you?'

'Don't know. Probably not. Once I get my degree I shall set about sorting things out properly. Might sell a picture or two.'

'I know someone who buys pictures. Or at least I know of him. He's in business with a friend of mine.'

'Really? I'll remember that. One hates selling to people one doesn't know.'

The tea arrived and they munched together. Bertie had a somewhat lugubrious face, Griselda decided, but his mournfulness was barely skin deep. He assumed a mask of bumbling and regrettable failure.

'There's a party tonight,' he said suddenly. 'Why don't you come?'

'At your college? Is that all right?'

'Absolutely. I'll pick you up, don't want you getting bashed on the head.'

'No.'

She hid a smile in the remains of her teacake. Such courtliness was almost unheard of in the university, where the girls evolved survival schemes amongst themselves. The door burst open and a couple more students came in, swathed in scarves. 'Hi, Bertie,' they said, and sat down.

'Griselda, this is Edwina Sharpe and Michael Brumfitt,' said Bertie, carefully punctilious. 'The Honourable Griselda Lemming-Knott.'

Griselda went scarlet. 'Call me Grizz,' she said jerkily. 'Everyone does.'

'Everyone except Bertie,' said Edwina, giving him an affectionate smile. 'What would we do without him to keep our standards where they should be?'

'There you are, Griselda,' said Bertie. 'I told you they think I'm a fuddy-duddy.'

'Our own pet fuddy-duddy,' said Edwina. She reclined in her chair extravagantly. 'I couldn't bear to stay in another moment. The trogs are having yet another appalling party, all shrieking and drunken yells. And they never invite me.'

'Or me,' said Griselda. 'I keep thinking I ought not to want to be invited.'

'They're never appalling if they're your own parties, are they?' said Michael. 'You are coming to ours tonight, aren't you?'

'She's coming with me,' said Bertie. 'Shall I collect you too, Edwina? I've got the car.'

'Is it the ancient Rolls-Royce? Then of course I'll be collected. So grand. You don't mind do you, Griselda?'

'No. Of course not.'

The afternoon was drawing to a close. Street lamps were starting to glow and shoppers were hurrying to catch the buses. Bertie ordered more tea and Michael told scurrilous tales of Mr Somers attempting to seduce girls in his tutorial group. 'He's an utter ram, of course.' Griselda felt her tangled nerves start to unwind a little. Thank goodness for Bertie.

The delivery van loomed at the gate, like a pregnant elephant. 'It says it's for you,' said the man, with a long-suffering air. 'This house.'

'I haven't ordered anything,' said Matty, repeating herself for the fifth time. 'Perhaps it's for the previous owner or something.'

The man scratched his head. 'Could be. I've got to deliver it, whatever. Can't take it back. Storage costs, you see. Someone's got to take responsibility. Can't bring things all the way from Italy and not take responsibility.'

'Italy?' Matty's voice rose in an alarmed shriek.

'Yeah. Know someone in Italy, do you?'

'In more ways than one. What is this thing?'

He shrugged. 'Damned if I know. It's big, that's for sure.'

A sense of doom came over Matty as she watched them unload. The thing was enormous, swathed in sacking and string. It was covered in various customs labels, some gloriously Italian and others British and functional. There were lots of long thin pieces and two large oblong ones.

'Where shall we put it, Missus?' demanded one of the men.

'I don't know. Does it go upstairs or down?'

They all contemplated the shapes. 'If you ask me,' said the foreman, rolling himself a fag, 'it's a four-poster bed.'

'Do you think so?' Matty brightened. 'We do need a bed. Oh, how wonderful. Then it's got to go upstairs. At once.'

But there was no 'at once' about it. The cottage hadn't been built with huge beds in mind. Eventually one of the men found a rope and they hoisted the base up through the bedroom window, following it with the lead-heavy horsehair mattress. Trust Sholto to be authentic, thought Matty ruefully. It probably had real bedbugs and they could easily have bought a sprung mattress to fit.

But, when at last it was erected, Matty hugged herself. It presided over the room like a flagship, the lack of draperies giving it an undressed appearance. The wood was heavily carved, with a light, burnished sheen. It quite lacked simplicity. There was an air of grandeur about the bed, of sensuous living.

'Bed and a half, that,' said the foreman, preparing to go. 'Must have cost a fortune to have it shipped, let alone to buy. Rich, your friend, is he?'

'Not if he goes on like this.'

She ushered the men out. She had been cataloguing when they called, making careful and comprehensive notes on each item of silver in her possession. Once she had begun buying it seemed more than possible to keep on, and her little collection now extended to three long shelves in the barn, and two chests full of 'smalls'. She was planning to write to Sammy's contact in America, which she hoped was ethical, and ask if he would like to offer for her teapots. She had ten now, all relatively good.

A fruitless half hour went by as she tried to concentrate on her lists. It was no good. She was quite distracted. Sholto was getting at her for hanging on to her silver for so long, but he must have spent a fortune on that bed. And somehow they never seemed to discuss money. His aunt provided it and although they both signed on the bank account, it was Sholto who received the statements. Matty knew that wasn't wise.

He was so profligate, that was the trouble. Money flowed from his fingerends like magic sparks; he spent and spent and spent again. If he wasn't making money he spent in the knowledge that he would tomorrow, and if he made it he spent to make up for all the tomorrows that might not pay off. No wonder people liked to have him as their broker, thought Matty. When you entrusted Sholto with a commission you could be sure he would find you dozens of things you never knew you wanted. And those you truly didn't want he kept, adding yet again to his collection.

On an impulse she picked up the telephone and dialled the bank. If she was to be given the balance over the 'phone she had to sound confident, so she began breezily: 'Matilda Winterton here. Can you give me the balance of my business account please? Winsham Specialist Antiques. Thank you.'

She waited with impatience. How much could there be? Sholto had sold his painting but the money hadn't come in, and the things in the barn moved but slowly. He placed them in galleries from time to time, and brought people to see them, as well as tucking some under his arm and visiting prospective buyers. Today he was talking to a museum; it was surprising how few had even the most minor example of Renaissance art. The girl came back on the 'phone. Matty wrote down the figure she gave, deliberately not thinking about it. 'Thank you,' she said airily, and rang off.

After a moment she got up and went to the cabinet to pour herself a stiff whisky. They had less than two hundred pounds. Out of all the money Sholto's aunt had lent they had almost nothing, and it was as much her fault as Sholto's. All the expense on the house, and buying silver and not selling it, following her own instincts as if she was collecting, not trying to make a turn. They said the best dealers were really collectors at heart. But the best dealers didn't run out of money.

Could they survive on two hundred pounds? It was almost Christmas, heralding the great British shutdown until well into January. And Simon was coming home, expecting all the things she had promised, presents, a tree, everything. How could this have happened? How could she have let it happen?

When Sholto returned that night she was sitting by the fire, wearing a long white robe, turning a glass in her pale fingers. He stopped in the doorway, caught afresh by her radiance. In the firelight her hair was dark and glowing, and her throat rose from her clothes like a young and slender flowerstem. Her fragility caught at him and he said rousingly, 'Don't sit in the dark, Matty! You look suicidal.'

He flung a folder on to a chair and flung himself down next to it. 'God, I'm tired. They want it but they've got to talk to the committees. Committees, committees. Give me an honest miser any time, he may hide the things away but at least he doesn't have committees.'

Matty said, 'I called the bank today. We're nearly broke.'

He glanced at her. 'Hardly. Cashless perhaps, but not broke.'

'I didn't think you knew.' When he said nothing she added, 'And the bed arrived today.'

Sholto sat up. 'Great! What do you think? I saw it in Florence and I knew it was magnificent. Original mattress – at least an old mattress – everything. Don't look so frosty, Matty. When you leave me for an accountant I'll let you take the bed. You can think of me all night, while he adds up balance sheets.'

In a low voice she said, 'Don't be silly, Sholto.'

'We could sell it tomorrow for fifteen thousand.'

'Then perhaps we should.'

He looked at her for a long, speculative moment. Then he said, 'I do so hate your practical streak. You never soar above the earth. You keep your feet firmly planted in the mud.'

'I could do more soaring if you would do less. It's both our faults. We've got to get some money in right away.'

'God knows why. We can manage.'

Matty spun round, flaring at him. 'No we can't! Simon's coming next week and he'll want a proper Christmas. I want to feed him well, and give him presents, and not have to count the cost. I don't want him to know we're on our beam ends.'

'We're not on our beams ends! We're in a cash flow crisis. In January I'll get the money from America, and you'll sell your silver, and the committees will meet and before you know it we'll be knee deep in it. What we really need is a bank loan.'

Matty shook her head. 'If you've got money you spend it. You know you do.'

He got up and came over to her, leaning down to kiss her nose. 'I can't help being lordly. Think back, Matilda. Did I ever say I was going to be thrifty and reliable? It's not something I recall.'

She looked up into his face. He had never promised her anything. 'I have to be responsible,' she said softly. 'For Simon.'

After a moment he said, 'It doesn't cost so much, does it? Christmas?'

'You know it does. Even without presents, there's the food. The turkey, the pudding, brandy butter —' She grimaced with horror. 'We'll be living on beans, like three drop-outs, when I promised him that this time I'd make it right!'

Sholto sighed. 'You and your blasted promises.'

'You and your blasted beds!'

He wandered across the room, jingling keys in his pocket. 'I can always get a turkey. Steal one, or something.'

'You couldn't. They live in sheds all locked up. And then you have to eviscerate them.'

'Too true. How about I scrounge one off the farmer in return for letting him run his daughter's pony on our field? In fact, he can supply sufficient poultry to see out Yuletide.'

She considered. 'We'll need tons of other stuff. Chestnuts, and brussels sprouts, and fruit — honestly, I'd better ask Henrietta if Simon can go to her. At least they'd give him a proper do.'

'Along with a set of building blocks suitable for his nursery years. Really, Matty! You can always shop at the market in town. They sell good, wholesome, cheap stuff that just needs peeling. It might not be the same as opening a freezer bag, but I've heard people can live on it.'

'Yes. That wouldn't cost much. We have got two hundred pounds.'

He laughed. 'We have bills to pay, my little pumpkin. When all the cheques come in we're going to be about two thousand pounds overdrawn. Let's hope the bank doesn't bounce anything.'

She was too stunned to think. As realisation dawned and she opened her mouth to protest he crossed the room, bent his head and kissed her. 'We'll talk about it later,' he said firmly. She knew they wouldn't talk about it at all.

'Hello, darling!' Matty could barely keep the excitement from her voice. Simon gave her and Sholto an oblique, embarrassed glance and said, 'Hi.'

They fell in on either side of him, aware that their demeanour now had to be creditable. Relatives were always invited to the Christmas carol service, subsequently to remove the relevant boy for the holidays, and any lapse in the manner of dress, speech or sneezing would only lead to teasing next term. 'I should warn you, Simon,' said Sholto, 'I sing rather loudly. Shall I just mime?'

'You don't do parts, do you?' One mother, operatic trained, had once soared into an unscheduled descant which had thrilled the music master and annihilated her son. The occasion had gone into legend. It was rumoured he'd tried to electrocute himself with the Christmas lights, which thankfully, as always, weren't working.

'He'll just sing the tune,' promised Matty.

'A couple of quid's more than enough for the collection,' Simon assured them. 'You don't want to look like someone who doesn't know what's what. Some millionaire or something.'

'God forbid,' said Sholto, absently.

He was looking at the paintings on the school walls. They were the usual collection of dark oils and obscure portraits. He paused at one next to the fire escape, although to Matty's eye it was too dirty for anyone to discern much. 'Not an undiscovered master?' she enquired sardonically.

'No. Just an unfashionable English painter who has lately become rather more fashionable. I might offer for this.'

'You can't! Don't!' Simon almost wailed in anguish.

'Not yet, duffer,' said Sholto scathingly. 'In January, when the school heating bills come in.'

Simon looked at him dubiously. It said something for the affection in which he held Sholto, Matty thought, that he hadn't complained about Sholto's dress. A cream suit, pale blue shirt and yellow silk tie were hardly the garments to ensure obscurity. Matty herself, in deference to Simon's feelings, had chosen a dress in navy blue. It was simple and well fitting, and she had slung Sholto's scarf across her shoulders. The effect was rather dashing, or so the boys thought. They concluded that Winterton's sister, or whatever she was, was easily the best-looking woman in the place, while Sholto was the absolute acme of style. Looking at their own parents, inevitably older and determinedly less glamorous, every boy in the place envied Winterton his connections.

The carols and readings went on their accustomed way. Matty was conscious of Sholto's restlessness. 'Don't you like it?' she asked, under cover of a shuffling preparation to pray.

He rolled his eyes at her. 'If you must know, I hate Christmas. I've never had a good one yet.'

The school chaplain began intoning his ritual beseechings, for forgiveness and the kingdom of heaven. Matty knew Sholto wanted neither. He felt no guilt for anything he did, and as for heaven, he wouldn't stay. Even the underworld would be preferable to all that goodness. Sholto had his own code, written in his own firm hand.

When, finally, they were released, they sank into the car and drove quickly out of the gates. 'That was OK,' said Simon happily. 'Pity you don't drive a Roller, though.'

'We'll get one soon enough,' said Sholto. 'Anything dreadful to report? You haven't set fire to the music room or anything?'

Simon shook his head. 'I can't wait to see the house. Matty sent me pictures and I put them on my bedside locker. Everyone says it looks great.'

'There's a pony in the paddock,' said Matty. 'It isn't ours, but you might get a ride. It belongs to the girl at the farm.'

'Did you get chickens? You said you would.'

'We have six,' said Sholto. 'But we weren't planning to get to know them. We're killing one each week, on Saturdays.'

'Yuk!'

He couldn't wait to see everything. When they arrived he ran straight up the stairs to his room and leaped on the bed, shouting joyously. 'I've got a cupboard! Two cupboards! And a mirror. Can I put posters on the wall Matty? With sellotape?'

Casually she said, 'It's your room. You can do what you like.'

He looked at her with delighted eyes. 'Yes. It is mine, isn't it? Thanks, Matty.'

She went hurriedly downstairs, sat in a chair before the dead fire and put her face in her hands. Sholto said, 'You're a disgrace, Matty. Soft as butter.' He rested a hand on her shoulder.

'I can't help it! He's so thrilled.'

'Yes.'

She looked up at him when he wasn't expecting it. She caught the expression on his face, bleak, and so cold she almost shuddered, while all the time his hand on her shoulder remained, comforting her. But then, Sholto never allowed his true thoughts to affect an action. It could take years to get to know him, patiently breaking the codes of endless locked doors and never knowing if this was Sholto, or that, or someone quite other. He was profligate and yet he was shrewd, loving yet cold as ice, devious and still in his fashion an honourable man. Matty was sure he slept with other women. When they first met he had been quite inexperienced, she thought, but as time went on he was acquiring tricks and techniques apparently from thin air. He was faithful when they were together, that at least she felt sure of. But who else, and how many? None of them could love him as she did.

They decked the house with great sheaves of greenery, and Matty used her silver as a means of storage. She filled up pots and urns, draped green garlands around lighted candelabra, hung teaspoons in a festoon from the Christmas tree. Simon took it all at face value, as an enormous joke, and it was fun, seeing if they could evade penury until the New Year. Matty surrendered the kitchen to Sholto without reluctance. His creations were intensely variable, sometimes inspired and sometimes insane. Charming the farmer's wife resulted in bottles of cream left at the kitchen door, and he used it liberally, until Matty complained they would all get fat and suffer from inflamed gall bladders.

'Don't be so revoltingly biological,' said Sholto, grimacing.

Matty wagged a finger. 'It's time you thought about nutrition. I never paid attention in a cookery lesson in my life, but even I know you shouldn't eat sauces containing five eggs and half a pint of cream at every meal.'

'I liked what we had yesterday,' said Simon, loyally.

Sholto beamed. 'The pheasant. Ah, yes. Who needs cream when we can do a little poaching in good red wine?' He caught Matty's eye. 'The cheapest plonk,' he added, and went to wield his corkscrew. Whatever their finances, Sholto was not about to give up drink.

Presents were a problem, though. Surrounded as they were with expensive antiques, it seemed churlish, let alone squandering, to press something from the business on each other. So Matty decided to be original. The hens they had been given were laying desultorily, unaware that their days were numbered, and she took four eggs, pierced the shells with a needle and blew them. Then she began painting, pale blue for Simon, dark royal blue for Sholto. There was nothing insipid about him. After that she cut each egg in two with a small hacksaw, hinged them with tiny strips of fabric glued to the shell, and set about making tiny mock Fabergé boxes. The jewels were plastic and the braid came from an old furniture tassel, but Matty was delighted. Lined with velvet they were delicate and strange. Then she spent as much as she dared on some Technical Lego for Simon, and lots of stocking fillers, the silly toys and games that he loved. She was so determined that Simon should be happy.

Simon insisted on having money to do his shopping, of

course. His presents were deliciously young. He went into Littlebury and bought Sholto a book on art collecting and Matty a set of electroplate spoons, and dropped hints about his brilliance ever after.

Christmas morning was wet. They were all disappointed, because the weather forecast had predicted frost, and possibly snow. But they gathered downstairs for presents, and Sholto opened a bottle of champagne. Matty felt herself bubbling just as much. This was Christmas, their first Christmas here, perhaps their only Christmas here. It should be wonderful.

She gave her eggs, received her spoons, and said, 'Simon, they're lovely. Perfect. And I know Sholto's going to find his book a great help.'

'Absolutely,' said Sholto, straightfaced. 'It tells me all the things I never thought I should need to know.' He got up, went behind the sofa and retrieved two parcels. One was enormous, one tiny. He gave the huge one to Simon. 'Here, Titch. For you.'

Simon's face was scarlet with delight. He scrabbled at the paper, printed all over with drunken Father Christmases. It was a vast, complicated, expensive set of electric cars. 'Wow! Sholto! You're the best!'

'Oh God!' Matty thought of the money, and shuddered.

'Don't you want yours?' asked Sholto. His eyes teased her. He knew she dared not utter a word. 'I've got you the most wonderful present.'

'Have you?' She looked at him fearfully. He tossed the package into her lap.

It was a small, exquisite jewel box. Inside, nestling on silk, was a heartshaped pendant. Beneath the pendant glass was a tiny miniature of a girl, not unlike Matty, with dark red hair. It was very old and very wonderful.

Matty began to cry. He knew how to twist her heart, that was all. He didn't mean what she was meant to believe. He wasn't hers, he wasn't anyone's. And she wanted him so much.

'Don't cry on your keepsake.' He squatted down in front of her. 'Have a little faith.'

'What in?'

He shrugged. 'Life. Art. Christmas. This is the best Christmas I've ever had. The only good one. Don't spoil it.'

Sholto cooked turkey while Matty wrestled with the electric cars. When her patience expired she took over in the kitchen and let Sholto lie on the carpet fitting track together and extracting fluff from the terminals. The smell of good food mingled with pine needles and burning logs, the rain hissed outside and a blackbird hopped on the window sill to shake his feathers and wish her good cheer.

Simon rushed in to fetch a knife to do something to his kit. He paused in his headlong dash and took a long, deeply happy breath. 'Oh, Matty,' he sighed, 'this is just great. Is it always going to be like this? You, me and Sholto?'

She put out her arms and hugged him, and he didn't resist. It was a day for embraces. And hadn't Sholto said she had to have faith? 'You, me and Sholto,' she repeated.

Chapter Fifteen

The post arrived early at Larkspur Cottage. Matty was making coffee and toast, setting out a tray to take up to Simon, still in bed. Sholto, muffled in an outsize grey jumper that made him look as if he had very long thin legs, scooped the envelopes from the mat.

'One for you, two for me. And one of those is from the bank. Happy days.'

She hung over his shoulder as he opened it. The letter was polite, merely mentioning that the account was overdrawn, and that it would be appreciated if this could be put right as soon as possible.

'I'll go and see them today,' said Sholto. 'Fudge the issue for a week or two.' Then he opened his other letter and his face changed. 'Forget the fudging,' he said with satisfaction. 'The American money's in. Matty, we're solvent.'

She let out her breath in an enormous explosion of relief. Sholto spread his arms wide and she fell into them, and he yelled, 'Didn't I tell you not to worry? Didn't I say it was going to be fine?'

'You did, you did, and I'm an idiot. Now we don't have to murder the hens.'

'Trust you to focus on the important things.' His lips brushed hers. His face was flushed, and suddenly young. It was a shock to realise that he hadn't been unworried at all, that he was just as relieved as she. He was not wholly irresponsible, then. He just took the most terrible risks.

Simon came blearily down, wondering what the noise was about. 'Have we won the pools?'

'Almost,' said Sholto. 'Eat some toast, have double marmalade. What are we going to do today?'

'Write to Ed McKeogh in New York,' said Matty. 'It's time I pulled my weight around here.'

Sholto spread his hands. 'Did I say that? Did you hear me speak? As if I'd object if you drank my blood every day of your beautiful life.'

'Oh, shut up,' said Matty, and kissed him.

Outside the rain was falling once again. It was a very wet year. Somehow it made the house seem cosy and safe, a refuge from storm and tempest. Simon picked up Matty's letter. 'It's an American stamp. It's from Carolina.'

'Lorne!' Matty seized the envelope and ripped it open.

Sholto said, 'Dear Matty, Surprise, surprise. I've dumped Greg Berenson and will be arriving on Tuesday.'

Matty raised horrified eyes to his. 'Not quite. She's marrying him. Like you said, it's on Tuesday.'

She rang Henrietta, but the 'phone was engaged. Henrietta was trying to ring her. Eventually they connected and Henry shrieked, 'Do you know? She can't do it! I haven't even seen the man.'

'If you saw him you'd be sure she shouldn't do it,' said Matty. 'Have you been invited?'

'Yes. Mother thinks I should go. I will if you will.'

'I don't know. Simon's on holiday. Sholto's here of course, but −'

He looked up from some papers. 'But nothing. I'm not a raging psychopath, I can be trusted to look after a boy of his age. Go on, Matty. The girl needs you.'

'What's he saying?' demanded Henrietta.

'Nothing. Everything. We'll go together. What about Grizz?'

'Which one of us is going to talk to her?'

'I'll do it,' said Matty. 'We should all go, you know. We can bring her to her senses.'

Griselda telephoned two minutes after she had finished talking to Henry. 'Pa says he'll pay for my flight. It is the vac after all. What about you, Matty, can you scrape up the bunce?'

'No scraping about it,' said Matty airily. 'Sholto and I are doing very well. Henry's going, of course. We'll go together.'

The morning passed in a flurry of activity and it wasn't until well into the afternoon that Matty had time to think. She went to look for Sholto and found him in his barn, amongst his paintings. He was cleaning something dark and unpromising, using a sable-haired brush. Where pictures were concerned Sholto had endless patience.

'I've been thinking,' said Matty, 'We'll never get her to call it off. Not the day before the wedding.'

'Stranger things have happened. She could turn tail at the altar and run. Wouldn't you, standing next to Greg Berenson?'

'Perhaps he isn't that bad. He's very good-looking. It just seemed she was throwing herself away before she'd done anything, tried anything.'

'What is there for rich girls to try? Different men, different parties, different drugs. Marriage and children in Hicksville might suit her. And he isn't unambitious, or rather his father isn't. She could end up in bed with the President.'

'But you don't think she'll be happy, do you?'

He looked up from his work. 'No. And neither do you.'

Matty sighed. 'I'll give her a teapot. And I'll stop in New York on the way back and sell the rest. I might do some buying, too.'

'Oh, aren't we getting businesslike? No stone unturned.'

'You're putting me in the shade, that's all. I didn't expect you to know what you were doing. I thought I should be the one working hard and doing everything, while you lived a dilettante existence, eating cream.' She leaned down and put her face close to his, and he exhaled suddenly, puffing in her face.

'You women are so vain.'

She wished he would stop work and talk to her; make love to her, perhaps. But he worked on, with absolute precision, and she was in the way. As she made for the door, he said, 'By the way, Simon's school is selling that painting.'

'They're not! Why?'

'Because they're greedy. Because it's run by little grey men who spend their lives with infants and don't see the virtue of keeping something you could sell.'

'Don't be bitter, Sholto. Not everyone cares about art.'

'How much better the world would be if they did.'

She steeled herself. 'You shouldn't have bought it, you know. We're knee deep in stuff, and I know you got paid but we've got your aunt's loan to think of. We're going to have to make a repayment soon.'

He sighed at her bourgeois anxieties. 'I'm not keeping the picture. I'll put it into a sale at Chester in February, and everyone will think they've found a provincial bargain. Relax, Matty.'

'All right. Clever old you.'

He was working with concentration, and she was in the way. Nonetheless she stood watching as he bent again over his work. If she dared, if he would let her, she would reach out and run her fingers over the scar on his cheek, marking every pucker, every crease, with love.

Matty made her way through the airport concourse, looking for her friends. She had come down on the shuttle from Leeds, and hopefully her suitcase with her wedding outfit would make it to the right plane. After losing her case on the way from Mexico she had no faith in luggage any more, and was wearing something that would do, at a pinch, for a wedding, if all else failed. It was a suit in pale green, with padded shoulders and nipped in waist over a flowing skirt. It made her look very curvaceous.

'Matty! Matty, over here!'

Henrietta, waving madly, but Matty barely recognised her. She was wearing a dress chosen by her mother, but in Henry's new, diminished size it no longer looked ghastly. Instead she was Alice in Wonderland, about to attend the Mad Hatter's Tea Party, ridiculously girlish.

'Henry! Darling! I hate the dress.'

Henry grimaced. 'I know. You've got to help me buy something for the wedding. I'm not turning up as an outsize Shirley Temple.'

'There's nothing outsize about you, darling. How's the vicar?'

The question was unwise. Henrietta's large blue eyes

suddenly swam with tears. 'I take it back,' said Matty hastily. 'Don't sob, you'll have elderly men offering you handkerchiefs and sweets. Oh look, there's Grizz. Grizz! Griselda!'

She was standing in the middle of the floor, turning steadily with her trolley, like some gangling waterbird inspecting the other occupants of a lake. She appeared to be growing her hair, for it stuck out from her head at a variety of unbecoming angles. Her skirt was both too short and too old, sagging in loops above her knees.

'You don't change, Grizz,' said Matty ruefully, enfolding her in a hug.

Griselda beamed at her. 'You do! You look incredibly sophisticated. As for you, Henry, you seem about to disappear. There'll be nothing left but your bows.'

'We're going to go shopping,' said Henrietta comfortably, linking her arm through Griselda's. 'You and me. We'll leave Matty reasoning with Lorne.'

'Oh, thanks,' said Matty. 'Don't you think a little joint reasoning should be in order?'

'We'll come in later,' said Griselda. 'I shall approve the marriage, of course. Lorne hates doing what I think she should.'

They all giggled. Their friendship had survived so well because of its tensions, perhaps. Acknowledged but left undissected, they gave energy and life to the quartet. They were friends and they were rivals, and they mattered to one another in many complex ways.

They checked in the luggage and went roaming around the airport shops, buying enormous scarves in case nothing could be found to clothe Henrietta and Griselda, when they would swathe themselves in fabric and make do. 'The oriental look,' said Griselda, utterly failing to achieve the correct chic draping. 'Lorne will know exactly what to do with this. In fact, she should wear it and I will have the dress. Like a bride of Christ.'

Matty gurgled with laughter. 'There's no one more un-Christian than you, Grizz. No, you get the scarf.'

The plane was half empty. The girls drank wine and exchanged news, revelling in each other's company.

'Now you can tell us about Peter,' said Matty to Henrietta. 'You must have seen him.'

Henry nodded. 'Twice,' she said in a voice full of heartbreak. 'And he was furious with me. He said I'd deceived him as much as my mother and put him in an impossible position.'

'Well, you had,' said Griselda. 'But what did he say when that was out of the way?'

'He said I should do as my mother wished and go to parties and have fun. He said he didn't need me. He said I'd probably marry a rich man and be able to sit on a committee. He said I'd probably turn out like my mother. And – and I was so angry I threw all the Mars bars on the floor. He yelled "Henrietta!" – and all the dossers got excited. Then I told him to eff off.'

'Wow!' said Matty, much impressed. 'And that's all?'

Henry shook her head. 'I went back the next day to apologise. The bishop was there. And Peter made faces at me. He was terrified I'd say something about doing the soup run, and the bishop would think he'd been seducing me. So I pretended I was a church member and had forgotten my gloves. Peter said – Peter said, "Miss Giles, you can rest assured that your gloves are safe with me." It was awful!'

'Peter, denying you thrice,' said Griselda lugubriously. 'Or twice at any rate. Oh, well. He might be right, you could meet someone wonderfully rich.'

'I already have.'

The others looked at her and she waved a hand dismissively. 'He's called Dominic, and he's kind and funny and hugely successful. Daddy knows him, he works for another broker. We go to the theatre and things.'

'Well!' said Matty. 'You are a dark horse.'

'A dark horse with a white knight,' said Griselda.

'He isn't Peter,' said Henry.

The little plastic wine bottles were empty. Matty waved at the stewardess, and she reluctantly brought some more. They were always quicker to serve the men, Matty noticed, although Griselda's imperious stare often brought results. It was odd, when the real Griselda wasn't in the least imperious.

258

'What about you, Grizz?' asked Henry, making a determined attempt to brighten.

'Oh, nothing much. Just Bertie Brantingham, and I've known him forever. He's wonderfully sweet. Found me moping in a coffee shop, making a terrible mess of everything, and he rather took me under his wing. Introduced me to people, took me to parties. Can't think why.'

'Perhaps he likes you,' said Matty.

Griselda smiled bleakly, 'Only in the sense that we're the same sort. Out of the same drawer, and all that. I'm generally considered to be clever but plain. And I dress so badly. But when I try to improve things I feel quite foolish, as if I'm aping all those shorter, prettier girls who spend so much time trying to impress Bertie. I'm sure he is impressed. He's just too nice. He shrugs them off and comes to chat to me, because I'm all alone and pathetic and he can talk about home. He's the sort of man who always chooses the runt of any litter, the one with the twisted leg.'

'Does he go out with them when you're not there, then?' asked Henry.

Griselda shrugged. 'One imagines so. But he's been so good. I think he realised that I was getting rather desperate. All work and no play. That sort of thing.'

Matty and Henrietta exchanged puzzled glances. 'Are you quite sure he's not smitten?' asked Matty.

'What? With me?' Griselda gave a hoot of derisive laughter. 'Be reasonable, Matilda.'

Matty wanted to hug her, but dared not. The gesture would be construed as sympathetic, and therefore horrible. The girls alone knew that Griselda's stiff, angular appearance hid a brave, loyal, acerbic and loving soul, but how was anyone else to know? Who else would spend years finding out?

The girls got out of the car and surveyed the Shuster home.

'Wow!' said Henrietta.

'I said it was big,' said Matty.

'Wonderfully smart,' said Griselda. 'I feel somewhat underdressed.'

Matty smoothed the creases in her skirt and went up the steps to the door. She knocked, but no one came. It was still early, not yet nine, but on the day before a wedding she would have expected much activity. She knocked again and an elderly gardener, passing with a load of hothouse plants in a barrow, said, 'Go right on in, Miss. They're in a fine mess just now.'

Matty turned the handle and went in. 'Lorne? Aunt Susan?' she called.

A maid bustled past. 'I always knew Lorne lived palatially,' said Griselda. 'It explains so much.'

At that moment Lorne came flying downstairs, her mother in hot pursuit.

'Just you come back here, young lady! I will not have you run out on me! I have things to say and I insist you listen!'

'No! No! I will not!'

'Hello, Lorne,' said Griselda.

Lorne stopped halfway down the stairs, transfixed. She put a hand up to her hair, drawn tightly back from her face to reveal sharp contours of clean bone. She looked very young and very beautiful. She was shaking.

'Girls! Thank God you're here!' She flew down the stairs to them, and Aunt Susan followed more slowly.

Lorne was in tears, hugging and kissing indiscriminately. She even clung to Griselda, which was an event unknown in history. Aunt Susan hovered on the periphery, saying, 'Matty, you have to speak to her. Griselda – Henrietta – Lorne's told me so much about you. I can't talk to her – she's more headstrong than any child I've ever known.'

Lorne cast a desperate look at her mother. 'You don't understand,' she said beseechingly.

'But, Lorne, if you won't talk to me, how can I understand?'

'We'll talk to her,' said Matty firmly. 'Come along, Lorne. We'll go to your room right now.'

But in the privacy of her room, Lorne fell silent. Her friends ranged themselves on the bed, just as they had at school, but Lorne folded her arms across her body, gripping her own narrow biceps with vicious fingers. She stood at the window, looking out across windy pasture, her face set.

'What's your mother upset about?' asked Henrietta.

Lorne shrugged. 'She thinks we should wait. We were going to get married in spring, but – '

'But what?' said Henry.

'But nothing,' said Griselda. 'You're pregnant, I take it, Lorne?'

Turning from the window, Lorne smiled. 'Trust you, Grizz. How did you know?'

'Your air of highbred tension. Besides, what else? But I can't imagine why you don't tell your mother. She must suspect.'

'She can't. She doesn't know.'

Matty said, 'I think she knows more than you want to believe. She's your mother, Lorne.'

'Perhaps I mean – I don't want her to know. I don't want it to be open between us. I want to be the sort of daughter she ought to have. I want to pretend to be that daughter.'

She flexed her back in a tense bow. She wasn't sorry she was pregnant, not really. She was escaping this house, the atmosphere that she had never before noticed. Her father went to see Berenson every week and when he came back he sat at his desk long into the night, drinking. Her mother didn't know, she was certain of that. Not all of it at any rate. Only she knew, and her father, and yet they could not speak of it. This pregnancy hastened the day of his release. If she untangled her muddled thoughts that led to muddled deeds and even more muddled conclusions, then she had meant this to happen. It committed her. It closed off her escape. It made her do what she knew she must.

'I don't understand,' said Matty doubtfully. 'How? You were the one who showed me what to do.'

Lorne said, 'I'm not so clever. I suppose anyone can get caught.'

'Is Greg pleased? He must be.'

'Greg?' Lorne looked vague. 'Yes, he's pleased. Worried about the dates. I think this baby's going to be fairly premature. It doesn't look so good to get married like this, so they're going to cram it in an incubator if they have to fold it in two.'

The girls chuckled. Griselda said, 'How far on are you?'

'Only two months. We've got to get hitched before I begin to show. And I feel so awful all the time. I'll probably throw up during the service.'

After a moment Matty said, 'There are alternatives, of course.'

With forced gaiety, Lorne said, 'Really, Matty! Greg's a good, strong, loving man and we shall be so, so happy. We'll have to live with his folks at first because the wedding's so rushed, but the house should be ready in three months or so. It's all going to be wonderfully exciting.'

'Does he love you?' asked Henrietta.

Lorne came across and hugged her. 'Of course he does, honey. Don't worry, any of you, I'm going to be fine.'

Under the influence of her friends, Lorne relaxed into her old, merry self. Aunt Susan was in a fluster, juggling caterers and interior decorators, not to mention droves of guests arriving to stay overnight. Shuster hospitality was at its best, with money no object, and welcome everything. Henrietta and Griselda were despatched to the shops after lunch, but Aunt Susan cornered Matty.

'Has she told you?' she asked urgently.

Matty's mouth opened and closed. Finally she said, 'Yes.'

'Is she quite determined? It's not that there's anything much wrong with Greg — he's a good boy, and he'll do his best for her — but Lorne's an unusual sort of girl. I want her to be quite sure that this is right. The Berensons can be difficult. We've dealt with them over years and they're not a family you mess around.'

Matty wondered what she could honestly say. Lorne wasn't going to change her mind for anyone, that much was clear, so was there any harm in putting Aunt Susan's mind at rest?

She said, 'I know she's very fond of him. And he adores her. Perhaps she needs to settle. And now — with things as they are — it could be the making of them both.'

Some of the anxiety ebbed from the older woman's face.

'I've been telling myself those same things,' she said softly. 'Thank you, Matty. Lorne and I are too close, we can't talk about hurtful things. Greg Berenson isn't a bad boy. But, when you've a daughter like Lorne, you want someone so special you can't imagine them. They probably don't exist.'

More flowers were arriving. Aunt Susan enfolded Matty in a brief hug and went to supervise their arrangement. Outside Drake Shuster was yelling, 'Well, hi there, Bick! Good to see you all,' as a man rode past the window on a bright bay horse. Matty felt a sharp stab of envy; how good it must be to be Lorne, daughter of this affluent, loving home. It was hard to imagine any real unhappiness, stepping from one sheltered existence to another. She was a fool to herself to make such a fuss about it.

The wedding was to take place in the house, under the great arches in the hall, with the couple surrounded by flowers and affectionate friends. It would be beautiful, Matty realised. A perfect wedding.

'Take it off,' said Henrietta coldly. 'It's foul.'

Griselda eyed her reflection. The dress was the wrong colour, the wrong style, the wrong length. 'It is quite a bargain,' she pleaded.

'Not if you don't like it, and you don't,' snapped Henrietta. She lifted a piece of green tubing on a hanger. 'How about something in silk?'

'I'm not buying a thing I can't wear later.'

'Then we should get you a boiler suit and be done with it,' wailed Henry. 'What about that nice wool dress? With the gathered sleeves and the braid? It is just about the only thing in this whole town we haven't tried on.'

Griselda eyed the garment haughtily. There was nothing obviously repulsive except the price tag. The assistant leaped on the dress and brought it over with unflagging enthusiasm, which had to be hiding despair.

'The dress is kind of close-fitting,' she said, hauling the zip up between Griselda's plate-like shoulderblades.

'Far too tight,' said Griselda. 'I refuse to go around in a straitjacket. Unfasten it, please.'

'It fits,' said Henry. 'Have a look, Grizz. It's the best-fitting dress you've ever had.'

Indeed, the mirror showed a tall woman, with terrible hair, in a beautiful dress. The waist arrowed down in a stomacher, outlined in black braid, and the same braided design was echoed at the neck and on the cuffs. But, incredibly, in this dress Griselda had something resembling breasts, hips, a waist. Yet for once the cuffs and hem accommodated her. For once in her life she looked half decent.

'We have a number of tall ladies around here,' explained the assistant, offering hats, gloves, a dozen extras that Griselda peremptorily waved away.

'I can't possibly afford all that! Henry, do you really think it's all right? I don't look ludicrous?'

'No! You look smashing. And when we do your hair you won't know yourself.' She turned to the assistant. 'And we'll have the hat,' she added.

Incredibly, Henrietta proved just as hard to satisfy. She wanted elegance, and it wasn't her style. She wanted lines instead of curves, linen and not lace, until Griselda roared, 'My God, Henrietta, I can see your mother's point. You're the most troublesome girl.'

The assistant said, 'Wouldn't you like to try this? I'm sure you'll find it more than appropriate.'

Henry eyed the pretty frock with distaste. It had a wide Puritan lace collar, a long skirt and a gathered waist. It wasn't a shantung suit, not by any stretch of the imagination. Yet she had to admit that it looked very well on her, very well indeed.

'But I wanted to look dignified!' she complained.

'Dear Henry,' said Griselda, 'girls with golden hair, blue eyes and curves don't ever look dignified. I content myself with dignity, not you.'

'There you go again, running yourself down,' said Henry, struggling out of the dress. 'I'll have it, thank you. Perhaps my other dresses could have lace collars. And I could get rid of the sash.'

It was a strange evening. The house was full of people the

girls didn't know, and Lorne herself wasn't in the mood to socialise. Quiet and thoughtful, she responded to every joke and question with the same preoccupied smile. After dinner the girls took her upstairs, and they sat in Lorne's room and ate sweets.

'Two down, two to go,' said Lorne, lying back on her bed. 'Who's going to be the next ex-virgin?'

'Not me,' said Henrietta. 'Not ever.'

'Not even the divine Dominic?' asked Griselda.

'Definitely not him! It's Peter or nothing. So it's nothing.'

Matty sat up and wrapped her arms around her knees. 'So you must be hoping to get things together with Peter. You can't seriously be thinking of spending the rest of your life at home. With your mother,' she added, as a pertinent afterthought.

Lorne said, 'She's being a martyr. Mayfair's answer to Joan of Arc. Don't you fancy one of my cousins, Henry? They're not as bad as they seem. If you like horses, that is.'

'Did I tell you Peter's got some other woman with him, doing the soup run?' said Henry in a strangled voice.

They stared at her. 'The man's a crook,' said Matty. 'A seducer. Just what your mother said.'

'He should be hamstrung,' added Griselda. 'By the way, how do you know?'

Henry sniffed. 'I saw him. Dominic was taking me home from the theatre and I saw the van. There was this girl — this woman — unloading pies. And that was my job! I always did the pies.'

'She could be from the WRVS,' said Matty seriously. 'Was she in a uniform?'

'How should I know? I was distraught. I went indoors and drank half a bottle of crème de menthe and now I can't look at the stuff.'

'Well, at least you educated your palate,' said Griselda. 'Was the woman in skirt or jeans?'

'Skirt,' said Henry.

The others exchanged glances. 'I don't want to encourage you, Henry, but she must have been an official,' said Matty. 'Anyone desirable would have turned up in jeans. I mean, no one would confront a load of dossers in a skirt unless it came with the job. She was probably in the Salvation Army. She'd left her trumpet in the van.'

A slow smile spread over Henrietta's face. 'Do you think so? Really?'

'You've been nobly renounced,' said Lorne. 'Are you sure you wouldn't like a cousin? We've got to do something with them. They're so troublesome!'

'He is noble,' said Henrietta dreamily. 'He gives up everything for what he thinks is right. I wonder if I can stop Mother coming to lunch with me? I could help with the lunchtime coffees. For now. And then later, when we've made up and everything – if you'll excuse me, I must have a bath.'

She wandered off, quite preoccupied. Lorne said, 'We shouldn't be doing it! Why don't we encourage her with this Dominic person?'

'I'm not sure we could,' said Griselda. 'Henry's besotted. I suppose she'll either grow out of it or into it.'

'Henry only ever lusts after the unattainable,' said Matty.

Suddenly Lorne said, 'How's Sholto?'

Uncomfortably aware of her line of thought, Matty said, 'He's fine. Looking after Simon. Mad as ever – madder, I sometimes think. Travels a lot, of course, but he's doing terribly well.' She smiled brightly, an excluding, confident smile.

There were some things you told no one, not even your very best friend. The night before she left Sholto had pushed her face down on the bed. He had coaxed her, shown her, made her lift herself up on elbows and knees. She was the beginner, he the habitué, and every move and every tremor told her something he wanted her to know. I have others, he was saying. They are better at this than you.

'You're so lucky,' said Lorne suddenly. 'You were the one we were all so worried about, and now you've got a home, a business, Sholto, everything. You had a reason to try, I suppose that's it. We all need a reason for the things we have to do.'

The weather was cold, with grey skies sometimes clearing to an unearthly, cerulean blue. The grass had lost its colour, giving the earth a brown, beaten appearance, although on close inspection the cattle wandered over thick pasture. On the day of the wedding flakes of snow drifted on the breeze, silently, but by mid-morning the sun was shining. It seemed a good omen.

The girls dressed early, to make sure they had time to help Lorne. Matty did Griselda's hair before her own, setting the wiry strands on rollers and forcing them into submission. 'You must grow your hair again,' she said, eyeing Griselda's reflection in the mirror. 'This is OK, but I much prefer your hair long.'

Griselda blew down her large nose. She hated her hair, and when it was long Matty always insisted on tying it back with a scarf, exposing the full horror of a strong-featured face, all beak and teeth. 'Long hair makes me look — equine,' she confessed.

'Maybe, but it's better to be a good-looking horse than a bad-looking poodle,' said Matty, coaxing Griselda's dreadful haircut into a neat shape beneath her ears. 'You've got a wonderful face. Not pretty, but interesting.'

Griselda wished she didn't need to hear such things. She wished she could truly not care that people looked at her and made judgments. Her happiest moments were spent at home, at Peregrines, walking the dogs in the wind, wearing gumboots and wax jacket, her hair tied up in a scarf because then it didn't matter what she looked like — people knew her and she knew them. Parties, particularly glamorous ones, meant that people dolled themselves up like advertising hoardings, offering this or that, promising the other. At parties, only the external mattered.

Matty only left when Griselda was all done. 'Very elegant,' she said, admiring her own subtle handiwork. 'When you grow your hair long you can wear it up in a bun.'

'I feel a fright,' said Griselda, flinging herself on the bed and succumbing to nerves. 'Why can't Lorne live in sin like you and save us all this?'

In her own room, Matty sat down. She had been up at six and felt quite weary suddenly. Her own dress hung on the wardrobe door. It was dark green silk. The neckline dipped over her breasts and the skirt swept her ankles, rising at the front to just below her knees. It was second hand, bought at an auction sale in a moment of madness. When she put it on, smelling the lavender in which it had spent years in storage, she felt as if it held the spirit of all the parties it had ever been to. Only happy dresses were kept, she thought. Like the sunshine, this too was an omen. Lorne would be happy.

The girls were all with Lorne when Greg arrived. They peered out of the window at him and he looked up, grinned and waved. Lorne, wearing nothing but a lace basque, waved back and he blew her a kiss.

'He's huge!' said Henrietta, opening her blue eyes.

'Enormously golden,' agreed Griselda. 'You'll be the most striking couple.'

'If I can only get ready!' wailed Lorne, stepping into her petticoat. It was many-layered and fastened around her waist with tapes. The short lace dress revealed the gleam of silk and satin beneath, and the hem of heavy diamond and pearl embroidery. But the dress would not do up. Half an inch resolutely divided both sides of the zip.

'What am I going to do?' Lorne wailed in justifiable panic.

'Lie on your front on the bed,' ordered Griselda. 'We may be able to force it.'

But no amount of struggle would do the trick. Lorne's waist had surrendered to pregnancy, and that was that.

'Is there anything in the seams?' demanded Henrietta. 'We can unpick the seams, Lorne, and sew you up again.'

'This dress cost a fortune!'

'We won't charge a percentage,' said Matty, attacking the other side seam with nail scissors. 'Get some thread will you, Grizz?'

Lorne's hands were shaking. 'Suppose my mother comes in?'

'We tell her you're getting fat! Honestly, Lorne, you're not fooling her for a minute, she's already bought a crib. Shut up and let us sew.'

The sewing mistress would have been astounded to see their concentration. In all their years at school they had between them completed two and a half cookery aprons, one disastrous blouse and a skirt that had eventually been donated to the guy on Bonfire Night. But for once they were all stitching. Downstairs they could hear the organ music begin.

'You must be done!' squeaked Lorne. 'Quick!'

'It's done.' Matty wielded her nail scissors to snip off bits of thread.

They dragged the dress over Lorne's head. It fitted. But her hair was flying everywhere and she had chipped her beautiful manicure. Henrietta did her fingers while Matty wrestled with her hair. Griselda contented herself with intoning a psalm, ' "By the waters of Babylon we sat down and wept, when we remembered thee, O Sion!" '

A knock came on the door. 'Are you ready, dear?' It was Aunt Susan. Her relief when she saw Lorne in the dress told its own tale. 'It fits,' she said breathily.

Lorne went pink. 'Yes. Only just. We had to unpick it.'

'Oh. Oh, I did wonder.'

There was an awkward silence. 'You don't have to go through with this,' said Aunt Susan. 'You do know that?'

Lorne nodded and Matty squealed, 'Keep still! I can't do it if you don't.'

Lorne met her mother's eye. 'It's going to be fine,' she said quietly. 'I'm getting married because I want to get married.'

Aunt Susan put her hands on her daughter's shoulders. 'That's all that matters, my darling. Be happy.'

Henrietta began to cry. 'Dry up and pass the veil,' said Griselda bracingly. 'Quick, or we'll all be in floods.'

The words were prophetic. When Lorne stood up, so small, still despite everything so slender, her face like marble beneath the mist of her veil, they all cried. She alone was calm.

'If you'd all go downstairs,' she said, 'it's time for Daddy to come and fetch me.'

Only her mother kissed her. Her friends felt suddenly distanced, as if she had stepped away from them, across a deep but invisible chasm. She was alone, and they could not go with her.

In the room downstairs, everyone was seated on small gilt

269

chairs. The three girls sat at the back, and people turned to look at them: Griselda, despite herself, striking, Henrietta golden and pretty, and Matty like a creature from another age, in her old-fashioned dress, with her creamy, ivory skin. The organist whispered out of the corner of his mouth, 'Is she coming? Soon?'

Matty nodded. And at last, like a tiny doll, Lorne floated downstairs on her father's arm.

As the service progressed, Matty felt a growing sense of unreality. The Shusters and the Berensons had combined to create a perfect wedding. Greg was immaculate from the top of his golden head to the tips of his highly polished shoes, and the Berenson tribe was ranged behind him, Sherwood in a dark suit and pale grey waistcoat, his wife in expensive but badly fitting purple crepe. Mrs Berenson worried Matty. She disliked the way her gaze went again and again to her husband, as if his approval must always be sought. Yet he barely looked at her. And Greg kept his eyes fixed on Lorne, like a great golden lion with his mate. Or with his dinner.

As soon as the ceremony was over, the party began. The Shuster cousins, confined until now by good behaviour and tight suits, drank champagne and practised Indian war whoops. The Berensons, a tribe of worthy citizens, gathered together in a corner, metaphorically circling the wagons.

'I told Mother she should have had it in the hotel,' said Lorne. She was looking reckless, her veil thrown back and her cheeks touched with colour. She loved Shuster parties.

'We'll go soon,' said Greg.

'No! We've done it, just like everyone wanted. Now we're going to have some fun!'

He took her hand, firmly. 'Lorne honey, you've got to take care of yourself. And it won't look good if I hang around wild parties. Next thing you know, folks will say we had an orgy at our wedding breakfast.'

'Why don't we have an orgy?' Lorne threw her head back, letting her veil swing out behind. 'We can behave well tomorrow!'

But Sherwood Berenson came across, and somehow Lorne was persuaded to go. It was strange to see him achieve what he wanted: a word to Drake, a hand on Aunt Susan's shoulder, an arm ushering Lorne in the right direction. 'Best let these children get some beauty sleep,' he said, with an understanding chuckle. 'Best they start as they mean to go on.'

'I do not like that man,' said Griselda thinly. 'He's altogether too determined to have his own way. And do you see how Lorne's father kowtows to him? All this smiling and getting him drinks. Anyone would think he was the boss around here.'

'Perhaps he is,' said Matty absently. 'You know what these small communities are like. The Shusters have the class but the Berensons have the money.'

'You don't suppose the Shusters are hard up, do you?' Griselda looked down her nose.

'What? After this lavish do? I've never known anything like a Shuster party. But probably the Berensons have more. That man looks the sort.'

Even after Matty had wandered away, Griselda toyed briefly with an idea. Something here wasn't quite right, and in her experience, things were so often not as they seemed.

The girls tried to get close enough to say goodbye. Somehow the crush of Berensons seemed to exclude them, and when they did get near they found Lorne shut away in the car, and Greg at the open door, obscuring her. 'Goodbye, Lorne,' called Matty, waving madly. 'Remember to write.'

'And telephone,' called Henrietta.

Griselda added, 'Best of luck. All love. Don't forget us.'

There was no sign that she had heard. The door closed, the car began to move, and Lorne was gone.

Chapter Sixteen

Something had changed. Matty stood outside the house, looking about her. Ah! It was the tree house. Ramshackle when she left, it was now an edifice of worrying solidity, bearing in mind the state of the tree. She went to stand underneath it. 'Simon? Are you in there?'

His face appeared, black with dirt, grinning from ear to ear. 'Hi, Matty. Did we know you were coming back today?'

'Yes! Where's Sholto?'

'Gone to a sale. He'll be back sometime.'

'But – he's left you on your own!'

Simon made a face. 'I'm big enough. Don't fuss, Matty.'

He went back inside, unmoved either by her absence or her return. She felt lonely and went in search of comfort, in a house that seemed warm and pleasantly lived-in. She made a cup of tea and leafed through her post. If only Sholto was here. She had sold her silver well and wanted him to know, and besides, he should never have left Simon on his own. Any eleven-year-old boy was a worry, but Simon was an anxiety attack. You never did know what he might do next.

Sholto returned at around six. He dropped a kiss on Matty's head, and said, 'Wotcher, Shortie. Want a drink? I could do with one.'

'Bad day?'

He poured two whiskies and took a gulp of one. 'The worst. Couldn't buy a thing. Someone always pipped me. I'm being followed.'

'Happened to Sammy all the time. You'll have to move around more, and shake him off.'

'There aren't so many good sales I can afford to miss. And it isn't always the same bloke. Very odd.'

Followers were the bane of any dealer's life. They lived off his judgment, bidding only when he did, always exceeding his top price. Sammy Chesworth had set up elaborate systems to avoid them, with surrogate bidders and secret signals, but it was less easy at country auctions.

'It was getting sent to prison,' said Matty. 'It's made you famous.'

He snorted. 'Like hell! No, I think someone's got it in for me. It's a set-up. Plants at all the big art auctions, waiting for me to bid.'

'Who do you think it is?'

He lifted his eyebrows and met her gaze. She looked away. The de Caruzons were not a family you could afford to upset with impunity, but surely they had no connections here? She said, 'They wouldn't waste their time with us, would they?'

Sholto sighed. He looked bone weary, she thought, bored and somewhat disillusioned. Yet this was the night she was home, when they should celebrate, just in being together. 'It could be Luca, he travels here a lot. Dark meetings in basements with factory owners who pretend they're not making guns. Christ, I'm so sick of all this! You struggle to get an inch up the ladder and someone big and powerful comes and stands on your fingers.'

'It's my fault,' said Matty.

He turned his blue eyes on her, dispassionately. 'Don't indulge in conceit. In Mexico we simply didn't make them any money. It was in Switzerland I actively took it off them. That's what caused the problem. It isn't down to you.'

'I still feel guilty,' said Matty. 'Shall I come to the next sale? I can bid for you. I did it for Sammy, lots of times.'

Sholto considered. 'OK. It might work for a bit, until they cotton on. You can come with me tomorrow.'

'I can't travel with you! We've got to pretend we don't know each other. And I can't leave Simon. Actually, Sholto, you shouldn't have left him today. I trusted you.'

She lifted her head, her eyes like clouds. He felt aggressive suddenly. Sooner or later women always made demands. 'You mollycoddle him,' he snapped. 'At his age I was wandering the Venetian alleys, getting propositioned by fat women. It was the days before my spots.'

'Suppose his tree house fell down? And he lay for hours in agony? I'd never forgive you.'

He gave a crack of laughter. 'Oh, how mortified I should be! Matty, he likes staying here on his own. Loves the place. You can try and drag him to this sale tomorrow but he won't thank you for it. He's got a home and he's making the most of it, and I for one won't stop him.' He took hold of her face, turning it to him with gentle force. He was tight with unexpressed anger. She felt bullied into silence.

He relaxed over dinner, and Matty showed him the wedding photographs.

'I missed you dreadfully,' she said boldly. 'All the Shusters wondered where you were.'

He changed the subject. 'Sell any silver?'

She nodded. 'Quite a bit. You know my first teapots? I sold one for nearly six thousand pounds. Much more than I thought. And I bought some things. I'll take some of them down to Sammy, I know it's what he likes.'

The atmosphere was uncomfortable, thought Matty. They weren't as close as before she went away. She felt a rising panic. Had he met someone else, had he decided he didn't want her any more? She had told him once she wouldn't cling, but she was more like Simon than she cared to admit. They both needed something constant in their lives. Sholto was her security, and without him she didn't know what she would do.

'Shall we go to bed?' she asked, licking dry lips.

He shook his head. 'I'll stay up for a bit. You go.'

Now she knew that something was wrong.

Simon complained violently about coming to the sale. He promised anything if Matty would simply leave him at home and not drag him round some dingy, draughty room where he couldn't touch anything.

'I've been to millions of sales,' he complained. 'I always hate them.'

'You could get to be an art expert. Like Sholto,' promised Matty.

275

'I hate art. I'm going to be an engineer. I'll stay home and not go near the tree house if that's what bothers you.'

'Suppose the house caught fire?'

He looked at her with surprise. Didn't she know he was quite invulnerable? Such things happened only on television, to people he didn't know. 'It won't. You're getting an awful scaredy-cat, Matty.'

So she left him. She and Sholto travelled together to within ten miles of the sale and then she caught a train. By the time she arrived Sholto had been there half an hour, and he left a twist of paper with his bidding instructions under the corner of Lot 23. Matty read them sitting in the loo.

But when she looked around the saleroom it all seemed foolish. There was a scattering of dealers, most of whom Sholto seemed to be on nodding terms with, and the rest were women interested in things which would look well at home. Sholto was after two huge canvases, and should get them cheap, because they were far beyond the scope of the normal householder. He would export them to Italy, or even Spain, where the taste for such things remained. They were by Dutch artists with a penchant for the macabre. There weren't many professionals would know what to do with such things.

To put any observers off the scent Matty bid for two or three small still lifes, allowing herself to be beaten a couple of bids before the last. Then, when Sholto's paintings came up, she waded in with enthusiasm, prepared to let it be seen that she would get them at any price. Every time Sholto bid she capped it, until finally he shook his head and dropped out, showing evident irritation. Grinning triumphantly, Matty waited for the hammer to fall.

'Two thousand four – do I hear five? No? Yes, five, at the back of the hall. It's against you, madam.'

She dropped out at three thousand, responding to a quizzical nod from Sholto. Her opponent, a thin woman in a mac, took that painting and the next. Matty and Sholto had nothing.

They caught up with her in the car park. She was hurrying to a battered van, not bothering to collect her paintings.

Sholto said, 'Excuse me. I wonder if we could talk?'

She looked nervous. She was poorly dressed, Matty noticed, she didn't look worth a bean. And yet she had just spent nearly six thousand pounds on paintings. 'I'm in an awful hurry,' she said, trying to unlock the van.

'Yes. I wonder if you could just tell me who put you up to bid?' Sholto came close to her and grinned. The woman flinched. He said, 'Don't worry, I'm not going to hurt you. But it's been happening a lot lately and I know I've never seen you before. Someone told you to do it, didn't they?'

She looked from Matty to Sholto and back again. 'He gave me five hundred pounds in cash,' she said. 'I deal in bric-a-brac mainly – he asked me at a sale here last week. Cash down, no name. And he came up to me again today and said you were together, even if you didn't look it, and I was to bid against either of you, as soon as it looked as if you were going to buy.'

'Did he give you a limit?'

She shook her head. 'I just went on until I won. That's what he said.' She licked her lips anxiously and added, 'Look, I'm sorry. But if I hadn't done it someone else would. You can't do anything if someone really has it in for you. And he must have. It's costing a packet. Some people I know have done it at other sales.'

Walking back to the car, Matty said, 'Who do you think it is?'

Sholto's face was stiff. 'Luca.'

'Why him?'

Sholto muttered something about the picture, and Matty lost her patience. She flared, 'For God's sake, Sholto! I think at least you could tell me the truth. No one gets that upset about a picture, and the de Caruzons can afford a thousand like that! What did you do? Get into bed with Eleanor?'

Her face was white as paper. A strand of hair had blown into her mouth and he reached across and removed it. 'Yes,' he said.

He thought she would hit him but nothing happened. Instead she went paler, if that were possible. She turned away from him, went to the car, tugged on the handle as if she couldn't wait another minute to be inside. He went and unlocked the door and she fell into the car, arms folded tightly over her breast.

He got in next to her and they sat quite still. 'I said there was no commitment,' he said finally. 'I never promised you a thing.'

'Yes, I know. Be quiet about it, will you?'

She sat utterly silent as he drove. Her eyes were wide, dry and unblinking.

Finally, as they neared home, he said, 'I'd better go away for a bit. Let things calm down.'

'If you mean me, I'm quite calm.'

He almost laughed. 'Like Vesuvius, an hour before the eruption.'

Matty swallowed on tears. 'Don't worry,' she said tightly, 'I'm not going to make a fuss. We are both of us free agents. Free as air.'

'Would you prefer me to have lied?'

She closed her eyes, because they had suddenly flooded. 'No. I knew anyway. I've known for months.'

'I haven't known her for months! Christ, it was only the once, in the summerhouse, a quick bang next to a load of ski poles and a rotting sleigh.'

'Don't pretend, Sholto. I know there are others.'

He glanced at her. After a moment he said, 'I'm not spending an hour in confession. I told you the first time, we do what we do together and what went before, what comes after, that means nothing. We're both free agents, it's a two-way thing. To hell with your weeping and wailing!'

'I am not weeping and wailing! To hell with you!'

She struck out at him and the car swerved violently. He grabbed her wrist and held it and she bent her head and sank her teeth into his hand. But he still held on, even though she bit until she tasted blood. When she stopped saliva and blood ran down her chin. He pulled the car to the side, one-handed, and then released her.

'Feeling better?'

'Sod.'

'You want to split? I don't, I really don't, but if you can't handle this we'd better.'

She couldn't bear it. She couldn't live if he wasn't there. 'I – don't want to split.'

'Right.' He wrapped his handkerchief around the wound in his hand.

She knew it hurt him and she was deeply glad. 'If you had any guts you'd outwit him,' she said tightly.

'But you know how gutless I am! Constant weaknesses and evasions.'

'Shut up!' she shrieked at him, and then her voice fell back to an odd, dull pitch. 'If you want to beat someone at auction then you can. All it takes is a bit of planning. You bid against yourself. You enlist the auctioneer in fake telephone bids, have him standing there with a phone with no one on the end. You bid in the hall, and when you drop out he goes on with the telephone. You have a sign, scratching your head or something. But if it goes too high on the telephone, then you pull your ear and he knows that this time you are dropping out.'

'You do know your stuff,' said Sholto. 'Sammy never taught you this.'

She looked at him coldly. 'My father taught me. He knew a lot about rigging auctions, one way and another. When we get tired of that we hire people. Two people, if you really want something. You can run them up against each other, which is a bore if you think you might get something a bit cheap. Even if it's spotted that one of them is bidding for you, they don't usually expect to have two. It can all be stage managed.'

Sholto grunted. Blood was seeping through his handkerchief, and he lifted his bound, bloody fist and wiped the mess from Matty's lips. 'I never meant you to know,' he said softly. 'Believe me, I don't do it to hurt you. What we have is different. Special.'

'I think about it,' she whispered. 'When we're in bed, when you're doing it to me, I know you think about them! I can tell!'

'No you can't. I don't care about them, Matty. Eleanor just wants amusement, she's restless as hell now she's off the drugs. All she wants is a cock, she doesn't care who's on the end of it – gardener, family friend – she doesn't give a damn.'

279

'Then why does Luca have it in for you and not them?'

His eyes seemed almost glassy. 'I couldn't say. But what we do in that bed of ours belongs to us, no one else, and what Eleanor thinks about me or I think about her has no meaning there. Believe me, Matty. If we have any future at all, you'd better believe me.'

'She loves you,' said Matty thickly.

'Does she? I doubt it. She's absorbed in herself, and I don't love her. There is no one I care about more than you.'

He said it in a voice as hard as metal, but her heart leaped suddenly. It swelled in her chest like a balloon of joy. The other women could do what they liked, he didn't care for them; he cared for no one more than her. If he had dozens of women in summerhouses full of ski poles it didn't matter, she couldn't let it matter. He said he cared only for her. Suddenly she seemed to hear Griselda's sardonic voice. 'Weasel words, Matty. Weasel words. Beware!' But what use was it listening to Griselda? In matters of love, Griselda knew nothing at all.

There was a photograph of Luca and Eleanor in the Sunday paper. He was listed as one of the world's richest men, and gazed out at them, nervous, cautious, the old Don's mean-spirited heir. Matty looked instead at Eleanor, not so thin as she remembered, beautiful in Yves St Laurent. She took the picture to Sholto. 'Doesn't she look nice? Tell me, was she any good?'

He leaned back in his chair and surveyed her, making her ashamed at even asking such a question. But she had asked it.

'An OK fuck,' he said shortly. 'On a scale of one to ten, she was a six. No extras, you see. Basic stuff. Surprising, when you think of the practice she gets.'

She went red and turned away. She would die before she asked him if he rated her as a six, or even less, in her boring, ignorant way.

He got up and followed her. 'Now are you happy? No, you're not! Matty, will you stop torturing yourself!'

She began to cry. 'You didn't have to tell me!'

'You didn't have to ask!'

Simon was going back to school that afternoon. Matty put on a front, making a special effort with lunch, laying the table with an arrangement of winter roses. They had a roast with crisp potatoes and carrots cooked with orange juice and pepper. She made bread and butter pudding, as her mother had done when she was young, when they made a point of eating Sunday lunch in style.

Simon said, 'You won't move anything in my room, will you?'

'No. It's a mess though. You'll have to tidy up.'

'Matty said when we moved in that she wouldn't do housework,' said Sholto in a brisk, housemaidish voice. 'We can't expect her to clean up after us, can we?'

Matty blushed. All right, she did fuss about the house more than anyone and now, with her life in turmoil, her only security was in orderliness. She seemed to have a lower discomfort threshold than the men. She could not endure rooms thick with dust or clutter, while they seemed barely to notice it. When the house was in order, so she felt was her mind, and she could concentrate. When it was in turmoil the chaos threatened her, like an advancing army of savages. Sometimes she felt as if civilisation itself, her very sanity, depended on clean floors, and though the others had their tasks she could seldom wait for them to judge that they needed doing. She did them herself.

In an ostentatious gesture of independence, she left Sholto and Simon to wash up. She could hear their chatter, Simon shrill and enthusiastic, Sholto lazy. He was very relaxed with Simon, she thought. More than with her. They might never be easy together again. She got up and went into the kitchen, saying, 'It's time we went. We don't want to get there in the dark.'

'You can stay for tea,' said Simon. 'If you want. You'd like that, Sholto.'

It was an honour. Always before Simon had leaped from the car, barely waiting for his luggage to be unloaded, and would have died rather than have them stay for tea. But Sholto said, 'Actually I think I'll let Matty take you. I've some work to do.'

Simon's face fell. 'But I thought – do come, Sholto!

Matty won't want to drive back all by herself. She might crash or anything.'

'Of course she won't!'

Matty said, 'He doesn't need to come if he doesn't want to, Simon. Sholto's got his own things to do, you know.'

Simon looked from one to the other. 'Aren't you getting on then? Is that it?'

Sholto drew in his breath. 'We're getting on fine. Look, if it means that much I'll come, even though I'd rather spend the afternoon in front of the fire. I'll come and eat poisoned egg sandwiches if that's what you want.'

'Right. Smashing. Thanks, Sholto.' Simon ran off to get his things.

It was a difficult afternoon. The headmaster joined them at tea and made arty conversation with Sholto, although he didn't know a thing. Besides, he kept referring to Matty as Mrs Feversham, and it never seemed possible to correct him. She found herself hiding her hands under the table to conceal the absence of a ring.

Afterwards, driving home, Sholto said, 'Simon was thrilled, anyway.'

Matty stirred herself. 'I don't know when I've seen him so happy. It makes me realise how miserable he was before.'

'Are you miserable, Matty?'

She didn't look at him. She couldn't. 'I don't know,' she said at last.

A silence developed. At length Sholto said, 'I will go abroad, you know. I've got the picture from the school in the Chester sale, but after that I'm going.'

'Because of me?' asked Matty, and her chest hurt with the effort of suppressing tears.

'No. Because of me.'

What did he mean? Night gathered beyond the windows of the car, turning ordinary houses into menacing heaps of shadow. Without Sholto the world was full of menace. It would creep up, inch by inch, and engulf her. How could she manage on her own? Secretly, not wishing him to see, she put her hand up to her mouth, hoping to gnaw on her fist and suppress the tears. He said, 'Don't, Matty. You don't understand.'

He turned the radio on and bright pop music blared out. Now they couldn't talk, and Matty let her mind cartwheel away from here, into dreams and impossibilities. Sholto loving her, Sholto wanting her, not wanting to go. Was he leaving forever?

They turned into the lane. All the lights were on in the house. For a moment Matty didn't understand. She wondered if visitors had come, perhaps. Then Sholto said, 'Christ!' and gunned the engine, screaming to a halt across the drive. The front door was wide open and rugs, broken glasses, even the odd piece of silver, lay strewn across the path.

She stood staring down at it, and now her tears were of rage, burning lumps of hot metal coursing in furrows down her cheeks. 'How could they?' she said, and it was a snarl of fury. 'How could anyone? I'll kill them!'

Sholto said, 'They're gone. It was the van we passed in the lane.'

'Let's call the police. Let's get after them!'

'Let's look at the damage first.'

They walked through the house, their feet crunching on shards of pottery and glass, picking up torn books and dented silver from the wreckage of chairs covered in syrup and sauce. A picture was slashed and the canvas hung in tatters, and a clock lay in a useless tangle of springs in the hearth. While Matty stood, nursing a silver flower vase beaten out of shape, Sholto went quickly from room to room. Finally he went upstairs.

'It's OK,' he called out, his voice light with relief. 'They didn't touch up here.'

He came down again and met Matty's stricken eyes. 'At least they didn't touch Simon's room,' he said. 'He wouldn't have got over that.'

She pointed to the hall. 'They smashed his cars. They opened the box, took everything out and smashed it. Luca hates us, Sholto. This man hates us all.'

'We don't know it was him.'

She grimaced. 'Of course we do.'

He went to check on the barns. While he was gone Matty began wearily to pick up the debris of what had once been her treasured possessions. Few of them were valuable, all had been selected with happiness and hope. And why had she brought silver into the house? The barn was the place for it, securely locked behind a burglar alarm. When Sholto came back she looked up at once.

'All shipshape and Bristol fashion,' he said.

'Do we call the police?'

He shrugged. 'They can't put it back together for us and we've enemies enough. I think we'd best keep quiet.'

'It's playing into the man's hands! I haven't done anything, he's no right to smash my home! I wish he was here. I'd tear him limb from limb!'

Sholto laughed. 'Don't be so bloody vindictive. It's only things.'

She didn't understand him. She stood and watched him bundle up the rug, shaking it in the garden, sending a shower of broken crockery everywhere. Then he got a sack and began tossing torn books into it, careless of what they were or how badly damaged.

Matty said, 'It isn't the things I care about. I just loved the way it was. I was safe here. We had a home, the three of us, here, with everything. Now everything's broken. And now you're going away.'

His hand raked through his hair in a familiar gesture of controlled fury. 'I was going anyway. Don't make a big thing of this, Matty, please. I give you all I possibly can and I don't need you trying so hard to make me feel guilty. I can't be responsible for your happiness. I told you at the start, I promised nothing. You can build your little nest, you can line it with pretty things, but you can't make me stay in it. And I never promised that I would.'

Matty sank on to the stairs again. She wasn't crying now. 'I know,' she said simply. 'And I haven't asked you to stay. If you feel guilty, that isn't my fault. I can't stop you feeling bad about me, although I can see that's what you want.'

'You should make some friends. Go out without me, have fun. I won't mind.'

'Won't you?' In the dim light her eyes shone like pale candles. 'Perhaps I'll do just that. Perhaps I'll find someone else to go to bed with so I can make you really happy.'

'I don't hate you, Matty!'

'No. I imagine you'd be happier if you did.'

After hours of tidying the house looked bare and scrubbed. The scent of polish and pot pourri had been lost to the stink of bleach and the piles of wreckage lay stacked by the kitchen door. It was late, almost three in the morning, and Matty's head was throbbing. Sholto put his hand through a slashed picture and said ruefully, 'Thank God this wasn't important. Madness, keeping good pictures at home.'

Matty didn't bother to reply. She trudged past him, going wearily up the stairs, past conversation, anger, everything. Crawling into bed she lay quite still, while her headache beat at her with every pulse of her heart. After a while Sholto brought her a mug of cocoa. He sat with her while she drank it.

'I'll get the alarm system extended to the house. We should have done it before, really.'

'You needn't bother. I won't love the house again,' said Matty.

'Are you so fickle then? To take your love away after the littlest bruise?'

'But you said it yourself and you were right. There isn't anything to trust in, anything settled. So it's best not to trust at all.'

He looked at her, huddled against pillows in the shadows of the bed curtains. Her face was white, with purple thumbprints beneath her eyes. She was drained of everything, worn out to the point of surrender. He felt a sudden apprehension. He didn't want Matty hard, armoured with cynicism. 'You can't mean that.'

She looked at him from beneath her lids. 'I wish I did,' she murmured. 'But you're right, I don't.' She turned on her elbow and nestled down to sleep. 'Goodnight, Sholto.'

In the morning she finished the cleaning with aggressive, raw energy. Sholto helped, making her laugh, playing games with torn pictures. He put his head through and said he was auditioning to be the picture of Dorian Gray, and Matty threw a cushion at him and said he was a warning to everyone. He was clearly a living testament to a life of shame.

'No shame about it,' said Sholto. 'Where's the point in sinning if you agonise afterwards?'

'Where indeed?' said Matty, and turned away.

They went together to the Chester sale, which was unexpected. She hadn't thought that he would invite her to come. So she dressed at her most elegant, in her green suit with a cream blouse, held at the neck with an antique stockpin. When Sholto saw her he blinked. 'Er — you look most toothsome. I can never resist your clean and virtuous look.'

She looked at him under her lashes. 'I thought we didn't do that sort of thing any more.'

'That was foolish of you.' He took hold of her lapels and brought her close, touching her lips lightly and coolly with his own. 'Later,' he murmured. 'After the sale. I shall unwrap you like a present.'

Perhaps after all the burglary, or whatever it was, had been a good thing. They were close again, or at least the gulf between them was no longer miles wide. She could think of him touching her and welcome the thought. He loved her best. He had almost said so. In the car they shared cheese sandwiches and Sholto grumbled about Matty's plebeian tastes. 'Take you to heaven and you'd put pickle on the ambrosia.'

The sale was large and well attended. Chester was always a centre of trade, attracting tourists to its ancient charms and dealers on their way to the less ancient attractions of Liverpool. On the way in Matty spotted a shop selling silver and relieved them of an odd set of forks that they were glad to see the back of. One day she would match them, if she kept on buying long enough. Her collection of odds and ends was growing, bought for a song.

Sholto said, 'Makes a change to be selling something. We should get a smart price today.'

'Why do you want to watch it though?' asked Matty.

He shrugged. 'Just to make sure. You never know. Oh, bloody hell!' She followed his eyes. Walking into the room, inconspicuous in a brown coat and soft felt hat, was Luca.

'He's set up a ring,' said Sholto urgently. 'He's going to screw up my sale. I'm taking my picture out.'

'You can't!' Matty grabbed his arm. 'Just stick on a hefty reserve.'

Sholto looked at her. Then he grinned. 'You're right. Let's see what happens. Let's see how clever he really is.'

'I'm going to bid it up,' said Matty decisively. 'I shall sit right where Mr Luca de Caruzon can see me.'

She removed herself to a gangway seat in the centre of the room. The sale began, running through a few low-priced lots quite briskly. Matty threw in a bid now and then, to see what would happen, and sure enough a man in a raincoat always topped her. An idea formed in her head. Had de Caruzon considered that she might bid for Sholto's picture? The possibility might have escaped him. She hoped so.

The lot was near the end of the sale, and after two hours people were becoming weary. Finally it came up. 'Lot two hundred and fifty,' intoned the auctioneer. 'A fine painting by a noted provincial artist, in excellent condition. May I have three thousand pounds?'

He could not. No one made a bid. Every single dealer was sitting on his hands. Out of the corner of her eye Matty saw Sholto lift his finger, and the auctioneer took the bid without a blink. 'And five?' Matty nodded. 'Four thousand?' Sholto. 'And five?' Matty.

They took it to seven and a half thousand, the new reserve. It was on the high side perhaps, but it gave Sholto a turn of fifteen hundred pounds. 'Seven and a half thousand pounds,' said the auctioneer, fixing Matty with a stare, 'in the centre of the room.'

And to Matty's delight, the man in the raincoat nodded. 'Eight thousand,' declared the auctioneer. 'Sold.'

She waited in the foyer for Sholto to emerge from the office. When he came out he glared at her in mock severity. 'You bad girl. You ought to be locked up.'

'Did the auctioneer know I was running up?' she asked in a low voice. He shook his head. 'Don't think so. Didn't know me either, thank God. Gave me a very funny look just now, mind you. We'll have to behave.'

She giggled. 'That's going to be hard. When everyone else is being so devious.'

At that moment the auction room door opened and Luca

came out. Matty's head came up. Sholto caught her arm but she wriggled free and stalked across the parquet, holding out her hand. 'How do you do, Mr de Caruzon,' she said in clear tones. 'I'm sure you must remember me? We met in Mexico, a lovely family party.'

He took her hand in a limp clasp and said, 'How do you do.'

'The gentleman in the raincoat,' went on Matty. 'He is a friend of yours, isn't he?'

'I'm sorry — I'm not sure I understand you.'

'Yes you do. We really did appreciate the mess you made of our house. In fact we appreciated it so much that if it happens again I think we shall probably return the compliment. With knobs on.'

The man looked from her to Sholto and back again. 'I have no quarrel with you, Miss Winterton. As yet.'

'You broke up my home!'

'Please don't accuse me of things you cannot prove.'

Sholto put his hand on Matty's shoulder. 'Leave it,' he murmured.

'Miss Winterton, are you aware that this man is a philanderer?' said Luca, almost trembling with suppressed rage. 'Deceiving women is his forte, the thing he does best. He enjoys hurting women. He enjoys destroying them!'

'Think that if you must,' said Sholto. 'But it would be better for you if you learned how to please your wife in bed.'

The smaller man seemed to tremble. Spittle seeped from the corner of his mouth. Suddenly Matty was sorry for him, because he loved Eleanor, despite everything.

She turned away, saying, 'Sholto, don't. Let's leave it, let's go.'

'I want to kill you,' muttered Luca.

'Then do it,' said Sholto. 'Do it, if that's what you want.'

Matty looked up into his face. He was smiling, taunting the man, and suddenly she realised he meant what he said. He wouldn't care if the man tried to kill him. To Sholto it would hardly matter.

Luca turned his back. For a moment he seemed to possess dignity, walking briskly from the building when Matty knew he had been an inch from tears. 'That poor man,' she murmured.

Sholto glanced at her. 'Save your sympathy. He's got no guts. Can't even bring himself to get out a gun and shoot me.'

He was almost regretful. As if life was a party which he suddenly wished to leave, missing out on the food, the laughter, the friends; he wanted to go, revolted by the crowds and the silliness; he knew only too well that it meant nothing, that in the dawn light there would be nothing important to remember. Suddenly Matty was afraid.

Chapter Seventeen

Sholto packed and left that night. Matty sat on the bed and watched him throwing clothes into a suitcase. This morning they had talked of making love, and now they shared nothing but silence. Night after night they had slept in this bed without touching. She wished she had reached out to him. Now it was far too late.

He said he was going to see clients on the Continent, but she made no pretence of believing him. He was leaving her, she thought, he might never come back. She offered love that he did not want, devotion he did not need. He said, 'I'll be a month, perhaps. It's better. He won't bother you if I'm away.'

She nodded, sunk in misery, and he lifted her chin and kissed her on the lips. For an instant she almost hated him, hated the easy way he enthralled her, as he enthralled all women, hundreds of them, whichever he chose. Easy promises, easy gestures. What fools women were.

The house was utterly silent without him. Matty prowled its rooms for a day or two, feeling restless, wondering if she would ever recover that old, warm thankfulness the place had given her. The house had been a symbol, a tangible representation of what she wanted from life, what she thought she might already have. She had been in danger of cherishing it beyond its worth, she realised.

Anger sustained her, against Sholto and herself. One morning she got up determined to tackle the world. It was time she visited London. She had some pieces she knew would appeal to Sammy, and she needed to go to sales and test her judgment against people who had forgotten far more than she might ever know. If Sholto had gone for good then she must work and make money, she must use her God-given wits.

Henrietta met her at the station. She was wearing tight black leggings and little black high heels, plus a battered leather jacket. She looked like an aspiring Hell's Angel, thought Matty, one still with some lingering scruples so not yet qualified for a motorbike and an axe.

'Darling!' Henrietta teetered down the platform towards her. 'You look so – expensive.'

Matty scanned her own restrained elegance. 'This is Sholto's choice,' she admitted. 'Neat and proper.'

'My mother will be delighted,' said Henry, in doomladen tones. 'You're just what she wants for me.'

In the cab, Matty said, 'Do you go out with Dominic looking like that?'

Henry nodded. 'I thought it might put him off, but no such luck. He doesn't mind how much people stare. He thinks it's just my adorably larky personality.'

'He sounds nice.'

Henry sighed gustily. 'He is. Utterly sweet. That's why I can't chuck him.'

They contemplated the sad state of affairs in silence. Matty rested her feet on her cardboard box, full of the silver she hoped to sell. She was determined not to think of Sholto, and yet somehow he constantly nudged at the edges of her mind. What was he doing now? He had given her an address, something Italian and unlikely, and she imagined him in a marble palazzo, drinking white wine.

Suddenly Henrietta turned and said, 'I'm going to go and see Peter. I've quite decided. Will you come?'

Matty blinked. 'Now? I've got a ton of silver to worry about.'

'It won't get stolen in a church. Come on, Matty.'

She leaned forward and rapped on the glass panel, and the taxi driver muttered under his breath and did a U turn. Henrietta's soft face was set in lines of rigid determination. Matty said, 'Suppose the bishop's there?'

'I don't care,' said Henry. 'This time I'm going to be brave.'

The church was dismal at the end of winter, with spring nothing but a few sprouting weeds between the paving slabs.

The tea and coffee sign was peeling, and when Henry tried the door it stuck because of damp. Matty lurched after her, burdened with a suitcase and her box. As the door at last gave way she was aware of the smell of paraffin, and air smoky with fumes.

Henrietta's heels rattled down the steps and across the floor. The dossers, mostly old men with beards, lifted their heads from their cups and stared at her as if she were an apparition, blonde hair, wriggling curves and all. The Reverend Peter Venables was filling the tea urn.

Henrietta said, 'Hello, Peter.'

He turned and went red. 'Henry,' he said finally. 'Goodness me.'

She perched one cheek of her bottom on the table and said brightly, 'Do say if you want me to leave. If the bishop's here or anything.'

He had the grace to look discomfited. 'Yes. I'm sorry about that.'

'Can't have you mucking about with the parishioners, can we?' said Henrietta nastily. 'Not that I am a parishioner. All I ever did was help you out!' Her small face puckered into anger.

He leaned towards her and hissed, 'We can't talk about this here.'

'Where else are we supposed to talk about it?'

Matty staggered to the table and dumped her box. 'I'm sorry,' she said breathlessly. 'I couldn't lurk in the background any longer. How do you do, Mr Venables. I don't suppose you remember but we met before.'

'I'm afraid I don't recall –' said Peter, bestowing a worried smile on her.

Henrietta said, 'You always were self-absorbed. I thought I might come back and help, actually. Not on the soup run, my mother would have a fit, but there must be something else. And if it's in daylight, so much the better.'

'Henry's a great philanthropist,' said Matty.

'What?' said Henrietta.

Peter Venables laughed. Henry said, 'I'm glad you're amused. I didn't think much of the way you behaved in front of my mother, actually.'

'I didn't think much of being lied to,' he exclaimed. 'I thought you were an ordinary girl. But you live in a mansion!'

'It's hardly my fault. We can't choose our parents. I mean, if they had the choice, who would choose my mother?'

'Me,' said Matty. 'I love being helpless. At least, I love it sometimes.'

'Precisely,' said Henrietta. 'You can't turn my mother off.'

One of the dossers came up and began poking in Matty's box. He unearthed a silver teapot and waved it at Peter. 'Make a brew in this, then, Guv?'

Matty tried to grab it from him but he held it above her head. She swore and kicked him in the ankle, retrieving her pot as he yelped.

'For God's sake!' said Peter. 'Henry, we can't talk here. We'll have to go for a drink. I'll pick you up at eight.'

'Really?' Her face lit up. 'Super! I mean – yes. Right.'

Outside on the pavement Matty said hysterically, 'Those horrible people – I know they're going to mug me for the silver. Why do you bring me to these places?'

'Don't be silly, they're harmless! What am I going to say to Mother? She thinks I'm going to a party. I'll have to be glamorous.'

'Be glamorous. Amaze the vicar. And get me out of here before I lose more than my cool!'

The Giles residence was, as always, a haven of calm. Henry's mother showed distinct interest in the silver, and insisted Matty unpack everything for her to see. 'It's very pretty,' she said, fingering a Georgian coffee pot. 'How much is this?'

'To you, four thousand pounds,' said Matty.

'Even to me?' Mrs Giles looked affronted.

'It would be nearly five to anyone else.'

'An extravagance at half that. I do hope you're not becoming mercenary, Matilda.'

Matty felt guilty. Four thousand was what she had paid

for the pot, and was she really supposed to take a loss? But Mrs Giles had been very kind. Her father had always said that friends expected bargains, and if you obliged you went bust and if you didn't you were lonely. Humbly, Matty rummaged in her box. She found a single potato ring, prettily chased with running greyhounds. 'Would you like this, Mrs Giles?' she said nervously. 'As a present, I mean. It's quite good.'

'A present, Matilda? Good heavens.' The older woman sat the ring on her hand and admired it. She smiled. 'How very kind.'

Because she was pleased with Matty, Mrs Giles insisted that she accompany Henrietta to the party. It was a grand affair, engraved invitations and carriages at two, but Mrs Giles was well known to the hostess. She telephoned and made arrangements, promising that the two girls would arrive just after eight. 'You can't stay in while Henrietta has fun,' she said to Matty. 'You do know about Dominic, I take it? A charming boy. I'm sure he must have lots of friends who'd like to meet you. Now that you're on your own once again.'

'Sholto and I are still business partners,' said Matty sharply. 'He's just travelling. On business.'

'Indeed.'

The two girls conferred in the privacy of Henrietta's room. 'You could have said you were ill,' fumed Henry. 'Now what am I going to do?'

'Go out with Peter,' said Matty. 'I'll go to the party. I can say you felt faint on the way.'

'I do feel faint. I feel terrible. Be nice to Dom for me. He'll wonder where I am.'

'I'll tell him you've got religion,' said Matty.

The evening proved more difficult than expected. Matty wore a dress of tight ruched crepe, in midnight blue, ending just above the knee. Mrs Giles thought it improper. 'Perhaps you've put on weight since you bought it, Matilda,' she said. 'It's very revealing.'

'It's great,' said Henrietta, staunchly. 'I should have a dress like that.'

'I think not,' said Mrs Giles, fixing her daughter with a firm stare.

Henry blushed angrily, snub-nosed and juvenile in ballerina-length pink satin, nipped at the waist and with a wide, stiff collar. As she and Matty waited for their cab she hissed, 'What's Peter going to think, taking me to the Coach and Horses in this rig?'

'If it's too much for him you can always come to the party,' said Matty. 'I shall keep Dominic warm for you.'

Henry gave her a quizzical look. 'You don't fool me, Matilda. Underneath that inadequate dress beats a battered heart.'

'Nonsense,' said Matty. 'I'm fine.'

When the taxi came they both got in, waving energetically to Mrs Giles. As soon as it rounded the corner Henry stopped it and jumped out. 'Blimey,' said the driver. 'Shortest ride in history.'

'I know he's going to be late,' wailed Henry. 'I shall freeze to death.'

'You've got more on than your friend, luv,' said the driver.

Matty snapped, 'Who asked you? Have fun, Henry. 'Bye.'

She turned in the seat as they drove away. Henry stood shivering on the corner, in high heels and gloves, clutching a small velvet bag. Matty was also wearing gloves, but hers were in dark blue lace and stopped at her wrists. What on Henry seemed quaint, slightly dated chic, on Matty became daring sophistication.

But it was strange going to a party with no one at all that she knew. It was a large white house, set back behind iron railings and a gravelled drive, gleaming with opulence. Her heart quailed as she paid the taxi off and ascended the steps. Suddenly she wished this was business, or that Sholto was here, because no one ever made him unwelcome. He was all insouciant charm; and you had to know him very well indeed to discover that his charm completely disguised him. There were some things that Matty herself was only beginning to suspect.

The butler opened the door. Matty pretended poise and inner calm.

'Matilda Winterton – Mrs Giles telephoned – Miss Giles was taken ill and couldn't come.'

It all sounded suspicious. When she repeated the tale to her hostess there was a surprised lift of the eyebrows. Clearly, if Henrietta was ill, her friend's duty was at her bedside, not at a party. But Matty was introduced to one or two people, and given a drink, some kind of punch. All the men were in bow ties and the girls in fabulous dresses. The man next to her asked what she did and she said, 'I'm a silver dealer. Antique silver,' whereupon he seemed quite taken aback.

'You're not called Dominic, are you?' she asked, and he shook his head.

'No. He's the one over there. Red-haired chap.'

She could see him now, freckled, watching the door. He had a kind face, she decided. Good-looking, in a boyish, conventional way. When she went across to him and said 'Hello' he looked over his shoulder to see if she was talking to somebody else.

'I'm Henry's friend,' she explained. 'She isn't very well, and couldn't come. She asked me to tell you.'

'Good Lord, poor Henry! It's not serious, is it?'

'Yes! I mean – no, of course not. She's not seriously ill at all. A slight – stomach upset.' She had been going to say cold, but people visited colds. No one ever went to visit a bad case of vomiting.

'We had prawn vol-au-vents the other night. I bet it was that.'

'Yes. Probably.'

He looked at her uncomfortably, taking in the dress, her curves, her considerable cleavage. Matty wondered if the dress really was too tight. He seemed to be finding the room particularly warm. She smiled encouragingly, and he said, 'I didn't think Henry would have friends like you.'

'What about me?'

'I don't know. I mean – you're very sophisticated, aren't you?'

'Me?' She almost laughed. Sophistication was what she practised, but she never expected to convince anyone that it was something she truly possessed. An air of poise and

297

cool detachment was her constant ambition. 'Do you think Henry's sophisticated?' she asked.

'Good Lord, no. She's a very jolly girl. Takes after her mother.'

Matty took a gulp of her punch. Was it possible that twenty years would see Henry turn into her mother? Was it to be considered that Mrs Giles had dressed in bomber jackets in her youth? Perhaps Dominic really wanted to marry Mrs Giles. She tried to decide if he had a weak chin and needed bossing, but her liquid stare unmanned him.

He said, 'You really are the most attractive girl, you know.'

Peter turned up in his old van. Henrietta flapped at it wildly, and ran into the road. He screeched to a halt and as she got in he laughed. 'Why are you dressed like that?'

'My mother thinks I'm going to a party.'

'Your mother's going to murder me. She thinks I've got designs on you.'

'Haven't you?'

He turned away and started the van. They drove in silence for some miles, until Peter said, 'I haven't a clue where we are. I suppose we ought to find a pub.'

'We could buy a bottle of wine and drink it in the car,' said Henry. 'I'm cold, though. You'll have to lend me your coat.'

He stopped at an off licence and gave her his jacket. It was worn at the collar with shiny elbows and threadbare pockets. Only one of the buttons remained. Watching him in the shop, she saw the customers notice his dog collar and usher him to the front of the queue. There was something other-worldly about the church, it set people apart from real life. She almost hated that dog collar. Peter wasn't so different. He couldn't be.

When he got back he said, 'We'd better go somewhere quiet. It wouldn't do to be seen.'

'No indeed,' she said, with heavy irony. He drove to a dark avenue, lined with trees. Houses stood well back from the road, behind fences and gates. They parked away from the street lamps, with only a faint glimmer of light on their faces.

'You have to be rich to own houses like these,' said Peter.

'Oh, loaded,' agreed Henry. 'You could fit a dozen Inkerman Terraces into one of these.'

'Your father could afford this.'

She considered. 'He wouldn't. It's too far out. Daddy would take forever to get to work.'

The wine was so cheap it didn't even have a cork. He unscrewed the top and sloshed good measures into two paper cups. It was disgusting. Henry said, 'Do you miss me on the soup run?'

'I've got someone else to help now. An ex-prison warder. A woman.'

'Is she lots better than me?'

He looked away. 'Actually, no, she isn't. Very tough. Not very funny.'

'I didn't know you thought I was funny.'

'Yes you did. We laughed a lot.'

'Yes.'

Despite the jacket it was cold in the van. Henrietta thought of the party she could be attending. Instead of bitter plonk she would be drinking champagne, instead of shadows there would be brilliant light. People would laugh uproariously and talk about France or Tuscany for the summer. Dominic would want to make love to her and she would say no.

Peter said, 'I was so excited about tonight I forgot a hospital visit. I had to telephone and say I was ill.'

'So we're both lying,' said Henry. 'I wonder why?'

Rather desperately, he said, 'There isn't any point in this, you know. I really don't want − I never intended to be in this situation. But you can't imagine the number of times I thought about calling at your house.'

'Why didn't you?'

'Well, your mother −'

Henry sighed. Heroes were few and far between these days. There could be no more dragon slaying when a man wouldn't even face a girl's mother.

'It wasn't just her,' he said.

'No?'

'I'm older than you. A lot older. I came to the church after a lot of struggle. I made commitments to – well, to God.'

'I imagine you did,' said Henrietta. 'But you're not Catholic or anything. You haven't renounced women.'

'I suppose not. But I do try quite hard to concentrate, you see.' Suddenly he felt foolish, embarrassed by his own faith. One of the things he had found hardest about joining the church was the necessity to talk openly about things he had kept private and apart. Henrietta couldn't understand. She was so worldly, so full of life and hope.

'I'm not going to upset your concentration, am I?'

'I'm not sure. Henrietta, dear Henrietta, I wish you could understand!'

'But I do!' She leaned towards him, her face anxious and unsure. 'You do like me, don't you? Just a little?'

'More than a little. I like you an awful lot.'

It was what she had longed to hear. Now that it was said she knew she should never have doubted him. She leaned back in the seat and sighed happily. 'I can come on the soup run tonight,' she murmured. 'I don't have to be in until two.'

'In your party dress? You look so pretty.'

'Now I'm thin. You wouldn't like me if I was fat.'

'I liked you just as much when you were.' He might even have liked her more. Hidden beneath rolls of flesh she had seemed sexless, he was protected from her attraction. Now he was uncomfortably aware of plump breasts, round, sweetly fleshed arms, buttocks like small pillows tempting him.

He put his hand on her arm, then reached across and took hold of her waist. Henry's mind detached itself, in a slow dance of deliberate thought. This was what she had dreamed of, night after night. It was here, now. If it wasn't what she wanted after all, what would she do?

His lips touched hers, inexpertly. She was better at this, veteran of a dozen lip bruising sessions in Dominic's car. It was as well she knew what kissing someone else was like. Kissing Peter, now, opening her mouth to him with a rush of sensuality, she knew she would never kiss anyone else.

'Are we really in love?' she murmured. He kissed her again.

Matty was dancing. Her partner was a friend of Dominic's, and he wanted to take her for a spin in his sports car. 'Just out to the airport. We can sit and watch the planes.'

'Why should we want to do that?'

He looked discomfited. 'No reason.'

She thought how much more fun it would be if Sholto was here. And yet the party was wonderful, with nice people and delicious food, moving to and fro in this elegant house like a tide. But this was Henrietta's world, not hers. At supper someone had tossed her a spoon and she had dated and priced it without thinking. They applauded her party trick and she was pleased with herself. Outside the trade, no one ever seemed to know anything much about silver, and within it, no one knew anything else. But she shouldn't have shown off. It marked her as trade.

At the end of the dance Dominic reclaimed her, and pinned her in a corner to talk. He kept saying how pretty she was.

'So you see, I've got to be London-based for at least another two years,' he said earnestly. 'After that I can get a place in the country. Do you like the country?'

'What?' Matty's mind had been wandering.

'I asked if you liked the country.'

Let him not see her professional self, she thought. Let him think she played at work. 'The country? Yes. Oh yes, terribly. Pheasants in the garden, and all that. And I like worrying about blackspot on the roses. And the rain, and the morning mists — I love that sort of life, really.'

'Do you? So do I.'

He chattered on, merrily, and she let her mind drift. Was Lorne a country girl? She was leading the country life. Henrietta was most definitely at her best surrounded by concrete and shops, and Griselda only liked Peregrines. But somehow Matty had always seen Lorne as fitted for chic New York, or Charleston perhaps.

She looked up mistily into Dominic's face. 'I really must go home.'

301

'Oh. I suppose it is rather late. Can I drive you?'

'Thanks. That would be great.'

Somebody's aunt was at the piano, playing 'John Peel', and people were singing. Matty found her hostess and thanked her, saying, 'It was such a lovely party. The greatest fun,' and the woman insisted that she have Matty's address, so she could invite her next time she was in London.

'I gather you're in silver. And we have so many christenings and things − I suppose you get asked for that sort of thing rather a lot.'

'Quite a bit,' said Matty, although she had never had any requests. Was this what Sammy meant about amateurishness, trading on friendship and social contacts? She needed the money, she told herself. 'Would you like to see some things? I'm in London for a week.'

So the diary was fetched and an appointment made. Matty left in a flurry of bonhomie.

It was almost four o'clock before Dominic dropped her at the Giles house. She scrambled from the car, and at the same moment Henrietta scrambled from Peter's van, parked across the street.

'You've been ages,' hissed Henrietta, getting out her key.

As they crept into the house Mrs Giles called out, 'Is that you, girls? Henrietta? Matilda?' and they dutifully called out, 'Yes.'

In the safety of their room Henry said, 'I did the soup run, but where were you? The party can't have been that good.'

Matty looked quizzical. 'It was OK, actually. But Dominic is − shall we say − keen? He stopped three times on the way home and I had to fight him to a standstill every time. He's rapacious!'

'Dominic? Good Lord.'

Henry threw herself back on the bed in an ecstasy of weariness. 'I'm in love,' she groaned. 'I don't care about anything, I'm in love!'

'Great, wonderful,' said Matty, crawling into bed. 'As far as I can tell you've been in love for months.'

'But this is special! Do you realise that the most incredible

302

thing has happened? Peter feels the same. He does, he really does!'

'Are you going to tell your mother?'

'What? Are you mad? Of course not.' Henry drew off her gloves and dangled them above her face, letting them drop and obscure her.

'We're going to do lunches together,' she murmured. 'And I've never been so happy in all my life.'

Matty lay in the dark, looking at nothing. Across the room Henrietta's sighs and little contented snuffles flicked her with irritation. It was easy for Henrietta, despite everything. She loved someone who loved her back, whereas Matty — she flung herself on to her other side. If Sholto loved her, if he did, why did he leave? He had cared more about her when she cared little for him, so it must follow that she couldn't win him with love, but only with indifference. And where Sholto was concerned, indifference was a word she didn't know.

Chapter Eighteen

It was odd to sit across the desk from Sammy, discussing silver, and to find that they were at crosspurposes. One by one he had discarded Matty's finds; they were too new, too old, too ordinary, too unusual. One nice set of table salts was damned with the words 'common as muck', whereas a lighthouse salt cellar, rare and very old, elicited no more than a sniff.

'So you won't want anything then?' said Matty humbly.

'Was that what I said?'

'No, but –'

'But me no buts. I'll take the three good teapots, all the salts and half the flatware. The Lord alone knows why I waste my time with such things. Me, Sammy Chesworth, with vaults full of silver. And no one buying. I have no customers, not a single one!'

Matty's spirits, which he had successfully lowered, bounced back happily. 'I don't want you buying from me out of charity,' she murmured. 'Since you are finding things so difficult.'

'Did I say that? I said customers were hard to find, and when were they not? I don't buy rubbish, never have and never will. And, it seems, neither do you.'

It took a few seconds for the compliment to register. Matty felt herself going pink. She wanted to rush out and tell Emily, Sholto, everyone. She looked up and met Sammy's beady brown eyes. 'I do what you taught me,' she said humbly. 'I think you must have taught me very well.'

'Don't think it will make you rich,' he snapped. 'I'm a poor man, a poor man all my life through silver.'

They looked at each other with rough affection. Matty said, 'How's Delia? Can I come and see her?'

He snorted and fiddled with his pipe. 'She is well. Learning Hebrew — wants me to go and work on a kibbutz. Me, at my age! I'm an Englishman, I tell her, old and past it, fit for nothing. She's lost weight, she's full of energy, I can't keep up with her.'

Matty beamed. 'That's wonderful. I'm so pleased. Could I call then?'

'No.' Watching the bewilderment on her face he relented. 'Perhaps you will never see her. I don't know. She has her weakness, like an alcoholic. We can't tempt her. In two years, three, who knows? Now — now she has me, and her bridge friends, and a little dog. It's best.'

It seemed the interview was at an end and Matty got up to go. But then Sammy said, 'Is Feversham behaving himself?'

Startled, she said, 'Yes! At least — I think so.'

'You surprise me. I heard about de Caruzon. Feversham was mad to cross him, completely insane. It should have been the finish of the boy. He should never have touched that picture, not in a million years.'

'That's been the only problem,' said Matty.

'The only one you've heard about,' said Sammy. 'He sails too close to the wind. Last week a painting left Italy on a forged export licence. Ended up no one knows where. And rumour has it that your friend was behind it, broking for some Arab with no scruples.'

Matty swallowed. 'How do you know?'

'How does anyone know these things? I want you to be careful, Matty. Watch yourself. Don't let him drag you into the mire. It's easily done.'

Matty nodded. Of course she would be careful, for Simon's sake if nothing else. She could feel Sammy's eyes on her and forced a smile. 'Thanks, Sammy. But don't worry, please.'

He grunted. And then suddenly he reached into a drawer and pulled out a card. 'Here,' he said gruffly. 'About time you got involved in something decent. Coverbridge House, Kent. They've a piece to sell. Wine cooler or some such great useless thing. Very like that I sold to Mrs Waterman some time ago. You could pick it up.'

'Oh, Sammy.' Matty sat down again. She thought her legs would give way. 'Are you giving up?'

He shrugged. 'Easing off, perhaps. The run of the mill no longer interests me quite as much as it did.'

'This cooler isn't run of the mill.'

'So? Can't anyone do you a favour? Get out of my sight.'

Outside the day was warm and scented with the aftermath of winter and the beginning of spring. Matty felt giddy with events, and somehow, walking, she found herself in the park. Dogs were playing on the grass and a child was chasing a ball, reminding her of Simon when he was little. She would buy this cooler and it would cost her dear. Suppose Mrs Waterman died, or changed her mind, or wouldn't pay? Could she afford the outlay, if it dragged on? Such a risk. She had a sudden cowardly desire to do no more than sell christening mugs to the upper classes, which would be easy and wrong. You could not play ball in the park all your life.

She thought about Sholto, and wondered if what Sammy had heard was true. Surely not. Sholto was sometimes reckless, but never underhand. Besides, he hadn't been in Italy long enough to forge so much as a train ticket. It was just that he looked up to the mark, and people assumed things. Luca probably helped them to assume them.

She hoped Sholto hadn't spent wildly. If she was to buy the wine cooler, then she must have sufficient funds. Suppose Mrs Waterman had sold her single piece? Collectors thrived on change, on the new and different. The old collectors, that is, veterans of a lifetime of acquisition. They started with furniture, until the house could hold no more, moved on to table silver and fine glass, bought Chinese vases to stand in corners and finally, when they had everything they needed for gracious living, they turned their attention to *objets vertu*; little, precious, probably useless things that would look well in glass-fronted cabinets and on polished mantels. Matty told herself that one day, when she had made enough money, she would move into *objets vertu*. She found a certain miserly pleasure in diamond-surrounded miniatures and emerald lockets containing a strand of Peter the Great's hair.

She bought a sandwich from a shop and went to munch it on a bench, bullied all the while by the pigeons. She toyed with the thought of marrying Dominic, and living a life of well-heeled convention, as prop and support to her man. Sammy would despise her, she thought. She would despise herself. She could not close the door on opportunity. A shower of crumbs sent the pigeons into a frenzy, and Matty rolled her sandwich wrapper into a ball. There was really no choice but independence.

When she brought home the wine cooler even Mrs Giles was impressed. 'Surely you can't afford something so expensive, Matilda? At this stage in your career?'

Aware that the potato ring present was about to be viewed in a new light, Matty said hurriedly, 'I've a buyer for this, actually. As long as I get paid quite quickly I should be all right.'

'How very risky. I don't wish to pry, my dear, but wouldn't it be best if I cast an eye over your accounts? You're very inexperienced. You could be making serious mistakes.'

'Er — that's awfully kind —' began Matty, dubiously.

Mrs Giles said, 'That's settled then. We'll have a little talk at my desk this afternoon.'

Casting around wildly for an excuse, Matty blurted, 'The books aren't here! They're at the cottage and really — the accounts are Sholto's territory. I find it much better to let a man get on with it.' She gave a sickly grin.

To her amazement Mrs Giles, who had never let her financier husband have so much as a peep at the family exchequer, said, 'I suppose that is best. Some girls wouldn't have so much sense, I'm sorry to say.'

Later, Henry said, 'Honestly, Matty, you nearly made me sick. You realise the only reason she's against female emancipation is because she thinks I might like a bit?'

'You've got it,' said Matty. 'She just doesn't know.'

'I haven't got anything. She's reduced me to lying and sneaking. As far as she's concerned I'm going to spend lunchtimes with Dominic, although he keeps ringing up and asking for you.'

'And he looks so harmless!'

'He was smitten by your fleshly charms.' Henrietta sprawled on the bed, looking equally charming, Matty thought. She was like a pink and white iced cake. But there was no accounting for the taste of men, or women for that matter.

'Are you sure you prefer the vicar?' she enquired anxiously. 'I mean, Dominic will almost certainly remember how much he likes you soon, and he's moving steadily towards a country house and a London flat and a dozen cars. A seamless progress, no less.'

'He's not tough enough,' said Henrietta disinterestedly. 'He'll be pushed out before he's thirty-five, I've seen it before. My childhood was littered with nice young men who didn't make it. They used to come round to see Daddy and sob. My mother sorted them out, of course. And I'm going to marry Peter.'

Matty felt a nagging disquiet. 'Does Peter agree?' she asked.

'He's struggling with himself,' said Henrietta. 'He's rather into suffering. Personal suffering that is, he doesn't like it for anyone else. Dear Peter. Dear, dear Peter.'

The next morning Matty went to a silver sale, and Henrietta came too, because she had nothing else planned. Mrs Giles was all for adding her weight to the party, and it took all Matty's diplomacy to dissuade her. She couldn't bear the thought of being loomed over.

It was a goodish sale, but she was judging by the catalogue, she hadn't been to view. Glancing around quickly before the start she discarded two or three things that on inspection were a little too battered. But a nondescript dish was added to her list of possibles, because it was simple and good of its type. As usual she marked the cutlery odds and ends, because they cost so little and she was sure that one day something would match. She was amassing trunksful of odd forks and spoons.

Henrietta said, 'Doesn't everyone look important? Who's that odd man glowering at you?'

Matty looked up. It was Sammy, in his brown suit, his battered hat on his lap. She dragged Henrietta across, saying, 'You must meet Mr Chesworth. Sammy, this is Henrietta Giles. She's a friend of mine.'

'Charmed,' said Sammy, and looked crosser than ever.

'You'll want to talk,' said Henry in fright, and scuttled away.

Matty said, 'Tell me what you're bidding for and I won't stand against you. Or we could share, if we're both after the same things.'

Sammy glanced at her. 'What a sensible arrangement. That way we won't force up the price.'

'Exactly,' said Matty. 'Now, I'm after the tray, those three jugs, the silver cow creamer and the coffee pot. How about you?'

'Only the creamer. It's very good and a little whimsical — it should sell well.'

'I'll leave that to you, then,' said Matty. 'Right, we'd better not sit together. Far too incestuous.'

But, as she moved away, he caught her wrist. She stopped and blinked at him, surprised. He was looking at her with fierce attention. 'You realise, Matilda, that we have just formed a ring?'

'What?'

'The little deal you just proposed. A sensible little deal, you might think. Helping each other out. I do you a little favour and you return it. You want to repay me for a small kindness, what could be more natural? It doesn't hurt anyone. Except the owner of the creamer, of course.'

Matty bit her lip. She hadn't thought — it was just that she couldn't challenge Sammy for something he wanted, not after all he had done. To compare this with dishonesty — but it was. She felt a fool, she went hot and cold. What a thing to have suggested! After everything.

She said, 'I didn't think. Of course I shouldn't have said — but I can't run you up for the sake of it. Now I know you want the creamer.'

Sammy shrugged. 'Such dilemmas are the very fabric of human conscience. If there had been three of us, good friends for years, we might have nominated one of us to bid and the rest would have bargained afterwards. A second auction, just for us. A knockout, in fact. The very thing your father did. And yet you judge him so harshly. Was it so bad?'

'It's cheating,' said Matty. 'It's what started him off. I can see how easily it happens, but — we have to behave well. As professionals it's up to us.'

Sammy said, 'But is it all up to us? Doesn't the seller take a risk, selling at an auction at all? He can nominate a good reserve, or he can advertise and try and sell privately. The auction is all about risk: for us, for him, trying to make a bit, trying not to get caught by buying too high and losing money. I should take it very unkindly if you bid for a piece you knew I wanted. Why should you do the seller, someone you don't know, more of a favour than you do me? Wrestle with that, Matilda.'

She went back to her place, next to Henrietta. 'You're awfully pale,' said Henry. 'That horrible man.'

'He's a very clever man,' said Matty. 'He's wonderful. I love him.'

Sitting, waiting for the auction to begin, she thought of all the things that could have prevented her learning her trade with Sammy. Lorne might not have telephoned him, and even when she did might not have seen beneath the gruffness to the man beneath. Indeed, Matty herself could have been stupid and frivolous when they met, and he would have hated her and sent her away. But, she was fatherless, he was daughterless, and the bridge on which they met was made of silver.

'Actually, I don't think he's very nice,' said Henry, boldly.

'No.' There was a chill in Matty's voice. 'I don't suppose you do.'

The room was filling up. The professionals nodded to one another, and to Matty's surprise, one or two of the older dealers acknowledged her. There was the usual sprinkling of private buyers, and the junk merchants, after the plate and the stuff that could be tarted up to be something it never was. A man in a dark suit moved into the chairs behind

Matty and tapped her on the shoulder. 'Have a look at the 1814 teapot,' he murmured.

Matty opened her mouth to say something, then closed it again. She got up and went to look at the piece. It wasn't something she felt she could sell. It was small and very plain, obviously naval. Certain men bought that type of thing, it was aggressively masculine. But it was in very good condition. As she studied it a small cluster of dealers lifted their heads to watch, like lions on the African veld, and the attendant guarding the pot twitched unhappily. Something was up, but he didn't know what.

Matty lifted the pot and felt the weight. Light, but not suspiciously so. The condition was spectacularly good, with the exception of one small dent on the lid. Then she looked at the marks.

They were as clear and sharp as if they were made yesterday. Sterling mark, maker's mark, town mark and date, all bright and new, with the surrounding metal puffed up from the strike. They were exactly in line, too, with none of the slight waywardness she might have expected. Matty looked up at the attendant, and frowned. 'I'm sorry,' she said clearly, 'but this looks very much like a forgery. This piece is new.'

The attendant looked wildly round and hissed, 'Could you keep your voice down, miss!'

Matty said, 'Why? You can't sell this as genuine. If you show it to Mr Chesworth over there I know he'll confirm what I say.'

The attendant signalled wildly and the auctioneer, preparing to mount his rostrum, came across. 'Is there a problem, Simpkins?'

'The pot's forged,' said Matty. 'It's spankers.'

'There's a dent in the lid,' defended the auctioneer.

'A pathetic attempt at ageing,' said Matty. 'And it's been dulled off. They've tried, but it isn't right.'

The man sighed heavily. 'Do we have to tell everybody?' he said in a low voice. 'I admit, I did think it was a little too good to be true. But it's so damned hard to get decent stuff these days. We can't be all that choosy.'

'You'd better be,' said Matty darkly. 'I'm buying off the

catalogue today and if I get home and find you've knowingly sold a fake I'll slaughter you.'

With a grin, he said, 'I can't think of anything nicer. We'll withdraw it. Now, can we get on?'

Matty went back to her seat. Glancing sideways she saw the little coterie of dealers smiling and whispering amongst themselves. They had set her up for that one, to see how she fared. Any one of them could have fingered that pot before now.

'What was all that about?' asked Henry, quite bewildered.

'I've just been blooded,' said Matty. 'And the elders of the tribe are well pleased.'

She slept badly that night. In the early hours she woke from a dream in which she was being chased across moorland, falling into ditches and bogs, never able to run fast enough to get free. Awake in the dark she listened to her heart thundering, and tried consciously to still it. But the fear remained, unreasonably.

She turned her thoughts back to the day. What would she do without Sammy? Sholto could say what he liked, but no one got anywhere without someone doing them a kindness. There was no such thing as total independence, and there shouldn't be. Everyone needed people. But she must remember, always, that a moment's inattention could lead to slackness and dishonesty. You had to guard against it like a robber, waiting to break down the solid walls of your integrity. Like the silversmith who had made the fake teapot, using his skills to serve a rubbishy trade.

She began to think about him. What sort of man was he? Skilled, obviously, every bit as skilled as the man who would have made a pot like that in 1814. What did you do with such skills today? There was little enough trade in modern silver. In the past it was made at the behest of great men, and under their patronage. Experiment and extravagance were permitted and encouraged, and the craftsman had the freedom to flourish. There was no such freedom now. And here was one silversmith reduced to making copies.

Early, before seven, she telephoned Sammy at home. He answered sleepily on a bedside phone. 'Yes? What? Who?'

'It's me,' said Matty. 'I've been wondering about something.'

'You tell me this at dawn? I should go on the kibbutz, they might let me have a little rest at night.'

'I think they make you get up even earlier. It was about the fake pot . . . I wondered if you might know who made it.'

He exploded in a snort of laughter. 'You think I know crooks? You think I know everything! Soon you'll say half my stock was made in Sheffield, yesterday.'

'Is that where it was made? Sheffield?'

She heard Sammy sigh, and murmur something to Delia. 'You know all the silversmiths,' wheedled Matty. 'They all do repairs and things for you. This one's so good he must stand out. Please, Sammy.'

'And why do you want to know?' he asked mildly.

'I'm not sure yet. I think I might get some stuff made. Not fakes, but original pieces. That's all.'

She could tell he was spreading his hands. 'You have only just learned what it is to deal in silver, and now you want to make it yourself? You want to be a tycoon, is that it?'

Matty laughed. 'I just want to do it. That's all.'

'And you won't lecture this man, and read him worthy tracts?'

'No. Promise.'

'Then you must go and see Richard Greensall. In Sheffield.'

Henrietta was in the bath when she went back upstairs. Matty sat on the edge and dripped bubblebath into the water while Henry stirred it with her hand. 'Want to come shopping, Matty? Come on. You've worked for days, you can have some time off. Afterwards I'm going to do the lunches with Peter, and then Mother wants me to go to an exhibition or something. You can come. Warm white wine and dry canapés.'

Matty shook her head. 'Actually, I'm off to Sheffield.'

'Really? Why? You're not into knives, are you? Can't you stay with the pretty stuff?'

'There's just someone I've got to see. A silversmith. Anyway it's time I went, your mother's getting tired of me.'

'She's tired of me too,' said Henrietta. 'But I'm a fixture, it seems. You will come back, won't you? I mean, if you find – if you feel – oh, Matty, don't you think you'd be better with someone else? I'm sure you could be more happy.'

Matty's smile was suddenly bleak. 'I don't know. It's fine when he's there, it's just – '

'He isn't there,' said Henry. 'You don't even know where he is. I'm sure all the agony aunts would advise you to Love Another. There's always Dominic. Or Dominic's friend.'

Matty splashed her friend with a double handful of water. 'Look after your own romance. I do quite enough worrying about mine.'

She went and packed her case, discovering that despite sales and vaults she still seemed to have more silver than when she came. It was odd, the stuff seemed to multiply without her noticing, as if teaspoons got together in the dark to breed and bring forth coffee pots and sugar casters. Like Sholto's pictures. Stopping in the very act of wrapping a candlestick in tissue paper, she felt a sudden wave of cold. Where was Sholto?

Chapter Nineteen

The room was painted pale apricot, although the plaster mouldings on the dome of the ceiling were gilded. The bed canopy hung down in a veil of white muslin, now moving lazily in the gentle morning breeze. But the scene on the bed was not gentle. A man and a woman were locked together, her legs around his waist, his arms pinning her shoulders to the sheets.

They were writhing, wrestling, fighting. She put up her hands to try and scratch his eyes and he let go her shoulders and held her wrists instead. She heaved herself up and they rolled over, to the edge of the huge bed, until she was on top and he underneath. He let go her hands and she sat back on him, panting and grinning. She had long black hair, tangled in her mouth. Her face was lovely, and had once been very beautiful.

Suddenly she reached back and swung her arm, slapping him viciously on the face. First one hand and then the other. At each blow he grunted. Then he reached out and took hold of both her fleshy breasts, closing each hand like a vice. Her nipples escaped through his fingers, like overripe cherries, and she threw back her head, letting out a guttural cry. He held her while she shuddered, and then, as she subsided, he let her go. Bruises stood out on her skin like the petals of a flower.

They lay on the bed in silence for a while. Then the woman lifted herself up on an elbow. 'You are getting better, my friend. Over an hour. Did you like it when I struck you?'

'You made me angry. Which I think was what you intended.' Sholto rolled over and grinned at her.

'But of course! You are too kind to me. Sometimes, when

I don't want you, you should make me have you. Hard, rough, quick. When you suck me you should use your teeth. When I scratch you, you must pull my hair.'

He looked at her for a moment, his eyes quite clear. Then he said, 'OK,' and came at her. Before she could move he had her face down on the bed, before she could speak he was forcing himself between her thighs. He groaned as he went in, sore from what was almost a weeklong orgy.

She was gasping and he reached out and pushed her face into the pillow. He was sick of her, endlessly at his bedside, in his bed. She had a strange habit of pushing things up inside herself for him to find, letters folded very small, jewels, a signet ring. He imagined ending up with it stuck on the end of his erection, and grinned. She was stupid even to offer that sort of present. It wasn't what he wanted.

Minutes passed. She was writhing again. Since she began his education he could go on like this for hours, until he decided he wanted it to end. He let go her head and gripped her thighs, forcing her buttocks into him. She was groaning, he must have half suffocated her. He held still for a moment, warding off his climax, and she muttered, 'For God's sake, aren't you finished yet?'

'I'm the tireless stud you made me, ma'am,' murmured Sholto, and half stood on the bed, she face down, gasping, supporting herself on her hands.

'Oh my God. Oh my God,' she was murmuring. He felt quite dispassionate about her, hanging there, obscenely. But he thought about it too long. His climax came, thunderously, and they fell together across the bed.

The dew was still on the grass when he walked there, later. He felt stale and drained, as well he might. He would have given anything then to be as fresh as the day, as unblemished as the daffodils with their brilliant perfection. Birds were singing, and he thought, suddenly, of Matty. She would love this garden, he thought, although little else about the place would attract her. It was beautiful, sensuous and alien to the very fibre of Matty's puritan spirit.

'Sholto.' Victoria was standing on the terrace, watching him. She had dressed in a dark blue frock, with a diamond brooch on the shoulder. Her hair was caught up in a heavy,

318

glossy bun. 'You look so serious. What are you thinking?'

He turned towards her. 'That I've got to leave. For the good of my health. And yours.'

He stood looking down at her. He was always surprised that she was so small. In bed she seemed his equal in every way. She wagged a finger at him. 'You are getting very wild, my boy.'

'So it seems.'

She tapped his hand, entirely the perfect lady, the Baronessa who had taken hold of her husband's crumbling firm and transformed it into an empire. She had four sons, three in the firm and the last still at school, and Sholto was of an age to be one of them.

They took tea on the terrace, served with perfect style by the Italian butler. Although the staff must know what went on upstairs, they never by the slightest hint betrayed disapproval. It was almost as if they expected it of their mistress. After all, the baron was old, past it, and spent his days in a tower by the sea, reading medieval manuscripts.

'Now,' said the Baronessa, 'have you everything you want?'

He grimaced. 'You won't sell me the Bertolini?'

'Of course not. It's a family treasure. But you have those things from the Montegros? They are in bad condition, but the family has been so poor for so long. It was time they acknowledged it.'

'And so they did. Once you leaned on them.'

'What an expression! I do not lean. Except perhaps on the goodwill of my so charming lover.'

She smiled at him and, as always, Sholto smiled back. The Baronessa was the most confusing woman. Insatiable in bed, impossible sometimes, she had only to come downstairs to be charming, witty, kind and level-headed. Outside bed he could imagine he might fall in love with her. Within it, never.

They had hardly begun well. Two years ago, before he had met Matty, before anything, she had enticed him with sex. He had been almost a beginner, with nothing but the odd brief tumble to his credit. He thought that was all there was to it. The Baronessa proved him wrong.

He left with the impression that she thought him callow. Some quiver in her voice gave him to understand that he was too quick and too basic, that it was all just too unimaginative. He was a little hurt, but more than a little intrigued. The next time – well, they had drunk champagne to the next time! In the end, inevitably, he had come back to her. Again and again.

Because he was leaving, he and Victoria toured the long gallery together. It was something they had in common, lingering over their favourite paintings, revelling in brilliant painted light glorified by centuries of time. He often wondered if these pictures were as remarkable in their own age. Probably not. There must have been so many more, when that was all there was. Thousands of paintings must have been lost – and there might well be thousands more yet to be discovered.

Victoria said, 'Soon you will forget me. When you have all your success.'

He laughed. 'Never.'

'You have a girl, don't you? Of course you do. I wish you – well.'

They stood in silence, although he knew he ought to be uttering soft words of reassurance. He knew what to say, he'd said it before, they were things people said, without meaning. All at once he had nothing to say. He hoped she would not plead with him, because pleading women were loathsome. Why did he always, in the end, long only to get away?

Victoria sat on his bed while he packed, making amusing, slightly risqué conversation. They were drinking thimblefuls of plum brandy, out of tiny crystal glasses. Sunlight dappled the old wool carpet, marking out deep, rich, painterly colours. 'I wish I had been born a painter,' said Sholto. 'My life would have had point. I should paint this room, now.'

'With me?' asked Victoria.

'I – was intending only a still life.'

She made a little face. 'I should have known. You are as your face, Sholto. Flawed. Not entirely, but enough. You don't love. Not even yourself.'

* * *

He thought about her as he sat on a train, one of the slow, halting Italian trains that meander through perfect vistas of sunflowers and terracotta roofs, stopping at quiet stations to let a single smiling priest on or off. He thought about a lot of things. He had a painting that might suit one of his patrons, dark, in need of cleaning. A minor masterpiece that had only to be recognised to be valuable. But he would not offer the picture. Like the country through which he travelled, it was gentle and serene; whoever had painted it, whether demented or corrupt or venal, he had found some corner of his soul that was filled with beauty, and he had tapped it for his art. Sholto loved that painting.

Victoria's words came back to him. He loved, of course he did. He just didn't love people.

There was a certain macabre relief in admitting it. The trouble was, years ago, something had died. Once, he remembered the old woman laughing when he brought her a little bunch of marsh marigolds he had found growing at the side of a canal. She had thrown them back at him. Again, on his birthday, watching him over the breakfast marmalade, demanding to know if he expected anything, did he, did he? A child, as yet unused to her, he had admitted that he did. She had demanded to know what he might like. A bicycle perhaps, a fine red bike that he could ride round the marble hall, and outside, in the square? Would he like that? 'Yes, yes please!' the little boy had cried, his eyes alight with anticipation. And she had smiled, so sweetly. 'You are a greedy little boy. For that, you will get nothing. Let it be a lesson to you.'

Oranges were growing wild by the railway track. They would be sweet, they would soothe a throat aching with the pressure of remembered tears. When the train stopped next Sholto got off, although there was nothing there, nothing but a few houses golden in the sun, a little church, a little street — a little comfort.

The church was open, and very quiet. It struck cool through Sholto's shirt as he entered, a cavern of blue glass and soft candlelight. He would light a candle, he thought, and petition God. He was damaged, and he wanted to be whole.

321

There was a girl in England who loved him, who needed loving in return. Matty. He conjured a vision of her in his mind, and lit the candle, setting it carefully on the topmost tier, where the wax hung in lovely stalactite fronds. He trusted her; he even admired her fierce integrity, her refusal to bend to the smallest degree. But beyond that he would not, could not, let himself go.

What would happen to him like this? He knew how it ought to be. He could behave with kindness, affection, even perhaps with love, but without the substance, it was all a sham. You pretended to be a whole person, and for a while the pretence held good, until suddenly, one day, you were surprised and found naked. Victoria understood. She came from the same sewer, the same stagnant pond. But Matty still believed in fairytales. He remembered loving, that was the trouble. The memory was there. But one day, if all he lived on was memory, conjuring up the appropriate response, the correct, loving behaviour, one day he would forget. Then there would be nothing there but anger, pain and cruelty. He kept himself hidden, kept himself under fierce and unremitting control, and it tired him so. Today, here in this church, he rested his weary head against the stone and offered up fervent prayers for strength.

There was a demon in his soul. A devil possessed him. If the peasants believed that, why couldn't he? Matty with her honesty, her courage, her clear grey eyes, her little, little concerns, did she never look and see who was in the bed beside her? She trusted herself to him. She forgave him. And she was so, so wrong.

As he knelt in the gloom he felt his eyes become hot. So, he might still be able to cry. Perhaps it was a sign. He hadn't cried in years, he hadn't thought he could. It was a sign, he thought. Here, in this beautiful place, he had been told what to do.

Matty approached the little brick building nervously. Her feet crunched on broken glass and at a distance, over the dull roar of the nearby road, men were shouting to one another. The place felt threatening and dangerous.

The windows were barred, but even so some of the panes

322

had been broken and filled in with wood. It gave what was otherwise a substantial structure the appearance of a shack. An iron door, heavily locked, bore a scrawled notice: 'No casual callers. R. Greensall'.

Matty took a deep breath and pressed a bell. It buzzed like a wasp in a jar, and after a moment a panel in the door clanged open. She glimpsed an unfriendly face. 'What do you want?' Young, aggressive, broad Yorkshire.

'Er – are you Mr Greensall?' She tried to smile, brightly, and managed only a sickly grin.

'Who the hell are you?'

'Matty – Matilda Winterton. I'm not an official or anything. I'm not the police.'

'I can tell that. You're not the type. So what do you want?'

She took a deep breath. 'I'm a dealer. In silver. And I want you to make something for me.'

All at once the panel slammed shut, but before Matty could blink the door was open and she was yanked inside. 'What you on about? Who's been talking?'

She pulled her wrist free of his hand and tried to collect herself.

Greensall was tall and bearded. His hands were stained black, leaving black marks on her wrist, and everything around was black too, a litter of tools and rags. A small gas flame was burning, above a flat tray filled with some kind of rock. The silversmith's hearth and lamp. On the bench next to it lay a bowl, as yet without its shine, but the chasing clear and perfect. Silver.

Matty said, 'Now whose mark's going on that, I wonder? By the look of it – Paul Storr, at a guess. Or Rundell's, anyway. To muddy the water. We don't want people thinking it's too easy. They might get suspicious.'

For a moment she thought she'd gone too far. His fingers clenched into a fist and she braced herself. But then he relaxed. 'You can't prove a thing.'

Matty said, 'I don't think proof's necessary. We both know what we know. I'm not telling anybody.'

'Who's the bastard told you?'

She considered. 'I don't think I want to tell you that.

323

Besides, it doesn't matter. Can you show me what you're doing? I'd love to see.'

'You didn't come here for a lesson in silversmithing!'

'No. But I'd like to see, just the same.'

He gave her a puzzled, sideways look. None the less he sat down on his high wooden stool. She could tell he was happiest there, that it gave him time to think. Putting the bowl to one side he picked up a tiny silver snuff box, the lid broken off at the joint. Quickly, neatly, he used pliers to take off the old fragments, dropping them into the morass of dust and rags on the floor. A tiny pot was set over the gas flame, and while it heated he painted the snuff box with clear liquid.

'Why are you doing that?' asked Matty.

'Flux. To get solder to take.'

His big stained hands were deft and sure. He held the pieces of metal with tweezers, fixing them to the box with tiny dabs of silver. Matty strained to see the work. 'Does your solder ever show?'

'If it does I'm the only one to see it. Can't let bad work go out, now.'

'How much will you get for mending that box?'

He shrugged. 'Fifteen pound, say. And the shop that sent it in will charge fifty. And complain about the time I took. You don't get rich silversmithing, not today.'

He was justifying himself. Even as little as a hundred years ago a man of his skill would have had it in him to become wealthy. He could make with the best of them, beating out flat metal into something lovely and rare. He would have had a business, patronage, loyal and enthusiastic customers, willing to interest themselves in his ideas and innovations. He would have been recognised for the artist he was.

But no one wanted that any more. He could make the most beautiful pot in the world and if it bore his own maker's mark, his own distinctive entwined RG, no one would be interested; but he had only to change that mark, even for that of a lowly and untalented journeyman living in provincial obscurity, and provided that mark was old, people would pay.

'Stop staring at me like that!' He brought his fists hard down on his bench. The flame of his lamp flickered.

Matty's eyes were fixed on him with a dreamy, thoughtful gaze. 'It isn't just the money,' she said softly.

'Of course it's money! I've got a family to feed, just like everyone.' But his hand went to the bowl, his beautiful, shapely bowl. His hands were calloused and filthy, burned here and there by the metal, but they had made this. He was damned if he would let it pass unappreciated.

'You get ripped off with the forgeries as well,' remarked Matty. 'I mean, whoever puts them on the market has to take the biggest cut for the biggest risk.'

'It's still more than I'd get if I marked 'em,' muttered Greensall. 'Besides — when you see sommat you made in the catalogue, great long spiel about it, talking about balance, and craftsmanship, all that about the hand of the master — well, it sets you up. Makes t'difference, like.'

'But if you sold under your own mark, surely you'd get a reputation?'

'If I sold at all! I had a few bits in Bond Street, few year back. Bloke liked my stuff and put it in his fancy window. Folk came galloping in off the street, panting to look. You could buy it for a tenth of the price paid for old stuff. But as soon as they heard it was new, they was off. No investment value, you see. At least not for a hundred year, and then who's going to care? They don't want to leave it to no one. They want to flog it when the tax man gets them, or the market falls, or their kids want to dump them in a home. My very best work, it were. And you couldn't give it away.'

Matty reached across and picked up the bowl. Greensall rumbled, like a dog growling, but she took no notice. She turned the piece in her hand, inspecting it. Then she put it down. 'You're going to have to stop, you know,' she said. 'The thing's perfect, but it's too perfect, and you've done too many of them. When a piece like that turns up, everybody starts wondering, and the patina's bound to give it away. You are getting yourself much too noticed.'

He said nothing. But he took up his bowl and ran his fingers over the chasing, the intricate and satisfying merging of leaves and flowers and texture. He looked like a little boy who has been told he can no longer use his beautiful, homemade catapult, just when he has become a crack shot.

'I was getting better at the patina,' he said suddenly. 'And I should have bashed them up a bit. If I'd engraved a coat of arms and then scrubbed it off, people would have believed it were repolished. But I'd made it right. I couldn't do it, see.'

Matty sighed. 'I do see. Really.'

'You want money or sommat? You going to turn me in?'

'Of course not! Good Lord, there aren't many men like you left. Men who can work silver as it should be worked. I'm going to send you my best pieces for restoration. And — I'd like you to make for me.'

'Make? You mean — make?'

'Yes. Flatware, to start with.'

She reached into her bag and brought out a jumble of cutlery. Some was all silver, some ivory-handled, some of it was chased, some engraved, some cast in elaborate and voluptuous shapes. 'I keep buying oddments,' she explained. 'They're always attractive, but they're always odd. And obviously because they're not full sets and can't be used, I get them very cheap. If I can make them up to full sets, they'll be worth — well, anything. They'd be part antique, you see. People can have the stuff and use it, and boast about the antique bits and the modern bits too. Once you've got a reputation, once people believe in your craftsmanship, you're made. "There's this wonderful silversmith, Richard Greensall, he has all the old techniques. Expensive, obviously, but the man's an artist. We were very lucky to get something by him, actually." '

For a second she was all the pretentious hostess. Greensall chuckled. 'Aye, that's the type. If they took to it you'd do OK. But there's work in this stuff. I'd have to make dies, I'd have to invest.'

'About time you did, if you ask me,' said Matty. She cast an eye around the mess and muddle of the workshop. 'You could probably buy old dies, I would have thought. And some of this is hammered.'

He blinked. Hammering from flat metal rather than

326

pressing in a die was the oldest, and the best method. It was also slow and expensive.

'You want me to hammer it up?'

'Yes. If that's how the original piece was made. And the price will reflect that, of course.'

He glared at her as if she had said something vile. Then he got off his chair, stomped across the room and fetched a battered kettle. He filled it with water, stuck it on his lamp and remained quite silent until the steam was billowing merrily from the spout. Only when the tea was made and they each had a steaming mug did he speak.

'How'd I know you're not some fool with delusions? I could make and make and never get paid.'

'You talk to Sammy Chesworth. He'll vouch for me.'

'Mr Chesworth? You know him?'

'He trained me.'

Greensall was impressed. He went to the cupboard and rummaged amongst thousands of tiny wooden blocks. They were marks, perhaps those of long-dead silversmiths, perhaps forged ones, acquired from heaven knows where. He brought out a small bottle of whisky and poured a generous measure into each mug of tea.

'Here's to us, then,' he said, raising his drink.

'So you'll do it?' asked Matty tensely.

'Like I said. Here's to us.'

Outside, driving home, she felt lightheaded. There was no air in that dark little workshop, and it was full of Greensall's intensity. Sitting there, day after day, working alone, he generated obsessive and single-minded brilliance. He wanted to be recognised for that, he wanted to be known, he felt it was his right. If Matty gave him that recognition, gave him his public face, then in return he would give her anything. She was sure of it.

Flatware to start with, she decided. She had left him to make a dozen forks in different sizes and four spoons, to complete a good set. If the sets sold as she thought then Greensall could move on. He would make to her own designs, small, beautifully crafted pieces that could take their place in people's modern lives. They would cost less than antique, but not much less. She would market them not as

327

reproductions but as new renaissance, the classical world once again calling to a new and hungry age. Her customers would see themselves as connoisseurs as well as collectors. She would honour them by allowing them to buy. She would let them know, subtly, that such things were never offered to the ignorant. Trading on snobbery and ignorance, because beauty wasn't enough, Matty was weaving her own version of the Emperor's New Clothes.

Chapter Twenty

Matty was in the garden when Sholto came back. The daffodils had been fooled into flowering by an unseasonably warm day, and the subsequent storm had knocked them down. She was gathering them, washing any dirt from the stiff yellow heads in the birdbath. Sholto saw her there, with an armful of flowers, and she was lovely.

'Sholto! You're back! I didn't think — you're back!'

'So I am. Back. Matty, you look wonderful. The flowers have turned your skin to gold.'

'To butter,' she said. 'I've been eating out of misery.'

'Then eating must suit you.'

She thought he would kiss her, but instead he stood back and drank her looks in. She was so fresh, as sweet and clean as any daffodil. There could be no greater contrast to the Baronessa. Matty was honest and straightforward and open, while Victoria was none of those things. And Sholto had tired of Victoria.

In the house, over cups of tea, Matty fell silent. She had almost believed he would never come home again. All the thoughts of the past weeks came back to her, all her loneliness. She dared not ask him where he had been.

'I wanted you to write,' she said shyly.

'I thought I had. Didn't I? A postcard?'

She shook her head.

'I'm sorry,' he said. 'I should have written.'

'I've been to London,' she said. 'I didn't stay here. I've been busy.'

'Good. Good.'

The silence once again developed, and soon it was

oppressive. Matty wanted to talk and knew that if she did it would only be prattle.

Sholto's face was lightly tanned, his eyes so blue that she could hardly meet his gaze. He seemed unbearably tense, she realised. 'Has something happened?' she blurted. 'Is something the matter?'

'There was something I wanted to ask you.'

'Oh.'

She looked out of the window, at the floor, anywhere that wasn't his face. Whatever he said was sure to hurt her. She tried to put up her defences, because she must not cry, not in front of him. He wanted to sell up, leave, and be done with her.

'I missed you, in Italy,' he said.

'You had your pictures, though.'

'I don't think they were enough. Nothing was enough. I wanted you. Matty, I want you to marry me.'

Her mouth fell open. Her expression of shock was comical. 'That's — that's ridiculous!' she exclaimed. 'You don't mean anything of the kind. I think it's cruel to play games.'

'It isn't a game, Matty. I want us to marry. Soon.'

'Why?'

He felt his whole body tense. He had to say it. It had to be true. 'Because I love you.'

She dropped her eyes and turned away from him, going to the pile of daffodils, picking up handfuls and stuffing them cruelly into jars. Tears showered down on to her hands.

'Matty, what's the matter?'

'Nothing. Everything. Why do you say things you don't mean?'

'I do mean it. I decided in Italy.'

'But you don't want ties. You don't want anything or anyone that makes demands on you. It's what you've always said.'

'Perhaps I've changed my mind.'

She lifted her head, with its heavy crown of hair. 'And perhaps you haven't.'

He felt a strong sense of unreality. This was not at

all as he had expected. 'Are you saying no? Is that it?'

'I'm not sure.'

'Matty, Matty!' He went to her and pulled her close, her hands still full of daffodils. 'Don't be silly! Say yes and love me. Please, Matty, love me. I need to be loved.'

'You know I love you. You know I do.'

'Then that's all we need. We'll be so happy. Darling Matty.'

She gave a strangled sob and flung her arms up around his neck. The daffodils were let fall, trampled to nothing under their feet as they kissed. The spring breeze, wayward as a young lamb, threw a shower of leaves against the window and Sholto lifted his head, and smiled.

They decided on a summer wedding, in June. Matty would have been happy with a quick civil ceremony, but Sholto wanted the whole production, dress, veil, bridesmaids, everything. Matty said, 'I don't need bridesmaids. Henry would be fine, but Lorne's married, and as she's pregnant I don't suppose she'll come, and Griselda would hate to dress up like a maypole.'

'Don't you have any little girl cousins? They could be charming, with posies.'

Matty made a face. 'If I had any aunts and uncles I should have cast myself upon them long before this. I've got a second cousin somewhere in Scotland, but he was at least fifty when last we met and I was about ten at the time. Really, Sholto, we don't know enough people to fill a church. Can't we slide off to the Town Hall and get it done? Please?'

He glowered at her. His scar seemed prominent today, making him sardonic and difficult. 'No. We'll have a small church wedding, then. But it must be in church. And I want you to have a dress. We don't want our children looking at the photographs and disapproving, now do we?'

'They'd think we had to get married,' sighed Matty. 'They do sound priggish. I don't think I shall like these disapproving children.'

Sholto laughed. 'We'll apply for approving ones. Docile little girls.'

'Girls aren't docile,' said Matty. 'They are so far from docile as to make one wonder how anyone thought they were.'

'I know dozens of docile girls!'

'You would,' said Matty.

Littlebury church was usually considered too small for weddings, holding no more than fifty people at a squash. But since Sholto and Matty could muster no more than thirty names between them, it was ideal. Sholto went into long discussions with the vicar about appropriate decorations. He wanted the flowers to be correct for the architecture. The church was very early, and he wanted blooms that reflected the Anglo-Saxon.

'What an interesting concept,' enthused the vicar. 'What flowers does Bede mention, I wonder? Flax? Saxifrage? Marigolds?'

'I'm not having a bouquet of flax and marigolds,' said Matty. 'Neither am I dressing in leather thongs.'

Sholto leaned lazily against a pew. 'How about Victorian extravagance, then? A crinoline and bunches of curls over each ear?'

'No thank you,' she retorted.

For some reason she felt tense. It was the suddenness of everything, she decided. When Sholto went away he had been close to leaving forever, she was sure. Then this. She didn't understand it.

That night, she sat in bed waiting for him to finish his nightly ritual of postcard inspection, turning over reproduction after reproduction of pictures that interested him. Some would be for sale, some he merely liked, some were things he hoped to get his hands on in due course. Sometimes a painting would seem to obsess him. Titian's Man with a Blue Sleeve, for instance. He kept that beside the bed, the man's sly gaze permanently watchful.

All at once Matty said, 'I don't think we should get married.'

He looked up. 'What?'

'We shouldn't get married. Not yet.'

Sholto put down his cards and sprawled across the bed.

332

'Why not, my little chickenheart? Don't you love me any more?'

'That's not the point. It's just — I feel odd about it, somehow. As if we shouldn't.'

'That is an unnecessarily fey remark. Explain yourself.'

'I can't.'

He rolled over and met her eyes. 'Then be still. All will be well.'

He came up the bed and took her in his arms. His mouth was hungry. He pulled her nightdress off her shoulders and sucked at her breasts. As always when he had been away Matty noticed the differences; the way he held her, the sense of controlled brutality. 'Stop it!' She pushed him away.

'Why? Don't you like that?'

'I — you seemed — I thought you were going to be rough.'

'I'm never rough with you.'

Did she imagine an emphasis that wasn't there? Who was he rough with, if not her? He pushed her pillows aside and laid her down on the bed. She looked up at him and he caught his breath, saying, 'Matty, you look like Bambi. I'm not going to hurt you.'

Suddenly he was all gentleness, stroking her hair, nuzzling her skin. He could change so quickly, bewildering her. She groaned and felt her hips lifting rhythmically, unable to do anything except respond. He touched her thighs, coaxing her, waiting until she wanted nothing so much as his hand. The sensations swept through her in waves. She was breathless, helpless, and yet some part of her kept thinking and wondering how he had learned to be like this. His fingers, inside her, pressed upwards. She gasped, her eyes wide open, and he said dreamily, 'I thought you'd like that.'

Someone else had taught him. Someone else had told him what to do. Even as she shuddered on the edge of orgasm she muttered, 'I don't want this. I want you.'

His face, inches from hers, tightened. Matty pushed at his hand, and suddenly, so fast he almost frightened her, he swung over her and into her. And this she understood. This was loving, kind, and entirely right. They were part of one another, locked for an instant in an ancient bond, giving each other everything.

As he finished Sholto let out a long, anguished groan. Then he rolled away, and lay panting, his arms outstretched. 'What a traditionalist you are, Matty,' he said at last.

'What an adventurer you are, Sholto,' she replied.

The word hung between them, unexplored. When at last she looked at Sholto his eyes were closed, and she said softly, thinking he might be asleep, 'What will it be like when we're married? Will you still go away?'

He smiled, without opening his eyes, and reached for her. 'I shall go, but you'll come with me. You shall be my talisman. My little currant bun.'

'And you are a fruitcake,' she murmured, nestling into his shoulder.

Griselda read the invitation leaning against the porter's desk in her college. She stood on one leg, storklike, gawky as ever in a faded print dress. Fortunately she had followed Matty's advice and grown her hair, wearing it in an as yet wispy bun at the nape of her neck. When her hair was long enough to give the bun weight she would be some way towards balancing her angular, beaky face.

'Going somewhere nice, Miss Lemming-Knott?' enquired the porter jovially. 'The duke taking you on his yacht now, is he?'

'The duke doesn't have a yacht,' replied Griselda. 'Which I'm sure you know. Don't be so curious, Higgins, you old devil.'

She walked away and left him chuckling. He was the scourge of the college, but somehow Griselda had his measure. 'You can tell she's out of the top drawer,' Higgins would say to his pals over a beer. 'No looks at all, chest like an ironing board, but she's got something.' He would sip his beer then, wait for his moment, smack his lips and say, 'Class. That's what she's got. Pure class.'

Griselda walked out into the pale spring sunshine. She felt very strange. She hadn't really minded when Lorne got married, because somehow they had always assumed Lorne would be the first. Beautiful and lazy, she was bound to be plucked from the tree. Henrietta too seemed destined to be the other half of a stockbroker who liked plump women, but somehow Griselda had never expected Matty to go. Matty. Her special friend.

They weren't as close any more, of course. Since she took up with this man Matty had closed the doors on girlish confidences. A few giggles over sex, the odd disclosure about how unexpectedly big it was, but there was the sense that nothing deeper would be said. If Matty had dark moments she lived through them alone.

Griselda was meeting Bertie by the river for a brisk, head-clearing walk. They often walked together, as an antidote to drink, coffee and late nights, although as Bertie said, it seemed a bit pointless without a dog. They had considered summoning a canine from the country, but it wouldn't have been fair. Why take a dog from his happy, rabbit-hunting days on the estate, just for their own whim? If there was a choice between their discomfort and the dog's, then the dog could rest easy on his worn fireside rug.

Bertie was waiting under a tree, his walking stick under his arm and his jumper hanging an inch or two beneath his tweed jacket. 'What a time of year!' he said enthusiastically as he saw her. 'Trees springing into leaf, the river full of fish, and a note from home this morning to say the wheat's green as grass in Long Acre. Good to be alive, Griselda.'

'Yes.'

Her quiet reply surprised him. He had expected a happy exchange about farming and the weather. 'Anything up, old girl?'

'No! Not really. I mean – my friend Matty's getting married. I don't know the man but she adores him and it sounds all right, especially since they're in business together and so on. But it isn't going to be the same, is it? Friends can't be, when they marry.'

'Well. Haven't thought about it. Do believe they come round again, you know. Once the novelty's worn off.'

Griselda chuckled. 'Really, Bertie! Will you get back to walking with me after six months with a wife in a frilly nightie? I don't believe it.'

'Frilly nighties! Makes a man go cold. Still, suppose it's

inevitable. Girls with money always seem to be relentlessly frilly, it seems to me, right down to their shoes. Bows and glitter and all that sort of thing.'

They fell into step along the bank. It was a good way to talk, with no necessity for eye contact or stillness. 'Got to be money then, has it?' said Griselda.

Bertie sighed. 'Not only money, of course. But if a nice girl comes along with a decent level of funds, then I suppose I'll pop the question. Least I can do, really, with Mother and the girls scratching along at home. Beef prices are well down, you know. And what do you do with huge great beef units if you don't rear beef in them?'

'A show ring,' suggested Griselda. 'For possible brides. You can parade them and take your pick.'

'Nine out of ten would take one look at me and decline! Thank God for the title, that's what I say.'

They laughed together. Idly Griselda wondered if her father was thinking about a similar match for her brother. She doubted it. Peregrines might be impoverished but they weren't as far gone as Bertie. The bank was so insistent that he had been considering selling land.

A kingfisher was darting along the riverbank, gaudy flashes of blue and red. They stood and watched it for a moment, barely able to follow the speed of its flight. When it rested they held their breath, until suddenly it was up and gone.

They began walking again. 'I was wondering,' said Griselda, 'would you like to come to this wedding? I mean, it says I can invite someone and I wondered − I thought −' She subsided into embarrassed stutters. She wouldn't dare ask anyone else, only Bertie.

'Why, that's awfully kind of you, Griselda! I should love to come. We can judge whether your friend is going to be lost forever or only until the wedding presents break. Terrible lot of people getting divorced nowadays.'

Griselda said, 'You'll like her. She's one of those people you know you can trust on sight. Pretty, too.'

'If you like her then I know I will. Stands to reason, really.'

They walked on, following the kingfisher, into the spring day.

They sat in the vicar's cluttered study, drinking lukewarm coffee and listening to the muffled sounds of the church bells as the bellringers practised. The vicar put his fingers together and leaned benevolently over his desk. 'Marriage is a sacrament,' he began. 'I'm sure you both understand that. It isn't something to be entered into lightly. There must be love. Deep and abiding love. Do you both agree?'

Sholto said nothing. Matty said 'Yes' in a shy voice.

'The thing is,' said the vicar, 'how can we tell what sort of love we feel? Is it strong and sure, ready to withstand all the world can throw at it? You'll be tested, I can promise you that. Illness, poverty, temptation, they are all tests. If your love is only frail, if it's based on some — well, today, we need hardly beat about the bush — on some sexual level of compatibility, then it will not survive. You must think about this. Think about it deeply. Even today I still believe that men and women find most happiness in a marriage that lasts to death, but we need sure foundations! We need our gift from God. We need love.'

When, at last, they escaped into the churchyard, Sholto was furious. 'What does he think he's doing? The invitations are out, the food's arranged, people are coming. And here he is telling us not to bother!'

'He didn't say that. You know he didn't.'

'He as good as said we didn't love each other.'

'He asked us to consider whether we loved each other enough.'

'And how are we to tell? There isn't a meter you can use. You either do or you — don't.'

They drove home in silence. Matty didn't want to talk, they only seemed to argue. Sholto was suggesting that they should change the car, get rid of the estate and buy something sporty and fashionable. His restless spirit was never content. He had to be changing, doing, buying, spending, endlessly trying to fill some void that Matty only sensed. When they were married it would be different, she told herself. Security would change him. When he knew that there was one sure, immovable constant in a world of shifting sands, then he would rest.

The soup was green pea, a luminous sludge that bubbled in the vat like a mud spring. Henrietta ladled it in bowls to the queue of people. One old woman, much reduced in circumstances and mad as a hatter, drew her moth-eaten coat around her and said, 'My dear, if I might suggest – shall we try croutons next time?'

'Of course,' said Henry, grandly waving her ladle. 'Croutons.'

'And,' said the old lady, leaning forward confidentially, 'do try and remove the clowns from the hall. They make it so crowded, with all that juggling. Most dangerous.'

It was a fantasy left over from some childhood trip to the circus. Henry almost envied her a world thronged with lions, tigers and liberty horses, not to mention the ringmaster, who sometimes leaned down in a kindly way and asked her to move on. Sometimes he took her to the police station, but they never kept her in. There was no place for her, since she was harmless and inoffensive. No place but this shabby church hall.

When everyone was served Henrietta took her own bowl of soup and piece of bread and went to sit down. They didn't get many at lunchtime, only the old and the kids who hadn't yet found something better. Peter talked to them, finding the money to send some home, finding a hostel for the ones who wouldn't go back. Henry watched over the old people, to see who was ill, who was desperate, who distressed. For a lot of them this life wasn't so bad. It was the one existence in which they could be entirely without responsibility.

Peter came across as she finished. He had been talking to a fifteen year old who was going back to Peterborough on the coach. 'What do you bet he spends the fare on drink or drugs?'

'You should give them tickets and nothing else,' said Henrietta.

'O ye of little faith.'

They grinned at each other. It was acknowledged between them that Henry's faith was pretty lukewarm. She sang carols at Christmas, and wasn't above begging God for favours when necessary, but as for any personal relationship

– well, she would pass. God could stay in his heaven and she would linger on earth. Peter, on the other hand, was nourished by belief. Sometimes, when she was with him, Henry could sense that he was listening, to something else, someone else, something other. It was excluding. Frightening. But it was Peter.

She reached into her pocket and brought out the wedding invitation. Peter read it and lifted his brows. 'Rushing into this, isn't she?'

Henry shook her head. 'Actually, I'm really pleased for her. I thought it was all going to fizzle out, and she'd have been heartbroken. I knew she adored him, she just wouldn't say. Anyway, are you going to come?'

'As your partner? I don't know. I'll have to check my diary.'

She made a face at him. He was never busy on Saturdays, his church being totally unpopular with the marrying kind. But, when he had his day off, Henrietta was always at the races, or in the country. And if she was in town she would go to the theatre in the evening, or to a party, and Peter would watch television alone.

'A whole day together – just think. We could even book into a hotel somewhere and stay the night.'

He looked at her from under his brows. 'Will you stop saying things like that.'

'Why? We could. I want to.'

'But it isn't right.'

'Who says? God? He doesn't care. You're just worried about the bishop. And my mother. But we love each other, and we should be able to express that! I want to be close to you. To show you how I feel.'

Her breasts pressed against her blouse. Plump, ripe fruits. In the van at night she would take his hand and put it under her shirt, forcing him to touch and feel. An aeon ago he had been an inept fumbler of girls, losing his virginity to a silent, gum-chewing slut who'd go with anyone. Since then there had been girls, women, now and then. But not lately. As his faith strengthened so did his demands on himself. It wasn't enough any more just to take easy satisfaction.

339

'No,' he said softly. 'We can't. It isn't something to be casual about.'

'Who's being casual?' She pushed her hair back from her face, like a schoolgirl, an overgrown child. He felt a sudden rush of desire. She was a lovely girl, the sweetest girl, and he would give anything — almost anything. She was too young to know anything of life.

'You don't understand, Henry,' he said desperately. 'I won't do something that's going to hurt you. And it would. I know.'

'I don't care if I get hurt. I want to be with you. Properly.'

'Do you think I don't want that? But — darling Henry, I don't keep in with the bishop because I want a better job, more money, status, anything like that, but because I need him to let me work here. I'm not going anywhere, I'm not progressing. I'm doing what I want to do. Always.'

Henrietta believed nothing of that. In her mind's eye she saw herself encouraging a move, a new parish, perhaps a rambling country vicarage. Peter was so talented, and ultimately he could even become bishop. Speaking cautiously she said, 'I know you think that now. But if we were married you wouldn't think that. You'd have a home and children, you wouldn't need — '

'I don't need it now! I want it. You see, Henry, this is what I want to do. It isn't some substitute for real life, it's the life I want, the life I choose. I shall never change.'

'Everybody changes.'

'Not fundamentally. Not right through. And I care for you far too much to subject you to a life you'd grow to hate.'

'There isn't anything I want to do more than be your wife.'

He caught her hand. 'I won't let you talk like that, Henry!'

He was suddenly aware that this was getting out of hand, that he was out of his depth. She was so utterly, passionately in love with him. He burst out, 'Perhaps I'd better not come to this wedding. Perhaps we'd better stop seeing so much of each other.'

'No! Peter, don't say that. Please, Peter. I won't be difficult, I won't say a word about sex. Peter, please.'

340

'I should think not, indeed!' It was the old lady again, elbowing her way through the crowd of clowns she saw surrounding them. 'He's a man of God! He doesn't need physical satisfaction. Every morning he puts his private parts in iced water and – '

'Thank you, Mrs Dodd,' said Peter, getting to his feet and taking her hand. 'How are the clowns? Many about today?'

'Well, of course there are,' she said testily. 'All this sex talk has addled your brain, young man.'

'Iced water on the head, that's what I need.'

Henrietta ducked over her soup. They never had any privacy, there was never time to talk. Did he mean to be rid of her then? She would die. And she at least knew there was no afterlife. Heaven was an earthly thing, and it was within her grasp, with Peter. Would he really take it away? But when she looked up, almost blinded by a mist of tears, Peter was watching. He winked at her and in response she gave him a tremulous smile. He would come to the wedding. He only needed time. It would be all right after all.

Simon watched them, munching his way through a cream cake the while. Matty was talking in short, brittle sentences, determinedly bright. Her left hand bore an antique ring, amethysts interspersed with tiny diamonds, like an underwater flower.

Sholto wasn't talking much. Every now and then he ran his fingers over his scar. When Matty's jacket fell from her shoulders, he reached out to wrap it around her once again, as gentle as a mother with a highly strung child.

There was a piece of cinnamon toast left, and since no one else was eating Simon obligingly cleared the plate. He wasn't unduly perturbed by the tense pair in front of him. Apparently it was common for brides to go to pieces before the big day, Cartwright's sister had called it all off a week before, but fortunately his mother hadn't cancelled the caterers, because she changed her mind by the Monday. Cartwright had been forced to dress up in a kilt.

'Do I have to wear a skirt?' he demanded.

Matty blinked. 'No. Why?'

341

'Nothing.'

Sholto stirred himself. 'You're an usher. You stand around showing people to their seats. Nothing to it. By the way, do you want another cake? You've only had four.'

'Can I take an eclair back to school? People might like it.'

'How many people?' asked Matty. 'You'd better take a few.'

Simon grinned at her. Sholto got up and went to buy the eclairs from the shop counter to which the tearoom was attached. Matty and Simon watched him.

'You are pleased, aren't you?' said Matty.

He nodded. 'I like Sholto.'

'Yes.'

She looked from Sholto's tall, almost gangling figure to the bright-eyed boy in front of her. She loved them both, so differently. There should be different names for such emotions, one so anxious and protective, the other full of jealousy and need. Did Sholto have one woman or many? One would be harder to bear. If she met her she would kill her, decided Matty, and felt her fingers tense into claws. It was humiliating to be at the mercy of such rage, and she pressed the cool stones of her ring against her lips. Sholto was marrying her. He had left the other one and returned to her. She must remember that.

He came back swinging a cake box from one finger. 'Right, let's get Simon back in time to smear cream on his Latin prep. And you, Matilda, have to get back to work.'

'She doesn't work on Sundays,' said Simon.

'Oh yes I do,' said Matty. 'I'm writing a catalogue, listing all my good pieces. I'm sending it to people I know, with pictures. Sholto's doing the pictures.'

'With my trusty box Brownie,' he admitted. 'Simon, did you know your sister now employs a silversmith to make for her? She's going to go bankrupt due to overambition.'

'And you are going to be ruined by foolhardiness,' retorted Matty. 'You refuse to sell good pictures, and then commit yourself to things you don't have the money to buy, in the hope you'll find a buyer in time.'

He raised an eyebrow. 'Which I always do.'

'So far,' said Matty darkly.

That evening she sat hunched by the fire with her pasted up catalogue. It was messy, with none of the gloss she wanted, although Sholto and the printer both assured her that the finished product would be fine. She didn't believe them. Sholto had insisted on arranging all the silver artistically, instead of the more usual single object display on a table, so the pictures had to have keys, explaining what was what. And he photographed in colour, which made it vastly expensive.

She stared gloomily at his representation of Richard Greensall's flatware. Sholto had draped a red cloth in a waterfall, and tumbled spoons and forks into it, in seemingly haphazard lines. Michaelmas daisy heads were scattered amongst them, and some feathers, while the strap of something in good leather intruded in the bottom corner. Classic silver photograph it was not, although it was undoubtedly attractive, in Sholto's extravagant Italian way. But would it appeal to buyers? She did not know.

Sholto wandered into the room and switched on the television, pressing the remote control like a gun, roaming the channels. He turned the volume up loud, too loud, and still switched channels. Matty got up and pressed the mute button. The sound ceased abruptly.

'Don't,' she said, putting her hands on his shoulders.

He reached up to unfasten her blouse and cup her breasts. 'Do,' he murmured, and she saw the hard, bright light in his eyes. If this was what he wanted, she thought, if he needed this, then she would give it to him. She lifted herself, engulfing his face in her warm, scented flesh.

Lorne said, 'Greg honey, do you want some more syrup?'

He glanced up and shook his head, then returned his gaze to the newspaper. She sat down opposite him, small, lovely, with a belly like a small protuberant football stuck on her slender frame. Resting her chin in her hands, lace folds of her housecoat hung down from her wrists. Pregnancy had added to her only in one place; elsewhere her bones were almost visible beneath her skin.

She watched her husband eat and read. He wasn't good in the mornings, but it was almost the only time they had alone together. By eight-thirty there would be Mrs Berenson, and in the evenings there was Sherwood. So Lorne got up early and tried to find a little time to put her marriage on a firm base.

She took a deep breath. 'I meant to tell you, Greg, I'm going to visit my friend Matty next month. She's getting married. Do you want to come?'

'Huh?'

His blue eyes focused vaguely on her. He wasn't listening. 'I'm going to England next month,' she repeated. 'Matty's wedding. Want to come?'

'You're pregnant. You can't travel.'

'I'm fine. I asked Doc Yates and he says I can go.'

'She's marrying that shit, isn't she? The one that took a shine to you?'

'He did not! And if he did, who cares? I married you. And I'll be back in a week.'

She got up and went behind him, rubbing his shoulders with her delicate hands. He leaned his head against her belly, and she rubbed herself on him, as sensuous as a cat. 'Don't be difficult, hon. I want to go. I want to see my friends.'

'You don't need them.'

'But I still want to see them! Please, Greg. Please, hon.'

She listened to her own pleading with a sense of disgust. But only a few months of marriage had taught her it wasn't wise to go against the Berenson family. They had a habit of making things hard. They had the money, they even had the cars, and if Lorne wanted either she had to go begging.

'I'll take you to dinner tonight,' said Greg, pulling away and standing up.

'I want to go to Europe, Greg.'

'You're not fit. You know that. Another time.'

When he was gone she fastened her hands to the edge of the table and gripped until she thought her fingers would pierce the wood. That man thought he owned her. He treated her no better than a cherished horse, taken out when it pleased him, left in the stall when it did not. She poured herself a cup of juice and drank it in short, furious sips.

'Howdy, Lorne.' It was Sherwood. 'Not often I see you in your night things.'

344

She tried to compose herself. 'You're early. Why's that?'

'Business meeting. Not only your folks in trouble these days, plenty of others in debt.'

'Do you issue lots of loans then?'

He looked at her over a coffee cup. 'Here and there. Here and there. You're looking peaky this morning, Lorne. Not your usual lovely self.'

If only she didn't dislike Sherwood so much. But Greg always listened to his father. She turned and smiled confidingly. 'Sherwood, Greg's being foolish. Thinks I shouldn't travel, when Doc Yates says it's perfectly safe. I want to go to England, to my friend's wedding. Will you tell Greg I can go?'

The small eyes watched her out of a genial face. 'Not right to come between a man and his wife, Lorne.'

'It is when you're asked. Greg listens to you. I'll do – I'll do anything!'

Her own desperation surprised her. It was only a wedding. But all at once it seemed as if she would die if she stayed here another moment, another second, in this grim house on this grim farm with limp Enid Berenson and Sherwood who scared her and Greg who needed sex night and morning. 'I do so want to go,' she said feebly.

Sherwood came across the kitchen towards her. 'You need some amusement, Lorne, that's your trouble.' He lifted her hand and patted it rhythmically with his own. 'I'll have a talk to Greg. He's worried about you, it's natural. Your daddy's worried too, you should run along and see him. About time he let us have his river meadow, and I've told him so.'

'The river meadow?' said Lorne, and coughed a little.

'I'll pay a good price,' said Sherwood. 'And he sure needs the cash.' His hand strayed down to her hard belly. He allowed himself a brief caress. 'After all, this is the Berenson we're working for now. All of us.'

Lorne went to the bathroom and took a shower. She dressed prettily and took the car to her parents' place, for lunch and a talk. In the evening Greg made love to her in the sagging bed under the eaves and when he was finished he told her, yawning, that she could go.

Chapter Twenty-One

Lorne emerged from the taxi in a flurry of bags, boxes and advice from the taxi driver. 'Now, don't you strain yourself, Miss. I'd better take that – you just look after yourself, I'll see to the bags.'

Griselda and Matty hurried out to meet her. 'I see you've lost none of your sex appeal,' said Griselda. 'I had the same driver, and he barely spared me a grunt.'

'It's my maternal aura,' said Lorne, waving a slender hand. 'It brings out the gallantry in men. All except Greg, that is.'

The girls embraced and went into the house. Matty felt a little light-headed. Events seemed to be racing along, bearing her on a giant wave. She felt excited and apprehensive all at the same time. 'I never thought you'd come, Lorne,' she said, sitting down abruptly on the sofa. 'I thought Greg would pin you to the marital bed.'

Lorne grimaced. 'He did try. But honestly, girls, if you knew how awful it is stuck in a house with nothing to do all day but avoid your mother-in-law and think about babies – well, I had to come!'

'It wouldn't have been the same without you,' said Matty. 'Just you make sure you have fun.'

'Fun? It's going to be a party!'

She flung out her arms and subsided on to Matty. There was a shriek and the pair of them slid giggling to the floor. Griselda said, 'Girls, girls!' and emptied a bowl of pot pourri over them.

'We'll smell like a hope chest,' squealed Lorne.

'A dope chest,' said Matty, smelling the leaves. 'I swear this is hash.'

'Henry would tell us,' said Griselda. 'She's an expert on all things squalid. She'll probably bring you a fumigation kit as a wedding present.'

'Just so long as she doesn't include the parasites,' said Lorne.

The girls climbed back on to the sofa, shaking petals from their hair. Griselda, very much at home after an hour in Matty's house, went to the tray and poured two glasses of sherry and one of tonic water. Lorne looked at her, as always hinting at challenge. She might have confided more if Griselda wasn't there. 'How's life with you, Grizz? Any sex?'

'Don't be ludicrous.' Griselda sat in the armchair, curling her long, jean-clad legs underneath her. 'I work, with result; I party, moderately; and I go for long and interesting walks with Bertie Brantingham. He's looking for a rich wife, so don't get any ideas.'

'Why's he walking with you, then?' Lorne gulped down her tonic water and held the glass out for more. Griselda obliged.

'He's not too good with women, generally. I mean, they all adore him, because he's quite a duck, but he can't relax. Feels he ought to give them chocolates and pay them compliments and so on. Doesn't have to bother with me, of course. But we've known each other forever.'

Matty said, 'He's coming to the wedding. We can look at him then and see if he's suitable.'

'Suitable for what?' Griselda looked down her nose, like an indignant horse.

'For you, darling,' purred Lorne. 'He can make money on the Stock Exchange or something. You, he takes to bed.'

Griselda's sallow cheeks flamed scarlet. She climbed to her feet, arms and legs everywhere, shaking with rage. 'How – could – you! How dare you! Bringing everything down to your own base level. Thinking everything's about sex, and fancying, and disgusting things. You don't understand anything that's decent and straightforward and above board, and I'm damned if I'll sit here and listen to you – spitting on my life!'

The door slammed behind her. They heard her thundering up the stairs to the scant privacy of Simon's bedroom. For tonight she was supposed to be sharing it with Lorne.

Matty said, 'Well!'

'I knew she was head over heels,' said Lorne. 'When she first spoke about him, I could tell. And I trampled on it.'

'Did you mean to?' asked Matty, sharply.

Lorne blushed. 'Of course I did! You know me, I was feeling mean. But she always thinks I've got everything easy, that I don't have to try at anything. But just now life doesn't feel easy. And she looks so – sure.'

They were silent. 'Are you scared about the baby?' asked Matty.

Lorne nodded. 'Some. More scared about my life. Matty, I don't know if this is what I want!'

Matty spread her hands. 'If it isn't, you get divorced.'

'If only it was that easy.'

Griselda came down a few minutes later. She had tidied her bun, and put a slash of lipstick on her narrow mouth. 'Sorry for that tantrum, Lorne,' she said stiffly. 'I must be tired.'

'And I'm bitchy,' said Lorne. 'Pax?'

'Pax.'

They were about to eat supper when Sholto came in. The sports car drew up with a spatter of gravel, and he burst into the house crying, 'Matty! Matty, look at this!'

It was a small, dark painting. One corner was cracked and the paint had flaked off, the colours had faded, and when at last you made out the shapes within the gloom there appeared to be a cherub with dislocated arms. 'From the school of Fra Filippo Lippi,' Sholto exclaimed. 'A pupil work, and rubbish of course, but it's things like this that show us the construction of the picture, the techniques the master was trying to teach. You see how bad the drawing is here? It's been corrected, and again here, and I'm sure if we use X-rays we'll see where the colours have been changed. What a find!'

'Can you sell it?' asked Matty.

He shrugged. 'Don't know and don't care. This I intend to keep.'

She let out her breath in exasperation. Sholto was off again, carried away by one of his enthusiasms. 'How much?'

'What? Oh, nothing to worry about. A bit. Stately home. They wanted me to buy some godawful hunting scene full of unlikely horses and even more unlikely squires.'

'Sounds marketable.'

'No doubt. Not my thing. And this was lurking in the passage. Quite ill-considered. Brought back by an uncle on the grand tour in the last century. Apparently he almost fell foul of Napoleon on the way home.'

Matty felt her head start to spin. The new car, the wedding, Sholto's inevitable monetary profligacy, and now this. She turned and saw Griselda looking stunned. The sight of Sholto in a dark gold padded jacket over tight black trousers was probably not what she had anticipated. 'Griselda – Sholto – if I might introduce –' she began.

Abruptly Sholto put down his picture. 'But of course. Griselda! I'm delighted. Matty's always wanted us to meet. How good of you to come.' He gave her the full force of his twisted, million kilowatt smile.

'It's a pleasure,' said Griselda, going pink. 'A great pleasure. I'm so glad you found your painting.'

'Yes. Wonderful, isn't it? Do let me know if you've got anything you'd like me to look at. Matty buys anything, of course, but I'm afraid I'm a little bit choosy. No horses.'

'I do not buy anything!' said Matty.

'No, it just seems like it. Tons and tons of metal, all over the place in that barn. She's wildly extravagant, you know. I shall have to work my fingers to the bone to keep her in teaspoons. My little currant bun.'

Inevitably Matty laughed. Lorne said petulantly, 'Are you ignoring me, Sholto?'

He put his hands on his heart. 'As if I could. As if I would. You could audition for the Madonna in the infant school play. How's beefcake?'

Lorne shrugged. 'OK. Keeps me close to hearth and home.'

'Well, you knew that. Jealous as they come is our Greg. Don't you know you fill up a gap in his lifeplan? Beautiful, intelligent and fecund. What more could a man want?' He put his hands on her shoulders and leered down at her.

Lorne chuckled and put one hand up to his face. 'Idiot.'

He went upstairs to change, and the room was empty without him. The girls swallowed down the sudden silence.

'My goodness,' said Griselda. 'Matty, you should have told me.'

'Told you what?'

'That man is − something other.'

'Isn't he just?' said Lorne. 'How did you do it, Matilda?'

Matty struggled for insouciance. Then she confessed, 'I don't know how I got him. He got me, I think. He is lovely, isn't he? Clever and sophisticated and kind.'

'Not kind,' said Lorne.

'He is. He is! Wonderful with Simon, and sweet to me. He's got the softest heart.'

Lorne's face turned away, just as Matty tried to meet her eye. She felt sudden anxiety. What did Lorne know that she wasn't telling? 'I don't think you should keep that kind of secret,' she said shrilly. 'Not now. Not when I'm going to get married.'

'I haven't got any secrets.'

'Then what? Lorne, we owe each other some trust.' Griselda was being judicial.

Lorne swung round, the folds of her dark blue smock swirling about her. 'He isn't stable, Matty. You know that. All I get is a feeling sometimes − and it's no more than a feeling − he's only just on the rails. He could go off them at any minute. Any way.'

Sholto's feet were on the stairs, coming back down. Matty looked at her friends, eyes wide and unblinking. Lorne had voiced her own vague thoughts.

Sholto burst into the room. 'We'll drink champagne,' he declared, striding through to the kitchen. 'Matty, is there any food in this house? I can't face salmonella in a basket at the pub. My digestion's applying for a transfer as it is.'

'I made lasagne,' she said. 'We can eat now if you want.'

He appeared in the doorway, bottle in hand, grinning wolfishly. 'I do want. Tonight I have three women at hand. I intend to make the most of it.'

Griselda said, 'I'm not handmaid material, I'm afraid.'

'Neither's Matty, as it happens. I bet she hasn't put any cream in the sauce. Look, I'll pour us all a drink and see what I can do to make this dinner a little less healthy.'

In the brief lull of his absence Griselda said, 'He makes me feel quite unbalanced. I don't know what he's going to do next.'

Matty giggled. 'I know. And I think you can keep stability. For now.'

The champagne flutes gleamed pale gold in the evening light; in the kitchen Sholto was whistling the unlikely notes of a Bach fugue; and Matty was suddenly certain.

The wedding was not taking the traditional pattern. Sholto was zipping up the wedding dress. 'This is very bad luck,' complained Matty.

'I think getting the zip stuck was the worst luck. You've got your camisole caught in the teeth.'

'I don't know why I bought one. I thought it would be romantic.'

'There was never anything romantic about a zip.'

Lorne sat on the bed, painting her nails. 'Having trouble with the dress is getting to be traditional around here. And Henry's going to be late.'

Matty turned round, ruining Sholto's latest manoeuvre. 'She can't! I won't get married if everyone isn't there. It was bad enough that Sammy wouldn't come, and now this. I won't do it. I shall refuse.'

'You won't have to,' said Sholto, turning her back with a firm hand. 'We'll postpone. Have the reception first and get hitched later. Or something. Let's have fun.'

She turned and put her arms around his neck. He looked wonderful in high collar and waistcoat. 'I do love you,' she said softly.

The light in his eyes seemed to flicker. It was as if, momentarily, she had reached past his defences and touched him. 'Behave yourself,' he whispered.

Lorne said, 'Do you know Griselda snores? I swear she didn't at school. Or at least I always thought it was that Thompson girl. The one with the buck teeth.'

Leaving the zip, Sholto joined her on the bed. 'Does the

infant snore? Let's have a listen.' He put his ear to Lorne's stomach, resting a hand lightly on her navel.

She said, 'Sholto, this is a great deal too intimate. Please desist.'

'Shut up, I'm listening. It's like plumbing. Matty, I think we shall have to reproduce. I know it means distasteful physical contact, but you women have to make sacrifices. Hell! We haven't room. We'll have to extend the house. I hate dust on the pictures.'

Griselda came into the room. She stood in the doorway briefly taking stock, then said, 'Do stop being provocative, Lorne. Matty, I'll do your zip. By the way, Henry just phoned to say the vicar's van broke down. They're on the train and she'll meet us at the church.'

'I take it this is her vicar and not ours,' said Sholto. 'I expect ours to have been up at dawn, getting the vibes right. I need God on my side.'

'Do you?' Matty put her head on one side.

He got off the bed, brushed her lips with his own, and said, 'Yes.'

Sholto stood at the front of the church, waiting for his bride. He wasn't unduly anxious since he had brought her in his sports car five minutes before. They had interrupted Griselda, Henrietta and Lorne indulging in excited giggling in the porch, while the two vicars chatted. It had resulted in Peter Venables being roped in to assist at the service, wearing borrowed robes.

The church itself was decked out with white flowers and green foliage, interspersed with great banners of red and gold fabric, hung in flat panels between the windows. Some friend of Sholto's, a photographer, was crawling about taking pictures of it, insisting that he could sell them to a magazine. Like Sholto himself, it was theatrical and witty. Matty, pausing in the doorway, alone because there was no one to give her away, felt herself smile with delight.

Matty's veil was of old cream lace, reaching to her knees. Her hair glowed like copper. As she walked, she was dignity vying with youth and spirit, straining against the slow pace of the music to which she walked. Sholto's aunt, turning to study her, thumped her walking stick on the floor and turned back. 'That girl is far too young,' she muttered to herself. 'She'll never cope with him.'

But as they stood together at the altar, and Sholto bent his head to speak, there was something so beautiful about them that people started to cry. Marriage was a sacrament, the vicar said. So it was. But to many it so often seemed a leaky boat. This boat, this little vessel, setting off in a skim of wind for no one knew where, must caulk its planks with love.

For himself, Sholto felt almost dreamy. Had he done it right? he wondered. Very nearly. The creation of pageant and ritual comforted him, he felt that he was making a sacrifice to God. Matty was his talisman, his hold on happiness. He had wanted always to be free — but this was better, this was safer. If he let himself fall, let himself plunge into that world he knew beckoned so insidiously, then he was lost. He looked up at the cross, fixed his eyes on that symbol, and prayed that all would be well.

The party was riotous. Champagne was everywhere, the popping of bottles at every open window mingling with birdsong in the garden. In the orchard the goat held court, receiving gifts of canapés from visiting fingers. Simon told everyone who would listen, 'It's a good thing I'm going back to school tonight. I had to lend My Room to Matty's friends, you know. It's got all my things in it.'

'We're awfully grateful, Simon,' said Griselda forcefully. 'I told Bertie you had a Scalextric and it was all I could do to stop him going and setting it up.'

Simon looked at her warily, in case he was being teased, but Bertie said, 'Don't be daft, Griselda! You need space for a track like that. Can't have it out with all these people trampling about.'

'It takes ages to set up, but everyone complains if you leave it out,' confessed Simon. 'If the barns weren't full of stuff I could put it out there.'

'We had a trainset once, at home,' said Bertie wistfully. 'Huge thing, permanent you know, in the orangery. Had to sell, of course.'

Griselda snorted and left them, saying to Henrietta, 'Why do grown men talk trains? Mystifying.'

Peter Venables, a little daunted by Henry's imposing friend, said, 'I never talk trains. I had a wind-up set once but I broke it. On purpose, I'm afraid. The boy next door kept coming round to play with it and he was stupid and boring and I wanted him gone.'

'So there!' said Henry. 'What a brute you were. No wonder you got religion, to be saved from breaking trainsets.'

He waggled a finger in her face. 'Contrary to your meagre expectations, Henrietta, I'm not in this business for what I can get, more for what I can give. As far as gifts from God are concerned, He gave already.'

Griselda, lost, said, 'By the way, have you met Henry's mother?'

Peter said, 'Certainly. Yes. Why do you ask?'

'No reason, really. Just − well, I'm surprised she hasn't had you posted to a missionary station in Luangwa. Or somewhere further still.'

'Oh. Er − um.' Peter looked thoughtful.

'She doesn't know about him,' said Henry. 'Or at least, she does, but she thinks he's done with. She thinks I go out with Dominic.'

'Sounds like lying to me,' said Griselda, looking down her nose. 'Is this Christian, I ask myself?'

The girls exchanged a look, and chuckled. Peter said, 'Don't think I don't feel very badly about all this. Henry and I are friends only. Nothing more. As I often say to Henry − it isn't as if I don't want to be honest with her mother.'

'Good Lord, nobody's ever honest with Mrs Giles!' declared Griselda. 'It would be fatal. Don't worry, Henrietta absolutely adores her, but she has survived to be the charmer you see today by never, never letting her mother win. It's the only way, I assure you.'

People were starting to dance, and Griselda went away in search of more champagne. Peter said, 'She's squiffy.'

'So what? So am I. Let's dance.'

Peter wasn't very good, putting enthusiasm in place of

style. He waved his arms rather a lot. Next to them Lorne performed an elegant boogie, accompanied by the photographer. He was saying, 'You really are fantastic. Why don't we try a few shots later? At my place?'

Suddenly Henry stopped dancing and went abruptly out into the garden. Peter followed. The apple trees in the orchard, in soft leaf, rustled like taffeta. Star of Bethlehem was glowing in the long grass, and there was dogrose in the hedges. Henrietta was crying.

'Go away,' she said, when Peter appeared. 'I don't want you.'

'Was it me? What did I say?'

'You know very well. You denied me. And you've done it a lot more than thrice. "We're just good friends — ", you say, to my friend, to my good friend, and you make me look a complete idiot! I hate you!'

He pushed at a piece of apple bark with his thumb. It was rotten and gave way, revealing pale wood underneath. 'I don't want people to think I'm taking advantage of you. That's all.'

'To hell with what they think about me, I suppose! It's your reputation you're worried about. Forget all this unselfishness crap — you think you know what's good for everyone, whether they agree or not. This isn't good for me, you only think it is. And I've had enough.' She waited for him to protest, to hold her and talk of love. But he said nothing.

The bark was rough and flaking. Peter crushed it between his fingers. He hadn't meant her to get so serious about things, he hadn't meant to get involved at all. He had shied away from harshness, and was tempted by desire.

He liked her so much; her ebullience, her generosity, her tremendous warmth. When he got up in the morning, if it was a day when he would see Henrietta he felt his spirits lift. If it was a day when he would not, there was an equivalent dip in his level of content. But he would not suffer if he never saw her again. Whatever it was she felt for him was not reciprocated.

He leaned his head against the tree. 'Don't pretend to be upset,' said Henry venomously. 'You don't care.'

'We're lying to people. That can't be right.'

'It isn't,' said Henry. 'We haven't done anything to lie about yet.'

'Henry, I don't want to marry!'

'I know that.' She moved closer to him. 'You think I won't live your sort of life. But I will. We'll be happy. I won't ever complain.'

'You know how fond I am of you.'

'Yes, but – '

'Henry, it isn't love!'

Henrietta sat down suddenly in the long damp grass. She felt sick, as if she stood on the edge of a precipice. The wide space of her vision terrified her. 'You don't mean that. You do love me. It's my mother – you're just trying to put me off.'

'No. There isn't anyone else. I doubt there will ever be anyone else. Henrietta, if I wanted to marry I should marry you, but it's not for me! It's not what I want!'

'You're not going to tell me this is some bleeding religious vocation, are you? There isn't a God! There never has been. You're going to waste your life serving something that isn't there!'

He turned from her, and in that gesture rejected her. She felt her heart stutter. If he felt as she did he could never do this. He didn't feel it then. Truly, she was unloved.

'I never wanted to hurt you,' he said.

Griselda leaned from the window and called, 'Do come in, you two! We're going to dance the Gay Gordons. Bertie's organising it.'

Peter put his hand up to his eyes. Henrietta said, 'We'll have to go. It's Matty's wedding, we can't spoil it.'

He let his hand drop. 'It's for the best,' he said. 'In time, you'll see.'

Her face was very pale. When he first met her, he remembered, she had seemed years younger than now. The girl had turned into a woman, at his bidding and under his hand. A sad woman. 'I'm sorry I've been so foolish,' she said, and walked stiff-backed into the house.

By eight, Lorne was the only sober person there. She fended

off the photographer once more, and hunted for a peaceful place to sit. Her back was aching cruelly, and her head hurt. The pregnancy was unavoidably making itself known.

Sholto was in the sitting room, building a tower of empty bottles to the accompaniment of bets and ribald comments. Matty was fuzzily telephoning, trying to get a taxi to send Simon back to school, and even Henry's vicar was insensible. He lay in a corner, eyes half-closed, muttering snippets of prayers.

The house was impossible. Even the wedding presents were in a jumble in the kitchen, topped by Sammy Chesworth's offering, a Queen Anne glass and silver rosebowl. Lorne went upstairs, seeking refuge in the bedroom she shared with Griselda, but the door was locked. She put her ear to the panel for a moment and heard someone moan. She was about to call out when someone grunted. Oh. That, then. She crossed the landing silently and pushed open the door of the room Matty and Sholto shared. No one there. Thankfully she sank on to the bed.

Behind the locked door Griselda lay beneath Bertie. She didn't quite know how this had happened, but they had both been very tired, and went to lie down, and suddenly Bertie's hands had been all over her front. The kissing came next, on and on, unbelievable, and then he'd been fumbling at her tights and things. 'Please old girl – sorry and all that – needs must!'

He'd been hanging over her with that incredible protuberance, just like a horse. She knew he was drunk. She knew they were both drunk. But it seemed quite impossible to do anything to resist. And now she lay there, his legs between hers, his belly against hers, his – him – inside her. Let it not be true, she thought suddenly, let this not be happening! Now that she and Bertie had done this, things would never be the same.

He was moving inside her, deliciously, incredibly. But oh, what was she doing here? Why was it her and not one of the pretty, easy, casual girls at college? He was grunting, his eyes shut, his big face twisting suddenly in near ecstasy. The sensation, within her, made Griselda gasp. He fell to the side, panting, and she was gripped by a sense of near

358

panic. If she got away he might forget, it might not be real. She slid from the bed, her head spinning, her breathing loud in her ears. She couldn't stand. Half crawling, she made for the door, unlocked it and headed for the bathroom.

Lorne, half-asleep, heard the scuffle. Probably Henry, she decided, which was why the vicar was in such a state. Weddings were like that, people getting in and out of bed with all the wrong partners. She, married and pregnant, was as chaste as Sholto's old aunt, if not more so, since the old woman was drinking like a fish and telling rude stories.

The door opened suddenly. It was Sholto. 'Oh, hell,' he said when he saw her. 'No privacy anywhere.'

'It's OK. I'll go. After all, it's your wedding and your bedroom.'

'Actually, it was the bathroom I was after. Stay put and look the other way.' He opened the window, unzipped and peed expertly into the flowerbed.

'That's disgusting,' said Lorne.

'Sure is. But essential. I'm carrying one hell of a load.'

He sprawled on the bed beside her. Lorne said, 'Are you going to try it on or something?'

Sholto laughed. 'I hope not. Although, I admit that a little thrusting where Greg Berenson has been before would not go amiss — but not on Matty's wedding day. And not with Matty's friend.'

'Damn,' said Lorne. 'I thought I was going to get a chance to make a moral decision. And you made it first.'

'I've made a lot of moral decisions lately. Bloody exhausting it is.'

Lorne sighed. 'Not nearly as exhausting as being pregnant. I can't even sleep for the kicking. And then there's the birth — can you imagine anything more disgusting? Somehow I never thought it would happen to me.'

'What? Not even in the barn, exchanging body fluids with golden boy? You girls need help!'

'That's the way it goes. And now I'm due to be torn bodily apart by something the size of my mother's sewing basket which seems to have taken up residence in a very personal place! Suppose I don't even like the kid? Suppose it's like

Greg's goddammed father? Why should I go through hell for that?'

Sholto yawned and put his hands behind his head. 'Couldn't be like Sherwood. God couldn't make the same mistake twice.'

'Even so,' said Lorne uneasily. Then she said, 'You are drunk, aren't you? Really drunk?'

'Absolutely.'

'Then tell me something you won't remember later. Have you ever slept with a woman who's had babies? Someone who's a mother? What's it like?'

He gave her a wicked stare. 'You mean, is it like a stick of salami in the Channel tunnel?'

She went very red. 'Yes. Though I wouldn't have been quite so coarse.'

He rolled on his stomach. 'Let me put your mind at rest. From some very recent experience with a mother of four, I'd say you haven't a thing to worry about. Although of course conditions do vary from time to time. What can be as tight as a nun's arse some days − do pardon the profanity − can be very cushioned on others. And it ain't the tunnel that changes size, more the salami.'

'Does Matty know about the mother of four?'

'Matty knows a very great deal.'

'But not that?'

'Not especially that.'

She grinned at him. 'Don't worry. I won't say. I like you.'

'Sure you do.'

He reached out and patted her bulge. 'I must be off to dispose of my aunt, God bless her. Following which, Matty and I will repair to bed in the village inn and I shall do my marital duty with the salami. Then there's no turning back.'

'Do you want to?'

He met her eyes briefly. He was very pale, she thought. 'I was thinking of Matty,' he said. 'I never turn back. Even when I should.'

When he was gone Lorne put her hands over her eyes. Sholto was shocking, and a little exhausting. For once she was glad to be married to Greg. A sudden chill ran through her as she realised what she had thought. Wasn't she always glad to be married to Greg? They weren't used to each other yet and it was difficult living with his family — but wasn't she glad?

No, she was not. If she could have waved a magic wand and had her life back again, she would have gone to her father and talked honestly about money, looked for loans elsewhere, looked for what they could sell. She would not have sold herself like this, lending respectability to the Berensons' shabby image, lending them her family's old world charm.

She put her hands to her head, trying to will herself into serenity. Life with Greg wasn't so bad. She didn't have to make choices or decisions, she need only react to things. Nothing need begin with her. All her life she had preferred to watch others take the lead: Matty, Griselda, even her crazy cousins, and now Greg. The destiny he laid on her was one she could adapt and mould to a degree. But she need not bear the responsibility of choosing it.

'You never knew what you wanted anyway,' she told herself. 'So there wasn't anything you had to give up. It's as good a life as any.'

She lay back again on the bed and tried to rest. Her heart thumped against her ribs, restricted by her pregnancy to a limited cage. If it was unbearable, beyond everything, she could always divorce. Until then, she'd get by, in her cage.

Matty lay in the big bed in Littlebury's only inn and knew she was floating. Her body was suspended a foot above the mattress, and her mind was two feet or so above that. 'I'm going to heaven,' she murmured. 'My body and I have parted company.'

'You can't die on your wedding night,' said Sholto. He swung across the bed and pinned her beneath his weight. 'Got you.'

'Now we're both floating,' said Matty. 'I think that was the most wonderful party I've ever been to. Wasn't it wonderful? Or wasn't it? The others might not have had fun.'

'The only person who matters is you.' He touched her closed eyelids with his lips.

'Griselda matters. And Henry and Lorne. And you. Most of all you.' Her eyelids fluttered open. 'I didn't see Grizz, did you? When we left, I mean? Was she all right?'

'Dunno. In bed with Bertie, I suspect. So that must be all right, don't you think?'

She let out a long, weary sigh. 'Probably. Yes. I never know with friends. Or me. Oh, Sholto, I do so love to have you close to me like this. It's as if the world could disappear and it wouldn't matter. I'd be safe. We'd be safe. Together.'

'I'll always keep you safe,' he whispered. And suddenly his face contorted in a grimace of anguish. But Matty, her eyes closed, didn't see.

In the morning, Bertie and Griselda drove home. At the crossroads at Bawtry he stopped the car and said, 'Griselda, I should like it very much if you would do me the honour of becoming my wife.'

Griselda said, 'Don't be a fool, Bertie. Just because — it was a mistake. We both know that. You don't want to marry me and you never will. Besides, you've got to marry money.'

'My dear, I can't possibly permit you to go on thinking — imagining —'

'You're embarrassing us both, Bertie! And even if you wanted to marry me, I couldn't possibly want to marry you. It isn't — it just couldn't be — I'm sorry, but it won't do.'

'I see. I — I feel so ashamed of myself. A moment's weakness —'

'We were both to blame. Champagne and too much excitement. I think it's best forgotten. Don't you?'

'Griselda, if there should be an unfortunate happening — something unexpected — you would tell me? It is important, old thing. I'd be so hurt if you didn't — if you wouldn't tell me.'

Stiffly, holding back tears, Griselda said, 'I'm sure there'll be no problem. We both know enough about horse breeding to weigh up the chances, and I'm happy to say that they are slim. Now, Bertie, please drive on.'

Peter and Henrietta parted at the station. She stood close

to him and pecked his cheek. 'Goodbye, Peter. Don't worry, I won't bother you again. I'm not a silly girl any more, chasing you into the vestry.'

'I never thought you silly. And you didn't chase.'

'I did, you know. But I liked the dossers. I'll find some of my own, perhaps. Goodbye. Good luck.'

'Henry —' He caught at her arm, but she pulled away, and to hold her would hurt her. He walked behind her for ten, a dozen paces, saying 'Henry, please wait —' but she wouldn't stop and kept walking with that odd, unHenrylike stiffness in her face.

And it remained, to the moment when her mother opened the front door, and Henry flung into her arms, sobbing, 'Oh, Mummy! Mummy! You don't know, but the most awful thing's happened!'

Chapter Twenty-Two

There had been no discussion of a honeymoon. Somehow Matty had expected that once the ceremony was over life would go on much as before. She had sales to attend, clients to see, and three more sets of flatware that needed Richard Greensall's attention. It seemed, incredibly, as if her business had gathered its own momentum, and she no longer needed to kickstart each day.

But, no sooner had they returned to the cottage than Sholto said, 'Right then. Off on Friday, OK?'

'Off where?'

He grinned, and she knew there was trouble. 'Somewhere – interesting. Romantic. You'll love it.'

She protested and complained, showed him the piles of letters she must answer, the bills they needed to pay, but it was to no avail. It was arranged, he said. She would love it. They had money, in stock, in the bank, enough money. Did she want to stay a grubby little shopkeeper all her life?

'My father was a grubby little shopkeeper,' she flared.

'Which must have been wonderful fun, darling.'

Matty banged out of the room. They must not row, not in their first week of marriage. Perhaps he was right, she thought. Perhaps she was in danger of becoming dull and boring. Just as she was preparing to capitulate the bedroom door opened and Sholto said, 'It isn't only fun, you know. It's a hunting expedition. For both of us.'

She looked at him, suspicion writ large. 'Where to?'

'Eastern Europe.'

Her eyes flew open. 'I am not spending my honeymoon eating cabbage soup and breathing poisoned air! And I hate queuing, even at the Post Office, and you probably need visas, and the whole thing sounds absolutely foul.'

'But,' said Sholto, crawling lionlike across the bed, 'think of the goodies. The art, the silver, the jewels. Think what a treasure house it was before the war, and since then – nothing. There must be tons of stuff about.'

Matty put a thoughtful finger to her lips. All her dealer's senses twitched in anticipation. Sholto certainly knew how to tempt. 'Can you buy the stuff? Is it legal?'

'Not for national treasures, no. But for other things – well, we'll pay a fair price. And pack it with our socks. Any objections, Miss Morality?' He reached up and pushed her sweater from her shoulder, mouthing the smooth flesh.

'Hundreds. But I'll go.'

She sank down and let him make love to her. It was wonderfully delicious. No more anxiety, no more pain, she told herself, because he had chosen her, finally and forever. He was sucking her breasts, moving his head from one nipple to the other, leaving each purple and engorged. Suppose he tired of her? she thought. He was her only lover, she knew nothing except what he had shown her. The women, the other women, knew everything.

Her thoughts were blocking out feeling. She surrendered herself to sensation, for Sholto knew when she was half-hearted, knew when she had no pleasure. You could never hold back, with Sholto. He demanded, insisted upon, commitment.

Krakow airport was small, dingy and congested. They stood in a slow-moving queue to have their faces and passports glowered at by an unfriendly man with a gun.

'Why you come to Poland?' asked people in the queue, students mostly, returning from study abroad. 'What is here for you?'

'We like to travel,' said Sholto innocently.

But Matty wouldn't prevaricate. 'We've come to look at your art.'

'You'll get us locked up, you will,' he murmured, hustling her out of the building towards a row of dirty taxis.

The place smelled of rain and low-grade petrol. Now, at twilight, the buildings seemed dark and ill-lit, the people dismal. Much of it was her own weariness, Matty realised. She looked for what she expected.

Her spirits lifted over a good dinner. They were in one of the town's two expensive restaurants, filled with the faded glamour of before the war, all cracked chandeliers and old scratched wood. Sholto peered beadily at the paintings on the walls, but there was nothing of significance. Matty tossed the forks from hand to hand, but they were thin steel and also lacking in interest. The glasses though – she twirled one in her hand.

'What did I tell you?' said Sholto.

'We won't find anything. We can't speak Polish and it's all so very – Polish.'

But, by the end of the evening, Sholto had four of the crystal glasses in a box and a promise from the head waiter to, 'Look see perhaps some of the arty, my sister, yes?' But she tried to sell them bad oil paintings of the Cathedral, and they bought nothing.

It was the oddest honeymoon. They hired a car and drove through fields farmed in strips, with horses. They stopped at lonely farmhouses and children peered at them fearfully from behind sagging shutters. At one of these, unexpectedly and without warning, Sholto was offered a medieval icon, painted with wax on wood, the picture of a saint. The gold of the halo was perishing through damp and decay. The farmer wanted twenty dollars for it, and was prepared to take less.

'You can't,' said Matty, in a low, throbbing voice. 'These people haven't shoes for their feet. The children work at school all day and herd sheep all evening, and look at this poor woman's hands! What's more, that thing you have there could well be a national treasure!'

'It'll rot to hell if I leave it here,' said Sholto. His long fingers stroked the disintegrating wood. 'Suppose I give them fifty, then sell this to the government? Best I can do.'

'You can't sell it to the government,' said Matty. 'Buying the thing's illegal in the first place.'

'So, what would you have me do? Leave them shoeless and the icon done for?'

She turned on her heel and left the dark, onion-smelling farmhouse. Outside the air was full of summer. The farm children, gaining confidence, came out to play with a cat and some lambs, and great brown hens scratched on a towering dungheap. There were flowers everywhere, but little birdsong. It seemed as if they had stepped back in time, that there were wolves in the forests and giants in the hills. Yet on the distant road, a lorry belched sour diesel fumes into the quiet air.

Sholto came out with a parcel wrapped in dirty paper. 'How much?' asked Matty wearily.

'A hundred,' he snapped. 'They think I'm mad. I think I'm mad. If they blab about sudden riches we will certainly get arrested.' He put the parcel under the front seat and Matty climbed behind the wheel. They drove away quickly, leaving the farm in stunned silence.

'How much can you sell it for?' asked Matty at last.

'Dunno. Can't sell it on the open market. Could get a quarter of a million perhaps. If it can be saved.'

'You're not serious?'

He nodded. And she knew, suddenly, that to him the money meant nothing at all. It was a fortune, and he didn't care. When Sholto had money he spent it, and when he had none he spent as if he had. Clothes, books, cars, houses, furniture – he would buy all and any of them, almost without thought. He didn't care about money, thought Matty. He didn't care about things. Sholto cared about pictures.

'Tell me you love me,' she said suddenly.

'What?'

'Tell me that if that icon was in a fire and I was too, that you'd save me and not the icon.'

He grinned. 'Don't worry, I'd save you. The icon may be old but it's very damaged. Not that wonderful.'

'Suppose it was a picture you really liked? Suppose it was – that thing, the girl with the junipers?' She quoted a Leonardo she knew he much admired.

'That's not fair! It's a masterpiece, irreplaceable.'

'And I'm not, I suppose?'

Sholto laughed, deliberately ignoring her anger. 'Don't be difficult. And put your foot down, we want to be miles from here by tonight.'

They went into the mountains, where the forests stretched black and limitless, and then, gaining confidence, to Warsaw. Matty bought some spoons and a jug covered with old European marks she didn't know. It seemed strange, in the midst of so much that was grey and utilitarian, to come across things of beauty. The uncertainty kept Sholto in a ferment. 'All these attics, all these people, hanging on to things,' he murmured, looking out from their hotel room over the city. But there was nothing else to be had in Warsaw.

They flew to Czechoslovakia next, and then to Hungary. They bought a dark blue painting of a woman, unsigned and without provenance, which Sholto's nose told him was good. Matty acquired a samovar, and put it in her suitcase, praying that it would turn up after every flight. A month went by, and Matty's clothes were grey from hotel washes. She was pleading with Sholto to go home.

He sat on the other side of the hotel room, watching incomprehensible television and drinking vodka. The carpet was threadbare, and yellow fumes from a factory chimney filled the air with an acrid smell. He wrinkled his nose. 'Home? No, not yet.'

'Sholto, why are we here? Why won't you go home? It's not Luca?'

He shrugged and turned back to the television, switching to MTV, with its endless stream of pop, beamed determinedly into Eastern Europe to infect its young.

'Sholto!' insisted Matty.

He swung round on her. 'If you must know, Luca is making things very tough. Got the cops following me like hawks, accusing me of everything under the sun. Forgeries, selling stolen goods, the lot.'

'Have you done any of it?'

'What dealer can ever be quite sure? Can you? People steal things and the things don't tell. I don't bloody know.'

He knew more than he was telling. 'Can't you buy him off?'

'Hatred doesn't have a price. His wife's left him and taken the children. He blames me.'

Matty felt as if she wanted to cry. 'We can't go on like this forever! Can't we ever go home?'

He shrugged. 'Sometime, I suppose. When I decide what to do. Until then we'll rattle around the world.'

But Matty was throwing things into a case. 'It's Simon's half term in two weeks' time. We have to go home.'

'He can go to Henrietta!'

'Damn it, no!'

She put her hands over her eyes. She should have suspected this. It was so dangerous to depend on Sholto. He was like an insecure fence, on which you dared not trust yourself to lean because one day it would fall. She stole angry glances at him, suspecting him. Was it really Luca who stopped him going home? Or was it Matty, with her demands and her expectations and her contentment? Suddenly she was crying. 'I've got to go home!' she wailed. 'I can't live like this!'

Sholto said, 'Why can't you be brave? Why can't you travel with me forever?'

She felt sudden sharp envy of Lorne, whose husband wanted her at home, kept her at home. And here she was, in this dingy hotel, rootless and insignificant. Sholto could travel forever but Matty was almost a refugee. She had the same desperate sense that without a base, a fixed and settled place, she was no one.

She went and poured herself a vodka. Sholto said, 'All right then! If you will be so bloody boring we'll go home. But first I want to go to Italy.'

'Why?' Although she knew why. Because he was angry with her.

'Why not? Because I love Italy. I have friends there. I can introduce you to people.'

'People?' A woman, she thought. He's going to a woman. To revenge himself for his new wife's stubbornness, he would insist on seeing her.

*   *   *

370

The undercurrents ran darkly through the days. They took planes together, took taxis, and hardly spoke. There was a certain restfulness about it, as if they were each alone and entering a private world of reflection. Matty watched her husband rouse himself occasionally, to charm a stewardess or a counter girl, easily, as Matty herself had been charmed. He was an expert.

They were given their first up-to-date British paper on a British Airways flight, and Matty devoured it avidly. Sholto couldn't be less interested. When Matty finally surrendered the pages, everything read, he said, 'Happy now?'

'It's all right for you. You don't care where you are.'

He grinned, that old self-mocking grin. 'Oh, I care. But not like you. I don't have to touch base all the time. Home is people, not places.'

'Home is — where you don't have to waste energy coping. Where you can think. Where you can work. I can't do that in limbo.' She gestured helplessly towards the cloud-filled space outside the window.

Sholto, for the first time in hours, took her hand in an affectionate clasp. 'Don't worry, sweetie,' he murmured, 'I'll take you home.'

So the demon had gone, for now. He was Sholto again, not the cold and uncaring stranger. And somehow Italy, with its shops and sunlight, vivid talk and fast cars, did not seem quite as alien as the grey east. Sholto breathed deep of the warm air, and said with satisfaction, 'Can't you smell the cooking? I know a little pasta place, you eat under a vine, we'll have spaghetti the way you've never had it before.'

Sitting there, drinking red wine and laughing at each other, with the proprietor alternately singing and rowing with his wife, Matty thought how foolish she had been. As if Sholto would ever let her meet one of his lovers. Suspicion is worse than whips, she reminded herself, it is endless flagellation. Why not believe in this sunlit day, in the good food, the love, the romance?

The next day Sholto picked up a small red car from

somewhere and drove very fast away from Rome. He called out things of interest that they passed on the way, but wouldn't stop, or even slow down enough for her to see. When he suddenly spun the wheel and sent the little car hurtling up a track, she squealed, believing they had crashed.

'Have faith, my currant bun,' Sholto sang out. 'How could you die on an Italian plain? You have your plot marked out in an English country garden.'

'I wasn't intending to die at all, ' said Matty jerkily. 'Do slow down! You'll kill a donkey.'

To her surprise he did as she asked. All at once he said, 'Look, we're going to see a friend of mine. She may ask us to stay. I know her as Victoria, but to you she's the Baronessa della Srebra. Hugely rich, and just as powerful. My most important patron. Ever.'

Matty felt a sudden leap of the heart. Another Mrs Waterman, then. And she had expected — what? So silly. So utterly silly.

They drove between olive groves, up into low, purple hills. The road twisted and turned, the houses were dark as blood. Lizards ran in fits and starts across the road in front of them. Matty got out her comb and lipstick, trying to make herself look in some way poised and presentable. Her skirt was creased and her blouse had lost buttons in some Czech washing machine. Yet Sholto, in blue silk shirt and creased khaki, looked as if he had stepped from the catwalk in a fashion show.

'I'm a mess,' wailed Matty. 'You could have warned me!'

'You'll do,' he said dismissively.

'You haven't even looked.'

He surveyed her with dispassionate criticism. 'Never mind. Victoria's maid can do wonders, I assure you. Let her have a free hand.'

'The last time I did that I ended up half-dressed. At the de Caruzons.'

'Ah. Yes. When I first came up against your steely resolve.'

He reached for her hand and gave her an affectionate squeeze. At that moment a donkey, ridden by a very old

372

and wrinkled woman, shot out from behind a bank and the little red car squealed, lurched and was saved from disaster only by the avoiding action of the donkey, which shot sideways at speed. The old lady's tomatoes abandoned ship, and soon they were all stopped, and apologising, and chasing tomatoes all over the dusty road. Sholto's Italian was quickfire, brilliant. Matty felt tongue-tied at his side.

They got back in the car and drove on. And then they saw the house; white walls under a heavy terracotta roof, dipping and swaying with the passing of centuries, now a turret, now a spire, now a turning weathercock. The gardens fell away down the hillside, green amidst brown dust, immaculately trimmed. Twin golden cherubs stood either side of the gate, and fountains played, out of the mouths of dolphins.

'I can't stay here,' said Matty throatily. 'I haven't the clothes. Sholto, how could you?'

He ignored her and sent the car spinning up to the house. A man came out and Sholto greeted him familiarly and gave him their bags.

'Matty, meet Alfredo. He runs this whole thing, he's a mastermind. Doesn't speak English, though.'

So Matty smiled and nodded, feeling uneducated and foolish. Why had Sholto brought her here? Why couldn't he come alone?

'Sholto.' His name was uttered like a caress. The woman stood on the steps before the door, and looked down on them. She was small and straight, deep-bosomed and olive-skinned. Her hair was a thick black coil at the base of her neck, as black as her eyes. Matty felt her mouth dry. This was no Mrs Waterman.

'Victoria.' Sholto exaggerated his purr, mocking her. She laughed and put out her hands and he sprang up the steps, took her hands and kissed them. 'I came to show you my bride. Matty, come and meet the Baronessa della Srebra.'

How could he? thought Matty, gritting her teeth on humiliation. How could he? Her hands were stained with dust and tomatoes, she was dressed like a tramp. She summoned every ounce of pride she had ever imagined she might have. 'How do you do,' she said, consciously imitating Griselda's centuries-old hauteur.

The Baronessa ignored the proffered hand and instead clasped her own together, saying excitedly to Sholto, 'Oh, but she's so sweet! A baby angel! That hair, those eyes, that bosom. Sholto, you naughty boy!' Matty wished the ground would open up and swallow her.

Sholto said, 'We'd like a bath, Victoria. We had a contretemps with a lady with a donkey, and had to pick up a sack of tomatoes. Sorry we're not at our best.'

'I did wonder about the stains,' said Victoria, making a face. 'But I thought, perhaps Sholto is up to his old tricks already, and we should not enquire! But I see it all now – a donkey, an English girl – love at once. The English are so sentimental about animals.'

'I don't think sentiment came into it,' said Matty stiffly. 'You can't run over donkeys just like that.'

'And you imagine we wicked Italians do so all the time? Of course, so it is. Our lanes are strewn with dead donkeys. So be it!' Again the conspiratorial smile to Sholto.

My God, thought Matty, watching them. They made a beautiful pair, dark-haired and dark-eyed. They looked like matching wickedness.

In their room at last, she turned on him. 'How dare you bring me here? How dare you?'

He flung himself down in a gold and white armchair. 'Don't be melodramatic. I confess, I didn't think she'd be quite so vindictive. But there you are. We won't stay long.'

He wasn't even prepared to deny it. She put her hot face in her hands and tried to grind the tears away. 'Have a bath,' said Sholto. 'You'll feel better.'

'Why did you bring me here?' she whispered. 'I think you just wanted to humiliate me.'

He got up then, and went to pour himself a drink. 'Damn it, of course I didn't! I thought – I need Victoria. I can't afford to have two powerful people against me, not if I want to earn money. And it seemed politic to put my relationship with Victoria on a different footing. I couldn't come without you or things might have got out of hand.

And how long do you leave these matters? She's done me a lot of good, recommended me to dozens of important Italian families. I thought a honeymoon visit would be a wise move.'

'So you threw me into the lion's den without even a pep talk explaining that I might get munched!'

He looked at her over his glass. 'You're no fool. I knew you'd cope.'

'Thank you so much.'

She went through to the bathroom and threw her clothes in a heap on the floor. Gold taps shaped like fish gushed steaming water. There was a glimmering heap of bath salts in a silver tray, and Matty knew that if she could, the Baronessa would lace them with acid. She got into the water, leaning back to trail her hair, amazed at the furnace of jealous rage that burned within her.

The woman must be fifty if she was a day. Older perhaps. But every inch of her was beautiful, expensive and poised. On her home ground the opportunities to savage Matty would be endless, and irresistible. Her one aim would be to entice Sholto back to her bed. If she succeeded, thought Matty, she would kill them both. In the act, a knife through both their hearts. And she imagined it, lifting her soapy arm high and plunging the blade.

She emerged from the bathroom hot-eyed. 'You've got to get me something to wear. And don't suggest the bitch's maid, because she'd turn me out in a pinafore. Find me something!'

'For God's sake, Matty, we're in the wilds here, where can I get you some clothes?'

'I don't care. You brought me here, you bloody well find me something to wear.'

He turned away, because he dared not laugh. Oh, but she was angry. Lately, sweet and loving, she had appeared to have outgrown her rages. But the volcano, long dormant, was emitting venomous smoke. 'I'll find something,' he promised. 'It might not be good, but I'll find it.'

'If it isn't good, you're dead,' snarled Matty. 'And that isn't a threat, it's a promise.'

He walked down the hall feeling a sinful enjoyment. If

nothing else, dinner tonight was going to be memorable. Oh, but it was good to be back in Italy, back in the sunshine, back in the hedonistic world of fun and beauty and emotion. How he wished he could go to Matty now and make love to her sweet flesh, and then go to Victoria, and punish her. He felt himself go hard at the thought of what he would do to the woman. What she would do to him.

He got into the car and drove quickly away from the house. What was he thinking of? That was over, he had chosen his path and made his decision. He wouldn't betray Matty, he couldn't. He had promised to cherish her, and he was putting her through this. If he had any feelings at all, he ought now to be feeling ashamed.

Instead he drove happily into the village and chatted to the daughter of one of the shopkeepers there, who worked in Rome for a designer during the week, but was fortuitously home just now. And he took a glass of wine with her father, pinched her mother's substantial cheek and offered the girl herself a heady flirtation. An hour later he drove back up the hill and gave Matty her clothes.

She showed him a note, just received. It read: 'Dear child, I know how tired you will be from your journey. Don't bother dressing for our meal this evening. What you had on today will be quite all right. V.'

'I conclude she'll be wearing a ballgown,' said Matty thinly.

Sholto lifted his eyebrows. 'That, or her old wedding dress, with a twenty-yard train. I don't think we should take her at her word, somehow. See what I've got.'

He held out the borrowed clothes. They smelled of another woman, but not unpleasantly. There was a black, full-length robe, with wide sleeves and thick gold embroidery from collar to hem. It was held at the back with a black sash, and managed to appear slightly Japanese. The other evening garment was a short red dress, that simply clung. Sholto said, 'She tells me you wear that with nothing underneath. Goes down very well in Rome.'

Matty grunted and looked at the day outfit. One perfect

linen blouse, thick and heavily woven, and a long, wrapover skirt in dark brown wool.

Some of her panic began to subside. At least, wearing these, she wouldn't feel utterly helpless. There would be nothing worse than sitting across the table feeling a wreck while the Baronessa queened it in diamonds and lace. Her eyes narrowed vindictively.

'You look like a cat,' said Sholto.

'A very angry cat. But not so angry as I was. You can't ever have liked her, Sholto. Don't say you did.'

He took her in his arms and kissed her nose. 'Be flattered. She wouldn't be like this if she despised you. We're married and she knows it's for good, and she's got her pride. She must not think I tired of her.'

'Did you?'

'Yes. I wanted you.'

He was so glib, he said these things so easily. Matty turned away and began to dress in the black robe, combing her hair into a thick brown curtain. When she was done Sholto inspected her, and turned her cuffs back irregularly, and tied her sash with a less firm knot. 'The Italian way,' he explained. 'The little touch that says you don't care.'

For himself he dressed in a white suit and dark silk shirt. As he was fastening his tie he turned and said, 'She can help me sell that icon. If it comes off I'll buy you some jewellery. To make up.'

Matty considered. 'All right. But not to make up. I should hate to wear it and be reminded of her.'

Sholto sighed. He wished very much that Matty would take this less hard. It wasn't so terrible, in any terms other than polite English, and she ought to be able to take it in her stride. Such confrontations happened all the time in Italy, they were the stuff of gossip and intrigue. He wondered just how far Victoria would dare go.

But they were not alone that evening. The drawing room was full of people, talking, laughing, drinking champagne from wonderful crystal glasses. Tall thin dogs wandered amidst the company, a greyhound and a borzoi, there to decorate and nothing more. Matty put back her head, set her teeth and walked into the fray.

'Sholto! Darling, you know everyone, come and meet them.'

Sholto hooked his free hand under Matty's elbow and bore her with him, until Victoria stopped and said, 'My dear, they only speak Italian, you'll be so bored. Who can talk to you? Ah yes, Hortense.'

Matty found herself confronted with a nervous, elderly lady who spoke precise English and talked about gardens. All the while Matty scanned the room, watched the Baronessa holding Sholto's arm, watched her patting him, laughing up at him, introducing him to all her friends. He knew far too many already. In a lull in her conversation about bulbs and autumn planting, Matty gently excused herself from her acquaintance and drifted across the room. People eyed her with curiosity, but no one spoke. They all knew what the Baronessa would think if they did.

She went to a side table on which three pieces of silver were displayed. With utter disregard for good form, Matty picked them up and studied them, ostentatiously tapping a candlestick and peering at the marks. Clattering them down carelessly she began on the pictures, walking round the room staring at each and every painting, now and then reaching up to scratch a fingernail across a corner of the canvas. Gradually people began to watch her, until at last, running out of pictures, she stopped at a small escritoire and began opening drawers to study the construction. Then she knelt down and peered at the underside, rapping noisily with her fist. Conversation, dying, fell quite away.

'My dear,' said the Baronessa in an icy voice, 'whatever are you doing?'

Matty scrambled up, dusting her hands theatrically. 'I hope you don't mind, Victoria,' she trilled. 'I was simply amusing myself. I can find no one here who speaks French or English, which are my two languages, although I have a smattering of Russian —' this was a complete lie, she knew nothing — 'and when I saw that rather sad silver I did wonder if you'd been deceived in anything else. Happily, I think the escritoire's genuine. But do take care when buying pictures on Sholto's recommendation. He can so often inflict works that are only of technical interest.'

'What on earth do you mean?'

'Well, if you look at the painting of, who is it, St John? Very worthy no doubt, but as a drawing room subject –'

'Not that, it's a family treasure. I mean the silver.'

'Oh.' Matty feigned surprise. 'Oh. Didn't you know the candlestick had been altered? The base is early, of course, but the rest is a later addition. I imagine the original was broken some time. Foreigners so often throw candlesticks about when they lose their tempers.'

Matty smiled beatifically. She hoped the old bat exploded with rage. But she had under-estimated her opponent. 'My dear,' purred Victoria, 'you are so, so sweet. Such an original, Sholto. You married a walking valuation expert.'

Sholto said smoothly, 'I've been neglecting her. Matty, let me take you to talk to Cesare d'Olini, I know he speaks –'

'We are to dine,' said the Baronessa, and rang a small bell very loudly.

Matty was seated next to Hortense, with her other side taken care of by an old man who spoke only Italian. Opposite and in the middle of the table stood an enormous flower arrangement which effectively prevented Matty from conversing with anyone. Through the soup and the fish she endured it. Finally she touched Hortense's arm. 'Do you think we could have the flowers moved? I find the pollen irritates me.' She sneezed unconvincingly.

'Oh.' A nervous glance at Victoria, seated at the head of the table, laughing with Sholto. 'I don't think we should.'

Matty sneezed again, and looked up hopefully to catch Alfredo's eye. He avoided her gaze with consummate skill.

'Sholto,' called Matty, in ringing tones. 'Sholto!'

'Yes, my love?' His voice was full of strangled laughter.

'Dear heart, would you remove these flowers, please?' trilled Matty. 'They're upsetting my hayfever, and I shall soon be an embarrassment. I keep trying to alert this waiter man, but you know what these Italians are. All emotion and no discipline.'

The faces of all English speakers froze in horror. Sholto got up and removed the offending arrangement, handing it to Alfredo with a few curt words of Italian. The Baronessa said, 'How strange for an Englishwoman not to like flowers. They do so like their gardening. All those worthy vegetables.'

Matty laughed shrilly. 'Are you all plums then, in Italy? How dreadful! When the sun shines you must all become a lot of old prunes.'

Victoria gasped in shock. Sholto's hand fell heavily on Matty's shoulder, and he said swiftly, 'Darling, do stop chatting. I think you're in the wrong place here. Yes, look, there are two men together over there. Change places with Giorgio, and you can talk to Cesare.'

The Baronessa sat in her place like a flame-cheeked statue as Matty rose and went cheerily to her new place. Sholto hissed in her ear, 'You are going too far, poppet. Steady on.'

As he leaned down to her Matty put her hand on his cheek and pressed a warm kiss on his lips. 'Take that,' she murmured.

Cesare d'Olini offered her the salt. 'For the Baronessa's tail,' he advised. 'That is what you are about, I think.'

'She — doesn't like me,' said Matty.

He chuckled. 'I wonder why? Well, Sholto must have expected it. You don't see Victoria at her best tonight. She can be charming. And you are very young and very beautiful. She thought he would marry money, I suspect. And then she would still not have lost him.'

Matty felt her hands tense. 'I don't think she's admitted defeat.'

'Oh, but she has! I am not often dragged from my home to a dinner with the Baronessa at two hours' notice. What is that but the action of a desperate woman?'

Some of the rage that had sustained her was ebbing away. Matty felt tired suddenly. She wished Sholto would stop sitting there letting that bitch of a woman hold his sleeve and chatter, while she — she felt like crying. 'We haven't been married very long,' she found herself saying. 'We're hardly used to each other.'

'Take my advice.' He tapped her sleeve. 'Have fun with him. Don't have a baby yet, don't get serious. It's enough for a man to marry. And Sholto – well, he has his problems.'

'Do you know him very well?'

Cesare shrugged. 'I suppose. Since he was fifteen or so. He was different then. He walked through people's lives as if he was watching a film. He caused things to happen and walked away. I often think – if he was not angry, then he should have been.'

'With his aunt, you mean?'

'Yes. And everyone. Because no one helped.'

When the meal was finished they rose and went chattering on to the terrace. Bats were flying, and some of the women called for scarves to protect their hair. Victoria was one of them. 'How very silly,' said Matty, loudly.

Sholto came up behind her. 'Not still firing all guns, are we? You won the first skirmish hands down.'

'But she means to get you into bed. Then she thinks she'll have won the war.'

He looked at her quizzically. 'Do you really think I would?'

'No! No – of course I don't.'

But Victoria stood there, in a beautiful white dress, with diamonds in her ears and her eyes full of knowledge. Sholto knew what she had taught him. Was it any wonder that Matty felt young and helpless?

She went to bed when she could no longer keep awake. Sholto made to go with her, but Victoria held his arm, saying, 'Come and talk to Hector. He has some good pictures for you to see, don't you, Hector?' It was the carrot, a house that Sholto had never entered, and he cast Matty a glance full of amused entreaty. She was too tired to care.

But in bed, she lay unsleeping and wondered where he was. The voices on the terrace had dwindled to nothing. Everyone had gone. And he wasn't there.

Victoria let down her hair and said furiously, 'How could

you marry such a one? Such a prig, such a harpy? Did she seduce you with her breasts and her big baby eyes? Is it so good in bed with her?'

'It's very good,' said Sholto.

He leaned on the desk, while Victoria sat at her dressing table. 'You know how to hurt me,' she said shakily.

'But you know I didn't marry for sex,' he said softly. 'You know that. I need Matty. I need to have her needing me. I need – something – someone – to be all mine. Someone to give a point to the whole stupid mess.'

She put her face in her hands and wept. 'She makes me feel old. She makes me wish I had never married, never had my sons, that I could be again what she is, have what she has.'

'Oh, Victoria.' He reached out and briefly touched her hair. 'I wanted you to know her. Because then you'd understand and we could be friends again.'

She brought her drenched, ravaged face into view. 'You only want introductions! All you care about is good pictures!'

'Yes – and no. We're friends. I hate to see you cry.'

He went back to the room he shared with Matty feeling drained. What a hell of a night. He had married Matty for peace, to insulate himself from all the sins he might commit, when a bit of sinning would have done them all a lot of good. To think he would have been spared all this if he had only gone and shagged Victoria in secret this afternoon. Matty could have had the night. And here he was, feeling randy and bad-tempered, and Matty asleep.

But she rolled over as he got into the bed and put her arms out for him. 'Don't worry,' he said bitterly. 'I sold the icon to Hector, it seems he collects. And Victoria covered me in tears, and nothing else.'

'We're not staying, are we?'

He lay back and let exhaustion wash over him. God, but he was tired. 'We'll go in the morning. I can't stand another day like this.'

She sank back to her side of the bed, but Sholto pulled her across. She lay on him, and then slowly sat up. 'Is this what she used to do?'

'I really can't remember.'

How she wished they had never come here, how she wished they were at home. She slid herself on to him and they made love, with Matty all the time wondering if he was thinking of Victoria and wishing it was her. Sholto knew it and couldn't come, until at last he caught Matty's shoulders and yelled, 'Damn it, she might as well be in this bed if you're going to think about her all the time! Think about me!' Matty cried out, and suddenly, he came. She had reminded him of Victoria.

Chapter Twenty-Three

They returned home to find Richard Greensall standing plaintively on the doorstep. He had a stubble beard, stained anorak and anxious expression. 'Have you been here for days?' asked Matty, pushing past him to unlock the front door. It jammed on a heap of letters and she struggled to push it open.

'I had to come. There's been trouble.'

'Not the police?'

He nodded, looking drawn and unhappy.

Sholto shouldered past them with the suitcases, saying, 'Hide him under the sofa, Matty. Criminals on the doorstep don't half give a business a bad name.'

'I've done nothing wrong!' wailed Greensall. 'Never stolen in me life.'

'Don't take any notice of Sholto,' said Matty wearily, and took him inside.

He pulled himself together over a cup of tea. Sholto was sorting through the mail, putting bills in one pile and more interesting correspondence in another. The house smelled cold and unlived-in, and a forgotten bunch of flowers stood now as a bunch of stalks in rancid water. Coming home was never as you expected, thought Matty. A home was a living thing, and when you left it, it died.

She looked at Greensall, hunched and miserable over his mug. Her first unworthy thought had been of her own involvement. If he went down, would it touch her? Possibly. Probably. She should never have gone near his dishonesty. 'Are you going to tell me about it?' she asked, her voice strained and accusing.

He looked up at her, a subject looking for guidance. 'They

came on Monday,' he muttered. 'Two of 'em. Did I know anything about these forgeries like, and they showed me this stuff, and it weren't mine. Crummy moulded junk, done from a cast of the real thing. One look inside and you can tell it's rubbish. No hammering up, it's all like porridge. But someone put them on to me. And they could see I was nervous, like. Next thing, me telephone went funny, and I thinks to mesen, well, they're on to me. And I upped and come along here.'

'Oh God,' said Matty. 'You would have been quite safe if you'd faced it out. Why didn't you just say it wasn't your work?'

He wrung his hands. 'It was the way of them! Menacing. Mean. You could tell they meant to have me!'

Sholto cast Matty a meaningful look. 'Isolation addles the brain,' he murmured. 'Oh look, another threatening letter from dear Luca. Accusing me of purloining religious treasures. Told you he was keeping a close eye. How good it is to be home.'

'Do be quiet, Sholto,' said Matty absently. 'Richard, have you the 'phone number for these policemen? I think I'd better talk to them.'

He quivered like a frightened rabbit. 'I was thinking maybe you'd pay for me to emigrate.'

'For goodness' sake, man, you've got a wife and children.'

'You're not getting out of it that easily,' said Sholto. 'If you could there'd be queues of men trying to knock up something dicky at evening classes. No, you can't go and live the life of Riley in South America without a major crime, preferably involving millions. Sorry, old son, no buxom foreigner with lax morals for you. You get to do community service in Huddersfield.'

Greensall began to bite his nails. Matty sighed.

When she telephoned the police inspector's number a soft deep, voice answered menacingly, 'Yes? Do you have any knowledge of Mr Greensall's whereabouts?'

Matty gulped. 'Yes, of course I do. And I'm not surprised he ran away – you sound as if you're about to hang him. I really must protest. My silversmith gained the impression that you were about to arrest him for some extremely inept electroplate forgeries.'

'The innocent have nothing to fear from us,' said the inspector.

'I'm afraid they do, Inspector! Mr Greensall tells me you tapped his 'phone!'

'We have our job to do, madam.'

'Look −' Matty dropped her voice confidentially, ' − Mr Greensall isn't the most stable man in the world. Obviously he's an artist and he spends a lot of time alone, and this does cause − contributes to − a certain attitude of mind.'

The voice on the 'phone snapped, 'You telling me he's bonkers?'

'Er − almost, but not quite. The thing is, he makes flatware for me. Cutlery, to you. He matches modern pieces into antique sets, all above board, assayed, his own marks, everything. But he has always believed that it might in some way be illegal. It isn't, of course, but being the way he is − well, I think you may have pushed him over the edge. He's sure you're going to arrest him for it. A married man with children!'

'Forging antiques is illegal.'

'And copying them isn't. Not if you mark them properly. Mr Greensall makes copies for me. And incidentally, if you are going round master silversmiths trying to pin electroplate on them, I'm surprised someone hasn't thumped you by now. Talk about an insult! Somebody makes a cast of the real thing and then electrically deposits silver on top − there's no skill at all. Not smithing skill anyway. I think the best thing is, if you have anything you suspect is forged, that you come and talk to me. I won't know who made it but I can tell you a great deal more than you appear to know at present. This is a complex business, officer.'

She replaced the receiver with a smirk of pleasure. 'You told him I was off me head,' complained Greensall.

'Yes,' she said happily. 'Get your 'phone number changed. You don't want any of your old friends ringing up and dropping you in it. Oh, how I do like this business. Have you finished the fruit set I gave you, by the way?'

'Weeks back,' said Greensall, still lugubrious. 'And the

others is sold. Bloke you sell them to keeps getting on to me trying to get some more, but I says to him, not without Miss Winterton's say-so. She calls the tune.'

'Mrs Feversham now,' said Sholto, and Matty thought with surprise, Yes, so it is.

She stood in the garden and watched him drive away. It was cold outside, and the late roses were whipping about in a stiff breeze. Italy had been softer, the sun more kind and the wind less chill, but it wasn't home. She felt herself calming.

Pigeons were clattering in the trees. They were growing fat off runner beans, unpicked and festooned in huge, tough strings in the vegetable patch. If she was here more often she would plant cabbages and onions, and be the vegetable that awful Italian woman expected, gaining sustenance from the soil. In the evenings she would sit in her garden and delight in it.

Sholto banged crossly out of the house. 'Bills,' he muttered. 'Bloody, bloody bills. And these for you.' He tossed her three envelopes, in three familiar hands. Lorne, Henry and Griselda.

'Where are Simon's?' called Matty, as he strode towards the barn.

'He wrote to both of us,' he shouted. 'He's top in maths and wants five hundred pounds to go skiing. Send him six, he can have the extra as pocket money.'

Matty grinned. There was a certain inevitability to that. Sholto denied Simon nothing, gave in excess, as if making up for his own childhood deprivations. If there was to be balance in their lives she would have to stop Sholto giving, rather than persuade him.

She was savouring the pleasure of her letters. There could be nothing nicer than catching up on news from them all. She tried to guess what they would be telling her — well, Henry was easy, she and the vicar would have come clean to Mrs Giles and would get married. As for Griselda she hoped — but rather doubted — that she was in a torrid relationship with lovely, bumbling Bertie, while Lorne would be a mother. Boy or girl? she wondered. She hoped it was a girl. She would send a pretty baby dress and a lovely piece of silver.

*   *   *

Lorne clung to Greg's hand with desperate fingers. He looked bewildered and uncertain. 'It can't hurt that much, Lorne honey,' he said. Oh, but it did. It hurt like – like – like nothing could stop it, like she was trapped in a vice, like her body had turned against her and wouldn't stop till she was dead. Where was the pain relief she had been promised? Where the avuncular obstetrician who had been comforting her all these weeks? Out on the golf course it seemed, and taking his time coming back.

'Can you get me something?' she moaned. 'Greg, please.'

He pressed the buzzer but no one came, and he went to find the nurse. Why had she consented to have her baby here, in this small clinic, when she could have gone ten miles further and had it in town? She gripped the sides of the bed and writhed as the pain came again. Jee-sus! That was bad. That was terribly bad. If the next one was worse she'd never survive it.

But suddenly all was bustle. Two nurses came, smiling and busy, setting up a drip, pulling down a mask, promising the doctor was coming. Greg was there and she clung to his hand, one sure point of contact in a frightening world. 'I'll go wait outside,' he said, and tried to free himself, but she hung on, she would not let go.

'I want you here. Stay here.'

'Lorne honey – I'll go find the doctor.'

He was gone, and she was on her own. A nurse said, 'Men are all the same. Get you in this mess but sure as hell don't stay around to get you out.'

They put a mask on her face and she took a long breath. Anything to dull the pain.

'Better now? Get control now, get on top.'

Oh God, why had she let Greg do this to her? The doctor came, people, lights. She didn't care, she didn't know, she was locked in struggle.

'Shall we call your husband back in? Want us to call your mother?'

Lorne shook her head. Greg was no use and her mother would be upset. Looking up at the masked faces, the many pairs of strange eyes, she felt like a specimen, an experiment. She felt completely alone.

At the end, at the height of the struggle, one thought recurred: five minutes out of this and she would be better. What she needed was a break. They were encouraging her, urging her on, and she heard the doctor say, 'If she doesn't make it in five we knock her out and operate.'

Damn them! She was failing even in this. Always a failure, so much promise and so little result. The nurse held her shoulders, saying, 'Come on, honey! Come on!' And with a huge and mighty effort, straining even the veins in her forehead, she bore down.

'Got it! Got it!' yelled the doctor. The baby, grey and slime-covered, slithered out of her and she felt sudden astonishment, a total wave of unbelief. Was that it then? Was this small thing the cause of all that pain?

She fell back, utterly spent. Someone gave her a sip of water. They asked if she wanted her husband now. She shook her head. Soon they brought the baby to her, wrapped in a blue cloth. 'A boy, Mrs Berenson. A lovely baby boy.'

She held him very close, still sticky, small pockets of moisture in the corners of his eyes. He blinked, very slowly, and spread his tiny hand. 'His eyes are so pale.'

The nurse touched the baby's downy head. 'Don't you worry about that now,' she said.

Mrs Giles put the letter temptingly beside Henrietta's plate. She had read it already, because Henry did nothing nowadays, even open envelopes. 'Lorne has had her baby, darling. Isn't that good news? I gather she's quite pulled down, so I suggest you pay her a visit. Daddy won't mind at all about the money.'

'When did Daddy ever have anything to do with money in this house?' said Henry. She picked up her breakfast cup and took a sip. Strong black coffee. She put four spoons of sugar in it, picked up a piece of toast, spread it thick with butter and munched.

'I shall book your seat on the plane,' said Mrs Giles. 'Really, Henrietta, this cannot go on! A failed romance with someone totally unsuitable is no reason to give up on living.

Why, I endured dozens of disastrous liaisons. Dozens.'

'You met Daddy in your first week of the Season and were married six months later,' said Henrietta dully. 'You dragged him down like a wounded stag. He hadn't a chance.'

Mrs Giles heaved on the reins of her temper. She was not used to Henrietta behaving in this openly independent way. It confused her. 'There are many nice young men you could get to know,' she wheedled. 'Dominic, for instance. Wasn't he terribly keen?'

'Keen on anything with breasts and a bum,' snarled Henry, viciously crunching another piece of toast. When it was all gone she got up and flounced away from the table. But even then she knew there was no point in putting up a struggle. Say what she might, if her mother wanted her to go and see Lorne, then go she would.

At least there she might stop thinking of him. Sometimes she saw his van, driving somewhere, and she had to clench her fists to stop herself waving, had to curl her toes into balls in her shoes to prevent her feet from running into the road. If she went away there would be an end to that. It might be a relief.

In the quiet of the college, with the tower clock chiming the hours, Griselda sat and worked. The pool of light on her desk seemed like a pond in which she swam, enclosing her whole existence. Indeed, she might be the only person alive in all the world. The silence was eerie, thick as butter.

Most of her year were living in flats this term, relishing the freedom. Griselda had rejected that. The girls she might have shared with all knew Bertie Brantingham, and inevitably they would have met and been forced to talk. The embarrassment hardly bore thinking about. Inevitably, after the wedding, he'd called on her a time or two, sending her flowers and so on; and that in itself showed how right she was to put an end to this. Flowers, from Bertie! When he brought her flowers she knew that their easy, companionable friendship was gone forever.

Linking her bony fingers on the page in front of her, she let her mind move to the future. A first class degree was in the offing, and there had been overtures from the Foreign

Office, who would like her to sit their exam. She tried to imagine herself in foreign parts, wrestling with local bureaucrats over passports, visas, trade delegations, her office hot as Hades, with a fan stirring a cloud of flies. Her father had taken them all to Cairo once, when she was small, on some trip or other, and she imagined it was still much the same.

Yes, she could see herself doing that. Her eccentricities would come to be seen as charming and droll. As the years went by the youngsters in the office would mimic her manner, and fall silent as she entered the room. For a plain, gangling, clever girl without any particular mission in life, it was as good a job as any. How sad that the rabies laws would make it so difficult to have a dog.

She unlinked her fingers and picked her pen up once again. If only she could have talked it over with Bertie. She so much missed his kindness and wise counsel, his down to earth understanding of what it was to be her. Those few minutes, those few, endlessly regretted minutes! She would have given the world to have them undone.

But there was no point in regret. She took out a new sheet of paper and began to write. 'Dear Matty, How are you? Blissful, of course. Do give Sholto all my best. I thought you should know that I have decided to have a shot at the Foreign Office . . .'

'Well, hi.' Lorne sat in the bed, surrounded by flowers and cards, the cradle at her side.

'Hi.' Henrietta sat down. For the first time in their lives there was constraint between them. Neither dared say what they thought.

'He's a beautiful baby,' said Henry, peering doubtfully into the cradle. In truth he had a squashed nose, was red as a tomato and had nothing in the way of hair.

'Don't you think he's kind of − red?' said Lorne.

'Aren't they all that colour?'

Lorne shook her head. 'In the hospital, mine was the reddest.'

'Well, at least that way you know you got the one that's yours.'

'Don't you think the nose would have been enough?'

Henry put up her hand to suppress a giggle. 'Or the hair! Oh, Lorne, I hope for your sake he improves!'

A gale of laughter swept over them. The baby stirred in his sleep and Lorne automatically reached out and rocked the cradle. 'You look different,' she remarked.

'Do I? You mean fat.' Henry sunk her chin into her hands.

'You're not fat yet. Just more covered. I like it.'

'You would. You're thin as a rake, already.'

Lorne nodded. 'It's the feeding. I eat it, he sucks it out. I could sleep for a week.' She yawned capaciously, stretching her long fingers like a cat's claws.

She was in her own house, at last. Sherwood had surprised her by getting it done, just when she was despairing of him. It was stark with newness, and she lay in the bed and made plans for it, with a pale yellow nursery and a hall in blue.

The baby stirred again and Henry said, 'Can I hold him?'

'If you want. He's not due to be fed.'

Henrietta cradled the warm little body, making smiling faces. 'He's got such pale eyes,' she said.

'Yes. Everyone notices.'

'He's the most beautiful baby I ever saw.'

'You know he isn't!'

'But he is! When you hold him, he is.' Henry felt like crying. Something about the baby touched her, she didn't know why.

Sherwood Berenson called that afternoon. He walked straight into the house, not bothering to knock, and Lorne hissed, 'Damn the man! He acts like he owns this place.'

'Doesn't he?' asked Henry.

'Yes, but it's still my home!' She pulled on her robe and went downstairs. 'Well, you're taking your ease,' he said when he saw her.

Lorne was crisp and unfriendly. 'Did you want something, Sherwood? My friend's here. We're talking.'

'That sure does sound fun.'

He smiled at her, mocking and infuriating. Lorne went into the kitchen and began to make coffee, and he leaned in the doorway watching her. 'Now, can you get yourself dressed for this evening?' he said. 'A party. Something stylish. We've got important people to meet.'

He often did this, summoning her at the last moment to some function or other, where her only role was to add class to the Berenson tribe.

'You know I can't go to any parties! Miller needs me.'

'I don't like that name. That's no name for a child.'

'It's a Shuster name. I like it.'

He let it lie, for the moment. She knew she hadn't won. That was his style, biding his time, waiting until he had everything on his side, when he could win. She waited, tense, for the next attack. 'You get yourself dressed now,' he said. 'We need you tonight, Lorne.'

She decided to be calm and reasonable. 'I'm sorry, I can't come. Your grandson needs to be taken care of, and there isn't anyone can do it except me.' A smile, to try and distract him.

'There's your friend. You've got work to do, honey. Being a good wife takes more than lying around the house eating cookies.'

'I am not lying around the house. Miller —'

'Why not call him Sherwood?'

Lorne bit back hot words. It never paid to lose your temper with this man, he never lost his own. He kept his head and manipulated people.

'His name's Miller,' she said again.

'Eight o'clock. Tell Greg now, don't be late.' He picked up his hat and left.

Lorne took a tissue from her pocket and shredded it, letting the pieces fall on the newly carpeted floor. Henrietta came in, holding the baby. 'You should stand up to him,' she said.

'I did.' Lorne sighed, and pushed at her hair. 'With Sherwood you have to give to get. I won't have this boy named after that man. I'll go to a hundred parties first.'

'But the baby's got to be fed!'

Lorne took the baby and rocked him, smiling down

tenderly at her red-faced, blinking cherub. 'You feed him. I'll leave a bottle. You never know, getting out might do me good.'

'You're not well enough, Lorne. And that man worries me. I don't like the way he looks at you.'

'No.' Lorne wandered through the kitchen. 'No more do I.'

The baby began to squawk to be fed. Henrietta went for a walk around the house, so newly finished that little heaps of sawdust lay in the corners of windows and boxes stood everywhere. From every side she could see empty pasture, without trees or softness. The Berensons farmed all their land like a blank page.

'You must plant trees,' she called to Lorne. 'That way you'll get birds.'

'We'll plant 'em,' called Lorne. 'This little fellow's going to want a tree house some day.'

A sudden wave of sadness rose up in Henrietta. Lorne had her baby, Griselda had her work. Matty had Sholto. She alone had nothing and no one. What's more, she knew what she wanted and simply couldn't have it. Ever. Peter didn't want her and that was that.

Later, in the kitchen, Lorne said, 'At school, we never once thought we were going to get things wrong, did we?'

'No. No, we didn't. And you haven't got them wrong. You've got a little local difficulty, that's all.'

Lorne chuckled. 'Sherwood Berenson, a local difficulty! Son of local difficulty stands for election. Hell of a campaign slogan.'

She got a tomato out of the refrigerator and munched, wondering if this was the moment to make Henry talk. But even before she opened her mouth Henry cut her off. 'There's nothing to say, Lorne. It didn't work out. And I've got to stop wasting my life and find myself something useful to do. If only I knew what.'

'At the moment you're helping me,' said Lorne. 'That's really useful.'

Henrietta smiled gratefully. 'Just you tell me the moment I start getting in the way.'

*　　*　　*

But in no time at all she found herself a necessity. Lorne was back in her social whirl, attending all the functions Sherwood thought appropriate for the wife of an up and coming politician. Henrietta took care of the baby while Lorne went to charity lunches and sat on committees, putting the name of Berenson right where Sherwood wanted it, in society. Her reward was the baptism, with the baby called Miller, after a General on Lorne's side of the family. Henrietta was godmother, and Aunt Susan gave her a cushion she had worked, with the date and Miller's name in needlepoint. The Shuster and Berenson clans were turned out in style and Greg was big, golden and smiling. Now and then he enveloped Lorne in a hug. 'Children bring you closer together,' he said, more than once.

At home Lorne never felt close to him any more. If he noticed it he gave no sign that he did, or that it bothered him. They lived separate lives, she with her committees, her house and her dress allowance, he less and less with the farm and more and more with his ambitions.

Even the sex seemed different, when he lay on her in bed and took his brief pleasure. They used to spend hours in the barn, she thought, in the days when winning her had been the goal. Now that she was possessed she was worth very little.

Soon afterwards he went on a trip. It was a regular thing, Greg and his father travelling around the state, talking to people and doing business. Sometimes they flew to New York for a few days, or Washington, and curiously, on these trips Lorne stayed at home. This time both she and Henry found it a relief. They could relax with the baby, doing baby things, looking at wallpaper and choosing paint.

The days drifted by, quite pleasantly. Henrietta became plump, and a little more than plump, on cake and Coca-Cola. One afternoon they went to Aunt Susan's for tea, but Lorne was restless. She walked around the room chattering brightly about nothing. Finally her mother said, 'Lorne, you'll wear yourself to threads and your milk will dry up. Sit down, and calm yourself.'

'I don't feel calm.'

Henrietta said, 'It's the wind. She's always in a state when the wind blows. It makes her nervous.'

'She grew up with this wind,' said Aunt Susan. 'Lorne, either sit down or tell us what's making you so jumpy.'

'It's nothing. It's not important.' She picked up a teacup and put it down straight away. 'Don't you think Miller's eyes are really kind of odd?'

Henrietta looked blankly at her. Then she said, 'They're just a pretty colour. Aren't they?'

'I don't know. I'm not sure. Sometimes I don't think he sees so well.'

'Babies don't see well,' said Aunt Susan. 'Faces, that's all.'

'He doesn't know my face. It's my voice he responds to.'

'You can't know that!'

'But I do.'

Henrietta went to the cradle and stared down at the sleeping infant. She rocked him a little and his eyes opened, his mouth making reflex sucking movements. He swam up out of sleep, and Henry passed her hand through the air in front of his face. Nothing showed that he had seen. In a low, anxious voice she said, 'Hello, Miller,' and his head turned, as if on a string. He began to kick.

'How could you suspect such a thing and not tell me?' Aunt Susan was glaring at her daughter.

'There was no point. And you've enough to worry you.'

'Lorne, you treat me like a deranged old lady! I won't crumble with a little bad news.'

'It wasn't all that! It might not have been that at all.'

Henry said, 'I don't suppose you wanted to admit that you knew.'

Lorne picked up the baby and cradled him. 'I think the hospital knew. I bet they're waiting for me right now, wondering when I'm going to come back. Don't suppose they like to break the news right away, and spoil the party. People get upset when they know their baby's blind.'

Her mother touched her arm. 'They might be able to operate. It could be something that happens, it could clear.'

Lorne turned away, closing her eyes on tears. Everything she did went wrong, even her baby was cursed. If only she could pretend she didn't know.

* * *

Henrietta accompanied her on the hospital visits. They moved up through the specialties, from senior man, to great man, to a stand-in for God. They took a plane to Boston to consult an expert in the field, and sat in a roomful of children, not one above six years old. Children with squints, children with eye patches, children with white canes and eyeballs turned up in their heads, like useless counters in a fruit machine. Miller was easily the youngest.

When Lorne was called in Henry waited, wondering if any of these children was going to be cured. Some of them, surely. She knelt down and helped a little girl make a pattern with bricks on the floor. The child said, 'Is that one blue? I can't see it. I don't see so well.'

Lorne came out and Henry got up and said goodbye to her friend. 'You going to give me some candy?' asked the little girl. 'I don't see so well.'

'Little brat,' muttered Henry, as they left. 'What's the verdict?'

'Congenital cataracts, and we know that already.'

'But? Don't be difficult, Lorne!'

Her friend turned to her, suddenly pink with joy. 'They can operate! This doctor's the best in the world and he's quite, quite sure. It won't be easy and he won't see at first because the eyes won't be used to working, but they can put it right!'

'When? Now?'

Some of the glow was already dying. 'Not now. Sometime. When he's about six.'

They walked through a park full of mothers and lively kids. 'Don't tell the others,' said Lorne. 'Matty and Grizz. I don't want them to feel sorry for me.'

'Oh, Lorne! You know secrets aren't good.'

Lorne grimaced. 'Griselda would be horribly sympathetic. And Matty might feel she should come out, and she's got things to do. Let's keep it a secret.'

'You'll tell Greg, won't you?'

Her friend shrugged. He would have to be told, she supposed. But whenever she told Greg something he didn't wish to hear he looked at her with a face as cold as snow. Anything she told him went at once to Sherwood, until sometimes she thought she'd married his father as well. Berenson men were very hard, she thought. They lived in an impenetrable shell made out of their own selfishness. Greg and his father shared a view of life that had no place for anything that couldn't be measured, had no time for anything that didn't pay off. Women were essential but unimportant, and children were owned. The thought of telling Greg that his son was sub-standard filled Lorne with horror.

It was their last night in the hotel. Lorne telephoned home and Greg was furious, because he had come home and found her gone. 'I'll be back tomorrow,' she kept saying.

In the end he growled, 'You get on the first plane back. And don't tell me you can't make it because I'll be there to meet you. You'd better, Lorne.'

She gibbered at Henrietta, 'When is the first one? Eight o'clock? Can we make the eight o'clock?'

'We're booked at twelve,' said Henry. 'Look, he's being unreasonable. I'll call him back and explain. We can't make an eight o'clock plane with a baby.'

'Yes we can,' said Lorne. She played with the fringe of her scarf, keeping her eyes down. 'Henry, don't try and interfere. I don't want to upset him, not when I've got to tell him his son's blind.'

So Henrietta found herself in the late afternoon crowds in a city she didn't know, trying to find the airline office to see if they could fly standby at eight the following morning. Even when she found the place the procedure was complicated, with fare discounts and transfer fees being freely discussed. The flight was almost full. They would be crammed on in discomfort at eight instead of travelling on an empty plane at twelve. It was ridiculous.

She came out feeling tired and hungry, as well as irritated with Lorne. The Berensons were getting things all their own way and she was letting them. The evening was cool after a warm day. It was getting late and few people were about. She hurried through darkened streets, looking for a cab, past offices that were empty and dark. A chill wind was blowing up, rustling papers in the gutter and making her jump.

Suddenly, too quickly for her to think, a man reached out from a shadowy corner and took hold of her arm. Her breath failed her. He grabbed her wrists and flung her back into the alley, pressing against her, grinding into her. It was unreal but the smell of him wasn't — sweat and booze and horror. She let out a scream of honest terror, a piercing shriek that split the grey evening like lightning. 'Bitch!' He hit her once, in the face. He was grabbing at her bag but it was over her shoulder, she couldn't let go, and suddenly he was gone, running headlong away down the alley. There were people, a man and his wife stopped their car, a caretaker came out of an office and stood worried in the street. Her mouth was full of blood. She felt a terrible embarrassment at being seen like this, a helpless mess.

It was a horrible night. She called Lorne and told her not to come to the hospital, but she found a sitter and came anyway. The doctor that tended her said she would need surgery on her nose, when the swelling had subsided. Two of her teeth were loose but he thought they would survive, and in the meantime her face felt huge, like a melon about to explode from over-ripeness. A desperate shivering kept coming over her, she kept wanting to cry. Lorne held her hand in the cab back to the hotel and helped her take painkillers and put icepacks on her face.

'And now we can't make the eight o'clock flight,' said Henrietta, speaking through thick lips.

Lorne looked up guiltily. 'No. No, I suppose not.'

'Call him and explain. You're not scared of him, are you?'

'I don't know.' Lorne thought about it. Sometimes Greg did scare her, almost as much as Sherwood. He could be so cold. She had married him thinking he loved her, but did he? Less than a year on, and she quailed at the thought of opposing him. Why had he stopped wanting to make her happy? When had he stopped? He'd got what he wanted, she supposed. Obediently, foolishly, she had married him.

When they got off the plane the next day Greg was waiting. He took their bags, listened to their explanations and said nothing. Lorne felt like a little girl, scuttling along beside his great golden bulk, trying to make him understand her little concerns. In the car he said, 'Why did you go to Boston anyway?'

Lorne took a breath. 'It was — haven't you noticed the baby's eyes? We had to see a doctor. He's got cataracts. Greg, Miller's blind — but he won't always be blind, they can operate! When he's older.'

He looked at her, at first disbelieving, then he glanced back at Henrietta.

'Is this true?' he asked Henry, and she nodded. He put his foot on the gas and sent the car roaring across three lanes of the Interstate.

Lorne squealed, 'Don't, Greg! It's all right, he's going to be fine. One day.'

He got drunk that night and accused her. He thought it was something Shuster, some evidence of bad blood, rotted by generations of good living. Henry sat up in bed and thought her head would split, with the yelling so loud and her own heart sending pulses like hammer blows. She heard Greg say, 'You bitch. You stinking bitch. You and your stinking friends.' Whatever Lorne said she couldn't hear. Then came the telltale grunts and groans, the rhythmic thumping, and Henry put her head beneath the covers. First thing in the morning she would go and stay with Aunt Susan.

Chapter Twenty-Four

The gentle charm of the Shuster home was balm to Henrietta. She lay in bed in the mornings, rising late to wander amongst the oaks and sweet chestnuts in the meadows. Her teeth recovered, and her mouth healed, and every day she stared at herself in the mirror, at her swollen, misshapen nose, and willed it to go down. Resolutely it did not.

The day came when Aunt Susan suggested she resort to surgery. She also suggested that Henry tell her mother, which the girl immediately vetoed. If Mrs Giles ever discovered the disaster which had overtaken her daughter the moment she was out of sight, it would be the last step Henry ever took on her own. Her mother was not a woman to make the same mistake twice.

'Can't we get it fixed here?' she asked. 'I've insurance, and if that didn't cover it I could work to get the rest.'

Aunt Susan called Lorne and they went into a flurry of discussion. Names were suggested, phone numbers found, until at last they had a plan. Henrietta was to go and live in town, with Darrell, a Shuster girl cousin. She would attend a clinic and work part-time at Darrell's art gallery. When told of the job, Mrs Giles wrote back: 'I always felt you would do well in a gallery, my dear. I am delighted to see you have at last taken my advice.'

It was strange to look in a mirror and hate yourself. Henry's nose had never been beautiful, but its old round snubness seemed something infinitely to be desired. In the clinic women with great noses came in and had them rendered characterless, and women with terrible noses had them tamed, and not one of them looked as bad at the start as Henry.

'Don't worry,' the doctor said to her. 'You're going to look better than before.' But the operation was painful and unpleasant.

Because she hated staying at home Henrietta went to work soon afterwards in the gallery, ignoring the stares that her nose splint inevitably attracted. One shy young man, buying a picture, said diffidently, 'Shouldn't you be in bed? Most people stay home after a nose job.'

'It isn't one,' said Henry thickly. 'I got mugged. It was broken, and didn't heal. They've done all sorts of horrible things, taking pieces of bone out and putting bits in. It hurts, so I'd rather work and take my mind off it.'

'Oh. I see. Well, good luck.'

He was paying a couple of thousand dollars for a small print. He was wearing a designer shirt, she noticed, and one of those big linen suits that cost a fortune. The only person she had ever seen them look good on was Sholto, who wore them creased and collapsing. This man looked as if he had lost a tremendous amount of weight and hadn't changed his clothes.

'Would you like a drink after work?' he asked suddenly.

Henry would have laughed if it hadn't hurt. 'With me? Like this? You can't.'

'If you don't want −'

'I didn't say that. I do want. Can it be somewhere dark?'

'Yes. Sure. Pick you up at six.'

He drove a Mercedes sports convertible with a white top. According to Darrell, his mother owned half Georgia and his father the other half, although they had been divorced for years and he had a succession of step-parents on both sides. Henry couldn't keep track of the relatives he seemed to half possess, there were dozens blowing in to borrow money and blowing out again. Tyler Cooke had a yacht, someplace, an apartment building, someplace else, and entrée to any party or gathering anyplace he wanted. The trouble was, he didn't want. He was a billionaire by default.

He kept Henry company when the splint failed and more surgery was required. He took her in his car and gave her milkshake through a straw, and went into the gallery and bought etchings, so that Darrell wouldn't complain that Henry's appearance was repelling business. In fact old ladies came in and gave advice on herbs, and kids with large noses lurked behind cabinets to ask Henry for an address, but they only bought postcards and dried flowers. It was Tyler who staggered out with four foot square canvases and tried to fit them in his car.

'We do deliver,' Darrell said, hovering anxiously after him. Tyler, always self-effacing, blushed and said he didn't want to cause trouble.

The day came when Henrietta's splint came off for good. The surgeon was nervous, because this had been a very troublesome case, but Henry felt detached. She was managing, wasn't she? What was a face? If the worst came to the worst she'd wear bandages forever. She heard the surgeon take a long sigh of relief. 'There! What do you think of that?'

She stared in the mirror in amazement. The nose she remembered had been ordinary — snub and a little crooked, a plump nose. This nose was different. Shorter, thinner, with a straightness that was almost geometric, it managed to alter the balance of her face. She was thin at the moment of course, since eating had been difficult for weeks, but it was more than that. Her new patrician nose gave her an air of quality.

'How are the teeth?' asked the surgeon. 'Eating apples yet?'

She shook her head. 'Not quite up to apples. You know, I don't look like me.'

'Sure you do. Everything back in working order. And better than before.'

That evening, having dinner with Tyler, he said, 'I never thought I was going to end up dating a beauty.'

Henry blushed. 'I'm not. Never have been. I'm usually really fat.'

'I don't believe it!'

She nodded. 'I get fat so easily. I've only been thin once

before. And I'm only thin now because I couldn't eat. And I don't belong with this nose.'

'It sure seems to belong with you.'

They were eating baby clams in pepper sauce, and Tyler was grinning from ear to ear.

'What are you smiling about?' Henry demanded.

'You. Us. This is so good.'

Henry's inner self recoiled a little. She liked Tyler, of course, because he was shy and generous and a little weak. He seemed to need her. But if he was in love, she was not. She couldn't be.

'I thought – perhaps – would you come and meet my mother? My father's in the Caribbean just now, but my mother's in New York. We could charter a plane.' Again the anxious quiver.

'That sounds fun,' said Henry tightly. 'If I can get away from the gallery. Darrell's been terribly good.'

'Shall I buy some more pictures? I mean – '

'No! No, Tyler, please. I'll talk to Darrell.'

But instead she went to Lorne. They knelt on a stool together, and studied the nose. 'Good,' decided Lorne. 'Better. But your mother won't know who you are.'

'Free at last!' said Henry. 'By the way, a man called Tyler Cooke wants me to meet his mother. Do you think I should?'

'Tyler Cooke's mother? My God!' Lorne fell off the stool. 'He's a zillionaire,' she said finally, when Henry picked her up. 'He's one of the country's most eligible men.'

'I think he wants to marry me,' said Henry lugubriously. 'In fact, I know so.'

'Then do it! Do it! If you divorce in a week you've got the money.'

'If Griselda was here she'd turn up her nose at that.'

'And hasn't she got a nose to turn.'

They permitted themselves a small, cruel laugh. Miller was crying so Lorne went to fetch him. The girls stood in the room they had decorated together, full of flowers and old wood and lace. 'I just expected to be marrying Peter,' said Henry in a small, sad voice.

'Yes. Well, things don't always turn out as we expect.'

'I don't think I know how to be the wife of a zillionaire.'

'You give money to charities and so on. People like Sherwood Berenson do as you ask. Nobody beats up on you in the street.'

Henry went back to looking at her nose. 'A new future for a new me,' she murmured. 'Well, I wasn't doing anything much else.'

'The engagement is announced between Henrietta Maria Elizabeth Giles, daughter of Mr and Mrs Geoffrey Giles, of London, England, and Mr Tyler Dartford Cooke, son of Mr and Mrs Silas Cooke, of Georgia, USA.'

Matty flung down her newspaper in disbelief. 'How dare she! Without telling us! Henry's engaged. I don't know how she could!'

Simon looked up from his breakfast cereal. 'Old Henry? Doesn't have to tell you every time she breathes, does she?'

'Oh, shut up!'

There was no point in expecting Simon to understand. He was at that tedious stage of growth when children have a great deal too much to say for themselves, she decided. Opinions on everything. 'Haven't you got some holiday work to do?' she demanded.

'Masses. Project on the ozone layer. You'll have to get me books out of the library.'

'I'll drop you at the library on my way out. It's not me doing the project.'

'And it's not me destroying the ozone layer. I'm the generation left to pick up the pieces because you've all been so irresponsible.'

'Oh, shut up!' said Matty again.

She was feeling thoroughly upset. Sholto had telephoned last night to say that he was in Bournemouth with his aunt and would be a day or two more. They were talking money.

If only she could make Sholto see sense! He spent with no limit, he bought what he liked, and only afterwards worried about a sale. Luca was stirring the waters of the art market, casting doubt on anything Sholto put up, so most of the selling was private, knocking on the doors of the world's richest men. It wasn't cheap and it wasn't quick, and Matty was sick to death of the air fares and hotel bills, not to mention the bottles of champagne and handmade shoes. He lived like a prince and would do no other, and the result was the meeting with his aunt.

Instalments on the loan were paid quarter by quarter, but they had missed two quarters now. Sholto said it was due to under-capitalisation, which Matty labelled extravagance. He had gone, alone, to persuade his aunt to lend another two hundred thousand, which would increase the repayments, of course, but should free them to trade. Matty was absolutely against it. She wanted paintings sold, at any cost, even at a blighted auction, but when she said so Sholto just looked past her. He didn't want to talk now. He had a project on.

Projects, projects. He had projects, she had work. Endless work. Sometimes she hated the silver that seemed to come in an unending flood. So much of it was substandard and ordinary. And she could guarantee that at least once a week she would find either a policeman on the doorstep, with something forged or stolen, or Richard Greensall, feeling insecure. He brought things over in person now, when they were finished. Then he stayed and drank tea, for hours.

Now, on top of everything, this. How could Henrietta not tell her? Matty felt tearful suddenly. Suppose she'd told everyone else and not her? He was an American so Lorne must know, but she might not have told Grizz, who was knee deep in exams.

She cleared the table with vicious efficiency, pushing Simon off the end before he had finished. He was reading the paper, precociously, because he liked to be able to quote things he didn't understand. And she didn't understand her own irritation. She loved him and yet he enraged her.

The telephone rang while she was in the barn, crouched over an inadequate heater, cataloguing silver. 'Hello?'

'Matty? It's me.'

Henrietta. Matty schooled her voice into cool disinterest. 'Oh. Hello.'

'What's the matter? Aren't you well?'

'Quite well thank you. And so must you be. If what I read in the *Telegraph* is correct.'

'What?'

'Your engagement. Good of you to let me know.'

'She didn't! She couldn't! She promised! Oh, Matty, I'm so sorry. I told her she wasn't to put anything in until I'd told everyone. Don't be cross, please.'

'I'm not. Honestly.'

'You sound furious.'

'You might at least have let me know it was in the offing. Who is this guy?'

'Tyler? A zillionaire. Very sweet. You're not so cross you won't come to the wedding, are you? Mummy's booking the Savoy Chapel and a reception the size of a Conservative party rally. Tyler's mother, Zena, is little and thin and beastly and she wants things like hanging baskets in the church, and Mummy's machine-gunning her at every turn. It's hell.'

'But you're still in America, aren't you?'

'Yes. Mummy came out.'

Matty's anger began to dissolve. It was so good to talk to a friend. She and Henry gossiped and giggled as they always did, and talked about Lorne and Griselda and themselves. 'It makes me feel very odd,' said Matty suddenly. 'You getting married, I mean.'

'Oh. Does it? We felt just as odd when you went. Not Lorne, though. We all expected her to go.'

'So it's just Grizz left now then.'

'Yes, Bertie didn't last. Still, she'll love the Foreign Office. We can all jet off in Tyler's plane and see her amongst the alien corn.'

'Amidst. You can't be amongst corn, you have to be amidst it.'

'Matty, you always were pedantic!'

The comment stuck in Matty's mind after the call was ended. She felt tearful and sad. The business she was in was no more than lists and detail, she thought, and at that moment she hated it, hated, hated, hated it! Her hand lashed out, caught a George III teapot stand and sent it

409

crashing to the ground. A leg fell off with a little, apologetic clang. 'Oh, shit,' she said. Value halved, just like that. Richard Greensall would have to mend it.

How ill she felt. A headache raged behind her eyes. She wanted nothing so much as to sleep. But Simon had his project to do, and the telephone would ring, and there was a shipment to Australia that had to be checked, parcelled and documented. Round and round the world the silver went, backwards and forwards, living its life. Matty hated to see a piece go to a museum. She felt it died there, untouched and unloved, never delighting anyone, never having fun.

Simon barged in. 'Aren't you supposed to lock this door? I could be the Mafia. I could fill you full of lead.'

'Go on then,' said Matty, hopefully.

'My project. Library. Remember?'

He chattered all the way to town. In the library it turned out that Matty had forgotten the tickets, and she had to produce identification and a pleading manner. Then, when she explained what she needed, the woman behind the counter said, 'Ozone? Everything's out. There isn't a school in the country doing anything else.'

So they went to the Green Party offices, and obtained some leaflets. They wanted Matty to join so they gave her a cup of tea, and it was good to sit down. When she stood up, agreeing to go on the mailing list, she stood swaying for a moment feeling strange. The feeling gradually identified itself. She took a sudden panic-stricken step forward, grabbed the waste paper basket, and was sick.

'Heavens,' said the girl at the typewriter. 'Are you pregnant?'

And she was.

The shock had abated somewhat by the time Sholto got home. In fact she was becoming reconciled to the idea, so much so that she had bought a ball of wool and was learning to knit. Simon, sour and unexcited, was at the door. 'It would be you,' he said with loathing.

Sholto swaggered past him. 'Yes. It would be. What have I done?'

'You might well ask,' said Simon, with a juvenile leer.

Sholto went into the sitting room. Matty was sitting looking dreamily into the fire, her knitting a tangle on her lap. Everything else in the room was a chaos of magazines, cups and bits of Simon's project.

'What's with the bombsite?' he demanded. 'This isn't like you, ma'am.'

'No,' said Matty. She had a strange, faraway look in her eyes. 'It isn't like either of us really. I was sick in town.'

'Congratulations. Salmonella?'

'Pregnancy.'

He went white. Then he went straight to the kitchen and got the whisky. After a large tot he said, 'Don't you think you could have taken a bit more care?'

'Possibly. I don't know. It must have been Italy, when I was upset. I thought you wanted children! When the girls were here once, you said something.'

'I didn't mean it! God, now we're really stuck.'

'What do you mean, stuck?'

'We can't get out of it. Even if we don't like being married we can't change our minds.'

The tears stung Matty's eyelids. She opened her eyes very wide to stop more falling. 'I knew we shouldn't have done it,' she whispered.

He gestured angrily. 'Of course we should! But this makes it rather permanent, don't you think? I had the feeling we had a bit of grace before the portcullis slammed down forever. And you've got a tadpole and we're stuck.'

'Don't you want a tadpole? Really?'

He looked at her, white and drawn. 'You know me. Never want what I should. Pity the poor tadpole that has to depend on me.'

He got very drunk that night. Matty and Simon went to bed, but in the small hours Simon got up and went downstairs. He found Sholto sitting in a chair, glass in hand, singing to himself:

> 'A-roving, A-roving,
> For roving's been my ru-i-in,
> I'll go no more a-roving
> With you, Fair Maid.'

'Gone off Matty, then, have you?' demanded Simon. 'You're making her cry.'

Sholto looked at him blearily. 'Get lost,' he said.

'Get stuffed,' said Simon.

Sholto sighed. 'Have I got to thump you one? No, I won't. Poor little devil. I mean, you're a case in point. Look what a mess you got into when your parents let you down. Disaster. And that's what I mean — kids should have reliable parents. Good, solid citizens. People with their heads together. Not people like me.'

'But you got married.'

Sholto nodded, sagely. 'So I did. Thought it would help. Tie up the escape routes, so to speak. It doesn't. Just makes you feel worse about wanting to go.'

His chin fell on his chest for a moment. Simon thought he was asleep, but then he took another drink of whisky and revived. 'Thing is,' he said, 'what does Matty want? Is she going to stay home rocking the cradle? Does she want me to stay with her? Because I can't.'

'We like it here,' said Simon, fearfully. 'Matty and me.'

Sholto realised who he was talking to. He passed a hand across his face. ''Course you do, Simon. If I'd come here when I was your age I'd have liked it too. But I didn't come here. I was — somewhere else. I didn't have anywhere I could call my own. I got out of the habit of needing it, you see. So now I don't need it. Won't ever need it. Which — might not be such a good thing.'

'I think it's stupid,' said Simon. 'We all need a home.'

Sholto looked at the boy. He was so like Matty. Same eyes, same hair, same panicky anxiety about being secure and safe. Oh, but these two twined themselves about him! And now the ultimate entanglement. 'Wouldn't you rather it just stayed the three of us?' he demanded desperately. 'Won't you be jealous?'

Simon shrugged. 'Probably. Who cares? Matty tries not to show it but she's really pleased. When the woman in town said she was pregnant she went bright pink.'

'You are — more generous than me,' said Sholto humbly. 'You have a much more generous nature.'

'But you put up with me. That's generous, isn't it?'

Sholto shook his head. 'I don't think so. I don't know what it is.'

Simon took away the empty glass and washed it. He put the empty bottle in the bin. Then he helped Sholto up to bed.

Henrietta's wedding was a production. Three hotels in London had their suites commandeered by the Cooke relatives and step-relatives, two florists had to work overtime, and the Concorde lounge at Heathrow requested a guest list, to help them direct their clients. Six small girls and two reluctant boys had been summoned from the furthest reaches of the family to do duty as bridesmaids and pages, the dress was handmade in silk and, as a wedding present, Tyler gave his bride half a million pounds of diamond parure. Then, with twenty-four hours to go, Henrietta ran away.

Matty and Sholto woke to hear her hammering on the door. It made Matty sick to leap from the bed, so she sat up and held her head while Sholto went down. Henrietta flung herself past him and into the house, mackintosh flying, blonde hair in a mess, her new, refined nose red from weeping. 'You've got to help me,' she declared.

'I do like the nose,' said Sholto, unhelpfully. 'Very chic. Matty has to take her time coming down, I'm afraid, or she throws up on people. She's pregnant.'

'She can't be,' wailed Henry. 'I need her to help!'

'Oh, she's fine once she's been up five minutes. Inclined to wander about with a foolish grin on her face, but we can't do much about that. What's the problem? Bloke's not gay, is he?'

'No.' Henrietta screwed up her handkerchief.

'Vicious? Drug addict? Hasn't got zillions after all and is running a very big overdraft?'

'No.'

Matty came slowly into the room. Henrietta looked up and let out a gulping sob. 'Oh, Matty,' she wailed. 'Will you come and see Peter with me? Please?'

Sholto said, 'Bloody hell, you're not pining for the vicar? You can't prefer cold soup to money.'

413

'Do be quiet, Sholto.' Matty sat down. 'Have you heard anything from Peter?'

Her friend shook her head. 'We haven't written or anything. But I can't, I just can't go through with this if I think there's just a chance he might – that we might – if there was any hope at all.'

Sholto leaned back and extended his long, lean bare feet. He was wearing nothing but a pair of green silk pyjama trousers. The muscles of his chest were in broad, flat plates, extending into long, corded arms. Henrietta turned away, colouring. 'I wouldn't mind if Tyler could just be my friend,' she said desperately. 'But it isn't. It's more. I keep thinking about it. I wanted to with Peter but I don't with him!'

Sholto said, 'Don't you think you should have given it a trial run? Suppose you can't stand it? Suppose you can't stand him? Marriage isn't like sharing a room at boarding school. There's nowhere to hide.'

'I don't know why we waited,' said Henry tearfully. 'Tyler wanted to do everything right, I suppose. He's so nice, you don't know how nice he is.'

'If you had to be nice to get girls into bed then I'd never have got past the knicker elastic,' sighed Sholto. 'But your American's bound to know more about sex than the vicar. Probably took classes in it at college – terribly thorough these American institutions. On any comparative test, Tyler would certainly come out top. If you'll pardon the expression.'

'You just want to go to the party,' said Matty dispassionately. 'You'll only try and do business. All right, Henry. We were driving down later today anyway. We'll just leave somewhat earlier.'

They telephoned Mrs Giles as they were leaving the house. Since she had been under the impression that Henrietta had gone for an early morning swim, she was more than a little surprised to hear that she had actually fled her home. Henrietta wouldn't speak, so she had to content herself with saying forcefully to Matty, 'I trust that you will return her here, in good spirits, before six this evening. I'm relying on you, Matilda. I refuse to have a

414

social event of this magnitude ruined by last-minute hysterics. At the very least she must go through with the wedding. We can always annul it later.'

Matty grimaced and replaced the receiver. Henrietta said, 'Don't worry, I can guess. Death before dishonour.'

'Just about, yes. Come on, Sholto's waiting.'

But the two girls went alone to the church. Matty remembered the first time they had come here, when Henry had been squawking about a coffee shop. Meeting Peter had changed her; plump little girl to elegant lady, and all due to him. The ebullience had turned to calm good sense, the jolliness into adult warmth. Indeed, if she was to be described in one word, that word would be warm. Was it any wonder that Tyler Cooke, in his expensive world, should want to have that source of fundamental heat?

The crypt had a new sign, newly painted. It still read 'Tea, Coffee, 20p'. It was early, not yet eleven, but the door was open and Henry pushed it and went inside. Matty followed, wrinkling her nose at the warm, dusty, human-smelling air. There was no one there except the vicar, setting out cups ready for the day.

'Hello, Peter.'

Pleasure, at first, unmistakably. A second later, he was struggling to conceal it. 'Henry! Good heavens – what a surprise.'

'Yes. I thought you might think so.'

'Yes. You look different. I don't know what it is.'

'No.'

Standing there, looking at each other, there was everything to say and no way of saying it. Almost reluctantly Peter put out his hand and took Henrietta's. 'I've missed you,' he said.

She pulled her hand away and walked across the room. 'Say hello to Matty,' she said shrilly. 'I wouldn't come without her. This is quite important. You don't know how important.'

'You're getting married tomorrow,' said Peter. 'I saw it in the paper.'

'Reading the paper?' said Henry. 'How frivolous of you.'

'I keep an eye on it. I knew I'd find out about you.'

Suddenly Henrietta couldn't bear it. In a low, throbbing voice she said, 'Why are you letting this happen to me? Why don't you care?'

'Henry. I explained.'

'But you know we'd be happy. You know it should be you and me.'

His green eyes held hers for a moment before he looked away. He shrugged, disparagingly. 'I suppose we'd do all right. We'd be happy enough. I just think we both deserve more than that. Don't you love this man, Henry?'

She wrapped her coat around her, as if dying of cold. 'I don't know. I like him, I think. But I knew what I felt for you. Right from the very first moment, and this isn't the same.'

Peter went back to his cups, rattling them into the saucers with desperate hands. 'What do you want me to say, Henry? I've decided how I want to live. Not because I want to, not because I don't want you, but because that's the only way it can be. I told you how it was. I'm not here to love you. I don't want to do it!'

'And what am I here for?'

'Perhaps to marry this man. I don't know.'

Matty, intruding, said, 'I don't know why you came here, Henry. He's one of those men who's best on their own. He thinks it's religion but really it's selfishness.'

'That's not what he is,' said Henry tearfully. 'We were close, weren't we, Peter? It wasn't all me?'

But he turned away, putting his hands in the air in a gesture of defeat. When he looked round again, they had gone.

He sat in the crypt for half an hour, thinking. He missed Henry more than he liked to admit. Looking around at the tables, the metal chairs, the detritus of hundreds of nights of boots and spittle, he felt nauseated suddenly. Was this really what he was supposed to do? Spend his life, his precious talents and years, in the service of this grim clientele of dossers and misfits and failures? At times Henrietta had seemed like a manifestation of sin, a temptation that he was meant to resist. But she might just have been his greatest opportunity. Which was she? He was never to know.

The girls ran out into the cold afternoon. Henry was sobbing. Matty took her to the park and they sat on a bench, watched by old men feeding the pigeons. 'If you don't want to marry, you needn't,' said Matty. 'You don't have to marry anyone.'

'Yes I do,' hiccupped her friend. 'I'm not clever, or talented, or anything. I'm just me. And Tyler's got to have someone, and he'll be better off with me. But I don't know how I shall bear it. I don't want to sleep with him.'

'Perhaps you should wait,' said Matty, thinking of the people, the presents, the food.

'My mother would kill me,' said Henry.

She unwound a little from her hunched sobbing. 'I don't know what I'd do without my friends. Lorne's bringing Greg over, did you know? It's a coup. Her father-in-law's furious. And Grizz is coming. Dear Grizz. And Aunt Susan's here, and Darrell, who I stayed with, and enough Shuster cousins to make the party go with a bang. I can't spoil it for everyone just because I've got cold feet. Can I?'

'Depends how cold your feet are,' said Matty doubtfully. 'One day you might find someone like Peter. Someone you feel the same about.'

Henrietta sighed, a long, regretful sigh. 'I won't. And that settles it, I think. If I can't have Peter then I must be happy with Tyler Cooke. I don't want to be single all my days.'

'There are worse fates,' said Matty. Then she looked at her dear, kind friend. 'But not, I think, for you.'

Standing in the Savoy Chapel the next day, Matty reached for Sholto's hand. She couldn't dispel her nerves. Should she have been stronger yesterday, persuaded Henry to quit? Mrs Giles stood in her place, majestic and immovable. Lorne stood with Greg, their baby left at home, and only Griselda was on her own, wearing the same dress she had worn for both Lorne's and Matty's weddings. She was

417

looking some indeterminate age, thought Matty, anything between twenty and sixty. Now that she had abandoned girlishness, Griselda had achieved a lack of style that was almost stylish in a raw-boned, colonial sort of way.

'Where is she?' hissed Matty between clenched teeth.

'Sit down,' murmured Sholto. 'Your ankles will swell.'

'Surely not yet?' Matty looked anxiously at her feet. They seemed just the same, it was her belly that concerned her, round and hard as a little melon. It stuck out against her silk dress as if she was running to early fat.

The organist began the march once again. Still no Henrietta. Tyler Cooke was staring over his shoulder, looking unhappy and strained. And finally, when they were all beginning to despair, Henry came in.

She looked as if she was drugged. Heavy eyelids drooped over her blue eyes, and she walked in a dream, each pace suspended for a brief half second. Tyler, anxious, reached out and took her hand and she gave him a lazy smile.

Sholto's eyebrow lifted. 'Sleeping pills,' murmured Matty. 'She never could take them.'

'The girl's half-conscious. The thing's probably not allowed.'

'If it gets her through — oh, Sholto, should we stand up and stop it?'

A look of delight crossed his face. 'Can we? Yes, let's!'

'No!' She dragged at his hand, never sure when he was serious. Griselda looked across and lifted a reproving eyebrow.

When it was done there were photographs, taking hours because Tyler's parents would not stand together and each required a set featuring the new partners. Finally Mrs Giles took command and despatched the photographer with a curt, 'My man, you have done enough!' Tyler tried to apologise and was briskly sent off to the wedding car, and Henrietta was given a sniff of sal volatile to wake her up.

'What on earth will her children think of those pictures?' said Sholto. He and Matty were ferrying Griselda to the reception. 'She looked stoned.'

'She'll be divorced in five years,' said Griselda coolly. 'Those sort of marriages never last.'

Matty stared at her in horror. 'Grizz! You are getting hard-bitten. He's a really nice man.'

'But the money! And he hasn't the stomach to stand up to his own mother, let alone Henrietta's.'

'Henry has. She's had years of practice. Only ever turns and fights when the odds are in her favour. It'll be wonderful.'

Sholto grunted. 'If they get through the first night.'

Henrietta took off the blue silk coat of her going-away outfit, revealing a tight silk dress underneath. It was tighter than it should have been, because stress always made her eat. Her mother had been getting at her about it.

She felt a sudden pang, and it wasn't hunger. She almost felt homesick. Here in this glamorous hotel, with a suite larger than some people's houses, she yearned for her father's gentleness and her mother's nagging.

Tyler came out of his bedroom. He was wearing a robe. 'Not undressed yet?' he asked tensely.

She shook her head. 'It all seems so terribly strange. I keep wondering why we don't behave normally and each go back home.'

'You must be very tired.'

Oh, but he was a sweet man. She turned and smiled at him and said, 'Of course I am. Just tired. I'll get undressed and we'll go to bed.'

In her own bathroom, huge and imposing, she wriggled out of the dress. It had left red weals at her waist and she spent minutes trying to rub the marks from her skin. Deciding that hot water might work best, she ran a boiling bath, emerging light-headed and beetroot red. In her flimsy, honeymoon nightie she put on her robe and crept back into the bedroom. Tyler was watching television, with the glazed expression of a man who is taking nothing in.

'Shall we have a drink?' said Henry. 'Champagne or something?'

'If you want — not for me. I had three glasses at the party and on top of everything —'

'I thought you looked a bit green. At least it's over. Now we can do what we like.'

'Yes.'

He switched off the television, and they each grimly took off their robes and got into bed. 'Have you done this before?' asked Henry.

'Er – yes. But I was always sort of – drunk.'

'We could always leave it till tomorrow and get drunk?' she suggested. 'I mean, it seems so odd, feeling obliged –'

'Let's do it. Let's get on and do it.'

He moved across to her and they began to kiss. Henrietta tried not to think about it. When he put his hand on her breast and her flesh jumped, she struggled to ignore the sensation. Let it just happen, she thought. She didn't want to take part in it, she wanted to be no more than passive. He was murmuring in her ear, words of love and reassurance. She wished they had turned off the light. When he pushed up her nightdress and swung on top of her she found herself biting her lip.

Tyler stopped. He lay for a moment on her body, breathing hard, doing nothing. 'I'm sorry,' he said.

'What?'

'I'm sorry. I can't do it. Perhaps it's the tension, I don't know.'

'What do you mean – can't?'

'I mean I can't! I can't get an erection! God, I knew this would happen, I've been dreading it. Every night I've been thinking, what's she going to think, what's she going to say. And here it is, and it's happened. What a bum wedding night.' He got out of the bed and went into the other room, returning with a Coke.

Henrietta sat up. Her nightdress was in a film of lace around her waist. 'I thought I was the one who was scared.'

'We're both allowed to be scared. But the man's supposed to be able to get it up.'

'But you have before. With other girls.'

'Oh, yeah. But not like this. Not with the whole world expecting it, my whole future depending on it. I so much want us to be happy, Henry. I want us to – I don't know, have five children, and dogs, and ice cream on the

420

furniture, and − and everything. I want you to be the happiest woman that ever walked this earth, and none of it can happen, none of it is even going to begin, if I can't − if we can't do it!'

'It can't be that hard,' said Henry. 'I mean − difficult.'

'You can't decide to feel sexy. You just do.'

Henrietta looked at his drawn face. Her heart went out to him. All week his mother had been nagging, all day his father had been belittling him. He was tired and worried, and she knew that if she said this was unimportant it wouldn't be true. Dear God, she thought, she was a half-hearted bride if ever there was one, and only hours after the wedding she was required to demonstrate commitment.

She got out of bed, dropping the nightdress to her knees. 'Does this make you feel sexy?' A Marilyn Monroe wiggle, accompanied by a pout. 'Or this?' The nightdress above her head, and a hand on her hip.

'Henrietta!' She was shocking him and she laughed.

'Aren't I supposed to do this sort of thing? Shall I dance for you? I always wanted to be Isadora Duncan but I was always too fat.' She ran around the room, waving the nightdress in a parody of the ethereal nymph.

Tyler was laughing. He laughed until his eyes watered, and Henry flopped on to his knee, quite breathless. 'I love you,' he said simply. 'I love you so much.'

Henry whispered, 'I won't ever be mean to you. I'm the one person in the world that won't ever try to hurt you, Tyler.'

He kissed her then, and she entwined her arms around his neck, letting a small moan escape. Her response excited him, and he kissed her again with true passion. Again she moaned and panted a little, copying every love scene in every film she had ever seen. It seemed to be working. The most extraordinary event was taking place in Tyler's lap and it took all her self-control not to stop what she was doing and inspect it.

He lifted her up and put her down on the bed. Henry closed her eyes, murmuring 'Tyler − Tyler −' in her best Hollywood style. His body was on hers, there was pressure, inaccurate pressure, and then − incredibly − invasion. Her eyes flew open. Ye gods, what was he doing to her? If her mother had known he was going to do this she would certainly have stopped it.

Small cries escaped her, of pain and astonishment. Tyler felt her hands on his back, flapping helplessly, and experienced a rush of excitement. He was harder than ever in his life, he rode a wave of confident sexuality. It was going on longer than she had expected. The whole thing took some getting used to, that was for sure. She tightened her muscles and lifted her knees, sending unexpected shards of feeling up from her groin. Wow! If her mother had ever done this, which she doubted, she had never felt that, no question of it. Gaining confidence she lifted herself up from the bed, feeling Tyler slide right into her, enormous, only to feel him − explode.

Lying together, exhausted and sweating, Henry said, 'You are not going to tell me that every person in the world was born because of that. A lot of people must be using test tubes. Think of the Queen. Think of my mother.'

'Our children will say the same about us,' said Tyler. 'They couldn't! They didn't! It can't be true!'

Henrietta ran a curious hand down his belly. This was all most unexpected, most surprising. Why hadn't she talked more to Matty and Lorne? Look at it now − good heavens!

'Isn't it bad for you?' she asked anxiously. 'Getting so big so fast?'

'No,' said Tyler, with justifiable smugness. 'Nobody has ever managed to say it's bad for your health.'

This time, thought Henry, I shall start wriggling straight away. She put her hands on his buttocks and held him into her, and braced her feet on the bed to push. If anyone saw me now, she thought wildly, aware that Tyler was near the end again, and she must − she must − the sensation was almost more than she could bear. It was intimate, and slightly lavatorial, the sort of thing that you should never, never do in company. She hoped Tyler wasn't looking. She heard herself cry out, a long way away, and every nerve in her body discharged itself in exquisite electricity.

Tyler was staring down at her. 'I don't think I have ever been so happy,' he said.

Happy. Henrietta looked up at him in bewilderment. Yes, when she got over the shock of this — this unexpected experience — she might well be happy. She said, 'Just don't let my mother know about this. I'm sure we're not supposed to have fun.'

Chapter Twenty-Five

Sholto was flirting with Lorne. They were all dining together, an arrangement made in the haze of the wedding party, when an elegant meal somewhere chic seemed a fitting finale. They had chosen a restaurant where the chef was a personality, and toured the dining room glaring at guests who had neglected to eat some part of their meal, be it the skin of the duck, a black olive, or even a mint leaf garnish.

'It's like school again,' murmured Matty, trying to divert attention from Sholto's blatant flattery. 'I can remember hiding burnt peas under my fork.'

'They were good at burning things,' agreed Griselda. Then she spoke sharply. 'Lorne, do stop giggling. Your poor husband is starting to feel neglected.'

Lorne batted her eyelashes at Greg. 'Are you, honey? But I don't feel neglected when you go off to your conferences. Or your meetings. Or your trips upstate, which can't be postponed, and on which I can never come.'

'You've had too much to drink, Lorne,' said Greg.

'Of course she hasn't,' said Sholto, and emptied a bottle of red wine into Lorne's glass. He signalled to the waiter for another. 'Get with it, my man. Now, Lorne, why does he keep leaving you like this? Don't you satisfy him in bed?'

'What do you think?' murmured Lorne.

'I don't do my thinking here,' said Sholto. 'It gives me blood pressure.' They chuckled at each other.

Matty leaned across the table and tried to talk to Greg. He was monosyllabic, watching Lorne in a state of steadily fulminating rage. 'Lorne was telling me that you're standing for election this year,' said Matty desperately. 'Isn't that going to take you away from home even more?'

'But he likes being away from home,' sang out Lorne.

'You know I don't, honey,' said Greg.

'But of course you do. That's the way it works. I stay at home minding Junior and you go off with your daddy and sleep around. You both do, and I wonder why? I can understand Sherwood but you used to love making out with me.'

Greg stood up and caught Lorne's arm in a murderous grip. 'Get up, Lorne. We're going.'

'Let her go, old chap,' said Sholto. 'We don't allow wife-beating in England. A sad reflection on progress, I fear, but what can you do? The women have tamed us.'

'I'll thank you to keep quiet,' said Greg. 'And you'll leave Lorne alone. You've always had the hots for her. But she's my wife and I'll kill the first man lays a hand on her.'

Lorne pulled her arm free of him. 'I'm not going back. I want some more to eat.'

Reluctantly, because he dared not make a scene, Greg went back to his place. Griselda said, 'I'm to start work in Whitehall at the end of the year. Then with a bit of luck, they'll send me overseas.'

'Paris,' said Matty. 'Ask for Paris. Lots of silver and lots of clothes. I should love to visit.'

'You're not going anywhere,' said Sholto. 'Nappies and maternity frocks, that's you.'

Matty flushed. She'd forgotten she was pregnant.

Lorne said, 'Then they leave you at home with the baby, and complain because you're boring. But I've got the answer – spend money. The more you spend the madder they get.'

'I'll take you away from it all,' said Sholto. 'To the ends of the earth in a peagreen boat. Adventure, excitement, and sex.'

'Divine,' said Lorne, and leaned back in her chair, arms outstretched. 'Take me, I'm yours.'

Greg, furious, yelled, 'Lorne, will you behave yourself!'

Sholto looked at him and said, 'Fuck off, beefcake.'

The fight brought the chef from the kitchen, waving a knife. Matty screamed, Lorne collapsed in laughter, and Griselda removed the offending implement with one decisive swoop. 'Please,' she said. 'Let's keep it clean.'

426

Greg was swinging haymakers at Sholto, who backed away amongst the tables, avoiding every one. When he reached the wall he laughed, ducked, and hit Berenson in the groin. The man fell, groaning.

'Damn you, Sholto,' said Matty, feelingly. 'Why?'

He shrugged and put his hands in his pockets. 'Because I felt like it.'

Griselda said quietly to Matty, 'Just take him home. I'll pay the bill and you can settle later. He won't hit you or anything?'

'Of course not!' Matty was appalled.

Lorne staggered over to her husband and knelt down beside him. 'You OK, Greg? I'll call an ambulance if you want.'

He looked up at her out of a grey face. 'You bitch. Get me out of here.'

The chef was raging volubly at Griselda, who was simply nodding and checking the bill. Sholto had his hands in his pockets, and looked bleakly across the restaurant at the astonished diners. He might have been looking at an exhibit in a museum, thought Matty. She took his arm and led him away.

The girls met at the Dorchester the following day for tea. Matty and Lorne paid their shares of the bill, and discovered that Griselda had somehow become a favoured confidante of the famous chef, who had sat with her in the kitchen and drunk brandy. She had found it difficult to ignore an apprentice sleeping in the corner, a collapsed relic from the evening service that no one had seen fit to remove, and what's more she and the chef between them had eaten all the puddings the party had ordered and not consumed. 'He said I was the most comfortable woman he'd ever met,' said Griselda. 'I think most women are afraid of him. But after the evening, nothing could upset me. My emotional well had run dry.'

'Ours hadn't,' said Lorne. 'I think Greg is going to kill Sholto.'

'Why not you?' asked Matty. 'After all, you were offering to go to bed with him.'

'Was I? Oh. But you know Sholto. He brings out the worst in me.'

Lorne looked restlessly about the room. She was wearing a coat in russet wool, and a small hat on the back of her head. Her slender hand reached for her cup, her legs crossed and uncrossed, and her attention seemed always to be about to slide away.

'If it wasn't for the baby, I'd leave,' she said suddenly.

Her friends sat in stunned silence. 'It's not that bad,' said Griselda. 'He adores you.'

'Does he? I play no part in his life. Or at least, only a decorative one.'

'What would happen if you left?' asked Matty.

Lorne shrugged. 'I don't know.' She lifted her hands in a fluttery gesture and then brought them firmly into her lap. 'Yes, I do. Sherwood Berenson would foreclose on my father. He's so much in debt, you don't know.'

'But you've always had so much money!' said Griselda, sounding shocked.

Lorne nodded. 'Borrowed money. Borrowed from Sherwood Berenson. I thought — oh God, I was such a fool! I thought marrying Greg would mean he'd forget it, but he never did. He never will. It's the sort of power he loves.'

'He's got you very well trapped, hasn't he?' said Griselda wonderingly. Lorne, thinking of Miller, nodded. She was more trapped than they knew.

'Greg's not so bad,' said Matty slowly. 'You shouldn't let Sholto make you think badly of him. He hates some men. The good-looking ones. The ones with everything. He takes things out on Greg because he envies him.'

Griselda sat with her eyes cast down. Matty might have been speaking of her. How often had she looked at Lorne and felt a dull fire of rage that Lorne should be beautiful, witty, confident, poised. But Lorne was in the briars, while Griselda had avoided them, through calm planning and strict self-discipline. There was no virtue in yearning for the things you could not have. No peace to be found in wishing.

'Greg isn't a bad man,' said Lorne desperately. 'I married too young, you know.' Her eyes roamed the room, looking at all the men she might have had, and were denied her. Young men, old men, men to make you laugh, men to make you cry. She could have dined and danced years away. And now she had a baby who couldn't see, and a husband she couldn't trust, when she would have given anything – anything – to have someone like Sholto.

Did Matty suspect? she wondered. No. Matty knew. But she rested in the stupid confidence that her husband and her friend would not betray her. Lorne put her hand to her mouth and gnawed a fingernail, praying that she would never find herself alone with Sholto, in a room with a door that locked. Because Sholto felt the same. Last night, in the restaurant, he had let Greg know that he could take his wife to bed whenever he damn well chose.

Suddenly Matty said, 'Good God. Oh no, it's him.'

'Who?'

'A man called Luca de Caruzon. I hate him. He does Sholto down at every turn, and all because – oh damn! He's seen me.'

Luca crossed the floor, a faint smile on his face. Lorne automatically draped herself more attractively in her chair.

'Mrs Feversham.'

'Mr de Caruzon. May I introduce Mrs Berenson and Miss Lemming-Knott? Girls.'

They inclined their heads disdainfully. Matty almost laughed. The girls had sided with her without question.

'I wish to talk to your husband.'

'Indeed? He's very busy.'

'I've got a picture that needs a good opinion. Normally of course I wouldn't ask.'

'I don't think Sholto will accept. I'm sorry.'

'I believe this painting once belonged to his aunt. I'm informed on the best authority that he alone can decide if this is genuine or not.'

'I don't think he'll do you any favours.' Matty's eyes blazed like a fire behind glass.

'I think the man can at least favour me with the truth! What is he, an expert or some damned charlatan?'

'An expert, of course! How dare you!'

'You know very well how I dare!'

They glared at one another. Matty was the first to drop her eyes. Was he trying to dupe Sholto into authenticating some dud? Or was it a genuine olive branch? Even Luca must tire of such feuds eventually.

'I'll tell my husband I spoke to you,' she said quietly.

'Thank you. Ladies.' He touched his hat and left.

Sholto was on the 'phone when she got back to their hotel. He was talking to another dealer in that extravagant, bulling-up way he used when he had a poor picture to sell. 'Exquisite brushwork. Superb form. You are familiar with this man's work, I take it? A little obscure, because not many folk have the guts to go off the beaten track and look for the lesser known –'

When he hung up, Matty said: 'The artist's obscure because he's useless.'

Sholto laughed. 'Yes, but how do you know?'

'The way you talk. I can tell. Luca asked me if you would look at a picture he has. It once belonged to your aunt.'

He lay back on the bed, hands behind his head. 'Can't have. She never sells a thing unless she's penniless.'

'Perhaps she is.'

'I live in hope. Where's he staying? The Dorchester?' She nodded.

Sholto got on the 'phone and spoke cryptically to Luca. 'Right. Got it. Take a look tomorrow, around ten.' He put the receiver down.

'Why are you going? It's playing into his hands.'

'He's got my aunt's Pissarro. I've got to see it.'

'He wants to ruin us and you're going to help him!'

'Who the hell cares if we're ruined? Christ, Matty, you think of nothing but sodding money!'

She gasped and sat down, staring at him in amazement. But he turned his back on her, getting out his damnable postcards again and working through them one by one, shutting her out. She felt as if he hated her. She felt as if at that moment he wanted her out of his life.

The next day, while Sholto went to see de Caruzon, she went in search of Sammy Chesworth. She found him, as expected, at Phillip's, viewing silver. Lesser mortals followed him, peering where he peered, causing him irritation. His expression became severe when he saw her.

'Matty, if you were with me I wouldn't have to do this. Everybody following me, looking over my shoulder. I'm an old man, I don't need this aggravation.'

'You sacked me, Sammy.'

'Me? You sacked yourself. Come and drink tea with me and cheer me up.'

They ate sticky buns together in a café. Sammy said, 'Business is very slack just now. Nothing about.'

'I heard you were buying for the Arabs. Moving into jewellery.'

He sniffed. 'Yes, a little. The odd five million.'

They chuckled together. Sammy looked around at the few occupied tables and as if satisfied, picked up his briefcase. It was an old, tattered specimen in concertinaed brown leather, at present expanded to its fullest extent. He took out a cardboard box a foot long and six inches wide, and put it on the table. 'Take a look at that.'

'What is it? Looks like a bomb.'

'Some bomb. Don't drop it.'

She lifted the lid carefully. Tissue paper had been carelessly wrapped around the object within, and she smoothed it fastidiously as she unfolded it. Sammy watched as her face changed. She looked at him with huge eyes, glanced around the room and whispered, 'You shouldn't have this here! We could be murdered!'

'No one knows I've got it. Like it?'

She looked down at a huge, perfect Fabergé egg. Diamonds and pearls banded it, encircled it, twined all over it like sparkling ribbons on a gleaming present. The egg itself was a light turquoise colour, enamelled to a brilliant sheen. 'It opens up to show some little eggs, a music box, that sort of thing,' said Sammy offhandedly. 'You can't see it here.'

'No. Did you buy on commission?'

He nodded. 'Of course.'

She wrapped the egg up again, and Sammy thrust it inconsequentially into his bag. It wasn't affectation; he had lived with precious things so long that their value did not

431

awe him. The Fabergé was good, but it wasn't silver, his love.

'Now, Matilda,' he said, 'let's talk about you. I'm getting anxious. A first-class reputation, of course, but where is the money? I don't hear it said that you are sharp, that people dread to see you at sales, that you drive a hard bargain.'

She shrugged. 'I do OK. I pay too much for things sometimes. And sometimes I don't like to sell. I've a barn stuffed full of silver, Sammy, tons of it. I don't keep it for no reason, but if I've a teapot I like to see if I can match it, and whole sets of casters are nice to have, and then there's the flatware — I've a lot of that.'

Sammy was shaking his head. 'You are not a collector, Matilda. You're dealing. Let others wait for the right piece to come up.'

'But I get a better price if I sell a set.'

'Your money wastes time in stock! Hold only those pieces you know are about to become fashionable. In twenty years' time you will curse me because you sold this or that for a song and now it's worth a fortune, but we can't keep everything twenty years just to see! Turn it over, Matty. Don't be a foolish woman dealer and let sentiment come before money.'

She looked down at her hands. He made her feel tearful, because of her pregnancy probably. 'Did you know I'm having a baby?'

'No! Matty! And I talk about business when soon you'll be giving all that up. The way of the world, the way of the world. I shall tell Delia —' he thought about it and changed his mind '— or perhaps not. Let's go and buy a teddy bear.'

'I'm not going to give up work, Sammy.'

'But your husband is doing well? I thought you said so?'

'Yes. Yes, of course. He's terribly sharp, is Sholto. I feel safer though, with my own business.'

He said nothing. Yet she knew he was old-fashioned enough to believe that women should devote themselves to children, leaving men free to devote themselves to providing for them. But if Sholto was at his postcards again Matty was not about to sacrifice her one claim to independence. She felt Sammy looking at her with old, wise eyes. 'When

432

did life ever work out easily?' he murmured. 'We're fools to expect it. The Lord means us to learn and He doesn't spare himself in teaching us. How hard it is.'

She put out a hand and covered his. 'Shall we go and buy that teddy bear?'

They bought a bear with a fat tummy and thin arms and legs. He looked out at the world with quizzical optimism, as if hoping at any moment to be offered something nice. 'A dealer in the making,' declared Sammy. 'Ever hopeful.'

Matty kissed him and hugged her bear. It was lovely to have someone else acknowledge that her baby would one day be here. She went happily back to her hotel, because they must pack up and leave that day.

Sholto was in the room. He was sitting on the bed, the scar on his face startlingly prominent, a clear sign that he was desperately tense. 'What's the matter?' asked Matty. 'Was it the Pissarro?'

He nodded. 'The real thing. And I told him so. So now perhaps he'll stop hounding me through the auction rooms of the world and I can make enough cash to keep you and your offspring in shoeleather. Does that make you happy?'

She felt her mood darken. 'I don't know. Are you sure the picture's good? It could be a trick.'

'I know that Pissarro better than I know you. It's authenticated and he'll make a million. And all it cost is my pride.'

'I didn't ask you to go!'

'No? You wanted the money. Now you'll get it.'

He made her feel mercenary and scheming. He made her feel like a dragging, nagging wife. She got up and began to throw clothes into a suitcase, but her anger burned, refusing to be quiet. She turned on him. 'Do you think I'm trapping you?' she demanded. 'Is that it? Because I'm not. If you don't want to stay and be married to me, if you don't want this baby, then you can go. I'm not going to cry and beg you to stay, I'm not going to tell you we can't get by. If you want to bugger off to that horrible Italian woman then I suggest you get up and go!'

'You don't mean that.'

'Yes I do! Ever since we married it's been the same, you're moody and difficult and I daren't say a word. I'm not asking you to keep me, I'm not asking you to live with me. So if you don't want to stay you can bloody well – piss off!'

She slammed the lid on the suitcase. She felt light-headed with the suddenness of her rage, welling up from nowhere to erupt at him. 'I am so tired of being tolerant,' she said thickly. 'I won't put up with it any more.'

Still he said nothing. She cast him a look under her lashes, and he was sitting on the bed, watching her. 'I thought you'd take hold of me,' he said at last. 'I thought you'd stop me falling. But I keep on going down, and if I hold on to you we'll go down together.'

'Go where? There isn't any down.'

'There is for me. Oh, Matty, don't worry, don't look so scared. I don't want to scare you. But you don't know me, Matty. Nobody does.'

'That's the same for all of us.'

'To some degree. But I feel as if I'm a fraud. A well-made, well-documented fake. People like it. Attractive, amusing, easy to know. Goes so well with the curtains and adds that touch of – well, a good fake's so often more glamorous than the real thing. And underneath there's a botched up, worthless piece of work.'

'You're depressed,' said Matty. 'It upset you, seeing Luca.'

'I'm always like this, Matty. But today I'm too tired to pretend.'

She flailed around for certainty, for some explanation of this odd, unpleasant mood. 'A man in Italy said you were angry. He said you never let it out.'

Sholto put a hand up to his face. 'Cesare. Well, he should know.'

'It isn't such a bad thing. You don't have to hide it.'

'It's not your sort of anger, Matty. Look at you. One moment furious, the next it's gone, like – like rain showers. What I have is different.'

'How different?'

His face was so white, except for the livid scar. His hands were so elegant, but for their long-fingered strength. She

434

had always suspected there was far more to Sholto than she knew. 'Sometimes,' he said musingly, 'sometimes I think I'm a balloon, filled with foul things. Hatred. Cruelty. A balloon stuffed full of horrors. People like you read in the paper about somebody doing something terrible, and you think, That could never be me. But it is me. I know it is.'

'Only a little bit,' said Matty, and her voice was a little girl's and full of fear.

'Oh, Matty,' he murmured. 'You're full of love and kindness and gentleness. And I copy you. I pretend. Don't you ever see that?'

Of course she did. Part of loving him was that frail balance between darkness and light. The black dog of his depression could never be outrun. He put his hands over his face and groaned.

Matty knew she was out of her depth. She had known it from the first minute with Sholto, the first day they met. 'I can't bear it if you leave me,' she whispered. 'That would hurt me so much.'

'You just told me to piss off.'

'That was then. I'm not cross now. Why can't you stay with me?'

'Because I'll hurt you, Matty. You and the baby.'

'I think we'd both rather wait until you do.'

The skin of his face was stretched tight across the bones. His eyes were sunk into his head, and all his movements betrayed restless unhappiness. 'I can't stay in that cottage,' he muttered. 'I've got to travel, I've got to get away.'

'I'll come,' said Matty.'

'You hate to come. And you're pregnant.'

'So? I'm coming anyway. You're not fit to go by yourself.'

'Me? Not fit? I'm fit for nothing else.'

'I've got to come to take care of you.'

She reached out her arms and hugged him. He was so big, so gangling. He tried to repel her and push her away. But she clung to him, face buried against his chest, until at last he wrapped his arms around her and put his face in her hair.

They stopped at home only long enough to change their

clothes. Matty scribbled notes to everyone, including a desperate plea to Mrs Giles.

'I wonder if I could appeal to you to take care of my brother Simon for the coming holiday? He's almost thirteen and very bright, and he may be something of a handful, but I simply have to go away with my husband and I have nowhere else I can turn. With grateful thanks, Matilda.'

Silver orders were piled up everywhere, cheques remained unbanked, the police had a call out for a stolen commemorative tray that she was sure she had picked up in a job lot at a sale. Everything would have to wait.

In the car, about to go, Sholto said 'This is the most stupid idea. Stay here and let me go, Matty. You belong with this house. You're in no state to go jaunting off with me.'

Dogged, determined, Matty said, 'I'm coming. You can't get rid of me.' With a sigh Sholto started the car and drove off.

Sholto made no concessions to Matty's presence. He didn't consult her about where they would go, never asked if she was happy with what they would do. It was as if he was showing her the worst of himself, the side he had resolutely kept concealed, the tortured, wayward wastrel he thought himself to be.

They went to France, to a houseparty in the Loire, in a turreted château set on a hilltop overlooking forests and vineyards. It was full of the international set, the rich and idle on their endless circuits around the world, filling the empty hours with empty sensation. They adored Sholto and his raffish ways, eyeing Matty with ill-concealed doubt. She walked the long stone corridors, listening to laughter and groans from here and there, waiting for Sholto.

He drank, as they all did, snorted cocaine, with the best, and flirted, Matty thought, with heroin. She was getting to know the signs. One of the girls was an addict, regulating her hours and days by the needle. She and Sholto disappeared together for one long evening, while Matty swam in the pool, exhausting herself. When at last she got out one of the French girls said, 'He is in the tower. I think perhaps you should go and look. The others, with all their laughing, they don't see.'

'See what?'

A shrug. 'How he is.'

'He's so terribly unhappy.'

She went up the circular tower stair, stopping twice to catch her breath. Pregnancy sapped you, unobtrusively, taking away the easy acceptance of strength and vitality. It was like suddenly being old, she thought. At the top of the stair she stopped outside a single oak door, and when she knocked there was no reply. She opened the door and saw them, lying sprawled on the floor, their faces dreamy and stupidly smiling.

'I hope you didn't use her needle.'

The girl rolled her lovely, idiot head. 'We're not amateurs. I pay for the best.'

'How nice for you. Silk cushions and all.' She flung open the window, letting a draught of cold air into this den of escapism and self-abuse. Sholto groaned. 'This is not pleasant,' he murmured.

'Good.' Matty pulled the cushion away and let his head thump to the floor.

'Bitch.'

He was coming round. She dragged him to his feet and pushed him, reeling in front of her, down the stair. The French girl stood at the bottom. She said, 'Sholto, you are cruel to your poor wife.' He leaned his head against the stone wall, and suddenly Matty was terrified at his despair. He was drowning, and she could not save him.

They left the next morning. Sholto was silent. He drove fast and dangerously. But when Matty asked him to slow down he did so.

'How do you feel?' she asked at last.

'OK. Weird.'

'Did you like it?'

'What? Oh. I don't know. Yes. But not enough to go for it.'

'Looked like a slow way to kill yourself to me. That girl was like Eleanor.'

'She was like me.'

They lunched on cheese and bread in a field by a stream. Cattle were grazing on the far side of the hedge, their feet plopping in the mud as they came down to drink. Watching Sholto yawn and eat, some of Matty's panic began to subside. He would get over this. He must.

But the big houses came and went, one after another. Sometimes Sholto did some business, but mostly he partied. Out of boredom Matty was forced to work, promising to send silver here and there, buying pieces she did not truly want. She acquired a giant silver clock, guessing at a price, a huge and ugly piece with gilded cherubs blowing trumpets on the top.

'Sell it to someone who will not hate the thing,' declared its owner. 'I cannot bear to look at it each day. It spoils my breakfast.'

Sholto never ate breakfast. He rose at noon and began drinking at four, returning to bed at dawn. Sometimes he smelled of other women and if he reached for her, Matty pushed him away. But he could not revolt her. It was all part of the same thing, the same collapse. She could only stay with him, the only person left, perhaps the only person there had ever been, who would always reach out her hand to help.

The pregnancy was becoming irksome. What's more, people were finding it more and more odd that Sholto should be so wild when his wife was six months gone and exhausted, poor girl, by the travelling. Even the brightest young things became a little staid when they saw Matty's state, and the parties began to degenerate into long broody chats about children. Couples went to bed together, misty-eyed, and in the mornings the girls drank mineral water and looked hopeful.

Sholto was living dangerously. If there were horses to ride he rode them, putting them at huge fences as if determined to die. But his lack of fear made the horses brave, and they always came back. He drove races on country roads in the dark, screaming round corners on two wheels, but he never crashed. One night he walked the crenellated battlements of a castle, for a dare. He put not a foot wrong, a hundred feet above the earth.

'Do you want to die?' asked Matty that night, in bed. He sighed, wearily. 'No. I don't think so.'

'Then don't do such things. It isn't fair to toy with death.'

'If it wants me it can have me. That's all. You'll be provided for. You can sell the stock.'

She pushed herself up on one elbow. Her belly, round and swollen, pressed against the thin cotton nightdress. Sholto put out his hand and rubbed the protrusion, feeling the creature within shift and stir. 'Why do you put up with me? I let you down all the time, let you both down.'

'It doesn't matter.'

'I don't know what you hope for. I won't change. You think this is the only time, but it isn't. This is what I'm like.'

'I don't mind. I love you just the same.'

The words seemed to transform him. The gentle stroking stopped as he grabbed her shoulders, forcing her back on to the bed. She let out a strangled cry and he straddled her, staring down into her face. 'How dare you! How dare you say that to me!' He lifted her up and flung her back down again, once, twice. Matty pulled back her hand and hit him across his scar.

He got off the bed and went, trembling, to the window. 'I knew this would happen,' he said calmly. 'It was only a matter of time. And if someone's going to get hurt, I would very much rather it wasn't you. There are an awful lot of women in the world who don't mind that sort of thing, but you're not one of them. And I can't trust myself. So that's it. I'll put you on a plane tomorrow morning.'

Matty, her head spinning, said helplessly: 'Where will you go? What will happen?'

He sighed, and smiled at her, his old sweet smile. 'I'll find somewhere. There's always somewhere for people like me. There's something about evil that attracts, I find. I wonder if that's why you stick with me?'

'Will you stop behaving as if you're some sort of monster! You're upset, that's all. You're tired.'

'Darling Matty, I'm tired of myself.'

She began to cry. He came back into the bed and held her against him, and their roles were reversed once again, he the comforter, she the comforted. He kissed her and stroked her hair, touching her breasts and body with all the familiarity of an old and trusted lover. She loved him then. This was the face he had always turned to her, the unblemished cheek and not the scar.

She didn't get on the plane. She waved goodbye to him and went to the gate, then refused to board and said she had changed her mind. Eventually, amidst argument, her ticket was altered. She got on a plane for Rome.

A week passed, and a few days more. She rested in her hotel, eating good food and walking in the back streets, buying expensive baby clothes and pricing silver. Soon she would have to economise, she thought, and wondered how long it would be before the money ran out. Sammy had said she must become tougher. When she had nothing but the money her silver made she would be tough indeed.

At last she thought it time. She hired a car and drove away from Rome, losing herself in the traffic and then in the hills. But eventually she recognised the village and the track. She stopped for petrol and the attendant said, 'The Baronessa, eh? The visit?'

Matty nodded. '*Si.*'

The house was as she remembered it, dusky rose in the sunlight. She pulled on the bell, and when Alfredo answered, she said, 'I've come to find my husband.'

He did not stand aside, but she pushed past him, and he followed her, protesting, through the hall. Matty turned. 'Go away,' she said clearly. 'I'm not staying, so please go away.'

He stood in the hall while she went on. The house was very quiet. There might have been nobody in it but herself and Alfredo, and she hoped quite desperately that it might be so. But she wanted to see him — she had to know.

The back stairs led discreetly up from the conservatory. Matty felt like a criminal, creeping about, looking at closed doors and wondering what was behind them. Then she heard someone moan. A woman. The baby inside her, sensing her own distress, began to kick.

Matty went forward slowly, her feet soundless on the thick carpet. The door at the end was tight shut, but when she

stood outside it she could hear them. Sholto, his voice heavy
and cruel. 'Bitch. Come on, you bitch.'

'You're killing me – oh – oh, my God!'

She turned the handle, opening the door the merest crack.
Sholto, naked to the waist, had his back to her. The woman
lay face down across the bed, tied to the posts, her rump
raised on pillows. He held a whip, and she bore the marks
of beatings. A small trickle of blood stained the pillows
between her legs. Matty pushed the door wider and said,
'Sholto.'

He turned in amazement. The woman on the bed twisted
her head around as best she might and, incredibly, began
to laugh. 'Oh, how exciting! We have an audience. Or have
you come to join in, my dear? We're having such fun.'

'I just wanted to be sure,' said Matty.

He was dazed, as if he barely saw her. He was doped,
drunk, something, and rubbed his hand across his eyes as
if trying to clear a mist. Then he shrugged, despairing. 'I
told you. This is me. This is what I'm like.'

'It's only a part of you,' said Matty. 'I wanted to see and
I wanted to tell you something. I know you now. All of you.
And when you want, you can always come home.'

She might not even have spoken. He turned back to the
woman on the bed. 'Go away,' he said. 'I've got things I
must do.'

She backed away and shut the door. The woman inside
the room began to laugh, but the whip struck and she
gasped. Recovering, she chuckled to herself. 'Dear Sholto,'
she murmured, 'I knew you needed this. I knew you'd come
back.'

The chill within her heart just would not thaw. She drank
hot coffee at the airport, cup after cup, but the cube of ice
remained. He was drowning and she had not saved him; she
had held on to his hands until his fingers slipped from hers
and he was gone. She could have held no tighter. She could
have done no more. Whatever happened to Sholto now was
down to fate.

Chapter Twenty-Six

Simon faced Mrs Giles across the breakfast table. They eyed each other like adversaries in a boxing match, sizing up the height, weight, reach and morale of the opponent. Simon concluded that she was less fit than yesterday, which was understandable. He decided on a subtle punch. He picked up the *Telegraph*, opened it at the leading article and said airily, 'Interesting Tory conference we're due for, don't you think, Mrs Giles?'

She smiled a steely smile. 'You know nothing about it, Simon. Don't show off.' A counter punch of creditable weight.

Simon opened his eyes wide. 'But it says here that the law and order debate could well influence policy for months to come. And last night Mr Giles was only saying that —'

'Eat your toast, Simon.' Cowardly, that. Sheltering from punishment in a clinch. He munched like a combine harvester, resolutely disposing of food. Was she now so sick of him that she would let him do as he liked? Or would it be some horrific activity once again?

'I thought we would visit Regent's Park Zoo today.'

He gulped. 'Today? But it's so cold, you won't enjoy it. Why don't we go tomorrow? I wanted to go to the Science Museum again, on the tube, and —'

'You know my views about young people alone in London,' announced Mrs Giles. 'It's kind of you to be concerned, Simon, but we will both wrap up warm and enjoy a good day at the zoo. What's your favourite animal? Shall we go and see the lions and frighten ourselves?'

A sickly smile slid off Simon's face. The woman thought he was a mentally retarded five year old!

When she suggested a picnic, Simon was beyond subtlety. 'In this weather? Let's have a McDonald's instead.'

'That's not good for you, Simon.'

'No E numbers but a lot of fat,' he retorted. 'We can make up for it by eating dry toast tomorrow. Anyway, your picnics aren't healthy either. You put in tons of chocolate biscuits. No wonder Henry had a weight problem.'

To his amazement, his idle swipe caused a knockout. Mrs Giles crumbled! Quite suddenly she pulled out an inadequate lace handkerchief and began dabbing at her eyes. 'Oh dear – Simon, I do apologise – it's just that I am so worried about Henrietta. And I do miss her so.'

Her tears defeated him. He felt desperately uncomfortable. 'I thought she was having a great time. In the Caribbean, isn't she?'

'Yes. It does sound fun. But she tells me – she's written to say she believes she's pregnant. I wouldn't normally discuss something like that with a boy of your age, of course, but with your sister in the same condition it can hardly surprise you. Can you imagine – my Henrietta, unwell, with no one to take care of her?'

'Doesn't her husband do that?'

Mrs Giles withered him with a look. 'That man? He can't take care of himself. She'll be on one of her silly diets again. She'll probably miscarry. And some ignorant native will let her bleed to death!'

A few more tears dripped into the handkerchief. Simon said, 'Actually I like the tigers best.'

Mrs Giles struggled to pull herself together. 'Do you? Then perhaps we'll see those first. Go and wash your hands upstairs, Simon – wash your hands,' she repeated, with a meaningful look. 'And be sure to put on a warm scarf. And you can change those awful trainers for your school shoes, I will not be seen out with a tramp. The worst moments of my life were when Henrietta was associating with tramps. I was in the constant expectation of being infested with lice.'

Upstairs, Simon had a morose pee and changed his shoes. 'Resistance is useless,' he muttered to himself. 'To resist is to die.' He speculated on the possibility of feeding Mrs Giles to the tigers, but thought that the tigers would come off

worst. But she wasn't so bad. Did he but know it he was
echoing his sister's view of Mrs Giles. There was a certain
relaxing security in having not one jot of independence.

The zoo was not as bad as he expected. Mrs Giles's
breakdown had rattled her, and she felt she must make up
to Simon for the trauma of seeing such a thing. They went
into the zoo shop and she bought him two relatively OK T-
shirts and some books, worthy tomes that would give him
an edge in biology projects for years to come. What's more
the tigers were in playful mood, and no sooner did Mrs Giles
approach the bars than they went into energetic copulation.

'What are they doing?' asked Simon, with shrill
innocence.

But she wasn't having that. 'Don't be ridiculous, child.'
She took him by the arm and frog-marched him to see the
sealions being fed.

'We'll take a boat trip on the river tomorrow,' she
announced. 'Very bracing. And nowadays you get a
commentary on historical sites of interest along the way.
Won't that be fun?'

By the evening Simon had had enough. He lay in his room,
sent to bed at eight-thirty after broiled chicken and rice
pudding, and plotted. He didn't want to run away. There
was nowhere to run except the cottage, cold and friendless
without Matty and Sholto. He wanted revenge.

The Giles household did not retire until almost midnight,
but Simon forced himself to stay awake. Finally, when all
was quiet and the clock showed a quarter to one, he crept
from bed. His first task was to switch off the newly-fitted
burglar alarm, the work of only a moment. It took slightly
longer to cut the wires, giving all the appearance of an
informed burglary. Next he took a rolling pin from the
kitchen and a large towel from the laundry and broke a pane
in the French doors leading to the garden. The glass fell with
muffled chinks on to the towel. He cleared that away tidily
into the dustbin, and replaced the towel, deducing that the
police would think it a very professional job. As a last act
he opened all the doors and cupboards downstairs, revealing
china, silver, wines and spirits, not to mention piles of linen

and books. He took nothing out. Yes, the police would think this a remarkably clean job.

He rose late, despite the confusion. A pleasant day was in store, with Mrs Giles far too busy to worry about him for once. No boat trip, no historical sites of interest, no nagging. Policemen were everywhere, asking questions and taking fingerprints, although obviously Simon had used gloves. What sort of idiot did they think he was? The neighbours were questioned, and the paperboy, and the staff were subjected to rigorous interrogation. Simon read, listened to his Walkman, ate sweets and enjoyed himself.

He came down once for biscuits and a drink, wandering with insouciance into the kitchen and threading his way unconcernedly between the sobbing daily, Mrs Giles and two policemen. Therein lay his mistake. Mrs Giles's eye fell upon him, and she wasn't born yesterday, oh no.

'I'm very worried that nothing was taken,' the policeman was saying. 'They may have been disturbed. Now they know what's here they may be back.'

'I doubt it,' said Mrs Giles in a chilling voice. 'Officer, you've done all you can. The alarm's being reconnected later this afternoon and in the meantime we must be vigilant. Thank you and good day.'

As the front door closed behind them, Mrs Giles let out a stentorian roar. 'Simon!'

He thought of pretending he hadn't heard. It wasn't any use. He came to the top of the stairs, but even from that perspective Mrs Giles looked formidable. 'Perhaps you would explain,' she asked, 'why you are looking so pleased with yourself? Or should I explain it for you? Or shall we simply content ourselves with giving you six of the best?'

'I – I don't know what you mean,' said Simon miserably.

'Oh yes you do, young man. I shall telephone my husband at his office and ask him to come home at once and beat you. I shall not, on this occasion, tell the police.'

'But –' Simon swallowed. Oh well, there was nothing else for it. 'Thank you very much,' he said.

When the deed was done, and Simon had been ineptly paddled by Mr Giles, he was sent upstairs to bed. 'You'll be sending him away, of course,' said Mr Giles to his wife.

He was having a restorative whisky and soda, because he'd never done more than smack a labrador puppy before and this business was a little too much on an empty stomach.

'I shan't do anything of the kind,' said Mrs Giles. She grinned to herself. 'I like a boy of spirit. I think Simon and I understand each other very well. The best thing for that boy is a change of scene. I shall take him with me to see Henrietta.'

Her husband knew better than to argue. He drank his whisky instead.

Matty felt disoriented. She had returned to find that Simon had been whisked off to the Caribbean and she had no one. She had been schooling herself all the way home for calm and clear explanation, but now there was no need. There was nothing to stand between her and a collapsed marriage, and she was pregnant and alone. The full extent of her desolation became clear to her. She sat in her home and experienced total despair.

Without Sholto her life was empty. Ever since they met he had given her a reference point from which she judged everything and everybody. He was the sun on which she depended, the warmth from which she drew life. Now he was gone from her and she mourned for him, mourning for herself too. It was all so impossible. She had given him everything and it hadn't been enough.

She spent a lot of time in bed, staring at the wall and brooding. She knew she had been at fault. She had driven him away. All that stupid, naive prattle about honesty, when what was honesty except conforming to someone else's rules? Why not break the rules, make your own rules, strike out and be someone different? She went out to the barn, still in her night things, and found her father's spoon. She took it into the house, into the bedroom, and hung it on the bare wall at the point where it constantly met her eyes.

Her father had cheated and his only mistake was in getting caught. If he had prospered she could be like Griselda now, qualified in something sensible. Instead she inhabited this little world of silver, where something was only worth money if it had those tantalising little symbols stamped on it to prove to the ignorant that it was good.

Nobody came to the cottage. Days passed, blurring one into the other. But one evening, as Matty was trying to eat something, anything, Richard Greensall called. 'I hadn't heard, like,' he said. 'I'm worked up.'

'Oh. Yes.' She hadn't sold his last work yet. No doubt she could, if she could summon the energy. 'What do you want to do?'

He spread his big, stained hands. 'Dunno. Sommat good. Big. Get your teeth into. Bloody sick of forks, I am.'

Matty sighed, letting her mind drift. Here was a case in point. A craftsman, one of the best, forced to copy forks for a living. If he had to copy, at least it should be something good. She got up and went to her desk.

'Here,' she said, tossing some photographs at him. 'Make that.'

'This?' He turned the prints with interest. 'Got someone wants this, have you?'

'I may have. Can you do it?'

'Oh, aye. Whose is it? Not Lamerie. Not Storr.'

'Sprimont,' said Matty. 'An unknown piece. Bet you a dozen pints you can't make it as well.'

The nearest thing to a smile she had ever seen on Greensall's face made a fugitive appearance. 'Get 'em lined up in around three months' time,' he said happily. 'Thisen's worth doing. Me own marks, like?'

'Don't mark it at all,' said Matty. 'It might be worth registering a new mark for work like this. To mark it as your best quality.'

'Aye. Good idea. I'll think of sommat with style.'

When he had gone she sat down again to her unappetising meal. The baby was kicking restlessly, as if demanding nourishment, and she forced down cold food. Her conscience, that over-active friend, nudged at her, and she gave a mental snarl, driving it back into the dark. She hadn't done anything wrong. Yet.

Days later she roused herself. She had a baby to think of. She had a business to run. But she seemed to have lost her bearings. She found herself wandering the house in a daze, unsure of the day, the time, the season. She started a hundred things and finished none of them, not even the washing up. One evening, waking from an afternoon sleep to disorientation and panic, she knew she had to have help. She telephoned Griselda.

She came up on the next morning's train. Matty met her at the station and they drove in silence to a pub where they could sit in a corner and toy with the food. 'I don't want to go back,' Matty confessed. 'I feel trapped in that house.'

'That isn't like you, Matty.'

She grimaced. 'No. I used to be such a coward — I couldn't live without my house. Not any more.'

She told the story in halting sentences. The part at the end, with the Baronessa, she left half said. 'I imagine it was very unpleasant,' said Griselda, making it clear that she needed no more. 'The poor man's having a nervous breakdown.'

'All my fault,' said Matty. 'I was too naive. I wanted the house, I wanted the baby, I wasn't good enough in bed. I should have been different.'

'He married you for what you are. Not even you can pretend you didn't know the risks. He's very clever, very attractive and very disturbed, and we all knew that. Even Lorne, who is the least perceptive girl I ever met.'

'She just doesn't see things your way, you mean.'

Griselda shrugged. 'Perhaps. Why she continues with that farce of a marriage I shall never know. She willingly placed herself in the Berensons' hands despite all advice to the contrary. Why?'

'Because her parents needed it.'

Griselda sighed. 'Yes. On top of everything else the blasted girl is admirable. Apologies to the absent Lorne.'

She went to the bar and bought them each another drink, orange juice for Matty and gin for her. The walk seemed to have clarified her thoughts. 'Sholto married you in an attempt to ward this off,' she said decisively. 'He knew this was coming.'

'Knew what was coming?'

Griselda gestured with a large square hand. 'The day of reckoning. The day when he could no longer pretend that his horrible childhood hadn't happened. Quite understandably, he doesn't want to face it. But he can't run away. He tried, and he's still trying, but it won't work. Eventually he has to turn and look those experiences in the face. That's all.'

'So I was just a preventative measure,' said Matty in a small voice. 'Like buying a nightlight because you're afraid of the dark.'

Griselda sighed. 'Possibly. But it's equally possible that he loves you. Rather a pointless emotion in his present state, of course. Don't think about it. The time has come to get yourself sorted out. You're a single mother, and you've got Simon to support. I imagine Sholto will send money from time to time, but he can't be depended upon. The first thing is to get back to your business and sort out how you're going to live.'

Matty gazed at her friend with awe. 'You really are terribly clever, Grizz. I'm sure you weren't this clever at school.'

A wry smile crossed Griselda's plain face. 'I had nothing to be clever about. Besides, other people's lives are easy. One's own is always so much more difficult to come to terms with.'

Under Griselda's direction Matty struggled to be organised. Her friend gasped when she opened the silver barn, astounded by the heaps and heaps of silver. 'Where did it all come from?' she demanded. 'You can't possibly have bought all this.'

'Yes.' Matty felt defensive. 'I sell quite a lot too. But good silver's hard to come by. If you see it you have to buy it — ' Her voice trailed off.

'It seems to me you've cornered the market. There's enough here to open a shop.'

Their eyes met. Griselda cleared her throat. 'I don't suppose — '

'Sholto always said we didn't want shops. He said they tied you down, with overheads and things.'

'You're going to be tied down anyway, with a baby. Why not have a shop? Somewhere in London.'

'It would cost a bomb.'

'Not if you were in partnership. With me.'

They went back to the house. Matty fervently wished she could drink. This was exactly the occasion on which she would love to have opened a bottle of wine. But they sat over mugs of tea and Griselda explained. She had landed her job with the Foreign Office and was to start work in Whitehall. That meant she needed a London flat, and as it happened her father had for years held the lease on a property consisting of a shabby apartment with a newsagent's underneath. The newsagent had gone out of business, and rather than let to another nondescript shop Griselda had thought of running something herself.

'I thought it would be an opportunity to supplement my salary,' she explained. 'And, of course, I might be a tycoon. It's always possible.'

'Yes,' said Matty. 'Would you run the shop then?'

'I'd put in a manager of some sort. You'd supply the stock. And, of course, when you visited you'd be able to stay with me.'

There was something proprietorial about Grizz, thought Matty. She was taking her over. It might well be something she would hate later on. At that moment the urge to hand her burdens to someone else was overpowering. The silver would go into the shop, and be sold.

'You'll need security,' said Matty. 'Proper alarms and things. And it is time I stopped supplying things for other people to sell. I should make twice the money that I do now.'

'Fifty-fifty on the profits, then,' said Griselda. 'After expenses.'

Matty blinked. She was buying the stock, transporting it, assessing it; Griselda was simply providing the shop. But she remembered how kind Griselda had always been, and how good to Simon. She sighed. 'Fine,' she said.

It did not take long to discover that Griselda's artistic sense occupied a space in her soul the size of a pea. Whenever Matty turned her back she discovered that Grizz had ordered inch-thick bars for the shop front, or yellow paint for the door, or a carpet in merry shades of red and green. Every order was resolutely cancelled. 'We're trying for elegance and charm,' she explained.

451

'What's inelegant about yellow?'

'In this setting, everything. And we shall put in toughened glass and fit a grille we can pull down when the shop's closed. Bars would make it look like the town gaol.'

'I thought security was a priority,' said Griselda huffily.

'It is! But nobody has bars and bells and things everywhere.'

Fighting tiredness, she worked through paint cards and carpet samples, finally deciding on black and gold for the exterior paintwork and a carpet of deep royal blue. Some of the inside counters would be lined with red, Sholto's choice for silver, and there would be pictures on the walls. She went into Sholto's barn and chose three small oils at random.

They were ready to open within six weeks. Matty was heavily pregnant, and her stomach seemed to have ballooned obscenely. At night, in the cottage or in Griselda's spartan flat, she lay in bed and stared at it. Boy or girl? His or hers? Sholto's child or her own?

She thought of him so often. The thought was like a constant thread, running through her days. He hadn't written or called, and whenever the telephone rang she half expected an official, telling her he was dead. Some days she felt such gloom that she was sure it came from Sholto. She loved him so. Inevitably if he suffered she must know it.

'I think you should have this baby in London,' announced Griselda one day. 'The cottage isn't at all suitable. You're there on your own.'

'It's all arranged,' said Matty. 'I just have to call the ambulance.'

'If you're here, I can call the ambulance,' said Grizz. 'Be reasonable, Matty! I can bring you things in hospital and everything.'

Matty felt reluctant. Griselda was taking so much of a hold. It was as if she had decided she would never have children and was staking a claim to Matty's, establishing surrogate parental rights. She said, 'All right. If you want. It isn't due for ages, though.'

'I thought it was next week.'

'Well, it isn't. The week after.' A lie, but it gave her space.

She went back to the cottage and sat in her four-poster bed. Sometimes she got up and walked around the garden, finding cuckoo-spit on the apple tree and willing the baby to come. A hedgehog, up early, blundered about in the warm afternoons and she bought a can of dog food and put dishes out to encourage it. Her love affair with her home wasn't quite at an end. The house was kind to her, she thought. It lent her strength.

One evening the pains started. She was sitting in bed, one of Sholto's sweaters around her shoulders, trying to decide which piece of silver should go where. It was tempting to keep the best pieces for Britain and offer the rest to buyers abroad, but they didn't want the second-rate. A piece bought by post had to be first quality or it would inevitably be returned.

Backache, insistent and unpleasant. She moved the pillows and still it remained. Then a new pain, spreading like a girdle, and retreating again. Calm certainty came over her. It was here, at last, and she was alone.

She lay back on the bed. No sense in calling the ambulance too soon. How good of this baby to come now, and avoid Griselda's proprietorial care. Another pain. She shifted uncomfortably, and suddenly, in a rush of anguish, she wanted Sholto. Why wasn't he here? Why hadn't he come? She needed him now as never before. If he couldn't be here then she wanted to be alone, she wanted to curl up in her bed and suffer.

An hour later the pains changed gear. Matty began grunting to herself, waiting with apprehension for each one to come. When did they say you should call someone? The bedside clock, an old wind-up model, was run down and stopped, so she wound it quickly and stared at it. There were three pains in ten minutes. Oh. She should have telephoned the ambulance earlier.

The number was by the telephone, and she stood in the hall to ring. A woman answered, unhurried and casual. 'Within the hour, OK?'

'Er — yes. I suppose so. Do they know where to come?'

'I'm sure they'll find it, dear.'

She went back to bed. Oh, but this was uncomfortable.

453

Suppose the waters burst here? She'd make a terrible mess. She went to the bathroom and got some towels, sitting on them carefully. Everything was beginning to feel very damp, but it was all so confused – she hobbled downstairs and telephoned again.

'I think the ambulance had better hurry up,' she said in a rush. Another pain came and she hung on the table, panting.

'What? I thought you were in first stage!'

'I don't know what I'm in. Oh God!'

'I'll get them to put the light on. Hang on.'

She was dripping on the carpet. She went into the kitchen, where the floor would wash, and leaned over the worktop, panting and sweating. This was unbelievable. This was a nightmare. Why wouldn't anyone come?

The ambulance klaxon shattered the night. Matty couldn't move, she couldn't speak, she hung over the worktop and fought every pain. When they hammered on the back door she moved with agonising slowness to open it.

'On your own, dear? Left it a bit late, didn't you. We'll never get her in, Trev, she'll have to have it here.'

'It's coming,' she grunted.

'We can see that, love.'

Her head felt as if it would explode. She tried to slide to the floor, but one of the men held her from behind, while the other one lifted up her nightdress. Were they supposed to do this sort of thing, she wondered? It seemed highly indecent. She braced her feet against the cold floor, gripping the shoulders of the man that knelt in front of her.

'Don't drop it, Trev!'

'It's not here yet – yes it is – once more, love – well done!'

The huge, painful burden was expelled from her. The man who held her drew her back until she was lying on the floor. He was fussing, worried that she'd catch cold, he wanted to cover her. She wasn't cold. Perhaps she would be in a while, when the shock went away. Because there it was, all slimy and upset. A tiny little girl.

They took her to hospital anyway. Matty made no objection.

She was utterly obsessed with her baby, looking at her now out of misty dark blue eyes. She had expected a baby, yes, but not like this; in an instant shackles of love and responsibility had been forged and fastened and she knew she would never get them off.

The child's face was Sholto's, she decided, with his clear features and wide eyes. But the hair was her own: dark, glossy chestnut, an unlikely thatch on that tiny new head. Nails like fragments of mother of pearl, and loose, buttery skin. She and Sholto had never talked about names, but now one popped into her head. Sasha. It hinted at the exotic. And this child seemed to Matty as miraculous a discovery as any rare orchid in a mountain pass.

Griselda materialised at her bedside the following day. Matty was very glad to see her. On all sides girls were being visited by husbands and lovers, mothers and friends, while she had no one.

'Have you told Sholto?' asked Griselda at once.

Matty shook her head. 'I don't know where he is. Or at least, I won't talk to that woman. And I won't write. She'd read the letter.'

'I shall write,' said Griselda.

She began to unload all manner of goodies, from clean nighties to perfume to boxes of sweets.

'You've gone a bit mad, haven't you, Grizz?'

'Have I?' Griselda blushed. 'Single women shouldn't associate with babies. It makes us quite foolish.'

'You can hold her if you like.'

Griselda gingerly took the infant into her arms. 'She's amazingly pretty,' she murmured. 'You're very lucky to have her, Matty. I hope you appreciate your good fortune.'

'She makes me very humble. She trusts me. And I must get out of here and get working or I shall never be able to look after her as I should.'

'Her Aunt Griselda will take care of her. Her Aunt Griselda will make sure she has lots to eat. Her Aunt Griselda will love her to death, won't she?' Griselda cooed at the little girl. Jealous fire ignited in Matty's chest. How dare Griselda assume that she had some claim over this child, that Matty's baby was in some way mutual?

'I'll have her back now,' she said carefully. 'She needs a feed.'

'But she looks so happy!'

None the less Matty held out her arms. Only when the baby was safely against her breast did she feel she could be calm. She was being unreasonable and she knew it, but for the first time in her life, albeit only for a second, she had hated her friend.

Looking back, it seemed to Matty that the moment Sasha entered her life, any semblance of order walked out of it. In the hospital she had entertained many a plan, but once free of that environment she sank in a welter of nappies and stained clothes. In theory it should have been possible to work and take care of a baby, but her nights were no more than snatched minutes of sleep and her days passed in a fog. The first thing to go was her overseas catalogue. It was so much easier to pile stuff in the car and take it down to the shop. Then she always seemed to be writing cheques, paying Greensall, house bills, auction settlements . . . so much more going out than seemed to be coming in.

The shop was prospering, fortunately, much to Griselda's delight. Her fifty per cent of the profits was a pleasant addition to her Foreign Office salary, but Matty found her own half little enough to live on. She felt as if she lived in the car, driving from this sale to that, Sasha asleep in her carrycot or wailing and miserable. Matty thought of hiring a nanny, but she hadn't the cash. Simon, now back at school, cost more than ever, and the bills kept coming, day after day.

The morning came when she received a letter from Sholto's aunt.

Dear Mrs Feversham,

I am sorry to draw this matter to your attention, but the financial arrangements I made with my nephew some time ago seem to have fallen into disarray. I am currently owed some twenty thousand pounds and I have heard nothing. Would you be so good as to ascertain whether my nephew means to pay and

456

continue our association, or if we must call it a day and sell up? I imagine the property you now occupy would go some way to clearing the debt. Obviously I have no wish to cause hardship, but I am of the opinion that this situation cannot be allowed to drift on unchallenged. Please let me know what you intend to do.

Sasha was muttering to herself in her cradle, prior to going to sleep. Matty automatically reached out and rocked her. Their home was going to go. She and Sasha would have no choice but to live with Griselda in her unpleasant little flat above a shop that drained Matty's funds and energies like a leech. Panic made her tremble. She found she was fighting tears. This was all so terribly difficult.

If only Sholto was here. If only there was someone else to share the burdens. She forced herself to wait until the baby was asleep, then she went out into the barns. Sholto had left about two dozen pictures in all, some black with dirt, some in need of restoration, one or two that looked saleable. They would go to an auction at once. As for her own barn, she ran a weary eye over a selection of poor purchases. Teapots, excellent of their type, but unfashionable. They stuck whatever she did with them, particularly some nautical examples, very plain and masculine. People didn't want understatement just now; flamboyant display was in order. The clock was another piece. She had bought it to oblige, but no one felt the need to oblige her. She had tried it in the shop and it had lowered the tone. She had put it in a sale and had it returned through lack of interest. What's more, she had the terrible feeling that silver was about to slump.

It happened from time to time. Fashions came and went, and with them the fortunes of those who lived by them. Many dealers would continue to prosper, but they would be older or better established. It was the newcomers who foundered, those without the solid broad base of customers built up over the years. She hadn't been in the business long enough to withstand any cold wind, and this one was icy.

She trudged back to the house, feeling exhausted. Money,

why did it always come down to money? She should have married it, like Henry, getting into bed between satin sheets instead of trusting herself to the dubious charms of Sholto. He was no damn good. He was utterly irresponsible. He always let everyone down.

He was sitting on the sofa, cradling the baby. For a long moment Matty stared at him, in case he was imagined. But he seemed real enough. Very thin, very pale, with deep lines scored from nose to mouth. One long hand was inexpertly patting the baby. 'She was crying,' he explained. 'Wind, or something. She burped milk all over me.'

'Oh. Yes. She does that.'

'Looks like you, I thought.'

'Did you? I thought she looked like you.'

Matty took the baby and put her back in her cot. Sasha began to wail, but after a moment or two she snuggled down and went to sleep. Her parents looked at one another.

'How are you?' asked Matty.

He shrugged. 'OK. Better. I can't get over how beautiful you look.'

'I look like hell. No sleep, you see.'

'There are beautiful shadows underneath your eyes.'

She went to the table and picked up his aunt's letter. He glanced at it. 'Yes. That's why I came.'

'How good of you. How kind to be so concerned. After all, a baby was nothing to come home for.'

'I was fit for nothing then.'

'And neither was I!'

She glared at him bitterly from across the room. A muscle in his face was working, and she thought, stupidly, that she would give anything for him to love her again. 'Would you like a cup of tea?' she asked.

'Yes, all right.'

They were together in the little kitchen. He seemed so close. He was wearing jeans and a big cowboy belt cinching a shirt in heavy Italian cotton. 'You smell of milk,' he said suddenly, and she blushed.

'I'll shower. I know I'm disgusting, all baby and nothing else. I'm a mess.'

He reached out and held her breast. She said 'No' feebly,

and he dropped his hand. The desire to have him touch her again was unbearable, a physical pain. At that moment she despised herself. He could do anything, anything, and she would still want him.

He said, 'I wanted to explain about the money. There might be a few problems.'

Her mind sluggish, Matty said, 'I'm going to be evicted.'

'No, no you're not! That's what I wanted to explain. I'm paying my aunt. I've got twenty thousand, there's no problem about that. It's just — there are difficulties.'

Matty grinned. 'You do surprise me. Can't you find someone to swindle? Some gullible woman?'

It was an unnecessary insult, born of pain. Sholto let out his breath angrily. 'You never grow up, do you? Let's all play by the rules and they've got to be your rules, and yours alone. OK, I'm not blameless. Who is in this world, always excepting your priggish self?'

'So why can't you pay the money?'

'Because Luca has an expert saying the Pissarro is forged. I'm being accused of deceiving him. It's a set up. The picture he's showing isn't the one I saw. My Italian assets have been frozen.'

Matty gulped. 'You idiot! I told you so!'

Sholto walked out. He slammed through the front door and down the path. Matty ran after him, calling, 'Sholto! Please, Sholto!'

He stopped at the gate. 'What?'

'Don't go. I didn't mean to be silly.'

'I can't stand you in your moralist pose.'

She took a long breath. 'If you must know, neither can I.'

He laughed and his entire face lit up. He had lost so much weight, she realised, his clothes hung on him like rags. She put her hands behind her back, because she must not reach out to him. He didn't want her, and she must learn not to want him.

They went into the house and drank tea. She told him about Griselda. 'She seems to think she's doing me such an enormous favour, and I don't seem to be able to object. If the rates and wages and so on came out of her fifty per cent, that would be fair, but she takes them off first and then splits the profit. And I invest the capital and do all the work!'

He looked nonplussed. 'I don't see the problem. Discuss it.'

'I can't. You don't understand, but I can't.' She looked at him helplessly. Griselda was the sort of friend you should never lose. She was loyal and steadfast and kind. She was worth far more than the entire shop enterprise in itself.

Sholto idly crunched on a biscuit. His spirits were rising, crawling back inch by inch from the ultimate low. Matty was so sane, such a far cry from the stunted and juvenile people he seemed to meet, who thought only of their own twisted natures. The very rich lost their humanity, he thought. Or perhaps it was simply that only the inhuman could ever be that rich. When the day came that you thought more of your possessions than your soul, then you were in trouble.

The baby woke and Matty changed her and fed her. Sholto was interested, but remained uninvolved. 'I shall come and see her again,' he said. 'If I stay out of gaol.'

'Surely you can just stay out of Italy.'

'They'd extradite me from almost everywhere. One thing they hate is a crooked art expert. Gives the treasures a bad name.'

A silence developed, an irritating, tense pause. Her breath became tight. He was going to say something, something she didn't want to hear. She looked up at him, frightened, tearful.

'I want to get divorced,' he said.

She blinked at him. 'Why?'

'Because — because it's best. I got married for the wrong reasons, because I wanted to be settled, to give up — my sort of life.'

'We're separated. That's the same.'

'There could be a call on our assets. Your things as well as mine. I want you clear of any involvement.'

He had her both ways. He didn't want her, but this way it seemed as if it was for her own good. Matty said, 'We're in business together. Divorce doesn't change that.'

'I'm making it over to you. A couple of the pictures in

the barn should pay my aunt off for a while. A pair of country scenes, in heavy frames.'

'I put them up in the silver shop.'

'Did you? They're worth about seventy thousand pounds.'

The baby had finished feeding. She gave her to Sholto and went upstairs, locking herself in the bathroom. The other women meant more to him than her. Matty Winterton had been tried and found wanting; she could not work the miracle and make him happy. Now he was trying elsewhere.

After a while he came and hammered on the door. Matty remained silent. Finally he broke the lock and stood looking down at her as she lay in the bath, her hair in wet streaks down her face.

'I don't know why you're so upset. There isn't anyone else.'

'Perhaps you should look for someone. You could find a younger version of Victoria, and spend your nights beating her up. I know you found me dull in bed.'

He squatted down beside her. 'I never said that.'

'You must have thought it. You kept learning new things, and I just stayed the same.'

'I never wanted you like her. I wanted what we had.'

She looked straight at him, her eyes accusing. 'So then you could go and have it all quite different with her!'

He looked at her and she was ashamed of her body. Once she had been lovely, but now she was stretched and sagging, her breasts bloated, her hair and her nails ragged and uncared for. She curled up in the water, hiding herself from him, and he reached out and stroked her hair.

'It's just a technicality.'

'Don't lie. You want to be free.'

The words of comfort rose automatically to his lips. Tell her you care, tell her you love her, tell her you mean to come back. He didn't know if any of that was true, and pretending was so endlessly wearisome. 'I've got to sort myself out,' he blurted. 'I can't do it for anyone. I can't do it with anyone.'

'The baby needs you now. She won't wait.'

'You find someone else, then. Oh, Matty, don't think I'm not sorry. I never expected it to turn out like this. You were

461

so alive, so hopeful, so innocent — I wanted to borrow some of that. I thought if I looked through your eyes, I wouldn't see my own nightmares. I'd share in your dreams.'

'You could try for some dreams of your own,' said Matty, and her voice quavered.

'That's what I'm doing.'

She got up from the bath in a flurry of splashing. Sholto stood and watched her dry herself. She thought she was ugly, but it wasn't true. The baby had left faint striations across her hips, and she had lost her boyishness. Standing in the bath, she resembled nothing so much as a goddess from a Renaissance canvas. The flowing curves of breast and hip and thigh delighted him, and it seemed as if all at once she touched some inner core of sensation he didn't understand. He turned away and went out, and Matty thought, He despises me.

Downstairs he was looking at the baby again. 'Shall I send money when I can or every month? What's better for you?'

'I don't want anything.'

'But you need it.'

'And you're making empty promises. If you've got a court case to fight you can't afford to pay me. Just ward off your aunt. Simon couldn't bear it if we didn't have anywhere to live.'

'Does Simon think I'm a complete shit?'

She shrugged. 'I doubt it. I haven't told him.'

He took the towel from her hands and began to rub her hair. It was bitter-sweet, as intimate as love. When it was done she threw her long, shaggy mop of hair back from her face and gathered her wits. 'I'd like you to go now.'

'Yes. I know.' He felt so tired. He would have given anything to go upstairs and sleep next to this lovely, fecund woman who would never wake him by biting his lips.

In the car he thought of Victoria. She had screamed when he left her. She had dragged rings from her fingers, clawed the jewels from her ears; she would give him anything, anything, if he would stay. She had gone gibbering to Alfredo and told him to bring the pictures, any of the pictures he wanted. It was repulsive and he wanted nothing. She hadn't loved him when he was innocent. He had been just a boy, one of the many, able to offer no more than passing satisfaction. But as he moved through knowledge, into sophistication and beyond, she changed. There was nothing he could do which would revolt her. There was nothing she would not do to keep him. It was as if when he cared for nothing, when all that had finally died, she could adore him. No wonder her sons feared her, no wonder her husband lived out his days by the sea.

He had hours to waste before his flight. When Matty was at an airport she wandered around exploring, like a little girl. Perhaps she wouldn't do that any more, now she was so evidently grown up. He thought of her as always full of this or that idea, some of them bullheaded, some of them good. Matty never listened to someone else's reason, but when things went wrong she felt aggrieved because no one had warned her. You never used to be able to tell Matty anything. That might have changed too.

His spirits, swinging like a pendulum, suddenly plunged. In years to come she would remember him as a youthful folly, one of those things that happen to girls who should know better. In a while she'd forget who fathered her child. There would be others, by other men. She would say to Sasha, 'Darling, he was my first lover, and you know how it is. One of those silly little marriages. I haven't thought of him in years, and neither must you.' He would be consigned to the rubbish heap, and forgotten.

Chapter Twenty-Seven

Lorne was tending her garden. It was, she admitted, an uphill task, since old man Berenson had only to notice she had planted a new shrub to organise a break-out of cattle through the electric fence, but she persisted. Miller needed flowers he could smell, sweet grass on which to play. One of these days she would persuade Greg to put up posts and rails, which would thwart the cows and Sherwood forever.

Sometimes she wondered if she was becoming paranoid. Not everything that went wrong in her life could be laid at Sherwood's door. When the car died on the way to one of her committees, one that he didn't like her to be on, she couldn't honestly blame him. When the nursery accepted Miller, but then decided a blind child couldn't go, it seemed unreasonable to accuse Sherwood. But accuse him she did. Some days she felt as if he was hovering invisibly over her head, watching her every move.

The sun was hot this early. She went inside to fetch a hat for herself and her little boy. He gurgled at her, a long burble of sound that meant nothing to anyone but her. 'You want some juice? Sure. Then we'll go and see the horses. You like the horses, Miller.'

He clapped his hands joyfully. A real Shuster, she thought, good-looking and mad about horses, even if he couldn't see what they were. If only her own father was a little less mad about them, they might have the money to live. She didn't like to ask her mother how deep they were in hock these days. It had to be deep. Two brood mares had gone to the sales last week.

Sherwood had developed a nasty little habit of staring at her recently. He didn't look away when she looked up, just kept on looking, as if he knew something she didn't. Something unpleasant. But why let him ruin a lovely day, even when he wasn't there? She poured the juice for Miller and watched with loving eyes while the little boy guzzled it down. He was thirsty, it wasn't greed. That was a Berenson trait. There wasn't a lot good that could be said about Berensons.

She gathered up their hats and they meandered down to the river, stopping at the paddock to feed apples to her saddlehorse and the hunter Greg never rode. The warm wind hummed in the grass, and the sky seemed to deepen in colour as the sun rose, as if a painter was washing it with blue. A rabbit scuttered away from them, which was unusual, here. Rabbits were shot on Berenson land. Nothing lived here that couldn't pay its way. It had probably come over from the Shuster property, which was a seething mass of happy wildlife, sharing what was going and paying not one bean.

Lorne let her mind drift. When Miller was five − or six, or eight, whenever he could see − then she might leave. There was no way she was staying here forever. She and Greg got along OK, so long as she did as she was told, but she couldn't imagine this going on and on, into grim old age. She hadn't done anything with her life! Matty was a businesswoman, Henry flitted between three homes, Griselda was sure to be brilliant at the Foreign Office, and Lorne was exactly where she had always been. Where she always would be, if she didn't do something, try something, go somewhere! If it wasn't for the money she would, she thought. If it wasn't for Miller.

Looking at his red-gold head as he played with blind caution with the pebbles at the water's edge, her eyes filled. How could she wish him unmade, want him undone? Without him her life would be worth nothing. If all she did in all her days was to give him sight, then it would be enough. She should not want for more. A cloud of rooks rose from a distant stand of trees. Shuster trees, where the rooks were never shot, where the bills were never paid. She let out a low, anguished moan.

'That doesn't sound too good.'

She spun around, stifling a shriek. A man stood there.

He was tall, almost gangling, and wore a suit with sleeves that were too short. His face bore deep lines, as if he was old, but his hair was black as coal and his eyes bright with youth. 'I didn't mean to frighten you,' he said, and took a step forward. He was very lame, she realised. The lines on his face were marks of pain.

'I was daydreaming.'

'More like a nightmare.'

She sighed. 'You could say that. What are you doing here? This is Berenson land.'

He looked quizzical. 'You going to run me off it at gunpoint?'

'No.' She laughed. 'But most people seem to think we might. We don't get trespassers. Are you from town?'

'Supposed to be there now. But on this beautiful day I played hooky and came for a walk. Haven't grown up much from his age.' He gestured to Miller, splashing in the rivulets at the river's edge. He squatted as only young children can, perfectly balanced. But the tilt of his head gave him away. He was unmistakably blind.

'Do you have children?' asked Lorne, tense, as she always was, when people first discovered about Miller.

'Me? No. Not married. I'd like to be, though.'

'Won't anyone have you?'

He shrugged. 'I'm choosy. All the nice girls went when I was in hospital. By the time I came out there wasn't a good one left.'

'What happened to your leg?'

'Cancer. Cured now. And I'm grateful to have two legs, even if one of them isn't so good.'

He moved with difficulty to the river's edge, and perched himself on a rock. Lorne took a seat on another stone, and they sat and watched Miller in the sunshine. 'I'm a lawyer,' said the man. 'James Belman.'

'Lorne Berenson. Shuster as was.'

'Ah! A Shuster. The wild bunch.'

She laughed again. 'They're wild all right.'

'Is that your nightmare? Or something about your boy?'

Lorne's head flicked towards him. 'You can't ask me that.'

'Of course I can. But you don't have to answer. Not if it upsets you.'

'It doesn't. At least — I do worry about him. Of course I do. And about my parents.'

'Don't Shusters ever grow out of being wild?'

'Some of them don't. And they take out loans and mortgages. And they won't tell their daughter what's going on so she worries herself half to death.'

'If they've managed this long without your help, surely they don't need it now?'

'I have helped them,' said Lorne tightly. 'In the past.'

She was playing with stones, tossing them from hand to hand. James Belman said, 'I was going to walk to those woods. Is it far? I can't do more than a mile.'

'It's less than that. I take Miller there sometimes to pick the flowers.'

'Don't you have flowers here?'

'On Berenson land. We do not. Everything here pays its way.'

He got up and began to walk, and because it seemed natural, Lorne picked up Miller and walked too. Belman told her that he lived in a collapsing clapboard house, and the lady who owned it would not stop visiting and cleaning up. Even his icebox wasn't his own. He could come home of an evening and find he had lost his salad and found a pie. 'And she moves my books,' he complained. 'That I cannot bear. If a book stays open at page thirty-three for six months, that's OK by me. I'll get back to it. But she shuts them up and dusts them. Makes me mad.'

'Are you doing OK? In your work?'

'I do a lot. Poor people mostly. Won't make me famous, but it makes me feel good. I have a need of that. Poor men's lawyers don't do it for love, they do it for adulation.'

Lorne chuckled. She put Miller down and held the rope by which she guided him, and she wished this walk could go on forever and a day. It was wonderful to talk to someone like this. Belman seemed so calm and intelligent. She felt as if she could stretch her mind for the first time in years.

'Do you have many friends?' she asked. 'I have only three.

From school. But if I needed any of them I'd just call and they'd come. Even Griselda.'

'That's a name for a witch.'

'Sometimes she seems like one. But she's not. She writes me letters full of sense and I depend on her.'

'Does she depend on you?'

Lorne considered. 'Yes. If she lets herself. But she thinks I'm a coward. She thinks I've taken the easy life. I should be in a city now, working myself to death, and I should marry someone working just as hard, and we'd see each other so rarely we'd never know we didn't get on.'

'But instead you married a Berenson.'

'Yes. Greg. It was a mistake.'

She never said that to anyone. The shock of it stopped her in her tracks. She turned and called to Miller, only a few feet behind, and her voice was full of fear. 'Miller! Miller, don't go away!'

'He's right here by you.' Belman held to her arm.

'I thought he was lost.'

'No. You're both fine.'

They went on to the wood. Here, in the shade, the grass was lush and damp. Bluebells lay in a thick carpet, as blue as the sky. Belman said, 'This is a romantic place. I'm glad we came here.'

Lorne nodded. They stood, inches apart, and she thought she could hear his heart and her heart, beating together. If she stayed quite still nothing would happen. This man would go, the day would end, and nothing would be different. All would be as before. She held out her arms. Belman, dragging his game leg, embraced her.

They met twice a week after that, in the clapboard house, locking the doors against the lady down the street. Lorne parked her car at the library in the afternoon, got her books and walked quickly away. The garden of the house was so overgrown that once through the gate she was free from prying eyes, and she would run to the door and fall through it, laughing. They made love in the hall some days. On others they lay in the bed, under the sagging bedroom ceiling, and led each other to paradise.

Lorne lived for those days. She closed her mind to the

469

wry comments of the maid, as she suddenly found it in her to leave Miller when she so seldom had before. She ignored the librarian's remark that she was reading a great deal these days, they didn't have many could read that fast, no ma'am. She turned a smooth cheek to the sideways looks at her exercise class, at her committees, the murmur of voices ceasing as she entered the room. Greg said nothing. He was rarely home, and they talked only of Miller, or the house, or the news. But she couldn't ignore Sherwood Berenson, in her kitchen on Wednesday afternoon.

'Well hi, Lorne. You're looking pretty today.'

'Thank you.' She had learned, over the years, to maintain stiff formality.

'Must be something mighty good to make a girl blossom this way.'

'The weather perhaps. I like the sun.'

'Don't want to have too much sun. Gives you wrinkles. Cancer. Best find something to do in the house on sunny days.'

Her flesh was beginning to crawl with apprehension. Why was he bothering with her? What was she to do? 'Why have you come here, Sherwood?' she asked bravely. 'Has somebody been telling you I've been sunbathing too much?'

He picked his teeth with a piece of grass. Even now, when he was rich and influential, with no need to think about the farm, he retained his farmer habits. It gave him credit with the people. 'You don't look too tanned to me.'

She permitted herself irony. 'That does put my mind at rest.'

'Did Greg say you were too tanned?'

'Greg has hardly been home except to sleep these past ten days. He can't see in the dark.'

'You make it good enough for a man and he'll come home.'

She spun around quite suddenly. 'I don't give a damn whether he comes home or not, Sherwood. I used to care but I don't now. And that's the truth.'

He levered himself off the table on which he had been resting. He was a heavy man, but it suited him. Some women even thought him attractive. 'A woman like you ought to care for a man.'

'I care for my son. Surely that's enough.'

'You ought to give a man some comfort. Woman like you.' He was standing very close to her now. She tried to move away but he caught her wrist. She saw their hands very clearly, hers small and clean, against the muscled strength of his, that she knew could crack nuts by the dozen.

'I'm giving you no comfort at all, Sherwood,' she said in a level voice. 'So let me go.'

He still held on to her. 'You've been doing too much comforting. You and this lawyer. Belman, his name is. A cripple. It's a desperate woman lies down for a man like that.'

She felt her face drain of colour. 'I have no lover. Least of all him.'

Sherwood let her go then. 'Good to hear that, Lorne,' he said cheerfully. 'I don't like to think of my son's wife catting around. If Greg gets to hear of it, chances are Lawyer Belman could find himself with both legs crippled.'

Grim, absolutely serious, Lorne said, 'I'd go to the police. You wouldn't get away with it, not for a minute. I'd ruin you.'

Sherwood, interested, said, 'And I thought you cared about that boy of yours! Counting the days to his operation, no matter how much it might cost. But the lawyer matters most. Well, that does surprise me.'

'I don't understand.'

'Operations cost money, Lorne. This one's going to cost more than you and that lawyer could ever hope to raise. My money. Berenson money.'

'You wouldn't deny your grandson sight just to get at me! Would you? Could you?'

He chewed his piece of grass. 'That kid's worth nothing,' he said. 'Time you had some more.'

Lorne wanted to kill him. If a gun was to hand she would shoot him then and there, she knew she would. 'Get out of my house,' she said softly.

Sherwood sighed. 'Well, Lorne, you're upset. And you and me haven't been seeing eye to eye lately. Best thing if

471

you take the boy and go to Boston for a week or so, have his eyes looked at again. Only the best when it comes to health, that's the Berenson way. Take some time, buy yourself some things, you've been getting stale around here. And it's time you and Greg went on vacation together. You've been apart too much.'

He came and stood very close behind her. He patted her shoulder in a fatherly way. She could feel the heat of his body, big, well fleshed, smelling a little of scent and whiskey. He frightened her so much. 'Greg's a good man,' he said. 'He's got standards, won't have his wife cheating on him. We don't want anyone to get hurt.'

'He won't be hurt, will he?' she whispered. 'I mean – if I promise –'

'Word of honour,' murmured Sherwood.

When he had gone Lorne fell, shuddering, into a chair. She didn't know what to believe, what to think. How could she have been so stupid, so blind! The word made her wince. If only she could talk to James. Talk to him she must. She grabbed the telephone and punched out the numbers.

'I'm so sorry, Mr Belman has been suddenly called away.'

Already? But of course. Sherwood had arranged it. Some case somewhere, some unexpected appointment. She felt hysterical and out of control. She had known it had to end, but not like this, not with Berenson making a lovely thing ugly and full of shame. Perhaps Greg really did not know. If she did as she was told and went to Boston, she might come back and find it had all died down. They would be more discreet next time. No one would ever know.

She went upstairs and began packing, trancelike and unaware. The day was hot but she was aching with cold, and when Miller toddled up and touched her she jumped. 'Don't do that, darling.' If Greg knew he might kill Belman and Miller and her. He could be a violent man; sometimes he got into fights in town and Sherwood had to pay to keep it quiet. Sherwood could buy anything.

She sat down and wrote the lawyer a note, writing 'Private' on the envelope in large letters. If it was found so be it, but she could not go away without telling him, warning him. What's more, he might think she didn't care.

Driving to the airport the sun reflected in brilliant white light from the road. She should have got pregnant with James's child and pretended it was Greg's. She should have left that first day and taken Miller, and found the money somehow, anyhow for the operation. She could do that now, if she wanted.

But the years had made her obedient. She got to the plane and endured the fuss over Miller, which held the usual tinge of horror and dismay; she ordered a drink and then another, and took Miller on her lap and rocked him to sleep. It would be cooler in Boston. She could shop and enjoy herself, the hotel always found her a nurse. But why, oh why, hadn't she stood up to Sherwood and faced him down?

In the hotel, two days later, a letter came for her. It contained a cutting from the local paper back home. 'The town is today in a state of shock following the appalling attack on James Belman, a law practitioner. Masked men assaulted him as he walked to his office last Tuesday evening, beating him so badly that it is feared Mr Belman may never walk again. Robbery is assumed to be the motive and police officers are asking for any witnesses to come forward with information, no matter how trivial. Mr Sherwood Berenson has offered a reward of five hundred dollars for information leading to an arrest.' Next to it, in the same envelope, was her letter.

In the midst of her rage and sorrow she had the wild idea that she would go back and tell what happened, go straight to the police and demand some Berenson arrests. But no one would listen. The Berensons owned that town, as they owned her parents, her, everyone. She couldn't win.

A day or two later Greg telephoned, full of 'Hi, honey!' and badly hidden triumph.

'I hate you,' she said suddenly. She heard him laugh, and she wanted to scream, because he knew she was helpless and her hatred meant nothing.

'I told you what would happen if you messed around. He's dead. Heart attack. See you soon, Lorne.'

She stared at the telephone in disbelief. Dead? James? They couldn't have gone that far, they wouldn't dare. Perhaps he died all by himself. She sat quite still and watched

Miller finding his way carefully around the unfamiliar room. They had even threatened this child. Was there anything they would not do? Possibly not. They had the power, they had the money, and she had nothing. Now her lover was dead.

Griselda leafed through the papers with crisp fingers. 'Are you going to agree?'

'He wasn't cruel. He's making it up.'

'He's making it easy. For you.'

Matty rested her head on her hands. She hadn't really believed Sholto would file for divorce. It was the sort of thing people talked about for years before they acted, they didn't mention it in passing and have done. 'I don't want to be a divorced woman,' she muttered.

'You're a grass widow at present. You can't go on like this, Matty. You can't waste your life hoping Sholto's going to change.'

How could life be wasted when you had barely a minute to call your own? Matty looked round the ugly little flat distastefully. Papers piled on the floor, boxes of silver in every corner, Griselda's files falling higgledy-piggledy off the sofa into an opened box of disposable nappies. She had the sudden feeling that everything, including the planets, was falling into chaos. Her hopes had gone, her dreams were blown apart, and soon the earth would spiral off into space and they would all be done with.

'Poor Sasha,' she said mournfully.

'She's got us,' said Griselda. 'Oh, don't mope, Matty. There's no need. We can have a lovely time.'

She smiled hopefully, but Matty didn't smile back. Griselda had moved into her life on what she seemed to think was a permanent basis, making plans for every weekend and becoming seriously cross if Matty insisted on staying at the cottage. 'I think after a week at work I deserve to have some family life,' she had flared, only yesterday. So Matty was here, amidst Griselda's disorder, feeling kidnapped.

She reached again for the letter but Griselda twitched it out of reach. 'I'm taking Sasha to the park this morning,' she declared. 'What are you going to do?'

'Well – er –' Matty fumbled for something to say. 'I was going to take her swimming.'

'You've been reading progressive literature again. At least let the poor child start to walk. No, I shall take her to the park. We'll give you a break and I shall really enjoy it. I might take a picnic.'

'She could catch cold.'

'It's lovely weather. Don't worry, I'll make up a bottle and everything. Don't fuss, Matty.'

Left alone in the flat Matty flung herself into tidying. When all was in order she read through the letter again. Damn Sholto. How could he do such a thing? Restlessness filled her. If she didn't do something to take her mind off this she would explode. Running her fingers through her hair she got up and went down to the shop.

The woman in charge became nervous when Matty was around, and fumbled and dropped things, so Matty didn't often intrude. Today, unhappy and directionless, she sorted stock and re-arranged the displays.

'How are we doing, Wendy?'

'Not very well this week, I'm afraid.'

'No. Nor last week.'

She watched people walking by in the street, glancing in at the window and going on. Sometimes it was hard to believe that anyone in the world wanted silver, as they all marched by with their bags full of clothes and food. Then a couple came in, and a girl on her own, just starting to collect. They sold two apostle spoons and one of Richard Greensall's renovated sets of flatware.

'That was easy,' said Matty in surprise.

'That's because you're here, Mrs Feversham. I've noticed before, people like buying from an expert. You tell them so much.'

Matty was perplexed. 'But I can't be here all the time. Do you think I should be?'

'I really don't know.'

Matty fixed Wendy with a distant stare, making the woman uncomfortable. An idea was forming in her head. If knowledge made people buy then knowledge they must have. She said, 'Do you want to learn about silver, Wendy?'

'Well — I do my best, but it's difficult.'

'I could teach you. And we could advertise. We could take a big piece in the paper and list lots of interesting things, for instance that coffee pot. We could say that it's George III but was damaged and was well restored early this century. An interesting piece at a modest price. We could list all our spoons too. Keen collectors always want to know if you've got this or that. At the end we'd put two or three things over ten thousand pounds, so people would know we weren't a junk shop.'

'And if you could give me notes on things,' said Wendy eagerly, 'the history of something, if you know it. People love to hear who something belonged to.'

'Yes.' Matty wrinkled her nose. 'I can never understand that. I'd rather not know that my teapot was drooled over by a country squire known for lack of charity. But there you are.'

They began working on a prospective advertisement. Oddly enough, the moment they decided to forget the customers the elusive creatures arrived. Matty found herself trying to discourage a man from buying a pierced bowl because she was listing it in her advertisement. 'Oh, have the thing,' she said crossly. 'I suppose I'll find another one somewhere.'

The man was about to haggle, but gave up at once. Wendy was wrapping teaspoons very neatly, glancing across at Matty from time to time. Mrs Feversham was very tense today. One moment laughing, the next as cross as two sticks. She only seemed calm when she was talking silver, bending over an object with true concentration, her chestnut hair swinging in a glorious bell. She was wearing cropped black trousers and a black overshirt with the cuffs rolled back, which again was odd. She never normally appeared in the shop except in neat suits and dresses. Wendy exercised her mind on Matty's obscure private life. She often wondered about Griselda.

A man in a suit came into the shop. Matty had at last finished the advertisement, and did not want anyone buying anything. She looked up and said, 'Yes? We're about to close.'

476

'It isn't a quarter to five yet. I understood you were open until five.'

'Normally, yes, but today I've had enough.'

'I imagine the owner would have something to say about that.'

'I am the owner.'

They eyed each other belligerently. The man said, 'Perhaps you'd be kind enough to help me with a purchase I wish to make? If you have time.'

Matty sighed. 'How much did you wish to spend?'

'I really don't know. As much as is necessary. I wanted some decent candlesticks for the dining room.'

'Decent?' Matty gestured dismissively at four candelabra, in the shop only until she sold them abroad or to another dealer. 'Twenty-five thousand for those. First quality, good marks, late eighteenth century.'

'That sounds about right.'

Wendy made a little mewing noise and Matty quelled her with a look. She felt ashamed of herself. Why did she imagine that no one wealthy would walk in off the street? If she had paid attention she would have seen that the suit was Savile Row and the shoes handmade, but she wasn't at her best today. Besides, millionaires often turned up in jeans.

She fetched the candelabra and talked the man through the marks. He remained cool. 'How do I know they're genuine?' he asked suddenly.

'I never sell anything else,' retorted Matty. 'If you buy these and take them to another dealer who disputes anything I have said, you can have your money back.'

'You're very confident for someone your age.'

'I started very young.'

At that moment Griselda came into the shop with Sasha in her pram. Matty went to pick up her daughter and Griselda said, 'Honestly, Matty, you don't trust me at all.'

'Of course I do. I've missed her.'

'But we've had a lovely day, haven't we, darling?' Griselda reached over and pinched the baby's cheek. 'She hasn't missed you one bit.'

'You wouldn't tell me if she had, I suppose.' Matty moved the baby out of Griselda's reach.

'If I might trouble you for a moment of your time?' said the customer testily.

'I can't tell you anything more,' said Matty. 'Either you want them or you don't.'

He seemed to take a long and constraining breath. 'Young lady, may I point out that if you wish to make a success of this business it is neither polite nor practical to treat your customers as if they are intruding on your life? Neither should you assume they are paupers, or that they are fabulously wealthy, until you have some indication of which is nearer the truth. You should not bring your offspring into the shop, you should not have barbed conversations with your childminder in the hearing of others, and above all you should dress as if you are serious about what you do.'

Griselda rose to the limit of her considerable height. 'And who are you, may I ask?' she demanded. 'Since you presume to lecture Mrs Feversham on her behaviour I trust you have some authority.'

'The authority of the customer,' he retorted. 'Have my card. I imagine you'll take a cheque, and I expect you to have it specially cleared so I can collect my purchase on Monday.'

Matty took the card and turned it in her fingers. It said 'Martin Sutherland, Bt., Locksley Hall, Hants'. The name meant nothing to her. She said, 'You may take the candlesticks now if you wish.'

'He certainly may not!' declared Griselda.

Matty said, 'Be quiet, Grizz. I run this business, not you. I believe in trusting people who look trustworthy, and I'm hoping this gentleman will overlook our lack of professionalism today and become a regular customer.'

He looked up from writing his cheque. 'I'm glad to see you have some sense.'

'I'm sorry we've behaved so badly,' said Matty. 'I've been a dealer for some time, but I'm new to shops. I don't wish to make excuses, but today has been trying. Please give us another chance.'

'I'm sure I shall. Some time.'

He replaced a gold pen in his pocket and stood waiting while Wendy wrapped the candlesticks. Then he put the parcel under his arm and departed.

'Really, Matty!' Griselda exploded with rage. 'The man's a con artist. You've been completely fooled.'

'I doubt it,' said Matty vaguely. She put her nose against Sasha's and burbled. The baby made little murmurs in return, telling her mother how happy she was to be back. Try as she might, Griselda could not disrupt this relationship. It was too intensely intimate.

'You should have told him to get out,' went on Griselda. 'How dare he lecture you on business ethics?'

'He was right. Wendy knows all about running a shop but I don't — all I know about is silver. So I shall teach her about silver and she'll teach me about shops. Then we might make a success of this thing.'

'It's doing very well.'

Matty eyed her thoughtfully. 'Shall we go upstairs, Grizz?' she suggested. 'We really have to talk.'

Sitting in the flat, knees to the chin on the uncomfortable modern sofa, Matty said, 'I can't live on the money I get from the shop, Grizz. If I sold all my stock I could get a better return by putting the money in a building society. You've got a salary as well, but I haven't.'

'If I sold this place I could invest the money,' said Griselda. 'It's not the same.'

'No, it isn't. You need a flat. But I don't need anywhere to live, I've got somewhere, and Sholto pays for it. So unless the shop does really well I shall go back to doing what I was before, only better.'

'Are you saying you don't like being in business with me?'

'I'm saying I don't like the terms. They're not fair. The man said we were unprofessional and he's right. The whole thing's on a totally unprofessional footing.'

Griselda's bun was coming loose. Wisps of hair were falling down around her long, horse face. All at once she began to cry.

'Oh, Grizz, please don't! We'll keep it the same, only please don't cry!'

'We won't keep it at all if you don't want. Oh, Matty,

I hate to be such a drip. But I've loved these past few weeks. It's been such fun. Someone to talk to at the end of the day, a baby in the house. At home it's so quiet. My father has his routine, and if the boys are home they only go shooting. And college was hell! Nothing but work and those terrible four walls, like a prison sentence. I know it's my own fault, Matty, but I can't seem to make a life for myself. I get so depressed.'

'Don't you like the job, Grizz?'

'That? Yes, I do. Very much a man's world, of course. I find it best to be one of the chaps. The trouble is I'm not a chap, but I'm not all fluff and frills either. I don't know what I am, Matty, and that's the truth.'

Matty gazed unhappily at her friend. She had never seen anyone more uncomfortable with her own undeniable womanhood. Brought up in an all male household, without even a mother to emulate, Griselda had utterly failed to find a way of living to fit her. Friends could impose clothes and hairstyles until the cows came home, but until Griselda came to terms with herself, they were just so much window dressing.

'I only wanted to say that we ought not to have a straight split of the profits,' said Matty mildly. 'I think I should get more.'

'Oh, have the lot,' muttered Griselda. 'Have it, if that's what you want.'

'I thought we'd ask the accountants to decide. Balancing rent against stock and so on. I thought that would be fair.'

Griselda sniffed. 'I suppose so. I take it you want to spend your weekends in the country again.'

'Only some of them. And you can come too. As long as you don't kidnap Sasha for hours on end and not let me near. I hate it when you do that, I get so jealous.'

'If only you knew how jealous I am of you!'

The silence spread out from them, like clear cold air. Beyond, in the street, cars were passing. The distant sound of an ambulance klaxon wailed hysterically. 'I know that I shall never have a child,' said Griselda. 'I don't know why that should upset me so, but it does. I've never thought of myself as maternal.'

480

'People don't. They just are.'

'So it seems.'

'But — didn't you have something going with Bertie? The man at my wedding?'

'Bertie Brantingham. Yes. At least — it was pure friendship. We were the very best of friends, or so it seemed to me. I've wondered since if he's just very good at being friends with people. You know, everyone thinking they're the special friend. Some people are like that.'

'Sometimes I think Sholto's like that.'

'Sholto? Oh no, he's quite different. But Bertie and I were so comfortable together. Walking, chats, even the odd dance at parties, though we weren't in the least good. You don't mind, with Bertie. And then, at your wedding — I don't know how it happened. Too much to drink, probably. We ended up in bed together. So that was that.'

'That was what? Did you get pregnant or something?'

Griselda shook her head furiously. 'No, nothing like that. But it was all such a mistake. Bertie's looking for someone rich, and someone who — who goes in and out like women should, with shiny hair and a pretty smile and all that sort of thing. Someone like you, or Lorne, or Henry. Not someone like me. And of course, after we'd — afterwards, he felt he should make me an offer, and I had to tell him no. So that was the end of our friendship. I realised then that I shouldn't expect a normal family life. That sort of thing isn't for me.'

Matty said, 'Wasn't he awfully upset? He must have thought he'd offended you terribly.'

'I imagine he was relieved not to have to marry me. The Brantinghams are on their beam ends. He has to have money.'

'Perhaps he'd rather have had you.'

Griselda sighed impatiently. 'Don't try and make romance where there is none, Matty. I learned a hard lesson, that's all. There's a side of life that I must learn to do without.'

'You can't have hated it that much!'

'I — I didn't hate it at all. It was unexpected, of course. I just wish I'd done it with someone other than Bertie. He was such a friend.'

Matty heaved herself out of the sofa and went into the kitchen. 'There's some wine in the fridge,' she called. 'Why don't we get a take-away and have a comfortable evening?'

'Stop trying to cheer me up.'

'I can't let you go on feeling miserable! Honestly, Grizz, you have nothing to lose but your own silly opinion of yourself. You can have friends, you can have sex, you can have marriage, you can have anything you want if you only try. You're not that much of a misfit. But you don't try so you never know if you might win.'

Griselda said, 'I am – a very ugly woman.'

'I don't think prettiness is nearly as important as you imagine.'

'Only a pretty woman could say that.'

Matty had the feeling that she had achieved nothing. But in fact the air had been cleared and they had gone some way to putting the business on a proper footing. As the evening wore on and Matty searched the television channels for comedy programmes and told amusing tales about Sholto, and silver, and deals, she wondered why on earth she was the one doing the cheering up. This was the day on which Sholto had asked for divorce. A terrible day. But life went on.

Chapter Twenty-Eight

In the early morning the sun was less harsh on the sand. You could walk to the sea barefoot, without creasing your eyes against the glare, without heat burning your head if you had come out unwisely without a hat. Henrietta loved the early mornings. She liked to watch the fishermen standing waist-deep and casting their nets, and the little boats coming in with their catch. Sometimes she bought fish and took it home for the cook to prepare for lunch. Mostly she gathered shells to show Tyler.

It was amazing how quickly she had become used to her marriage. Money made everything so easy, too easy sometimes. The mechanics of living could be taken care of in the space of a few hours each day, leaving the rest of it free for amusement. Henry had soon discovered that Tyler didn't know how to amuse himself. He jogged, he swam, he fished a little, all with the slight desperation of a man who fears that he will soon be done and will then face hours of unoccupied time. He was surrounded by people who did what had to be done far better than he could, so he didn't work, he didn't think, he didn't draw or paint, he didn't keep dogs or cats or monkeys – he simply gave away money.

Henrietta had stopped that at once. Tyler had been flabbergasted. For a second or two he thought he might have married a miser, who had utterly deceived him. But Henry put him right. 'You don't make undirected gifts. They're just wasted. Now, decide what you really want to do and you can get involved doing it. How about homeless people? You could build a shelter. Lots of shelters. You could decide on the plans and everything.'

'I have architects to do all that.'

'Then get them to draw up a selection of plans and choose which one you like. I bet no one asks the homeless what they'd like. And the people who run existing shelters will have something to say about alcohol and drugs, so you'd better talk to them. If that's what you want to do.'

Tyler brightened visibly. 'That sounds good.'

'Unless you want to help the starving in Africa more.'

'Do I want to do that?'

'I don't know. Do you?'

'Henrietta, you tell me.'

They laughed at each other. He wondered how he had managed to capture someone so beautiful and so sweet. Henry wondered how he had ever frightened her. He was such a gentle soul. In the wrong hands he could have been so miserable.

She looked up the beach towards the house, the terrace of which extended right to the sand. Servants were engaged in sweeping every last grain back on to the beach, a thankless task since each day brought further sandfalls. A figure stood amongst the men, waving authoritatively. Her mother.

Mrs Giles was impatient when she returned. 'I don't like you going so far, Henrietta. The baby could come at any time.'

'It's not ready yet, the doctor says.'

'I won't be happy until we get you to New York.'

'Then will you go home, Mother?'

'Don't be silly. I'm staying because you need me, as well you know.'

She hustled her daughter into the house. Tyler was at the breakfast table, desultorily reading the business news. With his own parents still with their hands firmly on the reins he had little to do except watch profits rise, but he liked to show willing. Besides, it impressed Mrs Giles. She thought he ought to be useful.

'Not finished yet, Tyler?'

'No – no, not yet.'

'He was waiting for me, Mother. We like to breakfast together.'

'Then you should breakfast earlier. We have a plane to catch.'

'Not until twelve. Please, Mother, don't fuss.'

She and Tyler exchanged patient looks. Henrietta's mother seemed to feel that unless she was in constant attendance on this pregnancy her daughter would die. Sometimes she went home for a week or two, but she always returned. Now she was dug in for the duration.

Relief spread around the table when Mrs Giles at last went off to bully the servants. 'We should have kept that boy Simon here,' said Tyler with unusual forcefulness. 'He gave her something to think about.'

Henrietta laughed. 'So he did. I'm sorry, Tyler.'

He filled her glass with orange juice. He loved to look at her as she was now, swollen with his child, her skin touched with sunshine freckles, her hair like sun itself. Emotion rose up in him. 'If the price of having you is putting up with your mother, then I'd pay it twenty times over.'

Henry chuckled. 'Can you imagine? Hell on earth.'

'The only hell is losing you.'

Sometimes he shocked her by his dependence. The responsibility of such love weighed so heavy. The baby would take some of it, she thought, and they would have more children for Tyler to adore. In the midst of busy family life Tyler would learn to spread his love around, releasing her from the terrible obligation of never being angry, or irritated or bored. It upset him so.

When she went upstairs to change, her mother was there. 'I don't know what that man does with his days. A man should have work. It does no good to have nothing to do.'

Henry said, 'Tyler has things he's working on. You're just used to getting rid of Daddy every morning. If it's not work it's golf. You like it that way.'

'Women have their own lives,' declared Mrs Giles. 'They can't live them with a man under their feet.'

'Tyler and I live the same life.'

'I don't like it. It's unhealthy.'

Henrietta felt a sudden wave of rage. Why was her mother always so critical? Why could she never accept any way of life different in any small measure from her own? Again and again Henry found herself opposing her mother when in fact she agreed with what she said. But if her mother ever saw a chink in the armour she would march on to absolute victory. Much as she loved the woman, Henry found herself fantasising about strangling her.

Mrs Giles burbled on, 'This man in New York, he has far too many qualifications . . . *a necktie around the throat should do it* . . . he can't have had any time for deliveries, unless you pay for letters after your name out here . . . *face down on the bed, and tighten the knot* . . . and that dreadful mother of his had better be kept at arm's length, I won't have you bullied!' *She would turn blue, stop breathing — and shut up!*

'Darling, you mustn't be too brave. You can ask for pain relief, you know. They may not let me be in the room, so you must ask for what you need. I know how shy you can be.'

Henrietta's rage dissolved. Oh, why did her mother put her on this rollercoaster? Why wouldn't she go home? 'I'll be fine,' she said feebly, and gave her mother a hug.

Any vestige of tranquillity vanished in New York. The weather was humid, the Cooke relatives were within reach and the doctor was over-cautious. He started talking about operating before Henrietta had made it through the door.

'If you think it's best,' said Tyler anxiously, and Mrs Giles crushed him beneath her wheels.

'Henrietta will have a natural birth. Unless there are problems, of course.'

'And what do you want, Henrietta?' The doctor gave her an encouraging smile, surprised that the girl seemed so calm in the midst of this.

'I'll have whatever's going,' said Henry. 'We'll see how we get on.'

Mrs Giles said, 'You'll do nothing of the sort, my girl! If intervention is required, then intervene we will.'

'There won't be any pain, will there?' Tyler asked.

'Mother —'

'Be quiet! Doctor, is there a proper alarm system in my

daughter's room? These nursing stations seem so poorly attended, and –'

'Mother, will you just bloody shut up!'

Henrietta was at last roused to violence. They all turned and looked at her in surprise. 'Go outside, Mother.'

With a look that spoke volumes, Mrs Giles rose. 'I will speak to you later, Henrietta.'

The consultation passed without further incident. Back in the tall brownstone that Tyler called home in this city, amidst rooms designed by other people, with furniture chosen by other people and books read by no one, Tyler and Henrietta retreated to their bedroom and conversed in whispers.

'You've made her really mad now. I think she's going to fire the cook.'

'If she does she can cook herself. At least it would keep her out of the way.'

'I won't let her bother you when the baby comes, I promise.'

'It's all right, Tyler. I know what she's like.'

Mrs Giles knocked on the bedroom door. 'Henrietta, I've had some camomile tea made. It's so good for your nerves.'

Henrietta, who hated camomile tea, gritted her teeth and opened the door. 'Thank you, Mother,' she said.

As the expected day of the birth approached hysteria rose in the household, in everyone except Henrietta. Tyler's mother took to daily visiting, and she and Mrs Giles staged pitched battles over the teacups in the drawing room. Two days before the expected date Tyler said desperately, 'There can't have been this much fuss over landing at Guadal Canal.'

Henrietta said lugubriously, 'This is Guadal Canal.'

That night, at around two, the pains began. In a conspiracy of silence the couple crept from the house, sneaking down the street and flagging a cab. They made it to the hospital undetected, but the baby went on strike and wouldn't come. At eight Mrs Giles beat the child to it, and arrived hotfoot.

'Let me see my daughter. I insist.'

'Mrs Cooke only wants her husband with her at present, I understand.'

'Nonsense! I promised her I'd be here and so I am. Where is she, please?'

'I really don't —'

'I'm sure you don't.' She swept down the corridor, peering into rooms.

'Doctor did say —'

'What that man said is of no consequence. Ah, there you are, Henrietta. How are you, darling?'

Henrietta, bathed in sweat, felt a sense of doom. She could travel to the ends of the earth, surround herself with rings of fire, and still her mother would find her. There was no defence! None! She moaned.

Tyler said, 'Henrietta wants to be alone, Mother.'

'Women can't be alone in childbirth. Draw that blind do, there's far too much sun in here. She'll be dazzled.'

'We just put the blind up. Henry's got me and the doctor, she doesn't need you.'

She eyed him distastefully. 'I knew you'd be difficult. Weak men so often are. Go and sit down and keep out of everyone's way.'

Tyler almost did as she said. But he looked at Henrietta, cringing on the bed, and the monitor pinging with about-to-be-born eagerness, and he stood his ground. 'We want you out of here, Mrs Giles.'

'Go away, Tyler.'

'Mrs Giles, if you don't go at once I shall pick you up myself and throw you!'

He had never roared at anyone in his life. He had never dared. But in defence of Henrietta he found he could. Mrs Giles raised her eyebrows in amazement, and almost smiled. 'You will find, Tyler, that a polite request is so often more effective than verbal violence. I shall be outside. Call me at once if you need me.'

Henrietta was laughing and puffing on the bed. 'I didn't mean to shout at your mother,' Tyler apologised.

'You can — shout all you like. I'm so proud of you, Tyler.'

'I'll make her go home if you want.'

488

'She's all right out there. She hasn't enough to do, you know. Do you think you could call someone, Tyler? The baby's coming.'

It was a boy, born without problems into a world full of love and money. There is seldom such a fortunate child.

'Henrietta's had her baby.' Matty tossed the letter across the breakfast table to Griselda. 'She'll have written to you at the flat.'

Griselda scanned the pages. 'A boy! Sasha can marry him.'

'He's too young. She's ages older. Besides, she'll be too tall, she's already enormous.'

'She's beautiful. So like Sholto.'

Matty stared at her daughter, sitting in the high chair making a mess of a rusk. Already she had Sholto's elongated fingers and toes. Her nose was an elegant arrow in the centre of an otherwise childish face. Sometimes she reminded Matty so much of him that it hurt to look.

'They're calling him Tyler Junior,' said Griselda.

'Surprised she didn't call him Peter,' said Matty.

'I imagine she's forgotten all about that. It was one of those silly things people get into, I imagine. Not serious.'

'She was deadly serious at the time.'

Matty yawned and rose from the table. Sasha was still waking in the night and she felt a constant desire for more sleep. What's more it was half term and Simon was home, with the resultant collapse in routine. She went to the foot of the stairs and yelled, 'Simon! Get up, you horror.'

He ignored her, as she expected he would. She went out to the barn, to begin sorting through sale catalogues and telephoning dealers who touched base only at weekends. She felt weary this morning, a fundamental tiredness that lodged in her bones. When she was tired she tried never to think about Sholto, because it made her want to cry. Exhaustion made her defenceless, with nothing to ward off despair.

She worked steadily for an hour or so, relishing the relief of uninterrupted thought. Griselda would look after Sasha forever if necessary, and today Matty was too tired to care.

She wrote notes in neat paragraphs, instead of the desperate shorthand which was her daily scrawl, and wondered if she should work all day and all night and try and get organised again.

Simon came in. He was wearing jeans and high-leg trainers, not done up. Teenage spots were starting on his forehead, and he wore his hair down to his nose to hide them. His fingernails were bitten to the quick. Matty wondered if she should mention any of this, and decided she had better not. She said, 'Hi.'

'Hi.' He wandered around, touching things she would rather he left alone. He picked up a hole punch and accidentally emptied it on the floor. Hundreds of circles of white paper lodged in the crevices of a pierced bowl and a copy of a medieval salt.

'Simon!'

'Sorry.'

She put down her pen and folded her hands. 'Did you want something?'

He hunched a shoulder. 'Can't we talk? I don't always want things.'

'No. Of course you don't.' But sometimes it seemed as if everyone wanted things. Griselda wanted Sasha, Sasha wanted time, and Simon wanted clothes, books, money for outings, the cinema, records — she felt like a bird, endlessly foraging to feed voracious nestlings who understood nothing but their own hunger.

'What did you want to talk about?'

'You. Us. Sholto.'

Matty said nothing. She wanted to say this was not the time, that she was too busy, even that he wouldn't understand. Perhaps he wouldn't. It was more than she understood.

'Sholto — isn't coming back.'

'You're getting divorced, aren't you?'

'Did Griselda tell you? Damn!'

'She didn't, actually. It was one of the kids at school. He's Italian, and there's a court case all over the Italian papers. I think it's pretty foul of you to divorce him when he's in trouble.'

'It was his idea, actually.'

'Of course it was! He's jolly decent is Sholto. And it's just like you to want to cut and run just when someone needs people to stand by them. You're such a coward, Matty. A stupid coward.'

He flung out, leaving the door swinging wide. Matty got up and went to shut it, and found that she was shaking. She cared for Simon's good opinion, more than she liked to admit. Yet he always judged her harshly. He expected his sister to be perfect, and she always failed.

After a while she locked the barn and went into the house. Griselda had taken Sasha out somewhere, and Simon was in his room playing heavy metal at full volume. The timbers of the old house shuddered under the impact and Matty went to the cupboard and poured herself a very large gin. There was no ease anywhere in her life any more. There was no one with whom she could utterly relax. That was the thing she missed most about Sholto, she thought, the feeling that here, with this one special person, she need not hide anything.

At one time the girls had filled that role. Griselda and Lorne might not always get on, Matty might occasionally find Henry a little bland, but collectively they had been solid in their support. Life moved on, they had all changed. Griselda was becoming acid, Henrietta had given up passion and Lorne had swallowed defeat. As for Matty – she gulped some more gin. The jury was still out. Was she going to be successful? Rich? Happy? It seemed to her then that everything teetered in the balance. What had been fun with Sholto now became terrible drudgery, what had been exciting before Sasha now terrified her by its risk. She had to find that fun again, she had to take those chances, if not with Sholto then without.

Her heart ached with a terrible physical pain. If only he loved her still. She didn't know if he had ever loved her at all. But she couldn't sit forever, frozen in longing for the past. She had to try, as best she could, to move on. The divorce papers were stuffed behind the clock. They had been there for weeks. She grabbed them, signing where indicated with a furious scrawl. Let it be done with then. Let Simon think what he might, she couldn't live her life by other people's standards. She bundled the papers into an envelope, stuck a stamp on crooked and walked a mile to the postbox at the end of the lane.

At tea, Simon said, 'I think you should go to Italy and try and help Sholto.'

Matty was silent. Griselda said, 'Matty's done what she can. At least if they're divorced there can't be a claim on assets in Matty's name. The silver, for instance. And the house.'

Simon absorbed that with surprise. Then he burst out, 'But we ought to be helping him!'

'Simon.' Matty met his eye for the first time in weeks. 'I can't help Sholto. He walked straight into this mess, as if he was determined to get into trouble. He wanted it and he got it. If he decides to extricate himself then I'm sure he will. It's up to him. And my life is up to me.'

'I just think you should stick by your friends,' muttered Simon.

Griselda said, 'We all think that. But there are times when friends can't help you. In the end, Simon, each of us has to go to hell or heaven, and we travel all by ourselves.'

'That sounds so lonely,' said Matty in a whisper.

Griselda sighed. 'Yes.'

Flies buzzed around the uncovered milk jug. Some syrup had been spilled down the leg of a chair and they buzzed there too, settling on the sticky pool of sugar on the floor. But Lorne sat at the table and did nothing. Greg had yelled at her that morning and he would yell at her again tonight but it was as if she hardly heard. They couldn't make her work. It was the one thing they couldn't make her do.

Another hot day. She would take Miller and go down to the river, where she had first met James. She liked to go there. In fact, she seldom went anywhere else. From the river she could see the wood and sometimes the smoke from the chimneys of the Shuster place. It reminded her of the days when life was good.

She got up, running a hand through her black hair. It was lank and dull, and her skin felt dull, and when her eyes looked back at her from the mirror she thought she almost looked dead. It had happened in an instant, in Boston, thinking about what they had done. They could do an awful lot, but they couldn't stop her thinking.

There came a knock on the door. Lorne didn't answer, not even when her mother opened the door and came in. 'Lorne? Lorne, are you there?'

When she came into the kitchen she looked around in silence before starting to clean up. She took the milk outside and fed it to a couple of scrawny cats that lived around the barns, she set the dishwasher going, she wiped up with disinfectant and put the towels in Clorox to soak. Finally she sat down opposite her daughter.

'Are you going to sit there in silence all day?'

Lorne stirred. 'I was going to take Miller to the river.'

'I'm going to take Miller with me this morning. You're harming that child, Lorne. He doesn't hear any talk. Do you want me to speak to Sherwood? We can get you a doctor, if that's what you want. Someone to understand.'

'I've had enough of doctors. I've had enough of it all.'

Her mother closed her eyes. Lorne frightened her these days.

'Miller needs you,' she said forcefully. 'I need you. Whatever it is that hurts, you must do something, Lorne! Leave Greg. Come home to us. Please.'

Lorne almost smiled. Her mother thought her home so secure, so free from threat. If she went back home to live, there would be no home. Sherwood Berenson would see to that.

Eventually her mother took Miller and went. Lorne still sat in the kitchen, letting her thoughts drift this way and that. The room grew hotter, but still she didn't move. She looked up only when Sherwood came in.

'Hi, Lorne. Greg said you were down.'

Lorne never even turned her head.

'He said you were letting things go again. But you've cleaned up in here. That's good.'

Still she said nothing. Her immobility seemed to fascinate the man. He rested one haunch on the table next to her chair, his knee an inch from her face. 'You're turning out to be good for nothing,' murmured Sherwood. 'You don't come out no more, and when you do you don't smile or wave. Greg needs a sociable wife, not a puppet.'

She turned her head a little away from him.

'I know you hear me, Lorne. You don't hear Greg. You don't listen to him. I listen to him. He tells me he puts his arms around you and it's like holding on to a dead woman. That's no way to be, Lorne. Not a woman like you.'

The kitchen was still as death. The flies buzzed idly against the window and water dripped. Sherwood reached for the buttons of Lorne's shirt, his big fingers slow and deliberate. His farmer's fist eased the material away and her breasts were naked and exposed. He took a nipple between finger and thumb and tugged it. Lorne gasped.

'So, you feel that, do you? Not dead after all.'

He stood up, pushing his heavy body between her and the table. He reached for his zipper, pulling himself out of his clothes with his usual calm determination. It was as if this was something which had to be done. 'Don't you hold back now,' said Sherwood. 'We both know this had to come.'

'Get away from me.'

'You want me to go to your daddy and tell him he's done? Can't make the payment again. Never can, these days. Tried to sell a horse and couldn't get his price. Foolish man, your pa.'

There was never any point in holding out on him. He got you in the end, and you paid for the delay. Besides, her body didn't matter any more, she had retreated from it, escaped. The smell of him came to her and she turned her face away, but he took hold of her chin and held her fast.

'You want that child to see?'

When it was over he was pleased with himself. 'No use telling Greg about this,' he warned. 'Go buy yourself something sexy. Just for me.'

'How often do you mean to do this?' whispered Lorne.

He came close to her and put his hand in her hair, rubbing her head with rough affection. 'You're a Berenson woman. You don't ask questions. You just do as I say.'

* * *

494

Matty was in the shop, talking Wendy through the new stock. She was attentive enough, but too often she missed the significance of small points, which could be the difference between an average piece and one of quality. Engraving, for instance, and clear marks, as well as the collector's desire for the oddity. If something was unusual, however ugly or useless it might be, then it commanded a premium. And it should be sold accordingly.

The telephone rang and Matty automatically picked it up. 'Winsham Specialist Antiques. Matilda Feversham speaking.'

'Mrs Feversham, this is Martin Sutherland. I bought some candlesticks from you.'

'Oh, yes. Sir Martin. Can I assist you again?'

'I hope so. I recently acquired my present home, Locksley Hall, and I should like you to come down and advise me on the silver. I inherited from an uncle and there's a terrific lot of stuff. Do you have a fee for this sort of thing?'

Matty wondered whether to instigate one, and decided against it. 'No. But I do like to be given the opportunity to buy anything you wish to sell. I don't take rubbish, of course.'

'Not even as a favour to a valued customer?'

She sniffed. 'Oh, sometimes, I suppose. It depends. Should I value you?'

'Undoubtedly! I'm in town, I shall collect you in the morning. Around nine.'

'Certainly. Goodbye.'

She relinquished the phone very slowly. Was he going to carry her off and leave her dead in a ditch? It was possible. She knew nothing about him, except that twenty-five thousand had passed from his bank account to hers without a hitch. She couldn't exactly remember what he looked like, except for sandy hair and pale blue eyes. Scottish ancestry no doubt.

Wendy cleared her throat. 'Are we finished then, Mrs Feversham?'

'What? Oh, yes, we are. Look, Wendy, can you look after Sasha for me tomorrow? I'll pay extra, of course, but I have to go to a house and do a valuation.'

'All day?'

'I don't know. Most of it, probably.'

'Oh. Just this once, then.'

Matty slunk back upstairs, feeling guilty. Having a baby and a job meant foisting things on people despite their reluctance. And what was she to wear? She had bought no new clothes since Sasha's birth. The ultimate humiliation was borrowing Griselda's, tying them at the waist with a scarf and putting up with trailing hems. She felt a wreck. A guilty wreck.

None the less next day she put on her best face. She wore a green skirt of Griselda's, sweeping the top of last year's boots, cleaned for the occasion. Her top half was taken care of by a cream silk shirt of Sholto's, with a scarf tied at the neck in a floppy artist's bow, and a jacket of her own hiding shoulder seams somewhere near her elbow. Her hair was brushed in a severe, shining fall. As a desperate resort it was quite successful, she reflected. She liked her hair these days. It was longer, almost as long as Lorne's used to be.

The thought gave her a twinge of anxiety. Lorne hadn't replied to her last two letters, or to Griselda's, and Henrietta often asked if they had heard. It was to be expected, she supposed. Not many people stayed in touch forever, they went their own way and whatever it was they had found in friendship wasn't needed any more. Lorne had a new life and new friends, no doubt. It was just sad that her old friends missed her.

A Rolls-Royce drew up at the door. Matty goggled at it. 'I think this is him,' she said to Wendy. 'Take care of Sasha, won't you? She's more important than the shop. 'Bye.'

Sutherland was driving himself. Matty got in the passenger seat, trying to look as if riding in a Rolls was an everyday event. It smelled of leather and good wax polish. Sutherland said, 'I'll bring you back at four, if that's all right.'

'Yes. Perfectly. Thank you.'

She cast covert glances at him as he drove. He was thirty-five, she thought, though he might be forty. Faint freckles covered his skin including his hands, and he wore no rings. 'Is it far?' she asked.

He shook his head. 'About an hour from here. May I ask how your business is going?'

Matty lifted her eyebrows. 'I hardly think it's your concern. But it's doing well. We'd be doing better, but I had a divorce and it was disruptive. I wasn't able to concentrate for a while. Are you married?'

'No. No, I haven't that pleasure.'

They drove on in silence. The traffic jams of early morning had eased, and the big car nosed its way out of town on to the motorway. Mist was clearing over the fields, and the sun was an egg in an autumn sky. Chamber music played softly on the radio.

'We're here,' said Sutherland, sending the car sweeping to the left. 'The house is only five minutes away.'

It was big, white-rendered and impressive. Banks of rhododendrons lined the drive, and Sutherland said he would clear those and open the place up. 'It's so dark in winter. Like a horror film. I can't abide it.'

Already leaves were thick on the lawns. Two gardeners were sweeping them into sacks, and Sutherland tutted angrily. 'They only clear up when they know I'm expected. Don't work at all when I'm away.'

'You need a manager,' said Matty idly.

'Actually, I think I need a wife.'

He stopped the car in front of the house and went to talk to the gardeners. Matty wandered around on the gravel, watching deer strolling on the still misty fringes of the park. Sunlight diffused through the foggy air, lending an air of spurious romanticism to the scene. Lucky Martin Sutherland, she thought. He lived amongst beauty.

The house itself was newly decorated and somewhat spartan. Colours were muted, and the walls looked bare, as if awaiting pictures and side tables. The silver was piled high on the dining-room table, a jumble of boxes and bags. Someone had wrapped everything in oily cloth, and Matty discarded it distastefully and told Sutherland his silver should be washed.

'I can get the housekeeper to do it if you wish.'

'Later. For now, I have to work.'

She settled down, sorting the good from the bad.

Sutherland brought her coffee and sat himself down, obviously hoping to be told what was what. Matty was feeling unsociable. But, business was business. She forced herself to talk.

'This fish slice is bright-cut, but it has worn badly. It does. But it's in a nice fish shape, with a good ivory handle. I'll make you an offer for that. Whereas the salts are all Victorian copies, and not in the least good. I won't buy them but someone will. Send them to a sale.'

The candelabra she had sold him were standing in window embrasures around the room. From time to time Matty looked up at them. 'They're the best thing you've got,' she mused. 'I sold them too cheap. I did you far too much of a favour.'

'Another dealer told me I'd got them cheap,' he said.

'Which other dealer?'

'A Mr Chesworth. But I think he knew you, so I didn't quite believe him.'

Matty chuckled and shook her head. Naughty Sammy. Always on her side. 'If you do get married you should buy jewellery from him,' she advised. 'He's terribly high class. Only the best.'

'You're two of a kind, then.'

'Are we? I hope so. Dealers don't come any better than Sammy.'

She found half a set of flatware, jumbled up in a box. 'Oh, I can do something with this,' she said enthusiastically. 'Can I take it off your hands or would you like the set made up to match? It's an unusual variation on fiddle thread and shell, quite uncommon but not impossible. Would you want silver-bladed knives or steel? Most people have steel — silver's too soft for general use.'

'I'll have steel then.'

'Good.'

Matty made a note in her book. There were cups minus handles, plates with parts of the rim broken off, meat dishes worn thin from use, and some bucolic tumblers. She offered for only four things, and gave an estimate for repair of the rest.

'It isn't a good collection,' she said regretfully. 'If you

want good things you'll have to come to me. Silver prices are falling just now, I can get you some bargains. Relatively speaking, of course.'

'I like good silver,' said Sutherland. 'I think it's an investment.'

'Good anything's an investment. But silver's fun.'

She was finished and went to wash her hands. When she came out Sutherland said, 'I've had some luncheon set out in the small parlour. Shall we?'

'Oh. Thank you. Yes.'

They drank crisp white wine in front of a small log fire. Designer curtains matched designer covers on the chairs, and the table was set with tediously co-ordinating napkins. It turned out that Sutherland had inherited two years ago, only to find the Hall falling apart with woodworm and dry rot. He had renovated it and commanded the decorations from a top-class firm. The result was less than homely.

'I need pictures and things,' he confessed. 'But I'm not an expert in art of any kind. When I came into your shop I didn't intend to buy silver, only to look.'

'Why did you buy, then?'

He grinned at her, for the first time. 'Because you didn't want to sell. And your shop was so obviously full of quality. What is the saying? "Of the first stare." Like the proprietor.'

'You said I was scruffy!'

'You said yourself, today: You can't disguise the best.'

Matty laughed and leaned back in her chair. This was heaven. Sutherland was the sort of man who would never do anything to surprise her. He was stolid, hard-working, snobbish, and perhaps a little repressed.

'Why haven't you married?' she demanded.

He shrugged. 'Perhaps I was too cautious. There were a couple of girls, but I always had my doubts. Now of course they're married to other people, and I see my doubts were quite unfounded.'

'What were your doubts?'

'I thought — one girl seemed a bit wild. I could see her running off with the best man. But she's a member of the Women's Institute nowadays, and running to fat, so

499

obviously I was wrong. The other was a wee bit extravagant. I thought she was after my money. But she's discovered she can't have children, so I'm very sympathetic.'

'I see you are,' said Matty ironically. He had the grace to laugh.

He showed her the house after lunch, making valiant efforts to steer the conversation round to her divorce. Matty resisted as best she could, ultimately resorting to a lie. 'He was an Australian businessman who went bust when he invested in mines,' she declared.

'What sort of mines?'

'Opals. Our marriage cracked under the strain. He's gone home to − Alice Springs. He left me with a load of debt.'

'Poor you.'

Matty opened her eyes. 'Yes. Poor me.'

On the way home they were caught in a jam on the M25. He drummed his hands on the steering wheel. 'I was hoping to get into the office for an hour.'

'And Wendy will want to get home. Damn!'

He handed her the car phone to let her call. She hated him sitting there listening to her grovel to an employee.

'You should have a nanny,' he said as she finished.

'I can't afford a nanny.' She chewed on a fingernail.

'If I hire one for the day, will you host a party for me?'

'What?' She blinked at him.

'I'm holding a big party on Saturday, at the Hall. A sort of housewarming. I wanted you to be my hostess.'

'On Saturdays Griselda looks after Sasha. And I'm your silver dealer!'

'You know about parties, don't you?'

'Of course. But is this business or personal?'

He looked straight ahead and drummed his hands on the steering wheel for a moment. 'Personal,' he said.

'How very incautious of you.'

'Yes. Taking up with the divorced wife of an opal miner.'

'But of proven fecundity,' retorted Matty. 'Are you planning a dynasty, or something?'

'At the moment, only a party.'

The traffic started to move. 'I haven't a thing to wear,' said Matty with relief. 'So obviously I can't.'

'I'll buy you something.'

'That would be improper.'

'You can give it back afterwards. Please, Mrs Feversham.'

'The name's Matty.'

'Matty. Please.'

How tempting it was. Life was so dull nowadays. She could wear something new and be delightful to people she didn't know. For a day she could play at being lady of the manor. She said yes.

Chapter Twenty-Nine

Her dress was rich russet wool, trimmed at wrist and neck with gold buttons. It wasn't the sort of thing she would have worn for Sholto. With him she had been younger. This was the dress of a woman.

She had no suitable earrings, so on impulse she went to see Sammy. He listened to her disjointed explanation and went to his safe. He lent her gold knots, heavy on the ends of little chains, swinging pleasantly against her cheeks.

'Sixty thousand pounds,' he muttered. 'Not insured. Don't lose them.'

'Sammy!'

He spread his hands. 'They suit you. They make you happy. Be off with you.'

Griselda was agog with excitement. 'Will he propose? You look smashing, Matty. Don't worry about Sasha, I'll take the very best care. He must have fallen in love at first sight.'

'Don't be so silly, Grizz!' Matty snapped at her. 'You're worse than Henry. Sloppily romantic.'

'Really!' Griselda went off in a huff. She was easily offended these days, when Matty turned on her. The arguments were always about the same thing. Griselda took vicarious pleasure in Matty's life, like a prying, doting aunt.

Repentant, Matty went to find her. She was reading. 'What's that?'

Stiffly, Griselda said, 'Background information on the African state of Limbowa.'

'Never heard of it.'

'Nobody has. But the king is putting it on the map by training everyone else's revolutionaries. He went to public school here, so of course he's an expert.'

Matty laughed. Mollified, Griselda put down her paper. 'Will he ask you to stay the night?'

'I don't know. I won't.'

'What if he insists? What if he won't let you go?'

'I'll hit him on the head with one of my candlesticks. If I'm not home by midnight, you can call the police.'

'You don't mean that, do you? I shall probably be in bed.'

Matty sighed. 'I suppose it will be all right.'

She arrived at the Hall in the early morning. The place was bustling, with caterers and trays, vintners with boxes of glasses and florists with unwieldy great bouquets. Sutherland himself was nervous, and getting in people's way.

'Good to see you,' he said, shaking Matty's proffered hand. Then he bent to kiss her cheek. 'You look magnificent.'

'Thank you.'

'Will you send me the bill?'

She gave him a sideways glance. 'I think after all I can afford this.'

'Please. I won't hear of it.'

He put his arm around her and drew her into the house. She was stiffly unresponsive. Such rapid promotion to the role of companion was difficult for her to adjust to. He assumed familiarity she did not feel ready to give.

The house felt less homely than ever, inundated as it was with people used to parties in hotels. Sutherland wanted to give her coffee in his study, but she resisted. 'I'm here to work, aren't I?' Instead she asked for the fires to be lit, and for pot pourri to scent the rooms, and for the caterers' boxes labelled 'MaxPax Best Before' to be removed discreetly from view. What's more she had brought some of her own good silver and set it out on shelves and in window embrasures, as if the master of the house was an avid and skilled collector.

504

He was lavish in his praise and without thinking, Matty said, 'I should have brought you some pictures. I didn't think.'

'You don't deal in art as well, do you?'

'What? No. They're just — things I picked up.'

Guests began arriving at eleven. Each one, as they were introduced, gave Matty a deep and searching stare. She responded with her own brand of welcome, warm yet slightly restrained. Gone was any girlish gushing, gone too the chill of shyness. She was too battered by life to care any more what strangers thought of her, and after Sholto's racketing no party in the world could cause her stress. It was Sutherland whose palms sweated.

'You really should relax,' she murmured to him in a lull. 'It's a wonderful party. Everyone's having such fun we needn't serve lunch till two.'

'They'll all be drunk.'

'So what? They can sober up this afternoon.'

His tension was affecting her. She drifted away from him, discreetly checking on glasses, fires and clean ashtrays, approaching the isolated and making efforts to introduce them to people neither of them knew. A grey-haired man leaned down from an immense height and said, 'Did I catch your name right, my dear? Feversham?'

She nodded. 'Matilda Feversham. I'm a silver dealer.'

'No connection with this Feversham chap in Italy, are you?'

Matty took in her breath. 'I don't know. Why? What chap?'

'Seems he's something of a celebrity out there. I was in Milan last week, couldn't turn on the television without seeing him. Italian public's taken him to heart. Seems he authenticated some picture and now there are claims it's forged. He says they've swapped the pictures, to do him down. All dates back to a row some years ago, but Feversham's winning hands down. There'll be a revolution if the court don't find for him.'

'What's he like?' asked Matty wistfully. 'He sounds very odd.'

The man chuckled. 'Tremendous charmer, actually. Has

a horrible facial scar, quite revolting, makes him look like a pirate. TV shows fight to get him to appear, but he plays hard to get, which is clever. Brilliant Italian speaker, full of wit. You speak it?'

Matty shook her head. 'A few words, only.'

'I picked it up in Sicily after the war. The British ought to make an effort with languages, we're so damned lazy.'

Matty murmured her agreement and moved on. Her heart was thundering against her ribs, and all her calmness had deserted her. How could Sholto? How dare he? He always managed to escape these things.

Her mind began to weave fantasies, of Sholto coming home. Sholto claiming her again. She was at the part where he said, 'Darling Matty, I shall never leave you again, not for a moment,' when Sutherland caught her arm. 'Do you think we should lunch now?'

Dragged back to the present, Matty was vague. 'I don't know. What time is it?'

'Half-past two.'

'Then of course we should eat! They'll be passing out soon.'

The guests fell on the food like starving wolves. Within minutes whole salmon were reduced to bones, great sirloins of beef became rags on a plate. Matty ate nothing, endlessly circling to make sure that dirty things disappeared to be replaced instantly by clean. Outside the park grew dark under a threatening storm. She ordered the candles to be lit.

Soft candlelight changed the mood. A string quartet began playing in the drawing room and since it was raining and the garden was impossible Matty organised skittles in the gallery. People began playing billiards too, and the older, drunker members turned on the television in the small sitting room and telephoned the local bookmaker to place bets on the racing.

Sutherland caught her arm. He was grinning, perhaps a little drunk. 'It's going so well. Thanks to you.'

'I haven't done anything.'

'You know you have. Everyone's talking about you. A

fellow just now said you were the prettiest woman here. And you are. You're beautiful.'

'Don't say that, Martin.'

'I must. If I don't say it now I might never say it. You look so lovely. I can't stop watching your hair, the way it rests on your shoulders. I want to touch it.'

'You're drunk,' she said desperately.

'Only a little. Only enough to tell you what I wanted to say the first time I saw you in that shop. Let's go somewhere private, please.'

He took her hand and led her through a door and along a corridor. At the end was a small sitting room, shabby and well used. This was where he truly lived when at the Hall.

He began to kiss her. She stood quite still and let him, aware of his hands on her back, touching her bottom, reaching up to tangle in her hair. She felt his lips, hot and rather wet, and his body seemed heavy against hers. Some part of her mind detached itself, maintaining a commentary on what was going on. This was nothing like Sholto — did he excite her? Was any of it the same?

Quite unexpectedly, she felt herself respond. There was pleasure in this. With Sholto it had been body and mind as one, but now it was only body, no more than that. She didn't know this man. She didn't know if she liked him. But there was heat between her legs, an almost painful engorgement, and she felt a desperate need to be touched.

'I love you,' murmured Sutherland. 'You beautiful, sexy girl.'

Her nipples were stiff with anticipation. At last his hand came to her breast, and she opened her mouth wide for his tongue. All it needed now — she got his thigh between her legs and discreetly pressed herself into him. Her orgasm came. She held herself rigidly against the shudders. He mustn't know, he simply mustn't know. He rushed on, still passionate, and her head cleared. She pushed him away.

'That's enough, Martin. I don't know you well enough.'

'For God's sake — Matty, please.'

'No. Not yet.'

He moved to touch her again, but she didn't need him now. She could be strong. She held his shoulders and kissed him on the nose, laughing and saying, 'You'll have to be patient, that's all. I don't go to bed with people I've only just met.'

'No. Of course you don't. Oh, Matty, you're such a darling.'

As they went back to the party she thought how little time it had taken Sholto to get her into bed. As long as it took to step out of her knickers. But she would give Sholto anything, while Sutherland was there to give to her. She hadn't known she was in need until now. Walking amongst the guests and chatting, she experienced a most pleasurable lethargy.

'How was it?' Griselda was on the end of her bed.

'I'll tell you in the morning. It's almost three.'

'Did you sleep with him? I had a bet with myself that you would.'

'Don't be curious, Grizz. I didn't actually. We had a wild snogging session in his study, that's all.'

'Do you think he's going to suggest marriage?'

Matty laid her earrings carefully down and let her head fall back on the pillow. 'Yes, I think so. He's being reckless, possibly for the first time in his life. He'd marry me tomorrow if I wanted.'

'And do you?'

Matty sighed. 'Yes. No. I don't know. I like the idea of stopping the struggle. My business could be a hobby again. I could stop worrying.'

Griselda yawned and got up. She was wearing a capacious white nightdress in unlovely winceyette. 'I hate to be practical, but you've tried marrying for love,' she said. 'He's in love with you, and that might be enough. It is for Henry.'

'I don't know,' said Matty again. 'Would you do it?'

Griselda snorted. 'I don't count. Chances are I shall be posted to Limbowa. Perhaps the king will take a fancy to me and keep me as a curiosity.'

'You're not really going, are you?'

Griselda paused. 'Possibly. I haven't said no.'

'What position?'

'Assistant to the Consul. A very lowly role, but one has to start somewhere. It's quite exciting really.'

Matty was silent. Griselda had moved into her life so completely that it was hard to imagine what it would be without her. Loneliness threatened again. She wasn't good at being alone. Was anybody? Sholto perhaps. Sometimes he could be the uproarious centre of attention and still seem alone.

In the morning she had a splitting headache. Sasha was cruel, squealing and throwing cereal about from her spoon. There was never any rest from babies, thought Matty, they kept on and on without considering the weakness of their parents.

'I'm going to miss you, Grizz,' she said suddenly.

'Rubbish. You'll be glad to get rid of me.'

'No I won't. I don't know what I'd have done if you hadn't taken me under your wing.'

'You'd have coped, the way you always do.'

'But not as well. Not as happily.'

Griselda's beaky face flushed. 'Thanks awfully,' she blurted. 'Even if you don't really mean it – thanks.'

Matty wondered if she dared tell her what she had heard about Sholto. She didn't want Grizz to know really, but she wanted to talk about him, to anyone. She was still thinking about it when the telephone rang and it was some moments before she realised who was on the line.

'Martin? Hello. Yes, I'm fine. Today? Actually I'd rather not, Sasha's got a cold and isn't well. Yes, isn't it? Yes. Next week, lovely. Thanks. You too. 'Bye.'

Griselda met her eye. 'Is this any way to treat him? The man's in love.'

Matty glowered. 'I don't care what he is. Shut up, Grizz.' He was nice enough. He was rich enough. He was a stopgap until Sholto came back.

'It won't happen, Matty,' said Griselda, and Matty curled up on herself, hugging her knees.

'Don't,' she whispered. 'Don't.'

Henrietta's figure had slumped again. She stood in her dressing room, looking at herself in the pier glass, Louis Quinze and priceless. This same glass had reflected queens and courtesans, women of the greatest beauty. Now it framed Henrietta Cooke, with nose job and flab.

Wearily she began to dress. Being grown up had its advantages, and being rich and grown up had many more. You could own clothes in hundreds of sizes, for one thing, and you could command the cook to serve only healthy food. What's more, you could then go down to the kitchen and pig out on cake and nobody could tell you off. A friend the other day had declared her to have an eating disorder, probably related to toilet training, but Henry took no notice. The trouble was, eating was fun.

When she was dressed she looked at herself again. Not so bad. Wide silk trousers hid plump little legs, and a long jacket disguised the unfortunate expansion in the territory between bust and hip. Shoulder pads and a tall hairdo gave an illusion of height and width to balance the fat little body, and her face – well, her face always looked OK. Fat people tended towards good skin, she reflected. A saving grace.

Tyler came in and said, 'Ready, honey?'

'Just about. I've got to get thin, Tyler. I'm getting gross.'

'Nonsense! You look perfect to me. You always do.'

She shot him a grateful smile. 'All the same, I'll be the only fat person tonight. They only let thin people in to these parties, they machine gun the fat ones on sight.'

'Honey, there'll be lots of fat people there tonight.'

'So you do think I'm fat!'

He flapped his hands helplessly. 'Who cares? Have another baby and forget about being thin.'

'You think about nothing but babies.'

'So, we'll have some more.'

He kissed her. She thought how lucky she was to have married him. Nobody had ever thought Tyler Cooke would amount to anything, but with Henry at his side, he did. Nowadays he did not hesitate to state his opinion. Nowadays he stood up to people. Nowadays he was getting

510

a strong reputation as a man of great wealth, judgment and charity.

They were going to a reception in support of Tyler's Rescue foundation, the organisation set up to build shelters for the homeless in some of America's most impoverished areas. Although still in their infancy, Rescue's projects were acclaimed by workers in the field and held up as models to the rest of the world. They were the only schemes to be fifty per cent administered by the inmates, some of the poorest and most difficult people it was possible to imagine. Brought in to jeers of contempt, they had not foundered. It was early to judge, but the media were beginning to talk of success.

'Let's go late,' murmured Tyler. 'We can start making babies.'

'It's our reception, we can't be late. And we haven't said goodnight to Tyler Junior.'

They went down the hall together to the nursery. It was a big room, decked out in yellow and white, with hand-painted murals of cartoon figures on the cupboard doors. The nanny stood up as they entered, and Tyler Junior shot across the floor towards them, crawling at the rate of knots. 'Mum, Mum, Mum!' he yelled.

'What about your poor old pa?' demanded Tyler, and swept the baby into his arms.

Henrietta suddenly caught her breath. This was her family, this her second best choice. It was all she could wish for.

Henry and Tyler didn't know too many people at the party. They were introduced to hundreds and made small talk as best they could, considering neither of them was much good at it. There were diamonds everywhere, and lean bronzed bodies, although since the scare about skin cancer it was fashionable to be pale. Three women were wearing the same diamante and lace frock, and to their credit they got together and did an impromptu dance routine. When they finished one muttered, 'And now I will go and kill my dress designer.'

Tyler began talking buildings with an architect. It was

a subject he knew about and he didn't need help. Henry forgot her role as supporter for a while and looked around the room. She caught sight of someone in the throng. She looked again. She began to make her way urgently through the crowd.

'Lorne? Lorne, it is you?'

A dark head turned. The hair was drawn back tightly from a face almost skeletal in aspect. Huge eyes in skin like white paper, with lips of blood. She wore a dress of violet satin, hanging in folds from fleshless shoulders, and her hands plucked at it, utterly transparent. She was eerily, unnaturally beautiful.

'It is you.' Henrietta stood amazed in front of her. 'Hi.'

'Hi. Yes, it's me. Look, hadn't you better go and do your great lady bit? People want to talk to you.'

'But I want to talk to you. Lorne, you look − you look like hell.'

The woman smiled a little. 'Surely not? Only last week a magazine said I was one of the great beauties of all time. That isn't looking like hell.'

'I've never seen you so thin.'

'A woman can never be too rich or too thin.'

'Claptrap from a woman who was both.'

They stood in silence. Lorne looked away, restlessly, as if she wanted to escape from her friend. A big man came up behind her and put a heavy hand on her shoulder. Henry recognised Sherwood Berenson.

'Well, Lorne, you chatting? Come over here, there's people I want you to meet.'

Obediently Lorne began to turn. Henry said, 'Actually, Mr Berenson, we still have much to talk about. I want to explain one of our projects to Lorne. She may be able to help.'

'Lorne's busy enough working with her husband,' said Berenson. 'She'll maybe have time for you later.'

'Where is Greg?' Henrietta hung on doggedly. 'Lorne, where is he?'

'He'll be here by and by.' Berenson tightened his grip on Lorne's shoulder and steered her resolutely away.

Henrietta couldn't get her out of her mind. During the

speeches she stood on the platform and watched Lorne flinch under Sherwood's hand. Again and again he touched her, that firm, proprietorial grip. And she was utterly, immediately obedient.

When it was over she and Tyler went off to eat, but for once she had no appetite. Tyler was worried and urged her to eat up, told her she shouldn't be surprised if one of her old friends had forgotten her.

'She hasn't,' said Henry. 'There's something terribly wrong. I'll phone Matty tomorrow.'

'She'll be worried for nothing,' said Tyler. 'You can't put the world right, Henry. Not even you. Sweet you.' He lifted her hand and kissed it.

That night, after they had made love, wondering if even then she might be pregnant, Henry made a decision. She had to see Lorne.

'Could you telephone Mrs Berenson and tell her Mrs Cooke is here to see her, please?' It was the front desk of a medium-priced hotel. The Berensons weren't in the Cooke league when it came to money, and they were careful. Henry looked around the lobby, wondering if she might see Greg, or Sherwood, or even Lorne. But there was no one she knew.

The girl at the desk relayed the message to the room. Then she hung up. 'Mrs Berenson's sick and too ill to be visited. She's sorry.'

'Oh. Oh, I see.' She hadn't expected that. But she had sneaked a look at the room number. She walked away, as if going out, but once out of sight of the desk she made for the elevator and the fourteenth floor. The hall was empty, and everything was quiet. There was not even a maid in sight. Henrietta went quickly to the door of room 1435 and rapped, calling 'Room Service' in her best bellhop voice.

'I didn't order anything – oh.' Lorne, in a robe. Her hair was a cloud around her face, released from the cruel knot of yesterday. She looked utterly weary. 'You'd better come in,' she said resignedly.

'Thanks. I know you don't want to see me.'

'It's not you. I don't want to see anybody.'

The room smelled of booze. There had been no maid service that day and there were bottles and glasses on the table and the television. Clothes were strewn everywhere.

'Is Greg out?'

Lorne nodded. 'The reason he didn't come last night was because he was drunk. He often is. I think he had a girl in while I was away.'

Henrietta took in her breath. 'You don't sound as if you mind.'

'Mind? Why should I mind? It keeps him off me.'

She sounded so bitter, so hopeless. Henry knew, without a doubt, that she was out of her depth here. Whatever was wrong with Lorne was deadly serious. 'How's your mother?' she asked. 'And everyone? Is your father still breeding horses?'

'Yes. Yes, he still is.'

'And Miller? I sent him a present for his birthday, do you remember? Did he like it?'

'What was it?'

'A boat. A toy boat.'

'Yes. Yes, I think he liked it. He likes to feel unusual shapes. And textures. He's got a bear made of velvet, he loves to feel it against his face.' She was oddly still. 'I don't know when they're going to operate. Some time. He sees light and dark, they say.'

Henrietta began automatically to move around the room, clearing up. Lorne said, 'People always clear up around me. It's all they do, clear up.'

'What do you want me to do? Do you want me to go, Lorne?'

The girl lifted her shoulders unhappily. 'I don't know.'

Henry's nerve suddenly snapped. She ran across the room and grabbed hold of her, yelling, 'Will you stop that? Will you stop looking like that? Will you for God's sake tell me what's wrong?'

Lorne's head rocked back on her stem of a neck, her hair hung down, her mouth was a rictus of pain. Small cries began in her, and tears started to trickle from the corners of her eyes. 'What is it? You must say!' yelled

Henrietta again, desperate enough for real violence.

'You can't know. You mustn't ever know.'

'Lorne, there is nothing, absolutely nothing, you can't tell me. I shan't think badly of you. I want to help.'

'I'm beyond help. You don't know what he does!'

'Greg?'

'No. Not Greg.'

'You mean Sherwood, don't you? Sherwood Berenson.'

Lorne let her head fall forward in a nod.

They couldn't talk there. Lorne was on tenterhooks, expecting Greg or his father at any time. Henry helped her dress, fastening every button and every zipper. It was as if Lorne had lost the power of thought, let alone action. She was shivering with fright. At last they made it to the elevator, and heard it ascending from the ground. A sudden hunch made Henrietta push Lorne to the stairs, and stand behind the door, waiting. Sure enough, Sherwood's calm, confident voice emerged into the hall. Henry steered her charge carefully down to the next floor and took the elevator from there.

She only felt safe back in her own house. Lorne was talking now, saying it was all a mistake, there was nothing to say, she'd best get back because they got mad if she wasn't there –

Henry said, 'I'll ring for some tea. Then we can sit quietly. They can't get you here.'

'They can get Miller,' said Lorne tensely. 'They can get my parents. They don't have to get me.'

'Shall I phone? Shall I say we're having lunch?'

'They know I don't lunch.'

'You do with me.'

She called her housekeeper and arranged for a message to be sent to the hotel. She gave the name of a restaurant out of town, to which the Berensons could not instantly repair. Lorne was sipping tea, holding her cup in trembling hands. 'Now,' said Henry calmly, 'no one but me can hear. What's going on?'

Lorne closed her eyes for a second. 'I had an affair,' she murmured. 'A good, kind man. I don't know if I loved him, but I wanted someone to love. Greg killed him. And after that, when I didn't speak out, when I didn't do anything, because of Miller and my parents, because I was just too damned scared, Sherwood knew he could do what he liked. And he does. All the time. With me.'

'He — he couldn't do anything to a child,' said Henry, in disbelief. 'Miller's Greg's son, Sherwood's grandson.' She wondered if Lorne was mad, paranoid perhaps.

'He can stop him having the operation. It costs money and he won't pay.'

'But I would pay! I'd give any amount, you know that!'

'Sherwood killed a man before,' said Lorne. 'At least, I think he did. I know he had him killed. Someone I cared for. Henry, he scares me so much!'

Henrietta was completely silent. A picture flashed before her, of Lorne last night, beautiful, ravaged, and that man's hand upon her. He had broken her. Lorne had been young and lovely, and year by year he had tightened the harness until at last the spirit was crushed. He was indeed dangerous.

'Why didn't you come to me?' she asked. 'You must know I can help.'

'I don't need help. My life's finished.'

'Miller needs you so much.'

'Not after his operation. When that's over I shall kill myself and be done. I've decided.' Calm, determined, terrifying certainty.

Henry burst out, 'Good God, Lorne, you're not even thirty!'

'I'm dead already. If I wasn't dead I couldn't endure it. Sometimes I think Greg knows what his father does and sometimes I don't think so. They don't either of them care. I just want Miller to have someone good to take care of him when I'm gone. Will you do that, Henry? I'll write it in my Will.'

'You're going to take care of him. This is going to stop.'

'Oh, Henry.' Suddenly Lorne was herself again, weary, bruised by knowledge, and a thousand years old. She stood up and took Henry's hand. 'You always wanted to make things right. You never liked sad endings. But sometimes

516

that's the way it is. I'm a sacrifice. Sherwood won't hurt other people while he can hurt me. And that's OK.'

Henrietta called a car for her. She stood at the door and watched her friend leave. And she clenched her fists and let out a string of curses that made the housekeeper reel back and exclaim, 'Mrs Cooke!' in tones of horror.

Henry screamed at her: 'I will not let her be! I will not! If I do nothing else in my whole goddammed life I will stop this!'

Chapter Thirty

Matty was at the cottage when the call came. She had driven up from London the evening before, while Sasha was asleep, but it was too much at the end of a long day. She felt drained and hopeless, surrounded by things she must do and unable to think about beginning. Even her third cup of coffee had failed to galvanise her into action and she picked up the telephone morosely.

'Hello?'

'Matty? Henry. Lorne's in trouble.'

'Is she indeed.' Matty was grimly ironic.

'Matty, this is serious!'

'I know, I know. But we've all got troubles.'

'Not like this you haven't.'

'Haven't I?' She sighed, thinking how little Henrietta knew. Then she pulled herself together. 'Oh, don't take any notice, Henry, I'm flaked out this morning. Sometimes it seems as if I can only run this business by driving up and down the country three times a week. And Griselda's gone to Africa and I've got no help.'

'You didn't appreciate Grizz when you had her.'

'Do you have to be right all the time?'

She heard Henrietta's sharp intake of breath. If it was anyone else she would have apologised, but she knew Henry too well.

'You are having a bad day,' said Henrietta gently.

'Too right. OK, tell me the worst. She's getting divorced.'

'If only she was! I saw her at this reception – she looks like a skeleton. Her family's up to the neck in debt to Sherwood Berenson.'

'That's old news. It's always been the same.'

519

'But lately Sherwood's started turning the screw. If she's difficult, her family get thrown out. You know her little boy, Miller, is blind?'

There was a pause. Matty said, 'I didn't know. When did you find out?'

Henrietta rushed on. 'Well, it seems —'

'Henry! How long have you known?'

A guilty silence. Then Henrietta said, 'It isn't permanent! There could be an operation, when he's six or so. Lorne didn't want you to know. You and Grizz. I think she was ashamed.'

'Henry! You traitor!' She banged the receiver down. She sat, fulminating, thinking that none of them had ever kept such a secret before. It was the death knell of friendship, then. The final blow. The foursome had dissolved into cabals and cliques, into four people separated by secrets. The telephone rang again and after a while Matty picked it up.

'I am sorry,' said Henrietta.

'Like hell you are!'

'But, Matty, you and Grizz are always the ones who have everything worked out! You're clever and successful. It was left to Lorne and me to fail the exams and get in messes.'

'Grizz and I get in terrible messes!'

'Yes. Independent ones. We're the stupid girls who can't cope.'

'Henry, that's a load of shit!' And this time, Henrietta hung up.

Matty called again later in the day. She had cried for a long time, and twice had decided never to speak to Lorne or Henry again. She picked Sasha up and studied her beautiful shining eyes, and felt petty. And she remembered school, when her father died, and the girls on her bed, trying to help.

'Henry? Me.'

'Oh. I am surprised.'

'No, you're not. You know I don't bear grudges.'

'People change. Matty, you should see Lorne, she's in such a funny mood. You don't know what Sherwood's like with her —'

520

'Does he make her sleep with him?'

A gasp. 'How did you know?'

'What else? He had a way of looking at her. I never could stand him.'

'Matty, I think she might kill herself! Leave me in charge of the kid and do it!'

'Oh God.' Matty knew she should promise to go out. She thought of Sasha and the shop, the auctions and the paperwork, Richard Greensall and Sammy Chesworth, and most of all Sholto, who might come back and find her gone. She couldn't afford to go out. Really, she couldn't.

'I'll come if you want,' she said humbly.

'Would you? Oh Matty, please!'

The call over, her weariness seemed to have vanished. She began to make notes and lists. Everything seemed possible. She must cable American dealers and make appointments, and a quick word with Sammy wouldn't hurt. He might like her to bid at auction on his behalf. Suddenly she stopped short. Martin Sutherland. It was his birthday on Saturday and she was absolutely sure he was going to propose.

She should have asked for Henry's advice, she thought. Clearly it was possible to think of one man and marry another. It was probably a sensible thing to do, since concentrating all hope and expectation on a single male was asking a terrible lot. One for romance and one for good living, she thought idly. Martin was so restful in comparison with Sholto, he was the ideal second husband. They would live out their lives in contented financial advancement, having regulated children at regulated intervals. Sadly, the start would be delayed. She composed a short affectionate note telling him she had been unavoidably called away.

A letter grinned at her, hidden at the bottom of her tray. She had known she would have to think about it sooner or later. It was another from Sholto's aunt.

'I regret to inform you that the latest loan repayment has not been forthcoming from my nephew. As I understand that he remains embroiled in legal difficulties I should be grateful if you would remit the necessary amount.'

This time no Sholto had appeared to rescue her. The money was due, there wasn't enough, and she had to go to America. For a wild moment she thought about borrowing off Henrietta but that would be shameful. Henry wasn't a liferaft for improvident swimmers who got out of their depth in the monetary sea. Lorne could appeal to her, even Griselda at a pinch, but not Matty. She had too much pride.

Setting her jaw, she went to look at her silver. Boxes of the stuff, shelves crammed with lovely things, knives, forks and spoons ranged endlessly around a table. This was her living, and money must be wrung from it, somehow. If she was travelling then some must travel too, in search of a market and a home. A thought occurred to her. She went to a shelf and took down a bowl wrapped in newspaper. It was heavy but not particularly large. The craftsmanship was evident, and she balanced the bowl on her palm, feeling the weight. Elaborate and extravagant chasing, combined with balance and flair. A bowl like this was very rare, and she needed money so badly. She put it into the box.

The flight was booked for Friday. She ended up in a panic at ten in the morning, due to take off at twelve, and still she hadn't loaded everything into the car. Sasha's bag of necessities bulged at the seams. She had a huge box of silver, a briefcase, two suitcases and a small print of Sholto's she was taking as hand baggage in the hope that it would sell quite quickly in the States. Sasha was fretful, two final demands arrived in the post and there was a disgruntled letter from a customer who had asked her to find him a good quality meat plate and had heard nothing. She had forgotten about him. What else had she forgotten? She rushed around the house checking switches she had already checked and caught herself in the act of switching off the deep freeze.

She stood in the hall and took deep breaths. 'Calm down,' she told herself. 'The plane will not go without you. You have plenty of time. Switch off the light, lock the door, go to the car and start.'

'Excuse me.'

She spun round. A man was standing in the open doorway. He smiled rather shyly. 'Matilda, isn't it? I'm sure you won't remember me. Brantingham. Bertie. Came to your wedding.'

'Bertie? Griselda's Bertie?'

'Yes, that's the one.'

'Hello.'

'Yes. Hello.'

They stood uncomfortably looking at each other. Matty said, 'Actually I've a plane to catch. Takes off at twelve, I'm so late —'

'I'm in the way. Knew I should be. So sorry. Another time, please —'

Matty followed him down the path. 'Did you want something? Were you looking for Griselda?'

He paused and half turned towards her. He was holding a tweed cap in his hands, and he wore a waistcoat in purple tweed stretched across his somewhat ample stomach. 'Her father said the other day she'd gone abroad. Poor old chap's getting on a bit, couldn't seem to remember quite where.'

'It's a place called Limbowa. Africa. She's assistant to the Consul, one of those dreadful posts they give people at the start. I've had a letter, it took a month to come.'

He looked quite shocked. 'Limbowa? Don't know what they're thinking of, sending a lady somewhere no one's heard of!'

'She seemed quite excited.'

'All the same, one can't approve.'

Matty's lip twitched. 'No. Perhaps not.'

She made another move towards the car, and suddenly Bertie was all attention, holding the door, shutting it behind her, making faces at Sasha whingeing on the back seat. Then he said, 'I wonder perhaps if you meant to shut the front door?'

'Oh my God! Yes please. If you could —'

He obliged, and brought the key ceremonially to the car. 'You aren't visiting Limbowa by any chance?' he asked wistfully.

'No. Of course not. New York. Look, I really must go. Goodbye.'

She drove quickly away, glancing in her mirror to see him standing in her drive, hand raised in a farewell salute. 'Oh, Griselda,' she muttered to herself. 'You should have stayed at home.'

Griselda sat opposite the King of Limbowa. He was of medium height with a bland, black face. The legs of his desk were made of entwined buffalo horns, and tribal masks and spears decorated the walls of this otherwise ordinary building. He wore loose white clothes and toyed with a fly whisk. It was very hot.

'It is so kind of you to receive me,' said Griselda.

The King played with his whisk. 'I was curious about you. I am told you found your accommodation less than satisfactory.'

'Merely dirty. I insisted that it be cleaned.'

'And now you are keeping goats at the Consulate? And hens and ducks?'

'Sadly the ducks died. I tried Aylesburys, quite stupid of me. Perhaps Indian Runners would be better.'

'Perhaps.'

Tea was brought in, with Sèvres china. It was rumoured that the King of Limbowa owned more diamonds than the last Tsar of Russia. Looking around her Griselda discounted that. With the occasional exception, the gloss was very thin.

'And how are you getting on with Mr Munro?'

The Consul was a grey failure of a man sent to Limbowa and forgotten. He was sick of the place and wanted to go home. 'He's enjoying our fresh produce,' said Griselda diplomatically.

'And the whisky! How he enjoys the whisky.'

'A traditional drink of our nation.'

They exchanged a meaningful glance. They each knew the conventions and they would stick to them. Only the tone of their remarks would betray them. The King leaned forward. 'Now,' he said, 'you have youth and energy. I wish you to intercede for us with your government. We want your army training. This we must have.'

'I gather you do quite some military training yourself.'

'We don't have the technology. For our brightest, they should go to Britain.'

'We should always be happy to receive approved people from Limbowa.'

'The black man needs to fight. It is no use to deny us the skills. It is the same as arming our enemies.'

Griselda felt sweat sticking her blouse to her back. She was supposed to be here to learn, not to conduct diplomacy singlehanded. She said, 'Limbowa has no enemies.' No one in their right mind would want to invade here, she thought.

He snorted. 'I am Limbowa.'

'Oh. Oh, I see.' So, there was a coup threatening. He wanted to send his bodyguard to Britain for training. Much would depend on whether he was considered a suitable king or not, and as far as she could see he was quite good. There was no more corruption than was usual for states full of tribal rivalries and the remnants of colonial rule, and much less than some. The King was ruthless in demanding medical aid and schools, but that was to his credit. He did have dungeons full of political prisoners, but few were tortured and most released within a year.

She rubbed her hands together. 'I'll write a report,' she said crisply.

'I should be much obliged.'

'You must let me know if anything causes you to believe this might be urgent.'

'Most certainly. And also I must inform the French. Should there be any urgency.'

She grimaced. 'If you must.' Surveying him down her long nose she thought he was getting off rather lightly. He shouldn't have threatened her with an alliance with the French. 'I gather some of the tourist safaris have been running into difficulties with poachers. I think they'd better have armed escorts for a while.'

'Escorts? For safaris?'

'Yes. I shall mention your forethought in my report.'

Outside the street was crowded with boys selling cigarettes and women taking goods to market. A huge poster advertised an English film, and Griselda thought she might

525

see it that night, drenched in fly repellent against the mosquitoes. She knew she was doing well here. The Consul disliked her, but that was to be expected. The people back home judged by other standards. This, her first posting, would be followed by a dozen others, and she would adapt to each and every one. She would take her English competence, her determination and energy, and create a small world for herself within this other world, that could never be hers. Her small spark of triumph flickered for a moment. She would give anything then to be back in London, with Sasha crying and Matty looking strained. Fish and chips in the paper, black taxis and traffic jams, and again, the unmatched beauty of English fields and hills in spring. The beauty of home.

An English voice cut through her thoughts. 'Hey! Hey, Griselda!' She spun round, looking for the joker who could so imitate that drawl. But there he was. Pushing through the crowds, red in the face and sweating, was Bertie Brantingham.

'By George, I thought it was you. Recognise that straight back anywhere.'

'Bertie! Dear, dear Bertie!' To her embarrassment she was crying.

'My dear girl!'

'I'm sorry. So stupid. Just so good to see you. Feeling gloomy, you know, the heat and far from home. Feeling sorry for myself.'

'Dear girl. Dear, dear girl.'

He patted her shoulder sympathetically. 'I'm working here,' Griselda explained.

'Yes. So I assumed. I'm on holiday. On safari.'

'You weren't with the lot that got shot up by poachers, were you?'

'Yes, actually. Absolutely terrifying – people running everywhere. Don't know if they thought we were game wardens or not, but our chaps were magnificent. Pitched battle in the middle of the night. They even gave me a gun and had me banging away at bushes. Couldn't see a dashed thing.'

'You could have been killed!'

'Have to admit, the thought did cross my mind. What else to do though? Bit of a problem.'

She took him back to the Consulate and gave him gin. He amused her for an hour with the tale of his exploits in the bush, and she showed him her hens and her goats. The mosquitoes were rising with the coming night, and they retreated back inside, dousing the rooms with fly spray. Griselda's cook served them both dinner, one of the hens in a stew, and they ate sweet potato and drank more gin. A little silence developed.

'You always turn up when I'm feeling at my worst,' said Griselda.

'I — can't say the same of you,' said Bertie. 'Fact is, you made me feel worse than I have ever felt. Made me feel like chucking the whole thing in.'

'I'm sure you don't mean that.'

'I was more ashamed of myself than I can say.'

'It was my fault.'

'Rubbish! I lost control. Ruined our friendship. Upset you. Unforgivable.'

Griselda nursed her glass. She felt like crying. 'Odd, really, meeting like this again.'

'Nothing odd about it. Asked your friend where you were. Matty. Nice girl, but a bit intense, don't you think? Hell of a job getting here. Had to come on holiday to get a visa, don't give them to anyone else. Nearly got shot for my pains.'

Griselda was looking bewildered. 'What did you want to see me about?'

He shrugged. 'Don't know, really. Mad idea that you might have forgiven me at last. Hated the way it was, you know. So ashamed.'

Griselda nodded. 'Me too. Moment of madness.'

'Total. Complete. Won't happen again.'

She smiled, but looked rather bitter, he thought. 'No.'

Sholto lay on the pool deck, long arms and even longer legs draped like awkward scaffolding. A fat German was sitting next to him, trying to make him talk. 'You will find me some good art? Some expensive art?'

Sholto opened half an eye. 'There is no guarantee of profit,' he murmured. 'I buy what I like.'

'Buy something for me! Something special! Go to Venice and see what you can find.'

Sholto retrieved his errant limbs, stood up and walked away.

He felt caged this morning. Yachts always had that effect, after three days he was desperate to get off and away. The drinks began before lunch and didn't end until dawn, the food was ever-present and the company relentless. He would jump ship tonight on a Greek island and head away from here. He was always heading away.

One of the women leaned down from the upper deck and waved to him. Was she last night's or the night before's? A bit of chat, a bit of laughter, and he could have anyone on this boat. The court case, with its curling mists of cynicism and celebrity, had made him very desirable, it seemed. They didn't mind his innocence; in fact, they might even have preferred his guilt. Sometimes he hated them all.

That decided him. He would get off as soon as he could. Hating women was very unhealthy. When they wanted things from him, when they needed things, he looked into their blank, soulless faces and hated himself for using them and them for being used. Where was the dignity, where was the love? None of them had it, least of all him.

He went to his cabin, and his postcards. The activity always soothed him, laying cool fingers across his brow. He stopped at a Virgin and Child, thinking of Matty, thinking of their child. He had never hated Matty. She had remained in his memory, bright and glowing, with her inner fire, her inner strength, lying like steel under a million weaknesses. And he always seemed to let her down.

He wanted to sleep but he knew he would dream. The dreams were a recent development, and one he would give anything to be without. Always the same. The old house by the quiet canal, the squeaking of water rats in the night. Hangings, heavy with dust, eating the sound of footfalls until someone was close enough to touch. How frightened he had been. How young.

His sudden rage astounded him. It was like fire, like dry

grass on a match, flaring, scorching him. That woman — that bloody, bloody old woman, with her cruelties and her strictures, her cunning, her easy use of terror to subdue a little boy! Tales of rats eating eyes while you slept, tales of horror and pain. Telling him always that he wasn't wanted, had never been wanted, had never been loved. What had she done to him? What had she done?

It was hard to breathe. The warm sea air was thick as cottonwool. Go to Venice, the German had said. He never went to Venice. Hadn't been there in years. If he wanted something there he wrote, or telephoned, or sent someone. He would not visit the place. But you do visit, his inner self told him. Every night. Every night that you dream, every night that you lie in this suffocating cabin next to some woman you hate, you are there again.

All at once he felt himself relax. Where was the point in fighting against something so strong? He would go to Venice, and he would go alone.

Matty fell on to Henrietta's doorstep clutching a pack of nappies, a box of silver and the baby.

'Dear, dear Matty!' said Henrietta, ushering her inside. 'You look like death. Nanny can take Sasha and I can look after you.'

'She cried all the way,' confessed Matty. 'I walked up and down the plane until I thought my legs would fall off. I have walked across the Atlantic.'

'You should have a nanny,' said Henry comfortably. 'Much better for your nerves.'

Matty felt poor and neurotic.

She revived after a bath and a meal. Sasha was staking her claim to the opulent Cooke nursery, galloping round it at a crawl. She and Tyler seemed fascinated with each other, and sat for minutes in silent contemplation, refusing to touch.

'She's very forward,' said Henry, feeling insecure. Next to Sasha's energy and fractiousness, Tyler seemed worryingly placid.

'She's hyperactive,' said Matty. 'At least, that's what it feels like. Hardly sleeps at all.'

'They have clinics for that over here.'

'We just have nervous breakdowns.'

But in this warm, pretty household she was relaxing. Tyler Senior was anxious to be the perfect host, and hovered, unsure if he was wanted. Henry included him with determined welcome, reminiscent of her mother. Every now and then she would tell him to do something, and off he would go, good as gold.

'You're very happy, aren't you?' said Matty, in one of his absences.

Henry nodded. 'We're blissful. I don't feel I deserve it.'

Her good fortune seemed very apparent just now. Matty was so obviously weary and strung out, with appointments and anxieties, and no one at all to turn to at night. 'You really should marry again,' she said.

Matty shrugged. 'Perhaps.'

They talked about Miller and the longed-for operation. 'In a way I don't want it to work,' said Henry. 'She lives for that kid. If he could see she wouldn't have a reason any more.'

'Course she would.' Matty was emphatic. 'People are so greedy. They always think if they get what they want they'll never want again, but they do. Five minutes is all it takes.'

'Not for something real! Not something this important!'

'Henry, you're still such a romantic.'

They were on edge again, and uncomfortable. Henrietta said, 'I'm trying to be sensible, Matty. To do the right thing. I could pay for the operation and everything just like that, but it seems to me this isn't about money. It's about Lorne's self-respect. It's all gone, you see. I know you don't understand but she hates herself, and that's awful, so ugly, so —'

'I know all about that,' said Matty.

'Lorne thinks you and Griselda will despise her. You were always so hard on people who didn't do the right thing.'

Matty said, 'I don't know about Grizz but I don't despise too many people any more. I grew out of it. I don't do the right thing all that often myself.'

Henry talked on, but Matty wasn't listening. Had she

530

really been so rigid in the past? She looked back on her young self with distaste, remembering how clear everything had seemed, with right and wrong as different goals on a football field, acres apart. It wasn't goodness that had made her so priggish. It was fear. The devil-may-care girl had entered adulthood with the curse of dishonesty to frighten her, waiting to bring her down.

'We ought to help Lorne get out of this by herself,' she said suddenly.

Henry made a face. 'If you could see her, Matty! She's in no state.'

'We can help her, but we shouldn't do it all.' Matty got up and walked around, restlessly. 'She made one bad move and had a lot of bad luck. She thinks it's all her own fault, when it could have happened to anyone. She needs to cheat those Berensons out of lots of money, and she needs to get something on them. Something big. Because then she'll be free.'

Henrietta looked plainly doubtful. 'I'll just give her the money,' she said quickly.

'No!'

'Then what do we do? I don't know!'

Matty chewed on a nail. 'Neither do I.'

The best way to approach Venice is from the sea. The city is spread before you like a medieval painting, and the sky is a limitless frame. But this time Sholto took the train. He didn't want to be seduced by the place. He had no use for its wiles.

He took the vaporetto from the station. It was very crowded, even so early in the year. As a child he had hated the summer, he remembered. He had hated the tourists clogging his streets, using his shops, admiring the backcloth that made up his life. So he had loved the place once, he thought. He had hated the consumption of something he thought of as his.

The dank, dead fish smell caught in his throat. He felt like crying. That was the trouble with smells, they transported you to another time, they made memories live. He looked around for his friend Alberto, who used to work the run from the station, but the men were unfamiliar to him. He wouldn't know anyone now.

Alighting, he was caught up in the crowd. They moved him with them, exclaiming and taking pictures, and he had to hold back, waiting until they left him behind, like flotsam in a wave. Someone called him.

'Hola! Sholto!' And Alberto it was, fat and going grey, his big hands greasy from the ropes. Suddenly Sholto was a boy again. He found himself blinking hard, and the man's arm was around him, the Italian like bubbles in a bottle, and suddenly he remembered it all, the journey that brought him to this.

'Old friend. Good friend.'

'So many years! Made your money, huh, at last to come back? Thought you were never coming back.'

'I wasn't. I don't know why I'm here.'

'To see your friends, to see me! Come, come, let's have a drink together. Let's talk. The old place doesn't change. More tourists and more stink, that's all.'

They went to a café and gradually men drifted up. Sholto shook hands, he drank red wine and then brandy. One old man, more daring than the rest, put a wizened finger against Sholto's scar. He whistled through his teeth. 'The old woman's still living, you know. Still at it.'

'Thought she must be. I'd have heard.'

'Wrong in the head, the old witch. Everyone used to say.'

'Did they? I never heard.'

'You were too young. We did what we could.'

He remembered. People had been kind. When he wanted to go anywhere, he always travelled free; if he wanted to look in a house the door was open. He had wandered through Venice guided by caring hands. They knew how it was.

He got up, shook hands and picked up his jacket. One of the men from the gondolas felt the material and waggled his head. 'Silk these days? Silk? I remember the days you had no seat in your pants.'

'He always had a brain,' said Alberto. 'We knew he'd do well.'

When he walked away from them he felt lonely suddenly.

The day had slipped away somewhere, it was late afternoon and cool. The wash of passing boats caused the water to suck at the old stones, and there was a slick of grease on everything. An old woman was dusting worn gilt panels on a door and always in the distance he could hear tourists, chattering like birds.

He knew the way so well. Every step, every stone was known to him. Here the cobbles, there the slabs, there the little shop selling curios. Not many shops here, for the houses were big and sumptuous, owned by people rich enough to have their shopping done by others. The windows at the front had the canal lapping at their sills, but at the back, they led to the shady street.

When he stopped at the door he felt exhaustion like never before. He felt as if he had climbed a dozen mountains, run a million races. He could not climb those steps. He could never knock. The paint had been worn before but now it was all gone, and the wood had turned a silvery grey. The knocker, in the shape of a fish, mocked him with a glassy stare.

Why hadn't he stayed on the yacht? Why couldn't he bury the years and have them stay buried? Why did they come back again and again? He was so tired, so terribly tired. Never once had he come willingly to this door.

He went up the steps and knocked. It echoed, as always, and in a while the maid came and slid the panel to look at him through the grille.

'Yes?'

'I have come to see my aunt.'

'I will speak with her.'

'No. You will let me in. If you don't she'll be cross.'

She was a new maid and frightened of doing the wrong thing. She unbolted the door and stood aside as he entered.

He felt dizzy for a moment, as if he might faint. The place even smelled the same, cooler than outside, a dark odour of must. The good bureau still stood in the hall, the gilding tarnished and the inlay in need of cleaning. He hung on to consciousness, fixing his mind on small things. The old woman must be feeling her age. At last. She never used to let good pieces go.

He pushed the maid aside and went down the corridor. Years and years of walking this passage, hating this passage, hating her. He had walked it in his dreams as often. It was as if he had never left. He had stepped here yesterday, a small boy, his hand too small for the twisted brass handle of the door. He had grown in a day, a boy to a man, and the knob was nothing.

She was sitting in her chair, like anyone. Like any old woman, even old Mrs Waterman who could hardly move. She seemed smaller, and her shoulders had bent. She had a folder open on her knees and it was full of postcards. Art postcards. Just like him.

After a moment she looked up at him. Her face became very still.

'Hello, Aunt Theresa.'

'Sholto.' Her hands trembled on the folder. She said, 'Damn you, boy, don't you ever go away?'

'I've been away for years. You must be losing your mind.'

She shut her folder with a snap. 'Don't be rude. You always were rude. Right from the first day.'

Rage rose up in him, almost too much to bear. He shook with the strain of holding it in. Even his voice shook. 'You bitch. You were a bitch then and you still are.'

She lifted her eyebrows at that. She had always had good eyebrows, fine and well arched. 'I see you have come here to berate me,' she said mildly.

She always made it hard for him to talk. He could hardly talk now. 'Perhaps I came here to kill you.'

'Don't be stupid! You never did have the courage.' She looked away, back at her postcards, as if she had lost interest in him, even in his threats. The familiar, so familiar helplessness came again. She hated him, she hated everything about him. All the hours in the dark, all the days without food, all the petty deprivations, had been because of that.

'You could have sent me away.' He sounded plaintive. He despised himself. 'I could have gone to school. To someone else. Why didn't you?'

She folded her old hands together. Her nails were long and still well kept. He loathed women with smooth hands, he thought. She said, 'I liked having you. I liked having you

534

run around trying to please me. And I liked it when you stopped trying, when you tried in your childish way to have your revenge. It was a war. A very interesting war.'

'You corrupted me!'

'I educated you. I taught you strength, such as you know, I taught you art! Don't tell me you'd be here now in all your finery if I hadn't taught you that.'

'I'm not so fine,' he said.

She almost spat at him. 'You never were! You just looked it. You looked like a beautiful, tragic angel. And I was never so happy — never so at peace — as the day I saw that beauty go.'

That day. Strange, it was never in his nightmares. Even now he could hardly remember anything, just the terrible, lurching drop when the roof gave way. The pain came later. Agony, of the mind as much as the body, cringing away from each and every clumsy stitch. Her eyes, brilliantly shining, watching him.

He reached up and touched his scar. The ridges, the puckers, mocked him every day. 'I knew you were pleased,' he murmured. 'Why?'

She looked thoughtful, and almost abstracted. 'How hard it is to understand one's own motivations. One should try, I suppose. I disliked your resemblance to me. I was beautiful as a girl. Very beautiful. But you were better. Those looks were better on a boy. Also, I disliked the effect of your appearance. On me. I have a natural affinity for beauty in anything, and to have a beautiful child in my home was disturbing. I knew I had to guard against you. Protect myself.'

'You don't protect yourself from children! You love them!'

She lifted her head then. He saw again the majestic figure of his youth, wearing her topaz brooch and her heavy lace, bearing down on him with a stone cold face. 'I only loved once,' she said. 'My brother, your father, sent him away. He was Italian and unsuitable. He caught pneumonia and died. As he came from Venice, I decided that here I would live. So wise a decision for a collector. I have made it my life's work to acquire beautiful things.'

He couldn't believe it. There had to be some better reason, some terrible thing he had done. Perhaps he had broken something, ruined a precious picture. 'Was that all?' he asked miserably. 'You hated my father?'

She shrugged. 'I couldn't hate him. He wasn't here. I hated you.'

The maid scratched on the door and brought in a tray of tea. 'You will take tea?' enquired his aunt. 'I have some paintings I wish to show you.' She was like any old woman, anyone at all. If they saw her now no one would ever believe what she had done.

'Aren't you ashamed?' asked Sholto. 'Don't you think you were cruel?'

She poured two cups of tea. 'I taught you what I know. Besides, you behave as if it was always. It was sometimes. When I felt — restless.' Her hand closed on the sugar tongs, a grip of cruel force. 'Sometimes I felt a demon. It came out and bit me and I needed to bite you. Needed to strike at your beautiful, beautiful face.'

'I have that same demon,' said Sholto.

'You? I doubt it. You never had the steel. All sweetness and kindness, that's what you were, like a sickly chocolate. If you have a demon then thank me for it. It adds interest to what would otherwise cloy.'

She had gone too far. Suddenly he had to strike back. He went to the wall, seized a picture and flung it down. He took another and another, smashing them against the furniture, leaving gashes and chips.

She put up her hands and cried out at him: 'You've gone mad! You're insane!'

'I want to do this to you! This is what I long to do to you!'

'Then do it! Do it! But don't spoil the art. Whatever you do, don't spoil the art. There's so little of it and it's so precious.'

He stopped, panting. One of the canvases was ripped horribly, irreparably. He ran his hand tenderly over the slash. 'See what you made me do.'

'Do you mean to torture me? Kill me?'

He shook his head.

It was night when he left. As the door banged shut behind

536

him he felt weightless suddenly. I don't have to stay there ever again, he thought. I can come out into the cold night air. I can go and I can come back, just as I please, when I please, never if that's what I want. Or I can come every day and see what she is; just a bitter, vicious old woman.

God, but he felt good. He hadn't felt so good in years. He would go to the big hotel where he used to stand looking mournful and hope the tourists would give him money, and he would pay a king's ransom he didn't have for a room with a balcony overlooking the canal. He'd have champagne and a good steak, served in his room. He'd watch television. Afterwards, dreamlessly, he would sleep.

Chapter Thirty-One

Griselda sat under her mosquito net, trying to read. Sweat was dripping off her nose on to the page and her armpits itched with prickly heat. Her drink, filled with crushed ice only two minutes ago, was now warm as tea.

The Limbowans claimed that the weather was unseasonal, but as far as she could judge this level of heat and humidity, together with a plague of flies, struck every year. No one made provision for it, merely expressing surprise that such a thing should occur, again. They seemed to live in the hope that one day it would simply not.

She sighed. Her spirits were very low today. It was just that Bertie's visa had expired and he had left for the airport this morning. It was awfully dull without him. If he was still here they would have spent this torrid afternoon at the river, since Bertie seemed able to repel hordes of curious Limbowans with one glare of his mild blue eyes. Alone, she did not dare swim for fear of being laughed at and embarrassed. It was good of Bertie to stay so long, she thought. Awfully good of him.

Another three months before she could go home. A lifetime. In actual fact there was little point in being in Limbowa during the hot − hotter − weather, because no one with any sense visited the place and all business closed down. But the King liked to summon the diplomats to his palace from time to time. It made a change. Different mosquitoes.

Sighing, she crawled from beneath her net and staggered into the shower. Refreshing as it was, the effect never lasted more than a few minutes, and at some times of the day they turned the water off. It was best to shower every hour if you could. As she emerged, dripping, she caught sight of herself in the fly-specked mirror. She looked terrible, gaunt, hollow-eyed, with flat breasts topped by big red nipples. Her ribs showed, her belly was almost concave and her pubic hair a nasty scrub of brown. Legs like spaghetti were terminated in big flat feet, to conclude a symphony of unattractiveness. Suddenly she felt aghast at the unfairness of it all, that she should have not a single good feature when people like Lorne had nothing but. Even Henrietta had graduated from plump girlishness into rounded womanhood, while Griselda only became more string and bone. If only, just once, she could be attractive, she thought. It would be something to look back on, like that time with Bertie, on which she based all her night-time imaginings.

There was a commotion in the street. She went to the window and looked out, although the pane was misty and the scene blurred. Men were running up and down waving clubs. The clubs did not surprise her but the running did. Something desperate must be happening for people to run in this heat. Griselda knotted the sash of her robe tightly around herself and went to the door. Men were screaming and rolling their eyes, beside themselves with excitement. There was blood on the dirt road and a man was crawling away, wailing and clutching his head. A riot, she thought excitedly. This is a riot.

'What's happening? What's wrong?' She grasped the arm of a passer-by and held him firmly.

'We kill the King! The King!'

'Good heavens.' She let him go. Had they killed the King, or did they only mean to? If the street were to be imminently raked with gunfire and teargas, what should she do? Set the goats free. It was only sensible.

She went to the rear of the house and out into the subdued jungle of the garden. The goats lived in a hut thatched with palm leaves and the hens scratched around them, periodically picked off by snakes, wild dogs and hungry natives. A small gate in the back fence led to strips of farmland. The goats would be safe enough there.

A man was crouched by the goat hut. She could see only his hunched back, but it was enough. One of the rioters, no doubt.

'I can see you. What do you want?' she said loudly.

The figure uncurled and stood up. Wielding his fly whisk, in stained white clothes, was the King.

'Miss Lemming-Knott, I am so glad it is you.'

'Er – yes. Your Majesty. Can I invite you – ?' Her mind buzzed with the problems of protocol. Should she at once summon the Consul? There wasn't much point, he would be drunk.

'If I could trouble your hospitality for a brief time?'

They went into the house. Griselda prudently drew the curtains across the windows. 'I imagine you'd rather not be seen.'

'Most thoughtful.' He sat himself down in her armchair and looked about him. 'I see you have some whisky.'

'Yes. Do you take water with it?'

'A little Perrier. Thank you.'

Outside the riot was growing. Men were chanting furiously. 'They'll tire soon,' said the King. 'Tonight they will start in earnest.'

Griselda sipped her own drink. 'Do I take it your bodyguard has deserted?'

'To a man. Bribed. But there you are, they were not trained as I wished. You took too long, Miss Lemming-Knott.'

'I am sorry.'

A rock crashed against the door. 'Dear me,' said Griselda.

The King looked quizzical. 'You are very calm. My wives are all in hysterics.'

'I'm not your wife.'

'I have often thought that you should be. Your wonderful intelligence! Your calm!'

'You're very kind.'

The noises in the street began to fade. Griselda said, 'Were you planning to stay long?'

'A few hours, only. A plane is coming at midnight. I shall have to try for the airport later on.'

Griselda got up. 'I shall give orders to have another place

541

set at dinner. I can trust my servants, there shouldn't be trouble.'

They dined together on goat and sweet potato with a warm white wine. When she went to ask for ice she found the house empty, for the servants had run away. Anxiety began to trouble her, but the gunfire was across the city, erratic and unthreatening. A light appeared in the sky and the King said, 'Now the palace is burning.'

'What about your wives?'

He shrugged. 'Most are by the sea with the children. The ones remaining are not important.'

She tried not to show that she was shocked. But he laughed and said, 'You English! So sentimental.'

The meal over, they drank more whisky, thankful for cooler air. The King loosened his sash, revealing three handguns and some exposed black flesh. Griselda was still in her bathrobe, and wrapped it around herself virtuously. 'How do you mean to get to the airport?' she asked.

He smiled. 'In your car, Miss Lemming-Knott. I trust that will be convenient?'

'I really don't — I'm not sure —' Aiding and abetting escaping leaders was not generally considered good policy for someone of her junior status. 'Perhaps we should consult the Consul.'

'We shall not. Don't worry, please. I am well armed.'

She looked at her watch. Not yet nine. The street outside was becoming active again, she had visions of being involved in a firefight. But the King was thinking of something else. He stood up in a swirl of robes and came towards her. 'Miss Lemming-Knott, I want you.'

She took a moment or two to understand. Then she waved her hands at him, quite without result. He advanced with determined purpose.

'Please! I don't think — oh, my goodness!' His hand reached unerringly for her breast. His palm was hot against her nipple, and she sat for vital seconds, rigid with shock. She had never before realised that he had such large hands.

'You know you excite me,' he said throatily. 'So thin. Like a starved lioness. I have loved a thousand women, but never one like you!'

If only it wasn't so hot. It sapped her resolve. 'Do stop it. Please,' she said feebly, as he pulled her robe open and exposed her. She should never have had the whisky. His black hands on her skin were outrageous − she felt a delicious resignation.

He pushed her from the chair to the floor, businesslike, as if she was one of the endless wives. The gunfire was close again, but Griselda didn't care. The King's big fingers were touching her, and then he grunted as he lay on her body. She could feel the guns against her skin, and he smelled strongly of gun oil. He went into her, like a gun into its case, and she groaned. God, but she needed this. Years and years of loneliness, and just that one night, when she had been too upset for pleasure. Outside the gunshots and inside the pounding, and her long fingers digging into his clothes, her bony knees spread wide, her flat breasts gripped by his hot palms as she suffered waves of crashing excitement. As it ebbed they fell away from each other. He got up and straightened his clothes.

'Very good, Miss Lemming-Knott,' he said briskly. 'I found you most satisfying. We shall now drive to the airport.'

He lay on the back seat of the car under a blanket as she drove. It was unreal. When a patrol of armed men waved her down she pulled up quite calmly and said, 'I'm from the Consulate and I've got to get to the airport. Is it still open?'

They didn't understand her and argued amongst themselves, debating whether to steal the car. 'Thank you so much,' said Griselda, and accelerated away, scattering them like chickens before her wheels. Gunfire followed her and she drove like the wind, past a burning truck, a gaggle of drunks, a machine gun mounted on a car that could not swivel in time to shoot at her. But she stopped when she saw the airport. It was in flames.

'I don't think you're going to get away,' she said blankly.

The King surfaced, and looked with interest at the conflagration. 'What time is it?'

'Almost twelve.'

'Then I must take my leave. Goodbye, Miss Lemming-

543

Knott.' He reached into his robes and withdrew a leather pouch. 'I give you the stone pearls,' he said. 'Limbowa's most precious jewels. They are given into the keeping of the woman the King most favours. Normally they are taken back with the favour, but I trust you to do with them as you see fit.'

'Of course. Certainly. Most flattered.' Griselda took the pouch in astonishment.

'Ah,' said the King. 'How I long for a hundred nights with you!'

'Indeed,' said Griselda. 'Couldn't agree more.'

He was gone into the night, heading across the fields to the ring of fire that was the airport. Briefly, outlined for only a second, she saw a small plane against the flames, touching down like a gnat on the furthest edge of the field. Minutes later it was up again, flitting away into blackness. She looked down at the pouch in her hand, and opened it. Two pearls, like long tears, lay gleaming in the darkness. They were lustrous, as long as her thumbnail, a gift of a king to a courtesan. This king, lover of so many, had thought her the best. She wrapped the pearls carefully and put them in her pocket.

An explosion in the distance made her turn. The city was blazing now, thatch and wood igniting in an instant. Now she dared not go back. She started the car again and drove cautiously forward, wondering if other foreigners might be sheltering somewhere. A roadblock stretched ahead, manned by white men with shotguns, and the Consul, hip flask in hand, flagged her down. 'Thank God you're here, woman! What took so long?'

'I didn't know we were evacuating,' said Griselda.

'Of course we are! Place is in turmoil. There's an American plane going in half an hour, and that's the last. The rebels are everywhere. Surprised you got through.'

'Good of you to worry,' said Griselda.

She parked the car and walked to the concrete building that served as a terminal. The lights had gone but it was lit by burning sheds and planes. A single American jet stood in the midst of everything, a fuel bowser urgently pumping gas. A small group of people waited restlessly, and one of them gave a cry of joy. 'Griselda! Thank God!'

'Bertie!' She put out her arms and embraced him.

He had passed an eventful day. His plane had been hijacked by rebels minutes before take-off, and they had been removed just before it was set on fire. After that the army stormed the airfield and then left again, the rebels shelled the runways and Bertie had climbed from ditch to shellcrater and back again, because there seemed nothing else sensible to do. 'Would have fetched you, old girl, but it wasn't looking too promising,' he confided. 'Almost resorted to prayer at one point.'

'I was fine,' said Griselda. 'Town was fairly peaceful in comparison, nothing until late afternoon. Do you think we'll get away?'

'No bloody idea.' He coloured. 'Don't care so much, now. If we're together and all that. Don't want to embarrass you and so on, but –'

'I love you, Bertie,' said Griselda.

He blinked his pale eyes. 'Yes. Rather what I wanted to say. I know it's not really your thing, but –'

'Yes it is,' said Griselda. 'I was in a muddle before. It is my thing. Absolutely.'

His heavy face lightened. 'Thank heavens for that! Rather starting to despair, if you must know. Get the whole thing legalised when we get home, eh? Sell the blasted house if we have to. Sell a farm. Something.'

Griselda fingered the leather pouch in her pocket. 'I don't know,' she said. 'Something may turn up.'

When Matty returned from a sale she found Henry agog. 'Look who's arrived!' she said excitedly. 'We wanted her and she's come.'

It was Griselda, brown as a berry, her hair grown long, and with a new, relaxed confidence. She was wearing khaki trousers and a washed out khaki shirt, giving her the slightly leathery look of a memsahib. 'You look great,' said Matty, moving to kiss her. 'How's Bertie and how's Limbowa?'

'You might well ask,' said Griselda. She leaned back in her chair with her hands behind her head. Matty and

545

Henrietta put their heads on one side, like a pair of ducks, and Griselda chuckled.

'You haven't!' said Henry. 'Oh, Grizz, I'm so pleased!'

'Bertie's gone home to talk to my father,' said Griselda. 'He's so old fashioned.'

'Isn't he just!' Matty flung up her hand as if in a swoon. 'How did he manage to convince you he wasn't simply doing the decent thing?'

Griselda snorted with laughter. 'I was a bit of a fool, wasn't I?'

'Total, complete and unforgivable,' said Matty. 'Have you heard about Lorne?'

Griselda nodded. 'Henry was saying. Really, that girl!'

'Grizz,' said Matty warningly. 'You can't be jealous any more, you know.'

She opened her mouth to deny anything of the kind. But it wasn't worth denying any more. The trap Lorne had fallen into wasn't laid for girls like her, so in the end she had been the more fortunate.

'Poor old Lorne,' she said simply.

They talked for hours about what they might do. They thought of blackmail, they thought of theft, and Henry even toyed with the unlikely possibility that they could saw through brake cables and have done with Sherwood forever.

'I wouldn't know a brake cable if I saw one!' said Matty in horror. 'We'd have to go to classes for weeks, and afterwards everyone would know.'

'We don't want to go to prison,' said Griselda firmly. 'No, we want to defraud the man with subtlety. We need to get him to part with a large sum of money for something worth not very much.'

Matty was silent for a moment. Then she got up and left the room, coming back a few moments later with a newspaper-wrapped parcel. She took out her silver bowl and set it on the table, all by itself.

'Wow!' said Henrietta.

'A little bit too much, Matty,' said Griselda. 'We want a pretend fortune, not a real one.'

'It's a fake,' said Matty, and put her head in her hands. It was the Sprimont bowl again. 'I saw this bowl years ago,' she explained. 'At least, a bowl like this. I don't know how the man got it but I bet it wasn't legal. Anyway, I took photographs and things. And then − well, I had an idea. A stupid idea. There's this man makes silver for me, lots of things, and I asked him − I didn't mean to sell it, I promise!'

'You must have done,' said Griselda. 'Really, Matty! You!'

'I know.' Matty ducked her head. 'But Sholto borrowed so much. He pays when he can, but his assets were frozen with this law suit so it wasn't any use to go crying to him. I thought we might lose the house. We still might. And Simon loves it so, and there's Sasha − I only meant to find some awful man I didn't like very much and relieve him of ill-gotten gains. I wasn't going to defraud a museum or anything.'

After a while Griselda said, 'Sholto had a terrible effect on you, Matty.'

But her friend blazed at her. 'No he didn't! If anything he showed me what was important in life, and it isn't money, or houses, or anything like that. It's inside. But I was tempted, and nearly forgot.'

Henrietta picked up the bowl and turned it curiously in her hands. 'Can anyone tell the difference?'

'Doubt it,' said Matty. 'Greensall took months to make the thing. In a way it was good, because I couldn't sell too much and it took up his time. He's a bit weird, you see, has to be busy.'

'There must be something says it's a fake,' said Griselda. 'If the real thing was here would nobody be able to tell?'

'I suppose I would,' said Matty. 'I mean, the patina would be different. And every craftsman has his style. This is more Greensall than Sprimont, and I think I can tell because I know Greensall. If you didn't you'd not have much of a chance.'

'The world could be full of fakes,' said Henry in amazement.

Matty nodded. 'It probably is. But as long as no one knows, everyone's happy.'

They digested this extraordinary piece of information.

'So,' said Griselda, 'we have our expensive piece. How do we make Berenson part with good money for it? Does he collect silver?'

Henry made a rude noise. 'Like hell. Only scalps.'

'He'd collect it if he thought it would make him money,' said Matty.

Griselda said, 'I think I have the germ of an idea.'

Much had changed at the Shuster place. When the girls got out of the car they looked around at the unkempt grass, the weedy flowerbeds and the unpainted fences with a sense of shock. Here was a farm fallen on very hard times. But there were still fine horses in the meadow, and Aunt Susan still came down the steps calling, 'Girls! Why, how good it is to have you come.'

They clustered around her affectionately. She was older, with lines crossing her forehead and cheeks. When they went in the house they saw spaces on the walls where pictures had once hung, and Aunt Susan said, 'I have Miller with me today. He's the sweetest little boy. Don't make too much noise or he gets scared.'

They stood in the doorway and watched him toddling around the room. He reached unerringly for what he wanted, rattling this and banging that, his head tilted upward as he sought for every last fraction of sound. 'Hello, Miller,' said Henry, and he stopped, putting his head towards them, quite sightless. Griselda put her hand over her mouth.

'Come and say hello,' said Aunt Susan, and they went to kneel on the floor with him and play.

When Aunt Susan put him down for his nap, Matty said, 'I take it back. Let's saw through Berenson's brake cables.'

'It isn't his fault the child's blind,' said Griselda.

'But to use that as a threat! To threaten to keep him that way!' Matty was appalled.

Aunt Susan brought them tea, and they sat in long chairs on the porch and talked to her. 'I remember this place as so prosperous,' said Matty bluntly.

Aunt Susan coloured. 'It always seemed so, didn't it? We haven't paid our way for years. When Lorne married Greg

Berenson we thought perhaps we might earn some grace, but it didn't work out.'

'Berenson charges you interest, I take it?' said Griselda.

'I don't think I can discuss our private affairs. If you don't mind, Griselda.'

'But you know that's why Lorne married Greg? And why she stays with him? To stop Sherwood turning you out?'

'She doesn't know about our problems,' said Aunt Susan. 'I have never told her and she doesn't know.'

'Sherwood Berenson told her,' said Matty. 'Before the wedding.'

For a long moment Aunt Susan said nothing. Finally she looked round at all three of them. 'I do know that,' she said. 'For a long time I've pretended that I don't. But I know. And I don't care what it costs me, or Drake, or anyone, we have to rescue her. Please.'

'That's why we're here,' said Matty.

Griselda leaned forward enthusiastically. 'You've got to hold a party. One last, wild Shuster thrash. Invite everyone, all the people you know.'

'We know half the State!'

'Make sure it's the top half,' said Griselda.

The guest list included governors and senators, old money and new, horse people and city people. Henrietta added sundry Cooke relations, Griselda threw in a few aristocrats who happened to be on the wrong side of the Atlantic, and of course they invited the Berensons. The girls flung themselves into an orgy of refurbishment, gardening, painting, scrubbing, borrowing, until the house looked something like the past. Matty spent a day excavating tiny weeds from the gravel, while Henry scrubbed white pillars with bleach and Griselda persuaded an antique shop to lend them paintings for the night. Aunt Susan sold a necklace and Drake a good horse, and the funds bought champagne and good bourbon. Then the Shuster cousins arrived and brought moonshine, and staged races in the paddocks even before the party had begun.

It was a wonderful night. Drake Shuster revived an old custom and set flaming torches along the drive, and a band played and people danced, and everywhere voices could be heard saying, 'This is just like the old days. We don't have parties like this any more.' But Matty chewed her fingers until the Berensons arrived. Greg, as good-looking as ever, Sherwood with his calm, blank face, and Lorne.

She almost failed to recognise her. She seemed so small, in a tight black dress that showed a waist so narrow it might break. Her face was nothing but eyes and bones, the skin stretched over her teeth.

'She looks horrific,' murmured Matty.

'The living dead.' Griselda went across and embraced her. But even as she tried to draw Lorne away, Sherwood put out his restraining hand.

'Now see here, Lorne, we've people to meet.'

'Griselda — I'm sorry, I'll come later. I must —'

'Nonsense!' Griselda bestowed a smile of glittering falsity on Sherwood. 'Lorne has her friends to see. Come along, Lorne.'

As she drew Lorne inexorably away, the girl said, 'Let go, Grizz! I've got to get back, you don't know how he is. He gets so angry — Grizz, please.'

'We want him angry,' said Griselda. 'Angry and irrational. We want him to decide to do us down.'

'What are you up to? Why are you here?' Lorne stopped and stared at her friend. 'You've come to gloat, haven't you? Because I've made a mess of my life.'

'If I ever gloated, I'm sorry,' said Griselda. 'I'm not doing it now. Really. We came to help, all of us. To do down Sherwood so you can be free.'

Matty and Henrietta joined them. 'It's bound to work out, Lorne,' said Matty.

But Lorne looked very old suddenly, and very tired. 'Suppose it doesn't? To you, it's just a game. But my parents could lose their home and I could lose my little boy. They could take him from me, you know. Get all their lawyers to say I'm an unfit person. Have you thought of that?'

'They wouldn't.' Matty was incredulous.

Lorne shrugged her thin shoulders.

Griselda said, 'Isn't it worth the risk? You can't go on like this. If it all goes wrong then we'll sort it out somehow, but suppose it goes right? Lorne, you could be free. Free to start again.'

Lorne looked at their bright, eager faces. She felt drained of strength tonight. The men did as they wished with her, pushed her here and there, and her only resistance was inertia. She had forgotten what it was to have her future in her own hands. There was no future.

'We've got someone we want you to dance with,' said Henrietta. She took Lorne's arm and steered her across the room. A tall man was standing by himself, broad-shouldered, prosperous-looking.

'Mr Stavinsky,' said Henry. 'This is Lorne Berenson.'

'How do you do.' He inclined himself from the waist. Mid-European, thought Lorne. Matty's sort.

He danced well, but she could not concentrate, aware of Greg's eyes following her around the room, and Sherwood's laugh booming out from his small coterie of influential men. They wouldn't be pleased with her. They always hated any evidence of independence, and afterwards they made her pay. Greg tonight and Sherwood tomorrow, in the long, hot afternoon.

' – and I hope very much that Mrs Feversham will buy it,' the man was saying.

'What?'

'My bowl. A family treasure. Mrs Feversham assures me she will buy.' He dropped his voice confidentially. 'We need the money, of course. I am from East Germany. It is best to sell for dollars.'

'Yes. I'm sure it is.'

The dance was over and he let her go. She was confused. Why did Matty have a customer here? Did her mother know him? She moved to Aunt Susan's side. 'Who's that?'

'Who, darling? Oh, someone of Matty's. She's trying to keep him sweet while she raises some cash to buy something from him. I don't know what.'

'He didn't have to come to the party!'

'Don't you like him? He seemed quite respectable –'

'Mother, have you gone insane? This must be costing a fortune! How are you going to pay?'

Her mother drew back slightly and quelled her with a

look. 'Not here, Lorne honey. If your father and I choose to hold a party that is our business and not yours.'

'But it is mine! Mother –' But her mother walked quickly away.

Lorne turned to find Matty bearing down on her. 'Why did you stop dancing? Lorne, will you please go and keep him sweet! It's really important.'

'Why? Matty, will you tell me what's going on?'

Matty looked around furtively. 'I can't tell you now. Just go and be nice to him. Please.'

Puzzled, Lorne went back to tall Mr Stavinsky. They danced again and he talked all the time about his bowl. 'Shall I show it to you? Perhaps you may wish to buy it? Americans are so rich.'

'Yes – er – thank you.'

He went out to the hall and pulled a cardboard box from under the coatstand. From it he extracted a large silver bowl. 'Isn't it beautiful? So fine. Will someone here want to buy it? Will you?'

Before she could stop him he was back in the party, bowl in hand, offering it to anyone who would look. Intercepting a horrified glance from Matty, Lorne tugged on his arm. 'Mr Stavinsky, this isn't the time or the place – shall we take it somewhere secure? It's a beautiful bowl.'

'You want to buy my bowl?'

'Er – Mrs Feversham wants to buy it, doesn't she?'

'Does she have the money? I must have a lot of money.'

Matty made faces, Aunt Susan mouthed at her, and everyone else watched. Lorne coaxed him out of the room, finally persuading him to let her put the bowl in her father's safe. 'I only want a million dollars,' he said.

'Only?'

'Don't you think it's worth that? Mrs Feversham will pay that.'

'Then probably it's worth it. I don't know.'

She got back into the room, away from him, and made straight for Matty. 'Why is that lunatic here? Why don't you buy his bowl if you want it?'

Matty made a face. 'Why not indeed? It's worth five times what he thinks.'

'What? Five million?'

'It's a Sprimont, but he doesn't know. And I haven't got the million he wants. I'm dead scared he'll go to someone else but Henry's funds are in trust or something, and no one else has a bean. What about Sherwood?'

Lorne stood back a little. 'This is your plot, isn't it?' she said softly. 'Who is that man?'

Matty shrugged. 'Mr Stavinsky. Go and tell the tale to Sherwood, Lorne. Ask him to lend me a million dollars. Tell him why.'

'He won't lend you a nickel. He'll buy it himself.'

Matty lifted her eyebrows. 'Will he? Oh dear.'

Lorne moved away. She half hid behind a curtain, watching the throng. Mr Stavinsky continued on his way, telling anyone who would listen about his bowl. Politicians were talking together, slapping backs, and Shuster cousins were everywhere, charming and wild. She had been like that once, she thought. The great family beauty.

Sherwood was planning to take this house. He had been planning it for years. He would do it quietly, forcing her parents to move out and moving the Berenson clan in, her and Greg included. She would give the move respectability, prevent all that nasty publicity he so disliked. She couldn't bear to see them here.

She moved from behind her curtain and went to Greg's side. The gleam in his eye told her he was drinking hard. 'Greg, can you ask Sherwood something?'

'And what would I want to ask him, honey?'

'To lend Matty some money. I know he lends money to people, he won't mind being asked. A lot of money.'

'You look real sexy tonight, Lorne. Everyone notices. I like you looking sexy.'

'Greg, will you talk to Sherwood?'

His eyes followed the backside of a young girl. 'You want to go home, Lorne?'

'It's all right, Greg. Forget it.'

He was turning into a real lush. She turned away, in search of Sherwood, hearing Greg catch a girl around the waist and say, 'Hey, but you're the pretty one!' The man was becoming an embarrassment.

Sherwood came up behind her, giving her a fright. 'You're getting all steamed up about something,' he said.

'Greg's drunk.' She looked past him, trying not to show that she was scared. He always knew what she was thinking, he saw through her little plots. He might see right through to this one. 'I want you to lend Matty a million dollars,' she said on a rising note.

He stook looking at her, half smiling, not very tall, and she felt a sudden, desperate urge to tell him everything. Perhaps, if she gave up even her little struggles, he would be kind to her. Their life together was almost like being married, and she was used to his humiliations. If she was very good and did as he said then everything might be right.

'I wouldn't lend that girl a gun to shoot herself.'

'But you must! I mean — that's why my mother's giving the party. If Matty can borrow the money she can make a huge profit, and I mean huge. They were going to share —'

'It's that man with his bowl,' said Berenson, and he rocked back on his heels in satisfaction. 'Sure is desperate. How much is it worth?'

Lorne licked her lips. 'I can't tell you. Matty needs the money.'

'Everyone needs money.'

'I can't betray a confidence!'

He sighed, and took hold of her wrist. He moved the bones against each other, making her eyes fill and her breath catch. 'Five million, Matty says.'

'Keep your mouth shut. Don't talk of this to anyone.'

He turned away and left her. Lorne felt her heart pounding. She thought she might faint. She thought, If I go home now I can get Miller and be gone. If only she could run away. When he found out the truth he would revenge himself.

The Shuster cousins were on horses, riding around the house, leaping from terrace to lawn and back again in a desperate race. Matty was at her side whispering, 'You did it! Well done, Lorne! Oh God, please let the cheque be OK.'

'What happens to the money?'

'We pay Stavinsky, who's an actor, and then we pay off your parents' debts. The rest's for you and Miller. Don't worry, he won't be able to sell the bowl. I'll put the word out.'

'He'll kill me,' said Lorne, in bewilderment.

'No, he won't, honey! You're coming to England with me.'

She went upstairs and sat on the bed. After a while Griselda came in, and sat next to her. 'I hope this is what you wanted,' she said.

Lorne stirred herself. 'I don't know. I don't trust what I want any more. I've made so many mistakes.'

'You'll feel better if you take some time.' Griselda put a long, strong arm around her shoulders.

Lorne said, 'I'm just so scared. You're never scared, are you?'

'Perhaps I would be, if I was you. People don't try and frighten big, ugly women. It's no fun.'

'We've never been real good friends, have we?' said Lorne. 'We just pretended.'

'I think we're friends now,' said Griselda. 'Anyway, I've got into the habit of pretending. Don't worry, Lorne. I won't let you down.'

Lorne travelled home in the car with the bowl cold and heavy on her knees. It was almost dawn, Greg was insensible, Sherwood triumphant. He looked over his shoulder at the girl. 'We're starting to go places, Lorne,' he murmured. 'This is a very good year for us.'

She nodded.

'Your friend was pretty angry,' he said. 'You see her face? Time you stopped that sort of friendship. She's nobody.'

Lorne nodded again.

'I guess I'll come up with you tonight.'

It was inevitable. Every triumph and defeat was celebrated on her. This is the last time, she thought. The very last time. I am a slave about to be set free.

555

Chapter Thirty-Two

At first the Sprimont bowl was an art world sensation. There was talk of it being the greatest silver find for two hundred years. Trade and antiques magazines began to draft articles on it and auction houses made approaches for the honour of selling the piece. Meanwhile, Lorne took Miller to Boston for another eye check, and failed to take the plane back home.

Only then did Matty let rip. She said she had seen the bowl, had been offered it, and had doubted both Stavinsky and the bowl itself. It was wrong both in patina and style. She had seen pieces like it in England, it was probably the work of the same man. There was a Sprimont bowl, she had seen it herself, but this was not it. Every headline in every paper with even the slightest interest in silver shrieked FORGED!

The bowl was impounded by the authorities, pending investigation. But Mr Stavinsky had vanished, his bank account was closed, and no one seemed to know how he had arrived at the party. One million dollars had disappeared with him, no one knew where. Although Berenson suspected. On the day Drake Shuster called on him and paid off his debt, he more than suspected. He knew.

He thought he would die of rage. Forget the years of toil, building a reputation, making friends – no one would remember them. This would be remembered. The whole world knew him for a sucker, a man too greedy to be careful. And Lorne was behind this. He went to Boston himself, looking for her, but she was long gone. Sherwood went to the airport and sat on a bench, watching the people come and go. This time no one would escape, he thought. Not

Lorne, nor Susan, nor the Feversham girl. He would put them all where they belonged.

Two days after Lorne and Matty arrived at the cottage, Simon's holidays began. Matty drove to collect him, unable to think where Simon and his clutter would fit into her life. Miller needed safety, Simon needed his home and Lorne needed time. They couldn't all be happy.

On the way home Sasha whimpered in her seat.

'Did you have to bring the brat?' Simon was all teenage intolerance.

'She likes to be in the car. Why shouldn't she come?'

'It looks so bad. Everyone thinks you're an unmarried mother.'

'That's OK nowadays. And I am unmarried. Briefly.'

'Oh God. It's Sir Martin again, is it?'

'Not again. Still. I'm seeing him on Saturday, actually.'

'Do you want the title then? It can't be him. He's an absolute creep.'

'You don't know him so you can't say.'

'Last time he picked you up he told you your nail varnish was chipped. That's creepy.'

'He's just particular!'

'Particularly vile.'

It was a Sholto expression. An unpleasant silence fell. 'Are we hard up again?' asked Simon at last.

'What do you mean, again?'

'I mean more than usual. I know you've got debts and things.'

'We're OK. I sold a few things in America. The prices are falling, that's the trouble. They'll come back.' But would she be there to see them? She hadn't made all the loan repayment this time. Eight thousand pounds was still outstanding, rolled on to the next quarter. It was only postponing the problem. She should put the house up for sale, but then where would everyone go?

Simon said, 'I wrote to Sholto, you know, and told him about your new friend.'

'What? How did you write? You don't know where he is!'

'Yes I do. He sent me a birthday present. Red and gold

silk shirt, everyone was green with envy. It was all tatty round the cuffs, like he'd worn it for years.'

'Decent of him. Sending you his cast-offs.'

'I wouldn't have worn it new!' He put his feet up on the dash, obscuring the wing mirror and leaving mud everywhere. Finally he said, 'He didn't write back.'

'Fine. Good. Don't talk about him.'

'Knew you were still smitten.'

'I'm not!'

'Says she. If Sholto was here you wouldn't give Sutherland the time of day.'

'Simon, will you please shut up!' She rammed the car into gear and squealed around a corner. Simon was impossible, and would get worse when he found out that Lorne had taken over his room. He was on the couch.

But the moment Simon saw Lorne she knew she had a different problem. He blushed to the roots of his hair and said, 'Hi. Hello. Nice to see you.'

Lorne said, 'Simon, you've grown tall and handsome. I'm so sorry to put you out of your room. I'll do anything to make up.'

'I'll move my stuff out and give you more room,' said Simon jerkily. 'I'll do it now if you like.'

Left alone, the girls exchanged a look. Lorne said, 'He's into older women, that's all. And he feels sorry for me.' She sank on to the sofa and lifted Miller on to her lap. He put his hands on her face, feeling her expression, and she nibbled his fingers to make him laugh. Just a few days had lessened her tension. She was wearing black trousers and a tight black top, and her hair was caught up in clips at the sides of her head. No wonder Simon was bowled over, thought Matty. Lorne looked utterly romantic.

Matty began to see herself as the workhorse, the one nobody cared about, the one who did the work and got the money for others to spend. She went out each morning and she came back each night, and sometimes she stayed over in London to see to the shop. It was exhausting and worrying. She missed Sasha, but with Lorne and Simon and Miller, Sasha didn't seem to miss her. If only Sholto hadn't saddled her with debt she would be fine, she thought. She had good clients now, who only needed care and time. But she never had any time, and the loan ensured she never had any money. She began to think more and more of Martin Sutherland.

One Saturday he took her to play golf. He wore smart golf clothes, the sort Matty disliked, everything too new and too well pressed. And his car was always immaculate, although he always complained about the valeting. She suspected he was one of those men who make unjustified complaints on the principle that it keeps people on their toes. She dismissed the thought as unworthy. It was good to be clean, determined and solvent. Martin Sutherland was a good man.

The day was bright and full of breezes and the long grass moved in waves, turning silver in the sunlight. Matty was preoccupied and played very badly.

'Never mind,' said Martin. 'Never mind.'

'You mind,' said Matty, who knew he hated messing about at golf. 'I'm spoiling your game.'

'It's not important. I've got things to think about myself.'

'What? What things?'

'You.'

She felt herself blushing. Here it was, then. She fought with an absurd desire to turn and run away, change her name, flee the country, anything! He reached in his pocket and brought out a ring box. 'I hope you like it.'

'Let me see.' She felt detached suddenly. Cool. She opened the box and viewed the jewel with professional scepticism. 'How much? Not above three thousand, I hope.'

'It was actually.'

'Really! Well, I suppose you were buying retail.'

'Matty!' He spoke with real irritation and she blushed again.

He was the right sort of man. Kind and good, strong and reliable. Henry had done well with her second choice. Perhaps second choices were always better bets, less flashy, more sound. Sound as a pound. Lots of pounds. No more worrying about Sholto paying up, no more struggling to make the shop work. Bliss.

'Shall we see if it fits?' She took the ring and slipped it

on to her finger. It was a trifle loose, but then she had lost weight recently.

Sutherland took her hand. 'Well?'

She tried to smile, the look of a woman delighted to be wearing a sapphire circled by diamonds. Women ought to be thrilled by such things. But she was a dealer and things were only things, you didn't love them as you loved your children, they could never be your lover. The response, though, that was important. She had to do it right. 'It fits perfectly. Lovely, Martin. Gorgeous. You really are a dear.'

'Does that mean yes?'

Matty tried to take a deep breath, but her lungs resisted. She struggled to speak. 'Yes,' she said at last.

He bent his head and kissed her. His appropriate response. Some people coming behind them and waiting at the tee shouted, 'Excuse me! We're waiting to play.'

Martin lifted his head and yelled, 'Sorry! I was proposing marriage. You come through.'

Matty looked at them against the sunshine, waving their congratulations, pleased for her. It was unreal.

They were married in a register office, a month later. Of necessity few people attended the marriage, but the reception at night was huge. Matty wore a gown of gold raw silk, the wide waistband woven in green and gold, the hem of the skirt shot with strands of green lustre. It dipped to her ankles revealing green and gold pumps, and she wore diamond clips in her hair, courtesy of Sammy. Sadly, her engagement sapphire did not match. She wished she could take it off.

Griselda was there, and Lorne of course, but Henrietta was having a difficult pregnancy and couldn't travel. Matty wasn't sorry. To have the same faces at your second wedding as the first seemed macabre to say the least. This time Lorne wore clinging white, and she wasn't the bride. Next to her Matty felt overdressed.

'You look wonderful,' said Simon eagerly. Matty didn't turn round. She knew he didn't mean her.

'Thank you, sweetheart. I shall dance with you. Only with you.'

'Will you? Great!' Simon adjusted his bow tie. He looked

older, suddenly. Almost grown up. If she hadn't married Martin he would have suffered the second great financial disaster of his life, before he had even begun to shave.

They were staying the night at Locksley Hall, after the reception. The thought of it put butterflies in Matty's stomach. She and Martin hadn't slept together yet, surrounded as they were with children and commitments, and they hadn't complicated the wedding with planning Matty's move. She would stay the night with Martin after the wedding, and then they would decide what would happen next. Sell the house, perhaps. But with Martin's money she need not sell it, and really, she'd rather not.

In the car back to the hall, Martin said, 'I'm amazed that I've got you. Someone so lovely. It's like a dream.'

And the whole thing was dreamlike. She could not escape the feeling that tomorrow she would go home and take up her business again, quite normally.

A band was playing in the ballroom. They were going to provide everything from classical selections to hip-hop, or so they promised. There were balloons in a net above the dancefloor, flowers for every lady and little gold dance programmes, which Matty thought the ultimate conceit. Most of the guests were friends of Martin's, and Matty had asked a great many business associates. They all wore wonderful jewellery.

Matty desperately wanted a drink, as so often nowadays. She was drinking every evening now, a shot to pick her up, a shot to relax her, another to send her to sleep. It was necessary. Sometimes she felt as if she was running to catch a train that was chugging steadily out of the station, faster and faster, the carriages whipping by one after the other, every door eluding her grasp, and she would never get on! The drink helped her run faster, she thought. And Martin was going to stop the train.

She downed a glass of champagne in one, and then took up her place to welcome the guests. Martin flicked through the list, telling her about people she didn't know.

'He's fine, she's a bore, talks about children. And she's all right – you'll like her, but the husband only talks business. Oh, and a friend from an auction house is coming, do you know him? Chap named Edwards.'

'I've only seen his name on the letter heading,' said Matty. 'I might know his face. Does he have anything to do with silver?'

'No idea. Look, here they all come.'

She felt absurdly nervous, when surely the worst was over. Her palms were wet. She stood in the hall, amidst the pillars and the newly acquired portraits, and wished she was anywhere else. Everything was so neat and well organised. From now on there would be squabbles at breakfast about putting the newspaper in the right place. They would have to send Simon on endless trips to stop him being at home. And what about Sasha's baby mess, inevitable and engulfing, a rising tide of talcum and plastic ducks and shoes? She felt an increasing sense of panic.

'Mr and Mrs Herbert Fisher,' announced the butler. Matty and Martin stepped forward in unison to greet the first of their guests.

The greetings lasted over an hour. Matty's legs ached and her face was stiff with smiles. Was it her imagination or did her own friends seem better quality than Martin's? They were certainly more flamboyant. One of the dealers had picked her up and swung her around, saying, 'Well, Matilda, you are going up in the world! Made it off the floor at last!'

Martin was not amused. It upset his sense of dignity.

At last it seemed as if everyone had come. 'Let's go and get a drink,' said Matty thankfully.

'I thought we'd dance,' said Martin. 'You know, lead it off.'

She would rather have a drink. They turned away, but before they could reach the door the butler intoned, 'Mr Gordon Edwards and – friend.'

Matty gritted her teeth and turned, fixing her smile back on her face. It froze into a grimace. Next to a chunky, grey-haired man stood Sholto.

He was wearing black trousers, a bright green shirt with a red bow tie, and a white dinner jacket. He looked Matty up and down, taking in everything, and smiled lazily. She hated that smile.

'Hope you don't mind,' Gordon Edwards was saying. 'Sholto blew in from Italy and was at a loose end. Art dealer, you know. Absolutely top notch, nothing under a quarter of a million.'

Martin looked nervously from one man to the other. Sholto pursed his lips a little, encouraging him in his misconception. 'It was really kind of Gordon to bring me,' he lisped.

Gordon shot him a look of horror. 'Er – hope it's OK,' he ventured. 'I'm so glad to meet you at last, Matilda.'

'Matty.'

'Yes – Matty. Very well known by our silver people, I understand. Perhaps you know Sholto?'

Matty observed the tall figure, now adopting a distinctly precious pose. 'I fear not,' she said coolly.

'But I never frighten anyone!' declared Sholto. 'Do I, Gordon? I'm the soul of discretion!' He made a little tiptoed run around the hall, flapping his arms like tiny wings.

'Bloody hell, Sholto,' said Gordon, who in fact was gay but kept it resolutely concealed. 'Have you gone mad?'

'It seems so,' said Matty. She turned on her heel and walked briskly away.

She had to have some champagne. She seized a glass from a tray and downed it in one. Her nerves eased in their relentless twanging. People came up to her to talk. One of her dealer friends glanced towards the door, did a double take and said, 'Good God, isn't that Sholto?'

Matty said 'Don't. I'm pretending I don't know him.'

Martin came to reclaim her. 'I don't blame you for running,' he said. 'That man's a lunatic. Can't think where Edwards found him.'

'It confirms what I've always thought,' said Matty. 'Auctioneers have absolutely no judgment.'

'There speaks a dealer!'

She twisted her mouth into an approximation of a smile. Out of the corner of her eye she could see Sholto bearing down on them. He would. He just would.

'My dear Matilda!' He stretched out his hands. 'I've discovered something wonderful! We have the same name.'

'I changed mine today,' said Matty distantly, avoiding his clasp.

'Oh! Oh, how sad! Still, we can be friends for a little while can't we? What happened to Mr Feversham, may I ask?'

Martin pushed belligerently between them. 'He was an opal miner. In Australia.'

Laughter bubbled in Sholto's eyes. 'How very – distant.'

'Extremely,' said Matty. 'He lives in Alice Springs now, I believe. It's best. It was a terrible mistake and I have no wish to see him ever again.'

'He must have been very cruel to you!'

Matty met his eye with a powerful stare. 'I never talk about it. The very thought of how it was is upsetting to me. I prefer to pretend it never happened.'

At that moment, for some bizarre reason known only to themselves, the band struck up with 'Tie Me Kangaroo Down, Sport', in strict tempo.

'The past will never stay buried,' said Sholto lugubriously. 'It leaps back at us like a rogue kangaroo.'

'Let's dance,' said Matty, and before Martin could say 'Yes' she had grabbed Sholto and hustled him on to the floor.

They tripped around the floor doing the quickstep. 'You bastard,' she hissed. 'How dare you come here! You owe me twenty thousand pounds.'

'Want a cheque now?' He paused, as if about to whip out his cheque book then and there.

'No! I want you to go.'

'What, and spoil the fun? Look at everyone. They are all absolutely fascinated. The only person who doesn't know is that poor sap you just married. Why, may I ask?'

'Because you didn't pay me the twenty thousand!'

He looked disbelieving. 'You could have said if you were desperate!'

'I would have died rather than say.'

He made a face. 'And you are such a little liar.'

She went pink. 'I only lied because – well, I wanted you to be down some opal mine in Alice Springs! If you had any decency you'd go there now and bury yourself.'

'Darling Matty! Is this the woman who told me she would ever be mine?'

Matty looked up at him then. Her eyes swam with tears. 'You didn't want me. So I found someone who did.'

He was silent. His hands gripped her with unnecessary force, as if he thought at any moment she would pull away. He swept across the floor with ungoverned brilliance, cornering with a dip and a sway, taking her breath and making her feet race. She felt she was flying. 'We are unfinished business,' he said suddenly. He wasn't laughing now.

'It's all over. I got married today. I didn't want to get divorced, remember? It was your idea.'

'I know — I know. I didn't know what I wanted.'

'Yes you did. The Baronessa, in a state of undress and an awful lot of pain.'

'It wasn't my fault you saw that.'

'Agreed. But there's no point in pretending that I didn't.'

The music stopped. Sholto held on to Matty for a moment, but she looked him straight in the eye, defying him to restrain her. He let her go. She walked swiftly back to Martin.

'Who is that man?' he demanded.

Matty shrugged. 'An art dealer. High on something, I expect. He looks the sort. Martin, everyone's hungry, why don't we eat?'

'Don't you think it's too early?'

'No. They're all drinking like fish.'

An ice sculpture dominated the table, a glistening dolphin emerging from icy foam. There was caviar and whole salmon, smoked pheasant and roast grouse, venison patties and little balls of something pungent that the caterer said was sushi. Matty moved amongst the crowd, her smile immovable. People's kindness unnerved her. One woman drew her aside and whispered, 'Do you want me to drag him upstairs and seduce him? It would keep him out of the way.'

Matty said, 'I couldn't ask you to sacrifice yourself,' and the woman giggled.

'Darling, isn't he wonderfully dangerous? I'm so glad you married Martin. You deserve it.'

Griselda bore down on Sholto, her face set. He evaded

her and went up to Lorne, standing alone in her white dress, remote and lovely.

'You look ridiculously vulnerable,' he said. 'Dumped Beefcake at last?'

She nodded. 'Took me far too long. Matty's looking after me, and my little boy. She's been wonderful. Why have you come to spoil everything for her?'

He shrugged. 'Actually, I think I add tone. Such a dull crowd. And this bloke's a complete no-hoper. Does she sleep with him?'

Lorne turned her shoulder. 'I don't know. She doesn't tell me. Sholto, you're just peeved because she likes him more than you.'

'Oh, but she doesn't. I'll swear she doesn't.'

'At least he never leaves her with bills she can't pay.'

He pushed his hand through his hair, the first gesture that hinted he was not quite in control. 'I always pay in the end. She knows I pay in the end!'

'You strung her out until she was frantic. Your aunt kept writing letters and she'd go into the barn at night and do the accounts. She'd be there until dawn, drinking too much, crying, trying to find some way to get the money. We all talked about it and decided she'd better get married.'

'You don't get married for money.'

'Oh yes you do! What did you get married for?'

For a moment he looked unsure. Then he said, 'Sanity. I married Matty to share in her sanity. But I find I didn't need it after all.'

He walked away, going out, sick of the whole thing, amazed at the impulse that had brought him here. But in the hall Simon ran down the stairs and caught him. 'Sholto! Sholto, please don't go! You didn't know I was here, I waved but you didn't see.'

'Hello, Simon. My, but how you've grown.' He rolled his eyes in a parody of the oft repeated phrase. 'Why were you lurking upstairs?'

'I was getting a handkerchief for Lorne,' said Simon awkwardly.

'Oh. The hormones are stirring, I see. She is looking deliciously tragic, I must admit.'

Stiffly, Simon said, 'She's had a terrible time. I help her as much as I can.'

'I hope she lets you look down her blouse occasionally. A toothsome little pair, it must be said. A tip, my boy. The first woman you go to bed with will seem like an angel. A sure way of checking is to try a few more and see if she still looks the same.'

A slow flush stained Simon's cheeks. 'I wish you wouldn't talk like that. You were horrible to Matty.'

'Tell you, did she?'

'No, of course not. But she was miserable for months. I only wrote to you because I thought you'd come back and make it right. But you're just interested in sex and − and having lots of women.'

Sholto put his hands in his pockets. 'I suppose it does look like that to you.'

'It is like that! I know Matty's my sister and that makes a difference, but she's been brave as anything. She loves Sasha but she hardly ever sees her because she's working so hard. She pays for Lorne, and Lorne's baby, and for me. I'm not going to be the sort of man you are. I thought once I'd like nothing better but I was wrong. I'm not going to leave someone like Matty in the lurch. She wishes you'd never been born.'

Simon's face was still so young, the bones masked by soft skin. His eyes were hot with the tears of rage and disillusion. Sholto said suddenly, 'I did my best, Simon. I tried. If she needed money I'd have found it for her from somewhere, I always do. I never wanted to hurt her.'

The boy paused, halfway to the ballroom door. 'But you came today. You're making a fool of her. I didn't want her to marry Martin, but now I want her to forget all about you and start again.'

Alone in the hall, Sholto went to the front door. He opened it and stood in the cold air, letting the night soothe him. Shadows of clouds passing across the moon drifted over the park before the house, and deer stepped one after another from moonlight into shade. The trees rustled in a puff of wind, a disapproving chorus. Why did I come? thought Sholto.

When he'd heard of this he felt outraged, that was the stupidity of it. He had thought of Matty waiting, like the Madonna, pure, inviolate. But she was a woman, like any other. In her absence he had forgotten the reality. How lovely she was, how brilliant her eyes, her hair, how heavy the breasts she had revealed to him when she was innocent. They had begun so well, in mutual joy and discovery, but he had strayed. The things he had wanted he could not take from her. In having them he had known he must give her up.

Why had her patience and love been such shackles? They demanded a response from him, something he couldn't give. He had wanted to shake her off, be rid of her, when just to look at her made him ashamed. When he saw himself reflected in her eyes he was forced to think about what he was. He had wanted to be free to sink and be done.

The trees whispered again in the wind. He shivered. Was that gone forever? He felt different nowadays. Before he left Italy he had gone to a church, to kneel in the candlelight and wait for the despair to come again. It always came in church, looking at the perfection of the Virgin, at her perfect love. Even as a child he had not shared in it. He had known himself alone, shunned, without hope. But then, for the first time, he had looked into those wonderful, painted eyes and seen humanity. He had seen pain. He had even seen the possibility of sin.

Sholto felt as if he had witnessed a revelation. Sin was there in everyone, even in her, and yet the actual sin was absent. Uncommitted. Neither she, nor he, nor anyone, not even Matty, was compelled to good or ill. They could choose. He had been given back the choice.

He turned on his heel and went back into the house, into the ballroom. When he entered conversations fell into a morass of hesitation and heads turned, watching him. He went straight to Martin Sutherland, standing with Matty under a giant chandelier.

'Martin? I'm sorry to interrupt your evening once again. I'm afraid I've behaved very badly tonight. I'm Matty's ex-husband, Sholto Feversham. Late of Australia and the opal mine. I came to disrupt things but I've thought better of it. You seem just the right sort to make Matty happy, and

I wish you both well. Take care of her. She's the most lovely girl.'

Martin gaped at him, but before he could speak Sholto had gone. Matty thrust her champagne glass at Martin. 'Hold on to this. I've got to talk to him.'

'What? Matty, come here. Matty, I want a private word, right away. Matty!'

She pushed through the crowd, unable to keep up with Sholto's long legs. He strode through the ballroom into the hall, and away. She fell through the front door after him.

'Sholto! Sholto, come back! You can't just walk out on me!'

He stopped and looked back at her. 'I just did. Go in and be happy.'

'At least you owe a duty to your daughter!'

He sighed. 'Look, I'll send the money tomorrow. Or do you want it now?'

'Now,' said Matty, who had forgotten the money, who didn't need it any more.

'I'll write the cheque in the car.'

She followed him across the gravel. It was cold, she was shivering. He said, 'Do you want my coat?'

'Yes,' she said. It smelled of old lavender bags.

'If you're in England you'll have to visit,' said Matty. 'That's what I meant.'

'She's got a new father. She doesn't need me.'

'Children go off the rails when people decide things like that. She's like you. Just like you. At least come and see her.'

He stopped at a Ferrari and unlocked it. How like him to have a bloody Ferrari, she thought. She sat in the passenger seat while he found a pen and wrote her a cheque. Her flesh was in goosepimples and she closed the door. His hands, so long and slender, seemed to her the most erotic things she had ever seen.

'I've been sleeping around,' she said suddenly.

He looked up at her. 'Why?'

'Why not? I thought I might learn something.'

'Did you?'

'Lots of things.'

He took a long breath and said shakily, 'I hate the thought of you sleeping with him. You do, I imagine.'

'Oh, yes, all the time. It's good. We're terribly adventurous. We don't use the missionary position much, he prefers to have me on top.'

'How nice.'

Matty warmed to her theme. 'Actually, he's not as tall as you but he's quite a bit bigger, if you see what I mean. And he always wants it twice. I hope he eases up a bit, because it's so exhausting, a man like that, especially when – Sholto, don't!'

He switched on the engine with a throaty roar. Matty fumbled for the door handle, but Sholto's elbow was firmly on the central lock button. He flung the car into gear and they were away. As she looked back she saw Martin Sutherland standing on the step, looking cross.

An owl was in the road, tearing at a rabbit. It blinked in the lights, beginning a slow flap into the air, and Matty shrieked. Sholto jerked the wheel and the car screamed across the grass, skidding sideways, deep in mud, before grinding back to the road.

'You're going to kill us!'

'And why not?' His profile was set in stone.

'Because of Sasha! At least let me look after her.'

He drove on, hurling the car recklessly around bends and through corners, like an Italian in Rome. But she could feel her words working on him. She knew him so well. The weak and the helpless never had anything to fear from Sholto. Suddenly he stamped on the brakes and the car shuddered to a halt. They were out of the park now, in narrow lanes pitch dark between the hedges.

Matty took her first good breath since he started the car. Perhaps she was going to live after all. 'Where did you get the car?' she asked.

He lifted his hands from the wheel, a gesture of helplessness.

'Exchange for a picture. Looks better than it is. Engine's shot.'

'It seems fine.'

He grinned mirthlessly. 'You of all people should know you can't tell by appearances.'

They sat in silence. Moths danced in the beams of the headlights. Matty felt her chest grow tight with the strain of sitting there with him. He was exactly as she remembered. He even smelled the same, of old clothes and new leather and soap. 'When we married,' she whispered, 'you said you loved me but it wasn't true. I knew it even then.'

'I don't know what love is.'

'That proves it then. You know what you feel.'

'You might. I never have.' He sighed, from the depths of his soul. 'I went to see my aunt, you know. The one in Venice. I thought – I thought it would kill me going back. I thought I might kill her. But we're both of us still alive. Something happened, but I don't know what.'

'Grizz said you'd have to face it in the end,' said Matty. 'Face her. She said you couldn't go on burying the past.'

'What do you do with it when you've dug it up? It's like a mouldering corpse, and I trail it around in a sack. I don't dream any more. I just think about it. Remember. I can even remember the night my – my mother died.'

He put his hand over his mouth, crushing the sobs. His eyes were tight shut, but still the tears squeezed through. His shoulders shook. She knew she didn't want to touch him, she couldn't bear to hold him close, but he had never cried, never once seemed as if he was capable of it.

'Oh God, let this stop,' said Sholto suddenly. 'Let me stop this!'

'No,' said Matty. She put out her arms and held his head, drawing it to her own, putting her face against his. 'Let's get it out for once. Let's be properly sad.'

His mouth opened in a silent howl of pain. Matty held him and soothed him, soothing tears from his cheeks with her fingers. Suddenly he pulled back and looked at her. 'She died. And I loved her. I loved her with all my heart.'

'But of course you did.'

'No – you don't understand. I'd forgotten that. I'd forgotten how. I didn't know.'

'Oh, Sholto. Poor Sholto. Poor little boy.'

A moment later he was calm. He pulled free of her and

wiped his face on his sleeves. He said, 'What a time I give you. Well, at least you can see how right we were to divorce. All we have to do now is make sure I stay right away and let you be happy. Incredible as it seems I only behave this oddly when you're around. The rest of the time I seem quite normal.'

'Do you feel better?'

He grinned at her. 'Better? No, actually I don't. Calmer, perhaps. But it's quite hard to see another man taking your wife, even when she's an ex-wife, even when she's got every reason to go. It's a primitive impulse.'

She sighed and folded her hands in her lap. 'I don't love him at all,' she said softly.

'But you sleep with him.'

She shook her head. 'Not yet. I only like Martin for his money and his house. And he likes me because I look right and can have children.'

'Better than nothing, I suppose.'

'Is it? He never does anything without thinking first. He thinks and thinks and thinks. He thinks I'm all the things I'm not. He thinks I'm sensible and reliable and honest –' her voice rose with gathering hysteria.

Sholto said, 'So you are. Sometimes. Anyone can be anything for a little while.'

She looked at Sholto's stained face. Her heart ached with emotion. He had been what she wanted, for a very little while. He was part of her life, part of her growing-up, but he could never be part of her happiness. It was all too one-sided.

'I'll grow to love Martin,' she murmured. 'And you'll come and take Sasha for holidays in Italy, and teach her Italian the way you speak it. But we won't talk, we'll write. Safer that way.'

'What are you afraid of?'

She laughed. 'Our groping hands! You know. You remember.'

'Oh yes. I remember very well.'

Suddenly he started the car again. She thought he was turning back, but as the hedges passed them endlessly and the miles went on, she realised he was doing nothing of the kind.

'Where on earth are we going?'

'Anywhere. Away from there.'

'Sholto, stop! You must stop. I can't leave Martin like this! Good God, can you imagine, everyone laughing, making fun of him? Go back. Sholto, if you ever want to see Sasha again, if you ever want to see either of us again, then you'll take me back.'

Sholto stopped the car and looked at her. 'You're not married to him. Not really. He might have gone through the motions but it was only a legalistic sort of thing. We were properly married. We still are.'

'We were properly divorced!'

'That was nothing. A formality, a legal fiddle. I can't leave you with a man like that. Ye gods, he's got no art!'

'What's art got to do with it?'

'Everything! He's nothing but a collection of bank statements.'

Matty began to cry. Sholto gave her a handkerchief and she sobbed into it, disjointedly accusing him all the while. He was cruel and spendthrift, he neglected her. He never wrote, he never telephoned, he was never there when she wanted him.

'I'd have come if you'd asked me. I thought you'd had enough. The last time — I knew it was over.'

'You thought I was ugly,' she whispered.

'You? Oh, Matty. My beautiful girl.'

Her glossy cap of conker brown hair fell forward as she wept. The forefinger of her right hand still bore the faint traces of ink and silver polish. She reached up and pushed her hair behind her ear and he fixed his eyes on that ear, so pink and perfectly formed. Every whorl and crevice seemed to be one that he knew so well that he could identify her from it, would know it anywhere. Sutherland would never know her that well.

He tried to think of something else and could not. He thought of Victoria, who had led him down a path further than she intended, until he left her once and for all. Desire always passed, he thought. His desire for Matty would pass one day. While there was love then perhaps it was fed from a spring that never ran dry, but in the ordinary course of events the flesh grew tired. Yet he was nearer loving Matty than anyone. Did he love Matty? Look at him now, a lovesick boy.

'I'll take you back to him if you want,' he said. 'But only if you want.'

She looked up at him then. 'You know I must. Wanting doesn't come into it.'

'Matty, Matty, when are you going to care about you for once? You care about everyone except yourself!'

She looked down at her hands and sighed. 'You don't understand. I can't live with myself when I let people down. I'm more selfish than anyone really. If I do it wrong then I can't be happy.'

'This isn't going to make you happy.'

A shudder ran through her. Her face was tight and pale. 'I know.'

He turned the car then and they drove in silence back to the Hall. Matty felt almost peaceful, savouring these few quiet moments, perhaps her last quiet moments with Sholto. As they turned into the drive all the lights in the house were blazing fiercely. People stood around on the gravel forecourt, unsure whether to go or to stay. When Matty got out of the car they stared at her and she walked quickly past them and into the house. Martin was standing by the stairs, his face drawn into carved lines of strain. When he saw her his eyes blazed with anger. 'Matty! At last!'

'I'm sorry, Martin. Really I am.'

'Sorry? What use is that? You're not some trollop, going off here, there and everywhere! I expect more of my wife.'

She hadn't expected such fury. He pulled her into the small sitting room and poured words on her head, a molten lava of reproach. Matty went to the cupboard and fetched the whisky bottle, doling out a large measure.

'Will you stop that?' said Martin, his voice rising hysterically. 'You drink far too much!'

'I came back,' whispered Matty. 'I thought you would want that.'

'You should never have gone! How could you humiliate me like this? In front of everyone.'

'I didn't mean to go. Truly I didn't. He made me. Why

don't we go out there now and behave as if it didn't happen?'

'Of course we can't! You're such a fool.'

'Martin, you're making this worse.'

He stood by the empty fireplace, shaking with pent-up emotion. Matty took another gulp of her whisky. Was she really to spend her life with this man? She had promised. But her soul felt utterly bleak.

There was a knock on the door. It was Lorne. 'Matty, do you know what you're doing?' she said in a low voice. 'Sholto's sitting under a tree in the park. He looks like hell.'

'I want that man off my property!' flared Sutherland. 'Matty's never to see him again.'

Matty raised her head. 'He's Sasha's father. I have to see him.'

'I forbid it! Matty, I honestly forbid it!'

Lorne said, 'I don't think that's something you can do, Martin. Matty's her own woman. She had her life before she met you.'

'I don't want that life,' he muttered. 'I want that to be ended, completely and utterly finished.'

'But it's my life,' said Matty. 'I lived it, and out of it came Sasha. It can't ever be finished.'

'Yes it can! Today was the day you started afresh. Living a proper life. Sensibly. With me.'

He wanted her so badly, this perfect woman who didn't exist. 'Anyone can be anything for a little while.' Sholto had said that. And she couldn't be what Martin wanted, not forever.

'Matty?' he said, his voice rising with the question. 'Matty?'

'I'm sorry, Martin,' she said. 'It wouldn't be honest to stay.'

The moonlight was silver on the grass. Sholto, slumped under his tree, looked up at her and laughed.

'Lorne said you were distraught,' said Matty accusingly.

'So I would be, if I thought you wouldn't come. I knew you would.'

'Then I think I'll go.'

But he stood up and caught her wrist, holding her tight. Such a deceiver, she thought, such a rogue. 'This time I won't ever let you go,' he said.

Almost everyone had left. They got into the car and drove away, numb with exhaustion. After an hour or so they found a hotel for the night, in a small town with cobbled streets and good pubs. They would sort everything out tomorrow, when it was all less stark. Matty felt helpless with weariness. She lay on her back on the bed and took off her bracelets, her sapphire and diamond cluster, her hair clips, and finally the wedding ring she had put on only that day. She felt free and unencumbered. But suppose she woke up in the morning and Sholto was different again? 'I want a drink,' she said fearfully. 'Something strong.'

Sholto climbed naked on to the bed beside her. 'Be quiet. You've got me.'

She looked up into his blue eyes, vivid and suddenly fierce. No one had ever hurt her so much and now she must lay aside all her defences, make herself open once more, and see if he would hurt her again. He put his hands inside the skirt of her dress, under the welter of silk and taffeta, pushing up until he reached the constricting waistband. He bunched his fists and forced them higher still, and the stitching tore with a noise like a dog's wild snarl. He touched her breasts and Matty gasped as he eased them free of the tight-boned bodice, ballooning upwards lasciviously.

'I hated seeing you in this dress,' he murmured. 'You looked as remote as any queen.'

'And what do I look like now?'

He pulled his hands free and knelt astride her. Slowly, voluptuously, he pulled her underclothes away and drifted long, cool fingers between her legs. Her whole body shuddered.

'My own dear wanton,' he murmured. 'I never hate myself for loving you.' He touched her again, sliding two fingers up inside, into the warm safety of her body. She watched him, excitement only a quiver away, and some part of her wondered how it was that he could never shock her. Together, anything they did was an act of love.

She pulled off the wreck of her dress and was done with

577

it. He held her from behind and pressed kisses on each and every bone in her spine, holding her breasts in firm hands. When she turned he put his face on her belly and whispered love to what lay beneath. She laughed, almost in anguish, until at last he pushed her back on the bed. He hung over her, breathing hard. 'It's been so long,' he whispered. 'This is too beautiful to be over.'

Matty, becoming desperate, reached for him. 'When it's over we'll begin again,' she said.

She rose up as he came down. Together they sank into the bed, locked in a bond that seemed as if it could never break. At last nothing was hidden and nothing held back, and for those few brief moments they felt unreal, beyond the normal scheme of things, like birds fluttering high towards heaven. It was unity and it was loss, gaining each other and losing themselves, and afterwards they were still. Matty felt a sense of awe and wonder, and knew that however often they met and kissed and loved it would never be like this again. Whatever it is that the spirit aspires to, whatever source of love and pleasure, it was one that they had reached up and touched.

Chapter Thirty-Three

At the Hall, Lorne and Griselda did their best to pick up the pieces. Sutherland seemed almost stunned, and sat silent, occasionally bursting out 'Why?' or 'I never thought –' and finally, 'If I'd known she was that sort, I'd never have looked at her!'

'What sort did you think she was?' asked Lorne. She sat back on the leather sofa, forbiddingly lovely.

'Is she like you? Would you do this?'

She lifted her shoulders in a shrug. 'For Sholto, I might.'

'He's a maniac! An ugly, badly dressed madman. I can't imagine anyone wanting to be with him.'

'He's the most sexy man I ever met,' said Lorne. 'If he ever asks me to go to bed with him, I'll say yes right away. No questions asked.'

Griselda came in and closed the door. 'I heard that,' she said. 'Don't get carried away, Lorne.'

'Well, wouldn't you?'

Griselda made a face. 'Before Bertie I might have done. Yes, I think I would. I don't know why, though. I mean, he's exhausting to be with, always doing things, saying things, being outrageous.'

'He's different with Matty.'

Griselda smiled. 'Yes, isn't he? More at peace.'

Martin said, 'You are talking about my wife! The woman I married today.'

Griselda came and took his hand. 'This must be very trying for you. So embarrassing.'

His mouth worked helplessly. He struggled to find words. 'I can't believe this is happening! I gave her everything – all this!'

'Balls to all that,' said Lorne decisively. 'The only thing that counts is what you feel. You didn't love her, did you? But she looked good and she behaved right and you could see her having your kids. That's all it was.'

He looked from one girl to the other, swamped by women suddenly, hating their easy sidestepping of his logic. They were capricious and unfathomable and difficult. But not Matty. She had seemed perfect.

'I suppose I'm not your sort of man,' he said suddenly. 'Too ordinary, too boring, too bloody rich! Ordinary things matter to me. Like − like not causing scenes, and paying bills on time, and behaving properly in restaurants. A man like him doesn't care about things like that, of course. But it doesn't mean I don't feel. It doesn't mean I don't love her. Because I do.'

After a moment Griselda said, 'Almost everyone's gone home. I'll get the butler to sort out the presents, shall I? They'll have to go back.'

He pulled himself out of his daze and said, 'Yes, if you would. A short note of apology is appropriate, I think. Signed on my behalf. I shall draft something.'

Almost laughing at his continued organisation, Lorne said, 'I think you're being very brave about this.'

His face was bleak, suddenly. He lifted his hands and let them fall again in an odd, fluttering gesture. 'Perhaps it's not much of a surprise. I knew she was in a mess, and I was a way out. But when it's someone like that, the sort of person you couldn't hope to have any other way, then it's all right. I knew it was risky, because she's clever and beautiful and I'm the sort of man who goes around buying things she wouldn't look at, and − I just thought we might get by. Children, and mutual friends and things. Tying her down. Stupid, really.'

Griselda buried her beaky nose in a handkerchief. 'I'm so sorry,' she burst out. 'I just think this is one of those times when you'll wake in the morning and think you've imagined it. We'll clear up outside and then tomorrow you can go on as if it never happened.'

But Lorne said, 'I'll stay and talk to you if you want.'

Sutherland tried to laugh. 'I'm not going to kill myself,

I assure you. Perhaps you'd like a drink? There must be gallons of champagne –'

'I'd like that,' said Lorne. 'My terrible moments have never had champagne. It's stylish.'

'Like the band playing on the *Titanic*.'

'Fiddling while Rome burned.' She kicked off her shoes and put her feet up on the sofa. She gave the still-present Griselda a surprised stare. 'Go on, Grizz! Go fetch the champagne!'

They left in the morning, a weary little cavalcade. Sutherland was still in bed, put there by Lorne at five a.m. She fell into the car beside the children, saying, 'Simon, the things I do for your sister! I saved that man from committing suicide with a letter knife.'

'He was probably trying to open his mail,' said Griselda. 'He's a very orderly man. Simon, come and sit next to me and navigate.'

The children were fractious and they only reached the cottage for lunch. There was no sign of Matty.

'I bet he's murdered her,' said Simon morosely. 'Bloody lunatic.'

Lorne said, 'I thought you liked Sholto. He's never hurt Matty, has he? I mean, physically.'

Simon shrugged. 'Don't think so. Actually – oh, he won't hurt Matty. Can't bear to see her cry.'

The girls relaxed and set about making lunch and lighting fires. The children, in some complicated team game, toddled around the room, Sasha as the eyes and Miller as the stability. Simon, ignoring all purposeful activity, lay on the sofa and opened the Sunday paper. He flicked through, looking for either naked women or motor racing, and suddenly stopped.

'Hey, girls! Look! Look at this!'

He spread the sheets on the floor, fending off erratic childish feet. Lorne came in and glanced at the article, stopped, read more carefully and yelled, 'Grizz, quick!' Side by side, covering a third of the page, were two pictures, each of a silver bowl. Below them were insets showing Matty, Luca de Caruzon and Sherwood Berenson.

Simon began to read:

Experts have been nonplussed by the appearance of two hitherto unknown silver bowls by the celebrated eighteenth-century silversmith Nicholas Sprimont. The bowls appear to be identical in almost every aspect, although some experts have disputed the patina. The question now being asked is whether either bowl is genuine; Matilda Feversham, a respected international dealer, went on record earlier this year claiming that the Stavinsky bowl, so called because it was sold by an East European of that name, was forged. She is understood to have seen similar high-class forgeries and to recognise the style, but her view is challenged by the present owner, Sherwood Berenson of South Carolina, USA, and several renowned silver authorities.

The position was complicated when Mr Luca de Caruzon, a Mexican with extensive Libyan and international connections, produced his Sprimont bowl. He claims that photographs of the bowl, taken by Mrs Feversham some years ago, were used to forge the Stavinsky copy. But he is unable to say how his own bowl came into his family's possession, only stating that it has been theirs for many years.

The argument is made the more poignant by the sums involved. One genuine Sprimont bowl could be expected to fetch in excess of five million dollars. If both bowls are genuine, unless it could be established that they were made as a pair, such a figure could be effectively halved. It is of course possible that both bowls are fakes, and the doubts cast by the wrangle over their authenticity may make it impossible to obtain a sensible price for either item. Tensions are certainly high in the silver halls of New York!

Lorne turned a towel in her hands. 'If Sherwood makes five million I will shoot myself,' she murmured.

Griselda said, 'I don't care how much he makes, Matty could go to prison over this. That actor fellow, Stavinsky, could talk. Or the silversmith. Luca hates Matty, and so does Berenson. They'll both be trying to do her down.'

Lorne chewed her knuckle. 'Where on earth is she? Perhaps she's seen this and run away.'

'She wouldn't leave Sasha,' said Simon. They all turned and looked down at the little girl. Matty's hair and Matty's eyes, but Sholto's long-limbed elegance. Matty would never leave her little girl.

Matty and Sholto appeared at six in the evening, still in their party clothes, yawning and apologising and unable to keep away from each other. Where Matty sat Sholto sat too, touching her hair or her hand; when he got up she was inexorably drawn to him, until Lorne said irritably, 'I wish you'd both take this seriously! Matty could go to prison and all you can do is moon about like a pair of kids!'

'They can't prove anything,' said Matty lazily. She wasn't interested in silver. All she cared about was Sholto's hand, Sholto's smile, Sholto's long, lazy kisses.

'They'll carve you up if you stay out of it,' said Griselda. 'They'll both do you down.'

'But I'm sick of New York. I don't want to go there. I want to stay at home. In bed.' She looked up at Sholto, and he grinned his twisted, wicked smile. Oh yes, thought Lorne, when Sholto wanted he could be so, so seductive. Until he stopped wanting. She felt scared for Matty suddenly. Sholto was such a risk.

But he said, 'You should go. We both should. It could be dangerous.'

She pouted. 'Luca always hated you, not me! And my actor was nice. He didn't know the bowl was a fake.'

'He knew you owned it,' he murmured.

'I suppose he did.'

A knock came on the door. Matty's eyes grew big, as if the police had already come to arrest her. But it was Richard Greensall, sweating and unhappy. 'Knew it weren't right,' he blurted. 'Knew it when you first asked. Told me right first day we met, not to make so much, not such good stuff. Told me the game was up. Bloody landed me in it now.'

Matty turned away. Sholto said, 'Have the police been on to you?'

He shook his head, dumb, miserable. 'Someone's going

to tell, like. People do. She found me because someone telled.'

They all stood looking at Matty, her lovely dress all crumpled, her hair a mass of shining, tumbled threads. She couldn't bear their accusing eyes and she turned and ran into the garden.

Sholto followed a moment later. He touched her shoulders. 'You silly, silly girl,' he murmured.

'Why silly? I parted Berenson from his money. He deserved it.'

'To put yourself at risk like this. To make the bowl in the first place.'

She turned to him and rested her face against his chest. 'I was tired of being good! Look where it got me. No money, no you. I was tired of it all and I wanted to do something – something exciting!'

'And was it?'

She looked up at him, a little smile playing about her mouth. 'Oh, yes. It was just a copy, you see, at first. No marks, nothing. And then I thought – well, why not go the whole hog? I made him stamp it just so, not too straight, not too crooked, and the polishing was crucial, because the original bowl has barely seen the light of day. It was an exercise, really. I never meant to sell it. Not really.'

He was speechless for a moment. Then he said, 'Matty, I have never done anything like that! I've passed on a few iffy things and I've fiddled auctions and turned a blind eye, but I would never sully the name of a great master! That is immoral, girl!'

She shrugged. 'Not if no one can tell the difference. Pretty things are pretty things. The rest's all hogwash.'

It was futile to argue. He doubted she believed what she said. Absolutes didn't exist in art, thank God. But to forge a hallmark was an offence anywhere, and he was frightened for her. They went back inside and he said to Greensall, 'Is there anything, anything at all about that bowl, that can trace it back to you? Some little thing, some idiosyncrasy?'

He thought. 'The leaves, maybe. Round the feet. One of his was set on not straight. Just a fraction, like. From what I could tell.'

'And that's all? Just one leaf?'

'Aye. What d'you think I am, stupid?'

Even when Greensall was gone the atmosphere was heavy and anxious. Sasha cried, a nagging wail, for no good reason, and Matty could not comfort her. All at once Sholto got up and put out his arms. 'Give her here. You're making her worse.'

Matty gave up the child, watching as Sholto put her to his shoulder, resting his scarred cheek against the baby's hot, unhappy head. The wailing lessened to a sad grumble.

He had such gentleness, Matty thought, as he gave the baby orange juice and wiped her face and little hands. Out of his own miserable childhood had come an understanding of children and their needs. Was Sasha special to him? she wondered. Let her be special. Let her not be just a child to him, any child, a passing interest. In Italy she had seen Sholto go into a shop and buy meat for a stray dog, to give it and be gone, the dog forgotten. If she wasn't there, thought Matty, if the baby were to live without a mother, Sholto must not pass on and forget this child.

'Do you love her?' she asked, in a low voice.

The child rested in the crook of his arm, almost sleeping.

'I would die for her,' said Sholto lightly.

'But do you love her? Sholto, you must. She isn't just any child, someone you know. She's yours. It's important.'

He turned his head then, lazy, almost amused. 'My darling Matty, don't ask such questions.'

The baby stirred and chewed at her fists. Sholto slid the tip of his little finger between her lips and with soft mews the child was calmed. In profile Sholto's face was stark, arrowing down in hard straight lines. But when he looked at his baby his face was different, she realised; as if an artist had softened harsh ink lines with crayon and wax. Indeed, thought Matty, she should not ask such questions.

In bed that night, lying next to Sholto, the baby in her cot, Matty said, 'I told them the thing was a fake. Won't that help?'

Sholto sighed. 'Perhaps. We'll fly out tomorrow and try and defend you. Do our lying face to face.'

His tone told her he was doubtful. 'I'm scared,' said Matty. 'Are they going to get me?'

'You're scared! Leave you alone for five minutes and you're committing major crimes. Don't worry, we'll say it was me. My idea. And you, trying desperately to stop a fraud.'

'You can't do that! You can't go to prison!'

He brushed her lips with his own. 'Better me than you, angel. Never you.'

She put her arms around him and thought, He loves me, he truly does. He loves us both. But it was all coming to nothing. Her little world, her little happiness, was about to fall apart.

Griselda stayed with the children while Lorne, Matty and Sholto flew to New York. Lorne insisted on coming, and seemed stronger now than for years. She took control of Matty, bolstering her nerve when it seemed most in danger of collapse. She bridged the silences, when Sholto retreated into thought and Matty into nervous imaginings. And at the airport Henrietta was waiting.

'Darlings! Everyone! I've brought the car, you must be exhausted.' Swathed in blue wool and diamonds, Henrietta was magnificently pregnant. Walking before them, talking and gesturing with her little plump hands, she looked like a balloon on legs. People opened doors for her, photographers took pictures and her chauffeur wrapped her up in cushions and blankets. She had turned into an adored great lady.

'Any news?' asked Sholto, settling himself into the car.

'Quite a bit,' said Henry. 'Everyone wants to talk to Matty and find out what she knows. She'll have to be good.'

'She's not going to say a word,' said Sholto. 'I am. This is all down to me.'

But Matty shook her head. 'It won't work, you know. You don't know enough. What's the date of these bowls?'

'Eighteenth century? I can mug it up tonight.'

She made a face. 'It took me years and you will take one night. Wonderful!'

She sounded exactly like Sammy Chesworth, she thought.

But you couldn't pass on skill in a few memorised questions. You couldn't fake competence as easily as you could fake bowls.

Henry said, 'She's right, you know.'

Sholto sighed. 'I know she is. But if it all comes out, I pose as the puppet master, pulling the strings. Little Miss Innocent gets off.'

'Tell that to the judge,' said Matty.

They went to the auction house first thing the next day. There was a modern art exhibition in place, and forms, shapes and garishness were set in a building of chrome and glass. Sholto felt his nerves being jangled. He wasn't up to a confrontation with twentieth-century style. Matty was very quiet but Lorne swept in on clicking high heels, bestowing brilliant smiles on men rushing to attend her. 'Your silver department? I do need to see the top man — why thank youall! So kind.'

It was her Southern belle act and Sholto muttered, 'Where is your leghorn hat, my dear? And where my gentlemanly charm?'

'You never had any,' she whispered. 'Or if you did, you didn't show it to me.'

He laughed, and she felt bitter suddenly. With men like Sholto in the world, why had she settled so easily for Greg?

Matty saw someone she knew, and shook hands. Men appeared from everywhere, a reporter took pictures, and they moved swiftly up a long flight of stairs. 'We'd like your opinion on the bowls, Mrs Feversham,' a gentleman was saying, a director. 'You seem to know them better than anyone.'

'She doesn't know them at all well,' said Sholto firmly. 'She is merely giving you the benefit of her extensive training.'

Matty thought grimly of prison. Perhaps she deserved it. Perhaps it was a family curse, something avoided only by death. Perhaps Simon could join the prison service and get round it that way.

'Now,' someone said, 'our Sprimont bowls!'

Two high doors were flung open, revealing a long polished table. In the centre, side by side, were the bowls. Every surface decorated, every line extended, excessive and yet never too much, they were a riot of leaves and curves and extravagance. 'Good heavens,' said Matty, despite herself, 'don't they look good?'

'Two remarkable pieces,' said the director. 'Shall we examine them?'

'Certainly.'

There was so little to choose. Perhaps the light reflected differently, and perhaps it was simply the angle from which it fell. The shape of one might be a little more bellied than the other. 'I think you'll agree,' said the director, 'that it really isn't possible to distinguish between them.'

Matty picked up one of the bowls. 'This is the fake. Sorry, but it is.'

The director dropped all pretence at friendliness. 'Mrs Feversham, I believe that's insupportable. Is there some mark, some distinguishing feature? How can you know?'

Matty licked dry lips. 'I — I just do.' She looked around at them all, Sholto's tense face, Lorne's white one, the nameless men, some of whom were certainly from the police. 'I saw the real bowl some years ago,' she confessed. 'Mr de Caruzon invited my employer, Mr Chesworth, to look at his collection, and I was sent instead. I remember Mr Chesworth telling me the bowl had to be wrong, he didn't believe another Sprimont existed. And I've looked at all the other Sprimonts, most of them in museums, and I think Mr de Caruzon's bowl is good. I have no idea how he got it, and Mr Chesworth didn't offer to make a purchase at that time. This bowl, the one I think is forged, is also very well made. But it's not by the same hand.'

The director said, 'So it could be an antique copy? Not necessarily modern.'

She nodded. 'Yes. Could be. We had one or two fakes knocking about salerooms in England and I thought it was one of those, but it need not be. To be honest, if it wasn't for the premium that Sprimont's name commands, I wouldn't care. It's a beautiful bowl.'

'But if Sprimont is the art and the other just a copy! Well, one was the master and the other the slave.'

'The end result's the same,' said Matty, and grinned.

That grin was in the papers the next day. It looked out of place. Matty was summoned by the police and spent three hours being grilled about photographs and hallmarks, her silver connections.

'We believe you have silver made for you in England. Who is your silversmith?'

Any desire to laugh had gone. She wanted to burst into tears. Instead she said, 'Greensall. Richard Greensall. He's — well, he's an odd sort of man.'

'How do you mean?'

'Odd. Unstable. I really don't want him involved in all this.'

'Is he capable of making a bowl like this?'

All her organs seemed to cringe from her reply. 'Yes.'

She was within an inch of admitting her crime. Why had she, who had always known that dishonesty was a loser's game, ever got involved in this? The door opened and she glanced up. It was Sholto.

'Sorry, officer, but she's wanted at the auction house. Incredible dispute going on, I'm afraid.'

As he rushed her out, Matty whispered, 'I was about to tell him everything! I'm no good at this, Sholto. I can't lie to save my life.'

'You think I don't know that?' He gave her hand a brief squeeze. 'Come on, love. You've got to be brave. Berenson and Luca are between them about to raise the roof.'

They were gathered around the polished table, the bowls before them. The short, stocky figure of Berenson was matched by the thinner shape of Luca, looking nervous and ill. They ignored Matty, each taking a glass of water from a carafe. Berenson took out a hip flask and added whisky to his.

To Matty's surprise, just as they were about to start, Lorne and Henrietta walked in. Berenson said, 'What's that woman doing here? That's my son's wife. She's trying to take him for every penny he has.'

Lorne faced him down. 'Don't tempt me, Sherwood. I might just tell them all about you.'

'You tell what you like, girl. I've got witnesses to your

behaviour. You were no wife to my son. Catting around all over the county.'

Lorne flushed dark red. 'You try that on and we'll see what comes out!'

'You threatening me, Lorne? You dare to do that?'

The director said, 'This is neither the time nor the place for such discussions. Do you have a reason to be here, ma'am?'

Lorne nodded. 'I do. It's important.' Berenson took out his handkerchief and ostentatiously blew his nose.

'Mrs Feversham.' The director came forward with his false bonhomie.

'Er — yes.' That wasn't even her name any more. She looked hopelessly back at Sholto and he gave her a wry grin.

'I regret to trouble you again,' said the director. 'These gentlemen both wish to hear your views in person. After much debate our experts seem to agree with you. These bowls were not made by the same hand. The Stavinsky bowl is not by Nicholas Sprimont.'

Berenson uttered a curse and Matty licked dry lips. 'That is my view.'

'Do you know how this other bowl came into existence?'

She could not lie. She could not tell the direct lie. 'That — that's not something on which I wish to speculate,' she said thickly.

Matty looked around at them all. Lorne avoided her eye, and Henry too, not looking at her. She wanted to shrivel and die.

Luca looked from Sholto to Matty and back again. 'She took photographs of the genuine bowl at the house of my wife's father, Don Paolo. I believe she passed these to a forger. If they were a pair they would be differently marked, and since they are not they are certainly a fraud.'

Matty said, 'Mr de Caruzon is not impartial, I'm afraid. He lost a law suit in Italy against my husband and pursues a constant vendetta. Now he's getting at him through me.'

'But is the charge true, Mrs Feversham? Did you copy this bowl?'

Blood rushed in Matty's ears. She thought she would faint. Smoothly Sholto said, 'If she had done such a thing

590

I doubt she would be here now, exposing this bowl as a fake. It wouldn't make sense.'

Sherwood Berenson rocked backwards and forwards on his broad feet. His gaze moved from Lorne to Matty and back again. 'It makes more sense than enough,' he said bluntly. 'She set out to do me down. Told me this bowl was genuine. I wouldn't have bought it without the say-so of an expert. I now believe Mrs Feversham was herself the owner of the bowl. It was a successful attempt to defraud, and she is only now admitting the suspect nature of the product because she can't stand to see me make a profit when she hoped to rob me blind.'

Lorne lifted her head. 'That isn't true. Matty told me she thought the bowl was fake, I told Sherwood it wasn't. I tricked him. I was the one who wanted him to lose. He's a man without morals and without heart, who has exploited me and my family for years now. This man is only interested in power. All he wants is power. I was determined to do him down. And Matty is too good a dealer to permit a bowl like that to circulate unchallenged. I capitalised on her principles, I'm sorry to say. I knew she wouldn't let that bowl go without speaking up.'

Lorne looked up and her eyes met Sholto's. Who was she doing this for? thought Matty. This was Sholto's idea.

'Is it true you owned this bowl, Mrs Feversham?' asked the director.

Matty tried to speak and couldn't. She looked at Lorne, she looked at Henrietta, and Henrietta smiled. 'In fact, the bowl was mine,' she said sweetly. 'I had made an arrangement to buy it from Mr Stavinsky earlier, for rather less than Mr Berenson paid. Part of the money had already been handed over. Mrs Feversham was horrified because she knew the bowl was a forgery, and Mr Stavinsky was so worried that I would stake my claim to the bowl and deprive him of his funds that he sold the bowl twice and then fled.' She smiled at everyone, the picture of affluent motherhood. 'A very tangled tale, I'm afraid. Mr Stavinsky appears to be the main culprit. My husband was so cross with me.'

A general buzz of conversation broke out, as people

591

discussed this. Berenson said, 'This is a load of hogwash! The girl's guilty as hell, just look at her!'

'You are upsetting my wife,' said Sholto, with menace.

'Upset! Upset!' Luca was purple with rage. 'You stole my wife from me. The man who broke up my home!'

'Does this have any relevance?' enquired the director with heavy patience.

Sholto said, 'Yes, it does. It's about time we had it all out in the open. I had an affair with his wife before I was married. Luca has never got over it. And it doesn't do to cross the de Caruzons. They make their money in arms deals and launder it through art. Luca's Sprimont bowl was probably obtained in exchange for a Russian nuclear warhead for a Middle Eastern state. He usually slides things on to the market through the back door, and I've helped him on more than one occasion, but this time the fake bowl brought him out of hiding. Couldn't let it go unchallenged, could you, Luca? Had to try for your fortune. That's the trouble with people like him, that's what brings them down. What they have is never enough.'

The room was silent. Sholto was doing himself no good, thought Matty. The sensible dealer never asked where the money came from. Luca was pale. His lips were trembling and a small tic flickered at the corner of his eye. Matty felt sympathy for him suddenly. Perhaps he had got into things, as she had, through circumstance.

'I am going to sue for slander,' he said thickly. 'I will not rest until I have broken you! I will not —' He seemed to jerk in mid-sentence. A look of surprise and then terror came over his face, and even his lips drained white. He fell forward across the table, sending the bowls crashing to the floor.

Matty sat in Henrietta's sitting room, a glass of brandy in one trembling hand. 'I thought they had me,' she said shakily. 'They were so determined to bring me down.'

'And look where it got them.' Sholto leaned back in his chair and stretched. 'Both bowls would appear to have been withdrawn. Now we have two discredited owners and one of them happens to be dead. I always thought Luca's temper would get the better of him.'

'Count yourself lucky,' said Henrietta, looking severe.

Sholto grinned. 'I do. Oh, I do.'

Matty said, 'I don't know why you were all so good to me. All of you, trying so hard to take the blame. I don't deserve you.'

'If you don't, no one does,' said Lorne. 'We stick together, remember?'

Henrietta got up. 'By the way,' she said, reaching behind the sofa, 'I bought a little something this afternoon. I just thought that with all the fuss he might be prepared to let me have it a little bit cheap.' She pulled out a plain brown bag. 'Voilà! Matty's own Sprimont bowl. Five hundred thousand, courtesy of Sherwood.'

Matty gaped. 'Henrietta! Why?'

For a moment she looked the mischievous girl she used to be. 'I don't know. I didn't like Berenson having it. Lorne's divorce is coming up and I always did think we stung him for too much. He wouldn't let it lie. And it's best if you can take the bowl, Matty, and hide it away somewhere. If you can find some use for it, fine, but if not – well, it's safer in your hands. Count it as a wedding present.'

Sholto said, 'Henrietta, you're an angel. I swear we'll pay you back. Eventually.'

Matty squeaked. 'Five hundred thousand dollars? We'll take forever!'

'Rubbish,' said Sholto. 'I shall think of a project, my little currant bun. We shall pay off all our debts and be millionaires.'

'Honest millionaires,' said Matty weakly. 'Honest ones. Please.'

Henrietta said, 'Actually, Matty, I think all this has done some good. Everyone's heard of you and everyone's talking about silver. You're the new silver queen. There's even a lady keeps calling the house talking about wine coolers, whatever they are.'

Matty spluttered. 'Wine coolers? Did you get her name?'

'I don't know.' Henrietta looked bewildered. 'It must be somewhere –'

'Mrs Waterman' murmured Sholto. 'Dear Mrs Waterman. I wonder what she's got her eye on now?'

'The woman's a bloodhound,' said Matty in amazement. 'It'll be something difficult, I'll swear. She probably wants this bowl.'

'Sell her something else,' said Sholto, extending his finger to brush the end of her nose. 'Persuade her. Making money need not come under the heading of sin, my dear girl, unlike hallmark forgery. Of which, I need hardly say, you know nothing.'

She made a face at him. Everything in life was more complicated than once she had thought. Good and bad persisted in entanglement. The Mrs Watermans of this world lurked everywhere with their impossible demands, and the good dealer had to go some way to satisfying them. Hopefully she would sell a nice piece and make a turn.

But it would take dozens of deals like that to pay off the debts. She looked ruefully round at them all. 'I wish I didn't like silver so much. It doesn't make enough money. I should never have started.'

'Perhaps you'll be rich one day,' coaxed Henry. 'Like Mr Chesworth.'

'God forbid,' said Sholto. 'I am not sleeping with Sammy Chesworth, not at any price.'

'I'm not giving up,' said Matty, looking him straight in the eye. 'I'm not, you know. Even if silver never made me another penny, I'd never give up.'

He blinked. 'Did I say that you should? You've got a first-class business, as it happens. Lots of contacts, lots of skill. You may even now have some sort of reputation. All we have to do is get rid of that load of debt. We must work together, my love. Distasteful as I know it must be, you're stuck with me.'

Matty made a face. 'Really? No escape?'

He encircled her throat with one long, gentle hand. 'None.'

Sholto and Matty stood in Richard Greensall's dark workshop. Matty removed a bowl from a brown paper bag and held it out. Greensall took it, rather sadly, and set it on the bench. Then he picked up a hammer and began smashing it, buckling and crushing it, ripping off the delicate

594

silver leaves, crunching the paw-shaped feet. When it was nothing but a tangle he set it on the hearth and began heating it, hotter and hotter, until the shape dissolved and ran together into a lump of nothing.

'There,' he said finally. 'That's it, then. My best work. Gone. I'll send this to the foundry and get it finished off.'

They stood in silence, looking at a lump that had once been lovely. It seemed an unjust end. Matty felt tears prick her eyes.

'From now on use your own marks and no one else's,' said Sholto.

Greensall looked glum. 'Aye. It seems as if I should.'

On the way home, Sasha in the baby seat and the roads quiet, Matty said, 'I should feel better, but I don't. Isn't it sad that something good had to be destroyed?'

Sholto shrugged. 'I suppose we need space in the world for the new.'

'It was new!' said Matty. Then she grinned. 'I think.'

'What do you mean?'

She swivelled in her seat towards him. 'Well, when the bowls fell on the floor I didn't inspect them. Someone else decided which was which. And I haven't looked since. So — Sholto, it may just be that we have bashed up five million dollars worth of irreplaceable Sprimont bowl, and Richard Greensall's effort has ended up as the treasured possession of some sleazy arms dealers in Mexico.'

Sholto started to laugh. 'You could have looked at the leaves,' he said desperately. 'Couldn't you tell by the leaves?'

'Yes.' Matty looked puzzled. 'That's the trouble. As he was hitting it I could have sworn one of the leaves wasn't on straight. But it was too late then. And now it's gone.'

They returned to the cottage in the soft grey light of evening. It was quiet, Simon at school and Lorne in Boston with Miller, seeing the eye specialist. Matty put the kettle on and leaned against the counter, waiting for the water to boil. Sholto leaned with her, smoothing the hair back behind her ear.

'Would you really have gone to prison for me?' she asked.

'You know I would. Like a shot. But I'm not sure they'd have had me.'

She smiled ruefully. 'No. Neither am I.'

Suddenly she said, 'Sholto, what are we going to do about Lorne? She needs to start something. She never really began her life at all, she got kidnapped. And now Berenson's discredited and she'll soon be divorced. What's she going to do?'

He opened the cupboard and helped himself to a handful of dried fruit. 'Easy. Silver dealing.'

'Silver? Lorne? But that's me!'

'You need an agent in New York, don't you? To see to the Mrs Watermans of this world. She's got all the style, and it's a massive market. She can learn as she goes along.'

Matty felt quite ruffled. She thought of Lorne taking her place, starting where she was leaving off, the glamorous lady dealer, with no need to start trading spoons. She remembered how hard it had been for her, with no one to tell her what to do. Despicably, she thought of Sholto. He and Lorne had always got on and this brought them all so close.

Sholto said, 'She needs a break, Matty.'

'I know. And she's my friend. I just don't know if I can trust you with her, that's all.'

He was silent for a moment. Then he said, 'We wouldn't do it, Matty. Either of us.'

'But you might want to do it. That's almost as bad.'

'No it isn't!' He ran a hand through his hair. 'Look, I may not have been saintly in the past but I have never, never propositioned your friend. I don't do it because I don't want you hurt.' He took her by the shoulders, making her face him, making her recognise that this time he was all steely intent. He couldn't afford to have her doubt him, now or ever. 'My dear girl, my dearest girl, I want you to believe what I say. Whatever stunted emotions I've got, whatever warmth there is in me, it's all for you. There's no one else and there won't ever be anyone else. I've learned all my lessons. So let's get out of that stupid contract you made to that stupidly boring man and get back into church and get wed.'

So it was that they stood before the altar once again.

Griselda, Duchess of Brantingham, was there with the Duke, looking decidedly prosperous. They had had a windfall of some sort. The Tyler Cookes were there, with their two children, accompanied by a nanny and a maid, on their way to stay with Mrs Cooke's mother in Mayfair. And Lorne Shuster was there, with her son in dark glasses after his operation. When the sun came out and struck through the stained glass, smothering the old stone flags with diamonds of colour, he reached out his hands and shouted, and nobody minded at all.

The bride wore a blue balldress she had had for some time, and was given away by her brother, resplendent in morning dress. The groom wore a white dinner jacket, to indicate pure intent, and broke open a bottle of champagne on the church steps afterwards, much to the vicar's surprise.

Everyone in the village thought it an odd sort of affair, although arty types were always a little strange. The children played on the grass and the groom gave them confetti and stood laughing as they threw showers of pink and white petals into the air.

Matty stood apart for a moment with her friends. Four of them, still.

' "We have not served the Fairy Queen – " ' said Matty.

' "But instead the jewel of friendship", ' added Griselda. They looked at each other and smiled, remembering.

'How young we were,' said Lorne.

'How innocent,' said Henrietta.

Matty looked at her friends, and beyond them to her husband. What she had learned from her friends she must bring to her marriage, setting out on a life together in kindness and loyalty and love.

Sholto turned and smiled at her, holding out his hands, confetti in his hair and the children at his feet. Matty left her friends and ran to him.

More Compelling Fiction from Headline:

THE COURT

ELIZABETH
WALKER

Vast, crumbling and magnificent, The Court has been the Yorkshire home of the Hellyns for centuries – it is part of them, part of their lives. But when the fifteenth earl dies, his four children are shocked to find themselves suddenly penniless and saddled with debt. Theirs is an awesome heritage – and it is one they doubt they can retain.

Mara, beautiful and sensuous, goes wildly off the rails. Men are attracted to her like bees to honey, but Mara falls for the one man she cannot have. The Hellyns may lose their home – now they face family disgrace. The younger sister, Lisa, forges an unlikely alliance with an Australian millionaire in a desperate bid to keep the family solvent. It isn't enough, for her or for The Court. Marcus, the heir, has his own demons to fight, and his twin, Angus, is forced to sacrifice his hopes to shoulder his brother's burdens.

The Hellyns are drawn back again and again to The Court. Through birth and death, triumph and tragedy, it shelters its children, but only one of those children loves it enough to save it . . .

'Earthy, exciting and well written . . . I was immediately hooked' *She*

Also by Elizabeth Walker from Headline
VOYAGE – 'Once you start reading you won't be able to stop' *Woman's World* – and ROWAN'S MILL – 'Whips along at a cracking pace – ideal' *Prima*

FICTION/SAGA   0 7472 3238 5

More Compelling Fiction from Headline:

CONQUEST
ELIZABETH
WALKER

A free spirit . . .
Enjoying her first, exhilarating taste of independence in
Nepal, Flora is hungry for new sensations. Accustomed
to a cocoon of wealth and privilege as the only child of
autocratic millionaire Malcolm Kincaid, she is
unprepared for the rigours of life in the Third World.
Unprepared, too, for the effect of Don Harrington.

A man with an obsession . . .
Big, confident and devastatingly attractive, Harrington
is in Nepal to conquer Everest. But he is determined
also to conquer Flora and when she is suddenly called
home to her father's bedside, Don follows her to Castle
Melchior, the magnificent Kincaid family seat.

A marriage of opposites . . .
Although they are in love, the couple hardly know
each other. There is a side to Don as remote and
inaccessible as the mountain peaks he is driven to
conquer; Flora is too young to give up her ideals
without a fight. Striking out for their individual needs,
they run the risk of losing each other for ever . . .

Don't miss Elizabeth Walker's other sensual sagas
Dark Sunrise, Wild Honey, A Summer Frost, Voyage,
Rowan's Mill and *The Court* also from Headline
'A wonderful, romantic read' *Annabel*
'A memorable book, and refreshingly different'
Woman's World
'The perfect holiday read' *Me*
'Whips along at a cracking pace . . . ideal for the escapists
amongst us' *Prima*

FICTION/SAGA   0 7472 3616 X

Free-to-enter competition
Win an Antique Silver Salver
and start your silver collection!

HOW TO ENTER

On the back of a postcard, answer the following three questions:

1. What do the initials 'NS' stand for on the beautiful silver bowl which Matty first sees at the de Caruzons' home in Mexico?
2. What is an epergne?
3. What percentage of silver is present in sterling silver?

Then, in no more than 30 words, tell us why you enjoyed reading *Hallmark*.

Make sure you write on your name and address, and send your postcard to: Dept WS, Headline House, 79 Great Titchfield Street, London W1P 7FN before the closing date (31 October 1992).

RULES

Entries must be received by 31.10.92 on a postcard or the back of a sealed envelope, and include the sender's name and address. This competition is only open to residents of the UK. The prize will be awarded to the entry with the correct answers and the most apt and original tie-breaker in the opinion of the judges. The judges' decision is final, and no correspondence will be entered into. The winner will be notified first week in November. Employees (and their relatives) of Headline Book Publishing are not eligible to enter. No cash alternative to the silver salver.